BAREFOOT TO
PALESTINE

A Novel

Loretta J. Krause

Copyright 2017 Loretta J. Krause
ISBN 13: 9780980021066
ISBN: 0980021065
Library of Congress Control Number: 2017905504
Loretta J. Krause, Wayne, NJ
This is a work of fiction. Names, characters, places, or situa-
tions are the product of the author's creativity and imagination
and are intended as fiction only.

DEDICATION

For my mother, who infused her love of literature and poetry in me when I was too young to realize she had. God bless, Mom. Rest in peace.

1

A CHILD'S IMPRINT

She climbs the rungs of her chair, this little three-year old with the chubby legs, and struggles a bit as she bends her knee; then lifts one leg onto the seat with two pillows. She doesn't quite make it, she's so little, but she tries again . . . and again. She never doubts she'll get there.

Fourth try. She makes it and grabs the edge of the chrome kitchen table with the red formica top. Then with all the strength a three-year-old can muster, she pulls up her other leg. She is kneeling on her chair. Halfway there. Her smile widens, little flecks of dimples peeking through, and her eyes twinkle with pride. Where's Mommy? Did Mommy see me do dis all myself? "Mommy?"

Mommy is leaning over the hot oven; its door is open wide. Heat rushes out. The little one sees it – shimmering, dancing its way to the ceiling – and she feels the blast. Hot! Keep away. Keep away, Mommy. "Hot!"

Her mom smiles at her. Mommy wears heavy potholder hands, and pulls a roast from the oven rack. With one graceful motion, she lifts the roasting pan from its rack to the top of the stove, planting it firmly on its cast iron surface. Fat sputters and explodes like embers from damp wood. Crackle. Splatter. Crackle. Splatter. Pop! One final explosion amidst a symphony of sizzles. Music. Like music. She inhales deeply. The aroma of food fills her nostrils. She drinks it in. "I hungwry Mommy," she says in her little three-year-old voice. Roasted leg of lamb. Pots burping steam from their lids. Big pots, little pots; it all smells so good.

She is hungry! Where is Daddy? They do not eat until Daddy sits. Twisting her little body on her seat, she straightens her legs and plunks her butt onto her chair. Now, she is settled; now . . . now she is ready! It is time for supper, and she is on her kitchen chair, the chair with two plump pillows on its seat so she can reach the table. By next year, she will need only one pillow. She is growing fast.

"When I four," she says and shakes her head, yes, "my chair reach me faster, and it have owny one pillow." She looks for affirmation from her mother and centers herself comfortably on the pillows, picking up her little fork, ready to eat. She knows Daddy is home; the faucet in the bathroom is running. She beams happily, and hopefully. Maybe Daddy is happy today?

"Did you wash your hands, Honey?" Her mom asks, her potholder hands pushing damp, hot strands of hair from her face, wet with perspiration from having been at the stove cooking all afternoon.

"Yes, Mommy." She holds up both hands, fingers wide apart. "I use thoap, too. I use lots of thoap, and I wub just like you tell me. Water, too. The water is warm. It takes all the thoap away. I dwry them really good. See?"

Her mom smiles and calls her "my little angel." Mommy always calls me angel. "I love you," her mom says, removes her potholders and sends a kiss to her little girl across the kitchen, to the little daughter with the golden hair, the almond-shaped eyes and the flecks of dimples when she smiles.

Mommy loves me. It's something she just knows in her heart. When you're young, you know when somebody loves you and when they don't. Same when you're old. It's the in-between years that get so confusing.

Water is still running in the bathroom. "Akh!' Her father's growl. Maybe Daddy hurts, she thinks, like my tummy when it's hungwry. Her mother is busy finishing up, frenetically putting a glass out for Daddy, a soup bowl, pouring juice in Daddy's glass, carving more slices of meat from the roast in the pan on the cast iron stovetop. Close to the bone, more rare, exactly the way he wants it.

Sis has climbed up on her chair with one pillow. They are in their proper places at the proper time. Her mom frantically stirs pots, tests potatoes still roasting in the oven; they have to be done now. Fork goes right through. Done. Now ladling hot soup into bowls. Lentil soup; hot home-made lentil soup. Daddy must eat soup, hot soup, with every meal. Bread is on the table. Daddy must eat bread with every meal. Mommy checks the juice at Daddy's place setting. Daddy must drink juice with every meal. Daddy always sits at that end of the table, close to the stove . . . and Daddy's hands must be clean. Very clean. He washes them long. We wash our hands long, too. Washing hands ith fun. Bubbles run down the drain.

No more running water in the bathroom. Daddy shouts. "This towel is wet! Get me a clean one!" Daddy is not happy.

Mommy puts down the carving knife. She hurries to the hall closet where clean towels and sheets are stored. She pulls out a fresh towel that has dried on the line today and knocks lightly on the bathroom door. The bathroom is in a tiny alcove directly behind the kitchen across from the hall closet. Five railroad rooms: kitchen, bathroom, living room, three undersized bedrooms. All align consecutively. With railroad rooms, where else can they go? The bathroom door opens several inches and a hand yanks the towel from her grasp.

Daddy is finished washing and will be out now. Mommy hurries back to the kitchen, to the roast almost completely carved. Two more thin slices and she carries the pan to the table. Roasted potatoes get pulled out of the oven and go onto a platter, green beans and cooked carrots go into serving bowls then onto the table. She glances around nervously, checking and rechecking. Has she forgotten anything? Anything at all? No . . . no . . . she doesn't think so. As far as she can see, everything is set. She ladles soup into her bowl and sits.

Daddy comes out of the bathroom; he walks to his chair and sits. "Daddy," she says. "I been a good girl today. I fill the thack with clothes pins and pick up all my toys."

Daddy does not respond. He picks up his soup spoon and begins to eat. "Akh!" He shouts, slamming his spoon down on the table. "This soup is warm! I want it *hot.* Hot! Do you hear me?! How many times do I have to tell you?"

Quickly, her mom gets up and takes the bowl away. "All right, George, I'll heat it up."

"Now I have to wait! When I come home from work, I do not want to wait!"

"It'll only take a minute. Talk to your children for a few minutes."

"Are you telling me what to do?!"

"No, George. The soup will be hot quickly." In one smooth motion, she grabs a small pot from the cabinet, pours the soup from the bowl and places it on the stove. It begins to simmer instantly. "Girls, eat your soup, please."

Daddy's face is red. He spreads butter on a slice of bread and waits for his soup. It's ready now. Daddy will be happy now. Mommy pours it back into his bowl and places it in front of him. A thin undulating strip of steam rises from it. "Daddy, where does steam go?"

Her dad eats in silence, never glancing at her. He takes another slice of bread, picks up his fork, and searches for rare slices of meat. He growls again. "It's all well-done. You cooked it too long!" Seconds pass; motion stills as he searches again. "You're home all day doing nothing and you can't make a decent leg of lamb?" He growls, throwing off the piece on his fork. Juices splash from the bottom of the pan over the table.

"The rare pieces are underneath," Mommy says. She ferrets them out with the serving fork. "Here, these pieces are very rare." She hesitates an instant, then puts them on his plate.

"Put 'em on top next time, so I can see 'em," he commands. Her mom does not respond. She is cutting meat for the girls. She removes their soup bowls, takes them to the white, enamel sink that sits on four enamel legs, and puts pieces of lamb, potatoes and carrots on the girls' plates.

The little girl smiles. Her Mom radiates when her daughters smile. She has done something right with her life. Success, when so much of her life has been failure. Her little girl beams. Her world is warm and safe when Mommy smiles. Her Mommy puts potatoes on Daddy's plate. He pushes her hand away and growls. "I'm not ready for vegetables. Can't you see I'm still eating meat? He has made the lamb slices and bread into a sandwich.

"I'm sorry, George."

"You're always sorry. Just get it right!"

"There was room on your plate. I thought you were ready for vegetables." Mommy answers back.

"I'll tell you when I'm ready." He glares. "Until then, don't think; you hear me?! He glances around the table searching for something. His gaze falls on the little one, trembling. Why Daddy mad again? She wonders, then shrinks away, making herself smaller than a three-year-old can already be.

"And get her away from me!" He bellows.

"George! She's your daughter!"

"I already have a daughter. I don't need another one. This child is good for nothing! Get her out of my sight!"

The little girl's tears flow as her heart begins to break. Daddy does not love her, she knows.

"Where's the salt! Damn it! There's no salt on this table! Do I have to get up and get it myself?"

Mommy gets up from the table, gets the salt and pepper shakers from the stovetop and takes them to Daddy. Then Mommy goes to her little girl with a great big hug. The little girl falls into her Mommy's embrace. She is safe again. "Mommy," she sobs.

"It's okay, Honey. It's okay. Daddy didn't mean it. He's just tired from work."

"I *did* mean it!" Daddy roars with uncontrollable fury. He jumps up from his seat. His chair falls back, crashing to the floor. His heavy strides stomp past the stove and across the kitchen floor. Mommy jumps back. Daddy grabs Mommy by the arm and hurls her against the wall. Mommy fights back. The little girl gets down from her seat as fast as her little legs can carry her and races to the corner of the kitchen behind the door. Her sister slides down from her chair onto the floor, crawls under the table, and scurries out the other side to her little sister. They are holding on to each other crying, crying and screaming.

Daddy has Mommy pinned against the kitchen wall. Daddy is shouting! His face is red . . . red! His left arm pins Mommy's head against the wall. His right hand is holding the butcher knife! He presses the point against the soft flesh under Mommy's throat. Mommy's eyes are bulging in fear! Mommy is scared! Mommy is scared! She is shouting at Daddy. "Put the knife down, George. Put the knife down!" Daddy roars. "I'll kill you!" His arm slams Mommy's head harder against the wall. Mommy's hands claw at the wall, as if she could dig a hole there and disappear. No place to go. Daddy's hand tightens around the wooden handle. "Go ahead!" Mommy screams. Kill me! Kill me in front of your daughters!"

For endless seconds and forever minutes, time hovers, suspended on the ceiling, around corners, and behind the kitchen door, where two little children are kneeling, gripping each other for survival, the younger one traumatized for the rest of her life, screaming, "Daddy, don't kill Mommy! Don't kill Mommy . . . Don't! Kill! Mommy!" . . . as Daddy suddenly explodes with rage and hurls the knife onto platters and plates, storming out of the room.

Mommy, swooning, still with bulging eyes, sinking to the floor, slowly sinking to the floor, breathing rough breaths, clutching her throat, suspending time, moving frame . . . by . . . frame.

Then, with outstretched arms, her little angels rush from their refuge behind the kitchen door into their Mommy's safe, warm embrace.

2

TAYLOR OTIS BARRETT

Taylor Otis-Barrett stares out her floor-to-ceiling windows that span the rear perimeter of her bedroom suite. She stares and gazes at the vast penumbra of natural woodland set more than three hundred feet back from her tennis courts, her gardens, her patio, her cabana and her pool. Beyond that, her stables. Hers. Over ten acres, hidden in this quiet Princeton suburb, where old money yawns lazily and new money rests smugly. Ten acres of Otis-Barrett dynasty established almost two centuries ago by two rival families, one, land-rich, that refused to relinquish its identity, having had three daughters but no sons, and the other, their political dominance in the territory satiated only by quenching its thirst for land.

Taylor, her second five o'clock martini in hand, had poured her first at 4:30, when the winter sky had begun to envelope the setting sun. She felt especially satisfied with herself this evening. No special reason. She surveyed her domain, all she had obtained and allowed her smug arrogance to unfold. She had become a woman of means with all the accoutrements like snobbery and condescension. Marriage had given her entitlement. Everything she had ever imagined when she was young, everything, she now had, and more, and she luxuriated in it, like bathing in a hot spa illuminated with the soft glow of ambient candlelight. Pampered with a personal chef and housekeepers, a mansion she could get lost in, garages with showcase cars, two-story closets straining from the weight of fine labels, shelves of shoes, cold storage for her furs, drawers of silk lingerie and accessories, jewelry of all kinds, diamonds, emeralds, gold necklaces, earrings, bracelets, rings, all asleep in her vault, much too much to ever wear; she was, unfortunately, bored.

That was the simple truth. Bored out of her mind, and nothing could dispel it. No matter how many trips to Europe, the Mediterranean, or Hawaii, no matter how many cruises south or north or in any direction, or flights in their private jet, nothing excited her. Not even the trappings of the Club. For her, they merely idled away time in a tolerable fashion, because, for Taylor, as much as marriage had given her, it had also taken away.

She missed the social ladder climbing, the conquests, the hunt, the chase and the kill. But to risk all she had for the thrill? She wouldn't chance it and that was the rub. Half, only half, if they ever divorced - her pre-nuptial excluded all assets before marriage, every one of them, including that multi, multi-million dollar trust fund his grandfather had established decades ago that would never be hers, married or divorced. That would go to her children. Thankfully there was only one.

She sighed. How many more years did she have before men stopped looking? Yes, there were some very attractive women in their sixties at the Club, well-coiffed and in great physical shape, but living into old age in this rut was not something she had thought through when she married. Tipping forty-one and stuck, settling for panache and old money. But, she thought, looking at the bright side, how much better to be bored rich than bored poor. "To panache and wealth." She toasted, lifting her glass for more than a sip.

Taylor's childhood had situated itself on the second floor apartment of a three-story clapboard house in five railroad rooms on Clerk Street in Jersey City. She was a daughter born to Irish parents who moved up in the world when she was eleven, into a brick house across the street from the park on the corner of Summit Ave. and Zabriskie Street, where the Polish landlord and his family occupied the first and third floors and screamed at each other at 2:00 a.m. in the morning on the second floor landing, sandwiching Taylor, her parents and younger brother in between.

This, the only world she knew until her father made a few wrong turns on their way to Atlantic City and drove through LBI. Wealth, stylish clothes, the hair, makeup, and most of all, the attitude and the sting of the snub. Another class existed. Another world existed, and she suddenly became nakedly aware of her petty, shameful place in society. A moment in time, just one brief moment, that's all it took. Then and there, she committed herself to becoming part of this perfectly pretentious panorama with which the wealthy adorn themselves.

Her goal was set, and Taylor had an uncanny ability to get it.

Her physical assets were outstanding: above her straight nose were large, round, Irish emerald green eyes, unexpressive, but widely set, complemented with dark thick lashes and arched eyebrows. High cheekbones added an exotic touch. Below her nose were full lips that invited more than perusal and a delicately chiseled chin. Below that, full breasts, a tiny waist and curvaceous hips.

But lots of young ingénues are stunning. What Taylor had, in addition, was a way-above-average IQ, and, for some unexplainable reason, a unique ability to understand men. Her mother, a puritanical throwback from the 19th century, married at eighteen and married "till death do you part." So Taylor knew, intuitively, she didn't get her ability from her mother, nor did she get the puritanical part. No guilt, no compassion, no conscience. If she connected to any characters in literature, it was a cross between Abby of Salem Witch Trial fame, and Cathy from *East of Eden.*

Time and again, she used her innate ability to dissect each male she met, define his singular weaknesses almost at a glance, and determine if he were worth the effort on the food chain. If he were, one step at a time, she broke him down and moved herself up.

She earned her cosmetology license at seventeen while simultaneously graduating from Snyder High School. She'd walk out the back door to Kennedy Boulevard, turn right, walk less than half a mile to the premier cosmetology school in three counties, and worked her butt off in the studio. When she graduated, she was placed in a salon at a pricey mall in Englewood Cliffs. Every day, she traveled in an old, beat-up Plymouth her parents had bought her. When she got to the salon, she'd park the old junk as far away from the patrons' lot as possible, walk to the salon and work effortlessly and enthusiastically. It was just a matter of months for her first opportunity to come along.

Late October, after torrential rains had soaked the roads and rivers overran their banks, her first worthwhile target hurried in. An emergency manicure, he claimed, but he needed quite a bit more. Vice presidents, lawyers and the CEO of his commercial realty company were convening at an executive business meeting that afternoon for his presentation, developing a strip of land along the Weehawken side of the Hudson River where the old railroad tracks lay abandoned. Maybe a good venture, maybe not. His presentation would be key, but not looking like that. This guy gets his car stuck off the mucky shoulder on Route 4 on his way from Kinnelon. What a mess.

He hurries in carrying the clean shirt he always keeps stashed in his trunk. Smart thinking. But the rest of him seems hopeless. She directs him to her shampoo sink where he cleans off his shoes. Better. His jacket? She could shake that down, dry the mud with her dryer then brush off the dried cakes. Wash down the residue with a damp cloth. After formal introductions had been made, he could take off the jacket and try for a more relaxed look. His hair needed a little touching up; he could get by with that, but his hands and nails? What a mess! He should have waited for AAA. Sometimes the most intelligent people have the least common sense.

Everything about him screamed money and her soothing yet artificial compassion induced conversation that corroborated it. Taylor took special care to give him exclusive attention despite waiting patrons checking their watches. But it paid off big time. "Any favor I can do for you, ever, just let me know," he offered as he paid, left her a huge tip and handed her his business card. Oh, yes, she thought, this guy could most certainly do something for me; Taylor accepted graciously but without hesitation. Reciprocity is the name of the game.

With this, Taylor had her start. Piggy-backing and leap-frogging from one prospect to another, she used her skill, honed in on the right targets and manipulated them to her advantage. The wealthy omniscient, the wealthy omnipotent, the wealthy self-absorbed wallowing in complete and utter hubris; these were the men she sought - solipsistic men who drew conclusions from myopic 'too big to fail' egos. Again and again.

At first, she found them though the salon. Later, she found them through night classes at Columbia, some business exec or prospective politician going for his PhD, but her best source? Political campaigning. Wealthy, married men who couldn't resist bedding what they perceived to be their conquest, no strings attached, not realizing it was the other way around. Until, of course, it was too late. Taylor kept a portable cassette recorder hidden away during every session, no matter where the rendez-vous. No married man yet had dared her ultimatum over wife, family, and political future.

Complete and utter victory, until she had amassed a substantial portfolio and established her "Manicures for Men" salon in this little sleepy, prestigious Princeton suburb. Then Vaughn walked through her door. Single, wealthy, so naïve and full of himself that her singular difficulty was not laughing in his face. So very easy to manipulate. He brought her into his obscenely wealthy world of old money despite objections from his parents, especially his mother, who somehow saw right through her. But Vaughn had never known sex like hers before, and he became Play Dough in her hands. Maybe it was time for Taylor to settle down. Easily, she maneuvered him into proposing and walked down the aisle to secure her future. A perfect plan, 100% successful. She got a dutiful husband . . . and a fantastic lover. She raised her glass in triumph, "To all the superficial, hedonistic pricks who have made me what I am," and sipped deeply.

Outside, what had been a hint of dribbling snow-flakes just minutes ago had become passionate bursts of icy pellets swirling through naked treetops, like bullets fired from chambered gusts of wind. "I am invincible," she laughed diabolically, forgetting that hubris and downfall were not indigenous to her victims alone.

The electric garage door engaged, its motorized hum the harbinger of the man she had married, the purveyor of all she surveyed. He was home.

"Vaughn," she murmured without a smile. She hurried though the sitting room and into its contiguous bedroom, an immense room that dwarfed a king-sized bed, an oversized armoire, two triple-dressers, two soft brown leather recliners set perpendicular to each other on the far wall, and her writing table between them. Vaughn's mahogany desk, when small amounts of paperwork didn't require his study, sat diagonally in the corner past his armoire, and a full entertainment system was walled to its right. But the centerpiece of the room was a gas fireplace the size of a 16th century hearth, cut from pink and gray sparkling granite, mantled with a white marbled crown. An eleven foot wide beauty, perfectly centered between glass window walls, protected from overuse by soft, plush snow-white carpeting.

Taylor placed her martini on the mantel and walked to the bed on which she had placed her fine lingerie before showering and dressing for the evening. She had chosen the black lace bra, so, she would not be wearing the pushups or strapless. Black lace bikini panties? No, she would not wear these tonight either. Pantyhose? No to those too. Folding them lovingly, she placed them on tissue paper in a dresser drawer, exactly where they belonged, and closed them in for the night. Another dab of Clive Christian No.1 and she turned to greet her husband.

"My beautiful, lovely, Taylor," Vaughn said effusively, walking directly to her and kissing her cheeks. He inhaled the sweet, musky scent of her perfume and gave her a callow peck on her lips.

Taylor pouted her sexy look, and drew her body against his. "I look and smell like this just for you and that's all I get?"

It worked; it always did. Vaughn's lips covered her mouth with as passionate a kiss as he was capable of giving and his hands left her neckline, roamed her breasts, waistline and hips, resting on her backside.

"Much better," she said coyly, "but save the rest for later, Darling." She pulled her head back, interrupting the intentions she had invited.

"For later? Why later? I'm ready now."

"Later," she remonstrated, "because I'm going out, remember?" And she slid out of his embrace.

"No." He said pensively, following her. "No, I don't remember. You never said you were going out." He took a closer look at her dress.

"Yes, I *did*, several times." She moved to the mantel; picked up her martini and took a perfunctory sip. "You must have been in your "Dean of the School" mode, because when you're there, you listen with your ears shut."

"Hmmph!" He grumbled dejectedly. Then more boldly, "When did you tell me? And, exactly *where* are you going?"

"Your brother's. Remember? Their twenty-fifth wedding anniversary gala? Brett wanted help?" She hid her impatience. "I'm sure you remember; he's asked so many times." She flicked his nose playfully with her finger, deception as usual. "As of this morning, your mother and I were supposed to take Hillary to an early dinner, remember now?"

Vaughn's blank stare held. "Me, your mother and Hillary, tonight, then Hillary to your mother's and me to your brother's to plan the party with Sharon and Veronica." Vaughn stood motionless, pondering his lapse of memory. "Invitations, menu items, linens, things like that?" She paused . . . nothing, "and I reminded you again last night in your study; you were perusing resumes."

"Hmmm, maybe." She must be right, he thought, because, unlike his brother, he hated stuff like that and most likely had ignored everything she had said. "So you're taking Hillary to dinner, at the Club"?

"As of 11:00 a.m., before Hillary called, that was the plan. But," she smiled, "Marcy, now three-months pregnant and *still* throwing up her guts, offered Hillary her ticket to this evening's performance of *Cats*. Hillary begged me not to be miffed." Taylor laughed. "As though I would be? It just makes the plan so much easier, *and* I get to be there all evening. Hillary won't be home till after 12:00 the earliest; so we won't have a thing to worry about," she added. We might get the entire party planned by then." She gave it a second thought. "No, that would be impossible, but we could get a lot done."

Vaughn removed his suit jacket. Even if he hadn't remembered what she had told him, he would have conceded and Taylor knew it instinctively. He draped his jacket over his valet. "I remember you were taking Hillary to dinner, but I didn't remember it was tonight. Hiring a replacement for Draggert has taken so much of my time I haven't been much aware of anything else. Sorry Darling." He paused, glanced out the window, and nodded towards the snow slapping their windows. "What about that?"

"What?" She turned towards the full-length bedroom windows and the sleeting tempest outside, snow and ice crystals still slashing against the glass. "That?" She dismissed it with the wave of her hand. "Insignificant," she replied confidently. "Weather reports say it's hitting the shore. Besides, temperatures were in the forties yesterday and it was thirty-four this afternoon. Unless we get a blast of Arctic air, this won't stick; the ground's too warm. But," she capitulated, "just in case, I'll take the Volvo."

"Have Thomas drive you. Take one of the limos."

"I don't need a limo to go to your brother's. The Volvo will be fine. It goes anywhere in anything, and this," she nodded towards the window, "is nothing. I'll be safe enough in that."

He nodded. "Fine, but be careful."

"I will be, Darling, so I can hurry home to you," she teased. Interrupted by the phone, "I'll answer it," she said.

"Leave it, Taylor. It does take messages, you know."

She answered sweetly; then her smile broadened. "Hi . . . What? They're already there? When? Yes . . . of course. I was just leaving. I can be there in about thirty-five minutes," and hung up.

"Brett's been home over an hour and Veronica and Sharon are there already brainstorming. If I don't hurry, I'll miss out on all the good stuff." She paused. Want to help?" She winked. Vaughn grimaced, giving his unequivocal silent answer, no.

Taylor laughed and hurried to the back of her two-story closet, both levels larger than the bedroom, one level larger than the apartment she had lived in as a child. She scrutinized racks of coats. Mink full length? No, too warm. Mink, knee-length? No. Mink jacket? Leather . . . suede? Hmm, which one? She browsed from one to another. Let's go casual, she thought, not wanting to take any more time deciding on a coat. She pulled out a three-quarter length cashmere with a hood, in case the weather prediction was wrong.

Going to the dresser for her keys, she took one more sip of her martini then paused. "Sorry, Darling, I forgot to ask. Did you have any success hiring a replacement for Steven?"

"Success?" Vaughn responded dubiously. His tie was off and he was wrestling with the top button of his shirt. "If success is possible. Draggert was an integral part of Chelsea for more than three decades. He knew the Elizabethan Age, Shakespeare's life, his plays, the Globe, cold. You don't have success finding a replacement for him; you just find a replacement, hopefully, with the best available candidate. And," he brightened, a thin smile of satisfaction turning his lips upward, "we hired one last week and finalized the paperwork this afternoon. She has her M.A. in English literature and has taught Shakespeare for over a decade. We lucked out, I'd say, finally. She starts Monday."

"That's positive." Taylor seemed to approve. "Any experience with the round table method?" She added. Her keys dangled from her index finger; she was halfway out the door.

"No," he shook his head, "unfortunately, "but how many teachers do? To her credit, she has done a lot of group work with high school seniors and college students when she was an adjunct."

"An adjunct? Taylor's patrician arrogance seeped through her thin veneer of politeness. "Vaughn, that doesn't sound very promising."

"An adjunct at a state college is more experience than any other applicant had. She's a city girl, somewhat experimental for us, but I think she'll present herself well."

"And what makes you say that, Darling?" Taylor's snobbery, now obvious to Vaughn, held.

"Taylor, she's teaching, not applying for the Club. There's no line on the application for pedigree." Vaughn's response was not his usually gesture of sophistication. "But to answer your question," he shrugged, "I think she can do it. There's something about her that's different, a tough crusty exterior displaying lots of knowledge and experience about life. She's cryptic and somewhat riveting. Whatever. I don't know." He gesticulated with his hands. "I can't find the right word right now, but it's there, and I think our students can learn a lot from her once she opens up."

"Vaughn," Taylor didn't hide her exasperation. "That's naive," she said crisply. "No one *ever* 'opens up.' But tell me more tomorrow, Darling. I've got to run." She blew him a kiss and was out the door, the click of her heels echoing on the marble stairs.

Heels? Vaughn thought momentarily. In this weather? She'll ruin her shoes.

3

A half hour later, Taylor steered her car into Brett and Hillary's long circular drive. Fieldstone pavers, intricately geometric in design, sparkled along a two hundred foot path from road to porte cocher. Taylor's house was the family's early twentieth century Victorian which Vaughn would never sell. "It stays in the family," was his mantra. Begun as an elegant country house in the mid 1800's, it had undergone three major additions in its lifetime, then completely gutted and modernized when she moved in. Big enough to get lost in, it was opulent enough to host a queen.

But Hillary and Brett's, built from the ground up with no detail overlooked, was spectacular. Modern Spanish, its clean stucco lines with faux nicks and patches, as though poverty, age or enemy attacks had torn away patches of its stucco, seemed unending. Marble tiles imported from Italy began in the gardens and wended into and throughout the house, and best of all, the Spanish tile roof. Southwestern, the flavor of Texas, Arizona, Mexico. Captivating.

She loved it. She slowed to a crawl and parked her Volvo between Victoria's Mercedes sedan and Sharon's Lamborghini, her husband's favorite car. Now that's a car, she thought. And she had to drive the Volvo when she could have driven her Porsche. Humiliating.

Taylor turned off the windshield wipers slapping hard and fast at nothing, then the motor and looked around for Arthur, Brett and Hillary's driver. No one. She'd have to let herself out. Despite icy flakes and heavy winds, the drive had been uneventful as she had predicted. Nothing had stuck to the road, and now, nothing was coming down. She could have taken her Porsche or the Mercedes, and been perfectly safe, but contending with Vaughn's melodramatic concern would have delayed a quick exit. She got out, slammed the door behind her, and quickened her steps through the front gardens into the foyer. No valet, no housekeeper. Brett must have given the staff the night off.

Then she stood in the foyer and inhaled. Tranquility, quiet, serenity, everything, even the soft flowing water; it was beautiful here. This place was paradise. Palms and tropical plants lined the entrance. Before her spread a botanical garden that rivaled the Rutgers' Gardens with its spectacular plant species. Angel's Trumpets, her favorite, were in full bloom; their pinkish red flowers that could grow up to eighteen feet, hung from bent stems, replicating upside down horns.

These and other eclectic species were fed by a gently cascading waterfall that rippled and fell from a twenty-foot-high stone monument, then wended its way around other exotic plants whose names Taylor would never learn. Its tributaries meandered past stones cut with Aztec relief, their destination, a natural pond supporting wildlife and several esoteric species of fish.

This place was soothing. She felt it every time she entered, and that presented her with a paradox: Taylor wasn't used to serenity. She had never sought it because it had never fit in with her goals. Serenity could weaken her, and she could never allow that to happen. Uneasiness overcame her and she shuddered, suddenly cold. Peaceful? Calming? Qualities like these could destroy her.

Quickening her steps, she reached the foyer's exit quickly, heard the chatter too late and almost collided head-on with Veronica as both women turned right-angled corners at the same time. They squealed in surprise and embraced amidst giggles and laughter. "Leaving? Already?" Taylor asked, realizing they were wearing their coats, keys in hand. She glanced from a very tall Veronica, close to 5'9," to Sharon, little over five feet, who was almost completely hidden behind her taller friend.

"We're finished for tonight," Veronica preened. "Everything's done, invitations, linens, colors, theme, a partial guest list – it's already over four hundred." Her hands were gesticulating above her head. "All of it. Done!"

"All this in what . . ." Taylor glanced at her watch. "in little more than an hour? Impossible!"

"Piece of cake," Sharon responded. "The social director of *The Love Boat* can't match us." They were effusive with self-praise.

"And the cocktail hour, dinner, desserts, cake, floral arrangements, an orchestra?" Taylor protested. She had assumed this, their first face to face work meeting, would have lasted hours.

"Other meetings; other times. Brett will show you. You can change anything you want, but tonight we're done," Veronica said with certainty, "and we've done a very good job."

"We even have the plan to get her there without a hint of suspicion," Sharon added, "the Club, week before their anniversary."

"That will *never* work," Taylor countered. "The second she hears she's going to the Club the week before her anniversary, she'll know, no matter *whose* party you tell her she's attending."

"You think so?" Brett responded, swaggering into the foyer, six feet four inches, barefoot, wearing casual slacks and a pale yellow tennis shirt which accentuated his most recent island tan, his face, and muscular arms. Brett commanded attention and he always got it. Two brothers so similar in facial appearance could not have been more different. "You don't think we can surprise her, huh?"

"That depends," Taylor challenged. "Tell me the plan and I'll answer the question."

"Come," Sharon said, taking Taylor's hand and hurrying her down the hallway into the right wing corridor which led to the great room, spacious enough to host a small ball. Color swatches and sample invitations lay in disarray on an oversized coffee table that could have served a small dinner party. Rough outlines of seating arrangements, guest lists and swatches of linens were strewn over two side-chairs and one oversized leather sofa.

"See, all done, and the outline of our surprise plan is somewhere in this mess." She giggled. "Brett will explain the details," she said quickly. "But we've gotta run. Patrick Swayze is dirty dancing!" They giggled like schoolgirls, hurrying through the foyer to their cars.

"You knew they were leaving this early?"

"Of course," he smiled. "I knew when they were coming, and I knew they'd be leaving now. And I also knew Marcy would be throwing up and giving Hillary her ticket to the play. I planned the whole evening well in advance." He took her coat. "I wanted more time with you. Perfect plan, don't you think?"

Taylor eyed him flirtatiously. "Absolutely."

Brett positioned himself on the armrest, enclosed his hands around the smooth curves of her butt and drew her down. "Staff is off; Veronica and Sharon are gone; Hillary is in the city, Vaughn is home reading a book, and you're here with me for the next five hours. Perfect don't you think, Mrs. Otis-Barrett? I've been waiting patiently for this all day. And you have too," he said with complete confidence.

"Now how would you know that?" She whispered, hiked up her skirt, forced herself down on him, devouring his ear. She shuddered and moved on him, bringing herself closer to orgasm faster than she had imagined. Pantyhose and black lace panties tucked away neatly in her dresser drawer. She smiled inwardly. Good decision.

Her mouth bit into his face and neck; her nails dug into his shoulders. She leaned into him. Heat engulfed her as she rode each savage thrust. Suspended in time for an endless moment, her breath exploded, her body shuddered, convulsing in waves of ecstasy, until she collapsed. She shivered in his arms, completely spent. Her hair was damp; her face was alive with sweat. "Again?" Her breath came in soft, bursts.

"Again, *and* again, Mrs. Otis-Barrett," he gave her a devilish smile, and in one fluid motion, swept her up and carried her upstairs.

4

CASSIE

Cassie navigated through silent Manasquan streets, crossing railroad tracks, passing Wilson Realtors on the right, Seven-11 farther up, and sleeping residents on little side streets, streets that had taken her onto route 34, and would now feed onto 33 heading west. The total distance would be little over sixty miles, miniscule if you plotted its latitude and longitude or marked it with 'to and from' dots on a New Jersey map, but emotionally, it would stretch past infinity.

The sky was dark, hints of sunlight not yet peeking through sinister clouds still on their westward journey after assaulting the denizens of Manasquan with pellets of sleet yesterday. Wishing yawns were voluntary, Cassie tried unsuccessfully to suppress her fourth and checked the clock on the Pinto's dash again. 6:07 a.m. Yup, that's 6:07, and on the road since 5:50. 5:50 a!m! On a Saturday! Oh my God! Who gets up this early on a Saturday?! Normal people are sleeping, but not us.

"I Can Feel It in the Air Tonight" ended and segued to "Thriller" without commercials or DJ interference. Thank goodness for Michael Jackson. If this song can wake up the dead, maybe it can wake me up. But we need more volume, and she turned up the sound.

Her favorite passenger, her precocious just-turned-nine-year-old daughter, was unmoved. Her head still immersed in a very thick book she continued to read by flashlight, ignoring her mother and the heightened volume. Cassie tilted her head in an attempt to check the title, but the book was open at dead center, cover down. From the driver's seat, she'd need a neck two feet long and her own flashlight.

She's shutting me out, Cassie thought, probably for making her get up so early. Or maybe for yanking her out of fifth grade two months after the school year had begun, or out of the elementary school she's attended since kindergarten. Or, if none of the above, maybe because she's leaving all her friends and we're moving to a totally alien destination. Anything else? Yeah. Maybe leaving the Manasquan beach and the ocean she's known since birth. And loved. Would I be in favor of this move if I were nine? Cassie, get real. You're over forty and you're not in favor of leaving it, not now, not ever. If I were nine, I'd hate it. So why am I doing this, she asked herself for the umpteenth time.

Her realtor had had tenants before their house, an expanded cape, was listed. They would be moving in the first of next month, transferring from North Carolina, security, credit check, first month's rent all pre-approved, all in order. No problem there, and Cassie lucked out with movers who had just enough time and space to add the contents of her small house to their truck on its way to Delaware yesterday. If the storm hadn't deluged Manasquan, Belmar, Point Pleasant and a few other neighboring towns, they would have been gone already. Either way, yesterday, today, her comfort level was still zero. She was uprooting herself and her daughter from all that was familiar, on their way to a new job and a new life, and she was still second-guessing herself.

Second-guessing was natural. From an idea that had been in the making for two years, then to reality in three weeks? Too fast! She had read the advertisement in the Asbury Park Press a mere three weeks ago, gotten her first interview the week after, hired the week after that and signed the paperwork this past Thursday. She would be starting first Monday in November, in two days. Guess Dr. Otis-Barrett, now that's a name, couldn't find anyone else who'd make such a rash decision; just her. So after a rush to find a mover, organize paperwork, get Stevie's transcripts, and decide what to take and what to throw out, here they were, on their way.

When they stepped out of their front door this morning, a clean, strong ocean breeze had greeted them, whipping through their hair and slamming their clothes flat against their bodies, like any bona fide strong ocean breeze would do. The Jersey shore had breezes with attitude.

Cassie gulped, her hands tightened on the wheel. She was leaving Manasquan, an address where she had played, laughed, and cried. Here, she had lived the happiest and saddest years of her life. Here had been her Never

Land and her refuge, but it had failed to be her catharsis. Time had whitewashed her surface pain, but the layers underneath? They still clung, like layers of old wallpaper, one pasted over the other, all hidden for eternity under fresh coats of paint.

These, time had not erased. And for this reason, she was leaving, to find a place for new beginnings in a pyrrhic attempt to reclaim whatever future remained. Tears had fallen. Yesterday, full of memories; today full of misgivings. Brian, am I doing the right thing?

Yesterday evening after the storm had run its course, mother and daughter had walked the beach in a farewell tribute to home. Sand had slapped their faces and slipped between tightly closed lips; it had filled their sneakers and socks with grit, as the raging, relentless surf dashed against breakers, lifting Jonathan Livingston seagulls skyward. Giant clams torn up from their beds littered the beach, inviting seagulls to an evening feast. Catering to gluttony, they challenged and battled each other for the biggest, proving that, despite having more than they could ever eat or need, the desire for power danced to its own savage drum beat. Life: beautiful, vicious and cruel. Such was the Jersey shore – as it was everywhere.

So, here they were, early Saturday morning, with a morning sun refusing to glance over its eastern shoulder despite the clocks falling back an hour a week ago, following a route that would take them to their new home and new life, none the worse for having camped out on their living room floor last night after the movers had taken their furniture and belongings. They'd be camping out again tonight once they arrived in Chelsea. No one could unpack in one night. Tonight would be soap, toothbrushes, clean clothes and cereal. No milk yet, but you could eat cereal dry.

The salty air had spring-boarded into their car with them when they had gotten in. Its scent lingered as they drove, but faded with every mile. Now, as Cassie took the exit ramp onto Route 33, it kissed them goodbye. I'll miss you, Cassie thought, choking back tears. I miss you every day, Brian, no matter how hard I try. I just can't say goodbye.

The first bars of "Leather and Lace" brought Cassie back to reality, but did nothing to assuage the pain in her heart. Soft music, delicate and sweet, a mellow alto voice and sensual lyrics about love and forever to follow. Damn, this DJ is reading my mind. "Thriller," my wakeup call, which I definitely needed, and now "Leather and Lace," which I don't!

"Stevie, listen, Honey, It's you." Cassie turned to her daughter. Stevie still had her head face-down in a book the size of a tome. She nodded indifferently. "Stevie? Listen; it's Stevie Nicks, "Leather and Lace," it's you, your song."

"No Mom, her daughter replied dismissively. "It's *your* song, not mine. And she's not me; she's just my eponym."

Cassie was taken aback. What a curt tone. "Stevie, that is definitely unfair. Your father and I named you after her, so it's your song too." Stevie's head remained in the book and Cassie turned down the volume. "And . . . 'my eponym?'" Her daughter's word choice registered. "What nine-year-old uses that word?"

"What, 'my'? 'My' is a possessive pronoun, first person, singular. Kids use it all the time. Adults too."

Cassie glared. "Don't get snippy, young lady. You know *exactly* which word I mean. And, I repeat, what nine-year-old uses it?"

"Well," Stevie replied curtly, "what mother tapes lists of Greek and Latin roots and prefixes on the shower stall door so they're in her daughter's face every time she goes to the bathroom?"

Cassie chuckled. "Okay, okay, you have a point. But I'm giving you tools so you can improve your vocabulary without having to use a dictionary or memorize words that don't have to be memorized. Obviously, it's working."

Smugly, Stevie put down the book, folded her arms mildly defiant. "Prove it."

The typical response from teenagers today, but Stevie wasn't anywhere near 'teen.' "How early does arrogance start in this generation?"

"Okay, Mom, *pleeease* prove it."

"I don't have to. You just proved it for me. You used the word, 'eponym' yourself. Break it down. You know 'Epi' means. . . ?

"Over or above," Stevie shot back.

And "nym?"

"Name, that's easy, like 'synonym,' same name."

"So you pretty much know what 'eponym' means without using a dictionary, just from that horrible list of roots and prefixes that stare at you while you're in the bathroom." A definite tone of victory in her voice.

Stevie's countenance expressed a mixture of impatience, disdain, and satisfaction. Satisfaction won out. Despite her tone, Stevie was a very rational child for nine, as of five days ago. "Okay, you win. I get it."

"Let's build on it," Cassie responded playfully, "and see if you really do. What does 'epiderm' mean?"

"'Derm' means 'skin.' Outer layer of skin."

"Dermatology?"

"'Logy' means 'the study of.' 'Dermatology' means the study of skin.

"Graphology?"

"'Graph' means 'writing.' The study of writing.

"Telegraph." Cassie was shooting words out quickly, and Stevie was responding with the answers just as quickly.

"'Tele' means 'far.' Telegraph means 'writing from 'far.'"

" Epigraph."

Stevie hesitated. This one stopped her. "I'm not sure,' she said, dubiously. Something written over something?"

"Excellent, Kiddo. Something written over or above something, like a short phrase written on a monument. But if your choices were phonograph, teleportation, inscription or pseudonym, you'd pick the right one just from knowing roots and prefixes." Cassie glanced at her daughter who was reluctant to admit her mother was right again. "It would be horrible to have to admit your mother was right twice in less than two minutes, wouldn't it?" Cassie teased.

Silence, except for the drum beat of tires against road and Stevie Nicks' soft crooning voice. They had gone about seven miles on Route 33 with about four to go. "Let me know if you see a sign for Route 133." Cassie changed the subject. "I don't want to miss our exit." The last lines of Cassie's song faded but she continued to sing.

"Mom, you okay?" Stevie asked, seeing that far-away look in her mother's eyes, sorry she had been rude and insensitive to something her mom was so passionate about. Her mom and dad had named her Stevie after her mother's favorite vocalist several years before this song had been released.

"I'm fine," Cassie replied, sneaking a sleeve across her driver's-side eye. A few seconds passed. "Hey," Cassie nodded, her curiosity now directed towards the book. What book *are* you reading? Looks like it's seven hundred, maybe eight hundred pages, or more."

"*Narnia*. Unabridged," Stevie replied with attitude.

"*Narnia*, unabridged, huh?" Oh, for the baby days when they'd put Stevie in a car bed and she'd sleep from one destination to the next. Cassie noticed a smile play on Stevie's lips. "You little pixie! You're just giving me a hard time, aren't you?" Cassie reached over and tickled Stevie's tummy, sending her into peals of laughter. "Now *that's* the way a nine-year-old should be laughing, not sitting here reading a book that's over seven hundred pages. Why not get another one from the back?'

"From the *back*? Of *this* car? Mom, are you serious?"

Cassie's mouth dropped a bit. Without glancing in her rearview mirror, she knew Stevie was right. Her '79 Ford Pinto wagon was not just stuffed, but *so* stuffed not even a tiny space existed to see out the rear window. There wasn't a thing either of them could have gotten from the back, which overflowed with cardboard boxes, a cooler, and plastic bags filled with shoes, clothes, toiletries, linens, cutlery, cooking utensils, everything they would need immediately before classes started Monday. Take one thing out, if that were even feasible, and the mountain could collapse. Grounds and Maintenance would be there to help unload and position furniture, and Dr. Otis-Barrett assured her he'd be there as well, but boxes did not unpack themselves. With tight schedules, lesson plans, students to meet, a total orientation required and no time to unpack and settle in, Camping 101 would be a prerequisite. Yes, they did need everything in the back. "Okay," Cassie capitulated with a smile, "read *Narnia*, unabridged."

She rolled down the window. Exit 133 straight ahead. A country breeze upwards of fifty degrees filled the interior, and Crowded House was singing "Don't Dream It's Over." Cassie turned up the volume and relaxed, heading towards Princeton and a completely new world.

5

FIRST DAY - NOVEMBER 2,
MONDAY, 1987

A little nervous. Yeah, you could say that. Wow, she hadn't felt this nervous since her first day of teaching, what, almost twenty years ago? Had it been that long? Must have; she had begun at twenty-one and here was forty-one. A few years off after Stevie was born, and a two year hiatus several years after that, and bookended in between were students and classrooms and the whole gamut of imparting knowledge and giving kids the tools to get it themselves.

Cassie had driven Stevie to the bus for her first day of school. She would have preferred taking her directly to her classroom, especially the first day, but this was her first day too. They had made one trial run last week. That would have to do. In kindness, though, Dr. Otis-Barrett, Dr. 'O'-'B,' as he was addressed by staff, had excused her from today's faculty meeting, first Monday of every month, which abbreviated each class ten minutes. This would give her ample opportunity to visit Stevie's fifth grade teacher later in the day and find out how day one went.

Right now, however, focused on subject matter, she was walking the quarter mile to Rand Hall where English and literature classes were held, to check out her classroom, a poster portfolio of the Elizabethan Period and early Stuarts, The Globe, and a few of Shakespeare's contemporaries in her attaché. If her predecessor had been as obsessed with the playwright as she was, and from Dr. O/B's description of Steven Draggert, he had been, maybe even more so, then she'd have no need of hers.

Hallways were still. Completely still. Without students, eerie. Empty schools were like morgues. She found her classroom, 110, down the main corridor and off to the right. The door was open. She peeked in apprehensively. Side windows were slightly open and fresh air was filtering in, an uncommonly warm November 2nd. She glanced around quickly and smiled, very pleased with what she saw.

The classroom was delightful. Aside from some blackboard space, colorful posters of the Elizabethan Age lined all four walls. Closest to the door, Shakespeare's profile greeted her ceremoniously. "Hey there, William, how you doin'?" Successive posters showed scenes from *Macbeth* and *King Lear*, the epitome of filial cruelty. *Hamlet* next, followed by *Julius Caesar*, stabbed in the back by his most trusted friend. Then *Othello* and *The Merchant of Venice*. Shylock; revenge foiled.

On the opposite wall were posters of Elizabeth 1, who ascended the throne in 1558. The Ditchley Portrait showed the queen, last of the Tudors, bedecked with diaphanous collar, exquisite brooches, studded crown, standing on the world; the queen, powerful, beloved and very kind to the theatre. Following these, smithies hammered horse-shoes against anvils, scullery maids cleaned and stacked dishes, cooks baked and tended a huge hearth, all in stark juxtaposition to the queen in her accoutered finery. Shakespeare's birthplace, Stratford on Avon, followed. Shakespeare, 1564-1616, master of the human condition through his plays. Contiguous to his poster was Anne Hathaway's family home. Ann Hathaway, Shakespeare's wife, eight years his senior, who bore him three children.

Passing the first Stuart, James 1, who succeeded Elizabeth, Cassie faced the back wall and pictures of the Inns of Court which provided the model for the first the-atres, and following those, detailed posters of The Globe. Suddenly her peripheral vision caught something in the rear far corner. Astonished, she quickened her steps. There on a round table sat a wooden replica of The Globe, as authentic in miniature as were documented drawings of the actual playhouse.

"Wow!" She uttered softly with reverence, like a kid who'd gotten the first present on her Christmas list, a gift so spectacular, she'd never believed she'd see it under the tree. "Look at this."

Hesitant to touch anything at first, she abandoned her restraint, dropped her attaché and began toying with movable parts. She lifted the trap door that would bring forth trees and trappings, the three witches in *Macbeth*, ghosts of Hamlet's father and Julius Caesar. She drew back the drapes where the musicians sat, then examined the boxes where the upper class sat, never to mingle with the groundlings, those unsavory people who stood in the pit and plied their trades. She picked up a few. Maybe she held a tradesman or a pickpocket; maybe a seamstress, weaver, or prostitute. Theatres were built outside city limits to avoid people like these, and were eventually closed by the Puritans.

She glanced at the wall clock; barely ten minutes before first period. She placed the groundlings in the pit, took her attaché to her desk, situated behind a huge round table, *the* round table, like King Arthur and his Knights. It was large enough to seat twelve or thirteen students who responded to each other and their instructor face to face. She pulled out notes, pens, pencils, class rosters, seating charts and her lesson for today.

A sense of anticipation bubbled inside her. She had studied her rosters carefully, memorized most of the names in her classes, and now had only to connect names to students and memorize the match. She was good at names. With the help of seating charts, she could have five classes, twenty-five students minimum per class, memorized by the end of the first week. One name on this roster, no, make that two, intrigued her. The first, Parker. Parker Otis-Barrett. If he didn't look like his father, she'd have a pretty good idea of what to expect from his mother. The other name, well, she'd wait and see. She could be way off base on that one. "What's in a name?" she thought. Well, we'll soon find out.

Other names intrigued her but for a different reason. Emelia Bronston, Rachel Greer, Elizabeth Stanack, and Gloria Morgan, these names were intriguing because this was the first year girls' names appeared on any faculty member's roster. Prior to this year, Chelsea Academy did not admit girls. Since its founding almost two hundred years ago, it had been boys only. For the first time in its history, the school had opened its doors to females. What an amazing time, and she and Stevie would be part of it.

Murmuring voices growing louder. Excitement surged; the wall clock read 7:55 a.m. Get ready, Cassie. You're their new teacher little more than a month after their iconic professor died. Be sensitive, she cautioned. This may be more difficult for them than for you.

Six feet of skinny, shock of red hair, freckles, khaki pants, careless long sleeved shirt, unbuttoned at the cuffs, hanging over his pants, entered first, followed by heavier, round-faced, brown hair with piercing blue eyes. They stopped when they saw her, nodded ceremoniously then apprehensively walked to their seats. Three girls followed in succession: the first had almond, dark brown, almost black, exotic eyes; deep brown hair; olive complexion, about 5' 6," dressed modestly in a tan sweater and deep brown skirt. Too monotone for most, but for her, stunning. Young males opposing coed might easily reverse their position because of her. A distraction? Yes, until she became a friend.

Next in line: pretty blond, perky, petite, cute, hazel eyes, no more than 5'3". The third - athletic, dirty blond, bright blue eyes, tall, with amazing posture. Cassie felt herself pull back her shoulders. Three more boys, one, buzzed hair, military look; another, Asian-American, the third, blond, muscular, stocky, walked in bunched together, followed by the fourth girl, blue eyes, almost violet, strawberry blond hair, with the tightest curls Cassie hadn't seen since high school. Lastly, tenth and eleventh, two more boys entered: the first, dark, tall, olive complexion, dreamy eyes, and the last one, distinctive. He was not quite like his father, but the resemblance was clear - very tall, fair, with a captivating smile. Of course, he'd be last. With his father dean of the school, he might be last every day were he so inclined, but no quick judgments. Maybe he wouldn't exploit his father's position. Let's see what the days bring.

Eleven students took their seats around the table, her seat closest to her desk. All eyes fixed on her. Same as public school, she thought, except there, she'd have a minimum of twenty-five pairs of eyes looking at her, seated in five or six vertical rows in five classes throughout the day. And business people think teaching is a piece of cake, she thought derisively. "Good morning." Her first address to the class. Lots of 'firsts' these past few days. Well, how did her voice sound? Too high, too low? Too impersonal, too conciliatory? Oh, come on, Cassie, just address the class and jump right in. This is your forte. Get on with it.

"Ironically, I can't welcome you, because you've been here since September; I'm the one who hasn't, so I hope you'll welcome me. I'm Mrs. Komsky, with a 'K,' replacing Professor Draggert, who will be tough to follow. My objectives will be to make the transition as smooth as possible and to continue the fine academic excellence he brought to the classroom. During consulting sessions, I encourage you to discuss any strategy you believe may make your experience in our class more comfortable and more receptive to learning about Shakespeare, his life, his time, his plays, and most importantly, his legacy about life to us all.

"He died in 1616, so, what's kept his plays alive since then and how do we relate to a playwright who wrote almost four hundred years ago? Customs, costumes, and accoutrements have changed. London is no longer a walled city; we are no longer an agrarian society; we don't plow our own fields, grow our own food, raise chickens, cattle and sheep, milk our cows, weave wool and make our clothing from it.

"Today, we shop at supermarkets, drive cars, use telephones, and watch television. What, then, could we possibly have in common with Shakespeare's age and the denizens he wrote for?" She paused, knowing she had asked a rhetorical question. "Think about it because we're coming back to it as soon as I connect you to the names on my roster. So, please, in alpha order, identify yourself when I say your name." She smiled. "And if I mispronounce your name, kindly correct me. I want to get it right."

An "A" began her list. "Jason Abrams?" The heavy-ish, round-faced, brown-haired boy with piercing blue eyes acknowledged with a nod, a smile, and a slightly raised hand at the end of the table. Cassie nodded affably. "Emilia Bronston." A wide, captivating smile emanated from the athletic, dirty-blond-haired girl with bright blue eyes and amazing posture. Cassie returned the smile and felt her shoulders instinctively draw back again. "Samir Gibran." Cassie pronounced the 'G' as a 'J.'

"It's 'Gibran,'" said a voice across the table, pronouncing a hard G as in 'girl.' "And he doesn't speak English."

Cassie turned. "And *your* name, sir?" Cassie responded.

"Parker. Parker Otis-Barrett." A thin, cryptic smirk was witness to his father's position in the school, and thus, by filial connection, his position as well.

"Thank you for your input, Mr. Otis-Barrett, but I believe the G is pronounced J.

"It's like the poet, Kahlil Gibran, *if* you're familiar with his book," Parker shot back, condescendingly, with emphasis on 'if,' and again pronounced a hard G.

"Yes, Mr. Otis-Barrett, I am familiar with *The Prophet*, by Kahlil Gibran, but the hard G which you've assumed to be the correct pronunciation is the G from *our* alphabet. However, that's not how it's pronounced in Arabic, which, I believe, would be the language of Mr. Gibran's heritage."

"He *is* Arabic. He's Lebanese," Parker said. But a G is still a G, not a J."

"Your reasoning is correct, but you're basing your pronunciation on the English alphabet, twenty-six characters, one of which is a G. The Arabic alphabet has twenty-eight characters," Cassie said emphatically, "but despite its having two more letters than ours, not one of those twenty-eight characters is a G, only a J. So," she said emphatically, "his name could never be pronounced with a hard G in his native language, unless, perhaps, you were in Egypt, where J is pronounced G, but not in Lebanon." She glanced at Samir, who was looking directly at her, then turned back to Parker.

"As I said, I'll do my very best to pronounce every student's name correctly, and the correct pronunciation for Samir's is a soft J as you'd pronounce 'gymnasium,' not a hard G as in 'girl.' But thank you for your input." She nodded ceremoniously and moved on to the next name.

Samir stared at her, a quizzical look on his face. Several students exchanged furtive glances amongst themselves, and Parker, somewhat chagrined, brooded, trying to come to terms with his error. Maybe he'd research his position on his own.

"Rachel Greer?" Cassie continued, and the perky, petite, pretty blond smiled. Samir bowed his head again and slipped deeper into his seat. Hmm, Cassie thought, something going on there?

She finished the roster and made some quick adjustments in her seating chart. Either Draggert had not placed them in alpha order or they had changed their seats in the last five weeks. It didn't matter. With such a small class, she'd know their names in a day or two. Now, to the lesson.

"Okay, roster complete. It's Shakespeare's turn, and yours. I began with a supposition that perhaps there's no reason to learn about Shakespeare. Hey, almost four hundred years? I don't keep a pair of shoes even four! Do you?" Several of the girls chuckled. More than likely, they didn't keep them more than one, but she had connected, even just a little.

"We're a wash and wear society. We cast off wearing apparel season to season, use a microwave to heat precooked meals, a washer/dryer to clean our clothes – or dry cleaning, and hop in our cars to go just about anywhere. Right?" A few shrugs; no contradictions.

"But, do we still love?" She paused not really waiting for a response. "Do we still hate? Do we still feel resentment when we want something, or someone, that somebody else has?" Now a few squirmed in their seats. She was getting close. "Do we still feel compassion, perhaps when a family member or even a pet dies?" More discomfort. "Do we still experience greed, excessive ambition, excessive pride? Still no verbal responses. "Ever been jealous?" This question was unsettling. "Ever want to destroy someone because you were?" She glances around, making direct eye contact. They were avoiding her eyes. "Think about your family, your friends, your everyday interactions with them. Anyone hungry for power? Anyone excessively proud? Anyone betray your trust? Anyone ever stab you in the back?" She said this with emphasis, and it provoked overt reactions. Parker stared at Samir; Samir and Rachel exchanged furtive glances, Gloria turned away; Matthew and Elizabeth averted their eyes. Yup, this one got to them.

"Because these traits are in Shakespeare's characters, and these same traits are in us all, all of us, centuries later, as I'm sure professor Draggert emphasized. That's what makes Shakespeare real. That's what makes him timeless, and *that's* why we read him today. Cut him out of the curriculum, and you cut out people who felt the same human emotions you feel. He lived just as we do, and so did his characters. And that's the greatness of Shakespeare, of any classic - timelessness."

She extended her hand around the room, "Except for some front board space, every wall in this classroom has a poster depicting some aspect of Shakespeare's life and time period: royalty, the queen; peasant life, cooks and craftsmen; theatre, The Globe, and an outstanding replica of the stage on which Shakespeare's plays were performed.

"I'd like you to study the posters that represent the plays. I'm sure you already have, but do it again as a re-fresher. Then take a problem, a conflict, or an emotion from your life, or create one, a plausible one, that par-allels a scenario from one of Shakespeare's plays, and substantiate it by referencing the act and scene, or the lines you're using to develop your scenario. We're read-ing *Hamlet*, which we'll start again at act 1, so you might want to stress him, but your syllabus says you've read *Julius Caesar* on sophomore level, *King Lear* as juniors, and be-gan this year with *The Merchant of Venice.* Reference any of these plays, including *Othello* and *Macbeth*, with which you're familiar from abstracts. Think about this individ-ually or collaborate, brainstorm, use the text, whatever. Take fifteen or twenty minutes. Make an outline, what-ever makes it easier for you. The parallel is what's im-portant. I'll walk around to see how you're doing. Any questions, ask. Then we talk."

Cassie paused, about to collect her papers and charts. "Oh, one last item before we start: Is there anyone who would not want to be addressed by his or her first name?" She expected one hand to go up.

It did.

6

CLASS CONTINUES

Cassie did a count-down at fifteen, seventeen, nineteen minutes, then redirected the class' attention to herself. All but Samir had worked in pairs or three's. As she had walked around the room, she had skimmed two good scenarios, but that was all. One described a materialistic wife pushing her husband too far up the corporate ladder – a contemporary *Macbeth*. The second depicted two deceitful sisters plotting against the third for their father's favor. *Lear.* Both were good parallels to Shakespearean characters and conflicts, but she had expected more. Thirteen minutes of class time remained. Let's approach the assignment in reverse, she decided.

"Before we read and discuss your responses, I'll present a scenario that parallels a theme in one of Shakespeare's plays, and you tell me which play. That will help you evaluate your scenario before you present it. Be sure to justify your answer by referencing the play and situation. Clear?" No objections. "Here it is: You've been elected captain of the football team." Emelia rolled her eyes. "Ladies, pretend it's captain of the field hockey team; but let's do football. Other than the objective being to get the ball in the opponent's goal, I don't know the first thing about field hockey. You can teach me another time." Emelia was satisfied.

"Stereotypically, a captain's veins are sprinkled with a little conceit." The emphasis on 'little,' was sarcastic, and they got it. Several laughed; Parker did not. "You're captain. In high school, that's a big deal. And, as captain, you start implementing new ideas that you believe will make the team better. They're your ideas; you're captain; you implement them arbitrarily; end of story.

"Dan, your best friend, is co-captain. Idealistic, he looks up to you, but thinks the team is fine as it is and that you're overstepping your bounds, pushing too hard, maybe for your own glory. Dan's friend, Jonathan, plays fullback. He's a little undersized for a fullback, so he makes second string. In his mind though, he's been cheated. He believes he's good enough to be a starter and that he didn't make first string because of you. He's in it for self-adulation, not the team, and he'll blame anyone so he doesn't have to face reality. Got a good picture of Jonathan in your mind?" Murmurings and nods tell her they do.

"Okay, so what does Jonathan do next? He plays on Dan's naivety. 'He'll ruin the team,' he complains to Dan. 'He's working us too hard. All he cares about is praise or getting a scholarship.' The problem is that Dan believes him, and he starts to undermine you 'for the good of the team.' Her fingers enclose an invisible phrase within invisible quotation marks. "Is this scenario plausible in your world or the world of high school athletics?"

Cassie waits for a response, heart beating a little fast. She has presented her case and thinks it's a good one, but do they? Does it make sense to them, and can they relate it to one of Shakespeare's plays? Her gut feeling says yes. She is positive someone will respond, even if it's just for a grade. They all need a grade, and that would come from her.

Emilia Bronston makes eye contact. Cassie responds with a smile and pulls her shoulders back. My posture will definitely improve by the end of the year, she thinks. Emelia returns the smile and sheepishly says, "Yes." Then she withdraws the contact, glancing at her classmates. But, gutsy, she adds, "Sure, it's plausible. I mean, it happens all the time. You get elected to something and somebody whose jealous tries to bad-mouth you or bring you down."

"It's not like they can do any better," Matthew Welsley, Asian-American on his mother's side, interjects, "because they can't. But they're jealous, like Emelia said. You have the position and they don't. Maybe they're jealous because they *know* they can't do it as well?" He shrugged his shoulders and ran his hand through jet-black, thick hair, without realizing his point has been so intuitive.

"That happens all the time; it doesn't have to be a sport or a club." Rachel Greer added. "It could happen if you like someone but the person you like likes someone else. Then you make up lies about that person, who has no way of refuting them except to say they're not true. But the damage is done and you can't undo it. All you know is the guy you like stops talking to you."

Perceptive, Cassie thought; maybe someone's done just that to her. Cassie notices Samir. So far, he hasn't said a word or made eye contact with anyone. Dr. O/B had given her essays Draggert had collected from his classes the first two weeks of school. From them, Cassie knew Samir understood English very well. His writing was excellent. So, although Samir wasn't speaking English, or anything, it was not because he couldn't.

"Anyone disagree with what's been said? Another viewpoint? Anybody?" No hands went up; no additional comments. "I'm concluding, then, that this scenario is plausible and that in some way, you've experienced something similar." No disagreement, not even from young Mr. Otis-Barrett. "So then," she began, "from your having read or discussed several of Shakespeare's plays, which play has something similar to the scenario I presented?"

Silence. The wall clock ticked second after second, loudly. Pencils thumped the table, some feet tapping. A few reviewed the table of contents, hoping for a flicker of enlightenment or to refresh their memory. "Look at the pictures on the wall. Take a close look. Reread your notes from Professor Draggert, skim through play summaries in your text and from those you've already read. Think. Analyze. Synthesize. Collaborate again, if it'll help."

Several students turned their chairs to examine the posters. A few paired off again. Six feet of skinny, shock of red hair with freckles, Mason Haworth got up from his seat and walked over to the posters, studying them closely. Interminable silence. His classmates turned pages, feet tapping out rhythms. The soft glow of overhead lighting illuminated the room, and a morning that had begun with bright sunshine was turning dreary. Cassie got up from her chair and walked around the table, peering over shoulders. What play were they reviewing, what scene, what characters, what lines? She had simplified it down to bare essentials for them. No spoon-feeding here. Suddenly, Mason blurts out, *Julius Caesar!* Comments, consternation, mumbled denials emanate from his classmates.

"Where'd you get that answer, Mason?" Zachary Wellington challenged. Zach's buzzed hair was typical military, unlike his peers. "I figured *Othello*, or maybe *Macbeth*. Iago's jealous of Othello, Macbeth and his Lady want the throne for themselves. Caesar? No way."

"Yeah, Mason," two or three voices challenged, "How'd you come up with that?"

Mason wouldn't be rushed. He stared at the poster of Marc Antony looking over Caesar's body. "Because," he said finally, each word deliberate, "Mrs. Komsky's scenario presented three characters, the minor one being the instigator. Right?" He turned to the class with attitude and they nodded approval. He was sure of himself, now.

"Iago's jealous, but he doesn't use another character to influence Othello. He does it himself. So *Othello* can't be the parallel scenario. Neither can *The Merchant of Venice*. Nobody talks Shylock into the 'pound of flesh' contract he makes. *Hamlet* is about indecision and retribution. Hamlet's father's ghost accuses his brother of his murder, but Hamlet is responsible for so many other deaths before he gets to his uncle, there's no direct cause and effect there, and there's no jealousy, either, and no idealism. So that's not the same scenario either. *Macbeth* comes close. Lady Macbeth does talk her husband into killing the king, but for a different reason. She's greedy for power, so you could say she's jealous, but idealistic? No. They don't kill Duncan for the good of Scotland. They want the throne for themselves.

"It's Brutus who's idealistic. He doesn't want to be king; he wants to save Rome from Caesar because he thinks he's become a despot, and Cassius just feeds his fears and idealism. Same with Dan. He doesn't want to be captain. He only wants to prevent the captain from hurting the team, and Jonathan feeds his fears." He turns to Cassie. That's why I think the parallel to your scenario is *Julius Caesar*. What do you think, Mrs. Komsky?"

Cassie chuckled. "What do I think? I think, Mason, if there's a time I can't be here, you can take my seat and be class facilitator." The class laughed, everyone except Parker, but he suppressed it. Mason had earned the class' respect in the academic arena, and, from her accolade, she had earned his. Well, she thought, it's a beginning.

7

FIRST EVENING

The volume was way too high. Hannibal Smith had just leaped from Murdock's chopper, hovering at second story level, to rescue Face from ground snipers holed up in a makeshift blind in some forsaken Central American jungle, Mr. T. picking them off from behind. All secure. Rush to the chopper. Lift-off successful; destination, the Texas border. A-Team safe. Another job well-done. "I love it when a plan comes together," puffs Hannibal.

Music was blaring from Stevie's stereo in the living room and Cassie was sparring with "Jeopardy" on her twelve inch TV in the kitchen. "Hastings, 1066," states Alex Trebek. "What is the Norman Invasion!" Cassie shouts. "Easy! Oh, no, don't pick science," she moans. "I'm horrible in science."

"Stevie, come help clear the table and load the dishwasher." She puts ketchup, mayo and other condiments into the frig and sponges the patches of table she clears. "I've still got lesson plans to do and it's 6:40!" No response.

Cassie glances into the semi-bare living room surrounded with cardboard boxes, cooking gear and vital necessities they had unloaded from their car two days ago. Everything that had overstuffed the car had provided them with towels, toiletries, cutlery, dishes, cereal for breakfast, hamburgers and green beans for supper. A grocery list was in the making for their first trip to the local market, but yesterday and today had been a success, except for her hearing, which was being challenged in stereo.

Stevie sat perched on the edge of the sofa, mindlessly watching commercials, surrounded by books and simultaneously doing the packets of back-work from September her teachers had given her for language, math and science. Stevie could study and learn through anything.

"I need help cleaning up and loading the dishwasher, Hon. Ten minutes max."

"Okay, Mom," Stevie said without offering any resistance. She pushed her books aside and got up to help her mom.

"And please lower that sound to a level that will allow me to think."

"Okay, Mom. I'll probably need to do that too when I am your age."

Cassie was startled. "You little imp! Consider that statement an act of war!" And without thinking, she splattered Stevie with sudsy water from her dripping sponge. Stevie squealed, raced past her mother to the kitchen and returned fire with water from her drinking glass, peppering her mother's hair, face, and T-shirt. "That's it, young lady. You're toast!" Cassie ran to the sink and grabbed the spray nozzle a second before Stevie. Forty-one and nine, dueling it out for the hose, both with hands on the trigger.

An uncontrollable nozzle can cover lots of territory, counters, walls, the floor, and each other. Hair, shirts, jeans, slippers. Nothing was out of bounds. "Let go!" Cassie shouted.

"No, Ma! You let go!" But neither would and neither did. The duel raged despite droplets of water falling from the ceiling. Just as the stalemate seemed interminable and the apartment would sink like Atlantis, the doorbell buzzed. They both froze. "Who? . . ." Stevie questioned, the only word she could utter. Cassie shrugged her shoulders, giving Stevie a one-second hiatus to break free and race upstairs. No one was going to see *her* like this. She'd let her mom do 'cleanup,' literally and figuratively.

"Great. Just great," Cassie grumbled, pushing straggling strands of blondish wet hair behind her ears, wiping water from her eyes and face with the only dry spot that remained on her T-shirt, and surveying the damage they had caused. What a mess.

Oh gees, she remembered, student visitations. Monday evening and her first evening to be on call. No, wait, Dr. O/B had excused her from the faculty meeting and this; so she hadn't expected anyone, not her first day. And weren't they supposed to give some kind of notification or use the office entrance accessible from the dorm? Didn't matter. She'd apologize for her appearance and make up some story to justify the flood in the kitchen. Whoever it was could wait in the living room or the conference room while she changed into dry clothes. She hoped it was one of the girls. That would make the situation less awkward. She walked towards the door, dripping, jeans sticking to her legs, her shirt clinging to her body, her feet squishing in their slippers. She kicked them off and, before opening the door, cautiously checked the peephole.

"Oh my God," she whispered, and backed away, shocked. "Oh my God! Dr. O/B! Oh my God, oh my God, oh my God, she uttered in rapid succession. "What do I do now?" Her heart raced like a schoolgirl's. She paced back and forth in front of the door. "Do I tell him to come back? Tell him to wait while I change? Tell him . . . tell him . . . tell him *what*?"

He pressed the buzzer again, a hint of impatience, implying, "I'm waiting and I don't like it." Well, here she was, the real her, the 'her' that people got when they dropped in unannounced. So, he'd get what he'd get, and deal with it. She steeled herself, held up her head and opened the door, boldly, with a broad smile and "Hi'!

In slow motion, she watched his countenance change from an initial smile, to slight consternation, to open-mouthed surprise and, finally, as his eyes dropped to her soaked T-shirt, which could easily have won her the wet T-shirt contest at Manasquan's Nor'easter Bar, home to ear-splitting music and drunken brawls, to shock. He emitted a slight gasp, stood transfixed in disbelief, his pale face turning red. Awkward? Oh yes.

In his hand was a small 4 x 5 booklet. "Is that for me?" She asked awkwardly. Say anything; say anything. She would have asked what the temperature was in China if it would have eased the tension.

Vaughn, about 6'4" with a slightly athletic build that needed serious coaxing, recovered a bit, shook off his initial shock, and stammered, "Y-Yes. I thought you might like to have this year's student handbook for a reference . . . or whatever. Sorry." He shook his head. "Sorry, I should have called. I should have waited for morning . . . I . . . I was in the area." Seconds passed. Seconds of silence. "Well," he rallied, "I've got to get back. Have a nice evening." He forwarded the handbook to her and she thanked him, taking it gingerly from his hand. "And if I can help you with anything, just let me know."

And just like that, he was gone, leaving Cassie bewildered, stunned, and shaken. She closed the door slowly and walked into the kitchen trancelike. Her robotic hands grasped the huge mug of tea she had left on the counter. Collapsing into a kitchen chair, still dripping, she sipped - warm, cold, whatever. Who cared? Her mind was scrambled. Had this been real? She held a small student handbook in her trembling hand; obviously, it had. "Oh, my God," she murmured. She put her mug down and her fingers laced through her hair. "Dr. O/B, dean of the school, here? With me looking like this?" This was way beyond real. This was *surreal*.

"Mom, who was it?" Stevie said softly. She had tiptoed down the stairs to her mom sitting in the kitchen. "I heard a man's voice. Is he gone?" In less than three minutes, she had changed into dry clothes and had damp-dried her shoulder-length curls with her diffuser. Her nine-year-old daughter, perfectly coifed, while she had just faced down a totally embarrassing encounter looking like a rat leaving the *Titanic*! Cassie did not reply.

"Who was it, Mom?" Stevie asked again, wanting an answer. She seemed bemused at her mother's behavior. It was unlike Cassie to be at a loss for words.

"Oh, just Dr. O/B dropping off this booklet," she answered sarcastically. "No big deal."

"And he saw you like that?!" Stevie squealed. She clasped her hand over her mouth, almost bursting into laughter. "Oh my God, you must be so embarrassed!"

Cassie leaped out of her seat as though she had been sitting on a tight coil, and raced for the spray nozzle. In her grasp, trigger depressed, she sprayed to its limit. Stevie barreled through the living room and up the stairwell, way beyond the reach of the nozzle pressure, laughing uncontrollably. "Mom, chill," she laughed. What's the worst he can think?'

"I don't know Stevie, "Cassie said sarcastically. "What *is* the worst he can think?"

"That you're a fox!"

"Stevie, do both of us a favor tonight," she shouted after her. "Stay in your room!"

8

CASSIE LEARNS ABOUT SAMIR

Tuesday and Wednesday proved as positive as Monday had been. All her classes had given outstanding anecdotes paralleling current experiences with themes and situations from Shakespeare's plays, and today they had begun *Hamlet*. Surprisingly, two students had stopped by to talk during yesterday's student consultations, Tracie Houston from period four, and Gloria Morgan from first.

Tracie's parents had divorced several years prior, and her mother had little time for this rebellious offspring who was blossoming into a beautiful non-conforming ingénue. Money no problem, off to private school she went, armed with the ability to speak eloquently and to co-captain a girls' field hockey team in its infancy. Did a girl who fit no prototype belong here? She had wanted to know. Easy answer - she was exactly the type who belonged here, as long as she was ready to cause polarization and be rejected by the opposing side. Hey, that was life. Go for it.

First period, Gloria Morgan, the girl with the tight, tight, strawberry blond curls, had come to talk, but not about herself. Gloria was hypothetically concerned about a hypothetical conflict between two hypothetical students whose parents would most likely hate each other. Okay, so we're dealing with a hypothetical Montague/Capulet situation, yes? Sort of, says Gloria, and then says no more. She has homework and she'd better get to it. "Gloria, let's talk about this some more," Cassie says. Gloria nods and her curls bounce up and down, highlighting a round face with high cheekbones and perfectly shaped lips. An effervescent personality gives the impression she hasn't a care in the world, but Cassie thinks she's deeply concerned about something. Pay close attention to the kids she hangs out with, she thinks.

Cassie was also pleased that she had not encountered Dr. O/B, not even in the dining center during lunch where she had seen him sitting with students Monday. That was a relief. She still had not overcome the embarrassment from her wet T-shirt debacle Monday evening. A little more time and it'll all disappear. Maybe he's hoping for that too. Even now, as she wove her way around campus using the buildings diagram she'd been given when she had been hired, she was consciously happy that she had gotten to the central office of Smythe Hall, the administration building, a two-story all-brick structure with Ivy League written all over it, without having run into him.

Her destination was Guidance, and no more than half the length of the first floor corridor, a brown door, opaque glass panel, large front door plate read, "Counselors Office;" no different from any other school she'd been in. The outer office had the same public school fit as well. George Washington and the Declaration of Independence on one wall, John F. Kennedy, Lincoln, and Martin Luther King, Jr. on the longer one. Long counters from one wall to the next, desks behind counters, one receptionist typing, three immersed in phone conversations and a fifth, impeccably dressed in a deep wine-colored pinstriped suit; underneath, a white tailored shirt with crisp pleats. She stood at the far end of the right counter, looked directly at Cassie and offered a smile. Such a warm feeling when you're met with a smile. People should do it more often.

"Hello," she said, walking towards Cassie with her hand extended. "I'm Melissa Donelly. Since I've been here for thirteen years and know everyone on the Chelsea faculty, I assume you are Steven Draggert's replacement." Thoughtfully, she grimaced. "Oooh, I imagine you've had your fill of that title by now. I would. Cassie. That's it, isn't it?"

"Formally, it's Cassandra, but everyone calls me Cassie." She smiled such a wide smile that her dimples came alive.

"Okay, Cassie, welcome. Do you have an appointment with one of the counselors?"

"No, but I should have called for one." Cassie indicated the frenetic secretarial pool. "Everyone's busy."

"Well, we have two senior level counselors, Dr. Goodman and Ms. Walsh. Let's see what we can do." She walked to her desk, the far one against the wall overlooking the athletic fields, and pulled up the computer screen that displayed the counselors' schedules. "You might be in luck. Dr. Goodman is available this hour for consultations and should be in his office right now. He has no appointments scheduled. I'm certain he could manage a few minutes for you. Let's see."

Cassie turned to follow, but her attention caught a glimpse of the football field. Practice seemed to be in high gear. At this point in the season, scouting reports had been done a number of times on the teams Chelsea played. So, first team offense was out there running against our opponent's defense. Did our reverse fool them? Did we protect the back side? Did our quarterback throw well from the pocket or from the run? Every play was practiced repeatedly; every play our coach felt would be successful against our opponents' defense to put the game in our favor.

Cassie knew this from years of watching every Giants game in every season for more than a decade, and from watching high school scrimmages and games when she taught. Now her focus was primarily on the quarterback, and she squinted to get a sharper look. Although helmets and distance made it impossible to see faces, there was something familiar about this tall fellow as he motioned the offense into the huddle and called the play. His gait, mannerisms, height, size - she could see all that from here. "The tall boy with his arm up?" Melissa asked, noticing Cassie's focus. "That's Parker Otis-Barrett, the dean's son. He's captain."

Cassie's sigh said it all. "Why am I not surprised?" She thought about the football analogy she had depicted Monday.

"No, no. He's good," Melissa replied, indicating merit, not nepotism, had earned Parker his position.

"Outstanding, in fact. He's being recruited by several top schools. Very athletic. He swims, too. Oh," she paused, "are you going to the game Saturday?" She asks as she motions Cassie towards the center hallway. Cassie considers Melissa's question. She had never thought about attending a football game, or any game for any sport. She knew Chelsea had football, basketball and other sports, but she never considered being a spectator. "You really should," Melissa encouraged.

They stopped halfway down the corridor. Two doors, two offices on opposite sides of the hall. "We're tied for first place and it's a sure thing for division champs. If we win our next two games, we win the Division Trophy. Weekend after this is Homecoming. You know that, don't you?" Cassie shook her head. She had thought of nothing except becoming acclimated in the classroom. "You have a daughter, I think?" Melissa added. Cassie nodded.

"Then you have to go. She'll love it. Sit with me. I'll introduce you to some of the gals. Some of the guys sit with us, too. Know anything about football?"

"Some," Cassie replied.

"Well, if you want to learn more, you will with these guys around. They eat and drink first downs."

A quick courtesy knock and Melissa led Cassie into the office on the left, Dr. Goodman's office. A tall, stocky man near fifty, full head of gray with a wave that plopped itself onto his forehead daring him to remove it, rose from his chair and nodded. He stood an inch or two over six feet. His pale yellow long-sleeved shirt complemented his ruddy complexion, deep green eyes, and fit him so well it telegraphed a man who kept himself in excellent shape.

Most likely works out daily or close to it, Cassie thought. Most likely was also athletic in younger days. Maybe he shoots hoops with the guys now. Or plays golf. Ugh! Such a proper game. "Dr. Goodman, this is Mrs. Komsky, Steven Draggert's . . ." and she stopped. "She's our new senior level Shakespeare teacher." She turned to Cassie and smiled.

"Please, it's Walter," he replied. His eyes were warm and expressive.

"Cassie," she responded.

Melissa started out the door. "Nice to have met you Cassie. Hope to see you at the game."

"Thanks, Melissa. Maybe you will."

Walter's office was brightly lit, and reflected light from outside. About as big as her bedroom, it was set against a panorama of the field house and the stadium, bringing the world of sports directly into his office. Sports. In high school, sports were not the sensationalized events the media showed, with glitz and megabucks contracts. Not even the high profile of college. At the high school level, it was the game itself replicating life in its basic setting around which a community assembled as one and poured their energy and life blood into developing character and morality into their kids, instilling character and the ability to strive. It was a game of intensity, its struggle, its dynamic; it was a metaphor being played out in front of you. It was here you picked yourself up if you got hit, were gracious if you won, accepted defeat if you lost, and went on from there. Work harder, go beyond your limits, practice, never stop improving; never let it defeat you, just as in the classroom; just as in life.

Sunlight streamed through the windows, between wide slats of all-wood blinds, not the old-fashioned aluminum kind she had grown up with when her mom had replaced worn-out shades. She shielded her eyes and scanned the field, trying to focus on Parker. Walter walked around his desk and stood at her side.

"I know," he uttered with self-absorbed satisfaction, acknowledging she had been focusing on the field. "Great view." He turned to her, his hand gesturing to the window and beyond. "It's one of the reasons I accepted the counselor's position here so many years ago. I could have made more money in public school and three or four times that amount doing private counseling, which I did when I *was* doing private counseling," he turned to her and smiled, "but the idea of working with kids who think they've got it all mapped out for them yet have no clue how tenuous it all is, and then have to fight it out on an athletic field of battle where everything levels out . . . I couldn't pass it up. It intrigued me. And so, here I am." He looked at her. "What about you, Cassie? What brings you to Chelsea Academy?"

His question surprised her. She had not expected to be questioned about herself, and she hesitated, unable to think of a reply. She knew why she had accepted the position, but did she really want to tell a stranger - or anyone, for that matter?

But for some reason, Walter expected a reply and intensified his eye contact. "I'm sorry," he added. "I don't mean to be forward or pry, but I like to know a little about the people I work with apart from their students, maybe something less formal than an application or a transcript."

At this point, most people would have said anything or redirected the question to something else, but Cassie couldn't; she had no response. She looked at Walter in silence as memories collided into a tragic montage. Realizing his two attempts had been non-productive, and the silence becoming awkward, Walter returned to the professional context of his job. "Okay, how can I be of assistance?" He gestured her to the side-armed, padded office chair facing his.

"One of my students concerns me," she began. "Samir Gibran." Walter's reaction was instantaneous, his facial expression confirming the problem. "He hasn't spoken since Monday, my first day. Not one word, and according to Parker," she paused, "Parker Otis-Barrett," she added, "in case there's more than one Parker on senior level, Samir hasn't spoken since the school year began." Walter nodded but remained silent. "Is there anything you can tell me that could help me help him?"

Walter returned to his chair. "I can give you a very succinct answer to that question without consulting my files, but to be as definitive as possible, give me a minute, and I can tell you a lot."

He presses a few keys and his desktop hums to life. "And no, there's only one Parker on senior level here at Chelsea," he adds as he types. "And everyone knows who he is." He opens a few files, pulls up the senior roster and hits "G." A roster of G's appears. He hits "S," and Samir's file appears on screen. Walter skims and scrolls, scanning write-ups, summaries and evaluations. Then he faces her.

"It's not pretty but here it is: Samir came to us this year as a senior; so it's his first year here, which means he's a senior drifting in a sea of kids who've interacted with each other for several years, some of them beginning as freshman, which is as early as a kid can begin. Used to be we'd admit eighth graders, but no longer.

"Anyway, when the term began, I attributed much of that to his reticence. But I was wrong, because we've admitted quite a few students beginning as seniors this year, especially girls who are all first year regardless of their level, because this is the first year Chelsea Academy ever enrolled girls, as you already know, and all of them have assimilated very well. Ms. Walsh and I keep a close watch on them.

"So, in Samir's case, the problem goes much deeper. According to his uncle, Ambassador Gibran, Samir's reticence is due solely to April of '83 when his parents were killed." Cassie gasps, bringing her hand to an open mouth.

"Oh, no," she uttered, gazing into nothing, momentarily, then looked at Walter, signaling more information. "How?"

"Are you familiar with what was happening in the Middle East in the early '80's, Lebanon specifically?"

Cassie nodded. "A little," she offered hesitantly. She had never expected Samir's narrative to go back to this.

"That's good. You'll have some frame of reference for his history." Walter refocused on his computer screen. "Our files are quite extensive, so I'll relate it chronologically. And I'll include my own research to provide a little more depth. Here goes:

"Israel invades Lebanon in '82 to drive out the PLO, which had dug itself into Southern Lebanon in the early seventy's. He looks up momentarily to see if Cassie is following him. She is. "Okay. They accomplish their objective, with about 15,000 civilians as collateral damage in the process, and Arafat evacuates Lebanon - gets all his troops out by the end of August. Of course this creates a vacuum, which is eventually filled by . . ."

"Hezbollah," Cassie interjects.

"Right," he smiles, a bit surprised. "Most people don't know that. In fact, most people don't know anything about what went on there, and that makes it even more difficult for Samir." He shrugs his shoulders. "You can't empathize when you don't know what the other person has gone through, but it is a safe way to go through life. You can't be hurt." He smiles bitterly, his experience showing through. But," he continued, "before Hezbollah becomes entrenched, Lebanon asks the UN to send in a multinational force to maintain peace. Unfortunately, this only increases hostilities. Then when Israel and the government-supported militia, the Phalanges, invade Beirut looking for PLO stragglers . . ."

"So they *claimed*," asserts Cassie softly.

Walter nods, "these two forces massacre the inhabitants of two Palestinian refugee camps."

"Sabra and Shatila," Cassie adds, averting her eyes.

Walter nods again, quite surprised, then returns to the computer screen, tracing his finger down to a specific paragraph as he continues. "So, the Lebanese government requests a multinational force to assist in reestablishing peace; we shell Shiite forces; our warm welcome turns to hate and . . . ." He is oblivious that Cassie is turning inward. "April, '83, a suicide bomber drives his car into the American Embassy in Beirut, killing over sixty people. One of them is Samir's father, a Lebanese diplomat, there on business; another is his mother, who had accompanied her husband. Samir had just turned fourteen, in his uncle's care at the time. He's been with his uncle ever since, reticent and absolutely unresponsive. The Ambassador contacted us in March. He was hoping an experience at Chelsea would help his nephew. So far, it hasn't." He pauses and reflects. "Living with that must be a nightmare for Samir, for American families who lost loved ones.

"And worse for us," he's still tracing his finger along the computer screen; he still has not looked up, "Talk about a nightmare, six months later, a suicide bomber drives a truck carrying over a thousand pounds of dynamite into Marine headquarters. Over two hundred Marines killed. Story made headlines for months."

Finally, Walter stops staring at his computer and turns to Cassie. Her hands are covering her mouth and her body is swaying. Walter sees an ashen face and hears her ragged breathing. She is a moment away from uncontrollable tears.

"Cassie? Cassie, what's wrong? I didn't realize this would make you so upset. I'm sorry." He hurries from his seat to her side, helpless, not knowing the right words and afraid to touch, unable to think of some way to console her. Twenty-five years of counseling, and he hadn't expected this. She rises from her seat and turns away from him, disoriented. "Cassie, please, sit down. Water? Would some water help?"

Cassie shakes her head but does not turn around. She is forcing herself to regain control, breathing deeply, not thinking, just breathing, just breathing, just trying to breathe. Her heart is pounding. She can feel it punching through her chest. She's alive, but why? Because, she has Stevie to care for; that's the only reason.

Gradually, she begins to calm herself, her breathing slows and she inhales deeply. "I'm all right," she says finally, her voice hoarse and a little shaky, but breathing evenly. "Sorry." She waves him off, pushing golden streaks of hair back behind her ears. Control. Regain control. She redirects her focus to Samir's problem. "May I have a copy of his file?" Her voice is raspy and weak.

"You okay?"

She nods. She looks so small and vulnerable. Aren't we all, when it comes to grief.

"I'd love to give you a copy, but these files can't leave the office, not for anyone – except the dean, of course." He offers a wan smile. But if you'd like, you can come in and read them anytime. I'll print out a copy and leave it with Melissa. Will that do?" She glances up at him. He smiles. "And you won't need an appointment."

She returns his smile. "Thank you. That'll be fine." She picks up her attaché and turns to leave. "Oh, I wonder if by some chance, and it may not be protocol, would Samir's academic adviser mind if I took him? Maybe we could do a student exchange?"

"Actually, Cassie, not only do I know she wouldn't mind, she'd welcome the exchange. She hasn't been able to make any progress with him at all. As I said, none of us have. We're all concerned, and," he pauses, "frustrated."

"Thank you, Walter. I appreciate that. Do I need paperwork for this?"

"Consider it done. From now on, you meet with him as your schedules allow – *if* he'll allow it, that is; consultations are not mandatory. I'll send you a formal transfer through inter-office memo by tomorrow. Any formal session you may have with him, document as much detail as possible and give it to Melissa. We'll be giving a copy to his uncle." He noticed her slight hesitation. "Something wrong?"

"Do we document every conference we have every time we meet with a student? I wasn't told that a report followed a conference."

He knew exactly where this was going. "No, we don't, but with Samir, we will because his uncle wants to know what transpires."

"Nothing will transpire, Walter, if he knows or becomes aware that I've submitted a form detailing our conversation. And you only require a formal report on him? How discriminatory is that? This kid is getting hit from all sides, don't you think?" Walter turns away, somewhat chagrinned. Cassie continues. "I could justify submitting a form that documents a meeting has taken place so there's a record of time and place, but not for any other reason. If that helps," she adds.

Walter grapples with this dilemma. "Then how do we keep his uncle informed?" He was asking Cassie for a solution. "Because that's his condition."

She thought for a moment, then candidly stated, "I'll call him." Walter didn't try to muffle his surprise.

"What, you're going to call an ambassador to the UN directly?"

"About his nephew who's in his charge? Of course I am. Give me his phone number. If I can even get Samir to talk to me, that'll be a major step. I'm not gonna ruin it by reporting to his uncle. If I detect anything relevant to Samir's health or safety, I'll let his uncle know; maybe include it in the form I hand in. Otherwise, it's just Samir and me, just as it would be with any other student." She gave her proposal a quick once-over. "And that's *my* condition," she states without equivocation. "What do you think?"

He was more than a little dumbfounded by her candor and her spunk, but he conceded, throwing up his hands up in a "you win" gesture. "Okay, I'll pass this new development onto Dr. O/B and will follow-up with a call to the ambassador."

"Thank you, Walter. I just hope Samir will meet with me." She turns to leave.

"Wait," Walter adds, looks at the computer screen and scribbles numbers on a notepad. "Take the ambassador's numbers now so I won't have to follow-up with it later. The top one's the embassy. You may want to try that first and have them connect you. The second one is his direct line, just in case." Cassie nods her appreciation and pockets the numbers. "Hopefully you'll never need them," he said, "but . . . you never know."

"Thanks." Cassie turns to leave again, pauses and looks back, directly into Walter's eyes. "Sixty-three killed at the Embassy; two hundred forty-one Marines at the barracks." And she was gone, leaving him stunned.

9

FOOTBALL GAME

November weather arrived Saturday morning with chilly, vapor-breathing cold, a white lustrous patent leather look, and a crunchy-when-you-walk feel on the hoar-frosted, crisp grass. But skies were clear. "Great day for a game," Cassie said out loud, and embraced anticipation. There was a sense of excitement about today, an exuberance inside her, reminiscent of high school football, red and black colors, a marching band with a halftime program, cheerleaders, "Fight team, fight." The everything, the all of it, turning sixteen and the hint of first love, if any boy would think she was worth it, her father's words in her subconscious.

She shook off a tear from a memory that had been imprinted on her brain so long ago. She had been so young, it was hard to recall, but pain surfaced, and a vaporous memory of a knife and her mom holding her close.

Where and how had youth and innocence left her? Unconsciously, while living her day to day tomorrows, they had vanished, one day at a time until they were gone, without saying goodbye. You didn't file them on a shelf or push them to the back wall in the pantry. You didn't take them down again to use at a later date. These puffs of time, like soft tufts she'd pull off a frayed blanket and throw away, simply left and found themselves new homes in a new generation, like the song, "Toyland." Devilish, impish sprites, teasing us in youthful years, mesmerizing us, letting us wish we were older – old enough to wear makeup, old enough to date, old enough to drive. Cruel. They never let us truly appreciate moments we could never get back.

"Come on Ma," Stevie prodded, way ahead of her mother. "We're late already."

Cassie abandoned her reveries and hurried after Stevie. By the time they walked across campus and got to the field, Chelsea had kicked-off, it was third down, and our offense was driving from our forty-yard line. "Up here, Cassie!" A female voice shouted. She searched the stands and located Melissa's hand waving her on and up, her smile reaching ear to ear. Cassie and Stevie began the climb, bleacher after bleacher, uttering an infinite number of "Excuse me's" until they finally got to familiar faculty two rows from the top.

"Doesn't anybody sit closer to ground level?" Cassie asked, a little breathless.

Melissa chuckled. "Nope. Can see much better from here. Besides, it's good exercise. Helps trim the waistline." She grabbed for what was supposed to be fat at her waistline, but there was nothing there. Melissa was in shape. "Let me introduce you to the gang. You know Walter." He was sitting directly behind Melissa; he nodded and smiled, "And this is Jeremy Harper, chemistry," another nod and smile from the portly man on Melissa's right. "Tasha Meyer, calculus," a light-skinned black woman in her late thirty's seated behind Jeremy; "Ronnie Collins," on Tasha's right, "Samir's erstwhile advisor."

"I sure hope you can do more for him than I could," Ronnie offered in a soft voice, a stately woman with graying hair around her temples, perhaps near fifty,

"And Alicia Walsh," Melissa completed the introductions, "the other half of Walter's department." Alicia's olive complexion was in strict juxtaposition with her flaming red hair that had to be natural.

Cassie nodded to everyone, introduced Stevie before sitting, and gave Walter a quick, "I got the transfer form. Thanks." Then she settled into the game. "Well, where are we with this game and do we have a chance of beating their butts?"

"Mom!" Stevie admonished, sometimes more proper than Cassie, who held up her hands in surrender. Stevie didn't grow up in Paterson, where vernacular was much less formal, especially when she went to high school.

"A great chance," Melissa responded enthusiastically, and Walter leaned forward with his thumb up. "We're seven and one right now," he said, so this should be a great game! Homecoming is next week.

On the field, third and long, Parker takes five steps back, looks for a receiver, and throws it down the field . . . will he connect? Breathing stops. Does he have a receiver? Yes! The receiver hauls it in at the twenty, an acrobatic circus catch between two defenders, evades a tackler and sprints down field into the end zone! Cassie is startled when she recognizes the receiver, Mason Haworth, six feet of skinny, red hair, amazingly fast, who can do Shakespeare *and* play ball! *Yes!*

The fans are on their feet clapping and cheering, with decorum, of course. "Great play,Vaughn. Outstanding! We'll take another one just like that!"

Accolades flowed easily after a play like this, but the name? "Vaughn?" There can only be one Vaughn here. When did he arrive? She leans forward and there he is, in his long woolen coat, collar up, his matching golf hat, and soft leather gloves. She sees him before he sees her, and when he does, she has to smile. Here he is, dean of the school, trying to shrink back into anonymity. "Hi, Dr. O/B," she offers. Parker threw an amazing pass."

"Thank you, Cassie. Yeah, he has a good arm." He moved forward a little.

Yeah? She thought, from Mr. Prim and Proper? Football will do that to a guy. Especially when it's his kid.

The kicking team takes the field. The snap; good hold, and the extra point is good. Another formal ovation from the fans, but Walter was right, we were in for one great game.

Now Chelsea kicks off. The Bulldogs return the ball to the thirty one-yard line – good play; our defense takes the field. The crowd is as ecstatic as private-school protocol will allow; the cheerleaders' black and red pom poms fan the air. Bulldogs attempt a reverse; defensive end seems to have the corner, but the outside linebacker isn't fooled; he stays home, tackling the runner for a two yard loss.

"Get him!" Cassie screams. "Get him! Bury him!" She is on her feet, her hands waving above her head! She is losing herself in the game and having a great time. Does she notice the faculty staring at her? The faculty *and* Dr. O/B? Nope. Not until she faces them exuberantly. Their faces show looks of surprise and admiration, but not Dr. O/B. Dr. O/B is staring with penetrating eyes. Then he stands, facing her.

"This is a highly prestigious private academy, Cassie." He says officiously. "I didn't expect to hear such a plebian outburst here."

Walter, Melissa, Jeremy are stunned, shocked. Melissa's mouth drops; Walter turns towards Vaughn and stares. Cassie is taken aback, frozen for a second or two. Then her spitfire personality, which most people never see, grasps the situation. She has been attacked, and her natural instincts to counter engage involuntarily. "I'm sorry, Dr. O/B," she says with feigned deference. "I never expected you'd be sitting amongst us. I simply assumed, obviously erroneously, that you'd be sitting snugly in your private box."

A shockwave reverberates through the staff as if Medusa had appeared and turned the group to stone. Frozen, speechless, wishing they were protected inside a bubble while a highly charged football game is playing around them. No one, except Walter, dared look at Vaughn and Cassie, who was confronting him face to face, eyes never blinking or wavering. No one, no one, had ever spoken to Vaughn like that. His countenance turns severe, then, with dignity, shoulders back, he turns and walks away.

Walter was the first to thaw. "So how long do you want to work here?" He asks humorously, breaking the ice. They laugh, and continue to laugh until Jeremy and Melissa are holding their stomachs in pain. "Best football game I've ever been to," Melissa manages to say between staccato breaths of air.

"Hey," Jeremy adds, "I've never seen Vaughn like this. We may be laughing because you really hit him hard, but it's your job that could be on the line."

"For giving him a retort? He deserved it."

"That he certainly did, but you've gotta understand the way the game is played around here, not just the football game," Melissa began. "We all know he sits with us at the games, but here's the thing: he *deigns* to sit with us. He doesn't do it because we're his peers. Not in the least. He does it because we know our place. Yeah, we're all equal hypothetically, and yeah, he invites us for Thanksgiving, which is a very nice gesture, but in reality, the obscenely wealthy, and Vaughn is in that class, simply condescend and pretend to be one of us . . . when they want to.

"You weren't too far off with that comment about his having a private box, either," Melissa continued. When I first got here, that topic actually came up at a Board of Directors meeting. Squelched, of course. Would have created too snobby an appearance for the academy and given us a bad image. Chelsea gives ten academic scholarships a year to kids who have proven themselves academically but who lack the finances. Having private boxes for the upper crust would seem counterproductive to kids from poorer districts.

"But hey, look at you?" Melissa's tone became light. "You sure do know 'a little' about football, don't you?" Melissa throws 'a little' back in Cassie's face and smiles.

"Just a little," Cassie laughs.

"So, until you get the ax," she laughs, "You're gonna fit right in with this crowd."

Fit in? 'Fitting in' implied trust. In her entire life, Cassie had only trusted once, enough to fall in love, and that had been purely coincidental. Fleeting childhood images flashed before her and she closed her eyes to squelch them. Brian had gotten behind her fortress who knows how, but he had. Trust and love; she had felt secure and nurtured. She could have lived the rest of her life like that.

And then, in a moment, he was ripped from her life and from Stevie's, because he trusted, because he cared about people and believed in doing what was right, what was moral, what was good. A disaster of cataclysmic proportions, and when she rose from the ashes, aside from still being Stevie's mother, she had become someone completely new and more afraid than ever to venture forth. Although she was trying to chip away at her barriers, could she ever succeed enough to fit in anywhere?

Halftime came and went and the crowd was back in their seats. Cassie's focus returns to the field. We have the ball. The scoreboard: Colts, 22; Bulldogs, 9. She relaxes, casually scans the field, getting a closer look at the band. Which ones are her students, and what instruments do they play? Then she focuses on the four cheerleaders who are facing the bleachers. Cute. Dressed in black tights and oversized red sweatshirts, they sure are keeping the action in high gear. But wait! It's Emelia, Rachel, and there's Gloria. Gloria Morgan next to Rachel Greer! That's the connection! Now she knows. The fourth cheerleader is

Megan, from her seventh period class, but they are all her students. She's overjoyed.

The kickoff teams take the field. The kick is high, taken on the five yard line, run out to the 28th. "Okay defense, let's get a stop!" Cassie yells! Cassie settles in to watch as Stevie taps her shoulder. "What is it Hon?" She turns. Stevie and three freshman girls face her with hopeful anticipation. They're in my house, Cassie thinks, but she doesn't remember their names, not yet.

"Mrs. Komsky," says the tiny short brunette with pixie hair cut close to her face, wispy bangs, wearing a red and black oversized Chelsea Academy sweat-shirt, "Stevie can sit with us if she likes; if it's all right with you?"

Cassie is pleasantly surprised. She didn't realize Stevie would be forming her own social group so soon and with girls four years older. But this is what she had hoped for, and here it was, happening. All were dressed in stone-washed jeans, and apart from the tiny girl speaking to her who was wearing the huge sweat shirt, the two other girls wore red and black school jackets that had a bucking colt decal on the left sleeve. They have light hair, big and puffy, and one seems very familiar, as though Cassie should know her – very familiar except for a dimple on her right cheek. All three wear makeup, bright but not overdone.

"We're sitting over there," the tiny girl offers, her sweat shirt almost to her knees, and points one bleacher down to their right.

"You want to go?" Silly question, Cassie thinks. Of course she wants to go. "Names, please?" She asks. She knows they're in her dorm because she's seen them sign in, but she hasn't connected names on a page to faces yet. The girls are Rebecca Greer, of course – Rachel's sister; that's why she looks so familiar, except she's taller and her hair is a darker blond. Stacy Bronston, Emelia's sister – not too much similarity there, except for the amazing posture. The tiny girl with black pixie hair is Millie. Last name begins with 'T.'

Names on a page now take on a different meaning. She remembers Rebecca signing in and her roommate, Stacy. Does Millie have an older sibling? She doesn't think so. Cassie didn't recognize her last name. This will be fine, Cassie thinks, relieved. "Sure, Hon; have fun." Stevie pecks her cheek, pivots and leaves without a backward glance. So this is how it is, she thinks, a tinge of nostalgia breaking through. Stevie is growing up, and I will be alone.

The crowd, still clapping politely, indicates action in our favor. "I missed it, Melissa. Wha'd we do?"

"Stopped them cold and recovered their fumble. Our ball; their 36-yard line. Here we go!"

Our offense comes out of the huddle. All eyes are focused on the center who snaps to Parker who hands off to his running back whose legs power him through the gap for a six-yard gain. The bleachers express themselves politely again. All eyes focus on the play, Cassie notices, except Rachel's. Who is she looking at, Cassie wonders, and her eyes follow Rachel's who quickly refocuses on the field and waves her pom poms.

Cassie leans forward and looks to her left. Nothing. Parents and fans of all ages. But there it is again! Rachel's furtive glance.

Cassie is determined. Her curiosity getting the better of her, she stands up and searches the crowd, bleacher by bleacher, following the trajectory of Rachel's gaze. She triangulates like a hunter honing his sights on his target. And there he is! Obscured by the crowd, way off, sitting apart from pockets of families, friends and cliques, his wavy jet black hair and his height telegraphing his presence, is Samir. Samir is at the game! Adrenaline shoots through her. She can't lose this opportunity. She just can't. She's gotta do something. Without forethought or hesitation, she excuses herself from her associates.

"Where are you going, Cassie?" Melissa asks. "It's almost fourth quarter and we're going to score."

"Other end of the bleachers. I'll be back shortly. Hold my seat, if you can." She smiles then begins to work her way through the bleachers, row by row, murmuring more 'Excuse me's.' Four rows down, then way over. Like any football stadium, two parallel sides are much longer than the two semi-circles. Her seat is on the home-team's 50-yard line; Samir's is at the far end.

Her destination seems endless as she works her way through crowded bleachers and prays Samir hasn't moved since she's seen him. Finally she's at the end zone. Not many people seated here; she sees him instantly. He doesn't see her coming until she steps from cover. He is less than five feet away from her; and five feet from the nearest spectator. Five feet of self-imposed isolation.

She waits. Patiently. He squirms, his discomfort is apparent. He is drop-dead handsome; blazing black olive-shaped eyes, a strong straight nose, slightly accentuated cheeks, full lips, a dreamy look, and a tall, lean, yet muscular physique. She inches forward, not wanting him to bolt. The rest of the world falls away. Now it is time.

"*Hal yumkinooni aljeloos huna?*" (May I sit here?) She asks, her tone soft and comforting.

His look is quizzical, untrusting, confused. How is it she speaks his language? Should he trust her just because she does? She waits. She will not move until he responds. She will make no assumptions, take no privileges until he responds. His eyes dart from her to emptiness; from her to sorrow. Then, very slowly, he nods. "*Na'am.*" (Yes.)

Her heart pounds. He has spoken! He has spoken! Oh my God, she thinks. Easy, easy, don't scare him away. "*Shukkran.*" (Thank you.) Again, she waits. It's all up to him. Calm down, Cassie. Calm down. But the significance of this breakthrough. It's miraculous! She has to fight to keep her eyes from tearing. His eyes continue to dart from her then away. Patience. Patience. Her words strangle her throat, but she holds them in check, inches forward, and takes a seat at the end of his bleacher.

"*Kaif ta'alamti Arabia?*" He asks. (How did you learn Arabic?)

She breathes again, still slowly. "*Jaa walidayee min Sureya.*" (My parents came from Syria.)

Samir nods. He is communicating with her.

"*Estattaee'a al takalluma qaleelan,*" (I can speak a little.) Cassie adds. Samir diverts his eyes again, this time, in Rachel's direction. She has stopped cheering and is watching them. Body language telegraphs her surprise. Happiness engulfs her face. She knows he has spoken. "*Bal arjoo an tatahadootha bil engleeziah.*" (But please speak English), Cassie says, following his glance. "*La yumkinaha an tefhemaka illa etha teqalemta engleeziah.*" (She can't understand you unless you speak English).

He nods. Silent, Cassie waits, then, "We will talk perhaps another time, yes?" He says. "Now I wish to leave."

A deep, mellow voice, masculine yet soft, expressing kindness and sorrow all at one time. English. He spoke English. Cassie realizes she has held her breath from Samir's "We," and finally exhales. She watches him walk away, then glances down at Rachel. Four cheerleaders had been on the field when she last looked down. Now, only three. Rachel is gone.

"If you have a few minutes Monday morning, please stop by my office." Cassie whirls. She knows his voice instantly, and also understands the directive, but when she turns to face him, instead of the disapproval she expects to see, Vaughn's countenance shows approbation and maybe a thin smile? She isn't sure.

Because he stood several feet behind her, her peripheral vision had missed him completely when she had looked towards Rachel. But there he was, several bleachers down standing on ground level, in his long tweed coat and Colts hat. He did look preppy, even for an older guy, preppy but classy, except for the Chelsea cap. That must be the Harvard look. Yale? No difference. They're both the same snobby elitist institutions.

He had seen her with Samir. That was obvious, and if he had stood behind her for even a few seconds, he had seen them communicate. Most likely, he had even heard Samir speak English.

So what was he thinking now, this man, so quick to judge by one sentence or one incident? Was it wealth?

Did that allow him to judge others so cavalierly? Most likely he thinks it does. Wealth bestows impunity and lets him believe he has it all figured out. And if not wealth, he still wouldn't care. Cassie nods. "I'm free after fourth period," she said. "I could stop by during fifth, if that's all right with you."

"That'll be fine." He walks on. She watches him as he circles the bleachers and sits with a couple on the opposite side. Not faculty. She knows this intuitively. Friends, donors, but definitely not faculty. He's followed through with his professional obligations towards Chelsea's faculty; now he's on his own time.

Cassie turns and hones in on the group with whom she's been sitting. Nice people. She would enjoy getting to know them better. But no expectations, she reminds herself. Expect friendship and loyalty from no one and you won't be disappointed. Stevie was seated one row down and several seats over having no inhibitions about making new friends. That's okay for her; she's young. As she gets older, she'll figure it out for herself. Her life will be different from mine, Cassie thinks. It already is.

10

VAUGHN

An evening at the Club was intended for fine dining, pretentious, insipid conversation, elegant table settings, expensive wines, top drawer whiskey and scotch and a dance or two so the wives could show off their new elegant gowns. It was the only game in town, but what a game. It was a watering hole where the obscenely wealthy gathered to strut their multi-colored plumage, recent trips abroad, upcoming vacations and galas, business deals, homes, second homes, third homes, the help, the housing market, a new diamond, a new yacht – as if one hundred twenty-one feet weren't long enough – stock exchange, commodities, Bull and Bear markets, the Federal Reserve, all were intermingled in the chatter. And golf, always golf, splices, hooks, and pars, the game of the genteel man, while wives prated about salons and spas, fashion and furs, cosmetics and cosmetic surgery, but don't tell. Much ado about nothing. Long live pride, may it not outperform their egos.

A wait staff in tuxedos hovered about, their presence invisible to diners and subservient to conversation. They existed to serve a member's every need, every whim. If one needed to blow his nose, they would provide the tissue.

Vaughn's table, number nineteen, was situated to the right of the wide-entranced foyer, the prime choice for Club diners. It offered a perfect view of the illuminated course and was positioned away from bustling kitchen doors. Near the dance floor, it was not so close that speakers could intrude on conversation. Vaughn and his family had had this table for decades, and when guests exceeded eight, the Otis-Barrett's would command the entire section. It had always been this way, ever since Vaughn and his brother could remember.

Vaughn enjoyed these evenings because it was customary to enjoy them; he talked the talk because it was the routine conversation; he drank his two, maybe three Highland Park Single Malt scotches same as always on a Saturday night, and he danced his obligatory one dance with his wife, maybe two if forced, because that was the way it had always been done.

But despite the evening, the conversation, the company and the glitz, Vaughn felt conflicted for the first time in his life. He had experienced disappointments in his past and had been confronted with situations he couldn't solve. They had existed; they always would. But this conflict was different and unfamiliar, and it troubled him for that very reason. Unfamiliarity caused him to feel unsure. Women had rejected him in his younger days. Rejected him soundly, flatly; they weren't interested. They'd find another man, another wealthy man who interested them more. This was a given, something he understood.

But no one, ever, had spoken to him as Cassie had this afternoon. No one had ever taken his words and hurled them in his face. How *dare* she! His position, his financial station in life, all seemed inconsequential to her. She didn't seem at all concerned about the consequences of her words. No trepidation, no deference, nothing from this insignificant bitch! Nothing. He had given her this job. At the very least, she should be grateful. At the very least, she should pretend. Was she that naive? He could crush her, this candid, feisty, non-conforming, unpretentious bitch.

How should he deal with her? How should he maintain equanimity, because thus far, his basic emotion with her bordered on fury. He could concentrate on nothing else as he had crossed the field this afternoon to sit with the Radfords, old friends from Harvard days who were now seated at their table with Brett and Hillary, drinking scotch. He finished his second as the male contingent's rare steaks bled into twice-baked potatoes and wives dipped slices of lobster tail into drawn butter, picked at watercress and cranberry salad, intermittently sipped vodka martinis and talked about seeing *Cabaret*.

Yet, she had gotten Samir to speak. Not only to speak, but to speak English. Miraculous! How had she done that? No one at Chelsea, no one in over two months had been able to accomplish that. Everyone had concluded it was impossible and had unwittingly written the kid off. But in a week, she had made contact and gotten Samir to open up, if just a little. But with Samir, a little was huge.

So what would he do with this unpretentious woman who was insidiously creeping into his thoughts every day and every night since he had knocked on her door Monday evening and seen her in that wet T-shirt. That soaked T-shirt that had clung to her body and outlined beautiful breasts, delicate nipples, a tiny waist and slender hips. His grip on his glass tightened. He had been unable to function since Monday night without her creeping into his thoughts like a silent cat, wishing she had turned around so he could have devoured a glimpse of her slender back and her sensually rounded ass.

Yet she still infuriated him, even this afternoon with her unrestrained, passionate outburst at the game, "Get him! Bury him!" Who does that? Does she have no sense of proper decorum? This woman, so passionate, and so uninhibited about expressing it. And that was another emotion he had never experienced - passion.

Passion was diametrically opposed to his rigid life. He had grown up rigid and had remained rigid, so much so, that until now, he had never realized or acknowledged he was. Cassie was pure passion, about Shakespeare, about teaching, about life, about happiness and helping people. Maybe that's what Samir had sensed. Maybe that's why he had opened up, not just to anybody, but to a very special person who happened to be passionate about understanding him.

But who jumps up from the bleachers and shouts at the players on the field? Who does that?! Chelsea Academy is a prestigious private academy, not a public city school. We're not just any place or any football game. We're not a forum for an Eliza Doolittle: "Come on, Dover! Move your bloomin' ass!" He almost smiled at the realization. Cassie was Chelsea's Eliza Doolittle, completely caught up in the game and completely uninhibited about expressing her emotions. He sighed.

He envied her insouciance. He envied her exuberance and loved it. He envied her absolute abandonment of norms and loved it. And he hated her for the same reasons, because she made him hate himself for his inability to be like her. And so, his cutting remark. Show her you're in control; show her you're better than she is; that you're above such undisciplined outbursts; show her you epitomize protocol and formality. But never show her she unnerves you. Never that.

The grip on his glass tightened until he realized even a thick rocks glass could shatter in his hand. But the triviality of his routine life plagued him; his routine days and evenings, his insipid, routine conversations; his routine mandatory dance with Taylor, maybe a second if his brother didn't come to his rescue; same two glasses of scotch, then home to the same bedtime routine. Was there more than this?

Home. Each to their separate bathrooms and into the same bed. Vaughn finished first, as always. No makeup, no jewelry, no fine lingerie, and waited for her. He knew what to expect, and it was good. Taylor never denied him, never gave him an excuse and never had a headache, unlike his colleagues and the stories they told about their wives. Unlike their grown-up, locker-room talk, Taylor never said no.

She was always horny when they came home from the Club, and tonight was no different. She glided from the bathroom, naked, and slipped between the sheets. She mounted him quickly, no preliminaries, no foreplay, just raw, unabated sex. She moved on him with grinding rhythm. Thrust after thrust.

She licked his neck and bit into him wildly. Her mouth devoured him, sucking feverishly. She slammed down on him hard and fast. Then her body tensed, her head fell back and her nails clawed his shoulders. Her breathing deepened until she stilled, held on, and hit. Deep gasps that gulped air and made her body shiver burst from her body. With one final thrust, Vaughn, held her down and exploded. Two bodies, linked in the savage embrace of mankind. Timeless. Universal. The universality of Man.

She stilled and smiled, collapsed on him and gently nibbled his face and neck. Her hair and body were slippery with perspiration and she smelled of lust and heat, raw primordial smells he loved. God, he loved being inside her. But for the first time in their marriage, something was different, not quite right, and he recognized it instantly. It was different because the image that crept into his thoughts was not Taylor's; the image was Cassie's.

11

MONDAY MORNING AFTER THE GAME

Gloria Morgan's violet blue eyes had begun to tear. She had related Hamlet's situation to her own life and her emotions had gotten a bit out of control. "My parents got divorced four years ago," she says, her voice thin and raspy, and my father figuratively died, because from that point on, I've seen him once, at my grandmother's funeral. "My mom was so hurt, she just gave up. She still doesn't date, and at this point I wish she would. But if she had married some guy within a month after she and my dad had split, I would have been crushed. And just thinking about her marrying my dad's brother?" She gives an uncontrollable shudder, "Yuk!' "So I can relate to Hamlet's turmoil. Anybody who can't, they've had it easy." She glances around the table somewhat defiantly.

"I'm sorry, Gloria. I wanted everyone to find a relationship between Hamlet's life and his or her own, but I didn't want it to upset you like this. I'm sorry this situation resurfaced."

"That's okay, Mrs. Komsky. My problem didn't resurface from reading *Hamlet*. It's always there, day, night, weekends, all the time. My dad left. He threw me away, me, my mother, and my little sister for someone eight years older than me. I live with that just as Hamlet lives with his inner grief. Guess Shakespeare's characters really do live in us."

"Good characterization lives on in any play or novel because we're all human. You empathize with Hamlet because you've been hurt by your father. Hamlet was hurt by his mother, and so much more. His father dies suspiciously, he knows this after he talks with his father's ghost, his mother remarries almost immediately, *and* to his uncle! Three horrific events. How bad is that? If any of you disagree, if you think he's whining, showing 'unmanly grief,' as his uncle puts it, speak up." She glances from student to student. No one disagreed, but maybe because it was so cold jaw muscles weren't working properly.

It was a frigid morning, temperatures much colder than forecasts had predicted. Saturday's frosty bite was tropical compared to today's single digits, and unfortunately, the new heating system that had been installed in Rand Hall during the summer was dragging its heels. Her students were freezing, as was she, making class participation close to impossible.

Mason, Zach and the girls had put on their coats, and anyone who had spurned heavy outerwear thinking a short walk would get them to a warm classroom sat shivering, teeth chattering. Dr. O/B had stopped in unexpectedly to assure them that maintenance was on it, that the boilers would be pumping heat up any minute, but if they preferred, they could hold class in his outer office. A kind offer, but she was relieved when the class had opted to stay put. Despite the cold classroom killing concentration, no one relished the idea of being that close to the school's ultimate authority for warmth, not even Parker. *Hamlet* was set in Denmark; it tied in perfectly.

"I don't like Hamlet," Zach's voice broke the chilly silence, "but I get why he's brooding. "His father dies, his ghost says poison; his mother marries his uncle right after, tells him he's stubborn because he's still grieving for his dad, and his uncle calls him unmanly. Here it is, act 1, scene 2, line 94. I agree with Emelia. I'd feel completely abandoned and alone, and I'd probably hate my mother for doing what she did."

"Tell us how you really feel, Zach," Matthew Welsley interjects good-naturedly, adding a touch of levity. His Asian eyes twinkle.

"So, two of you would feel alone; the rest of you haven't answered. I know it's cold, and maybe that's part of the reason . . ."

"It's the whole reason – for me, anyway," Rachel interjects.

"Ditto for me, Mrs. Komsky," Jason adds, with approval from the others.

"Understood," Cassie replied, "but if you can be verbal enough to tell me why you're not contributing to the discussion, you can be verbal enough to contribute. How about that?" Grumbles and more grumbles, but they got the message.

"One additional point as a reason for Hamlet's anguish. A cultural one. We agree that the interlude between Hamlet's father's death and Gertrude marrying her brother-in-law was unethical, correct?" They nod. "But was it, as Hamlet says, incestuous? And I'm stressing, 'as Hamlet says.'"

That made them pause. "Think. Thinking will keep you mentally alert. Don't want that brain to become dormant, do we? Get active and collaborate. Move your seats, partner up, get up and do jumping jacks." They eyed her apprehensively on that one. "Just move! And come up with an answer."

Most partnered up. As they did, Cassie observed them as individuals. Teens fascinated her. It was a tough time, balancing emerging identities with collective acceptance, a war game she wouldn't want to relive.

Shy and quiet Jason paired up with Matt who had paired up with Connor, but they seemed to merely tolerate him; Emelia and Rachel paired off, reaching out to Gloria who leaned past self-absorbed Zach, who moved over to give her room. Elizabeth moved her seat to be with the girls, intuitively knowing, without hesitation, she'd be accepted; also knowing Samir who sat on her right, would work alone. Parker and Mason were still basking in the glory from Saturday's win, books open, exchanging football plays, oblivious to the assignment. After Homecoming this weekend, win or lose, she wondered if they'd be able think at all.

But Cassie had finally connected the bright red and black posters hanging in the main hallway of Sanders House and in the cafeteria to Homecoming, and was leaning towards going. The rivalry of the game would be unparalleled and the elegant dance that followed, boys wearing suits; girls wearing fancy dresses, was a major event at Chelsea, one of the two biggest all year. She might go to that, if she could find someone to be with Stevie. She wouldn't want her to be alone.

She stopped digressing and refocused on the class. Jason and Connor were perusing the preface, both on the same page, both in the same paragraph but without interaction. Mason, finally coming down from his football high, thumbed through act 1, hoping to trump Emelia's response or preempt one from Zach. Samir, very tastefully and conservatively dressed in a heather gray Henley in sharp contrast to the bright, bold colors surrounding him, sat quietly flipping pages. Cassie watched the four young ladies who were now seated next to each other. She was so proud of them - new school, new environment, the first of a female line at Chelsea, building a strong foundation for all future female students. Tenacious, vivacious, and beautiful.

Elizabeth's dark hair is feathered; Gloria's tries to be, but with her tight curls, a can of spray wouldn't hold them back for more than an hour. A little phys ed plus a little sweat, and they'd be back to kinks. Emelia's blond hair is short, pixyish, highlighting her bright blue eyes. Rachel is petite, blond, hazel eyes, turned up mouth that forms a perpetual smile.

Cold as it was, they were actively engaging her question. Zachary puts his head down, either deep in thought or close to freezing; Rachel and Emelia cup their hands on their chins; Gloria Morgan twists a strand of hair around her finger, as if it weren't curly enough; Parker turns away and slouches down in his seat, seemingly unperturbed by the cold or the assignment.

"Well," Jason begins apprehensively, "that's a little creepy, but I don't think it's incest like Hamlet says."

"Why not? "Cassie responds, happy Jason initiated the answer.

"Because there's no blood relationship there. Claudius is Gertrude's brother-in-law. That relates them through marriage, but they're not related through blood. They're not brother and sister like the Ptolemies."

"But Claudius *is* Hamlet's uncle, right?" Cassie countered. "And remember, Hamlet says it."

"Claudius *is* Hamlet's uncle," Elizabeth Stanack comes into the discussion, "but that's not incest for Gertrude and Claudius. Not through bloodline. I agree with Jason." Jason was pleased.

"But I presented the condition, 'as Hamlet says.' Anybody read the preface?" Cassie asks. Zachary's hand shoots up before Jason can respond. "Just say it, Zach, you don't need to raise your hand."

Zachary smiles. He feels empowered. He has beaten out Mason, Matt, Elizabeth, and Emelia on this find. "The preface says that the Medieval Church denounced the marriage of a widower to his sister-in-law, and a widow to her brother-in-law, as incest. Here, page 4, second column. It also says that by the sixteenth century, eight Catholic universities invalidated the marriage of Henry V111 to his brother's widow."

"Good call, Zach." Anyone else see this?" Connor raises his hand; he had been reading the preface. Jason raises his hand slightly saying he did but wasn't sure, or should have spoken up faster. "I saw you leafing through the preface, Jason, and figured you may have found it. Don't hesitate to say what you find or what you think, even if you think it may be wrong. More than likely, you might be right. And you can always change an answer based on new information." Jason beamed. "You too, Connor. You were right there.

"Okay, then," she focuses on the group, "could we say the definition of incest is either broader or more confined based on what a culture accepts in a given era?"

They nod approval. "So we qualify our statement and conclude that, although Gertrude's marriage to Claudius may not fit our definition of incest in today's culture, it was incest according to the church during the Elizabethan period when Shakespeare wrote. Yes?" A nod is the best she's going to get.

"So we accept the definition of incest based on Hamlet's era. *Now* how would you feel if you were Hamlet? Worse, despite the era considering it incest, how is their marriage received?" No answer. "I can be patient," she says with good-natured sarcasm. "But not for long, especially when it's a simple question. And if I can talk when I'm freezing, so can you."

"Yeah, but you're the teacher," Mason counters with a smile. "You get paid to teach."

"And you get graded to participate," Cassie rejoins.

"Hey, Mason, she got you." The class was picking up steam; maybe the room was too. The smell of heat was filtering in.

"Nobody cared. Only Hamlet." Elizabeth Stanack picks up the challenge.

"Correct. Nobody cared, only Hamlet, and for that, he's criticized."

"But he can't change it; so why not just get over it?" Parker's first contribution to the content of the class discussion. Cassie is a bit stunned. His classmates are a bit stunned.

Cassie keeps it light. "You're correct, he can't change it, but some things take time to get over. Other things you can never get over, so they change you. Forever. But if you've never experienced a life-changing situation, consider Hamlet's dilemma from a moral position."

"Like?"

"Ever say or do something because it's right or moral and get penalized for it?"

Parker smirks. "No, I never have. My father's the dean."

"I sure have," Mason states. My father sells life insurance. I don't get a pass for much."

"I have too," states Matt. "And there's some pretty big bucks in my family.

"Me too," say Zach and Connor in unison, and the rest of the class, except for Samir, agrees.

Cassie looks at Parker. "Okay," he says, reluctantly, "I can empathize." Not only has Parker Otis-Barrett contributed, but he has admitted he can empathize with humanity. Amazing! And on a day without heat!

"So, he alone adheres to moral principles and he alone is castigated for it. It's hard being moral; it's hard being good when the masses are against you. Agree?"

Everyone is quiet. Everything is still, only baseboard heaters emitting a clanking sound, and the smell of heat permeating the room. Cassie inhales deeply, gulping in warmth. "I'm taking silence as 'yes;' interject if you disagree. No one did. "So you all relate to Hamlet's internal conflict, and from this one scene alone, you all see Shakespeare's universality? Stop me now or your position is indelibly sealed. Do you all relate?"

"Yes, Mrs. Komsky," from Rachel; yesses from Jason, Matthew, Zach, Emelia, and yes from Parker, and everyone else follows, except Samir, but he makes eye contact. Will he respond? She knows he relates. He has to relate, but will he respond? She gives it a second. There it is, a slight almost imperceptible nod, more with his eyes than anything else. But she gets it. He has communicated in class. Woah!

"Thank God for heat," Cassie interjects. Laughter. A wonderful sound. "Okay, then, tomorrow we'll factor in what Hamlet's father's ghost tells him and its edict for revenge. That finishes act 1. In act 2, analyze how Hamlet presents himself to Ophelia, and the letter he writes her. Also consider the concept of his insanity, feigned or real; include his letter to Ophelia in your response. Do these developments give more credence to Hamlet's soliloquy in act 1, scene 2, beginning with line 129, and," she pauses, "let's tie in Hamlet's response to Guildenstern, the lines, 'What a piece of work is a man,' lines 273 to the end of that passage, act 2, scene 2. If we have time, let's talk about his scheme to catch his uncle using the players. Does it confirm or refute his purported madness and cowardice? Okay, any questions?"

"So this is all due next month, right?" Matt Welsley asks masking a smile. At this the class broke into unrestrained laughter, joined by Cassie after she realized she had assigned much too much."

"Okay, we'll hold off on Hamlet's dialogue with Guildenstern and talk about the players Thursday or maybe even Friday. I know, I know. Homecoming is Saturday and there's tons of stuff to do. Guys, keep up the good work on the field. Ladies, I love the cheers." That seemed to give them pause, as though they had never expected her to notice them as people outside the classroom or to care about their other interests when nothing was further from the truth.

"See you tomorrow, then. Have a great day."

Cassie collects her things amidst chairs scraping the floor, books leaving the table, and footsteps shuffling out the door. She turns just as the last students, Mason and Parker, pause by the doorway. "You coming to Homecoming, Mrs. Komsky?" Mason asks apprehensively.

"I've been thinking about it, Mason. You think I should?"

"Of course. Nothing's better than Homecoming. The game, we're gonna win, of course, and get the District Trophy; then the dinner and dancing. We even dress up, big time. Guys wear suits; girls wear dresses," he added. Best event all year."

"Okay, Mason. I will give it serious consideration."

As they exit, Mason turns, "And I'll save you a dance, Mrs. Komsky; my dance card fills up really quickly." With that, he was out the door, leaving Cassie in stitches.

12

APPOINTMENT WITH VAUGHN

By the end of fourth period, Cassie's room was a toasty seventy-one degrees, and Maintenance had risen to man-of-the-hour status. She hated to leave and brave the frigid cold, but she had that appointment with Dr. O/B looming over her head, and, even though his demeanor was affable when he offered his office to her first period class this morning, his motivation was most likely appearances for the students. After Saturday's game, she expected nothing but reproach, but, she was a big girl. She could handle it.

She made Smythe Hall in record time, running over brown, ice-encrusted grass, covering her face and mouth with gloved hands, her attaché slung over her left shoulder, giving her a perceptible lean that was slowing her down. Couldn't be much more than fifteen degrees out here, she thought. Boots for warmth, not just for style, and gray woolen pants topped with a gray woolen sweater, embellished with shades of deep red and violet flowers embroidered with woolen gold-flecked thread and tiny gold beads. Dry-clean only. She hated that, but she had loved this sweater the instant she had seen it. Macy's. Sometimes, they had just what she was looking for.

Passing Guidance on her left, she took a quick peek in to see if she could discern shapes and shadows of Melissa or Walter. Distorted they would be, but that was the characteristic of beveled glass. No one in sight; she hurried down the hall to Administration and the dean's office, where another brown door, another beveled glass panel faced her.

She let herself into a spacious front office, peopled with several secretaries seated at huge deep cherry wood desks, each with her own PC, file cabinets and drawers bordered by counters and more file cabinets. Mrs. Charlotte Grayson's metal nameplate was firmly planted on her desk, which was stoically taking up guard duty in front of Dr. O/B's inner office. Cassie announced herself to the woman wearing the deep purple knit dress, high collar complementing a long graceful neck, gray hair pulled back strikingly in a chignon, and was told, without a glance, to go right in. Cassie had no doubt Charlotte knew exactly to whom she had approved entrance, or Cassie would never have made it through the swinging half door, especially since Charlotte was not a small woman, and Cassie was a mere 5'3."

Cassie entered a modestly appointed foyer that seemingly bifurcated into two inner offices, one left, one right, both doors slightly ajar. She walked right and knocked with formality, not too loud, not too soft. Did she have the right office or did he occupy both? It didn't matter. Vaughn's deep voice replied immediately, "Enter." The office was huge, not palatial, that would have been too ostentatious for a dean, but opulent in moderation. Now what the hell does "opulent in moderation" mean, she asked herself. She didn't know exactly, but she knew every piece of furniture, every lamp, every bookcase, every armchair, every desk, Vaughn's and the smaller one set to his right, was elegant and outrageously expensive. She had worked as a summer nanny at an upper-crust estate in Upper Montclair during college, and these furnishings were of the same ilk.

Vaughn put his paperwork aside, looked at her and smiled. She had to admit, he did have a captivating smile. It was his best facial feature. Cute, like the smile of a bashful little boy, the way he tilted his head sideways and smiled a great big, open-mouthed smile showing perfectly aligned teeth. A smile that said, "Hey, I've gotcha," and it did; a smile that should have melted into dimples, but didn't; it was a smile that invited trust. Careful Cassie, there's no such thing.

"Hi," he said disarmingly and she detected a slight hint of a blush. Or did she feel her own face warm a bit? Nah, she dismissed the idea. "You should take off your coat, or you'll melt. It's seventy-two degrees in here, and the thermostat's set at sixty-eight. And please, sit."

Cassie let her heavy attaché fall, unbuttoned and removed her coat, draping it over the chair, then sat in the seat facing Vaughn, hands folded neatly in her lap, right over left, feet together, the proper sitting position for a lady. Had she been less naive, she might have noticed Vaughn's eyes studying every curve of her body when she turned and spread her coat over her chair. Had she been prescient or telepathic, she might have read Vaughn's thoughts as he lost himself in her sensuality, studying her body and imagining more. His wife had an exceptional body, without equivocation, but he had never seen one like this. This body was more than sensual; it moved with liquid grace. It exuded soft, hypnotic, devour-me moves, moves that mesmerized, moves she seemed unaware she had.

Was she that oblivious, he thought, or is she teasing me? Then she sat with such propriety and smiled such an ingenuous smile. He looked directly at her and recognized her complete innocence. He was stunned. Taylor had assets and used them to get exactly what she wanted. Cassie had assets she didn't even know she had. Taylor was dangerous because of what her assets could get her; Cassie was more dangerous because she had no idea what she could get, and, unless the guy were a eunuch, she could get just about anything. She sat in anticipation. He had summoned her here for a reason; he'd better get to it.

"I asked you here for several reasons," he began, and . . ."

Nineteen minutes later, to be exact, she stood outside his office recalling one of the most, if not *the* most, convoluted conversations she had ever had. A confusing, disjointed, unfocused exercise in circumlocution. He had begun by talking about proper decorum at a Chelsea football game, but perhaps Chelsea spectators were a bit stiff and her enthusiastic outbursts could liven up the crowd; he talked about the absurdity of having a private box then admitted it could offer protection from inclement weather. However, since it would only be for himself and his family, it might be a bit pretentious; he had lectured about the responsibilities her tenant status required, but stated that while she occupied her apartment, it was legally hers to do with as she wished; he explained the difficulties Parker had being the dean's son, but that he was required to adhere to the same academic and behavioral standards as any other Chelsea student, and then he got to Samir.

Don't get too close to him; but get close so you can identify his problem. His uncle, most likely a billionaire, is concerned; we need to help Samir as much as possible, provide his uncle with some positive feedback. Yes, I know detailed reports would derail his trust – I've spoken to Walter, and that's a good point, but let me know anything that you think even hints of danger. I'll give you the number to my mobile phone. Talk to Walter if you need professional counseling to assist you. Our goal is to get him to communicate more. Why did he open up to you? Just you and no one else . . . and please, keep up the good work.

She stood in the hallway, stunned, recalling every word of their meeting verbatim, again and again, wondering how, after his nineteen minute expostulation, she walked away with the number to his mobile phone, a directive that she was not to miss Homecoming and, an even greater directive, an invitation to his home for Thanksgiving dinner that he expected her to accept. What?!! She stood shell-shocked in the hall, outside the dean's door, wondering what had just happened. And how?!

Oh-my-God! Dr. O/B's house for Thanksgiving dinner! How am I ever gonna get out of this one? She inhaled and exhaled deeply, calming herself, shaking off the shock. Well, she decided cavalierly, nothing to stress about - you get an invitation from the dean, you go. Simple as that.

13

HOMECOMING

Exhilarating! No other way to describe it. The game, tied again and again from third quarter on, each team gaining and losing no more than a field goal at any given time, racheted up to maximum intensity near the end of fourth quarter. Spectators screaming, mimicking Cassie's outbursts in one short week. Pom poms decorated the air; cheerleaders and fans in sync. Tension, pressure, guts and glory interwoven and pushed beyond reason, beyond limits, past physical endurance into overtime, with the Colts finally pulling it off: one pass, one leap that defied gravity, and one amazing reception that culminated in the winning touchdown. And the stands exploded, regurgitating spectators onto the field - parents, siblings, uncles, aunts, in-laws, friends, everyone, pouring onto the field, surrounding the team, suffocating the players with a blanket of uncontrollable ecstasy. Euphoric bedlam on the field; Parker and Mason riding high on teammates shoulders, District Trophy held high in their hands.

Cassie had hung back in the stands but mentally had floated with everyone else, reflecting on the passion and the ecstasy that had played out on the field; the epitome of limitations and man's ability to go beyond.

Cassie appreciated sports because they challenged human limits, but her sport was football because Brian had loved it. He had played as a seven-year-old in Pop Warner, then in high school and college. From fourth grade, he had followed every Giants game avidly. After they had met, they had watched the games together, him with such passion it had seeped into her, slowly, insidiously, until it had found a home.

Football replicated life. You got hit; you got up; pushed back and beat on. On the field, these kids were no different from the Paterson kids she had grown up with. Kids without a nickel for a candy bar, whose parents struggled every day to provide for their families; parents who wouldn't take a handout or government assistance; they earned what they got, regardless how much or how little; they earned it themselves, with pride, and their kids were the same. Tough, resilient, never backing down from a fight. No matter how outclassed, no matter the odds, they fought through, took a beating if they had to, got up and moved on. Win or lose, tenacity and honesty earned the respect of their peers.

And these kids on the field were the same. They had earned this win themselves, with pride, guts, determination and merit, without parental intervention, without mom or dad to stop a tackle, prevent an interception, or stop the opposition from pushing them back or throwing them to the ground. These kids had fought to the last tick of the clock and had never given up. This was life; they had lived it on the field and they had won, graciously.

That was morning, and the exhilaration of victory was still in their blood as they entered Landon Hall, the erstwhile cafeteria, now transformed into a breathtaking ballroom shimmering under a panoply of night sky and the awe and majesty of the stars and their constellations in full splendor.

Breathtaking. Cassie paused at the entrance to breathe in the ethereal nighttime scene. She had been told that professional set designers had created and constructed the setting, and this confirmed it. Anything she had imagined paled in comparison to what appeared before her. The ceiling had become the heavens, not pale, muted amorphous heaven, but star-studded heaven adorned with thousands of brilliantly twinkling mini-lights, used as a backdrop for larger lights that formed the major constellations in the night sky. Nothing she had ever seen, no Broadway set design, not even the Planetarium, replicated this. She gazed in awe, completely enraptured.

"Beautiful, isn't it?" He asked.

"Absolutely breathtaking," she responded, not breaking her focus. She knew who it was.

"We hired the set designer from *Pippin*. The designers from *Cats* are all pretty busy, but we got a great talent. Parents here know some outrageously gifted people," he said with pride. "We got a crew, illustrations, more than a fair price, and we said, 'Go.' It was somewhat of a dedication to Fosse." He glanced around and up at the heavens. "Outstanding."

Cassie was still awed by its beauty. "That's Orion, the hunter," she said, pointing to the constellation crossing at the far end of the northern sky, "Poseidon's son. The myth says he hunted with Artemis, but he touched her, so she poisoned him with a scorpion's sting. Did you know that?" She turned and looked at him, not with conceit, as one would to say, I know something you don't. On the contrary, her tone and expression were apologetic, saying, I'm sorry; of course you knew this, but I wanted to share it with you. She turned to the sky and her hand swung left. "Pegasus, born from Medusa's blood, and . . ." she turned her hand further left in the northern sky; "that's Hercules."

"I'm impressed." Vaughn stepped forward and looked at her, amazed.

Cassie smiled. "Don't be. It's just some leftover mind-clutter from a course I took one summer. The professor was so obsessed with astronomy and Greek mythology that he integrated both into the microcosm/macrocosm theory from the Middle Ages and Elizabethan period. I remember it though, because, on clear nights, I'd step out onto my back porch and the stars would be so close, and the constellations so bright and alive. I'd talk to them out loud." She giggled. "Sounds silly, doesn't it?"

"Come," he replied, in a soft voice he had never heard before, ushering her forward, "let me show you the rest." Other than that, he said nothing, allowing himself to digest the pure innocence of what she had just shared with him.

They walked slowly through the main ballroom and dance floor, the area of the cafeteria that would be serving lunch and dinner come Monday. "Constellations," the DJ, had set up at the far end. A very appropriate name for the evening, she thought. His music choices were soft and romantic from the 50's, her era. "Earth Angel" was filtering throughout the room. What a beautiful song. A starlit night; music for lovers, and she was taken back to a past time, a past life, when her fears and apprehensions had been tinseled with hope. She felt her lower lip tremble and she fought back memories peeking out from her subconscious.

At Landon Hall, each grade level had its own seating in its own individual section off the main cafeteria where meals were served cafeteria style, and the Starry Night's motif flowed into each of these. Vaughn escorted her from one to another, from wide-eyed freshmen who sat awkwardly with friends, to senior students, hers. Young adults seated with their dates or friends, dressed up for the ball. The young ladies wore elegant cocktail dresses, intricate, sophisticated hairstyles, diamond necklaces and bracelets, most likely their mom's but maybe their own. Cassie had to remind herself that this was far from the Paterson socio-economic strata. The young men wore suits, Parker and Mason even sported bow ties - very stylish. No sneakers, no T-shirts, no sweat shirts, a very different image. Nice.

"Lookin' good, Mrs. Komsky," Elizabeth said, smiling. She wore an all beaded, black strapless gown beautifully accented by her olive skin tone, and did she ever look gorgeous.

"Thank you, Elizabeth, so do you." Strapless was not something Cassie would have worn, she was much too conservative, but her finely woven mohair knit, accented with bursts of silver thread and beading running from the shoulders down the sleeves, then from her sides to her hips, accentuated her tiny waist and her well-rounded backside, where it flared just a bit so it flowed as she flowed. Diamond stud earrings and a single diamond choker provided just the right touch of elegance. From their expressions, the young men in her classes were quite aware that their forty-something-year-old Shakespeare teacher had dynamic physical assets. They also noticed that their dean was in no hurry to leave her side. Did Parker notice this too? Cassie greeted each of them, telling them how elegant they looked and that she was proud to be their teacher. Then Vaughn escorted her across the hall to her table under a bedazzling night sky and a shimmering floor that glistened reflective light from above. Magic.

Walter, Melissa, Alicia and most of the football crowd were already seated at their table when Vaughn and Cassie arrived. He assisted her with her chair, said his hellos and took his leave to the Board of Directors' tables across the room where the trustees were seated with their wives. Dr. O/B walked to the head of the first table and sat. "Why isn't his wife with him?" Cassie asked quizzically.

"She never comes to school-related affairs," Walter replied.

"But Parker is here. You'd think she'd want to see her son and be with her family."

Walter shrugged. "You'd think, but whatever their arrangement is, it works for them. You'll see her during the day if it pertains to Parker's academics, but not at any football games or nighttime affairs. Her evenings are reserved for the Club."

Melissa added, "Vaughn's fine going solo; he's been doing it for years. Actually, we'd all be suspicious if she did accompany him." Some of the group agreed. "Is this spectacular or what?" Marissa asked rhetorically, changing the subject intentionally. "I've been to every Homecoming since I've been here, almost fourteen years, and I've never seen a Homecoming ball this spectacular. The others pale in comparison. And this DJ is perfect. The songs are a bit before my time," she injected with flippancy, "but I love the fifties and the rhythm and blues from the sixties."

"Tonight's the Night," segued into "Oh, Girl," a seventies song with sensual lyrics and rhythm. Senior level couples hit the dance floor. Cassie was finding it difficult to stay seated. Music this beautiful was meant for dancing. It was intoxicating, and involuntarily, she began to sway. Again, flashes of Brian and a tear interrupted her blinking.

She turned away so no one would see, and inadvertently faced the dance floor. Oh my God, she exclaimed silently. Elizabeth was dancing with Matt, a nice comfortable fit; Gloria and Zachary had partnered up, and amidst all the other dancers on the floor, were Rachel and Samir. He's here, she thought, shocked. He wasn't here when Dr. O/B had escorted her to the senior dining area, but the seat next to Rachel had been empty, her handbag and scarf warding off any would-be sitters. She must have been saving it for him, right next to her. Well, Cassie thought, my suppositions have been confirmed. Samir held Rachel gently, but unmistakably, telling the world she was his. His left arm around her waist; his right hand cradling the nape of her neck, her head resting in the crook of his neck. Oh, yes, she was his all right, and it was just where she wanted to be.

"Walter," she whispered, tapping his hand, "look." He glanced over and saw.

"Oh my God," he uttered, "I never expected." He looked at Cassie. "But *you* did, didn't you?"

She smiled, "I had an idea. A male and a female don't put so much effort into ignoring each other unless it's love or hate. Thankfully, they got past that." The music played on. The heavens smiled; the setting embraced them, and love suspended time.

Dinner was delicious: hearts of palm salad, shrimp baked in phyllo dough and bacon-wrapped scallops for appetizers. Prime rib, chicken or sole francaise for entrée selections. Napoleons, cream puffs, mini torts, and cheesecake drizzled with raspberry sauce for dessert. The ladies would not be stepping on scales tomorrow morning.

Dinner over and plates cleared, the DJ let loose with music to move by. "Hungry Like a Wolf," set the dancing tone, igniting the students, and the faculty at her table sang along. Jeremy, portly and kind of staid, a geeky kind of chemistry teacher, howled out the chorus. Surprisingly, Tasha leaned in and joined him. Who would have thought two brainy nerds would have even known this song existed.

Then the DJ kicked it up further. "She Works Hard for the Money," and the dance floor overflowed. When "Thriller" permeated the room a few minutes later, Cassie could hardly stay seated, shoulder and neck action she couldn't control, her hands beat the air.

Walter stared at her. "Having a little trouble sitting still?" He asked, humorously.

"Doesn't anybody dance around here?" She countered. Seconds later, "Billie Jean" filled the room, and Cassie was on the dance floor before Walter had answered, in the middle of it all, dancing solo, until Mason saw his English teacher moving in perfect rhythm to Michael Jackson's beat, absolutely stunning and as graceful in motion as pure silk on glass.

And that's when the Board of Trustees stopped talking about red-line items and golf tournaments and turned their attention to the most recent addition to Chelsea's faculty who had just been hijacked by Chelsea's second most prestigious senior, matching her footwork and her rhythm step for step. Cassie's innate rhythm had taken control, and God, but she did have rhythm, becoming one with the beat, unaware of anyone watching, unaware of do's, don'ts, should's and should nots. Cassie's feet slid her across the floor, hips gyrating, arms swaying above her head and she, rotating in a circular motion, pelvis following curvaceously, seductively, so lost in the rhythm that she was unaware of the males in the room gazing at her lustfully, and the women in the room gazing at her jealously.

She became aware of her surroundings only when a strong hand grabbed her arm and pulled her off the dance floor into the corner behind her table. She looked into Vaughn's flaming eyes, she breathing heavily from the dance, he breathing heavily from anger, and what else?

"*What* do you *think* you are doing?" He hissed through clenched teeth. She was startled. More than startled; more than surprised. Was she that naive? No one could be that naïve. "Cassie," he tried to calm himself a bit, "we don't dance like this at Chelsea Academy."

"Like what? Everyone else is dancing the same way."

"No, they're not."

"Yes, they are. Look." She pointed to the dance floor where hips, bodies, extremities were engaged in a primordial ritual.

"It's not the same," he countered, "you didn't look like that . . . you're a faculty member . . ." he stammered, at a loss for words. "You're older!" He shouted, trying to save himself, until her facial expression told him he had just given her a reason no female wants to hear. "Look," he began, attempting to redeem himself, the Trustees are very proper, and we accommodate them, administration and faculty alike. No other faculty member was dancing like that, just you. And there's a reason for that. We give the Trustees the propriety they expect." Had he mollified her or heightened her indignation?

She considered his comments before speaking, and when she did, it was not the diatribe he had expected. "Maybe you try too hard, Dr. O/B. I, we, the kids, we're having fun and enjoying the music. I love to dance – can hardly sit still when a great song comes on – and my students in Passaic showed me how to loosen up. Maybe you and the formal faculty here might do the same. But," she caught his pained expression, "if you prefer more formality, I'll comply. It's your academy. I'm not out to break any established mores here. I just don't know what they are. You'll have to be a bit patient and explain them to me as I go along. Just slow dancing from now on. That should work. Maybe Walter will dance with me."

"I'm sure he would," Vaughn signed, relieved. "I'm sure any of the male faculty would. Thank you. I appreciate it." He nodded and returned to his table, the Trustees and their proper wives, as Cassie returned to her table and eight pairs of staring eyes.

"What?" She asked, looking directly at Walter, then to each of them in turn; all continued to stare. "You want to know what he said, right?" Yes they did. "Okay," she stated, "he said he didn't like my dancing. That what you wanted to know?" That's what they wanted to know, and more as Melissa indicated by rotating her hand, saying, "Keep going."

"He also said I have to give the Trustees the propriety they expect, so I'll be slow-dancing for the rest of the evening. There," she said emphatically. "You wanted to know what he said? Well, that's it."

"Cassie," Walter replied thoughtfully, with no disrespect in his tone, "Chelsea has a stellar reputation and Vaughn has to make sure it's upheld. Propriety and prestige are two of the major reasons we have such a huge endowment, and it's his responsibility to keep it that way. So don't take it personally; he'd say the same thing to any of us."

"Any of us when? If you were dancing with a student or the way I was dancing?" Walter blushed. Even in the ambient light she could see his face turn red. "Walter, I understand the political nature of education. Even though public schools don't operate on endowments, they do operate on taxpayer money, so they're beholden to the taxpayer, which is just as bad. We get parents' groups that insist on sitting in on review boards that are charged with hiring a superintendent simply because parents pay our salaries, and the BOE concedes because they want to get reelected or get the next budget passed.

"Suppose a parent group insisted on having representation on a medical board that was hiring the chief medical administrator of their hospital, parents with no more medical knowledge than how to apply a band aid, demanding representation because the hospital gets state and federal funds. Absurd, yet that's the intrusion education suffers because of politics. It all gets down to money, and the way we have to behave to get it, or keep it. So, no more 'dirty dancing' from me." She threw her hands up humorously.

"Walter suppressed a laugh. "Cassie, you can't change the world, or the influence of politics."

"I'm not trying to change anything, Walter, I'm just me, but maybe that's a bit too uninhibited for this place. I don't want to cause Dr. O/B problems, but I hope I can still say what I think and what I believe is right or not."

"Nothing wrong with that, Cassie, but when something you say or think offends or threatens the big guys, be ready to take the consequences when they push back, because they do push back, and they can get ugly."

"I've seen big guys push, Walter, and I've seen ugly. But might doesn't make right; it only lets you win even when you're wrong. Even in the days of King Arthur and his round table, idealism failed. It's great in theory, but only in theory, not in the real world."

A commotion on the dance floor interrupted their conversation and turned heads. Angry shouts; a young lady's screams; shuffling feet and dancers running for cover, leaving Samir, eyes blazing, shielding Rachel from Parker's and Mason's angry epithets. "I said, I want to dance with her!" Parker shouted threateningly at Samir.

"And she said no! Leave us," Samir countered emphatically. He had spoken in front of every onlooker, his anger as apparent as was his courage. Nor was he to be intimidated. He stood face to face with Parker, grounded, feet firmly planted, not a hint of trepidation by Parker's extra two inches and twenty pounds. Eyes were solely on them, their classmates wondering who this handsome foreigner was and why he had never spoken until now. Rachel was shouting at them to leave Samir alone as he stood firm, defending himself and protecting Rachel.

A stand-off thus far, but if Parker or Mason became physical, Samir would counter. This Cassie knew instinctively. He would never back down.

Suddenly, Parker swung with his right! Samir side-stepped, protecting his face and delivered a calculated, well-trained swing that connected with the left side of Parker's jaw. Parker went down; Mason tackled Samir low. Losing his balance, Samir countered with double fists pounding on Mason's back, kicking his assailant off from his supine position, slamming his fist into his face, rolling and leaping to a standing position, arms and fists protecting his face, clearly a trained fighter. At this point, Walter and Vaughn descended on Samir, grabbed his arms and held him back. Rachel became hysterical.

"They started it!" She screamed, pointing at Mason and Parker, both on their feet, Parker's jaw red; Mason's nose bloody. "They started it! Let Samir go!" Unrestrained, with Samir now an easy target, Parker and Mason went for Samir, helpless within the grasp of the head of Guidance and the dean of the school, until Cassie, from nowhere, threw herself in front of Samir with a curdling "No!" Everyone froze.

With fury in her eyes, she shouted, "No! You are *not* going to hurt him!" She glared at Parker and Mason, who froze where they stood, caught off guard, hesitant to move. "And neither of you" she glared at Walter and Vaughn, "are going to let them! They're wrong! "They started it. You both saw that. We *all* saw that. If anyone takes a beating for this, it should be *them*." She pointed emphatically at Mason and Parker. *"Not* Samir!"

Dumbfounded, Walter and Vaughn loosened their hold on Samir. Seizing the opportunity, he slipped away, racing for the side exit, Rachel running behind him, her hand in his.

"It's over, everyone," Vaughn ordered, regaining composure. "Please, kindly go back to your tables or the dance floor. He nodded to the DJ to resume play, and directed Cassie to the same corner again. She waited for Vaughn to begin, as Crowded House began, "Hey Now." The song's irony was almost palpable – the lyrics begging the world not to build a wall between the two lovers. She imagined Samir and Rachel, running from everything and everyone, finding succor nowhere, a 20th century Romeo and Juliet. Be ready to take the consequences, Walter had just said, and here she was, facing her consequence.

"You have superseded your authority, Cassie." Vaughn seethed. "You are a mere faculty member at this institution and at this function. Nothing more. You neither administer justice nor dispense it."

Cassie's sense of indignation, from all the novels and drama in literature she had read about man's inhumanity to man, propelled her now. "Do not misinterpret my intentions, Dr. O/B," she hissed. "I was neither attempting to administer nor to dispense the 'justice' I was witnessing. You would have allowed Parker and Mason to beat Samir, who was clearly in the right, by holding him down for them?" She glared at him. "I'm sorry Sir, but what I saw didn't even approach the definition of that word!"

"I will give you thirty days notice and you will be dismissed before Christmas!" She did not bother to look for clenched fists. His countenance was sufficient enough.

"If you wish to dismiss me because I prevented your son and his friend from attacking Samir, who was unequivocally the victim here, that is your discretion, but . . . if the situation were reversed, and Parker were in Samir's place, would you have allowed Samir to do the same thing to Parker while you and Walter held *him* back?!"

Her analogy stunned him. Stunned him. "How dare you!"

"How dare I? How dare I what, present an analogy you can't refute because Samir is the one who is right and Parker, your son, is wrong? That's favoritism, Dr. O/B, and discrimination. That's not justice."

"You see favoritism! You see discrimination?! I see two all-American kids, one of whom is my son, fighting a kid who clearly does not belong here and does not want to belong here, and what I see from you is blind devotion to that kid!"

"Blind devotion! Yours is the premise operating from blind devotion, not mine! I'm defending Samir because he's right! My analogy asked you to switch the students, to hold Parker while Samir attacked him, but you can't. You won't even allow yourself to do that because you'd have to admit Samir is right. And to arbitrarily characterize Samir as a kid who clearly 'does not belong here' versus 'two all-American kids' is wrong, clearly wrong, especially because you have to alter the definition of justice to make your interpretation right. Can't you see that?"

Vaughn's temperament was not suited for this. In his lifetime, he had barely experienced a "no," had hardly ever met with a contradiction, and had never, ever witnessed open defiance. "Cassie, how can you defend him! Have you no sense of loyalty?"

"Loyalty? How does loyalty play a part in this? Loyalty to what! Loyalty to whom?!" She asked, completely dumbfounded.

"Cassie, are you so naive? . . . Samir is an Arab!"

She became oblivious to time, place, the twinkling sky and the magical night. Her mind whirled; her senses, in a state of delirium, separated from her like an out-of-body experience. She became Dorothy, holding on to something that was grounded to nothing as a tornado ripped her from her foundation and lifted her to some metaphysical destination she could not comprehend, the epitome of existential man – alone, unguided, swept any way, but she knew she would not wind up in Oz, and she doubted there would ever be a happy ending. "No," she murmured, her voice a tenuous whisper, and uncontrollably, she started to cry.

"He's an Arab," Cassie. He has no loyalty to this country. Why are you so upset?"

"Because he's a human being, a person with feelings, a person who bleeds. 'If you prick us, do we not bleed? If

123

you tickle us, do we not laugh? If you poison us, do we not die?'" Tears filled her eyes. "Why am I so upset? Because you give your son rights you flagrantly deny Samir and justify it with, 'he's not loyal to this country.'"

Vaughn seethed. "Do not quote *The Merchant of Venice* to me! This is *not* the same thing!"

"This is *exactly* the same thing! We're all human, Dr. O/B. We all have feelings and we all hurt. Yet with Samir, you choose to forget that. You claim his reticence frustrates you and the faculty; you tell his uncle everyone's trying to help him, and you take his money, but you don't care if he opens up, do you? To you, he's just an Arab," she challenged. "So what do you care? What does it matter? And you think he doesn't sense that alienation? Doesn't sense the ostracism? This 'Get out, you're not one of us,' stereotype? But if he weren't an Arab, Dr. O/B, if he were Irish, or Italian, then he'd have rights? What if he were a Jew? Would you justify taking away his rights and say, "Cassie, he's a Jew?"

Vaughn gasped, clearly shaken. "Enough, Cassie. That's enough!"

"Not enough, Dr. O/B. You can't even say what I've just said. You might lose your position despite your family's standing in the community. You might lose it because of political pressure, because the statement would be unmentionable, anathema. But to switch the words around, exchange Jew with Arab, two little words, that's fine, isn't it? Isn't it?" She challenged, in tears.

"Cassie, what does it matter?!" He stared at her with penetrating ferocity. "He's one kid we can't help!" He was furious; his patience with this mistake he had hired had overpowered him. She conformed to nothing! He was a fool for taking her on. "What! Does! It! Matter!"

"It matters," she shot back, "because *I'm* an Arab!" She hurled the words at him. "I'm an Arab, Dr. O/B, and your statement demeans us all! But I'm damn proud of my heritage and its contributions to Western culture that we're never taught in this country. Just make those Arabs into pariahs; then it'll be easy for us to take their oil, depose their rulers, or help Israel invade Lebanon and confiscate more Palestinian land. Won't it?!" Vaughn's face went from bright red to ashen and elements of shock crept into the crevices of his countenance. "And the biggest irony of all?" Cassie, almost snorted her disdain. "The *only* person in this entire institution who saw through Samir's hurt, his isolation and his pain, and who cared enough to get behind his walls, is Rachel, a Jew. The only person who offered him succor, and love. That's situational irony at its best. I'll have to include that in a future lesson."

She turned, ran back to the table, grabbed her purse, and, without looking at anyone or saying goodbye, hurried out. Walter got up from his seat and watched her rush past him. He had heard it all. For a brief moment he let the shock of her words penetrate, forcing him to wonder, in disbelief, how he, head of Guidance, with degrees in psychiatry and medicine, could have allowed himself to participate in holding Samir down, vulnerable prey to Parker and Mason. A second of incredulity, then he left too. Vaughn remained glued where he stood, his face a "whiter shade of pale."

14

VAUGHN'S REACTION AFTER HOMECOMING

Vaughn drove home in a stupor and let the darkness envelope him. He had always welcomed driving at night so he could disappear into his own thoughts, which usually dwelt on finances, work, or golf, and he enjoyed the quiet time night-driving provided, coveting it as his own. He used Thomas, their driver, for formal occasions or Broadway shows where front door service was mandatory, but to and from work and about town, driving was his quiet time to meditate and relax.

But tonight, his thoughts were on none of those topics and his time was definitely not quiet, for, inside, his stomach was churning and he was seething with emotional turmoil, consumed, obsessed with a teacher he had hired no more than two weeks ago whom he had hoped would, in time, open up and become part of the faculty and the Chelsea experience. What he had learned in these two weeks was that her opening up to become part of the faculty and the Chelsea experience were mutually exclusive - she would never fit in.

Yet, he could not expunge her words from his mind. If the situation had been reversed and Parker had been the one who had been attacked, would he have for a second allowed his assailants to continue their assault while he and Walter held him down? Never. So, Cassie had been right. Her analogy had been perfect and his bias blatant, but until tonight, he had never viewed it that way, and he had never admitted his prejudice against Samir. He's an Arab. Subconsciously, that made it easy, but Cassie hurling his words against him? That made it so different. He had judged her from appearances; she looked European; her name was Slavish, English was her dominant language, and she was an American. All this, yet she was an Arab.

She was correct; schools taught nothing about the Middle East; so he would research her heritage. But he would rethink his Thanksgiving invitation to her and her daughter. He was certain she'd say or do the wrong thing since she had shown repeatedly she was capable of doing both. Taylor would react with venom. Taylor appreciated Walter, whose estranged family lived in Oregon, and she liked Melissa, widowed at a young age, childless, who never remarried. Others on the faculty who were alone or isolated from family she welcomed for the holiday's sake or the sake of her husband's position, but this female, this Cassie . . . if she held to her inimitable manner, she would never be tolerated. Taylor would brook nothing that would tarnish the family's reputation, one of the reasons Vaughn adored and respected her so much. Her devotion to the established Otis-Barrett dynasty was unimpeachable.

So he continued to ponder, continued to think, and the peace he associated with night driving never materialized. As he turned into his driveway, he was as far from the solace he was seeking as he had been when he had inserted his key into the ignition.

15

CASSIE AFTER HOMECOMING - BRIAN

Cassie cried herself to sleep. She cried for Samir, for the hurt and isolation she knew he felt; she cried for Dr. O/B's shocking insensitivity, and she cried for her acute and relentless loneliness. She was a beautiful, kind and sensitive person who felt for others. Her biggest weakness was her inability to overcome feelings of worthlessness imprinted within her from childhood, feelings that, at some unpredictable event or time, would resurface involuntarily. Some place inside, she would hear four words, "You're good for nothing," and she'd be confronted with the inner battle that kept her apart from others, until Brian. Brian was the one time, the only time in her life her feelings of insecurity hadn't prevailed.

At twenty-one, she was about as naïve as a twelve-year-old. Celebrating her twenty-first birthday five months late, Cassie walked into the Nor'easter Hotel's Bar in

Manasquan with college girlfriends and wished she had driven her own car so she could have turned around and walked right out. Horrible! What was this place with cement floors awash in beer, up to several inches in some places, depending on the slope and the slant of the floor, where guys and girls alike seemed impervious to sloshing through this indoor surf? Dim lighting, a band screaming hard rock at deafening volumes, plastic glasses of foaming beer traveling high above heads wending their way to drinkers and revelers grabbing a glass or two en route - who would want to be here?

Obviously, everyone, since, when she turned around, she discovered all her friends had abandoned her, had completely disappeared, had dissolved into this suffocating crowd that opened and closed its maw to allow its captives to fight their way to the bar or a tiny place on the dance floor to make contact with someone, anyone.

"Hey," she shouted as some big guy in a sloppy T-shirt grabbed her ass. She slapped his hand away, but he came after her with a condescending laugh from a mouth that stunk of beer, and hands that closed in on her. He was drunk, stinking drunk. She squirmed her way free, taking advantage of his loss of balance. She forced her way through the crowd in search of a safe haven, to be confronted by more hands pushing, more prodding amidst laughing and mocking. Two hundred pound guys feel mighty empowered when accosting a single female half their weight.

Almost beside herself, she began to scream. It didn't help - everyone was screaming. Unlike hers, though, their screams were part of the ritual. "Get away from me! Get away!" She knocked beers into faces, twisted, squirmed to break free. Slobbering guys accosted her, pushing her one way and another like some beach-ball being bounced from one player to another. Her fist smashed a nose. A crunch, maybe a possible break, nothing more than a minor victory. She was being devoured by guys who had gone beyond reason, and she would lose this battle. How could this be happening? In public, she was being mauled, and no one cared.

From her peripheral vision, she saw a huge bartender wearing the Nor'easter Hotel's blue T-shirt leap over the bar and barrel through the crowd, heading in her direction, a wake of falling bodies at each side like bowling pins going down. Was he coming to assist her? Oh, please, let him help. Her screams were uncontrollable and she was crying hysterically.

But he was coming to her aid, this wall of muscle, tossing assailants aside with one blow, smashing faces, pummeling chests. Although drunk beyond rational thought, they still felt pain, and instinctively turned away. Fight or flight, they chose flight. "Mike!" Her savior shouted to the bartender on his right. "Cover my hook!" A thumbs-up from Mike said he had it covered; then this guy ushers Cassie through the parting crowd and outside into the cool, refreshing night air of Memorial Day weekend, opening season for the Manasquan bars and all the Jersey shore bars. The frenzied drinking orgies had begun.

"What are you doing here?" He demanded softly as if to say, who gave you permission?

"I came with my friends," Cassie stammered wiping back tears, her insides racing, her stomach jumping. She was still trembling.

"Did your friends tell you what this place is like, because you sure as hell don't belong here." At this, Cassie became indignant. Who was this guy telling her she didn't belong here, even though he was right. "Hey, you have the right to be here," he replied, reading her thoughts, "but you don't belong here."

He softened and she capitulated with a nod. "Wanna go home?" Cassie couldn't stop trembling and her knees were weak. "We're a little short on bartenders and bouncers tonight, as you can see, but I'll drive you to wherever you're staying if you can wait till my shift ends. That'll be in about ten minutes. I can't leave Mike to hold down the fort alone. Even a full roster of bartenders and bouncers can hold off a drinking frenzy for only so long. This is the first weekend of summer and these guys are getting smashed," he said with conviction. You can sit behind my hook until I leave."

She liked him. She liked him immediately. Her instincts told her he was okay, but did she trust him, a stranger? Hell, no. Just because he had saved her from a total disaster didn't mean he would be any more trustworthy than the others, maybe just as bad using a different tact?

Again, he read her mind. "Look, I get off in ten minutes, but I only have a twenty minute break. I could stretch it a few minutes because I manage the hook when the manager is gone, but I gotta be behind that bar in twenty-five minutes after my break. I need this job. So, if you're thinking I could drive you off somewhere and you'd never be seen again, don't. I'd have a rough time taking you home, fighting you off from the untoward advances you're imagining, and coming back, all in twenty minutes."

He smiled, but it was the word that got her. From a muscled guy who she'd expect to be all brawn and no brains, "untoward" was not a vocabulary word she had expected.

"Of course, I could always leave you here for the pack of wolves that comes out to get some air, regurgitate or take a leak. Prefer that?"

He was insulting and offensive. "Listen Romeo, find yourself another Juliet," she retorted angrily, walking off in a direction that would take her farther from her rental unit rather than closer. Cassie never knew where she was heading even if she wore a compass on her wrist.

"Hey," he uttered softly. "Sorry. I was being a jerk. But unless you live on the beach, you're going in the wrong direction." He waited for reason to take over. "Come on. Come inside, sit behind my hook until my break, and I'll take you home, wherever that is. Okay?" He asked, adding, "And I'll be a perfect gentleman."

She considered it. Maybe his apology was sincere, maybe it wasn't but she had no choice. "Okay," she answered weakly. "I'll wait. Yes, I'd like to go home."

And that was it. He was the only guy she couldn't run from, couldn't throw away. He was persistent, and always a gentleman. They married three years later, set up home in Union City. She taught English lit and Shakespeare in Passaic; he taught biology in Weehawken, Jersey reserves on the side. Stevie came along in '78, after years trying to conceive, and later that year, they bought what was to be their first home in Manasquan. Brian could be closer to the Nor'easter during summer months, and she and Stevie would be there for summer vacations. Small, well-built, a cape, Meadow Ave, end of the block.

Those years were the happiest years of her life. Laughter and love filled their house. Like kids, they'd run around furniture playing tag, hide in shower stalls and closet nooks playing hide and seek, take long walks in the park, day trips to the shore to eat at the Lobster Shanty or the Shrimp Box, walk the surf with Stevie in tow, gather clams for chowder, have long talks about dreams and future plans, and their permanent move to the shore.

And they'd talk about life, his life, her life, and her childhood. Just about everything. And when the child-hood fears she could never shake crept from their hiding places and darkened her thoughts or her dreams, Brian was there. He was always there to wrap his arms around her and whisper, "It'll be all right." And she would feel safe in his embrace. So safe, like nothing could ever hurt her, and she'd snuggle into his arms and fall asleep.

She would say he was her salvation; he would say she was his. He had never known anyone as kind, as generous and goodhearted; someone who would offer a helping-hand to a stranger, and who had, upon too many occasions, gotten herself near danger for having done so. He had been her rock and her fortress when her naivety couldn't quite be contained, and in turn, he had learned from her that giving and helping others linked him with humanity.

And this willingness to help had taken him from her. So, for all of this, for the obstacles she had faced in her past, for the prejudice she had faced tonight, this night of Homecoming that had begun so beautifully, and for Brian who could no longer be there to hold her and tell her everything was going to be all right, she cried. You can only be strong for so long before you break down.

16

MONDAY AFTER HOMECOMING

C assie walked to Rand Hall with heaviness in her heart she had not experienced in years. She did not doubt she'd have a one-year tenure at Chelsea, if that long, but how she'd endure it pained her. Her outburst at Homecoming was honest, and as shocking as it was to Dr. O/B, his statements were equally as shocking to her. She had visualized a slave being brutalized then hanged for the fun of it. Not as a human; not even as a domesticated pet. A thing, to be used for one's cruel folly or sport, a practice accepted, condoned in the culture. She was resolved. She'd lose this job, but she would not lose her humanity.

Yesterday had turned exceptionally warm, and the thermometer hovered in the low forties. Bright sunshine peppered the grass, filtered through brown leaves of juvenile oaks that rustled slightly as gentle breezes nudged them in one direction then another. She'd go home early as she could today and spend some quality time with

Stevie. Maybe make up for a very poor performance at motherhood over the weekend. Stevie was her daughter, her family, and Cassie had cheated her this weekend by letting the vagaries of this place and its dean manipulate her emotions. She'd stand up for what was right and take the consequences, as she had told Walter, but she would not allow her emotions to deprive her and Stevie of precious moments that could never come back. Life was too short. "We strut and fret our hour upon the stage and then are heard no more." Shakespeare was so right.

Eight o'clock arrived as did eleven students, hushed and apprehensive. A real eye-opener when they discussed Hamlet's first soliloquy - a metaphor of the world and all that reeks in it: "an unweeded garden that grows to seed; things gross in nature possess it entirely." Homecoming had given them a heavenly panorama of the beauty and talent man possessed, juxtaposed against an unforgettable image of man's inhumanity to man. The discussion was muted, voices were silent because they understood. They had seen it up close, personal and ugly.

Towards the end of class, the discussion lightened a bit when it segued to Hamlet's father's ghost. A few jibes about the Elizabethan period's belief in ghosts until Elizabeth countered with *The Exorcist*, Zach referenced *The Crucible*, and Connor mimicked the ghost by shouting, "Swear . . . Swear!"

That provided some much-needed levity, but Cassie also reminded them not to laugh at another peoples' cultures, past or present. "We have enough idiosyncrasies of our own. What works for us may seem as absurd or harsh to them as their ways seem to us. Sure we're more advanced with industry and technology today, but to think we've always gotten it right might be a bit solipsistic. Some great cultures existed while Europe's culture was still in diapers." They liked the imagery.

Cassie gave tomorrow's assignment and ended the lesson a minute early. As books closed, Parker slowly rose from his seat and stood at attention. "There's something I need to say," he stated stiffly and he looked at Rachel and Samir. "My behavior was unacceptable Saturday night and I apologize." Short, curt, practiced, most likely sternly motivated by his father, but nevertheless, any admission of impropriety was a sign of maturity and Cassie was pleased.

Mason surprised her even more by following Parker's apology. Mason was a day student, so he drove to school, but football tied him closely with Parker. Although he had an aggressive personality, he followed Parker's lead concerning proper decorum. His apology was a bit softer than Parker's: He had less to lose; he wasn't in love with Rachel. But his touch of informality and genuflecting earned him a thin smile from Rachel. Samir's countenance remained non-committal.

Cassie was relieved when they left. Three more periods passed, and by the time period five, her free period, came around, she sat, more like collapsed, in her seat, head down, too tired to reread Hamlet's letter to Ophelia. Discussing whether Hamlet's insanity was feigned or real just wasn't her top priority right now. Quiet and peaceful. She sensed the ticking clock, the warmth from the heaters radiating throughout the room, the buzz of florescent lighting, and the smell of a classroom, books upon books, their musty pages, the chalkboard and the remnants of fragrances left behind by her students' perfumes and aftershaves.

She was subconsciously aware of all this because she had taught for so long and the classroom was her second home. So here and now, she was at peace. Hamlet's letter could wait; it all could. The tension fell away as she held her head in her hands and inhaled the silence one breath at a time, unaware that Dr. O/B had quietly approached her room and was standing in her doorway, arms raised above his head, holding onto the lintel; his body leaning in a very relaxed stance.

Suddenly she looks up and emits a spontaneous little gasp. He makes no effort to move, the quiet she had been enjoying vanishes in a second. Am I dismissed? She thinks, her mind whirling. Is he here to say, forget Thanksgiving? No need; I already know that. Is he here to harass me, observe my classes three, four times a day? Gotta be some type of punishment for Saturday's outburst. Her mind raced in a loop, like a hamster propelling the wheel to nowhere.

Though he looked composed, Vaughn's thoughts were as convoluted as hers. If he began with mundane topics like the weather or classroom temperature, he would lose whatever credibility he still had. Things had gone too far to avoid the topic. If he began the topic belligerently or pedantically, with an "I'm right and you're wrong" posture, he would turn her off in a heartbeat, and she would have no respect for anything he had to say . . . . Don't be insipid or mundane, he thought, and so he began.

"I only have one book in my library about Arabs, and I'd better apologize for that, since it's a pretty big library.

Huge, in fact. I'll get more on the topic, though." He stood fixed in the doorway, and Cassie thought he was actually hesitant to come in. She had thought from her first interview that he had a captivating boyish smile, and it peeked through at that moment. "But, I was wrong Saturday night. Wrong . . . and biased. I never thought I was, and I never doubted my thoughts or actions before, but I did think about them this weekend and realized you were correct." He dropped his hands to his sides then sought out his pockets to hide them there. Then he looked away, somewhat bashfully. Looked back at her; looked away; looked back at her. Cassie tried hard not to smile; the encounter had passed from tense and strained to somewhat humorous. Here was the dean of the school slightly nonplussed. "I'm sorry," he finally blurted out, staring at her, and, seeing her feeble attempt to squelch a smile, laughed.

Cassie smiled broadly. "That is the nature of being biased, is it not?" she offered. "or brainwashed, to use a more aggressive term. You don't know why you think a certain way about a topic. You only know you do. And in this case, as in most, the brainwashing is intentional."

He gave her a quizzical look.

She shrugged slightly. "Have you ever heard a report on the Israeli/Palestinian situation that presented the Arab side by someone speaking English coherently or at all, dressed in Western attire?" He paused a few seconds then shook his head. "Neither have I. The media presents us with raving madmen screaming some foreign, seemingly primitive language, while the Israeli proponent is calm and speaks perfect English."

He was contemplating her question as she continued. "For years, I was a strong, unconditional supporter of Israel, until I began listening closely, and finally realized I was hearing only one side, the side I was supposed to hear.

"That's when I deviated from mainstream media and branched out on my own, reading everything I could about the conflict there, beginning with the Balfour Agreement and going way back to the Arab culture during the Golden Age of their empire.   Only then did I learn what an amazingly, highly-developed culture it had been, and how much it bequeathed to the West that we simply assume is ours. You'd be amazed if you knew how much." He looked at her quizzically, as if to say 'What?'

"What? You mean give you an example?" She asked. He nodded. "That's easy. I can give you dozens but you're going to be surprised."

"Well, go ahead, then. Surprise me."

"Okay. I noticed a chessboard in your office when I was in there. You play?"

He nodded. "Love the game."

"Thank the Arabs. Chess originated in India, was played by the Arabs who carried it into Europe via North Africa. Backgammon, one of the oldest, if not *the* oldest, known board game came directly from Egypt, approximately 5000 B.C."

"I've never heard that."

"And you won't because no one concerns themselves with Arab contributions to Occidental culture, and they're not taught. But they exist everywhere." She paused briefly. "You drink coffee?" Another nod and a facial expression that said, who doesn't? "Would you be surprised to learn that coffee is an Arab contribution?"

"I thought it was all-American and from South America."

"Maybe today, but the earliest credible evidence of coffee drinking came from Yemen in the fifteenth century. By the 16th century, it had reached the rest of the Middle East, Persia and Turkey, picked up by the Venetian merchants and . . . here we are today! But, again, no one knows this." She paused briefly. You have a PhD." He raised his eyebrows as if to say, not quite the whole truth. "Two?" She added apprehensively. He smiled demurely. "Three?!" She said in disbelief. He nodded. "More's the pity," she added. Vaughn laughed a full guttural laugh. "Because if you have three PhDs and you know none of this, think how little the majority of our population knows."

"I will admit I know nothing about what you've just told me."

"You've gotta read, Dr. O/B, she added informally. Another question. How do you drink your coffee?"

"What, you mean black, cream, sugar?"

She nodded. "Uh-huh."

"One sugar." He shook his head. "No; you're not going tell me I'm drinking sugar in my coffee because of the Arabs."

"I am *absolutely* going to tell you that. Sugar's history may have begun in India, but Arabs established the first sugar mills, refineries, and plantations. The Crusaders brought it back to Europe with them. Prior to that, Europeans used honey. And this country certainly can *not* do without sugar. Think of the pastry and packaged junk food Americans eat. All full of sugar. Cheese. You eat cheese, but you can't make a cheesecake without sugar. Ice cream. You may like cream in your coffee, well, you don't," she interjected good-naturedly, "but you can't make ice cream without sugar. And who doesn't like ice cream?

"It's foods too, not just desserts. Yogurt, hummus, pita, pomegranates, apricots, dates, to name a few. And it's more than food." Vaughn was captivated by Cassie's enthusiasm. "It's fabric like muslin; it's learning, like the University of Cordova and Baghdad. It's libraries, poetry, literature, algebra and the concept of zero! Algebra! From the Arabs, those primitive desert people who know nothing about anything." She paused, shaking her head in frustration. "Things we accept as part of our culture, as though they began with us and were always here. How ethnocentric."

"I didn't know any of this, Cassie. In this area, I'm pretty illiterate."

"None of this is taught in this country. We live in a time capsule that dates us from 1776 to the present, and all our advances we believe are our own, or European, but the Arab Golden Age? Amazing. They had sophisticated medicinal cures unheard of by Europeans. Hospitals in every major city and mobile hospital units that served distant places and battlefields."

"Similar to 9-1-1 or an ambulance," Vaughn interjected, showing he understood.

"Or a Red Cross unit," Cassie confirmed. "But they had them, surgeons and doctors, well over a thousand years ago, who had to pass oral and written examinations to become licensed. Some hospitals had separate wards to treat different diseases. All this, while Europe's state of the art at that time was mud or thatch housing, disease, no sanitation or running water."

She leaned her hand on her chin and thought she detected a touch of empathy in his eyes. She wasn't sure, but he was no longer standing in the doorway looking in. He had entered the classroom slowly and was now leaning against the wall, arms folded across his chest, very much intrigued by her exposition.

"Wouldn't you be more comfortable sitting in a chair rather than leaning against the wall?" She smiled, and her smile was so inviting and non-intimidating, Vaughn casually walked over and took a seat at the table. Cassie rose, came around her desk and sat at the other end. The two faced each other on friendly terms.

"I can get a little long-winded when I talk about this," she smiled, "and, as you can see, I don't need much prodding to get me started." She openly laughed. "But I also realize this can get pretty boring to someone who has never heard any of it. So I'll stop. Thanks for listening."

"On the contrary, I don't find it boring at all. I find it quite fascinating. But what happened to all of this? What happened that turned them into the backward culture they are now?"

"Wars for power and the Ottoman Turks. Over four hundred years of clock reversal, and the Golden Age and all its contributions were transferred to Europe, then England and assimilated into those cultures who claimed possession of the Middle East. All credit to the Arab world was forgotten, or ignored, a slate wiped clean. Now, they're intentionally forgotten. The only image we're given of an Arab is a wild terrorist who's blowing up busses and buildings and killing innocent civilians, women and children.

He glanced at his hands and squirmed a little. "But, unfortunately Cassie, they are," he replied. "You can't deny that."

"Now? Yes, terrorist groups are doing that. But the PLO, Hezbollah, these groups first began after the Six-Day War when the Arabs felt all hope was lost. That's why they exist. The *original* terrorists in the Middle East were the Irgun, the Haganah, and the Stern gang, Zionist terrorist gangs that led a campaign of terror against the Arabs and the British, doing the very same thing we accuse the Arabs of doing today.

These original terrorists bombed Arab busses, Arab trains, Arab cafes, marketplaces, buildings, houses. Innocent men, women, children, blown apart by Zionist gangs. The King David Hotel, bombed, over two hundred people killed. Or, The USS Patria, loaded with Jewish refugees. Jewish refugees, Dr. O/B, their own people, bombed, over two hundred fifty killed. Then the British exit, the establishment of Israel and continued systematic cleansing of Palestinians from their land. Research Israel's attack in 1947 on a little village called Deir Yassin, a village that had signed a non-aggression pact with its Jewish neighbors, approved at Haganah headquarters. Attacked anyway; villagers massacred. Just the threat these gangs were going into a village caused a mass exodus because of what happened in Deir Yassin. I've never seen press coverage on that. Have you?"

Vaughn shook his head. "No. Never."

"Then please read something other than mainstream media. Read the Balfour Agreement of 1917, passed to Baron Rothschild, a Zionist, who passed it to the Zionist Federation of Great Britain. It stated the British government was favorable to establishing a national home, not a state, for the Jewish people in Palestine with the caveat that nothing was to be done that would affect the civil and religious rights of the existing non-Jewish community. But that didn't happen, because, with ethnic cleansing and settlements, Zionists made sure the Arab population would change.

"Their long-term agenda was realized with the state of Israel. Read the McMahon-Hussein Correspondence, ten letters, not long, and read the Sykes-Picot Agreement, or books written by 20th century scholars to learn how Palestinian land was usurped by terrorism. Read *They Dare to Speak Out*, by Findley, *The Arabs* by Phillip Hitti, and the opposition many Orthodox Jews had regarding the state of Israel; many still do.

If you look at a map of that area, before and after the Partition Plan of 1947, you'll see the amount of land Israel got. Then look at a map from 1949-67 or to the present, and you'll see how much land Israel has taken and settled, all against the Geneva Convention. When the Palestinians began to fight back, they were and still are, demonized for it. You'll read about attacks on Israelis and *their* causes, but nothing that represents the other side. It's a sorry mess."

She paused, caught her breath and sighed. Then, looking up at him, added, "And you wonder why Samir doesn't open up. Samir was orphaned at fourteen by an Arab terrorist attack against our embassy in '83, an indirect result of Israel's invasion of Lebanon and the massacres at Sabra and Shatila the year before. He's here now, amongst people who know nothing of what his country and the Middle East have experienced, in a country that offers unconditional support for everything Israel does."

Vaughn nodded, beginning to understand Samir's reticence, guilty in knowing he had been complicit, subconsciously, in keeping Samir isolated. "It had to be a nightmare, his parents caught in the middle of the attack."

"Yes," she said softly, "and not just for Samir." She avoided his eyes and looked away. "For everyone who's lost a loved one in that bombing, and all the bombings in that region. They've all suffered. Sons, daughters, spouses. For what? So some military can confiscate land with impunity. And hundreds of thousands of Palestinians lose their lives or become refugees because they're fighting a monolithic power they can never defeat."

"Come on, Cassie, I'm sympathetic to innocent civilians being killed on both sides, but Israel's no monolithic power."

"I didn't mean Israel, Dr. O/B, I meant us, the United States."

Vaughn was startled; his countenance showing shock. "That's a serious charge, Cassie. You make it sound as though we're responsible for the rise of Arab terrorists."

"In a way, we are. We've involved ourselves in the Middle East for decades, manipulating governments and heads of states for whatever our own interests were at the time, never thinking of the ramifications or the consequences to the people, theirs and ours. Never caring. Our government cares about power and money. Most politicians only care about getting reelected. Give them those two things and they'll vote any way donors want."

"That's a very strong statement, Cassie. How long would you stand by it if you were pressured?"

She thought about it. She was taking his question seriously and weighing her priorities. Her principles versus her failing point. "As long as I could until it hurt Stevie. She's my life, my life and my husband's. I would give up my principles, overtly only, call it hypocrisy, to protect her." She turned her head. She had responded to something personal and was embarrassed because she had revealed it. She had made herself vulnerable unintentionally.

Vaughn paused, equivocating. Should he push just a little or back off? "Divorced?" He uttered, surprising himself at the audacity of his question.

Cassie's eyes turned red and she breathed a little heavily, looked into his eyes . . . "widowed."

"Oh, Cassie, I'm so sorry." She forced herself to recover, but the wound had been reopened, and Vaughn knew, instinctively that the conversation had ended.

"I'm sorry, Dr. O/B, but I should leave. I should eat something before my next class. Can't have a serious discussion about Hamlet with a growling stomach."

She forced a laugh, started for her desk, then turned back in his direction. Her expression read equivocation; she paused momentarily, but pushed forward: "Every now and then," she began, "when I'm in a nostalgic mood or when I have the time, I make Stevie an Arabic dinner or a dessert. She has several favorite desserts. When I do, say within the next few weeks, maybe for Thanksgiving, would you like to try one?" She was apprehensive, not knowing if she were transgressing over the limits of propriety. But he smiled a smile that drew her in.

"I'd like nothing better." He said, ran his hand through his hair uncharacteristically, and left.

17

WEEK BEFORE
THANKSGIVING: VAUGHN

Vaughn was changing. On his way home that evening, he detoured to Barnes and Noble and purchased Philip Hitti's short history of *The Arabs,* a small book, less than three hundred pages. He could knock that off in a few days. And he ordered another book by Hitti the store didn't stock. "Not much demand for books on this subject," the clerk had stated. Vaughn wasn't surprised. Rather, he was pleased that the order went through at all and the book was still in print.

That evening, he made another decision. Checking himself out in his full length mirror, he thumbed through the yellow pages and ordered a set of free weights, a workbench, and a suspension bar for pull-ups. He was forty-three to his brother's fifty-two. If Brett could look as good as he did at fifty-two, Vaughn could build up his body too, at least a little. Dressed in sweat pants and a T-shirt, he hit the floor optimistically to start a set of pushups, exercises he had not done since college.   What am I thinking, he wondered as he rolled onto his back after struggling with five. These things are hard! Amazing how difficult it is to pick your entire body weight off the floor on your palms, then take your body down to perpendicular elbows and back up again. And he only weighed a trim two hundred five. Make that a thin two hundred five.

But he kept at it, and on his third attempt, completed ten, no small feat, since his total from his three attempts was twenty-one. Not bad, he thought. That'll build up the chest muscles, deltoids and triceps; now the abs. He rolled over, clasped his hands behind his head, pulled his right knee up as far as tolerable, and started bicycle rotations.

"Vaughn? She asked quizzically. "What on earth are you doing?"

"Hi, Dear," he replied, not breaking stride, but already breathing hard. "Day one of my exercise routine. I am not in shape."

"Vaughn, Darling, I do not want my husband to have a heart attack. Don't you think you're a little old to start such strenuous exercise?"

"Brett is nine years older and he works out every day."

"My point. He's been doing it regularly."

"I have to start somewhere. Don't worry Taylor, it'll be gradual. I give it six months and I should be in pretty good condition."

"Are you going to sweat on this beautiful plush white carpet when there's a gym downstairs?"

"No, Taylor, I've ordered equipment and will work out in my study. Parker uses the gym. Let him have it for his own space. And why concern yourself with the rug? It gets professionally cleaned every six months anyway. Where were you?" He asked, an afterthought.

"I did two manicures at the shop then had a light dinner with your mother, Brett and Hillary at the Club. I got a chance to sneak Brett away from Hillary for a few minutes to put some additional touches on her surprise anniversary gala. It's coming up soon; February is less than four months away."

"How do you plan on surprising her?" He began a series of crunches, counting softly.

"Here's the plan." Taylor's eyes sparkled with enthusiasm. "She expects the Club. Nobody holds an affair anywhere else. So, we go to an early dinner at the Club, and that's all there is, just the Club. She'll be so disappointed, looking and waiting for something more. But no, nothing. We start to leave, we take the elevator to the parking garage and Brett realizes he's left his wallet on the table or somewhere. That'll be the only suspicious thing because we always do valet parking, so why would we park our own car that evening. But we can't think of anything else, not yet anyway." She paused a moment to contemplate other possible scenarios.

"Anyway, he stops the elevator to go back up to the dining hall, but presses the button for the ballroom floor, supposedly by mistake, because renovations aren't supposed to be completed until early February. Maurice has assured us he won't be taking bookings until furnishings are complete and every detail perfect. And even if he's off by a week or two, who cares? The plan will still work, we'll still have the maiden voyage, and Hillary won't suspect a thing! The elevator will stop on the ballroom floor. We'll get out to see how renovations are progressing, then voile! Surprise!" She gestures with a flair. "What do you think?"

"I think it's a great idea and it may work . . . thirty-one, thirty-two . . ." he uttered between breaths. "Hillary's curious and she knows something's in the works, but to eat her entire dinner at the Club a week before their anniversary, and then leave? It'll burst her bubble completely. She'll be so disappointed she won't even see Brett push the wrong button."

"That's what I'm thinking too." She paused. "You think she'll suspect when we park in the garage?"

Vaughn gave her question some thought. "Set it up in advance so something or someone's in the queue for valet parking one of us doesn't want to see. Maybe the Stauer's. Everyone knows you hate Allison, or, she hates you, but Trevor's a nice guy. He'll play along."

"That's such a fantastic idea! Yes, Trevor *will* play along. I'll speak to him personally." She allowed herself a brief moment of exhilaration. "I am so excited, but all this intricate planning just means more of my time, Darling."

"Take whatever time you need. I won't interfere. I'll be doing push-ups and crunches. Maybe by February, I'll see some tangible results."

Taylor walked past him smiling. Vaughn, so trusting and so naïve!

18

A CRUEL, HARSH WORD

Widowed. What a cruel, harsh word. It ripped your heart from your chest, and, worse, if you weren't expecting it, tore your world to pieces in one breath. Seven letters; one word. No, do *not* remember the visit; do *not* remember the quaking knees and the sinking down and the goodbye to yesterdays and tomorrow, tomorrow and tomorrow. Do not remember the unbearable sorrow, until she could crawl to a stagger, take baby steps though an hour, then a day, day by day. Do not remember.

But she had remembered it all with his one piercing question. She had remembered the memories she had lovingly tied up with brown paper and string and placed on the forget-these shelf in her mind. Like a lance, his question had ripped her heart open and shredded the stitching she had used to patch it up so tenuously four years ago, just enough so she could tell the world, "See, I can make it. I can make it on my own." Vaughn's question had reopened the gaping wound in her heart, and she had bled. She bled from mankind's cruelty, its injustice and its lust for power, for mammon and the insatiable beast that craved it. How many lives had been ripped apart for the big-time players? We were all just pawns in their game.

She wiped off tears as she sat at the kitchen table, turning the pages of her recipe book, and forced herself back to the mundane, yet happy aspects of reality. Every day was another day until the last tomorrow. Either make it a happy one or stay in bed. And she'd do her best to make it happy.

Cassie had Stevie to care for and protect. Stevie, the child she and Brian had waited eight years to have, with the hope of having more. Cassie was determined to make every day as happy and as positive as she could for Stevie; so, back to the treasured recipes that reminded her of her youth and the protection of her mother's nurturing arms. This always calmed her. "Which one do you want, Stevie?" Cassie asked making her voice sound as casual as possible as she flipped two pages back and forth, each one honing in on her two favorite desserts, nemura and beklowe.

Even though these desserts had been part of her mother's Christmas tradition, they had become Cassie's all-time favorites three hundred sixty-five days of the year. She could have eaten them anytime, anywhere, as an appetizer or an entree, and she had passed that peccadillo on to Stevie, because, ironically, these had become Stevie's favorite desserts, too, including chocolate, of course.

Cassie's mother had died long before Stevie was born, long before Cassie had finished high school and started college. Deserted by a husband who disappeared from their lives one October day while strong winds and freezing temperatures heralded an early winter, subsisting on rent from a first floor apartment and a grueling job as a seamstress in one of Paterson's many factories, her mother had taken ill and her health had deteriorated quickly.

She passed one cold morning when the apartment stayed cold; when she had not gotten up at five to light the wood-burning stove whose heat eventually permeated the hallways into the adjacent bedrooms by 6:00; when the sisters stayed under their covers and wondered why there was no heat. When Cassie got up to look for her mother, she knew. She didn't know what death actually was, but she knew her mom was still and would be forever still and cold, that she wouldn't be holding her or cradling her in her arms, telling her she would love her forever.

How long is forever, a little child asked, and the answer was always, past upon past; today and tomorrow, a life without end. The little child listened, and then asked again. But how long *is* forever? Her mother replied, well, not quite so long that nobody dies.

And her mother had died. Cassie was eight; her sister ten. Her sister chose her favorite paternal aunt in Massachusetts; Cassie remained in Paterson with her mother's sister who took her in and tried to nurture her young niece as Cassie's own mother had. Their two-family house on Grand Street sold for twenty-one thousand, split two ways; it was enough to help her aunt bring up Cassie until college, then pay her way through, as Cassie worked weekends for book money and gas to keep an old second-hand Chevy running.

And because her aunt had known tradition and memories were all Cassie had left of her mother, she had encouraged her determined niece to keep her mother's Christmas tradition alive. So, baking nemura or beklowe, sometimes both, every Christmas from the year her mother had died, long before there had been a hint of marriage and family, continued the tradition Cassie's mother had begun.

Here they sat, mother in the kitchen and daughter in the living room, pondering the question Cassie and her mother had debated weeks before Christmas that would lead to a day of mother/daughter baking. Tradition needed work to stay alive. Hadn't T.S. Eliot said something like that, maybe in relation to talent or poetry? Well, even if he just meant it for that, he should have said in all of life too – tradition of any kind takes work.

"Hmm, which one do I want?" Stevie asked out loud, interrupting math homework to consider her decision. Tough one; she loved them both. "Nemura has that rich cream in the middle. Yum. That's so much better than Napoleons, and beklowe has the chopped nuts." She thumped her finger against her cheek, legs crossed, sitting on the couch, pencil in hand, notebook and math book open, contemplating variables, constants, and dessert.

"And you would prefer . . . ?" Cassie asked slowly and deliberately, awaiting Stevie's reply.

"Nemura!" She said emphatically. "And can we make extra cream?"

Cassie laughed. "Nemura it is, and yes, we can make extra cream. We'll make a whole bowl-full if you like," she conceded, "and we'll make the syrup this weekend.

"Gotta love Christmas." Stevie was ecstatic.

They both loved Christmas and the special memories that resurfaced when she'd take out a childhood decoration or one she and Brian had bought together. Happy memories they'd always have as they went through life.

Making nemura was a time-consuming process, and making the syrup took forever! Stirring water and sugar until it simmered slowly to a sweet, syrupy reduction? Hours! A lost art that had almost disappeared through two generations of assimilation into American culture. But it was just the thing to keep her mind off painful memories that Vaughn had stirred up. She and Stevie would share the kitchen this weekend, drink hot chocolate, make popcorn, just as Cassie and her mother, then Cassie and her aunt, had done decades ago.

We'll shop after school tomorrow, she thought, and we'll be ready for the weekend. Vaughn! Damn his question and the scar it had opened. She'd do her best not to let that happen again.

19

Tuesday into Thursday kept her exceptionally busy and her spirits were high. By Thursday evening, she and Stevie were watching "Cheers" and eating popcorn smothered in garlic butter and walnuts, the healthy part of the snack. Before bedtime, they had had a classic pillow-fight with polyester-filled pillows - no chance of errant feathers. Something they hadn't done in months. That had helped more than words.

And here it was Friday, and her classes had reviewed Hamlet through act 2. Of the topics they had discussed, the majority of her students had been motivated most by Hamlet's inability to kill his uncle, nothing unique about that. Period 1, her most outspoken class, issued one diatribe after another about his cowardice, especially the guys, except for Jason, who tried to be more reasonable.

"All he had to do was kill him," Zach ranted passionately. He's an unequivocal coward. Hamlet even asks that question about himself – here, Hamlet's soliloquy after he hires the players, end of act 2, scene 2. He asks if he's a coward, and five lines down, he answers his own question. He says he's 'pigeon-livered and lack gall to make oppression bitter.' Then he says, 'Oh vengeance! Why, what an ass am I!' He sure is a coward," Zach stated firmly, "and an ass!" When else do you get to use the word "ass" in class with impunity. But Zach was no wimp when it came to conviction.

Jason was the only male to defend Hamlet and was Cassie ever pleased that he did. In a few short weeks, he had gone from a student who quivered at making any statement, to challenging the entire male contingent. "The Elizabethan period ushered in the Renaissance," he challenged, "a period of learning and art that distanced itself from Seneca's tragedy of blood where everybody just kills everybody else for revenge. It wasn't that simple for Hamlet. He's a product of transition; his character is mellow, far from avenging a death with more blood. He's caught," Jason continues with surety. "It says it in the preface. 'His father's ghost represents the old-line act of blood for blood, so Hamlet's caught between these two eras and their opposing philosophies and does nothing.'"

"Good point, Jason. In fact, it's excellent." He was speaking his mind easily and with conviction. Great progress.

But Elizabeth Stanack, prescient as usual and never hesitant to speak her mind, countered with the number of deaths that had resulted from Hamlet's indecision. "Hamlet may have been a product of two different eras at odds with each other, but he doesn't 'do nothing.'" She gets that supercilious look on her face then says, "You missed the point. Look how many deaths he causes in the end."

"How many?" Cassie asks. "How many people die because he doesn't 'do nothing'?" You've all read the introduction. Without finishing act 5, you should know this.

Most of them were counting on their fingers. "Eight," Mason blurts out.

"Name them."

"Ophelia, Polonius, Laertes, Gertrude, the king, then Hamlet." Zach calls out. "That's only six. Who am I forgetting?"

"Rosencrantz and Guildenstern," Connor jumps in, "when Hamlet switches letters."

"Eight people dead, because he couldn't follow the edict instructed by his father's ghost. If he had, there would only have been one death, his uncle's," Elizabeth says in disgust. "All because he's a Renaissance man!" She adds with condescension.

"What a mess, huh?" Cassie adds. So you think it would have been better if Shakespeare had let Hamlet follow the Senecan model, kill his uncle and save seven lives?"

"Yup," Elizabeth concurs, followed by Mason and Zach.

"Vengeance?" Cassie blurts out. "Simple, raw vengeance? An eye for an eye? Just go kill him?"

Elizabeth pauses. Cassie had stated her question with passion and a hint of anger, or was it vengeance? Elizabeth nods. Zach, then Parker, Mason, Matt, Connor, and Gloria; they all nod.

"So Shakespeare would have written another *Macbeth* and the play would have ended with act 1: his father's ghost says, kill Claudius; Hamlet kills Claudius; end of play. Right?" No response; Cassie's premise was accurate. "True, Hamlet's genteel character creates its own blood-bath, but Shakespeare wasn't looking for revenge, or it would have been another *Macbeth*. Shakespeare wanted us to go deeper. He wanted his main character to go deeper. He wanted Hamlet and the audience to search their souls for morality, for humanity, for justice, not just revenge, and the effects of melancholy and depression.

"And Hamlet's indecision does just that. Through his soul-searching, we see the complex character who can't reconcile revenge with justice, or at least who needs absolute proof of Claudius' guilt before he enacts revenge, even though his father's ghost has given him the murderer and the motive. Proof would make it justice. What Shakespeare did was to give us a psychological character, a thinker at odds with himself. I can relate to that big time. Can't you?"

"At first I saw him as a prince who's afraid to avenge injustice," Emelia states, "just another someone who can't make up his mind. Like us; no one makes up his mind all the time. But it's much more than that."

"You're right, Emelia, so much more. Consider these examples where we simply can't make up our minds: Do you wear brown socks or black with this outfit, a bow tie or a tie with this suit; do we go to a movie or a watch a game, order a burger or pasta, call a friend or stay in. We all do that; we all waffle; we all tergiversate, don't we?"

"Woah! Mrs. Komsky. Watch the vocabulary or you're gonna lose us," Mason interjected good-naturedly.

"Bet my daughter would know what that word means," Cassie countered.

"Yeah, she's got you for her mother!"

Laughter, continuous, ingenuous, and Cassie laughed with them, thinking of the lists of roots and prefixes on the shower stall door.

"Good one, Mason," she offers as the laughter subsides. "But back to the topic before class ends. Are the situations I've presented on the same plane as Hamlet?"

Jason shakes his head. "Not even close," he says. Your examples are about mundane things. Hamlet's conflict is profound."

"Big difference deciding between black or brown socks or deciding between what's morally right or wrong. Doing the right thing when it's not popular, or doing the wrong thing to fit in with your peers. Big difference between speaking up for the truth when it'll hurt you, or telling a lie that'll make it easy. Hamlet can kill – he finally does in the end – but he struggles with it, really struggles with it to do the right thing. He wants to know, he *needs* to know, what the truth is before he commits murder. Tremendous difference. Tremendous inner conflict. And the machinations he goes through to divine the truth, to feign insanity, to destroy Ophelia, to use the players, everything regardless of consequences, that's his dilemma and that's what creates the problem for others. Justice? Vengeance? Huge difference. Either way, the outcome is not always pleasant."

And then it was Friday and the week was over. Hamlet's first soliloquy, done. Hamlet's letter to Ophelia, through Hamlet hiring the players to perform the play that will catch the king were all done. Essay for Monday: one type-written page comparing Hamlet's, "What a piece of work is man," lines 315 to 322, act 2, scene 2, with Macbeth's "Tomorrow" soliloquy, and begin with act 3 Monday. Busy, busy, busy. Her classes had kept her so busy, in fact, that she had forgotten she was a widow. She was back in the present and enjoying it.

And they were still invited to Thanksgiving. That invitation had not been rescinded. In fact, Dr. O/B had stopped by her room Wednesday morning before first period and, very boldly and confidently, announced, "cotton," both his visit and the word so completely unexpected that it left her disorientated for a few seconds. Cotton? What was he doing here; what was he talking about, until she realized he was announcing another Arab contribution to Occidental culture. He's reading, she thought, and responded with a broad smile that lit up her face. No words were needed. He returned her smile, pushed himself off the door jam and was on his way.

She collected her books and papers after her last class and shoved them into her attache. A quiet Friday evening and Saturday with Stevie was just what she needed. Do some lesson plans, read some essays, finish collating first quarter grades and make syrup for nemura Sunday.

I've made it through another week, she thought, humming "Leather and Lace" while cutting through student housing for home, but time is going quickly. Christmas is about five weeks away. Christmas! Oh my God, five weeks? Christmas will be here in no time. Too early for a tree, but shopping? Never too early for shopping. Perfect! We'll go shopping. And that was the end of a *quiet* Friday.

And one other thing she knew she had to do, she had let go far too long. She had waited for Samir to initiate a conference with her, as was the customary procedure, but he hadn't, and now she realized he never would. Here it was a full week after Homecoming's fiasco and he had not sought her out. She'd simply have to break protocol and go see him. Even though his demeanor had not changed in class, too much had transpired and she would deal with it face to face, the way she handled most issues, except when it came to Brian. She promised herself, this weekend, on her brief "to do" list, she would meet with Samir.

20

VAUGHN AT THE MALL

"**M**oth-er!" Stevie stated emphatically. "I *can* not, I *will* not wear these jeans! Everybody's wearing stone washed. These are blue, like what sailors would wear and just as big. These make me look like a tank, or a farmer. I hate them. If you're gonna buy me new clothes, at least let me buy what I like. I want to go to Bamberger's . . . or Old Navy if Bamberger's is too expensive. This store is for people your age."

Ouch! Cassie thought. She still didn't view herself as old, but she was getting there. No longer the young fox her students in Passaic used to call her when she first began teaching at twenty-one. Gray flecks took up residence at her hairline and she noticed little permanent lines closing in on her mouth. It was an insidious, ineluctable assault, but she still had her shape, for whatever that was worth. She checked her look in the mirror as Stevie reentered the dressing room to take off the ugly baggy farmer jeans. "Okay, Old Navy," she conceded. "Maybe you'll find something form-fitting there."

Cassie could get lost in a mall, both figuratively and literally. She loved to window shop and look at clothing and accessories she didn't need or never could afford. A designer handbag, for instance. A thousand dollars! Are you kidding me? That's about nine hundred fifty dollars more than any handbag deserved. She didn't care who made it or anything else for that matter, happiness came from inside. A drawer full of these things wouldn't bring back the happiness she had found and lost.

But Godiva chocolates? "Come on, Stevie; let's hurry before I lose every shred of will power I have. I could eat the whole box in one night."

"Half, Mom. You eat half; I get the other half." They both loved chocolate; chocolate cake, chocolate milk, chocolate ice cream, chocolate cheesecake, brownies. If it even resembled chocolate, it would be devoured. To stave off temptation, Cassie never bought it.

Sears, Macy's and Bam's were the anchor stores in the mall, but Catharines, for exquisite costume jewelry, Hallmark for collectibles, Footlocker and Champs for athletic wear, and a bunch of satellite stores gave the mall some flair. Not what Paramus offered, or even Willowbrook in Wayne, which boasted a pretty good food court, but this mall offered enough for her. Although eateries like Subway, Danny's Pizza, Burger King or Brooklyn Bagels were plentiful, she tried to avoid the calories. She preferred a family restaurant or something she'd make at home.

They passed all of these, where families and teens gathered inside, releasing a week's worth of energy geared towards whatever they did from Monday through Friday that sapped their strength and required a Friday or Saturday night hiatus: work, taking care of kids, studying, all held in abeyance for two plus days, two days that allowed the working class to unwind a little.

Cassie slowed down when they passed Radio Shack. "Look, Stevie. Mobile phones. I've read this is the wave of the future. Individual phones you can take with you wherever you go. No cord; attached to nothing. You just plug it in to recharge batteries. Actually," she remembered Dr. O/B's office, "Dr. O/B has one. I saw it when I was in his office a couple of weeks ago. Big, though. Can't put that in your pocket."

They'll get smaller, Mom. Technology fixes things to make more people buy them."

"Well, listen to you," Cassie said, amazed. "Going into marketing technology when you're older?"

"Mom, it's simple. Look at music. Radios used to be four feet high. Today, we walk around with them. Same with records. That was your day. Our day is tapes and CD's." Bet most people will have a computer in their homes in the next ten years."

"Sounds highly improbable to me." She nodded towards the store. "Wanna go in?"

"First, pleeease," she importuned, "I wanna get jeans that fit. Maybe on the way back?"

"Sure." Cassie and Stevie locked arms and walked past vendors, a GNC, familiar to Cassie for supplements and digestive enzymes, Hallmark, and several stores that catered to teens before they got to Old Navy. "Here. Let's see what they have."

Lots of fashionable clothes for teens was what they had. Baggy jeans, ripped skinny jeans, coveralls, colored jeans, blues, reds, neons. Racks of baggy tops, off-the-shoulder tops with cut collars paired up with leggings, made popular by "Flashdance," on mannequins wearing multicolored Converse and bright red jelly shoes, big hair and brightly painted faces, bright eye makeup, lipstick - red or blue. Stevie's face lit up. Just what she was looking for. "Oh, Ma, wait till my friends see me Monday!"

"Get what you want, any pair of jeans you want. And get a matching top. Have fun."

Stevie was overjoyed, but she controlled her excitement, going from rack to rack, taking her time, placing tops up against jeans or leggings. Jeans with high waists, tight around the hips and thighs, or black leggings with sweatshirts that fell off the shoulder, the entire collar cut away as though it had frayed and your mother had cut off the edging before she cut it up for rags. In the end, happy beyond measure, Stevie chose black leggings with one of those off-the-shoulder sweatshirts, the word "Everlast" printed in bold blue letters across the front. Stevie carried her new purchases with pride; she was in style.

On the way back, they made their way to Radio Shack so Cassie could look at mobile phones. At least she'd learn a little about them. The article she had read listed the cost at close to three thousand dollars. Not something your average teacher's salary could afford.

To her dismay, the salesman confirmed it. "They'll come down though," he said encouragingly. "This is the future and they're in demand. Once that happens, manu-facturers will have to mass produce and that'll bring down the price." He reiterated Stevie's words almost verbatim.

Cassie turned to leave, but stopped when a familiar voice at the other end of the counter explained to the salesman that he was purchasing one for his wife. "Hi, Dr. O/B," she said good-naturedly, "I didn't expect to see you here." He was dressed very casually, almost incognito for him, wearing a pair of jeans and a golf shirt under a Columbia jacket. That's about as casual as he'll ever get, she thought. But nice.

"Cassie," Vaughn returned a smile, "what a pleasant surprise. Nor did I expect to see you. My wife, Taylor – you'll meet her Thanksgiving – wants one. She sees mine and suddenly decides it's something she must have. A quick trip here and it's done. How about you?"

"One of these is not in my budget."

"I'm sorry. I didn't mean here, in this store. I meant in broader terms, like what are you shopping for in general?"

Cassie nodded to Stevie who was two counters over at the far end, looking at cassette players. "Clothes shop-ping, and you know how traumatic that can be."

"No, Cassie, actually, I do not. I have a son, not a daughter. Parker wants nothing to do with clothes shop-ping. As long as his mother dresses him in what everyone else is wearing, he's fine."

"So you miss trying on two dozen tops and rejecting them all, with comments like, "This is ugly. I wouldn't be seen dead in this," and other similar outbursts? No tem-per tantrums and "This makes me look fat?" She laughed.

"None of that," he smiled. "Now if he were trying on football cleats, that could cause frustration, but in the sartorial category, total disinterest."

Cassie smiled, then realized she was in an out-of-school setting with the dean and enjoying it just a little too much. Actually it was worse than that. She was actually feeling like a person, a woman. "Enjoy your evening, Dr. O/B," she interjected quickly. "We've been here since 3:30. Way too long. Ready to go?" She called out to Stevie, still two aisles down, not her usual manner, but without knowing why, she needed to escape. Stevie turned and started back.

"Wait a minute," Dr. O/B interrupted. Cassie glanced back with a questioning look. "Let me take the two of you to dinner." He saw Cassie's hesitation immediately and interjected, "My wife is at the Club. When I go home, I'm sitting down for a heated plate left by Sarah, our cook, then TV. Why not dinner?"

"I don't know, Dr. O/B, Cassie stammered. "Maybe because I'm a faculty member and you're the dean. Isn't there some line of protocol here that's not supposed to be crossed?"

"Stevie's not on the faculty." He smiled.

"But you couldn't take her to dinner without me."

"Exactly my point."

Good comeback, she thought. He was quick. Or was she slow tonight? "I doubt she'd want to go."

"Maybe she would. Let's ask her and see."

"Neither of us eat fast food," Cassie protested, searching for a way out.

"The Italian restaurant in town doesn't serve fast food."

Cassie replied in surprise. "You mean leave the mall and meet you at Scarbello's?

"So you know the restaurant?"

"Only from the outside."

"Then it's a perfect opportunity for you to see it from the inside and try their cuisine."

What else could she think of? They'd get home too late? It was Friday. They'd already eaten? Obviously not, since it was 6:00 p.m. and she'd already admitted they'd been shopping for over two hours. What about, I don't want to drive in the dark? She had to drive home whether they went to eat or not, and it was already dark. What else could she say? She threw up her hands in surrender. "Only if she says yes. Just a straight yes/no question. Fair?"

Vaughn nodded. "Fair."

"What's fair?" Stevie asked, approaching them at the last sentence.

"Are you hungry, Stevie?" Cassie asked.

"Famished."

"Dr. O/B has invited us to Scarbello's. Would you like to go?"

"Would I?!" Stevie said ecstatically. Cassie had lost. No way to avoid it now, and Vaughn's smile showed it. Cassie felt herself blush, and Stevie looked at her in a weird way as though she had never seen this mother before.

"Then let's go," Vaughn concluded, making light of an awkward moment. He ushered an apprehensive Cassie and an excited Stevie forward. Stevie, happy because it was a cool place to eat; Cassie, confused because a barrier was slipping, and Vaughn, in complete denial of what his subconscious had just designed.

21

AFTER THE MALL; SEARCH FOR SAMIR

"He's here somewhere, Mrs. Komsky," Matt Welsley offered. "I just don't know where. He signs in on time, but he only comes here to sleep. Really, we've been roommates since September, but we never talk. In fact, he's never said one word to me."

"Funny, it never entered my mind that you were Samir's roommate. Do you get along?"

Matt laughed. "Other than we never talk? We get along fine. No arguments. Can't have an argument if you never talk. There's no conflict over quiet time, or study habits or anything. He does his thing; I do mine."

"Do you have any idea where I might find him?" Cassie had hoped to find Samir in his dorm by now. Almost 8:30, most students would gravitate to their rooms after curfew. Just the natural thing to do. Kick back, grab a soda or coffee, open a book, whatever, but obviously not the natural thing for Samir.

She stood in the middle of Matt and Samir's dorm room and examined the striking difference between the two sides. Matt's side, typical of a college dorm student's, a bit untidy, desk messy, books carelessly covering dust, bed unmade, topped with an open bag of chips. Samir's spotless, meticulous bed made with hospital corners, books in two ordered stacks on his desk, one opened to . . . hmm . . . *Romeo and Juliet*, a copy of Kahlil Gibran's, *The Prophet*, topping the other stack, and of all things, a mobile phone, like the phones at Radio Shack, sat at the far end of the desk, the side closer to his bed.

Matt shook his head. "Having Samir for a roommate? It's like I live alone. Even when he is here, he's not. All I can tell you for sure is he's in the building. He has to be, or his signature would not be in the register. No one would sign in for him and violate protocol, especially for someone you hardly know. Sorry Mrs. Komsky. I know you're concerned about him, and I would help if I could. But I can't."

"That's okay, Matt. Thanks anyway. Oh," she added, "would you mind if I put a note on his desk?" Cassie felt around in her purse, more like a satchel, found a small pad and held it up. "I'd appreciate it."

"Go right ahead, Mrs. Komsky. Whatever you think will help."

Cassie scratched a quick note, and put it in the crease between the opened pages of Romeo and Juliet, act 3, scene 2. And that concluded what was to have been an informal conference with a very reticent young man who reached out to no one, neither in class nor out. No one, except Rachel. She wondered how Rachel had gotten in, how she could ever have gotten Samir to open up and trust her. Her appreciation for Rachel increased exponentially with that one thought.

On her way home, she considered where he could hide, and that troubled her. Where could he go and disappear from everyone's sight? She pondered the possibilities as she made her way past brick buildings lined with hedges and covered with ivy. If I were Samir, she thought, where would I escape to on a daily basis after classes were through? He eats his meals in his dorm and has an occasional dinner at the dining center, retreats to the library after or before that, and spends time somewhere on campus. But it's winter and it's cold! A week, less than a week, before Thanksgiving and the temperature is frigid. Ugh. She shivered and hugged her quilted down coat. He could never stay out in such cold very long and she knew the library closed at 8:00. Besides, he's gotta sign in by 8:30, and he does. So where can he be?

She had promised herself she would seek him out this weekend, and after dinner with Dr. O/B seemed like a perfect time to find out how he was doing since Homecoming, but she didn't expect him to be this hard to find. She did learn that Jeremy Harper was housemaster at Damon House. That might provide a lead, and she'd follow up with that next week. Hopefully, her note would bring Samir to her. Two possibilities, both weak. Keep your fingers crossed, girl, she thought, and took off-the-path shortcuts to hurry home to Stevie and warmth, her thoughts diverging from Samir's plight to conversation and laughter at Scarbello's, not nearly as serious an issue as Samir's, but causing uneasiness, specifically because she had had such a thoroughly delightful time. Had Stevie not been with them and had Vaughn not been married, she would have likened it to a date. Scary.

She wished she had the opportunity to conference with someone. An old friend, a girlfriend, someone she could trust, but there was no one here she could do that with, not yet anyway. She'd default to avoidance if that was possible, but Thanksgiving would not make that easy. In fact, Thanksgiving would make that *im*possible. You can't avoid someone when you're their guest. Forget it, Cassie. You're making more of it than is necessary. Go, enjoy the holiday and be grateful for the invitation.

22

DAY BEFORE THANKSGIVING

Classes came alive with excitement and anticipation. Tomorrow was Thanksgiving. Many students were going home, drivers or parents picking them up for the four-day holiday, but most, those who lived too far to travel home, would be sharing the holiday with those who lived closer. A four-day holiday was not the same as a two-week break like Christmas or Spring break, when the academy shut down.

Chelsea's enrollment drew from almost every state in the country and from countries abroad, blending a wonderful mix of traditions, life-styles, regions and geological differences, customs and speech. But because of this, proximity to home became a detriment at Thanksgiving. Fortunately, Thanksgiving meant sharing, and Chelsea students opened their homes to anyone who couldn't get home. Good will towards fellow students made it exciting in itself, and it became contagious for everyone, including

Cassie, where it transferred to classes. First period discussion had ramped up to heated debates.

"And Ophelia pays the price, for all of it!" Gloria had blurted out. "You guys are so busy dealing with Hamlet's problem that you're overlooking her tragedy. She becomes everybody's pawn. The two people she's trusted most in her life betray her. Claudius & Polonius use her to spy on Hamlet. Polonius, her own father, uses her as a foil to ingratiate himself with Claudius, and Claudius uses her to prove Hamlet's insane. And Hamlet, this guy who supposedly loves her, whatever that is, drives the knife right in. Gotta love his finesse: 'Get thee to a nunnery?' Unbelievable. Oh, and for her dowry, a plague of chastity, 'be thou as chaste as ice,' he says. Here, lines 139 – 140. Nice guy. No wonder the poor girl goes crazy. He never loved her or he wouldn't have used her for his own ends."

"Act 3, scene 1, let's address these lines and the situation Gloria is referencing. If her father loved her, if Hamlet loved her, would they have used her for their own agendas, because it's obvious they did." Cassie searches faces around the table for reaction. No one. "Want to write a take-off on *Hamlet* using Ophelia as the main character and showing her tragedy?" Heads turned at this one.

"That's a good idea, Mrs. Komsky," Gloria replies. "We could do that, couldn't we girls?" She looks at Rachel, Elizabeth and Emelia, who nod.

Cassie returns an "It has possibilities" nod. "Maybe a project; we'll be doing them after we finish *Hamlet*, most likely the week before Christmas, and that might be an excellent topic. But let's stay on point, here. Consider this question: You support the premise that you don't use someone for your own agenda if you really love them. So, point two, if Hamlet were crazy, would that exonerate what he did to Ophelia?" They shake their heads. No.

"Why not? Haven't people who've reached their breaking point gone over the edge? Couldn't we make a case that Hamlet, with all he's gone through in the past two months, has gone over the edge?" They shake their heads, no, again. "So you believe that his betrayal has no justification for what he does to Ophelia? Not even insanity, if it were real?"

"Not to me," Emelia says emphatically.

"Maybe real insanity, if their mind is gone and they can't recognize who they once were," Rachel says, "because then they're really not the person you fell in love with or who fell in love with you. Then you have to pull yourself up and go on, accepting things for what they are, and they don't always go your way." She pauses then gains momentum. "The thing is that we never know if Hamlet's insanity is real, because he tells Horatio that his behavior will seem erratic. Doesn't he say this early in the play?"

Cassie nods. "End of act 1."

"So how can we trust him, or his behavior, or his love towards Ophelia?" Rachel concludes. "I agree with Emelia. He's too devious and too concerned with his own agenda. And maybe he has become partially crazy from his obsession with his father's death and everything that followed, but he sure does use Ophelia, and he sure doesn't care what happens to her. He's sane enough to know that."

"Rachel makes a good point," Elizabeth adds, "especially about trust. When it comes to trust, does it matter if it's a boyfriend, a husband, or a friend? Someone who encourages you to trust them, nurtures that trust, then knifes you in the back for their own agenda is inhumane. Somebody who can do that doesn't have a conscience."

A hush pervades the classroom. "That's happened to me," Jason whispers softly. A very courageous statement from Jason, Cassie thinks. "It happens to guys, too. Guys just don't talk about it openly. We're men. We're supposed to be strong and not be hurt by emotions. But that's not true. Betrayal is betrayal, and it hurts."

"Like a knife," Gloria adds. And do you ever need support then. Someone who's never deserted you. The problem is, you wonder, if you were so blind before, can you ever trust anyone again? Or worse, can you ever trust your own instincts again?"

Shakespeare had a gift for getting into humanity's souls, and Gloria's comment had cut right to the core of his universality. Human emotions transcend time; all people want to trust and believe in sincerity. Once you lose trust in someone, or in your own instincts, do you ever get it back?

"But then, what do we do, Gloria? Shut ourselves off from everyone? Build a wall around us so high that we let no one in, ever, to prevent ourselves from being hurt again?"

Gloria stared at her teacher for seconds that seemed interminable. "What would you do, Mrs. Komsky, if someone hurt you like that? Would you ever let anyone in again?"

Cassie was thunderstruck. Without realizing it, she had invited the question. Also without realizing it, she had asked herself this very same question repeatedly for as long as she could remember, as far back as her teen-age years when she first became aware of what insecurities were and realized she had needed protection from hers. And here she was, decades later, asking Gloria what she'd do, when Cassie had never been able to overcome her own internal conflict except once, completely by accident, when fate had simply placed a determined Brian in her path. To intentionally be secure enough to let someone in, to trust? You'd have to feel confident to do that; subconsciously, Cassie was not confident. She was feisty; she could defend herself quickly, but confidence stem-ming from that subconscious feeling of worthlessness was always lacking.

She could easily give to a stranger or help someone she hardly knew. Kindness and generosity did not require trust. No need to tear down walls. But to open up and let someone in and let them know how scared you were? That had always been her insurmountable hurdle, and Gloria's question had just asked her to address it, directly in the firing line.

Cassie paused for seconds that knocked on eternity while her mind whirled. How should she respond? Would she respond? She had prodded the question never think-ing that any student would turn it on her. What irony. Well, she breathed deeply, she had expected a fair and honest answer from Gloria; Gloria deserved nothing less from her.

"I wouldn't want to," Cassie began. I'd be afraid, afraid of getting hurt, being used, again. And I wouldn't feel that pain if I lived behind a wall. I'd be safe. But if I let my feelings take up residence behind a wall, would I be living . . . or just existing?

"Khalil Gibran, *The Prophet*, says of sorrow, 'When you are sorrowful look again in your heart, and you shall see that in truth you are weeping for that which has been your delight.' It's a paradox which may not make sense at first, but it's the reason for sadness. We hurt when we realize someone who loved us, or was supposed to love us, doesn't, and we hurt when we lose something or someone who made us happy. We may never get the object of our happiness back, but if we have the courage to live outside the wall, we might be able to get happiness back from something else."

In her peripheral vision, she caught Samir's focus. Her hands went to her head and she tangled them in her hair, unsure if she should continue, but she put her hands down and finished her thought. "As frightened as I'd be of coming out from behind my wall, I wouldn't want to merely exist. It would be too empty there. Too empty, too cold. If you lock away all the love you feel, doesn't it become worthless? It's like hanging the Mona Lisa in a closet. Why have that masterpiece if no one can share its beauty. So, Gloria, I think, and I can only say, 'I think,' I'd take the chance, and whether the results shatter or uplift me, I'd have to go on from there and do the best I could, as Rachel said."

Eleven students sat mesmerized as they pondered the depths of their teacher's comment. She had opened up to them, and she didn't seem afraid. But inside, if they knew, she was scared to death of what she had just revealed to them and admitted to herself. Now what would she do with this knowledge? Putting words to it had made it palpable, and she knew instinctively she didn't want to live behind her wall anymore, did not want to let her father's denunciations dominate her life. She wouldn't go searching, but if trust or love punched a hole through that wall, she wouldn't lock these intangibles out.

This was Wednesday. She sat at her desk at the end of the day and reflected upon the week and what had transpired during period one today. This is what teaching literature is all about, she thought. It opens insights into the character's soul, and into our own. Phew, that's tough, but you can't do this teaching physics.

Today was also the precursor of Thanksgiving, where she and Stevie would be sharing the day with Dr. O/B, his family, which included Parker, his extended family and several faculty members she had come to know.

This afternoon, she and Stevie would bake nemura; it was on their calendar. The syrup had been in the frig since Sunday. This evening they'd put it all together. It was going to Dr. O/B's tomorrow, and that was good. No cheating, no nibbling one tiny piece, then two, then, oops! All gone. Nope, except for a full bowl of cream she had made for Stevie, this sweet, sticky dessert made with layer after layer of buttered phyllo, with a centre filled with sweetened heavy cream, thickened with corn starch and smothered with the thick, sticky syrup would all be going to Dr. O/B's tomorrow. It, and all its calories, could disappear there.

23

CASSIE'S AND SAMIR'S LINK

A slight tapping on her door and she was in the present, her classroom, quiet, still and empty, her only companions the hum of radiators, the smell of books. She glanced up, and there he was. Seconds of uncertainty; she motioned him forward. He entered apprehensively, and, honing in on his comfort zone, took his classroom seat. "I was hoping you'd contact me," she said cautiously. "Thank you."

"Your note." He held the note she had left with Matt Welsley Sunday. "It is the same passage you quoted today." She nodded, but let him continue. "You think you know my feelings, my thoughts?"

"Not necessarily, but I know mine. And you and I, I believe we are not so dissimilar. But my primary concern is if you're okay after the way you were treated at Homecoming."

"'Okay' is relative, is it not? My history is in my files. You know it. Better to ask if I was okay after my parents were killed after the embassy bombing in Beirut. I have lived behind your metaphoric wall since then. Homecoming was simply the manifestation of unilateral prejudice my people have lived with for decades; only now the American press has stereotyped us all as terrorists. They report only one side, while your government dictates policy in our countries." He stared at her. "How is it you have escaped that label?"

Cassie remained at her desk momentarily; then moved to her seat at the table. "Unintentionally," she replied. "My maiden name is Haddad, but that meant nothing in the Italian neighborhood in which I grew up. My first name is more Slavik than anything else, and I look European, fair skin, hazel eyes, honey blond hair, lighter in summer. Must have been French influence when Napoleon ensconced himself in the region."

She smiled. "But while I was a kid, and into my late teens, no one had heard the word "Syrian" or "Arab" until the media selected Arabs as their object of persecution after the Six-Day-War. Basically, I slipped in under the radar without even knowing it."

She waited for him to reply, but his reticence held. He glanced around the room slowly, as though just noticing the posters; then turned his head away. "We, in this class, talk about courage and cowardice, trust and betrayal, ethics and revenge, as though they are juxtaposed for all people, and we all have some of the good and some of the bad, a balance, just varying in degree. But in my country and in Palestine, there is no balance; there is only bad. 'Good' is real for the country or the people in power. In Palestine, for decades, busses, homes, villages have been blown up by an occupying power that claims self-defense.

"In my country, political chaos and military conflict have existed for years. Lebanon's government represented each religious group well until Israel was established. After that, so many Palestinians fled to my country it changed the religious balance between Muslims and Christians. Fighting, the PLO, and more fighting. Syria and Israel invading, more fighting. Hezbollah filling the vacuum after the PLO left, more fighting, more war; UN forces sent in to restore peace, attacking Shatila and Sabraa. Three thousand civilians massacred. Is that restoring peace?" Israel invades Beirut; seventeen thousand civilians killed. Is that restoring peace?" He shook his head sadly. "No, only more fighting; more bloodshed, more war. All have destroyed my country.

"Ethics, morality, humanity do not exist for us. To the world, we are superfluous, invisible, a non-people to be exterminated when your government or Israel deems it. And that breeds hatred, hatred manifesting itself in the only way it knows how. And my mother, my father, and I paid the price.

"As Gibran says, I weep for what has been my delight. Yet, despite my loss, and my sorrow, I understand it. Even though it took my parents, I understand the hatred, the feelings of helplessness. It is those feelings of utter hatred and futility that destroyed the embassy, and your Marine barracks."

Cassie winced almost imperceptibly, but Samir caught it. He was used to subtle body movements and their meanings. "I'm sorry we have had to undergo such persecution for so many decades, and that a country whose appetite for conquest goes unchecked because your Congress allows it, under the pretense of establishing peace. Is this not the epitome of hypocrisy?"

His head fell to his chest and he remained downcast until Cassie spoke. "You've kept yourself so sequestered, how is it you made contact with Rachel?"

At her name, a smile danced around his lips. "It was she who initiated contact." This young man, so full of emotion and sorrow, for once, was speaking freely. His voice had a lovely melodic resonance that would captivate any listener regardless of religion or ethnicity. "Professor Draggert was in poor health when the term began, and he was kind enough to explain this to us, to inform us that he had become seriously ill late August, that the administration would have to look for a replacement.

"He told us he had not read all our profiles and was going through them slowly. Mine was one he had not yet read. I know this because he paralleled a child's death in *Romeo and Juliet* to the death of a parent and indicated how much worse the former was. His analogy and analysis may have been accurate, but it opened deep wounds for me.

"The housekeeper of Rachel's mother has a friend who works in Administration. I do not know who she is, but over the summer, events in my life became public to some of the personnel. Rachel knew my past." He paused, most likely reminiscing because when he continued, a wistful smile appeared on his face. "When she sensed my pain, she reached out and put her hand on mine. She did not care who stared or who understood. Her concern was to comfort me.

"When class ended, she left. I sought her out that evening. Until Homecoming, she was the only person with whom I communicated, the only person who had heard me speak, and speak English." He smiled, remembering Cassie's words at the game when she had said Rachel couldn't understand him if he didn't speak English. Then he became pensive. "When Parker said hurtful things about her, I drew away from her: I could not bear to have her hurt because of me. But she faced all of it with such courage; she withstood her world for me." Then he glanced up. "She taught me how to be courageous. For her, I would do anything. For me, she is an angel."

His sadness became palpable, but Cassie did not interrupt. She sensed he had more to say.

"But tell me, Mrs. Komsky, you talk about coming out from behind walls and being able to face our own internal conflicts instead of letting them destroy us like Hamlet, who's afraid to do what his father's ghost commands. We all go through life with fears, do we not?"

Cassie nodded. "We wouldn't be human if we didn't."

"Then is it not hypocritical for you to tell me I should come out from behind my wall when you, who have much more experience in life than I, have had difficulty coming out from behind yours?"

Cassie sat back and turned silence into discomfort. This young man, so prescient, had made her transparent. To speak or not to speak, she thought, using a play on words; that is the question. It was time. She nodded and began. "Kind of ironic that your life-altering experience occurred four years ago as did mine. Ironic that yours happened in Lebanon as did mine. Ironic that yours occurred from a terrorist bombing as did mine. Only difference is that your nightmare occurred at the Embassy," she paused for a brief moment, realizing the import of what she was about to admit, "while mine occurred at the Marine Barracks."

And the import of what she had told him sunk in. His eyes held hers and she realized how completely he understood her feelings. "Your husband was a Marine?" He asked apprehensively.

"Yes," she uttered softly and gulped hard. "The biggest irony is that he wasn't supposed to be there. The weapons analyst the unit needed had undergone back surgery ten days before deployment. Brian volunteered to transfer from his unit, which was part-time, and assist temporarily until the analyst had completed rehab." She put her head down and tears fell. "His last letter arrived after the military brass, along with a chaplain, paid their visit to the 'widow!'" Her hands went to her face and tears flowed through her fingers as she tried to wipe them away. Nothing could keep them confined.

"Forgive me," Mrs. Komsky. I had no right. I will leave."

"That's okay, Samir. It's something I have to live with and overcome."

"As do I." He stood up, gave a slight bow, and left.

24

THANKSGIVING DAY

Cassie had seen affluence before. She had been in
the homes of some very wealthy families when she
worked as a summer nanny in Upper Montclair.
Both estates had been Victorian, with deep gabled roofs, a
turret here and there, rounded facades, but neither came
close to this magnificent edifice that appeared before her.
This, this was more than wealth; this was obscene, mammon at its worst.

"This is a house?" Stevie exclaimed. "How many people live here?" she asked, with the emphasis on *here*.

"I think," Cassie said, her response slow as she absorbed her surroundings," Dr. O/B, his wife, and Parker.
Full-time staff, if you include them. Must be servants'
quarters somewhere though, maybe out back. Did you
notice the iron or bronze stallion posted at the drive?
Maybe even stables."

Stevie's eyes widened at the immensity of it all.
"Unmitigated opulence," she said disgustingly.

Cassie laughed out loud. "Good choice of words, Stevie. Keep studying that dictionary."

Cassie's Ford Pinto had come to the end of an intricately paved drive lined with leafless oaks that shivered in the frigid chill, and at the end of the drive, where it had curved and widened into an immense cul-de-sac, she faced the largest and the most elegant house, make that "mansion" she had ever seen, except in magazines that touted Homes of the Stars. Dr. O/B had used the word "house" incorrectly, perhaps as a misnomer to be modest, but definitely deceptively. This was not a house. This was a mansion, and the five railroad rooms she had grown up in could have fit into a corner room easily.

Two stories, all stone, extended from a massive entranceway bordered by two colonnades on each side, to section after section of wings, with a hexagonal . . . what? . . . at the end, if that were actually the end. She could see nothing beyond it. Not a game room, not in front; not a study; not an all-season sunroom; billiards, a smoking lounge, maybe a gigantic indoor hot tub? She had seen pictures of huge indoor hot tubs that opened to nighttime views and wood fireplaces. But whatever it was, it stood elegantly at the far right end of the house, the far, far right end, glass encased with stone, its roof ending in a spiked turret. To the left, an expansive wrap-around porch characteristic of the traditional Victorian that didn't seem to end. The lovely "painted ladies" at Cape May, well-appointed with peacock flare, were miniature doll houses in comparison to this.

Cassie knew very little about architecture, but she knew no one needed this much room. Did Parker have his own wing? Was there an indoor basketball court? Did he have intermittent contact with his parents as he passed through the kitchen, unless he opted for room service or used an intercom? She hoped this opulence translated into happiness.

Cassie recognized Walter's car several spaces down and pulled in next to it. Either valet parking attendants were on break or Dr. O/B had given them off for the holiday. That wouldn't hold true for the wait staff. She could never imagine the dean and his wife wearing aprons.

Once out of the car, a huge tray of nemura in hand, she and Stevie hurried up four immensely wide, stone steps to the front entrance and rang the bell. Should she have used the gargoyle knocker? Whatever, as long as someone answered quickly and let them in from the cold.

Warmth radiated from the inside as soon as Dr. O/B's tuxedoed butler opened the door. He ushered them into a huge foyer, decorated with a floral centerpiece in reds, yellows, oranges, and browns set on the marbled table top, as tall as any Christmas tree, and took their coats. From the vast expanse of the foyer and its vaulted ceilings, she realized she had been wrong; the five railroad rooms in which she had grown up could have fit in *here*.

The foyer led into the great room which had been set up buffet style to rival the cocktail hour at an elegant wedding. Four stations, one at each corner of the room: a carving station, a raw bar, pasta station, and closest to them, cheeses, vegetables, relishes and condiments of all kinds, and, what was that . . . caviar? This, was Thanksgiving? Cassie felt stupid holding a tray of nemura, which the butler had deigned to hold while she wiggled out of her coat then returned to her. Did he consider it low class? At this point, she wished Dr. O/B had retracted his invitation, but she was here with Stevie and she would not be intimidated by this atmosphere. People were people. Not really. Some people floated above the rest. A snap of their fingers and you became chafe.

Just as she was digging in her heels, Walter appeared from a knot of guests milling about the carving station. He smiled broadly and headed towards them, Melissa close behind.

"Hey, you made it," he said warmly. "We thought you had gotten lost. "Happy Thanksgiving." He touched Cassie on the shoulder and offered his hand to Stevie. "Your mother is an excellent Shakespeare teacher, and yes, I am flattering her."

"I know she is," Stevie smiled. "I'm sure she'll teach me all about Shakespeare's universality and the highlights of the Elizabethan theatre when I'm older. *Hamlet* is one of her favorites, I think, but I'm not quite ready for a 'To be or not to be' soliloquy yet."

Walter tried hard not to laugh.

"Oh my God," Melissa said, stunned. "And you're nine?" She asked dumbfounded.

Stevie nodded. "I turned nine last month. Maybe in another year I'll be ready for Shakespeare. I'd like to begin with *Romeo and Juliet* so I can compare it to *West Side Story*. I've never seen the play, but I have seen the movie. That should be sufficient for comparison and contrast."

"Right now," Melissa said, trying to opt out of the conversation casually, "I think I'd like to do some comparison and contrast between the shrimp and the lobster tails over there. Would you like to join me?"

"Sure," Stevie replied. I'm hungry."

"So," Walter began, once they were out of earshot, "what, do you read her your lesson plans as a bedtime story?"

"No, silly, stop being facetious."

"Ya think?"

"Sometimes when I prepare my lessons, I talk out loud, just to hear how it sounds, and Stevie, well, she just picks up on it. Hey, if she asks questions, I answer them. I don't shove Shakespeare down her throat." By now, the tray was getting too heavy for Cassie to hold. She was about to ask Walter to take it from her, when a male voice came from behind.

"Is this the nemura I've been expecting all week?" Vaughn asked, taking the tray from her hands.

"Thank you, Dr. O/B. My arms were getting tired. I've gotta do more push-ups. Increase my upper body strength."

"Nothing wrong with your upper body strength," he said as she passed the silver tray to him. "This tray is heavy, and I do pushups too." He exited, leaving Cassie and Walter talking about kids, school and a touch of his own family. When Vaughn returned, he was swallowing the last bite he had sampled and was uncharacteristically licking his lips.

"Cassie, that is delicious. I've never tasted anything so good. You'll have to tell me how it's made some time, so I can pass it on to Taylor . . . and our cook." He corrected his error, knowing Cassie had assumed Taylor did not cook, or bake, or participate in any culinary activities, although he loved to putter around the kitchen during any excess time he had after work and golf. He could make a mean lasagna that he and Parker both enjoyed, and occasionally on a Friday evening, he would skip the Club and roll up his sleeves. "Come," he ushered Cassie forward, "let me introduce you to everyone."

Since Walter knew everyone, he gave her a see-ya-later wave and peeled off to the carving station for another slice of prime rib. Cassie made a mental note to grab some food from this sumptuous buffet in case no traditional Thanksgiving dinner followed. People have different traditions. This might be Vaughn's. Stevie, plate of peeled shrimp in hand, joined her mother from group to group, and became the center of attention in each one, everyone wanting to know her interests, her sports, her hobbies, books she was currently reading, if she liked or hated math, and how she was getting along at Chelsea Academy, her new home.

When Vaughn ushered them to his mother, his aunts, one uncle, his wife and Parker, Stevie was ready for a break, and fortunately for her, Parker supplied it once he learned she liked football. "Want to see my memorabilia of the Raiders"? He offered, and wasn't offended when she agreed, with the warning that she was a Giants fan like her Mom. Parker escorted her to another wing, leaving Vaughn to introduce Cassie to Taylor, Brett, and Brett's wife, Hillary.

The first thing anybody noticed about Taylor was that she was outstandingly beautiful. Her features were almost sculpted, without imperfection, and her figure flawless as well. Whether it was the deep green silk dress, scoop neckline, shirred bodice, fitted waistline nicely accentuating her figure, or her figure that accentuated the dress, it didn't matter. She was beautiful and it was easy to see how Vaughn would dote on her. "Vaughn has told me so very much about you and how you infuse your classes with a love of Shakespeare," were Taylor's first words to Cassie, words said with perfect formality, but there was something cryptic in her tone. Were her words meant as a generous compliment or was there a hint of ice there? Was it Cassie's imagination, or was there animus behind those words? Cassie dismissed it. First impressions weren't always accurate.

Dr. O/B's brother, on the other hand, was effusively attentive and overtly fawning, sickeningly so. About 6'4" of lean muscle, Brett had charisma and magnetism and he used it to do and say anything he wanted. "My brother was distraught with the Draggert situation until he hired you. It's extremely difficult to find a replacement in such short time for a man who's had so much experience teaching Shakespeare. But he found one. And from what Vaughn tells me, he hasn't been disappointed." He smiled and took in more than her facial features.

Cassie's dress didn't come from a top designer's line. It was an off-the-rack fine woolen crocheted sheath, deep purple, with a self-slip underneath. Form-fitting but not clingy, it was designed for the perfect shape with a little flexibility here and there to fill in where a B-cup might be a C, or a well-shaped and well-toned backside would want a tad more to adhere to propriety. Cassie's assets qualified in both those areas; she looked outstandingly good and Brett noticed.

His smile, charming like his brother's, made Cassie uncomfortable. "Thank you. I'm happy the transition has gone as smoothly as it has. This academy has remarkable students and excellent achievements in athletics and non-curricular activities." She winced, remembering her loud outbursts at the football game and her passionate response at Homecoming. Had Dr. O/B told him that?

"I also hear you love football." His smile intensified and his gaze bore into her eyes. How could she not notice this? "That's surprising," he continued, either missing the cold glare from Taylor or not caring. "My wife, Hillary," he nodded towards his wife, an attractive, petite woman in her late forty's perhaps, chestnut brown hair worn in a top knot showing off high cheekbones and deep blue eyes, stood between him and Taylor; she nodded affably and Cassie returned her smile. "My wife," Brett continued, "hates it. When I watch a game, she leaves the room. When, or how, did you become such an avid fan?"

Not a question Cassie wanted to hear, and not a topic she wanted to discuss. If she referred to Brian, and she would have to if she were truthful, the next question would be about him, why he's not with her. She couldn't do this, and fortunately, Vaughn sensed her reluctance and ran interference. "Brett, no 'when,' no 'how,' no football. Not now. Relax a bit before you talk about statistics and Super Bowls." He directed Cassie away, unaware that Brett's smile had transformed into a smirk. Now he understood his brother's enthusiasm for Draggert's "outstanding replacement."

"I sensed this was not a conversation in which you wanted to engage; so let me escort you to Melissa and

your colleagues where I'm sure you'll feel quite at ease."
Dinner is at 4:30."

She smiled and melded into the faculty where
Jeremy, Tasha, Melissa, and Walter were talking about
beaches and island vacations, a topic she could appreciate. Oh, for warmth this time of year. Joe De Biasso, the
band director she had seen only on the field, was with
them, talking to Ronnie Collins and Alicia about Mozart.
Distinctively thin, Cassie wondered how he could keep
his balance on the field when the howling winds whipped
through the stadium. For whatever reason, he had not
been at Homecoming. He was a new face she was now
meeting, which pleased her, but after a few pleasantries
and some light conversation, she honed in on Jeremy and
asked how Samir could possibly be in his dorm yet hide
from everyone all evening.

"That's a good question, Cassie. I'll give it some
thought, because until now, I had no idea he wasn't in his
room."

"Matt says Samir always signs in."

"He has to. Most of the time I look him in the face
as he's writing his name. No communication of course,
but where he could go and still be in the building without
being in his room is puzzling to me as well." His finger
traced his chin in thought. "I could check the building
schematic," he offered. "Maybe that would help? And if
you'd like, we could go room by room, floor by floor, for
any possible hiding place."

"You mean both of us? We could scope it out, like
detectives?" Cassie smiled.

"We sure could," Jeremy nodded, eager to put his sleuthing idea into effect. Being housemaster of Samir's assigned dorm, Jeremy was quick to involve himself in the dilemma Cassie had presented. Call it not wanting to be outdone on his turf or feel foolish because he didn't know the answer to what Cassie had discovered; he wanted in.

"What are you two contriving?" Melissa asked, seeing Cassie and Jeremy deep in conversation.

"Nothing much. Just trying to discover where Samir secludes himself after 8:30. By the way, I have a *very* short write-up about my first consultation with him. How's fifth?"

"Oh my God, you talked with him?!" Melissa squealed, causing heads to turn. Not proper decorum for the Otis-Barrett's Thanksgiving feast, but too spontaneous a reaction to have controlled.

"Uh-huh," Cassie nodded, whispering to keep volume down. "Very brief, yesterday after last period."

"What did he say? What did *you* say?"

Cassie smiled. "I *can't* say. But would you be available Monday after fourth to take my report and sign my copy? I'm adhering to protocol with date, time, and signature."

"Of course, Cassie. But you met with him? Oh my God, how did you accomplish that?"

Cassie demurred. "Sorry, Melissa. But unless I feel it's something that could hurt him, it's strictly a confidential thing."

Melissa nodded. "Understood. Well, good for you, and for him. If talking to you can help him in any way, it'll be huge."

"What am I missing?" Walter asked, another slice of prime rib on his plate. He wasn't waiting for dinner. "I heard the squeals."

And in less time than it took for Walter to receive an answer, Vaughn joined the conversation. "What did I just hear? You met with Samir? Amazing. And what did he say?" Cassie gave him her "We agreed I can't talk about it" look, but she was saved by the dinner bell.

Four-thirty on the dot, the chief butler summoned them to the dining room. "Dinner is served," he announced, and the entourage began working their way into the dining room.

"I am impressed," Vaughn stated emphatically with a smile, missing another glare that emanated from Taylor across the room. This time, though, Cassie read it perfectly. A cold stare, laced with vitriol. She almost shuddered. What is the matter with her? She thought.

Placards placed Cassie next to Walter on her right with Stevie on her left and Melissa on Stevie's left. Tasha, Joe, and Jeremy sat across from them. Good, she'd been bundled with people she knew. Dr. O/B sat at one end of the immensely long dining room table that could easily have seated thirty. Dr. O/B's mother, his aunts and uncle were seated on his side. Taylor sat at the other end surrounded by Brett, Hillary and the friends contingent. Faculty had neatly been placed in the center. As they were taking their seats, Parker switched placards with his uncle so he could sit across from Stevie.

Cassie's gaze swept the room, noticing every detail. It was pure elegance: decorative window panels, window treatments of rich brocade, golden cords and scalloped valences. Layers of crown molding edged the vaulted ceiling and the hardwood floors; a centered chandelier boasting hundreds of crystals, maybe more, in raindrop clusters illuminated the room, each one meticulously dusted to reflect optimum light. That chore alone must have taken hours, maybe an entire day. She could grade three sets of papers in that time. Odd how everything is relevant to one's own individual priorities, lifestyles, and social class.

China, is anything better than Lenox? If so, this had to be it. Gold cutlery, formal place-settings: Cassie was glad she had taught herself proper etiquette in her teens. Not that she ever imagined or fantasized about being the wife of an outrageously wealthy CEO. It was just a phase in her life when formal place settings interested her. But the knowledge had never been lost and fortunately, she had taught Stevie. Stevie could mix it up on any social class. She could eat chicken with her fingers, yet know the difference between a cocktail fork and a salad fork, a soup spoon and a dessert spoon. No intimidation on her part. She could handle it all.

But aside from the place settings and five exquisite equally-spaced floral arrangements, the table was bare. So, it was a formal dinner served by the wait staff, not family style as she was used to. Vaughn tapped his champagne glass, picked it up and stood for the welcoming speech from the host. "I'm not addressing the Board of Directors, nor is this a business presentation for land acquisition, for which our family is famous, as you all know. . . ." He nodded towards his mother, a stately woman with an ingenuous smile. "This is better, because today I am surrounded by the most important reason for Thanksgiving: family, and good friends. To have these is to be wealthy indeed. And so, to all of you who have chosen to spend this day with us, I thank you, sincerely." His gaze went around the table, and centered on Taylor, who nodded formally, then to his family, the faculty, and lastly, on Cassie. Then he raised his glass and sipped. Everyone followed.

"And now," he continued, we come to the second tradition in the family, carving the turkey!" Everyone applauded, everyone except Cassie and Stevie who seemed a bit confused. "To the newcomers," he nodded towards them, you may think there's no food on this table because we've already eaten . . ."

"We have, Vaughn," Brett interjected loudly, accompanied by laughter.

"Or because we don't serve until I carve the entire turkey, but not so. Our tradition dictates that the host of the O/B Thanksgiving," he points towards himself, "makes the ceremonious first cut of a turkey, which our staff then takes to the senior complex. Everything we eat has already been carved. It's just waiting for me. So," he motioned to the head butler, "bring it on."

What appeared from the kitchen was the largest turkey Cassie had ever seen. It had to be close to fifty pounds, set on a huge silver tray that two female servers carried into the dining room, each holding one side. They set it in front of Vaughn as a third server removed his place setting for the traditional turkey carving ceremony.

And then it appeared, carried aloft by the head butler, a good fourteen inches of carbon steel, sharp as a razor, ending with a rounded point at the tip, set into an unfinished yet intricately carved wood handle, like the one, like the one, like the one. . . .

"Uh," a muffled yet sharp gasp emitted from Cassie's throat, from her lungs, from her mind, from her heart. She squelched it, she thought. But again, it appeared, like an apparition, like the dagger Macbeth had seen before him. Again Cassie tried to control it. She brought her hand to her mouth to stifle what she could not silence. She turned away from the knife so she could not see it, but the image played in her head, danced around and opened the gateway to her past.

Suddenly she was three, crying in her mother's arms, her dad shouting, "She's good for nothing!" Her mom comforting, her dad bellowing, throwing back his chair, coming at Mommy with the sharp butcher knife, hurling mommy against the wall, the pointed blade against her neck, Mommy screaming, "Kill me in front of your daughters," two little girls huddled in the corner behind the kitchen door, "Don't kill Mommy; don't kill Mommy!"

"No . . . no!" Chair falling back, seeing nothing, seeing everything, remembering nothing; remembering everything. Running, tripping, running from the dining room, suffocating, running, where, run to where, where to hide, bathroom, where, where is it, passing a server coming from a door, kitchen, maybe kitchen, run, into the hallway, down the hall, opening a door into the kitchen, the look on her face saying it all, the look of complete and utter terror, a server pointing her towards a door, running, a pantry, food, flour, cereals, rice, pasta, row after row of canned foods, jars, bottles, juices, soda, run, run, to the back . . . collapse, hide, tears, let the tears flow, can't hold them back, "No!" emitting from her soul, and the final acceptance of the horror. Why can't it die, why can't it die!?

Still the nightmare, as vivid as though she were never thirty-eight years older. Thirty-eight years ago, sixty-eight years ago, if she lived that long, and it would still haunt her. *I'll never forget it. Never! It'll always be with me. Why can't it just die*!? "So we beat on, boats against the current, borne back ceaselessly into the past." Everyone has a Gatsby.

And then, Vaughn, standing at the door of the pantry, staring at her down this long aisle of shelves, pale, worried, fearful. Without hesitation, he went to her, sunk down on the floor next to her, took his handkerchief from his pocket and dabbed at the tears falling from her eyes. "I'm sorry," she uttered. "I'm so sorry. What you must think of me."

"Hey, it's okay. Something upset you. Nothing to be embarrassed about. Everyone has problems every now and then. Even me," he said humorously, "and I'm considered omnipotent, and omniscient. By myself, of course." She looked at him and smiled. Then she laughed, and slowly, the image from childhood faded, then disappeared like an apparition, like Hamlet's father's ghost. "So, what do you think?" Vaughn said, when he saw the Cassie he recognized come back to life, "Who's had the worse day, you, or the bird?"

And suddenly she was laughing. Through the tears and the emotional trauma, laughter, and he laughed with her. The most informal thing she had ever heard him say, and it had saved her.

"Thank you," she said softly. Thank you so much."

"Ready to go back?"

"Uh-hum," she nodded. "I hope Stevie's okay."

"She is," Vaughn replied. "Maybe just a little worried about her mom." Vaughn leaped to an upright position and offered his hand to help her up. She was wearing heels, not her comfort zone.

"Mrs. Komsky," a detached voice uttered, "do you prefer the classroom, or the pantry?" Taylor, with livid eyes, even colder than they were when first greeting Cassie, stood, arms folded, glaring at her and her husband.

"Sorry, Darling," Vaughn replied. Something upset Cassie." He looked at her, "but she feels better now." He gave no notice of his wife's glare. Was he used to this, Cassie wondered.

"I would hope so, Darling. Our guests are waiting." With that, she turned and left.

"Shall we?" Vaughn asked good-naturedly, guiding her forward. Cassie sensed something very unsettling, but nothing seemed to bother him. Must be me, she thought. My instincts must be off, way off. But that glare? She shook it off and walked back to dinner.

25

SUNDAY AFTER THANKSGIVING

"Three floors in this house?" Cassie asked after Jeremy unrolled the schematics for Damon House and she took her first quick glimpse.

"In this house, yes; it's old. The newer houses have two, and their footprint is much larger, like yours, Sanders, which was built last year. Damon's footprint is 80' by 200,' but you can see from these drawings that some rooms are not occupied. They're either used for storage or simply vacant. Look." He ran his fingers along the extremities of each floor and the third floor, whose footprint was smaller than the two lower floors. "None of these rooms are for student occupancy."

"How do you know that?" Cassie asked, perplexed.

"Because they're not numbered." He paused. "At least that's what I've always assumed." He looked at her intently. "But since I can't say for certain, and since chemistry is a discipline that seeks absolutes," his eyes glimmered with mischief, "want to find out?"

"You mean now, 4:30 on a Sunday evening, search them out?"

"That's what I mean," he emphasized. "How else do you find out what's in them? Besides, now's as good a time as any, unless, of course," he added wryly, "you've got something better to do, like lesson plans or grading tests?"

Cassie paused briefly, thinking of three more essays she had to read before tomorrow, then digested the sardonic smirk on Jeremy's face and let the spirited side of her personality have free rein. "Lead on Macduff," she said with flair and a wave of her hand, hooked and ready for adventure.

Jeremy stopped. "I thought it was *Lay* on Macduff."

"You have *got* to be kidding me!" Cassie was shocked. "It *is* Lay on, Macduff. It was misquoted around the mid-19th century and it stuck. But you? I thought you just knew chemistry. Silly me. Big mistake!"

"You'd be surprised what this chemistry teacher knows. Besides, I played a pretty good Macbeth in high school," he smiled proudly.   "But we can talk 'me' and Shakespeare another time. Let's get started with these blueprints before curfew check."

Blueprints in hand, they passed room after room of young men who had gotten back from Thanksgiving weekend in the late afternoon. All unpacked by now, some were sitting at their desks with open books; others were writing papers, playing chess or bridge. A few were relaxing with popular fiction, a newspaper, or a magazine. A few rooms were empty, others packed, football reruns in full swing, popcorn, pretzels, chips, Cokes. Cassie and Jeremy passed the game room, ping-pong and pool competitions on heavy. Warm hello's from Cassie's first period students, Parker, Matt, Connor, and Zach, and smiles from the others. As they continued deeper into the hallways, voices faded and activities became sparse. Jeremy was matching the schematic to each room and they were near the end of the hallway.

"Let's open this one. No label on the drawing."

The door opened on creaky hinges; Jeremy flicked on the light. The room was about 30' by 40', with four large never-been-washed windows at the back wall, filled with nothing but cardboard boxes and dust, dust and dust. Dust on the boxes, the molding, and the floors. "Unbelievable, Jeremy. I feel like I'm entering Miss Havisham's parlor; she's seated in a high-backed chair, calling for Estella." She moved about the room slowly to avoid touching anything. "I can actually see my footprints in this stuff . . . yours too."

"This room hasn't been used in years. And I have to apologize because I've been housemaster at Damon for five years and I have never opened this door until now."

"Nothing unusual about that Jeremy," Cassie laughed. "Until I moved to Chelsea, I hadn't opened a few closets for at least that long!"

"You have a good sense of humor, Cassie," Jeremy commented and looked directly into her eyes. "Never lose it," he added seriously.

Cassie scrunched up her face. "Wow, where'd that gravitas come from?" She added, still laughing.

"Nothing specific, Cassie. But I've known a lot of people in my lifetime who won't let someone who's genuine and sincere be happy. Don't lose it, Cassie. Too many people would love to see you be miserable like themselves."

"You see happiness?"

"Yeah, I do. Maybe a little tarnished, but I see a lovely, warm person who's happy and wants others to be happy, and I haven't known you very long."

Cassie pondered Jeremy's comment as they continued towards the end of the first floor hallway. No one had ever said that to her; no one except Brian. They opened three more rooms like the first, all so laden with dust they could have written their names on the walls and drawn hop-scotch grids on the floor. The last one was so cold Cassie shivered.

Climbing the stairs to the second floor, they found the same layout, the same student activities throughout the central rooms, same lack of activity in the extremities, where there were two vacant rooms instead of four. Both were much larger, almost double in size from the vacant rooms downstairs, and each had a small room off the far wall used for excess building materials. Cassie opened boxes of tiles and stepped around broken window frames, ladders, piles of ancient texts, old desks, chairs, copiers. Why not just throw this stuff out? Cassie thought. What a waste of space.

"See any place Samir would be able to hide, or would *want* to," Cassie asked, throwing down two dusty volumes of an old set of encyclopedias. "No one could breathe this stuff in for long. Really, Maintenance has to do some serious spring cleaning."

Jeremy, smiling, shook his head. "One more floor to go, no students up here, though."

Up the stairs to the third floor, which was barred by a set of heavy metal doors. Unlocked, they opened to a narrow center hallway that bifurcated into two very large rooms, one on each side. Cassie peered into the room on the right, Jeremy took the left. "I think this was a music room, Jeremy," Cassie called out as she opened sliding doors where derelict music stands piled one on top of the other, discarded from disuse. A few abandoned instruments leaned against closet walls, trumpets, a clarinet, one trombone, and some yellowed sheet music.

"These instruments must have cost a small fortune back then," she said.

"Lots of Chelsea students have small fortunes to discard," Jeremy shouted from the other room. "Come in here; you're gonna like this room."

Cassie closed the closet doors, leaving the dead-file room exactly as she had found it, and walked across the hallway. "Why am I gonna . . ." She paused in the doorway. Before her at the far end of the wall was a stage which was large enough to present Shakespeare's plays. Two curtains in the back could hide the orchestra or be a marshalling area for witches, ghosts, props or changing scenes. Cassie nodded with approval. "Yeah, I like this. Classes could come up here and rehearse for a project, write their own plays and rehearse here without having to schedule the auditorium. Completely impromptu. And certainly enough space for a small inner-core audience."

Jeremy smiled. "I thought you'd like it." Cassie had gotten absorbed in the possibilities of the room and was forgetting the reason she and Jeremy were here. "Do you think Samir would find refuge here?"

Jeremy's question brought her back to the real world. "Sorry, Jeremy, I got sidetracked."

"I can see that, but it's understandable. I'd feel the same if we had discovered an abandoned chemistry lab."

She was appreciating Jeremy more and more. "Yes." She nodded. "I think Samir could find solitude and solace here. It's isolated, quiet. It would let him adhere to protocols, yet stay apart and detached. Dusty though, so whether he has or would, that's something we wouldn't know unless we found him here."

Cassie began to examine closets. Nothing but folding chairs and some dusty old costumes on hangers hung there. She tried to recall plays from time periods the costumes would match, but nothing came to mind. She closed the doors and moved on.

At the far end of the room was a door. She opened it and peeked in, nothing much, just a small vestibule, a window on the far end and another door on her right. Cassie opened it and was surprised to see a narrow flight of stairs going up. "Jeremy, where do these stairs go? Any other room up there?"

Jeremy shook his head and rechecked the schematic. "Nope, fourteen stairs lead to a door that leads to the roof."

"The roof? Wow, this building *is* old. The last time I saw stairs like this was in the house where I grew up. I'll never forget it. You put the stairwell light on from a wall switch before you unlocked the door. My parents always kept it locked; then you climbed eleven steps to a dark attic that had two windows, one on each side. Sometimes my dad would climb out onto the roof to repair a shingle or something, or adjust the TV antenna. Never imagined I'd see something like that again, especially in such a prestigious private academy such as this."

"This academy was founded almost two hundred years ago. Can't modernize the whole campus."

Cassie nodded. "But," she gave something a second thought and pointed to the door, "shouldn't this door be locked?"

"Why? Who uses it but Maintenance? It gives them access to the roof if they should need it, you know, to repair a shingle or adjust the TV antenna." He looked at her with a mischievous smile. "Gotcha," he added as she rolled her eyes. "Besides, it's been this way forever."

"I know, but . . ." Cassie gave Jeremy a pleading look.

"Okay, if it bothers you, I'll write up a work order to have it bolted this week. Will that assuage your paranoia?"

"Yes, it would. Thank you. And now," she announced, dusting off her hands in finality as much as to slap off dust, "I'm going home to a relatively modern condo, kept clean by a fanatic who can't stand dust and who does all her own cooking, make that 'almost' all."

"You've got me on the cleanliness part, but I'll go head to head with you in the kitchen, except for that nemura," he added with a smile, "which was better than ambrosia. "So, choose your weapon: Chicken parm or linguine with white clam sauce? Or both?"

"What are you suggesting?" She asked, thoroughly surprised by his challenge. "A cook-off?"

Jeremy nodded with conviction. "Yup!" He had seemed meek to her. He wasn't.

That gave Cassie a moment's pause. "Do I have to steam my own clams?"

"Canned is fine."

"You're on - for both! Me and Stevie versus you. Name the time and the kitchen."

"Next weekend, Saturday or Sunday; my kitchen; we invite the football crew."

"Saturday. Sunday to recuperate. They bring wine and dessert."

"Done."

26

MONDAY AFTER
THANKSGIVING, NOV 30

Monday after Thanksgiving. Her students were back in class physically but mentally they were anywhere else, alive with left-over excitement from Thanksgiving weekend. The guys were rehashing football wins, losses, and plays, and as guys do, they pushed and prodded each other good-naturedly. The girls, of course, leaned towards more feminine pursuits, highlighting dinner, desserts, and weight gain, shopping, and movies, giggling with enthusiasm.

As if Thanksgiving conversation weren't electrifying enough, Elizabeth Stanack had come to class wearing a necklace of green holly, dotted with red berries and Santa bells, a stunning contrast against her soft woolen, off-white sweater. The holiday spirit had begun. It was in their speech and their affable manner. Oh, the travails of being a teacher between Thanksgiving and Christmas, and keeping your classes focused. Public school or private, no difference.

What students failed to realize, though, was that their teachers were as excited and happy as they were. Most of them anyway. Inwardly, Cassie was; she just couldn't show it. Otherwise, they'd never focus on a lesson.

"Like my necklace, Mrs. Komsky?" Elizabeth asked proudly, looping her thumb and finger through it, holding it out so Cassie could see. "I made it myself. I'll make you one if you'd like."

Cassie's smiled broadened. "Thank you, Elizabeth. I love your necklace and I appreciate the offer, but I have more than enough Christmas jewelry, and decorations. In fact, I'm smiling because my daughter and I just brought out two boxes of Christmas decorations yesterday evening, getting ready to decorate the house."

"Oh!" Elizabeth exclaimed, picking up on what Cassie had just said, "Can we decorate the room?"

Gloria, Emelia and Rachel jumped right in. "That's a wonderful idea. Can we?"

This was one question she was 99.9% sure of that no instructor at Chelsea Academy had ever heard before, before girls were admitted. "Will it interfere with Hamlet?" Cassie asked feigning skepticism.

"Ask me anything about act 3, or 4, or even act 5. I know it cold," Elizabeth challenged.

They were all seated by now and enjoying the exchange. Even Parker was smiling, perhaps remembering a different Mrs. Komsky from Thanksgiving, or from his lively conversation with Stevie, which he had enjoyed thoroughly.

"First let me return your essays," Cassie replied. "That might curtail some effervescence."

"Were they bad?" asks Jason; "Oh, no! How'd we do?" Asks Elizabeth, Gloria, and Matt. "No way; I aced it!" from Parker.

"Okay, okay," Cassie gestured a downward motion with her hand. "They were good. I'm just teasing."

"How good? . . . Yeah, how good?"

"Settle down and let me pass them out. Then you'll see how good," she smiled wryly. "Or not!"

"Mrs. Komsky, you've got a very playful side to your personality," Emelia commented.

"So, you have discovered my secret!" Cassie's laughter bubbled out like seltzer when the cap comes off too quickly. "Here, read them; read my comments, and of course, your grade. Two grades; the first is logic in thought - sequence and whether you supported and proved your premise; the second is paragraph development, transition, cohesion, introductory and closing paragraphs, grammar, all that good stuff that allows the reader to follow what you're saying."

They reached for their papers; some grabbed for them amidst, "great" and "darn." A hint of a smile played around Samir's lips. His paper was excellent. He had interwoven the miracle of man which Hamlet ultimately reduces to dust, to the insignificance of all mankind as told by Macbeth: We strut and fret our hour upon the stage and then are heard no more. "Any questions? Quick ones, ask me now; if you need more time, see me after class or during consultation. Anybody have a serious disagreement with my comments?"

"Better than I thought," said Mason. "Thanks, Mrs. Komsky."

"I grade it as I see it, Mason. Never expect an inflated grade from me if that's what you mean." She turned her attention to Elizabeth. "That's done; here we go, Elizabeth, the deciding factor as to whether you will or will not decorate the room." The ladies rubbed their hands in anticipation. "Drum roll, please." Cassie was in rare form and her students knew it. If anyone had to be contained today, it was her, not them. "Okay," she put on her serious face, with difficulty, "act 3, scene 2. Hamlet tells Horatio he wants another set of eyes to observe his uncle while he watches the players perform. Why Horatio, why that choice for the play, and does it work?"

Elizabeth beams. "We are so gonna decorate this room," she says with super confidence. "Horatio because Hamlet trusts him, and only him; the play is Hamlet's deception to see how Claudius reacts to the part where the actor puts poison in the king's ear, and yes it works. Claudius gets up and walks out, clearly proving his guilt and Horatio confirms it." Elizabeth knows it cold.

"Nice work, Elizabeth. Wear any Christmas decoration you like, and come in early any morning to decorate," Cassie replies. "I'm usually here by 7:30." The ladies are ecstatic.

"Wait, Mrs. Komsky." Parker objects. "Wait, that was way too easy. Any of us could have gotten that. If the guys answer a question that easy in January, can we decorate the room for Super Bowl?"

"With what?" Emelia chides amidst the laughter and hooting. "Dirty jocks and cleats?" And the class roars!

Cassie was laughing so hard she was holding her stomach and wiping tears from her eyes. Thirty seconds of uncontrollable, stomach-holding, gulping-for-air laughter.

"I'm sorry, I shouldn't have been laughing like this, but the answer to your question is no," Cassie finally manages to eke out between tears of laughter. "Absolutely not, and you can call it discrimination or whatever. A few football posters is as far as I'll go."

"That's good enough," Mason comments. "We'll take it."

"And ladies, you can start as soon as you like. Just keep it simple; don't overcrowd the room. A tree, ersatz gifts, okay? And include Hanukkah, it's two weeks away." Boundaries were established and accepted.

"Now, let's *try* to continue," emphasis on 'try.' If we overlap with previous discussions, stress your point and move on; hopefully we can get Hamlet and the cast killed off and get into *Othello* before Christmas. If not, we'll begin *Othello* first day back."

Who was this teacher and what had this replacement done with her? "Mrs. Komsky, you feeling okay today?" Jason asked quite seriously, almost breaking down the serious veneer Cassie was trying hard to maintain. She had no idea what was wrong with her today, but her witty humor was percolating up and out.

"Quite fine, Jason. I should have been a bit more formal. Sorry about that."

"We're not," Matt added. They all made it very clear that they liked this playful side and could learn *Hamlet* anyway, maybe even better, maybe even faster, if she stayed this way. She said, quite affably, she'd consider it, and the discussion began.

Back and forth from the play within the play achieving its purpose, giving Hamlet the proof he desperately needed, to Zach still labeling him a coward, and now stating his mother was as well. "She appears sympathetic to his statement that Claudius murdered the king, but she turns on him in the next scene." Zach's explanation was sound.

"Hamlet knows Claudius is guilty now; now he has his proof, so he can kill him. But he doesn't. He passes him right by when he sees Claudius praying because he doesn't want to kill him while he's purging his soul, because Claudius would be . . ." Zach flips a few pages "'season'd for passage.' Come on. It's more cowardice. He's a joke."

Mason concurred. He supported Zach's statement showing Hamlet had no problem killing Polonius, who was hiding behind the arras in his mother's room, without knowing who he was, "but he won't kill Claudius because he needs concrete, absolute proof," Mason argues, clearly correct.

Cassie agrees. "You're right, Mason. He was just hoping it was the king, sight unseen. Anybody think he's lost his ability to reason, since he can't dispute Claudius' guilt any longer?"

"Maybe the madness he begins as a pretense takes over, and he doesn't know he's become mad?" Rachel introduces an insightful possibility.

"Excellent hypothesis. Let's expound on this a bit."

"That would mean what he told Horatio way back at the end of act 1, you know, about putting on an antic disposition, has taken control of him; so what Rachel had said about Hamlet hurting Ophelia for his own agenda is no longer his agenda, because insanity has taken control, despite Hamlet's original intention to pretend." An outstanding and insightful contribution to the lesson from Parker.

"Parker," she nodded with admiration, knowing he had asked to be called by his first name a week before Thanksgiving, "outstanding contribution; outstanding reasoning. Take it a step further. Does his mother believe he's acting?"

"Wait, Mrs. Komsky, before we answer that, what about the reappearance of his father's ghost who his mother conveniently can't see," Jason asserts. "When Hamlet talks to it, his mother thinks he's mad, but he tells her he's not mad, only mad in craft. *That* follows through with his antic disposition."

"Maybe that's Shakespeare's genius," Parker is still in it. "Maybe the reader will never know for sure. Maybe Hamlet's been 'mad' so well that when he does say it's just craft, the reader doesn't believe him. His mother certainly doesn't. She thinks he's nuts, and everything she says to him after that she must have said to appease him, because she tells Claudius in the next scene Hamlet's 'Mad as the sea and wind when they're vying for power.' That's line 7, act 4, scene 1. She also tells Claudius how Hamlet killed Polonius. I understand how she can believe he's mad, because if he is, he did that to himself, but I can't understand how she can just throw him to the wolves. Some mother!"

"And," Parker is not finished, "that means everything she said to Hamlet in her room was a lie. She's two-faced. She doesn't feel any guilt at all about marrying her brother-in-law, and she doesn't believe Claudius poisoned Hamlet's father. She could have said this to Hamlet's face, but she didn't. She didn't have the courage. Just like Hamlet, no courage. Zach's right."

"Great analysis, Parker. Glad you came to class today." Parker smiled. What a transition, Cassie thought. "Class, what do you think? Hamlet and his mother, both cowards in their own way?"

Yes, by acclamation. Not one dissenter, not even Jason, whose sympathy to Hamlet's plight had dissipated.

"But don't most people do this? In some way, don't we all, sometimes? Not to such an extreme, but in less dramatic ways? Don't we all avoid the truth, hide from it, lie to others or worse, lie to ourselves and surround ourselves with acquaintances and friends who validate the same lie, the same charade. Don't a lot of people continue a deception rather than face the truth?"

Parker shrugged. "Don't know, Mrs. Komsky. If you don't see the truth, or don't recognize it, it's understandable. But when you've been told, or once you become aware . . ." his gaze fell on Samir and the two stared at each other, face to face, for more than a moment, "then I think most people, not all, but most, would get it."

"Last year you read Conrad's *Heart of Darkness*?" Lots of nods. "Remember the scene at the end of the story? I almost choked on it." At least six hands shot up amidst yeses and I remember! "Describe the scene. What was it saying to the reader?"

Jason reaches for it but doesn't quite pull it from his memory. "His, his . . . I can see the scene," he states in frustration, his hands circling the air.

Gloria and Emelia are struggling with the same problem. "I can see it in the text," Emelia says, "I can see him
standing there with papers in his hand . . . it's when the
guy who finds Kurtz gives her those papers that say and
mean nothing, and she lets herself believe they're proof
Kurtz loved her. What's she called . . . what's she called?"

"His Intended, with a capital 'I!'" Connor shouts.
Connor, who rarely contributed in class, nails it. "And
Marlowe's the guy who finds Kurtz. He lies, a blatant lie,
when he tells her that Kurtz's last words were her name."

"And she never asks Marlowe what her name is!" Zach
adds. "I couldn't believe that part either. How stupid
could she be? All she had to do was say, 'What's my name?'
and she would have known Marlowe was lying."

"But she also would have known her fiancé didn't even
think of her when he was dying. So she didn't want to
know." Rachel confirms. "That's what Mrs. Komsky is saying about Hamlet's mother. Maybe Gertrude didn't want
to know what she'd done." She becomes pensive, then
whispers, "How can anybody live like that, always walking
around with your head in the sand?"

"More people than you'd want to believe, Rachel,"
Cassie says softly. "More people than you'd want to believe. Living a lie is sometimes a lot easier than facing the
truth. For Kurtz's Intended, knowing she wasn't even a
thought in her fiancé's mind as he was dying might have
killed her. Maybe the lie allows her to live. And as you
said last week, it takes a very strong person to pull yourself
up and go on from there. Marlowe's Intended couldn't.
Maybe Hamlet's mother couldn't either."

27

FIFTH PERIOD, CASSIE TAKES REPORT TO GUIDANCE.

Cassie almost skipped to Smythe Hall. She was ecstatic! Period one, great class; great classes all day. Best part of all, Parker actively participating, at times even dominating the discussion, with great insight, thought-provoking questions and non-verbal interaction with Samir. The best reason in the world for teaching. She reviewed almost every word, every question, every discussion, every everything as her steps carried her to Guidance and her enthusiasm propelled her through the door to Melissa's desk. She was, proverbially, walking on air.

"Well, what's taken hold of you?" Melissa asked when she saw Cassie beaming from ear to ear.

"I've just had the best class discussions today, and period one was outstanding!"

"And why was that any different from the usual fantastic discussions your classes have?"

"Because Parker volunteered and was so motivated in the conversation."

"You are creating a remarkable rapport with your students. What's your secret?"

"I don't know, Melissa. It's just happening. That's what rapport is all about, isn't it? We don't go into a situation saying, 'I'm gonna create a rapport with this person.' It just happens."

"Pat yourself on the back. You're doing something right," Melissa said.

Cassie propped her attaché on Melissa's desk and began searching for her very, very brief report about her meeting with Samir. "I sure hope so, but I am so psyched, and . . ." she was interrupted by, "I hear you and Jeremy have thrown down the gauntlet for cooking?"

She whirled. "Walter. I didn't hear you creep up on me."

"That is the nature of being stealthy, and I was being stealthy."

"Proof there's a little child in all of us, no matter how old we get," she teased.

He pretended to be insulted. "Are you implying I'm old?"

"Well…" she replied with an impish grin.

"Child or not, I can't wait for Saturday's cook-off. Linguine with white clam sauce is one of my favorites."

"Oh my God, Jeremy invited you already, and he's told you what we're making?" She looked at Walter, then at Melissa who wore a Cheshire cat smile as she held out her hand for the report Cassie had just pulled out of her attaché. "I guess he told you too?"

"He's told everyone," Melissa added, initialing Cassie's report then taking it to the copier.

"How many people did he invite?" Cassie gulped.

"You're safe. He invited the football crew, but he's *told* everyone – everyone who's not too busy to listen. And that's a lot of people," she added good-naturedly, "since Jeremy can be quite loquacious when he wants to be. I wouldn't be surprised if he has a crowd of spectators outside his apartment watching the event. We might even call the local media."

"You guys are unbelievable."

"We aim to please," Melissa teased.

"I guess it's okay, as long as he doesn't announce it at today's faculty meeting; then he might have the entire faculty, a crowd of spectators *and* the local media."

"Warn him before the meeting starts or he might do just that," she laughs, takes a closer look at Cassie's report and passes the copy back to Cassie. "You weren't exaggerating when you said it would be brief."

"Time, place, that's about it. That's all Dr. O/B expects, with a brief comment about my tour of Damon Hall with Jeremy, which is what got me into this cook-off. Believe me, it wasn't my idea."

"But it's a great one," Melissa said. A cook-off. Now that would never have entered my mind. But then again," she put her hand to her mouth as though she were announcing a secret of the highest order, "I don't cook."

"This is what happens when you do!" Cassie said. "You get roped into a cook-off with about ten hungry judges." She slides the copy of her report into her briefcase.

By now the entire office staff was listening and enjoying the banter. "Well, not quite ten." Melissa began to count. Let's see, there's you, Jeremy, Walter, Tasha, Joe Biasso, he was invited too. You met him at Thanksgiving but not at the game because he's always on the field with the band. Then there's Stevie, me, Ronnie Collins and Alicia Walsh. Only nine." Now, Melissa's smile was wider than a Cheshire cat's, if that was possible.

"What are we counting?" The laughter stopped immediately, like a popped balloon. "From everyone's reaction, I'd say I wasn't supposed to hear the discourse that just transpired?" There he stood, at the door's entrance as it closed behind him on its tight hinge. He panned the group then focused directly on Cassie.

"No, not at all," Dr. O/B, Cassie offered awkwardly. "We should have waited and discussed it after school. Sorry." She was embarrassed.

"Cassie and Jeremy are having a cook-off Saturday night," Melissa blurted out, "and we were counting the number of guests Jeremy's invited." Cassie glared at her. "There are nine."

"May as well make it ten," Vaughn replied. A nice, even, composite number, divisible by 2 or 5, whichever way you look at it."

"Or, divisible by ten," Cassie added playfully, "whichever way you look at it."

Vaughn paused, always surprised at the candid comments that emanated from Cassie's lips. "You do have a way about you," he replied, staring at her. You could hear the clock tick. Suddenly he laughed, hard and from his gut, shocking his audience. "You amaze me, Cassie," and for a few seconds, he just stared. Then he turned to Walter. "I came in for college application forms." He looks at Cassie, "and I'm glad I did."

Cassie threw up her hands in surrender. It seemed to her that she usually said the wrong thing when Dr. O/B was around, but, then sometimes, he seemed to encourage it. Perplexing and a bit disturbing, although she couldn't figure out why. He's the dean, she thought, but he doesn't always act like it. Am I the only one who notices or am I being paranoid?

"It's a bit early for college forms," Vaughn continued to Walter, "but several senior parents have requested them. Charlotte says you haven't sent the new ones over. I needed the walk, and then I hear this interesting conversation." He turns to Cassie. "But I can see no invitation is forthcoming," he pauses, as Cassie's mouth drops and her face turns bright red from embarrassment, "so I'll leave. Send over the forms as soon as you can, will you Walter?"

"You'll have them in less than an hour." And Vaughn is gone. Walter stares at Cassie, still in shock and still embarrassed.

"Oh my God," she stammers, once she gets her voice back, "did he just about invite himself?"

"Not 'just about.' He *definitely* invited himself, and you, Cassie Komsky, turned him down flat."

"How could he do that, Walter? I didn't turn him down; I just never expected anything like that! He's the dean; he doesn't hang out with faculty. He's always at the Club! Didn't you say that once?"

"I've said it more than once, and it's true," Walter confirmed. He's always at the Club with Taylor, Brett, Hillary, the family, friends, every Saturday, and most Friday evenings, unless they're traveling."

"Then why would he try to include himself on a get-together for staff?"

"Beats me, and it's out of character for him too, because I've never seen him in this office before. Have you?" Walter looks at Melissa who shakes her head, no. "Charlotte conducts all his communications with us, and I respond directly to her. If we have to deliver something to his office, I might walk it down. Sometimes Ronnie or Melissa will walk something over, or we use inter-office boxes. This visit is uncharacteristic."

"Is it just me," Melissa interjects, changing the subject, "but is he a little broader?" They look at her quizzically. "You know, beefier, like more muscle?" Getting no response, she adds, "Forget it. I'm seeing things."

"Well," Cassie figuratively brushes off Vaughn's comments, "whatever it is, it is. See you Saturday. And don't come too early. Stevie and I have to carry the food to Jeremy's and do some touch-up cooking. If you see what dishes our food is in, you'll know whose it is."

28

PREPARATION WEEK FOR THE COOK-OFF

Monday, Tuesday and Wednesday already, but an exciting Wednesday. Today she and Stevie were shopping for the cook-off. Shopping for cans of whole peeled tomatoes, chopped clams, fresh garlic, linguine, three boxes - must have enough, even though Jeremy thought if they each made a pound and a half, three pounds total would be plenty. Cassie wasn't sure. Maybe she'd make two pounds herself. But for that much linguine, she'd need at least six cans of clams, no, maybe seven, even eight, and an extra bottle of clam juice, just in case. Parsley. Fresh parsley, an absolute necessity. She'd get that Friday so it would be as fresh as possible. Let's see, what else? Chicken cutlets, she'd get those Friday too, for the latest sell-by date. Mozzarella cheese and extra sharp provolone she'd grate herself. She had read an article about additives in grated cheese. Nix to that.

Their shopping list was long enough for a weeknight. Stevie had homework and Cassie had to put some final touches on tomorrow's lesson. The guys would focus on Claudius' and Laertes' scheme, a poisoned rapier. Of course their plot would work; they all knew the play's ending. In fact, Matt, Mason, and Zach were looking forward to it. The end of Hamlet would make their day.

Cassie threw out the word 'honor,' but neither the male nor female contingent sympathized with Hamlet. They couldn't wait to see him die, and Ophelia's insanity and subsequent death were key, especially for the ladies. Shakespeare had taken a completely innocent young girl, her whole life before her and, through no fault of her own, had destroyed her.

The success of any work of fiction is how well the reader empathizes with the characters. Their strong resentment towards Hamlet and their complete sympathy with Ophelia proved they had empathized. Trust and betrayal, two of the most powerful emotions motivating the human psyche regardless of gender, regardless of age; these they understood without equivocation. Ophelia had been a victim of love and trust, and their betrayal had destroyed her. Betrayal could bring us all to our knees. As Rachel had said last week with such perception, do we get up and move on? Ophelia could not.

So, shopping would be a quick trip for essentials, then home. Up and down the aisles she and Stevie hurried, dropping boxes of pasta, cans of tomatoes and clams, fresh garlic and other essentials into their cart. They finished their list and were through check-out in less than an hour, looking forward to all the fun this cooking challenge would bring. Friday and Saturday couldn't come fast enough.

29

THE COOK-OFF

Jeremy's condo smelled like an Italian bistro. The aroma of tomatoes, garlic, onions, basil, parsley, and sharp, aged cheeses emanated from his kitchen into the foyer; and most likely had permeated his entire condo. Breathe deeply; you'd become intoxicated.

Cassie stood in the middle of the foyer and inhaled. "Jeremy, this is heavenly."

"I know. One of the reasons I love to cook. Better than any perfume. I love the aroma of the spices and the way they comingle. Most people air out their houses after they cook. Not me. I sit, have a glass of wine and absorb."

"Doesn't this aroma seep into the dorm rooms?" Cassie asked; she and Stevie put their food on the foyer table to remove their coats.

He chuckled. "Their problem. They've got cafeteria food. Don't get me wrong, it's very good, but I always prefer mine."

"I'm surprised you chose chemistry. This smacks of culinary arts."

"Actually, cooking is a form of chemistry, and vice versa, for me, anyway. I zipped through chemistry tests way back in high school, identifying all kinds of knowns and unknowns, feeling like I was in a kitchen. Put in a little of this, and it bubbles. Add a little of that and it changes color. So I'm at home in the kitchen, and obviously," he took the huge tray from the table, "so are you. And you, young lady," he nodded to Stevie, "you must be too. Let's take your dishes into the kitchen and see what we've got here." Jeremy led the way and they followed.

Jeremy's apartment was more open than Cassie's, and his foyer led past the living room on the left to the dining room beyond, which accessed the kitchen from the back. When Cassie passed the living room, she stopped. "You've decorated for Christmas," she squealed in delight, "and you put up your tree! Oh my gosh, I'm so jealous! We haven't even taken ours out of its box!"

"I exploit the entire month of December for Christmas. Come into my house December 1st, and you see Christmas, whether it's a wreath, tabletop ornament, garland around the mantel, something. There's gotta be Christmas in my home starting Dec 1st. My mother did that for as long as I can remember, and I carry on her tradition. Everything else is up by the first week; nothing comes down until New Year's Day."

"Do you mind?" Cassie started towards the tree, like a little kid to look at the beautiful ornaments.

"No, no. Go. Look. Enjoy. The tree is one of my obsessions, and I love it when people make a fuss over it. I'll put your dish in the oven with mine to keep them warm, and Stevie, I'll take that bowl from you in a sec."

"That's okay, Mr. Harper. I'll put it on the counter for you." Stevie placed the Corning Ware bowl filled with clam sauce on the counter, then joined her mother, with Jeremy a few seconds behind.

"These are beautiful." Cassie pointed to the miniature glass lamping figurines that were exquisitely crafted and detailed. "Look at the precision, the artistry; they're absolutely exquisite," she said, rotating a tiny, delicate reindeer with spud antlers and a red nose.

"Rudolf, of course," Jeremy replied. "I add one to this collection when I can't walk out of the store without it. I love the little poinsettias and the elves." He touched a few lightly. "When the tree lights are on, the glass glistens and creates a gossamer, almost mystical, aura. Some soft Christmas music, a glass of wine, that's all I need."

"So there are other people out there like me who disavow the glitz and hype of the Christmas season."

"Hype is definitely overrated. It just sends us on a never-ending quest for happiness out there that you can only find inside yourself."

"From experience?" Cassie asked quietly.

"From experience," Jeremy nodded. "But let's get that pasta boiling and the table set. Our guests will be arriving in fifteen minutes. Stevie, want to set the dining room table for me? "

Stevie nodded eagerly and began putting out place settings as she moved and hummed to a medley of Christmas music and Oldies. Her mother liked the 50's but her favorites were from the 70's and early 80's, and this station was playing them all. If "Leather and Lace" came on, Stevie knew her mother would cry. She always did.

Sometimes Stevie would think of her dad and remember times when he'd carry her high on his shoulders and the three of them would walk the surf. She couldn't have been more than three, maybe four, because he was killed when she was four. But she remembered certain memories as though they had happened last summer; her little voice laughing and squealing as he'd swing her above the waves. She'd hold on to him like she would never let go. Then he was gone.

Leaving Manasquan and her friends was not what she had wanted, but Mom needed a different life, away from memories of her dad that still hurt. Stevie knew this instinctively. And here wasn't so bad. She was making friends from public school, and Rebecca, Stacy and Millie were nice too. She was glad her mom was making some too. "Oh, oh," she murmured out loud. "Billy Jean" had come on.

"Hey Mom, wanna dance?" Stevie yelled into the kitchen. Cassie had told her Dr. O/B had dragged her off the dance floor at Homecoming when this song had come on. Not surprising. Stevie knew her mom could really move, and at nine, she and her 9th grade friends understood Dr. O/B's reasons better than Cassie. Her Mom was so naive.

"We, and I use the royal, 'we,'" Cassie yelled from the kitchen, "are never dancing to that song again, so remove that smug look on your face I can't see from here but I know is there."

Just then the doorbell rang and the football crew tumbled in as one cohesive unit, carrying cheeses, crackers, nuts, olives, wine, beer, cherry pie, apple strudel, and ice cream. They unloaded everything on Jeremy's counter, taking over a good part of his kitchen. Then they put ice cream in the freezer, pie and strudel on the back counter, cheeses and crackers on cutting boards, chips in wicker baskets, nuts and dips in bowls. Beer went into the frig. All was done, ready to be devoured.

"You guys brought so much stuff you're not going to be hungry for all this food," Jeremy chastised.

"Oh yes we are; don't worry about that," Walter replied. "Which one's Cassie's?" He searched the kitchen for a clue, lifting aluminum foil from dishes. "Hey, where's the chicken parm? I thought we were having chicken parm?"

Cassie gave him a playful glare, hands on her hips. "You know you are not supposed to know, so stop searching and get out of the kitchen, now!" She scolded, with emphasis on 'now.'

He pouted like a little boy who had just dropped his ice cream cone, but he left. "Hey," he called, will this be better than Vaughn's Thanksgiving dinner?"

Jeremy threw a wooden spoon in his direction. "Much better, and if you don't like it, we'll give you a pre-packaged frozen dinner."

"Just kidding, I *know* this will be better. Great food *and* I can wear jeans."

He was right. It was better, exceptionally better. The laughter, like the wine, flowed unabated. Conversation was casual, fit for any age and Stevie fit right in with comment after comment. Topics segued from academics and the problems with New Jersey's public education system to tenure, good or not; the pension system; the Department of Health Education and Welfare and government control, and how money dictated policy. Then conversation turned to public education in the northern states, how its origins emanating from religious institutions to produce the magnificence of a middle class, and how they believed it was devolving.

Fascinating and somewhat scary topics, because individualization in education was being threatened and compromised for state take-over testing. The teacher's ability to individualize was getting lost, even though that was purportedly the state's focus. Can't individualize if there are twenty-five students in the room, special-needs mainstreamed and state tests to be passed; can't motivate kids to learn if there's no support from the home; can't do much if an administration is more concerned with getting a budget passed than keeping standards high; can't do much if colleges are lowering their standards to maintain enrollments, producing a society that has trouble reading past a fourth grade level, a society in which the news stresses sensationalism and sports and a society that spends more time per day watching TV than it does all year reading a classic. What happened to Cooper's *Last of the Mohicans* or Dumas' *Count of Monte Cristo*? Do we still teach, or does anybody read, *Animal Farm* or *To Kill a Mockingbird*? Classics were timeless because humanity and its emotions were universal, but classics were being shelved for TV programs and canned laughter.

As they talked, they ate, helping after helping, pass this; pass that, until they noticed an obvious discrepancy between two casserole dishes: One tray of chicken parm and one of linguine with clam sauce had been consumed

much more than the others. Reaching for another helping of chicken from the almost empty tray, Walter suddenly paused. "Who made this? I am definitely voting for this
one, and so is just about everyone else because I'm taking
the last piece." He looked from Cassie to Jeremy. Neither
claimed ownership. "Well? Whose is it?'

"Name's on the bottom of each platter," Jeremy said.

Carefully, he tipped the platter as far as it would go
without spilling sauce and crooked his neck to look under.
"Ah hah!" He exclaimed. "I knew it! I knew it!"

"Whose is it? Whose is it?" Melissa and Tasha asked
excitedly, reaching for the other plates and tipping them
sideways.

"Jeremy, yours is good," Walter began, "and I sure
hope my saying this doesn't preclude other dinner invitations that may have been forthcoming, but . . ." he looked
at Cassie with admiration, "this is the best chicken parm
I've ever had. And I've eaten in a lot of Italian restaurants."

Cassie blushed. "Don't forget Stevie. She's my
backup."

"So noted," Walter added, and they all raised their
glasses to toast Cassie and Stevie. Jeremy included.

"I agree," Jeremy said as he raised his glass. "Glad to
be bested by someone who clearly excels in the culinary
arts. So what's your secret?"

Cassie shook her head. "Then it wouldn't be a secret."

"Stevie, what's her secret?" Jeremy asked.

They roared. Stevie shook her head.

"So you're not a traitor, huh?"

"Never," Stevie stated emphatically.

And with that, Jeremy stood and announced it was dessert time. "Everybody, bring in a dish and we'll get this table cleared real fast."

Off went dirty plates, serving platters, cutlery and napkins into the kitchen. Cassie began cleaning plates and loading the dish washer; Stevie wiped down the table; Jeremy got down dessert plates; Melissa took out dessert forks and spoons; drip coffee pot was on and working hard; Alicia took down cups and saucers, Joe and Tasha began slicing strudel and cherry pie, Ronnie putting them onto serving platters. Ice cream came out of the freezer, giant serving spoons for scooping; Ronnie got out sugar and the creamer. Like the hierarchy in a beehive, each played his or her part effectively.

Cassie got lost in the rhythm of the running water and the Righteous Brothers singing "Just Once in My Life" filtering in from the living room, and the other sounds simply faded into the background of the evening and her life. She was happy from inside out, and she hadn't felt this way in so very long. The ambient sound of the doorbell simply melded with the music.

30

THE COOK-OFF, THE CLUB
AND VAUGHN

Vaughn sat at his table, number nineteen, as usual. He was there, but he wasn't. He picked at his dinner without relish. He had eaten lobster but it had no appeal; most of it lay discarded on his plate. He stared at his vodka, swirling it again and again, no urge to drink; he watched his wife dance with his brother and thought, thank God for Brett. He felt nothing but relief that Taylor wasn't urging him onto the dance floor. He listened to his mother talk about Otis-Barrett holdings and how his great, great, great, or maybe add another 'great' grandfather had cornered some market that had launched the family into land holdings and the established dynasty.

But his mind and his fantasies were at a two story apartment where a group of faculty and its amazing recent addition were holding a cook-off, a cooking competition, and most likely having a wonderful, informal, dinner party filled with laughter, lots of wine, a few beers, and great food. All without him. Was he jealous? Of course not . . . maybe . . . no . . . yes. Damn it! Yes! He had no doubt Cassie was a great cook, and that the dinner would be delicious. If her food rivaled her nemura, she'd make head chef at the Club. But that's not why he wanted to be there.

She was getting under his skin, and he was beginning to be aware of it, not something he could excuse or dismiss anymore. He wanted to be there instead of at this sterile Club that patronized the same sterile people with the same multi, multi-million or billion dollar portfolios, his being one of them. Did he want to be poor? Of course not, but did wealth mandate you had to talk the talk and walk the walk of that ilk? Come on, Vaughn, he chastised himself, you married Taylor, from Jersey City. You are not just another rich snob.

But he married Taylor because he knew she'd fit in. She'd never be outspoken like Cassie. He also married her because she looked great on his arm, and because no female had ever shown him so much attention and given him such unconditional sex. Was there any other reason? Did he love her? Did she love him? Had there ever been any love there or was it simply suitable, convenient, for both of them. What is love, anyway? Vaughn lived his life doing and making others do whatever was convenient for him. Was that love? No. He never considered how he managed other people because he never cared enough about anyone else to consider them. What did he care if his actions were good for someone else as long as they were good for him. But he thought about it and he wondered why, after all these years, these questions were emerging now?

Enough, he thought. Enough of this. I do *not* want to be here tonight. He stood up, walked to the kitchen and heralded the head chef, whispered in his ear, walked onto the dance floor, and spoke into Brett's ear. Brett and Taylor smiled, Taylor gave him a kiss and Vaughn turned, walked back to the kitchen where the chef handed him a huge pastry box for which he was tipped handsomely, then he summoned his car and was off, removing his tie and undoing the top button on his shirt. He'd be there in less than tewnty minutes.

31

VAUGHN ARRIVES AT JEREMY'S

And then this familiar male voice was talking to Jeremy, Walter and the others welcoming him, shaking his hand, taking his jacket and a pastry box from him, and Jeremy was bringing it into the kitchen.

"Who brought this, Jeremy? Who's here?"

Jeremy avoided an answer. "I have a large platter I can use for these. Let's see if it's in here."

And Cassie knew. She instinctively knew. "Oh, no. Jeremy, is Dr. O/B here? He is, isn't he? Oh my God, he came without an invitation?"

Jeremy placed his finger across his lips in the universal 'shush' symbol. "Well, not exactly." He looked chagrinned. "He came to see me yesterday about putting that lock on the door to the attic steps, what I wrote in a work request and you put in your report, remember?"

"I remember," she said emphatically, but how did that get him an invitation to this?"

"He sort of steered the conversation to our cook-off. Don't look at me like that, Cassie. What was I gonna say, no? To the dean? Basically it's his school."

"So he used intimidation to get what he wanted."

"People use a lot of things to get what they want, and intimidation is one of them. Life's not such an enigma, Cassie. You know that from literature. Go back to King Arthur. All that talk about a round table making every one equal. Even he learned might makes right. If you fight too hard for every ideal, you'll not only lose, you'll lose hard. Save the fights for the big ones."

Cassie dried off her hands, opened the box and almost swooned. "Jeremy, these are absolutely decadent," she exclaimed softly as she transferred the desserts onto the huge platter Jeremy handed her. Then she carried it into the dining room and placed it on the table in front of Dr. O/B who Jeremy had seated opposite her. "I'm so glad you could come, Dr. O/B," she said with a detectible hint of flippancy in her voice. These desserts look delicious. You must have been baking all day, yes?"

Vaughn didn't even try to glare. His eyes bespoke of a much deeper emotion that made the other men wince. "I wish I could say yes, but unfortunately, the best I do in a kitchen is a pretty good lasagna . . ."

"Woah! Next cook-off is his!" Jeremy shouted. Everyone pointed to Vaughn and roared, diffusing any tension between him and Cassie. She was happy for that. She could be antagonistic in self-defense, but she was a softie at heart. Her smiled was automatic, and without her knowing it, Vaughn melted.

"Look at these," Melissa said. "Eclairs, napoleons and . . ."

"Oh my gosh! Mom! Black Forest cake!" Stevie became nine again. "Chocolate! Mom, can I have a piece?"

"The biggest one goes to her," Vaughn ordered and picked up the largest piece with the serving tongs and, as he was about to place it on Stevie's plate, looked in Cassie's direction. "That is, if it's all right with your mom." Cassie nodded her approval, relieved he had asked, and Vaughn transferred it to Stevie's plate.

"An epicurean delight!" Stevie announced, initiating peals of laughter from everyone.

"Stevie, where do you get your vocabulary? Does your mother shove big words at you before you go to sleep each night, maybe a tape, played for osmosis?" Walter asked facetiously.

"Not exactly Dr. Goodman," Stevie giggled, pushing dark blond strands of hair behind her ear, like her mother. "But she's had lists of Latin roots and prefixes on the bathroom wall since I was in second grade. I pick up words from them, and I leaf through the dictionary when I'm bored."

No one spoke. All eyes were fixed on Cassie. "Okay, everyone, coffee's getting cold." Cassie began to pour. Everyone passed plates around for éclairs, slices of cheesecake and pie, strudel, cream and sugar, and everything else on the table. Huge dollops of ice cream topped cherry pie. Joe and Tasha added it to their cheesecake. Cassie took half a napoleon and Vaughn took the other half. This did not escape notice, neither hers, nor Walter's.

"This is delicious, Dr. O/B," Cassie said as the sweet cream filling slid off the fork and passed her lips. Then she slid the fork between the pastry layers and dug out more of the filling.

"What are you doing, Cassie?" Jeremy asked, perplexed.

"What?" Cassie diverted her focus to his question. "Oh, this? I love cream, any cream. So I eat the middle out of napoleons or éclairs, or cream-filled donuts, just to get the cream. I really don't care that much for the pastry itself. In fact, I leave most of it. That's why I only took half, so I wouldn't waste too big a piece when I left the pastry on the plate."

"Cassie Komsky, you are a unique individual," Melissa commented.

"We all have our idiosyncrasies," Cassie shrugged playfully. "This is one of mine."

"There are more? Why am I not surprised," Walter jibed.

"Lot's more," Stevie interjected. "Right, Mom?"

"Stevie Komsky. Keep that up and you'll be finishing that cake at home."

"Anyone who can cook like you deserves a few idiosyncrasies," Joe said, usually listening rather than talking. "And that nemura you made for Thanksgiving is as delicious as any of these."

"Here, here," all echoed in agreement and raised their wine glasses. Stevie raised her ginger ale.

"So, Cassie," Dr. O/B began, "I spoke to Jeremy about the lock you mentioned in the report you submitted. It's a good call. Jeremy's written up the paperwork. Maintenance should get to it this week."

"Thank you, Dr. O/B," Cassie replied. "That's one less thing I have to worry about."

Vaughn questioned her again. "You actually think Samir would go up there?"

"It sounds farfetched. It's winter; it's cold; it's dangerous. But he's alone. Who knows where he would go. I try to think of the degree of isolation I'd seek." Suddenly she realized she was talking from real-life experience when she had shut herself off from humanity.

"He makes himself be alone, though," Ronnie commented, not noticing Cassie's sudden hiatus. Having been Samir's adviser until Walter transferred Samir to Cassie, she could validate her statement, although she may not have gotten to the reason as had Cassie. "If he reached out to just one person, he would have someone with whom he could share his feelings, but he doesn't do it."

"Didn't you see him with Rachel at Homecoming?" Cassie noticed Vaughn wince; she had forgotten the fight. But she pushed on. "Going to that dance was a major hurdle for him to overcome, but he did it."

"That's once, and it was a start, but if he communicated more, lots of kids would open up to him."

"What would he communicate for? He doesn't seek friends, athletics, clubs. He seeks peace."

"You can't cry forever for a tragedy you couldn't control," Ronnie stated with finality.

Her statement hit too close to home. "Depends on its cataclysmic proportions, Ronnie. Give someone a tragedy too overwhelming and they'll rise from it a completely changed person, if they rise from it at all. That's what happened to Samir. His country was and still is, steeped in civil war, innocent civilians massacred by one faction or another. Consider our own country and our own Civil War, a war of devastating proportions. You think parents who lost kids in that bloody war; wives who lost husbands;

siblings who lost brothers, soldiers who lost limbs; do you think they arose from the ashes the same person they were before the tragedy, like a recreated phoenix? Or were they a different bird, merely colored with the same plumage?"

Cassie's response caused them to equivocate. She seemed to have such a deep perspective about life and tragedy. Ironically, only Vaughn knew she was a widow, no one else, which led them to be a bit cavalier. Even though Walter was estranged from his family, Melissa had been widowed, Alicia divorced with two grown kids, theirs were the normal, the typical, tragedies, not the tragedy of cataclysmic proportions. No one here had had both parents or a spouse blown up in terrorist attacks, taken so cruelly and by such vicious assaults nurtured by inbred hatred. She stared into her past and shivered at the prospects of loneliness in her future.

"You say that as though you can relate to his tragedy more than we can," Alicia countered, "but everyone has some kind of tragedy in their lives."

Cassie completely ignored the first part of Alicia's response. For her to explain why she could relate to Samir's tragedy more than anyone else sitting at the table, she'd have to explain how it felt to have her husband, torn to pieces in a foreign country fighting foreign factions who hated us, wondering why we were there in the first place. Oil, money, Israel? She'd have to explain how it felt to have your future taken from you, to have Stevie's father taken from her, for a cause that Cassie believed never would have existed if our government had supported just one UN resolution that gave the Palestinians credibility as a people or condemned Israel's ethnic cleansing. No, she would not mention how her life had changed after a tragedy of cataclysmic proportions from whose ashes she arose, a completely different bird simply colored with the same plumage.

"Alicia, death at a young age or a terminal illness is tragic enough. But Samir's parents were killed, blown apart, in a civil war initiated way back that had seeped into the present, initiated from promises given to Arab leaders when the Allies asked for their assistance against the Ottomans. Promises made way back before 1920 that were all lies. There's history involved in Samir's sorrow.

"When the French Mandate in Lebanon ended in 1946, Christians and Muslim sects were given a set quota of seats, with power pretty much evenly distributed: The president was a Maronite, the prime minister, a Sunni Muslim, and Speaker of Parliament, a Shia Muslim.

"That may have maintained peace in the long run, but there was little time to test it. When Israel was established shortly after, a hundred thousand Palestinians fled to Lebanon, and the entire demographic balance shifted towards Muslims. Couple that with the expulsion of the PLO from Jordan early in the 70's, and you have a breeding ground for Palestinian recruits into the PLO. Lebanon's army could not hold them off, and war among the factions escalated. The Lebanese Front, the Lebanese National Movement, the PLO, Hezbollah, factions at war with each other destroying a beautiful westernized country and the city of Beirut, once considered the Paris of the Middle East.

"By the late 70's, Beirut had been split into a Christian East and Muslim West. Over a hundred fifty thousand people killed. The president, a Maronite, asked for assistance from a Multinational UN force and the legacy of that decision became Sabra and Shatila. Over three thousand massacred by the Maronite factions, with Israel shooting up flares to help the Maronite army find human targets.

"As Samir said, his people are non-entities. Who cares what happens to them. If you're gonna be labeled a terrorist even when you're the victim, retaliation becomes your only outlet. 1983, they brought it to us and bombed the American Embassy, and more." She could not reference the Marine barracks. "That is Samir's life. That is his tragedy, quite different from the world as we see it."

"I remember the American Embassy, but not anything else you've said," Ronnie conceded. "But why do you read so much about Lebanon?" She asked. "Why do you even care?"

"Why? Because all of it concerns us. Our Embassy is bombed; our troops are sent there and die." She was quivering; no one caught it. "That concerns me. And if I didn't 'know so much about Lebanon,' as you say, then I'd have to believe everything the media tells me, because we sure don't teach anything about the Middle East other than the negative indoctrination the media gives us." She glanced at Vaughn. His focus was on her alone, and his gaze was penetrating.

"Why is it surprising that I want to know? You all should, so when the news tells us Hezbollah is entrenched in Lebanon and the State Department invalidates US passports for travel there, you'd know about Hezbollah and how it got there." She glanced around the table at eight blank adult faces. "Mostly, you'd understand the background from which Samir came, and he would take on a persona, have an identity for you. You'd empathize with him and perhaps understand why he doesn't speak, and doesn't want to."

No one responded to this. They were digesting information they had never before heard, trying to accept a lesson in foreign affairs they did not want to hear, but perhaps opening a window of understanding to Samir they had never considered. Cassie focused on Samir because everything she had said would have meant nothing if it were not relevant to him.

"Do you still believe his tragedy is your normal tragedy?' She asked softly, and their silence and expressions told them they were reconsidering their cavalier perceptions. "Unless you understand a tiny little piece of what Samir lived, especially knowing his parents had been blown to pieces, you can never empathize with him, and he can never communicate what he's experienced to people who have never experienced anything even close. We would nod our heads in sympathy, but it would simply be a social reflex and that wouldn't help him communicate, would it?"

Her question was rhetorical. Cassie shakes her head. "No, it wouldn't. Nothing in our background could possibly relate," she adds, using that statement as a shield for protection. "But you might think about what he has lived with for the past four years and the hell he has experienced." She shook her head, "I can tell you his tragedy was most definitely not typical." She had inadvertently referenced herself again, and she realized she was losing control of her emotions. The discussion had become too intense, too close to home. She felt her face flush and her hand begin to visibly tremble. She needed to escape, quickly.

"I'm so sorry," she apologized. I get overly emotional when I talk about this subject. I'll be back in a few minutes for another cup of coffee – and the middle of that napoleon if no one's going to eat it." She managed a wan smile, pushed her chair back and walked down the hall.

There was a long interval of quiet, then Melissa spoke. "Stevie, your mom seems really upset. Will she be all right?"

Stevie nodded and dug out the last bit of cream from her Black Forest cake, picking at it the same way her mother had ferreted the cream out of the napoleon. "She'll be fine," Stevie reassured them.

"Maybe you can help her, calm her a bit?" Walter suggests, wondering why Stevie was being so casual.

Stevie shook her head with certainly. "No, Dr. Goodman. The best thing for her when she gets like this is to leave her alone. You'll see. She'll come out of it in a few minutes."

"She gets like this often?" Vaughn asked, riveted on Stevie's words, 'when she gets like this.'

"Not so much anymore. She's a lot better than she used to be. I don't remember it all. I was just a little kid."

"Why, Stevie?" Vaughn asked, perplexed. He looked around the room at his staff. Their expressions replicated his. "What happened?" He uncrossed his legs and leaned forward.

"It happened when the Marine Barracks were bombed a few months after the American Embassy. My dad was a Marine. He was there. That's where he was killed."

Nothing, nothing, could have prepared them for that. Nothing, nothing, had prepared Cassie for that, and nothing, nothing, could ever take it away.

32

Walter poured himself vodka, turned the gas fireplace on high, started his stereo, and sunk into his favorite leather recliner. Then he replayed every aspect of his interaction with Cassie since the day Melissa brought her into his office.

How could he have missed it?! How could he?! His degree in psychiatry, his certificates, plural, authenticating advanced training and validating his ability to analyze a person's speech patterns, inflection, tone, body language, nuances, to divine behaviors, emotions, and problems stemming from some aspect of their background, some tragedy, some upbringing, some whatever. Yet, with all his training and degrees, he had completely missed Cassie's problem.

She had come about Samir, no other reason. She had been sincere, candid and forthright. No ulterior motives, nothing secretive, everything about her was genuine. When she reacted to Samir's history with such emotion, so traumatically, he should have realized the cause went deeper. He reassured himself that he had. At least he hadn't been that ignorant, but he should have pursued it. As the head of all Guidance issues amongst the student body, and with his medical experience, it was incumbent upon him to seek her out and at the very least, invite her to talk, to open up about her reaction. Even if she had declined, it was still his responsibility to encourage discussion. As a professional, he should have written it up and included a description of her reaction and an evaluation of what he had witnessed. But he didn't.

So the Marine Barracks was the reason; now he knew; now it made sense that she knew exactly how many Marines had died there – her husband had been one of them. He took another sip and let the vodka work its way through his body, easing his stress. The American Embassy and the Marine Barracks. She was inextricably linked to Samir, head to toe. Despite being thousands of miles apart, their tragedies stemmed from the same root: different colors on the color wheel, but the same spectrum.

How inadequate did he feel now? He had seen her face, its beauty marred by unabated grief; he had witnessed her horror emanating from the mention of these two tragedies. The summary of Samir's history had gotten to her more than if they had been news stories on television or in the press. No one would have reacted as she had if they had not been personally involved. Samir's response had been alienation; Cassie's was mainstreaming herself into a semblance of normalcy. Both suffered in their own way. Hands to her face, backing out of her chair, trying to run, escape the memories while being caged in his office, debating how to flee and remain professional at the same time; how to flee and maintain her primary focus, Samir, all while losing it, yet trying to maintain control, and him asking, do you want some water? What a jerk! What a complete jerk he had been.

The sensual rhythm of "Oh Girl" washed over him and he pictured Cassie swaying to it at Homecoming. She had been trying so hard to remain seated. Like the lyrics of the song, he realized he'd be in trouble if Cassie left him now, because he was falling in love. Being alone was okay until you wanted to be with someone you couldn't. Only then did you feel lonely. And it was now that Walter felt lonely, for the first time in decades.

He reminisced about his life. It hadn't gone the way he had planned, but whose does? When he married, he thought it would be a lifetime commitment. For him, it had been, but not for her. His wife had left him seventeen years ago, after he had given up his medical practice for the Guidance Chair at Chelsea. She had wanted glitz and money more than she had wanted him. Once her objectives for marrying him were gone and their lives were relegated to school functions and counseling, their marriage was over. She had packed up, took the kids and left for Oregon. If she had to be poor, as she saw it, she had wanted to be poor there. Her announcement had come as a hard blow, but he had adjusted quite well over time, calling the Chelsea football crew his family. He had never considered remarrying, never even caring to date. But something tonight had left him empty, and it was unsettling.

Had he been younger, he would have run. Packed it all in and made a new life, a new state, new job, maybe even go back to private practice. Now he sat calmly and relived the memories he had stored, like quick clips on a video. There were many. Too many, but he honed in on the recent past and highlighted Homecoming, when she was screaming at Vaughn, "I'm an Arab." This should have triggered something. He should have connected her reaction right then to her reaction to Samir's profile. And helping Vaughn hold back Samir so Parker and Mason could beat him? He had actually done that. He winced at the memory. Oh my God, how could I have done that? How unprofessional; how inhumane. What is wrong with you, Walter?

Coming to Chelsea? It made sense now. She had come here to get away from memories, her tragedy of cataclysmic proportions. And here we were, me, Melissa, all of us, challenging her perception of Samir's grief, disagreeing with her when not one of us had ever come close to the depth of their feelings. How arrogant we are. Of course Samir could relate to her. He could see it in her eyes; could feel the depth of her tragedy and knew it rivaled his. Coupled with her ethnicity, approaching him at the game, defending him at Homecoming; of course he'd open up to her.

And then there was Cassie the woman. How could you not notice her, not be mesmerized by her vivacity, the warmth she exuded, her goodness and the way it emanated from her so naturally. No guise, no deceit, no dissembling, just herself. You'd have to be a fool not to notice, and Vaughn was no fool in this regard.

Walter had observed him since Homecoming. He had been watching Cassie dance. God, was she sensual.

Vaughn had watched her from his table. Walter had seen him push back his chair in anger, walk across the dance floor, grab Cassie's arm and usher her off the floor. Anger, with a touch of violence, subdued but present, a guttural, raw, primordial presence. He was not angry because she was dancing, but what her dancing was doing to him and how he was powerless to do anything about it. He had to stop her.

Walter had also heard their conversation and observed Vaughn's body language. Walter knew Vaughn's anger did not stem from protocol. He had watched Vaughn fume as Cassie ran back to the table for her purse. He had watched him at Thanksgiving and yes, he wondered about her invitation to Vaughn's family gathering. The football crew had been invited to Vaughn's house for years because they were established faculty, most were on staff before Vaughn had accepted the dean's position. All knew he hated the corporate aspects of his family's dynasty and was glad to sit at the helm of this prestigious school.

Vaughn's invitation to him and the other faculty was almost as traditional as the holiday itself, and somewhat of a payback for their having weaned him into his position. But to include Cassie was an anomaly. Walter had watched him escort her from guest to guest with one-on-one introductions when he could have let her join the faculty group and meet others willy-nilly throughout the evening. That was not the typical Vaughn. Taylor caught it and reacted with venom. Vaughn missed it completely.

Too many anomalies though. Vaughn in the Guidance office this past week while they talked about the cook-off. Never had Vaughn ever entered Guidance to casually request anything. Why now? Granted, he didn't know Cassie would be there, or did he? Did someone at another desk just happen to call him? Even if it had been pure coincidence, to invite himself to the cook-off, such a plebian gathering compared to the Club? This was not Vaughn, this man staring at Cassie throughout dessert knowing she was feeling uncomfortable; then insisting he walk her and Stevie home after she returned from the rest room? No, this was not Vaughn. Walter hoped Stevie would honor her promise not to tell her mom that the entire gathering now knew why she was widowed. Knowing they knew would probably have destroyed Cassie.

So what was he feeling, he asked himself, finally facing his own demons. Why did it matter what Vaughn was doing? What was eating at Walter that was making him drink vodka alone to mellow music, and ponder how the dean of Chelsea was behaving towards one of his faculty? Did it matter that Cassie's reaction was discomfort? She was a big girl; she could handle herself. But could she? Was she capable of disarming someone in a position of authority especially after rearranging her whole life, and her daughter's, to come here for a new life, hopefully a better one, away from tragedy? Furthermore, why should she have to? Why put her in this compromising position to keep her job?

Walter was certain this could not end happily, and it was cutting him up inside. Vaughn was using his position to his own advantage and inevitably he would hurt Cassie. Whether Vaughn knew it or not, whether he'd ever admit it or not, the results would not be good. Vaughn wouldn't care a whit about her feelings. He was into convenience, and she'd be just that, a convenience, until it no longer benefitted him. When that happened, she'd be conveniently discarded. This was unequivocal; this was what Vaughn was all about. And when it happened, as Walter was certain it would, he had a good idea how Cassie would respond. How much longer, he wondered, would she be in his life? The answer saddened him.

33

MONDAY AFTER COOK-OFF

Cassie dragged herself halfway out of bed Monday morning, 5:30 a.m., bleary-eyed, to Wham's, "Last Christmas," and sat for a moment on the edge of the bed, reflecting. Sleep had not been easy since Saturday night. Too many memories resurfacing; too much emotion that evening; too much tension and stress about Vaughn's presence. Worse, his hovering over her after she had gotten back to the table while she was trying to be nonchalant, worming her fork between pastry layers from the last piece of napoleon no one had taken, eking out cream.

Then of all shockers, insisting he walk her and Stevie back to their condo when all she wanted was to be alone. What do you say to the dean when he escorts you home, in the dark, in the cold, takes your arm with one hand while he holds the casserole dish in his other. She didn't need his help. He had to know that. She had carried the dish to Jeremy's when it was full. She certainly could have carried it home once it was empty.

So what do you say? How many times do you say, "No, thank you," when he insists repeatedly? Tell him she doesn't need his help? It was what Jeremy had said about fighting too much for an ideal you'd lose anyway. Besides, it would have been kind of crass telling him to his face what he already knew.

So what's his reason? He's married, so it can't be that. Can it? Nah. His wife is beautiful and seems to fit his lifestyle perfectly. If nothing else, she certainly seems to complement his money. But Cassie dismissed it, not wanting to think negative thoughts especially about someone unrelated to her life. Nor did she want to ponder why such a beautiful woman was so cold inside. Not someone she'd have as a friend.

Anyway, got to get up, shower, dress for a nice, crisp December day, a week closer to Christmas, and see what her students say about the culmination of Claudius' plot. Let's kill off the whole bunch of them today and see where the discussion goes. How close to life is it when one person's actions or lack thereof can be the cause of such total devastation, the destruction of so many lives. Anybody at Chelsea ever live through that, she wondered? Well, she could give them an example. So could Stevie; so could Samir.

A quick shower; get Stevie off for the bus, and head to class.

34

TO DIE FOR HONOR

The morning turned from crisp to raw and damp, dark clouds casting a dreary pall over what would have otherwise been a beautiful wintry frost. Although no rain had pattered on the windows last night, a light layer of ice covered tree branches and bushes and everything glistened like the glass lamped figures on Jeremy's Christmas tree. Maybe she and Stevie would put up their tree today, at least start it.

And then the first flake slapped her in the face, followed by a blast of frigid air that nearly pushed her off her feet. Woah, she thought, steadying herself. Where'd this come from? Nothing in the forecast about this.

It was Monday, December 7th, 7:15 in the morning, a bit early for her, and her classroom door was open and the room brightly lit; not only bright, but active with chatter when she walked in. She had heard it down the hall. Confused at first, she wondered if Maintenance was repairing heating units again. But no, not that at all, she smiled as she got closer. She knew exactly what was going on.

There they were - Emilia, Gloria, Rachel and Elizabeth, surrounded by open boxes of Christmas tree ornaments and lights, working furtively to put together an artificial tree of modest proportions, not too big to overpower the room or occupy too much space, but Elizabeth was struggling.

"He promised me he'd be here to help," Elizabeth said more with disappointment than anger, her dark brown hair covering her face as she tried unsuccessfully to connect the middle segment of the tree to its bottom. "I don't think I can get this without him."

And as a deus ex machina, Matt, Mason, and Parker burst through the room, breathless. "Sorry I'm late, Lizzie," Matt offered apologetically, "but I conscripted two grunts who can make up for my tardiness." He gave her a genuine, flirtatious smile that lit up Elizabeth's face and his dark Asian eyes gazed only at her.

She pulled back her hair and her exotic dark eyes almost danced. Her response was a flirtatious command. "Come here, fella and help me put up this tree."

Matt loved it. He and Elizabeth worked in unison connecting tree parts and articulating branches. Mason and Parker strung lights, top to bottom; Rachel opened all the boxes, checked all ornaments for hooks and handed them to Gloria and Emelia who hung them in sync as the lights worked their way down, the precision of a well designed assembly line.

Cassie loved it but she was apprehensive. "Will all this be done by 7:50?"

"Not a problem, Mrs. Komsky," Parker said, with his father's glint in his eye. "And if it's not, you can call the dean."

Everyone laughed. She was getting to know these kids as people, not just as students, getting to know them and to like them. That was her fear in life. If you don't know someone, you don't miss them when they're gone, or, when you're gone. As Gibran said about sorrow, "You weep for that which has been your delight."

True to their word, when 7:45 rolled around, the tree was up, surrounded by a beautiful felt tree skirt trimmed with red, gold and green brocade. Rachel had punctuated the Christmas decorations with two menorahs, one on each side of the tree, and she and Gloria had even decorated the Globe. Zach and Jason had come in early and got right into helping with clean-up. By 7:50, empty boxes and bags had been folded and stacked into the back corner, ready to be carried out after school. Then Samir and Connor filtered into the classroom, with Connor's added ooh's, ah's, and Samir staring at the tree in admiration. Then they all took their seats and sat quietly, appreciating its beauty and its meaning.

"Kind of cruel to take such a beautiful sight as this, that represents happiness and love, and juxtapose it with a play that symbolizes nothing but deceit and bloodshed." Cassie's voice was a whisper.

All was silent, as though a prayer was being said in that moment for all the cruelty in life to disappear.

"Is it not better to have cruelty juxtaposed with love than not have love at all?"

No one spoke; no one moved. They were frozen, dumbfounded and speechless, in unison. Focus slowly turned towards Samir. Shy, eyes somewhat averted, he looked towards Rachel for guidance. Her eyes were tearing, as were Cassie's. Not just theirs; Emelia, Gloria and Elizabeth were tearing up too, and she actually discerned emotion from some of the guys. Rachel placed her hand over Samir's as he fought back tears, tears bottled up so long he hardly knew they existed. But he did, and they fell; he got up and left the room; Rachel followed.

Cassie needed a tissue. She had cried from destruction and horror; it was beautiful to shed tears for love, and, maybe, forgiveness.

They returned to class about ten minutes later, after the class had quickly glossed over Claudius' plot to have Hamlet killed in England. A murder plot is a murder plot. Simple as that, but now, when Hamlet finally becomes empowered with courage and purpose for the sake of honor, this got to them.

"It's like a light bulb went on, an epiphany," Matt concludes. "Once Hamlet finds out the captain of Norway's army has just gotten permission from Claudius to march his troops through Denmark to fight for a worthless piece of land in Poland, he realizes these men know they're going to die. But they'll fight and die anyway, not for the land, but for honor. Then he gets it, at last."

"Zach, I'd like your position on this." Cassie turns to Hamlet's biggest detractor. "You've attacked Hamlet for being a coward throughout the entire play. Any change now?"

Reluctantly, Zach nods. "A little. When he says 'to find quarrel in a straw when honor's at stake,' I think he finally becomes a man, willing to fight and die for what he believes is honorable."

"He's seen his father murdered by his uncle, his mother 'stain'd,' and he's taken no action. But when he sees twenty thousand soldiers marching to their deaths for a worthless plot of land, he realizes he's been a coward and vows to take action. 'From this time forth, my thoughts be bloody or be nothing worth,' act 4, scene 4; he knows what he has to do. That's how I see it," Jason says, and Connor, who had become comfortable pairing up with Jason, concurred.

"So does he overcome his tragic flaw?" Cassie asks.

"Yeah, at this point, right here, he does." Emelia adds; everyone nods.

"Well, here's where the real tragedy emerges, because Hamlet overcomes his flaw a bit late, and he and a lot of other characters are going to suffer the consequences for his procrastination and his tergiversation." She looks over at Mason and smiles.

"I know that word, Mrs. Komsky. I know what that word means!" Mason announces proudly, his red hair accentuated by his pure white cable knit sweater.

"Good memory, Mason." Cassie teased. "And yes, Stevie does know what it means. Ask her some time."

"I'll make it a point to do just that," Mrs. Komsky. I might even throw one at her she'll never get."

"Don't be too sure of yourself, Mason. My daughter studies the dictionary when she's bored."

"Anything else she's interested in, other than the dictionary?"

Cassie glanced at Parker who was enjoying this repartee as much as the rest of the class. "Football."

"The Giants," Parker interjected, and Mason groaned.

"No one on this side of Jersey cares about that team," Mason stated.

"You'll have to start, Mason, if you want to talk to my daughter about football."

Mason put his hands up in surrender amidst the onslaught of laughter.

"All right, everyone, we didn't get as close to the end as I had thought we would, but that's okay. We have the whole week before Christmas break for your presentations. Maybe we'll even have time to start *Othello*, but no problem if we don't; we'll begin that after Christmas break. Remember, if you haven't submitted the topic for your presentation yet, deadline's today.

"Tomorrow we'll discuss Ophelia's plight, Laertes' arrival from France, his plotting with Claudius to use poison to kill Hamlet, Ophelia's drowning, and the significance of Yorick's skull and, most of all, how you interpret Hamlet's saying, 'I lov'd Ophelia,' and the rest of that line." She glanced up at staring faces. "What, too much? Again?" She didn't need an oral reply. "Okay, study-read through Hamlet and Laertes fighting in Ophelia's grave. We'll discuss what we can, no pressure to finish it all tomorrow. How's that?"

They nodded, smiled, closed their books, packed up and filed out in good spirits, glancing at the glistening lights on the tree, genuinely happy. Samir and Rachel were last to leave, and Samir nodded to her before they exited. Cassie felt herself swell with happiness. She wanted all good things to last. She hoped this would.

35

MONDAY'S LIFE-THREATENING DECISION

By the time classes ended and Cassie had begun her trek home, about two inches of snow had fallen. Not much, considering it had had all day to become a major snow storm. Obviously, it had missed its opportunity, but that didn't mean it was over. Wet flakes clung like a loose tablecloth over the ice encrusted branches from the morning. Lower temperatures coupled with blasts of frozen air would quickly transform them into icy flakes, turning wet snow into a white crunchy crust over ice, kind of like the caramelized sugar topping on creme brulee. That would be dangerous. She wasn't exactly old, but she didn't want to fall and break a bone or two. She wasn't the pliable kid she had been at twelve.

But what she did want to do was visit Damon Hall again and search for Samir. Opening up today for the first time ever, and in front of his classmates, took boundless courage. She wondered if she had that much. Could she have ever made a statement like that and overcome her inhibitions? She didn't know, but she did know she had to seek him out to tell him how beautiful a person he was and how much character and honor he had.

And something else. Intermittently, what had continued to plague her was Samir's hideaway. Something about her search with Jeremy Sunday after Thanksgiving had nagged at her. Finally, she thought she knew and was determined to check out her hypothesis. No better time than tonight with snow on the ground. And to make it even easier, protocol at night when snow covered the ground dictated a 7:00 curfew. Everyone would have to sign in an hour and a half earlier. After dinner, she'd get Stevie settled in with homework and their bedtime routine, and go out on the prowl. Take a good flashlight too.

Three hours later, not wanting to use Damon House's entrance, she knocked on Jeremy's front door.

"You're crazy; you know that, don't you?"

"Maybe . . . a little?" She gesticulated with her thumb and index finger about a half inch apart. They exchanged smiles and she began her search. Once through the kitchen, living room, back room, the dorm's office and into the dorm itself, she headed directly towards the vacant rooms. She had hoped Jeremy would have joined her, but he had insisted they had searched every crevice and that no other possibility existed. There was simply no place anywhere Samir could hide.

"Let me know if you find anything," he had said. "Otherwise get yourself home ASAP. It's snowing hard and getting colder."

"Yes, Mother," Cassie had replied mockingly. She followed up with, "Okay, okay," when he gave her a big-brother look she couldn't ignore.

Everything replicated her last visit here. Boys were either studying, watching TV, or in the game room. Parker and Matt were aggressively at ping-pong again, and this time Mason was with them. Chelsea made accommodations for day students on certain occasions and during inclement weather, and this sure looked like inclement weather. If this snow kept up, Chelsea would cancel classes tomorrow.

They nodded a quick hello, Matt waved, and Cassie pressed on, anxious to check her hypothesis and get on home. Now into the first floor wing, she opened the first door, switched on the light, gave it a quick once-over and left. Not this one; she doubted it would have been. Next one, she repeated the process and crossed this one off her list. No surprise here either. Two more to go and she was more sure of herself than ever. Third room, again, dark. Lights on, dust all over, just like the previous two, lights off, door closed, down to the fourth and final room. She stood in front of it, paused, inhaled deeply then opened the door.

Standing directly in the doorway, even before flicking on the lights, she knew she had the right room. She flicked the light switch, saw footprints on the floor, then walked directly to the back windows. Her hunch paid off. She had felt something was different about this room but she couldn't figure out why, until she realized this room had made her shiver. And here was the reason: the window to the far left was open an inch or two, and not for air. It had been left opened by the resident who had used it as an exit to insure his safe entry back. This is what Samir had done, why he couldn't be found in the building. Because he wasn't in it. Where he had gone, Cassie could pretty much guess.

Now the big dilemma: follow him and track him down? His footprints were an obvious give-away, outlined clearly in the snow, or confront him when he got back? Either way, this she would definitely have to report; it concerned Samir's safety.

As impulsive as she had been as a kid, she glanced at her watch. It was 7:05. She extrapolated quickly. It had taken her barely ten minutes to scope out each room, confirm her hypothesis and start back. She had approximated an hour. She still had close to that to work with. Yeah, why not, she thought.

She retraced her steps into the active part of the dorms, past the game room where Parker, Matt, Mason, and now Connor were in a four-way competition, through Jeremy's office. A quick knock announcing her entrance, she hurried into his living quarters, through the dining room, kitchen then foyer, on her way out the door.

"Cassie, where are you going?" Jeremy shouted as Cassie almost sprinted through his apartment.

"I found him, Jeremy! Almost, anyway. I know how he disappears and I'm sure I know where he is. I've just gotta prove it."

"Cassie! Cassie! Come back! It's dark! It's freezing, and it's snowing like crazy!"

"I'm prepared. I have my flashlight!" She shouted as she waved her flashlight towards him. Her voice faded with the wind and the snow and the starless sky covered by marauding clouds.

"Damn it!" Jeremy cursed, feeling powerless and unsure of what to do. She could be in serious danger. "Damn it!" Then running on instincts, he called Walter.

36

CASSIE IN PERIL

Thirty-five minutes later, students heard the sweetest sound known to school kids throughout the entire northern states: "Due to inclement weather, and the forecast for more snow throughout the night, tomorrow's classes are canceled . . ." and the wild roar emanating throughout Damon House and every other house on campus drowned out any words that followed. They didn't need anything else; they knew what it meant: sleep late; ignore assignments, forget essay deadlines. Freedom! Freedom from academic restraints for a whole day!

Ecstatic, Parker, Mason, Matt, Connor, and most likely everyone else in every other dorm at the academy raced to the windows to look at this wondrous occurrence. To look, stare in awe. And then . . . then Parker saw it. He saw it and strained to focus. It was a light that didn't belong there; a mound he didn't remember being there before.

"What the hell is that?" Parker asked.

"Where? What is what?" Mason followed. "What are you looking at?"

Parker, an inch or two taller than Mason, turned to his favorite receiver, put both hands on his scalp and positioned his head around. "There. Straight ahead. That light. There's a light in the snow, and . . . it looks like it's blinking!"

"You're right. I see it. You see it Matt? Connor, you guys see it?"

"Yeah," Matt strained. I do. What the hell could it . . . oh my God! Oh my God!"

"What?" What?" Parker and Mason still confused as Matt whirled around and raced for the door, Parker and Mason right behind him. Connor still straining to see.

"It's Mrs. Komsky. Mrs. Komsky! We've gotta find Dr. Harper! "She had that flashlight, remember?" Matt shouted.

"What the hell is she doing out there?" Parker challenged, defiantly, as if that would change anything.

"I don't know, but if she doesn't get back soon, she's gonna die!"

Connor caught up to them in time to hear this. They froze, their faces turning ghostlike as fear, real palpable fear seized them. This was true. This was real, not some story or play where characters die in words, but real. If Mrs. Komsky were actually stranded out there, she could die.

Matt raced through Jeremy's office first and reached the back door first. He pounded on Jeremy's door frenetically, screaming for their chemistry teacher's help. Once his comrades joined him, the place sounded like ramparts being assaulted by mortar and cannon. Jeremy's face showed his rage as he opened the door; rage at their horrible manners, until he picked out the word 'trouble' from Matt, 'Mrs. Komsky' from Parker, 'snow'. . . 'flashlight' from Mason, and 'die' from Connor. Then his face mimicked their horror. He knew where Cassie had gone and now he knew she was in serious, life-threatening danger.

Jeremy's thoughts whirled. What to do? What to do? His call to Walter had been a good move; Walter was medical as well as psychiatry; his help would be invaluable. But what next? What next? Think, Jeremy, think.

He leaped into action. "Parker, call your father. Connor, call Mrs. Donelly. Her number is on the Rolodex on my desk. Tell her to get here ASAP. Then to Mason, Parker, Matt, he turned to include Connor who was already holding the phone, "I need your help. I can't bring her in alone. Are you with me?"

Their reaction was instantaneous. "Get your heaviest coats, gloves, boots, flashlights, goggles, anything. Everything. Back here in sixty seconds; then we go!"

That headstrong, stubborn, recalcitrant, tenacious, insane woman! He fumed, then prayed. He prayed they wouldn't be too late.

37

VAUGHN GETS PARKER'S CALL

This hadn't been a day of tranquility for Vaughn. Today, the weekend, everything since Saturday's cook-off had gnawed at him. No peace, only anguish since Stevie had revealed how her father had died. Blown apart at the Marine Barracks in Lebanon, his death was his widow's link to Samir. No wonder she could empathize with the young man, a student he had only castigated. Not only were they the same ethnicity, but their tragedy had arisen from the same country. He should have pried deeper; he would have had a better understanding of their plight. But he would never have thought of doing that, since Vaughn's primary concern was always for himself and his own wants.

Nope, this had not been a day of tranquility nor was it a night to go home. Weather had been iffy all day and the heavy snow had only begun. He had stayed into the evening for the latest forecasts, preoccupied with Cassie until the impending storm worked its way to the top of his priority list and he now contemplated cancelling classes.

That would be the safest measure, but before he did, he'd have to check Maintenance, on foot in addition to the phone. If this storm turned out to be close to the predictions stations were indicating, it was going to be one hell of a crippler. He couldn't risk even the slightest oversight. Maintenance had to be ready to roll early tomorrow morning or this evening, if necessary.

To be on top of everything, he had stayed in his office to track the forecast and keep in touch with the community to see how they were handling it. He had spoken with local and district school board presidents and the police department. They had been tracking the storm as well and all districts were leaning towards closing. Vaughn would not hang back and wait for their decision. When it came to the safety of his students, his decision would be on the side of caution.

This would not be the first time Chelsea had been snowed in. Twice during his tenure as dean, the academy had shut down. It hadn't been a problem then; he doubted it would be a problem now. A pair of heavy winter boots in his office, heavy outerwear and blankets were always stashed in his back closet just in case. For him it was like camping out, whatever that was. Elitist boys from obscenely wealthy families did not camp out. Maybe they did in this generation, but not in his.

He checked his office frig. A couple of snacks would do, and he could hike over to Landon Hall in the morning to get whatever the cafeteria ladies would make for him, if they could get in. He hoped a few of them could; they could make one hell of a delicious breakfast. Thinking about it, he almost welcomed his predicament. He made more calls, dressed for the storm, braved the heavy winds and freezing flakes that were now slapping down hard and headed for Maintenance. It was a little after 5:00.

Two hours later, he stomped back into his office, beating off stubborn clumps of snow still stuck to his boots. Finished. Everyone and everything was ready. Plenty of fuel; plow trucks ready; food in place; generators ready to perform if necessary. Not only was he too tired to drive home, but who'd want to drive in this. Roads were probably snow covered and slick. And even if they weren't, they would be soon. Besides, why drive through crawling traffic or risk an accident. He called Taylor on her mobile phone. She had one last manicure to do.

He made one final call to the county school board president. Chelsea would close despite the community's decision, but not surprisingly, public schools were closing, and all public institutions as well. It was approximately 7:30.

He notified the key people to work the phone chains for administration, faculty and staff, then used the public address system, which went out to all buildings and dorms. "Due to inclement weather and the forecast for more snow throughout the night, tomorrow's classes have been cancelled. Stay indoors and keep warm. Any emergencies, see your housemaster. Updates regarding food services to follow."

Done. He called Taylor again to tell her he'd cancelled classes. He'd see her tomorrow. She was finishing her last manicure. Close up, go home and stay warm.

He poured himself a cup of coffee, rechecked emergency plans and called Brett in case Taylor needed help in any way. Then he reclined into his office chair and sipped his coffee, not quite energetic enough to lean down and pull off his heavy boots. He was forty-three. Was he getting old? He chuckled, thinking Maintenance should have been built closer to Smythe Hall. Then he wouldn't have had to walk so far. It was good that he had begun to work-out.

He situated himself deeper into his cushions, thought of Chelsea, of Cassie, that beautiful woman in Sanders House, and finally relaxed. And then Parker called.

38

CASSIE IN FROM THE COLD.

When Cassie had raced through Jeremy's kitchen heading for Samir, Jeremy's instinct had told him to call Walter. Although Walter lived a good thirty minutes away and the roads were risky, Jeremy knew if Cassie had come back cold, Walter could help. Now, Jeremy was certain he had made the right decision. Walter's medical skills would be vital.

In less than five minutes that felt like hours, four students and one housemaster, dressed for a rugged storm, were trudging through darkness held at bay with five narrow beams of artificial light. With each step they fought howling winds and ice-encrusted snow. Their flashlights scanned the path Cassie had taken. Only one set of footprints was distinct, and another set, much larger, was almost covered with fast-falling snow. It had to be theirs.

Samir had left the dorm little more than twenty minutes before Cassie arrived. Samir had signed in at 6:42 and Jeremy had made direct eye contact with him, almost daring him to disappear for places unknown. Cassie had raced in minutes before 7:00 to search the rooms and had left the dorm to begin her hunt for Samir about ten minutes later. Vaughn had announced school closing around 7:35; it was now 7:50. Cassie had been exposed to the storm at least forty minutes. Oh my God, Jeremy thought. Could she freeze in that amount of time?

"There! There!! I see her! I see her light!" Connor shouted, wiping snow from his goggles to be sure. His powerful voice was almost lost in the wind's blast. Connor, a muscular fireplug no more than 5' 9" and as tenacious as a bulldog, would be a tremendous help bringing Cassie back.

They reached her moments later; Jeremy gulped: her body supine, covered with a thin protective blanket of snow, head turned sideways, almost as though she were sleeping. But clearly, she was in mortal danger. Even in the darkness, their flashlights detected a whitish tinge on her face.

"Two on each side!" Jeremy shouted. Lock arms together, under her! Then lift! Gently!"

Parker and Mason positioned themselves on opposite sides of her lower torso; Matt and Connor, the two shorter, placed themselves on each side of her shoulders. Balance well distributed, they lifted Cassie's body very gently. Jeremy held five flashlights awkwardly, trying to direct light where it was needed most. Once Cassie was securely hoisted, Jeremy lighted their return route. Not an easy task. Tense, tired, scared, four young men managed one synchronized step at a time, slowly very slowly.

Jeremy remained especially vigilant in order to backtrack in whatever footprints remained so they wouldn't lose the path or fall into a depression, maybe trip on a snow-covered rock or stump. The young men held Cassie gently but securely. They held her life in their hands and they knew it. Minutes passed; time seemed infinite; their rescue insurmountable. Could they get her back in time? The howling wind hammered against their senses, hammered their faces, their heads, their hands. Goggles, gloves, hoods, hats . . . didn't matter. The storm had turned into a monster, and they were mere mortals. Stay focused Jeremy, he thought, boosting his confidence. Stay focused; stay oriented. Five lives are in your hands.

And then, floodlights. What? Where? What was happening? And Vaughn's muted voice shouting through the storm, calling their names, calling Parker. Two snowplows flanking their perimeter, lighting up the night even through the storm, and Vaughn racing towards them as quickly as the snow would allow. Walter right behind him.

"Son, are you all right?" Vaughn shouted as he reached the brigade, his voice clearly shaking; Parker nodding. "Are all of you all right?"

"We're all right Dr. O/B," Mason shouted, his voice like an echo even at this close distance. "We're not sure about Mrs. Komsky. She looks blue!"

Walter swung around to look at Cassie. Completely unconscious. "Inside, as quickly as possible!"

With the extra lighting, they increased their pace and were back in Jeremy's condo faster than they had hoped. Walter took over. "Put her in the guest room down the hallway, first floor. Jeremy, got a plastic cover? A plastic tablecloth?" Jeremy nodded. "Quick. Put it over the bedding so her outerwear doesn't soak through. We want her on dry bedding once her wet clothes are off."

Jeremy raced to his linen closet and came back with a felt-backed plastic table cover which he spread over the sheets. Then the boys placed Cassie gently on the bed, like placing fine stemware on a counter, afraid it would break. Very carefully, under the watchful eyes of Dr. Goodman, they unlocked their hands and slid them from under her soaked body. They stood by the bed transfixed, too shocked, too frozen to move.

"Boys, go. Get yourselves warm," Vaughn ordered. "Get a hot cup of tea or soup. We have to go out again." They looked puzzled. "Cassie can't leave here, and we can't leave Stevie alone."

Suddenly they realized Cassie's precocious daughter was home alone. Stevie, a kid who could define words from roots and prefixes and who studied the dictionary; to Parker she was the kid who could talk a streak about the Giants. To Mason, she was his teacher's daughter who could define "tergiversate" when he couldn't. But she was still only nine, and by now, she must be panicking, especially in this weather, when she had expected her mother to walk through the door over an hour ago.

"I'll go," Mason called out. "Me too," three voices followed in unison.

"She'll be scared to death if you all show up at her door," Melissa said from the living room hurrying towards the guestroom. "Sorry I'm late. The roads are icy and visibility is terrible. Traffic is at a crawl."

"We can't stay here talking," Walter said. "We need warm water, lots of towels. We have to get Cassie out of these wet clothes. Melissa, call Stevie. It'll be best if she hears a female voice. But don't scare her. Tell her that her mother fell and wants her here. Tell her Parker and Mason are on their way." Then you two, go." He nodded to Parker and Mason. "Quickly, Melissa. I need you here. Connor, Matt, get some bowls or pans of warm water; test it with your elbow." He glanced up at Vaughn, transfixed on Cassie. "Vaughn, you've gotta leave, too."

Vaughn walked out, staggering as if in a stupor. Walter could hear Melissa reassuring Stevie, telling her Parker and Mason would be coming for her in about fifteen minutes. Telling her to pack her pj's, toothbrush, and dress warm.

"Melissa, I need your help, now!" In the few minutes it had taken Melissa to make the call, Walter had started to remove Cassie's coat. "It's soaked through the lining. We have to take this off and get her dry. Be careful, very careful with her hands. If we have to, we'll cut the coat off."

Very gingerly, Melissa and Walter worked to remove Cassie's water-laden coat. Both sleeves had to be cut down the middle and the left shoulder cut through the collar before the coat would come off. Her boots and snow pants slipped off more easily, and Walter began examining her skin, keeping her hands elevated on pillows and her upper body and torso under warm dry blankets as much as possible.

Her skin color was very pale, parts of her face whitish, some patches red, but not bluish, thank God. Two little blisters were developing on the right side of her face, the side that had lain against the snow, and on the thumb and two fingers of her right hand. "These are filling with clear liquid. They'll blister and break, but they're not filling with blood. That's good, but she's shivering big time." He took her hand and gently palpated the flesh over her hand and forearm.

"My call is superficial frostbite," he said to Melissa. "Her skin has no blue or yellow tinge; the liquid in the blisters is clear, and most of all, the underlying tissue under her skin can move over the bone. If it were worse, the underlying tissue would feel hard and solid. We can keep warm damp soaks on her face and hands. No direct heat; no heating pad, ibuprofen for pain, which she'll have as the nerves come back to life. She needs rest. We'll see how she is in the morning." He looked directly at Melissa. "You might want to go home, but I'm staying."

"If it were ninety degrees outside, I'd stay." Then she looked at him and giggled nervously. "That is, if Jeremy would let us."

"Let you what?" Jeremy asked, carrying a pot of water in each hand.

"Stay the night." He nodded towards Cassie. "Watch over her."

"I would be at the door blocking your exit if you even tried to leave."

A commotion in the kitchen interrupted them. Vaughn's voice, sharp and belligerent, overpowered a softer one. Jeremy quickened his steps, entered the kitchen and faced Samir, covered with snow dripping over the floor, feet planted squarely, facing a seething dean.

"Reports of Mrs. Komsky have traveled into every house," Samir addressed both Vaughn and Jeremy formally yet politely. "I am responsible for what has happened. It is I who has put her life in peril. This would not have happened but for me. I accept all consequences meted out at your discretion and have informed my uncle of such. He is in agreement. We will abide by your decision. When Mrs. Komsky revives, please tell her I ask her forgiveness." And he headed for his room to stay, perhaps for the first time since his arrival at Chelsea.

Vaughn seethed, his hands balled into fists, but he maintained control, taking a seat on the sofa. Jeremy sighed. Despite his anger towards Samir, he had a soft spot in his heart for him. Connor and Matt were in the kitchen filling more pans with warm water. "Guys, I'll do the rest," Jeremy motioned to them to put the pans down. "I can take over from here. You've already done so much. If it weren't for you, for everyone, I could never have gotten to Mrs. Komsky. Thank you for your courage, your selflessness, for everything." Pride and embarrassment showed on their faces. Chelsea was indeed honored to have such fine young men at its academy.

You should go home," he said to Vaughn, who was visibly distressed. "You have a wife at home. She might be nervous if you're away on a night like this."

Vaughn shook his head. "I've called her twice. Taylor understands and she'll be fine. I've stayed the night before. She dismissed the staff hours ago, and if there's an emergency, Brett can stand in for me. I called him twice too, before and after Parker called. He has a Unimog that can navigate these roads as easily as our plows, and a lot faster. He can get Taylor home if she needs help. I'll go back to the office after Parker and Mason come in. Maintenance is plowing a path for them and lighting their way. Once I know they're back safely; I'll be okay."

Jeremy nodded. Although he had never married or had kids, he understood that bond.

They arrived fifteen minutes later through the house-master's office, their laughter and stamping feet announcing their entry. Obvious from their levity, Parker and Mason had not told Stevie about her mom. Good.

"Hi, Dr. O/B," Stevie announced ingenuously when she saw Vaughn. She was a delight, and, despite the tragedy of not having her father in her life, her cutting wit, which had to be genetic, kept her companions on their toes regardless of age. But tonight, she would be reduced to a child who would be lost without her mom. "Hi, Dr. Harper." She glanced around. "Where's my mom?"

It was the lack of response that triggered her apprehension. When Melissa walked out of the guest room and her mother had not appeared, something sank in the pit of Stevie's stomach. She knew instinctively something was seriously wrong. "Mrs. Donelly? Where's my mom?" Her voice quivered. She looked around; she looked at Parker, who had talked to her about the Giants; she looked at Mason, who was teasing her about prefixes; she looked at Vaughn, Jeremy, and Melissa, and suddenly she screamed, "Mom! Mom! Mommy!" Her breath came in gulps, her hands pulled at her hair, then she raced to Melissa and held on. Melissa held her tightly. "Where's my mom, Mrs. Donelly?!" Stevie cried. "Where's my mom?!"

"In here, Stevie. Your mom's in here!" Walter's voice called from the bedroom. He was struggling to keep Cassie still, who, through her subconscious, had heard her daughter's screams and was willing, fighting her body to go to her rescue. "She's okay, Stevie; she's okay. She's here. She's safe." And Stevie was at the bedroom door.

"Mommy!" she cried, and raced to Cassie's bedside, her mother opening her arms to her daughter, fingers bandaged with gauze, and Stevie jumping up on the bed and nestling in tight. Crying. She was with her mom; she was safe.

"Easy, Stevie," Walter cautioned. "Be careful. Your mom's hands and face are frostbitten. Try not to touch them. They need warmth and careful monitoring."

Stevie's look showed she understood. "What happened, Dr. Goodman?" she asked, wiping back tears.

"We found her in the snow. We think she fell or became disoriented when she left the dorm to find Samir. There are no broken bones or sprains, and that's the good news. Dr. Harper, Parker, Mason, Matt, and Connor brought her in." He glanced towards Parker and Mason and nodded in appreciation. "She's had a rough time, and she'll have more pain during the night as her nerve endings regain feeling, but she'll be okay."

He changed the subject. "Did you bring your pj's?" he asked, lightening the tone. Stevie nodded. "Good, then you're all set for the night. Help keep your mom warm." Walter stood. "I'll check in on the two of you throughout the night." He closed the door on his way out.

They'll be okay. Thank God; they'll be okay, this headstrong woman and her beautiful daughter. He'd do everything in his power to make sure of that.

39

Cassie had trouble holding her attaché and her handbag. The fingers in her right hand still tingled and every now and then, a painful spasm seared through the thumb and index finger of her right hand where she had gripped the flashlight. She had held it so tightly and with such tenacity that her circulation would have stopped even without the numbing cold. But as minutes had ebbed and she couldn't get up, she knew her only hope depended on someone sighting her light. She had held on, and held on, until the slashing wind pushed her down, and her consciousness slowly dimmed.

She remembered familiar voices. She had been lifted, then carried to an unfamiliar place, a room, a warm room, then placed on a bed. She remembered shivering and being unable to speak, as people hovered over her with trepidation and concern. She might die, but that was all right. She'd be with Brian, and this nightmare they call life would be over. This loneliness and this fear would all be over.

Death would be all right, until she heard Stevie's voice crying out for Mom. Then suddenly it wasn't all right. It wasn't all right to die, because she had unfinished business, and their daughter needed her. She sensed Brian telling her to live, to live no matter what, because she had their child to raise. And she remembered struggling to rise and Stevie snuggling in close just as she had done so many nights after Brian was gone. So many nights when Stevie had cried herself to sleep because Mommy couldn't tell her when Daddy was coming home. She was snuggling again. Something she hadn't needed for several years, she needed now.

Cassie had awakened yesterday morning holding Stevie and staring into Walter's drawn face. She smiled weakly and his eyes lit up. The worst was over. "Where am I?" She mouthed, feeling completely disoriented but not wanting to wake Stevie.

"Jeremy's spare bedroom," Walter mouthed back, with a thin smile; Cassie felt safe.

Hours later, after she had awoken sufficiently, Melissa helped her into a set of clothes she had brought just in case. A little big, but clean and dry! Warm and dry were top priorities for Cassie and would be for a long time. Parts of her fingers had frost nip, thank God only that, but her thumb and index finger were worse, as was the side of her face that had lain in the snow. The few blisters she had would scab in a day or two. Maybe leave a mark. No big deal. Would remind her how stupid she had been. Going after Samir would have been fine in May or June, but in December and in the heart of a severe blizzard? Just plain stupid. She had put so many people in danger with her spontaneous, stupid decision, one person's stupid, foolish decision. Foolish choices not only bring us down but bring a lot of innocent people with us, a spiral that can suck us all into the maelstrom, like *Hamlet.* That's exactly how she'd apologize for her actions tomorrow.

All these thoughts played in her head as she dressed for work. Dr. O/B and Walter had pleaded with her to stay home, but she had fought them tenaciously. As though they had expected something different? Not from her. Most likely, they knew what her answer would be before they had asked, but they couldn't force her.

So, she was up early, taking more time to get ready and dress. Stevie was up earlier than usual too, helping her mother whenever she could. Plows had labored all day yesterday to clear roads and sidewalks, which were clear for walking and driving, but tons of snow lay piled high along the sides. They'd need the extra time just in case. And this morning more than ever, both needed to know the other was okay when they went their separate ways. They laughed, joked and listened to music as they breakfasted on boiled eggs with buttered toast and raspberry preserves, easy for Stevie to make. Their laughter continued as Cassie drove Stevie to the bus stop.

After Stevie had safely boarded the bus Cassie concentrated on the new people in her life. Walter, Jeremy, Melissa, they were all wonderful people. She never thought they would have risked so much for her. Even Dr. O/B bringing the plows. He had saved her life. They had all saved her life. No way she could thank them. And the young men in her first period class: Matt, Mason, Connor and Parker. Parker, who had wanted no interaction with her whatsoever when she had first arrived, calling his dad and coming to her rescue with the others. How do you ever repay something like that? Maybe you never do.

She drove her car to Rand Hall and parked in the reserved space she hardly used; then she walked into the building, to her classroom, and placed her attaché on her desk. When she flexed her right hand, burning pain shot through her fingers. Ouch! She was glad for the round table method of teaching where a small group of students interacted with a teacher facilitator who related literature to the universality of mankind. Blackboards and chalk did not dominate the scene. She wouldn't have been able to hold a piece of chalk now. Life is strange, it takes you where it wants you to go, no matter how hard you protest or head in another direction.

She glanced out the window. The day was gloomy, without sun, without brightness. Not so different from the setting Shakespeare had given Hamlet. Melancholy sent a shudder through her. Focus on the good things in life, she thought, not the negatives. She gazed at the shimmering tree. Its beauty and its light glowed, tinseling the world with hope and love. Young men and women who would take over the reins of society in ten or fifteen years had decorated this tree. She focused on that and felt renewed.

They entered quietly, eleven of them, tiptoeing reverently to their seats. Most nodded respectfully, with heads down, not looking directly into her eyes. They saw the broken blisters on her face and the bandages Dr. Goodman had changed for her yesterday. Four of them had witnessed death up close and personal. One considered himself the direct cause. Another implicated herself in the blame. And Cassie, the catalyst of it all, stood before them and spoke.

"My fault. Completely and utterly mine. Not yours in any way. I made the decision to leave the building and head out into the storm. It was the epitome of foolishness and recklessness. Had it not been for Dr. O/B's quick thinking, bringing the plows to find us and to light our path, five of us in this room, and another staff member, might not be here. I am truly sorry and I ask your forgiveness."

The tick of the wall clock, the hiss of heat; that was all. Magnified sounds of inanimate objects, marking off silent seconds in a silent room, no student had found his voice. And then, one student did.

"It is I who caused this, Mrs. Komsky. Not you." Samir spoke with sorrow and dignity as he rose and faced Cassie; then addressed the class. "I have avoided all of you; I have avoided life, because my heart felt sorrow and despair from the loss of my parents and the destruction of my people. I never allowed myself to feel that again. But that has become impossible," he looked at Rachel with compassion and love. Her eyes teared but she did not turn away, "I have placed myself in a position where I can be hurt again. Willingly. So, hurt will be inevitable. But I had no right to put anyone else in danger. It is as Khalil Gibran said, you cannot have sorrow unless you've known delight, but in seeking my delight, I placed so many ohers in danger. For that, I ask forgiveness." He sat slowly and placed his hand over Rachel's.

"Mrs. Komsky?" Gloria's soft voice spoke. "This may sound trivial, but I get what you mean now about how our decisions and our actions affect so many others beyond our control. And as silly as it sounds, I get the theme of *Hamlet, really* get it, like I lived it. So many people were destroyed because of him. Decisions we make don't affect us alone. They affect a lot of people in ways we never know.

"Gloria, your point is not only *not* trivial, but it's a major lesson we learn from reading this play. We all make decisions or we don't make them, which is a decision in itself. And the ripple effect, and all the concentric circles it forms, affects a wider and wider perimeter, as my foolish decision affected so many others; same as Hamlet. His inability to make a decision caused the deaths of eight people. If Shakespeare had taken the play further, who knows how many others would have been affected. But he took it far enough. He made his point about humanity."

"Then aren't we all just doomed?" Mason asked in earnest.

"Why Mason? Why doomed?"

"Because we all have to make decisions, but we never know how they'll affect other people, or ourselves."

"You're right; decisions are a concomitant of life, and we all have to make them every minute of every day. Whether it's to eat breakfast or not; study for a test or not; run for class office or try out for a team; go out with the guys or stay in. Come to class or not. Simple, innocuous decisions. We make them all the time. Robert Frost, "The Road Not Taken," he took the road less traveled by, and that made all the difference. It makes all the difference for us all.

"We can take the road most traveled by, or the road least traveled. We have to take one. But I think the difference is in how we make our decisions, or, why. Remember the first example I gave you on my first day of class? The two characters - Dan, the co-captain who wanted the captain to make changes but only for the good of the team, and Jonathan the fullback, who tried to undermine the captain through Dan because he was jealous? Hamlet didn't try to hurt someone; he tried *not* to. That's what caused his tragedy.

"I tried to help, albeit in a rather foolish way, and that put others in danger, plus myself. But my intentions were good. So if we make decisions with good intentions, then whatever falls into place is the way it goes. If we always avoid decisions because something bad might happen, we'd live in a cave and never come out."

She stopped talking and they fell silent again. A Christmas glow filled the room. This was the beginning of another beautiful holiday season. Cassie felt it; she hoped they did. She also hoped they'd learned from her experience: decisions always confront you, life confronts you, and you have to go with it and live with the results. Like Hamlet, Brian and Cassie, like Samir; regardless of social status, regardless of place, regardless of century, we live the destiny of Man.

40

SAMIR & RACHEL VISIT, WEDNESDAY, DECEMBER 9

Senior year methods class in college had taught its prospective teachers that the most effective way to teach literature was to relate it to some aspect of real life, because all fiction is a story with characters, plot, setting and theme that are seemingly real. Everyone lived varying degrees of the agony and ecstasy of these four components, and Cassie's story had leaped off the page and tied in perfectly with the tragedy in Hamlet's life.

Hers had been a real-life narrative. Not set in Denmark, nor in a castle with a king and queen who lived hundreds of years ago, not from a folio printed in 1623, or from words from a 20th century anthology, but set here, now, 1987, in the present, in an academy involving real people, faculty and students living now.

It was a real-life narrative founded on a foolish decision that had been meant for good, wrought with potential disaster. The conflation of a single flashlight, a school-closing announcement, seniors rushing to the window to see the storm, a series of seemingly totally unrelated events, each individual on its own, had coalesced to bring about her rescue. Hamlet and Ophelia hadn't been so fortunate.

Cassie's original lesson plan had focused on Ophelia's plight and the collusion between Laertes and Claudius to poison Hamlet as a last resort. But her close brush with death made death so palpable that the class empathized immediately with Hamlet's graveyard scene, holding Yorick's skull and postulating about the significance of man.

That dominated the discussion all period, relegating Ophelia, Laertes and Claudius to second place. Ashes to ashes, dust to dust, "and all our yesterdays have lighted fools the way to dusty death." Monday night's averted tragedy had spread through the dorms. Every student knew what had happened and all her classes, not just period one, expressed their apprehensions and fears about life. Her classroom had become the perfect venue.

They had talked openly, and Cassie had listened closely, reading between the lines to sense danger, always stressing tenacity and forbearance for them and for herself. Although her students had strong family support and guidance, for the most part, when decisions confronted them, especially with their peers, they had to make choices on their own, there and then, and they alone were responsible for the consequences. The road not taken might be nostalgic, but it, as well as the road taken, would travel with them through life's journey.

This was the aura that hovered around their discussions which monopolized Cassie's thoughts as fifth period, her prep time, began. She needed a few minutes of meditation before taking her brief report about Samir to Guidance. Get your act together, girl. Her palms supported her chin; she was especially careful to insure her bandaged fingers did not engage the scarring blisters on her face. While she was deep in thought, someone quietly knocked at the door. She shook off her reverie and saw Samir with Rachel by his side.

They walked several steps into the room, but that was their limit. Cassie motioned them in further, but Samir declined. He was focused, as usual; determined, as usual, reserved, polite, deferential, but never intimidated. He had come for a purpose, his manner indicating he had something of importance to say. One decisive glance at Rachel and he spoke.

"*Samaheenee lee enanee alsebab fee eyetha yekee.*" (Forgive me because I am the reason you were hurt.)

"It wasn't your fault, Samir. It was mine."

He cast his eyes down and hesitated. "*Ana Ahubha.*" (I love her.) He nodded towards Rachel.

Cassie nodded and smiled. "I know." That they loved each other was easy to see. No other emotion surpassed the power of love. But their visit was a little perplexing. Samir knew she suspected or was certain of his love for Rachel. He had overcome his solitude to attend a football game to be near her and he was with her at Homecoming, not only with her, but fighting off the school's two biggest and most dominant seniors in the class. So why this, here and now? Yes. He had something else to say.

Samir's countenance went from apprehension to a hint of a smile. He breathed heavily and his eyes almost teared. *"Heeya zowjatee,"* he said proudly. Cassie leaped from her seat. Her chair toppled over and hit the floor with a resounding thud. Samir beamed, took Rachel's hand, and guided her out, leaving a stunned Cassie speechless. Oh, my, God, she muttered in disbelief. Oh. . . my. . . God. Never had she expected this.

41

CASSIE SUBMITS REPORT ABOUT ACCIDENT AFTER CLASSES

It took her a while to digest Samir's revelation and, as she hurried to Smythe Hall to submit her report to Melissa and thank her and Walter again for everything they had done for her, she gave a second's consideration whether to include it. To report it or not to report it, that is the question. She punned Hamlet's soliloquy.

No, absolutely not. It was none of anybody's business. Samir had told her this in confidence; she'd never betray his trust, and further, his love for Rachel had motivated him to interact with his peers. What a beautiful effect she had already had on him. Nope, she would never disclose their secret to anyone, and since Samir had vowed he would never leave the dorm after curfew again, regardless of weather, regardless of reason, their secret would not affect his safety in any way.

Report what concerned Samir's safety, nothing else. That was the deal. His secret, their secret, would be safe with her; his secret, his reason for leaving his dorm in such horrific weather was the most wonderful reason she could have imagined - he wanted to be with his wife.

Cassie glowed, almost skipping to Smythe hall; that's how lighthearted she felt. The sky had turned bright blue, with foamy white clouds accentuating the contrast. White against bright blue, like a pretty summer day, except for the stark white mountains of snow abutting sidewalks, buildings, and dorms, with a few scraggly, dried brown leaves scuffling along the cleared sidewalk paths, dragging their heels in nascent puffs of wind. Maintenance had done an outstanding job, especially concerning her life.

Hurry, hurry, hurry, she encouraged her feet to move faster, a tough job for them after the beating she'd put them through. But it was cold. Her hands were even colder, and they felt awkward in mittens, which made holding her attaché difficult. Mittens didn't allow for dexterity or a secure grip, but her bandaged fingers wouldn't fit into gloves. Come on, Cassie, she chided. You're lucky you still have fingers. Enough with the griping; hurry and get inside where it's warm! And that she did, directly to Guidance and Melissa's desk.

"Well, look who's here!" Melissa voice rang out as Cassie, beaming, approached the counter. "Back to the old grind, huh?"

"And very glad to be," Cassie replied with an ear to ear smile. "Thank you again, for all you did for me." Melissa smiled bashfully as Cassie gave her the report. It covered the vital info about Samir's leaving through the window, her following, and his promise never to break curfew again. One sentence at the end asked to be apprised of the communication Dr. O/B had had with Samir's uncle. Nothing else, and following protocol, Melissa's signature went on the report and she passed a copy back to Cassie.

"Walter and I were just saying that you haven't replied about the faculty Christmas party." Cassie looked perplexed. "You're the only one in the football crew who hasn't. Everyone else is going."

The football crew? The only one of the football crew who hasn't responded? Cassie was confused. First she was elated because Melissa had included her in the football crew, but secondly, what party? "What Christmas party?" She stammered.

"You *do* read the daily bulletin that's in your box every morning, don't you?" Walter's deep voice reprimanded. She turned. He sure did look good in casual Hagger slacks and a soft cotton, pale blue dress shirt that had a velveteen look to it, more casual than dress.

Cassie opened her mouth to speak but no sound emanated. She had been aware of absolutely nothing regarding a Christmas party. "It's been in the bulletin since the first week of December," Walter continued. "We didn't talk about it at the cook-off because we were too busy eating, but there is a faculty party."

"And too many other interesting conversations at the cook-off in addition to food. We didn't remember the Christmas party," Melissa interjected. "The brain can only focus on so much and last Saturday our brains were focusing on chicken parn, linguine with white clam sauce, and, and Vaughn's desserts! Umm!" Melissa's eyes closed and her hand kissed her mouth. Delicious . . . and fattening. I jogged three extra miles that weekend."

"Outside?" Cassie asked, astounded. "In wicked temperatures like that?" Then she gulped, realizing how much worse her decision to go out in the storm had been.

"Treadmill," Melissa replied. "No reason to go out in bitter cold weather if you don't have to.

Cassie hung her head. "Yeah, most people are smart enough to know that."

"Hey, don't beat yourself up," Walter remonstrated. "We all make foolish mistakes every now and then."

"There's foolish, and then there's stupid, Cassie replied. "But," she smiled, I was able to tie my mistake to Hamlet and the analogy was perfect."

"Good save, but verisimilitude does not have to be taken to such an extreme," Walter chided good-naturedly. "So, are you going?" Too many topics were colliding. "To the faculty Christmas party," he added.

Cassie paused, digested the question and responded. "Where is it; when is it; time, place, and if I can find company for Stevie."

"It's at King George's Seal, Saturday, the 19th. Huge log-burning, stone fireplace, enormous tree, great food and a DJ. I'll put the flyer in your mailbox. So read it, please? We need to know by Friday. Money has to be in then; Friday's the 11th, and it's already the 9th."

Why not, she thought as she left the office. This should be fun; Christmas decorations, a huge tree, a log-burning fireplace. She could almost hear the snap of dry wood and crackling cinders, almost smell the aroma of burning wood. She inhaled involuntarily and sighed, "Hmm." A good buffet, or maybe a sit-down dinner, and a DJ, without Dr. O/B pulling her off the floor? Yeah, why not, King George's Seal, someplace in West Windsor, where ever that was, Cassie had no idea, but why not?

She checked her mailbox after school and the flyer was there as promised. Thankfully, the party's location no longer mattered, because Walter had scrawled the words, "I'll pick you up - Walter," along the bottom of the sheet. That was a relief, because, aside from Main Street's quaint antique shops, the Bagel and Bakery next to Manicures for Men, two luncheonettes, a small grocery, the Colonial Bank and Lina's Bookstore, Cassie didn't know where anything was. Oh, and the local supermarket half a mile away. And she had to include Scarbello's, where Dr. O/B had taken her and Stevie for dinner after their shopping excursion at the mall.

That was it, all she knew of her surroundings. Not bad, though, for someone who had pulled into town for the first time, November 2nd and had steeped herself in lesson plans, meals, moving herself and her daughter into a new apartment, and students. One student in particular.

Since getting to King George's was settled, the only problem might be if Walter wanted to leave before she did, or vice versa. They could work that out. And thirty dollars? Not too steep for her budget. I'll go, she thought with conviction. She'd see how things would work for Stevie. Next Saturday night, the 19th. Me at the Christmas party, and Stevie with Rebecca Greer, Stacy Bronston, and Millie, the tiny girl whose last name began with 'T.' Stevie would have fun. Thompson; Millie Thompson. That's her last name.

Two and a half days to put this all together. She could do it, depending on how much she wanted to go, and surprisingly, she found herself wanting to do just that. In fact, she realized somewhat disconcertingly, she wanted to go very much. Yup, for whatever reason, she wanted to go!

42

Friday had come and gone with a renewed anticipation for life Cassie had not known in years. Mostly confined to her subconscious, it was percolating up towards everything. Her classes were psyched and discussion had become electrified with the play's last scene.

Shakespeare had done the job stupendously. Gertrude's, "I will drink, my lord." Did she know the drink had been poisoned? Laertes, stabbed with the same poisoned rapier he had used in his duel with Hamlet, then implicating the king and their nefarious plot to poison Hamlet, and finally, finally, Hamlet running Claudius through with the same poisoned rapier that both he and Laertes had used on each other. Redemption, the ultimate triumph. What a scene. They loved it. Trust and betrayal, jealousy and deception, love and hatred, each a clash of paradoxes that can either lift us to new heights or take us down further than we have ever gone.

Hamlet had been tested to his limits. His character had allowed ambivalence until he committed himself to his fate. Once committed, he could do no less. A tragic, yet honorable way to live and die.

December 11th, the play was finished, and she recalled the outstandingly prescient discussions she and her classes had had. *Hamlet* had been her baptism into Chelsea and the lives of sixty-two students, eleven of them in her first period class. She knew at this point in her life, that no matter what or how or where life took them, she'd never forget them. They were indelibly fixed into her memory.

Next week they'd present their projects. The ladies had rewritten several pertinent scenes from Ophelia's perspective. She had a good idea what they would say and was eager to see their approach. Zach and Matt had honed in on weapons of war during the Late Middle Ages, like swords, cleaving weapons, spears, from a different perspective they wouldn't divulge. Theirs would be an interesting presentation, too. Jason and Connor would analyze Hamlet's development as a psychological study, a good fit for them. Parker and Mason would be comparing *Hamlet* to Seneca's tragedy of blood. They'd love that.

Samir would, as usual, work alone, although all his male classmates had encouraged him to join their groups. How beautiful was that? But he had honed in on the twenty-thousand Norwegian soldiers who had gone off to die for honor, comparing it to the factions in Palestine and Lebanon who are branded fanatics and terrorists by the West, but continue to fight for dignity and justice. In his abstract he stated his presentation would be analogous to past atrocities of ethnic cleansing. She wondered how he would tie that in, but she knew his would be an amazing presentation. They all would. Cassie looked forward to next week, anticipating greatness.

And she was also looking forward to next week because a little spark had been rekindled deep inside her. She was happy. She didn't quite know why; she couldn't piece it all together, but she was simply happy, and because of that her feet carried her quickly to Smythe Hall. Aside from her first trip there, when Dr. O/B had called her in after her outburst at Homecoming, she always seemed happy when she headed in that direction. It flashed into her conscious for an instant then quickly receded.

A Christmas party. Wonderful, like Cinderella at the ball. Whoa, don't get carried away; there's no such thing as Cinderella. But she thought about what she'd wear, what shoes would go with it, what earrings and bracelets. She let herself be creative. She was playing big-time dress-up; something she hadn't done in years, and she was floating.

Consciously rather than unconsciously, she was aware that she could have talked herself out of going; she could have easily begged off: It's too close to Christmas; there's too much to do, some excuse, but she didn't. For the first time in four years, she didn't want to. Enjoy the moment; life was short. Brian would not have wanted her to sequester herself from people for the rest of it. He would have encouraged her to make a new life and be part of the living. He had always told her he had never known anyone who was so full of life and good will, and from the hundreds, maybe thousands of people he had met or known from years of working at the Nor'easter, his saying that was significant. She knew he would have expected her to go on without him, and to go on happily. It was that last part she still questioned.

Her $30.00 check in hand, she skipped around tree branches that had broken from their strong trunks and littered the walkway, potential stumbling blocks if she weren't careful. Her hands were feeling better, bandages still on, but almost no pain. Her feet almost ran to Guidance, finally applying their inner brakes when she faced Melissa, who was standing directly behind the counter five feet from the doorway, wearing a soft beige suit over a white blouse with a ruffled bodice. It looked good. A bit breathless, Cassie placed the check in Melissa's hand.

"Since this isn't a report on Samir," Melissa stated facetiously, "I guess you're going."

Cassie nodded emphatically. "Yes. I have decided to go. Finally, get out and mingle."

Melissa pressed a button on the phone next to her. "Good for you. It's about time." Melissa almost bit her lip when she said that, wishing she hadn't, remembering too late that Cassie didn't know the football crew knew her tragedy.

"You're right, Melissa. It *is* about time."

"Do you know how to get there?"

"She doesn't have to; I'm picking her up."

Melissa looked a bit surprised. Walter had entered the main office at her cue; so his presence didn't surprise her. What did surprise her, though, was that he had never offered to take anyone to a party before, or anywhere, preferring to drive solo, just him and his radio, especially at night. Maybe there was something here Melissa had missed? But if there were, Cassie's expression didn't indicate it. She exuded nothing but appreciation and warmth.

"You sure it's not an inconvenience?"

"Not in the least," Walter added.

"What if I want to leave before you do?" That was her one apprehension.

"Then we leave."

And it was decided, that easily.

"It starts at 7:00. How about I pick you up at 6:30?"

Get Stevie dinner; make sure she's ensconced with her friends, and be ready by 6:30. Do-able. "Fine, I'll be ready." Next Saturday, she thought, a Christmas party, and she just about twirled like a little kid, her platform heels clicking her backwards then spinning her around on her way out, taking her to the door partially backwards on a collision course directly into Vaughn, the force of the impact careening her backwards. Cassie emitted a yelp of pain and her hand went to her forehead.

"Oh my God!" She squealed, in the throes of pain. "Oh my God!" Then, completely forgetting his position and hers, "Again? You're here, again? Do you have radar?"

She realized what she had said and to whom she had said it, too late, but it didn't matter. Vaughn's face had turned a bright red, as red as the bump forming on his jaw. Attempting a recovery, Vaughn muttered, "I came to tell you, informally, that I want to speak to you about Samir. I did not expect to be assaulted by a strong forehead with a sharp tongue beneath it." He had given himself away without realizing it, and Cassie was too ingenuous to be discrete.

"How'd you know I would be here?" She asked, perplexed.

Vaughn stammered again, then, recovering his veneer of decorum and his latent arrogance, went on the defensive. "I haven't received a copy of Monday night's situation with Samir. When will it be ready?"

"I submitted it Wednesday. Whatever the proper channels are, it's in one of them, one channel at a time." So he was back to the condescending Vaughn?

"I received it yesterday, filed it and sent it inter-office memo this morning. It should be on Charlotte's desk as we speak," Walter countered. Cassie detected a tone of defiance in Walter's voice, nothing that she had ever witnessed before.

"Thank you, Walter. I'll check on it later." He nodded curtly; then turned to Cassie, and, with a complete metathesis, "And what meeting are you attending at 6:30 for which you'll be ready and about which I have no knowledge?" Walter bridled; Cassie fell for it.

"It's not a meeting, Dr. O/B," Cassie smiled broadly with a hint of defiance. "It's the faculty Christmas party. I've decided to go, and Walter is picking me up, since I don't know my way around this area yet. Actually, I have trouble knowing my way around anywhere. My husband used to say I could get lost coming out of our driveway." She smiled for the first time when she mentioned her husband. "And he wasn't far from wrong. I come off an elevator in a department store and don't know where I am." She laughed pleasantly, not noticing Vaughn's snarl that he quickly morphed into a smile. But Walter noticed.

"Well, have a good time," Vaughn said curtly.

"Thank you, Dr. O/B. I'm looking forward to dancing, *my* way, without any interference from the upper echelons of society, if you recall." She smiled coyly but not flirtatiously. Vaughn gave her a formal smile and walked out. Then, suddenly realizing how gauche she was being, she followed him out the door. "Dr. O/B, I apologize. That was a bit flippant of me. I'm sorry. Sometimes my mouth speaks before my brain kicks in." Her smile was glowing, and a soft hint of warmth and sensuality exuded from her that made Vaughn hurry down the hall. "And thank you, Dr. O/B, for everything you did for me Monday evening. I put a thank-you note in your box. I hope you got it." Her voice trailed after him but he didn't look back.

Vaughn left Guidance but he did not leave the encounter. Even more so, he did not need her comment about dancing to recall Homecoming. It stuck in his mind like a mosquito bite midway between his trapezius muscles that was impossible to scratch. He replayed her twirling backwards in that light grey pants suit and colliding with him hard, her forehead into his chin. He rubbed his jaw and actually welcomed the lump that was swelling on the side of his face, a token of the physical contact he could only dream about, and he was doing that a lot. And her apology. The softness of her voice; the rapture of her smile and yes, he had gotten her note, tucked away in his desk drawer. He was drowning and he knew it. No, he would not succumb.

He swaggered to his office to compensate for a sense of inadequacy he had never felt before. Inadequate? Him? Otis-Barretts *never* feel inadequate. But she'll be dancing in her uninhibited, inimitable fashion, doing that

313

gyration he had never seen anywhere, anyplace, anytime in his lifetime; she would be dancing like that without anyone pulling her off the floor. Would Walter? Would he pull her off the floor? No, no one would, and he, Vaughn, omnipotent Vaughn, would not be there to see it.

Why did it matter? Did he want to be there, at that Christmas party? No . . . yes . . . no . . . maybe, damn it, yes! Vaughn, what the hell is the matter with you? It's a faculty social function. You don't attend those things. And since he had never attended one, there was no reason why he would now. But there *was* a reason, now. Damn! No, he would give the matter no further thought, waste not one more second pondering it. I must be losing my mind, he thought, walking into his outer office.

"Charlotte, the file with Cassie's, Mrs. Komsky's, reports on Samir. There should be two. One after Thanksgiving and the one she submitted this past Wednesday. When you have them, please put them on my desk."

Before he passed her desk, Charlotte reached over to a short pile of manila folders, yanked the one second from the top and handed it to him. "Walter sent this over this morning; both reports are in this folder."

Vaughn took the folder into his office, poured himself a mug of coffee, sat in his reclining chair and read.

43

"Full House" was about to begin. Stevie got comfortable on the sofa with her math book, crossed her legs and propped the book up on her knees, notebook at her side, pencil in her hand. For Stevie, the program was all about John Stamos, Mr. Cutie, as Stevie and her new friends called him. For Cassie, the show was about a widower who was trying desperately to raise his daughters. She could relate to that.

Stevie had been doing the bulk of the cooking and cleaning since Wednesday. Surprisingly, for nine, she could make a great meatloaf. She loved to mix the ingredients and get all that gook, as she called it, over her hands, then shape it into a football. Sometimes her Mom would add tomato paste, sometimes cheese, sometimes onion and parsley. Tonight Stevie had added mustard. "Let's add a dash of celery salt, too," Cassie had suggested after Stevie insisted on mustard. If we're gonna experiment, why stop there?" Cassie had set the oven, supervised the final preparation and suggested the pan to use. Other than that, Stevie had done it all.

Well done. The meatloaf had been excellent, with roasted sweet potatoes and green beans for veggies. Stevie had been a strong second in preparing the chicken parm and linguine for Jeremy's cook-off. She could do a roast chicken too, crispy skin, juicy meat. In a few years, she'd be making that and more without any supervision at all.

After dinner, all that remained was stacking the dishwasher and doing some superficial touch-ups; Cassie could finish those by herself. Stevie needed more time for homework; she wanted to finish it tonight rather than let it go until Sunday. After a little polishing here and there, the kitchen sparkled. Leftovers had been put away for a quick Saturday lunch. Done. Next she put on the kettle and took down cups and saucers for tea. Walter was coming over at 8:00 to change her bandages and help them finish decorating the tree.

Using her left hand to put up the tree had been a problem, but stringing lights had been nearly impossible. The bottom strand lay on the carpet and the top strands were hanging in disarray. With Walter's help, they could do it quickly. Cassie also hoped that, when he removed the bandages, she'd no longer need fresh ones. She glanced at her watch. Eight minutes late. Hope he hasn't forgotten, she thought. She shook off her doubt. Walter would not forget; he was not that kind of person. He'd be here.

"Wanna watch "Full House" with me, Mom?"

"Thanks, Honey, but I'm making tea and putting out nibbles for Dr. Goodman. Nuts, some sharp provolone, a chunk of cheddar, and crackers. Even if he's not hungry, he'll most likely nibble. I'm sure I will"

"Me too," Stevie added. "I'm always hungry."

"That's because you're as thin as a rail." Cassie was getting out the cheese board and a jar of salted cashews; pulling cutlery out of drawers. "I'm also looking at the calendar," she added, glancing at the month of December displayed on the cabinet door. Are you aware that Christmas is less than two weeks away? I can't believe it. Where did the month go?"

"The cook-off one weekend, and. . ." Stevie hesitated.

"I know. My searching for Samir the other. You're being polite. Thank you. Next time I want to practice for the Iditarod, remind me of the potential consequences."

"What do you know about the Iditarod, Mom?" Stevie asked, surprised at her mother's analogy.

"Not much." She thought for a second. "It's in March," she paused, "and it commemorates dogs and mushers who delivered an antidote to a village somewhere in Alaska decades ago, maybe the '20's. That's about it, only what the media says when they cover it. What made you ask?" Cassie looked at Stevie, her head in her math book, pencil moving quickly.

Stevie shrugged. "No reason. We read something about amazing animals in English class last month, and one story was about two lead dogs that ran in it." Then doing a complete metathesis, "When's Dr. Goodman coming? "Is he going to help us finish the tree?"

"He said he would be here at 8:00, but he's late. I hope nothing's wrong."

Stevie looked at her mom. "You like him, don't you?"

Cassie almost dropped the serving bowl she was filling with cashews. "Whaaat! Where did that come from?"
No response. "Stevie, what made you ask that?"

Stevie responded with a shrug. "Just wanted to ask."

"Saved by the bell" was never as applicable as it was
now, and when it buzzed, Stevie pushed her books away,
jumped off the sofa and hurried into the kitchen as Cassie
took the whistling kettle off the burner and started for the
door, rolling her eyes at her daughter. "Garlic-buttered
popcorn?" Stevie asked as the bell sounded a second time.

Cassie nodded, "Sure, but not another word about
what you just asked me, promise?"

"Yup," Stevie replied convincingly and began searching the bottom cabinets for their popcorn pan, throwing
one pot on top of another, creating one hellacious racket.
She pulled out a deep, black rectangular pan with a mesh
wire lid and hoisted it to the stovetop. Then she reached
for the corn oil to coat the bottom of the pan so the kernels
would slide back and forth easily and not burn, wondering
why Dr. Goodman wasn't coming inside. In the time it took
her to reach for the jar of kernels, open it and sprinkle a
layer into the pan, she knew: The man's voice she heard
from the doorway wasn't Dr. Goodman's; it was Dr. O/B's.

You like him, don't you, replayed in Cassie's head as she
walked to the door. She smiled, wondering if she actually did. Maybe, but sometimes she hardly knew her own
feelings; it had been so long since she'd had any, any feelings except sadness. But the thought of it, the thought she
might like Walter lit up her face, and the smile was still
obvious when she unlatched the bolt and swung the door
wide open. There, in the middle of, "I wondered when

you'd . . ." she froze. She was not staring into Walter's face; she was staring into Dr. O/B's. Suddenly there was only a void, a vacuum, and the contemplation of any action at all wouldn't surface.

"You were expecting someone . . . someone else?" Vaughn's smile faded.

Cassie was speechless. Disoriented; shocked. "I . . . yes, I . . ." she stammered. Of course she was expecting someone else. She certainly wasn't expecting him! Besides, why would it matter to him? What was he doing here, anyway? Friday night? Here? Not at the Club? He should be anywhere, but not here.

"I wanted to talk to you about Samir this afternoon, but I didn't get the chance. Our encounter turned somewhat negative and I still have a bump on my jaw." Cassie blushed. "Charlotte had your report on her desk when I left Guidance and I read it. There are some gaps, and yes, I know you only report succinctly unless something concerns his safety, but I also wanted to talk to you about the conversation I had with his uncle, Ambassador Gibran. I thought it important you should know."

"Dr. O/B, it's Friday night." How do you tell a guy who's saved your life, and the dean of the academy, he shouldn't be here? "I don't mean to sound aloof, especially after what you did for me Monday evening," she had been caught off guard, and she felt uncomfortable, wondering why he was here, liking it, not liking it and no longer knowing which feeling dominated the other, "but shouldn't we be doing this Monday?"

She had put him on the spot, not a place he liked to be, but he had expected a challenge. She had gone face to face with him at the football game, at Homecoming and this morning. He didn't doubt she'd resist him now, and here, but since he had convinced himself he was justified in being here, he only had to convince her. And if all else failed, he was the dean. But to be fair, not autocratic, he had rehearsed almost every possible scenario she could present, determined to get inside without exercising authority.

"As you can see by my dress, I was at the Club, as usual; you know, that snobby, elitist, ostentatious establishment for the gathering of the obscenely wealthy and egotistical upper class, and I noticed the chef had something very special on the menu; so I brought it for Stevie." He presented a big, white, dessert box from behind his back.

Cassie stared at it. "Oh no," she murmured, knowing exactly what it was. He was trying to lessen the shock of his presence with levity and a bribe, and it would have worked if she had not steeled herself against it.

She looked at the pastry box, then at him. The power of wealth, its unabated, raw power stared back at her. She had been aware of this power since college, but mostly in theory. Now here it was, staring her right in the face. The problem was that he could be so nice when he wanted to be, and he had a tender side to him, a tender and caring side which showed this past Monday when he went beyond obligation to consummate her rescue. Yet the other side, the powerful side, the side that showed his wealth, always trickled through. Wealth made him omnipotent, simple as that. It didn't make him *feel* omnipotent, nothing subjective or affective about it; it actually *made* him omnipotent, and infallible. He could do anything, say anything, hurt anyone; he could be wrong, and, via the power of wealth, he could make himself right.

Wealth conditioned you to believe everything in life was about you and for you. It was a way of life, assimilated with upbringing, indoctrination so pervasive and so strong it was almost as if it had been implanted in your DNA. Do anything you want, manipulate people, view them as commodities, use and discard. With or without his charming smile, Vaughn expected to knock on her door Friday evening, unannounced, and get exactly what he wanted, regardless of her comfort level, without any consequence to himself.

Monday evening, November 2, her first day at Chelsea flashed through her mind. Delivering that student handbook had not been a lack of judgment on his part. It was simply his way. He could have brought it to her classroom after school, or he could have waited until the next day. But functioning as an omnipotent ruler, he had arbitrarily brought it when *he* had wanted - a wealthy man who thought he had everything all figured out.

But what differed from her first evening when spontaneity from a water fight had left her and Stevie drenched, and a relatively unknown dean had presented himself at her door, was her reaction. This time she was not embarrassed, nor was she angry; she was confused.

His arrogance and conceit still offended her, but his pedantic demeanor had softened. He had recognized his bias and his quickness to stereotype. Not many people would. And he had been open-minded enough to research things to shatter his stereotypes. Most people never would do that either. His Thanksgiving invitation had added dimension to her internal conflict, but he had also been instrumental in saving her life, literally. So, this time, as much as she had decided she would not let him in, it was not a simple, Thanks for the handbook, goodbye. This time, she forced herself to admit, Dr. O/B held a special place in her life, and subconsciously, this put her at a big disadvantage.

You can't just turn someone away once they've saved your life. But then again, how could she let him in? He was her boss, her employer, and he made her uncomfortable by chipping away at boundaries of propriety between employer and employee. Did he sense her discomfort? Did he have any clue as to how he was making her feel? Or was he doing this intentionally?

She didn't know; she couldn't tell, but despite his having saved her life, despite everything she owed him, she couldn't acquiesce. She had to stand firm. Letting him in would not be good. He belonged at the Club with his wife and his family. He did not belong here on a Friday night with an employee who lived completely out of his world. She'd send him away; she had to, regardless of the consequences. Their discussion about Samir would have to wait until Monday.

Vaughn, knowing he was on the brink of having the door shut in his face, "And to be honest, I wanted to ask you how you were doing." He nodded towards her bandages. "I could not, would not, bring that up in Guidance today, but when I finally got the chance to stop by your room yesterday after classes to talk to you, it was 3:10. You had already gone. Also, I was touched by your apology this afternoon and wanted to thank you. We don't get many opportunities to talk, me being the dean and you being faculty."

Woah, he's good, she thought. He is totally disarming her. He had stopped by her room yesterday afternoon? She thought quickly. He must have; otherwise, he would not have known she had left early and was not there at 3:10, since she always stayed until 3:30. Now what? Her internal conflict increased exponentially. Let him in, tell him no, close the door? Damn it. He had no right to intrude on her like this. And then it was all settled by a third party.

"Dr. O/B? It's you? What are you doing here?" Stevie had left her popcorn to check the situation at the front door, and she had left it at the point where the pan had to be kept in constant motion or the kernels would burn. From the front door, you could hear the cacophony in the kitchen as it reached a crescendo, little explosions of kernels coming faster and faster, until the whole thing sounded like a bundle of firecrackers exploding all at once in a back alley garbage can.

Stevie spun off quickly and raced back to the kitchen. She took the pan off the burner and immediately raced back to the front door. What was Dr. O/B holding in his hand? "What's in the box, Dr. O/B?" She asked, breathless, looking for some sign to confirm her supposition, and Dr. O/B's wide smile did just that. "Black Forest cake? Oh my God! Twice in two weeks! Can I have a piece? Mom, can he come in?" Stevie looked back and forth at her mother then at Vaughn.

Unbelievable, Cassie thought. He wins. He wins! Damn it! "Of course he can," Cassie responded, and with that, her stomach churned and her internal conflict sky-rocketed towards infinity.

44

DISCUSSION IN CASSIE'S KITCHEN

Cassie ushered Vaughn into the kitchen and he placed the cake box on the counter. It stood high and white and proud, tied with double string knotted into a bow, proclaiming to all it stood supreme in the world of confection.

"Want some popcorn, Dr. O/B?" Stevie asked ingenuously. She pushed back the mesh lid of the popper, took a huge scooper from the drawer and began funneling fluffy white popcorn into a huge wooden bowl. Every few seconds, a kernel would pop and shower the counter with four or five errant kernels. When the bowl was full, she sprinkled melted butter over it, mixed it up gingerly and placed it on the kitchen table. Light, fluffy kernels of popcorn seasoned with salt, a dash of pepper, melted butter and a sprinkle of garlic powder. Yum.

Tempting, thought Vaughn. He actually liked popcorn, and his cook, Sarah, would make it for him and

Parker whenever they had the opportunity to watch a movie in their entertainment studio. "I'd like nothing better," he said. "You eat the cake, Stevie; I'll dive into the popcorn."

Cassie took down a fourth cup and saucer, four dessert plates and four bowls and put a place setting in front of each of them, and the fourth for the empty chair. Cassie was still expecting Walter and the number of place settings did not go unnoticed. Then she turned for the kettle. "The water's still hot, Mom. I checked for steam."

"Thanks, Hon." Cassie filled the ceramic teapot, already holding two tea bags, and brought it to the table. She put out the bowl of nuts and took the cheeseboard from the frig. Crackers, too. Stevie took Vaughn's bowl and filled it to the top with white clouds of popped corn that overflowed onto the table. Vaughn picked them up and popped them into his mouth, what any normal person would do.

He's pretending, Cassie thought. Just another average guy who would casually pick up stray kernels from the table and pop them into his mouth. But Dr. O/B is most certainly not another average guy. People with homes the size of castles, with yachts – she knew he had one at least – stables, and foyers the size of her apartment, with garages stocked with more cars than she had shoes are not average. She knew it; he knew it.

Stevie untied the string, opened the box's lid, turned down its sides and removed the most luscious Black Forest cake Cassie had ever seen. Then Stevie slowly carried it to the table. Three layers of cake, its top exquisitely decorated with dollops of whipped cream shaped like roses topped with fresh, dark cherries soaked in kirsch. Tiny shavings of dark chocolate covered its sides in an overlapping shingled pattern. Either they had a master pastry chef at the Club who could work miracles in minutes, or Vaughn had ordered this special. She'd go with the latter, which made this entire evening even more bizarre. Surreal. There was that word again. Absolutely surreal.

Cassie took a cake cutter from the drawer, sliced a medium wedge for Stevie and placed it on her plate. Stevie sat at the table and began to pick at the cream and the cherries from the center, just like her mother. Stevie brought the fork to her mouth and savored her first mouthful, decadent and delicious. Then she looked at her mother and Dr. O/B, alternating her gaze between the two. At this point, conversation was non-existent.

I'm being rude, Cassie thought. I invited him in; so I've got to make the best of a very awkward situation. "What did you and Ambassador Gibran discuss?" She asked, wanting to add, that could not have waited until Monday, but she held back.

"Well," he began, loosening the top button of his shirt and taking off his jacket, making himself more comfortable than Cassie felt, "He knows why Samir left the dorm that night, and why he's left the dorm every night. But you know that too, right?" Cassie nodded, pouring tea into his cup. She was implying she knew about Rachel. That was enough. She was not obligated to mention 'wife.' "Samir told his uncle he would accept Chelsea's consequences, including expulsion."

Cassie's eyes widened. Even though she knew Samir had agreed to this, how would he handle such a punishment? He had a wife, a wife who lived here. How could he see her if he were expelled? And see her, he would. If Cassie knew anything about Samir, he would be on this campus one way or another to see Rachel. Or, she would find a way to get off. "What have you and the Board decided to do?" She asked, trying to mask her concern as she casually pushed the sugar bowl and creamer in his direction, remembering too late he did not take cream.

"No student has ever done this before, on a continual basis, that is. A few have had clandestine rendezvous to commit some prank or break a rule, but no other student has ever been able to sneak out consistently without anyone even knowing he was gone. Actually it was quite ingenious. It took a lot of sleuthing to find the weak points here, like finding the weak points of a castle before you plan your attack. But find them he did, and he used them wisely. The fact that he talked to no one, ever, helped, because it made him invisible; so no one even missed him when he was gone."

Cassie became pensive at Vaughn's description. Invisible. She remembered Samir describing himself and his people as invisible when he was talking about the thousands of people the UN's peace-keeping force had killed, supposedly to establish peace. 'Ethics, morality, humanity do not exist for us,' he had said. 'To the world, we are superfluous, invisible, a non-people to be exterminated when your government or Israel deems it.' So he had used his invisibility to leave the building without being missed.

"He had once told me that about his people, Lebanese and Palestinians alike," Cassie began. "Our press, our Congress, our society treats them as though they're a non-people, invisible, so to speak, which makes it easy to bomb them, civilians, women and children alike. In this case, he used this invisibility to his advantage."

Vaughn nodded, added sugar to his tea, and remembered how prejudiced he himself had been at Homecoming, never giving a second thought to Parker and Mason beating Samir until Cassie forced him to reverse the situation. "Apparently, he did. But, to the point, he has five months until graduation. His actions didn't *intentionally* hurt anyone – and I'm stressing 'intentionally,' because unintentionally, they did hurt you, and could have hurt many more, my own son included."

"Dr. O/B," she thought perhaps it was good he had stopped by, although she'd never say that, because now she could thank him properly for his heroic efforts in saving her life, something she had yet to do, "I've been remiss in not seeking you out to thank you personally for what you did for me that evening. A thank-you note is insufficient for saving a person's life. My decision to follow Samir was foolhardy, and your actions were commendable. No, they were brave . . . no, actually they were heroic." Her eyes glazed with tears and she turned away.

She did not want him to see tears. It was bad enough he had sat on the floor with her in his monstrous pantry, in his monstrous kitchen on Thanksgiving Day when she sobbed uncontrollably at the memory of a butcher knife at her mother's throat, but for him to see her in tears again would have been too embarrassing, because the feelings she felt were not fear and agony from a horrific childhood memory, they were emotions of gratitude and appreciation for something he had done for her personally.

Something dangerous and life-threatening to save her life. What's happening here, she thought. Why can't I sort out my emotions?

"Mom, you okay?" Thank God Stevie was sitting here, a buffer between her emotions and the inexplicable reason for them.

With a thin smile, Cassie nodded. "Yes, Honey, I am." She glanced at Vaughn who was staring at her with his own emotions.

Then he cleared his throat. "He's staying," Vaughn announced. "Samir is staying. No expulsion. Early curfew and early confinement to his room after curfew. Jeremy will check on him every hour after 7:00 pm until lights out. The Board will allow him to stay under those conditions, and Samir promises to comply. His uncle suggested he rent him an apartment or a condo off Chelsea's grounds, but that would add time to his day. As long as he doesn't break his word, everything will be fine."

"He won't break his word, Dr. O/B. That he won't do."

"You say that with such certainty. How can you be so sure?"

"I know Samir enough to know he would never break his word." Cassie knew Samir's word was inviolate, once given. She also knew he would do nothing to jeopardize his ability to be with his wife.

So, Stevie, how's the cake?" Vaughn changed the subject after glancing at Stevie's plate, a good reprieve. A bite and several crumbs remained. Stevie's fork finished off the last bite, and the tines mashed into the last crumbs, taking them directly into her mouth.

"The cake's amazing, Dr. O/B. How's the popcorn?"

"Just as amazing."

They both laughed. Stevie took her plate to the sink and retreated to the living room to watch the rest of "Full House" and finish her math, leaving her mother and Vaughn to face each other without any protective buffers. "I finished *History of the Arabs*. Very informative. My next goal is to find articles or books about the injustices perpetrated by the European powers after World War 1. What you said about the past being the cause of today's problems makes sense."

"Yeah," Cassie stated informally. The past makes the present understandable. If you want documentation about trust and promises broken, read the McMahon-Hussein correspondence, between 1915-1916, ten letters. McMahon accepted the regions Hussein stipulated, which included Palestine, if the Arabs fought the Ottoman Empire for the Allies, which they did. That was the T.H. Laurence era. The Arab leaders committed; they succeeded, and, behind their backs, Balfour issues his "Declaration" and the Brits and France secretly carve up the Middle East. That's the Sykes-Picot Agreement. Complete betrayal, just like Hamlet's uncle, just like Brutus, just like Iago."

"Any other Shakespearean character you want to throw in there?" Vaughn smiled.

"There's always Macbeth, and his 'lady,'" Cassie added humorously.

"Okay, I will read the McMahon-Hussein correspondence."

"It's short, and if you've got extra time on your hands," she added teasingly, "you might want to read a synopsis of the King-Crane Commission report, which occurred in the summer of 1919. Woodrow Wilson commissioned Henry King and Charles Crane – one was from Chicago; I can't remember where the other was from," she paused, trying to recapture some vital point that had eluded her. "Maybe Michigan."

"You mean you may have forgotten something about this topic?" Vaughn asked with good-natured sarcasm.

"Stop mocking me," Cassie retorted; then smiled realizing there was a playful expression in his eyes. "Anyway," she stated adamantly, refusing to be dissuaded, "King and Crane are sent to areas throughout the Middle East where they spend the summer of 1919 interviewing economic, social and political groups, and religious groups in the region to get a feel from the Arab side, rather than the West, which was determining the outcome of all these peaceful people who wanted self-determination and freedom from Turkish rule. Their interviews included Christians, Jews, Muslims, Druses, a total of almost four hundred fifty various groups. They concluded that, although sympathetic to Zionism, there should not be Jewish state. Arab sentiment was that, if there had to be a mandate, they wanted a U.S. mandate, not British or French, because they believed they could trust the United States. Some trust. Anyway, the report was ignored."

"I'll do my best to read as much as I can. Cassie, you're a real taskmaster."

"No harder on my students than I am on myself."

"So I am your student?" Cassie's face turned beet red. "I didn't mean that changes our positions, but I could easily learn a lot from you about this topic." He paused. "By the way, who were you, are you, expecting?" He motioned towards the fourth place setting isolated at the end of the table.

Cassie poured herself more tea and topped off Vaughn's cup. "Walter. Walter is, *was* coming over to change my bandages." She held up her fingers and tried to wiggle them unsuccessfully. "And to help us finish putting up the tree. But," she added glancing at her watch, "he's late, very late. Hope he's okay."

"I could help with those bandages," Vaughn offered.

"Oh my God, Dr. O/B, no. I would not be comfortable with that, at all."

"Why? I can change a bandage."

Cassie shook her head emphatically. "No, absolutely not."

"Then let me help with the tree?" He asked as the phone rang. Cassie just about leaped for it, taking it into the dining room. "Hi . . . What? How? Will you be okay?" Then a hearty laugh. "Can you come by later . . . All right, if it's not too late. Otherwise, tomorrow? Sounds good." Cassie returned the phone to its cradle.

"What's happened?"

"Walter cut his thumb, badly. He was slicing an apple and the knife slipped. He's at Princeton Medical and it's busy. He's next. He said if he could stitch it himself, he would, but he's not that ambidextrous." She smiled at that. "He also said we'd have matching bandages, only difference is his would be on his left hand and my bandages are on my right. He has a good sense of humor." She smiled broadly. "He makes me laugh."

And I don't, Vaughn thought to himself, angry that he could not voice it. He was the dean, her employer. He'd always be playing it on the edge. He changed the topic, completely. "You think Samir's statements are justified?"

His questioned surprised her. "Justified? About what?"

"About being invisible; about being a non-people, to be exterminated whenever our government or Israel feels like it'?"

Cassie gave a cautious nod, thinking the question through carefully. Then she nodded emphatically. "Pretty much," she said with conviction. One last nod, "Yes, yes, I do."

He surprised her with a smile. "What?" She asked quizzically.

"You don't have many Jewish friends, I presume."

Now it was her turn to laugh. "As a matter of fact, I do, or I should use past tense. No Jews on my side of Paterson when I was growing up or going through high school, but I've had Jewish friends since college. Several actually agree with my views. They couldn't voice them though or they'd be labeled anti-Semitic like anyone else who opposes Israel's military actions, but, you're right, most did not agree. They did respect what they called my 'courage' to say what I believed. Too many people are intimidated by the anti-Semitic charge. They were amazed I didn't buy into it. They're good people, but I haven't seen them since . . ." she paused, "in a few years."

"So you argued?"

"We vehemently disagreed, but, wait, that's not why I haven't seen them in a few years," she said, thinking he was referring to the Palestinian issue. "I moved." She stopped abruptly. She had said more than she needed to say. The reason was none of his business, and she had no idea the football crew knew about Brian's death.

"Referring to the Palestinian/Israeli question, they didn't see the logic behind the data. Everything showing a negative picture of Israel, its invasions, occupation, killing children, demolishing homes, more and more settlements, taking the water, all those acts of inhumanity are omitted by the press, and what my friends did read they justified by saying it was Israel's right to defend itself. They never went into history far enough to know Israel had the first terrorist groups. Maybe it wouldn't have mattered if they did."

"Brainwashed?" Vaughn asked. Cassie nodded. "Like me?" Vaughn added. She nodded again.

"If your primary source of information has a pro-Israel bias, you're only going to get filtered news and biased journalism. If major donors to political campaigns are generously supported by AIPAC, which lobbies for Israel, Israel will get away with things other countries can't. And we'll excuse it using some euphemism, like Israel is our special friend. You'll even get government committees doing some fast stepping around a blatant act of war committed by Israel that another country would be held accountable for."

"Act of war?" Vaughn asked somewhat defiantly. "What are you talking about? Most of what you say makes sense, and when I research it, I find you're correct, but this charge sounds preposterous."

"Then research this too."

"Like what? What act of war are you talking about?"

"The USS Liberty. Our ship, flying the American flag, clearly marked, attacked by Israel's jet fighters and torpedo boats, jamming the Liberty's calls for help and strafing our sailors while they were swimming for their lives. A blatant, cold blooded attack, covered up. American fighter planes, launched from our aircraft carriers several hundred miles away, were recalled for no logical reason other than to prevent President Johnson from having to confront our friend. Thirty-four American servicemen killed and over seventy wounded, because Israel claimed it mistook the Liberty for an Egyptian vessel, while the American flag was flying and the Liberty was in international waters. *That's* our government for the sake of our friend."

"You really get heated over this issue." The words were out before Vaughn remembered why Cassie was a widow. He turned away without another word.

"Wouldn't you? What if it were your son, your spouse, your relative? Too many people never question our own government or what it does, even though challenging government is the very principle on which this country was founded. This lets the government get away with any explanation it wants. Anyone who challenges its findings is labeled crazy or a 'conspiracy theorist.' So we have to believe the Liberty attack was just a mistake and dozens of sailors being strafed was just a mistake and our fighter pilots being recalled was just a mistake and thirty-four dead was just a mistake. What else is our government going to do or tell us about something it determines, or wants us to believe, is just a mistake?"

Vaughn pondered her concepts. "Even if what you say about the USS Liberty is true, and I will research that myself, it's hard to believe our government would lie about it not to offend Israel. Why would we have to? America is the strongest nation in the world."

"It appears the Biblical prophecy about Greater Israel is stronger; that's the goal of Zionism. They're not going to stop until they have it, and they're not going to let us get in the way."

"You're really serious, aren't you?"

"She's very serious, Dr. O/B," Stevie shouted in from the living room over the elevated sound of a commercial. "I've heard her argue down four antagonists and not give an inch."

"So how's "Full House?" Cassie called from the kitchen.

"Over in five minutes. "Dallas" is coming on. Wanna watch?"

"No thanks, Honey. I'm doing my own Ewing war here with Dr. O/B."

Vaughn chuckled. He could just imagine how alluring Cassie would be if he weren't the dean and she weren't his employee. But that was a fantasy. "Show me," he said emphatically.

She shrugged her shoulders, gesticulating with her palms. "Show you what?"

"Show me something that supports this Greater Israel is intent on taking over the entire region."

"Well, I can't show you the Balfour Agreement which was written by a Rothschild . . ."

"I've read it; it's what, sixty words." Vaughn stated flatly, surprising Cassie. "Show me something else."

She hesitated for a second; then she picked up the cake server, carefully removed the dollops of fresh whipped cream studded with dark cherries, placing them carefully on a clean plate, transferred the last one to her fork, plopped it in her mouth, and smoothed the top of the cake. Studying its perimeter, she began drawing imaginary cuts on its surface, talking as she worked. "Okay, let's see, in 1920, some committee of the League of Nations, I can't remember its name, reports there were about seven hundred thousand Palestinians in Palestine and approximately seventy-five thousand Jews. That's close to a 10:1 ratio, not exactly, but for expediency, 10:1 will do. So let's go with these figures, because that's about when the British mandate was going into effect."

She hummed as she cut into the top of the cake, then she pushed it towards Vaughn. "Here, see this? Aside from the wedge Stevie had devoured, Cassie had made nine cuts in the remaining cake to show ten sections, as equal as the eye could proportion them. Stevie's missing piece was the eleventh portion and she pointed to it. This represents the number of Jews in Palestine in proportion to the Palestinian population in 1920." She glanced up at him. "Small," she stated, "in relation to the rest of the cake, which is all Palestinian, don't you think?

Vaughn nodded. "Yes . . . definitely, without question."

"Okay, that's 1920. Let's go to 1931. In 1931, the total population of Palestine was approximately one million, a little more, but I'll round down. Of that the Jewish population was approximately one hundred seventy-five thousand. I've rounded up. That's a ratio of 6:1." She smeared the frosting and marked off six slices to one. The number of settlers is larger than it was ten years prior, but there's still an obvious difference, favoring Palestinians, yes?"

Vaughn nodded again.

"Now, let's forward to 1948. A UN study shows the population in Palestine had increased to approximately one million nine hundred thousand. About 68% of that number were Arabs, 32% were Jews. Lots of settlers coming in and taking Palestinian land; lots of Israeli raids and attacks driving the Palestinians out. So now, that's about a 2:1 ratio, or close.

"Which means," Cassie explained as she smeared the frosting again and repartitioned its top, "if the UN were dividing Palestinian land to fit the population in 1948, a state for Palestine should have been approximately 66% of the original Palestinian land, with 33% to Israel."

Cassie's completed sections now showed a cake divided into three sections, depicting a 2:1 ratio. "Of course the Arabs would have a gripe, since they were promised Palestine in total and then promised their lands according to the population almost thirty years ago when the Palestinians had ten out of eleven wedges of this cake. "What do you think, Dr. O/B? Does my art work show the confiscation of Palestinian lands somewhat adequately?"

"If your data is correct, your model shows it more than adequately." He paused, smiled and added, "but I'll research it myself."

"I sure hope so. Okay, here's the biggest slap of all, and remember, all this is from a 10:1 ratio in 1920." Vaughn nods okay. "The UN recognizes the state of Israel in 1948, same year as this UN study, but the final result is that the Arabs don't get two-thirds of the land as the population shows; they get this much. She smears the frosting again. This time the results show an almost 50-50 split, one side being slightly larger.

Vaughn looked, with some consternation. "What, the Palestinians get a little more than 50%?" His question showed his surprise.

"An obvious error on your part, but no, Dr, O/B, the Palestinians did *not* get a little more than 50% of the land. They got *this* side." Cassie points to the smaller side. "About 43% of their original land. Israel got the rest." Vaughn's surprise was obvious. "Now," Cassie continued, "how would *you* feel if somebody took over *your* estate, and in all the squabbling and fighting that ensued, the court awarded you with 43% and gave the rest to the intruders? Think *you'd* be angry . . . or worse?"

He didn't have to answer. His facial response and his silence were clear. He let Cassie continue; she was visibly upset. "One month after the massacre of Deir Yassin, which drove out hundreds of thousands of Palestinians, David Ben-Gurion, then head of the Jewish Agency, and Israel's first prime minister, declared the establishment of a Jewish state in Eretz-Israel to be the state of Israel. All the Palestinian land taken by military aggression and all the lands they left when they fled for their lives after the massacre, were confiscated and settled; no right of return. All this is against the Geneva Convention.

"But the thing you never hear is that this takeover was intentional. About ten years before Deir Yassin, Ben-Gurion said, 'We must expel Arabs and take their places.' Those were his exact words, Dr. O/B. The irony is that their conquest was acceptable to the UN and it was acceptable to the

U.S.; but when the Palestinians organized and *counter*-attacked to get their land and their homes back, suddenly that was not acceptable, and they were labeled terrorists. Our media tells us *nothing* about what they've lost, but it does a great job condemning them for fighting to get it back."

She looked at him with sorrow. He could see it in her eyes; he could see it on her face; and he could almost feel it in her soul. Her spirit, along with her countenance, drooped. She was living inside herself, back to the destruction she had lived, the horror in the Middle East that had destroyed so many lives, including her own.

"I should go," Vaughn announced softly, letting her retreat into nostalgia undisturbed.

"Here, take the rest of your cake. I will not let Stevie eat any more; she's too young to 'drink.'" Cassie smiled as she said that. "Besides, Parker and Mason, and Connor and Matt could finish this in one sitting."

Vaughn stood up slowly, yanked his jacket off the back of his chair and started for the door while Cassie transferred the dollops of whipped cream onto the top of the cake. Then she boxed it and tied the string to secure it. "Not even one more piece?" Stevie importuned, coming into the kitchen as her mother was tying the knot.

"Not even one more, tiny, tiny piece. Wait, Dr. O/B; don't leave without your cake." Cassie did a quick scuffle and handed the box to Vaughn who lingered at the door. As he opened it, Cassie thanked him for bringing it. "You've made Stevie's evening just about perfect." Her own words sounded strange.

"Good. I'm glad." He took the box. "But what about you? Did I make your evening just about perfect?"

Cassie was stunned; she paused a few seconds, not knowing what to say, how to respond.

"Well, then how about making *my* evening just about perfect by calling me by my first name."

Had she been holding the cake, she would have dropped it. Was she hearing him right? Did he just ask her to call him by his first name, and that would make *his* evening perfect? This had become scary. "No," she replied, shaking her head decisively, "I could never do that."

"Why not? Everybody else in the football crew does."

"Because, Dr. O/B . . . because I wouldn't feel comfortable and, well, because we're not friends." She gulped down her words.

He stared at her with a mischievous grin, this ultra wealthy man who believed he could get anything he wanted. "No, we're not," he flashed his charming smile, "but we *could* be," he stated conclusively, and he walked into the night, leaving Cassie dazed.

She shut the door, leaning against it for support. She had known him for what, less than two months, as her employer. Maybe the football crew called him by his first name, but there was no way she could do that. And even if he had known them for decades, had he ever stopped by their homes unannounced, on a Friday evening, to bring them a cake? What was going on here? Here he was, this same man who had saved her life, asking her to call him Vaughn. How old do you have to be to stop being confused?

She glanced at her watch, 9:20. It's not too late to call Walter. Maybe he'll be home.

45

WALTER REACTS

One of the stupidest things you have ever done. Walter berated himself for the hundredth time as he pulled into the garage. A white bandage covered half his left hand. He could have been helping Cassie put up her tree if he hadn't peeled that apple wedge with wet hands. Did you not realize your hand could slip, you with your psychiatry degree and a medical degree on the side? And you couldn't figure this out? He castigated himself with venom.

The knife had slashed through the underside of his thumb directly above the lower joint. Blood had gushed from the wound instantly, splattering the sink bright red, droplets running in rivulets down the drain. Pressure didn't help. Paper towels didn't help. Blood seeped through every one he applied. Without a doubt, this cut needed stitches, and stitches he could not do himself.

He had cursed himself all the way to the hospital, realizing he had ruined the potential for a great evening with Cassie. Just to change her bandages and help with the tree would have been enough, if that was all she was ready for. Wary himself, he hadn't been ready to ask her out on a formal date, preferring to take it slow. But this cut had ruined even that. Hopefully, it would be a temporary setback.

The phone was ringing when he got out of his car. How many rings? The fifth would go to his answering machine. He hurried through the garage to answer it as, "Hi, you have reached Walter Goodman," played. Just in time.

She was confused. When she explained Vaughn's visit, he understood why. "I'm coming over," he said, after she got to Vaughn's, "Call me by my first name." Walter could have kicked himself. Maybe if he had asked her out on a formal date, word would have gotten around and it would have given Cassie a shield that Vaughn would not have trespassed.

"Now? Doesn't your thumb hurt?"

"Sure it hurts, but it'll hurt whether I'm here or there, and I'd much prefer there."

Cassie's okay confirmed it was a good decision. He grabbed his coat and keys, backing his car out in less than a minute. He could make it in thirty if he made the lights. His thumb would hurt no matter where he was, and he wanted it to be there, not only for himself, but for Cassie. After the confusion he had heard in her voice, it would be better if she talked it out. What a stupid stunt Vaughn had pulled.

Without realizing it, he was driving faster than usual. Every time he thought of Vaughn's behavior his foot pressed the gas pedal harder, until he finally got a grip and slowed down to a few miles above the speed limit. The Vaughn Walter knew and had known for almost two decades was a man who had evolved from a wealthy effete young man in his early twenties, who hated the corporate life bequeathed to him by his father, to the dean of Chelsea, one of the top ranking private academies in the country, where he could subsume his inability to manage global corporations beneath the simplicity of administrating one prestigious academy. Quite a difference, and a difference where he could find success easily.

When Walter first met Vaughn, it was common knowledge he, unlike Brett, had not been especially attractive to women. The only females interested in him had looked at his family's power and money, nothing more. Young women of the same financial stature wanted to maintain the same affluent life-style they had with daddy, but not with Vaughn. Taylor had noticed that weak spot, his multi-millions, and had honed in.

She was easy to read, except for Vaughn who had convinced himself Taylor desired him for himself. Everyone saw her intentions, even Mildred, matriarch of the family. To protect the family fortune, she had insisted on a fine-tuned pre-nuptial contract which Taylor's sexiest pout could not deter. Taylor or no Taylor, Mildred would not let her younger son, such an effete man, risk their fortune for his need to believe he was desired. Taylor would marry him for much less.

Walter smirked but chastised himself for that. Trained not to be judgmental or denigrating, it was difficult for him to hold back innate human responses towards someone as feckless as Vaughn who was using his professional shield in order to toy with Cassie. Maybe he wasn't aware of it because he was so used to using power and money to obtain his goals, but he was. Power and money, tools of the O/B trade.

But Vaughn's money could never seduce Cassie. That was indisputable. She was too feisty, too idealistic, and too outspoken, but she might, subconsciously, be compromised by his power. She had the spunk to get in his face when his arrogance was downright disrespectful, but she was also a widow who had lost her husband tragically and was raising their daughter on her own. Cassie was sensible enough to know her priorities, and she knew Vaughn could destroy her life and Stevie's if he chose. That, Walter believed, was the underlying cause of her distress now.

Vaughn, you sick bastard. He fumed, and stepped on the gas. Hell with the speed limit. He pulled into Cassie's drive in twenty-three minutes.

46

FRIDAY AFTER VAUGHN LEAVES

Friday evening had not begun well but it had finished better than expected. Walter had arrived a little before 10:00, just after Stevie had finished her math and gone to bed. While Walter changed her bandages, they drank three cups of tea in quick succession and talked about getting-to-know-you things, like childhood, parents, siblings, marriage, kids. They talked a little about everything, except how Brian died, and then Cassie talked about Vaughn.

"It's not paranoia, Cassie, Vaughn has definitely overstepped his bounds. He's muddying boundaries. That's what's getting you confused. We, the football crew, we were all, well most of us, were at Chelsea before Vaughn accepted the dean's position; so it was easy for us to call him by his first name and even easier for him to let us. But your situation is different. You're a new arrival. You have no problem fitting in with the football crew because we're your peers, but to fit in with Vaughn that way, well, that's another matter, and no, you're not going to feel comfortable with that kind of approach." He paused. "Vaughn shouldn't be pushing himself into your life." It was obvious that you don't drop in unannounced carrying a Black Forest cake you know Stevie loves unless you've got an ulterior motive.

Talking helped, and by the time they had finished a fourth cup of tea, Cassie was her old self again, happy and delightful. She wiggled her fingers under the new bandages Walter convinced her she should wear a bit longer. Not a problem; she could wait. Together, they finished the lights on the bottom of the tree and adjusted the strands on the top rows. Between the two of them, they managed quite well. Where she couldn't do something with her right hand, he could, and conversely, when his left hand faltered, hers was there. Low-playing Christmas music and a glass of wine added just the right ambiance, and the tree glimmered with hundreds of lights, all done before midnight. "I'd like to save the decorations for tomorrow when Stevie can help put them on." She looked at him with a little apprehension. "Would you like to come over and help? We'd love to have you."

This time, Walter was not ambivalent. He accepted her invitation and jumped right back with an invitation for her and Stevie to spend Christmas at his house. He'd cook dinner. He marketed himself as a pretty good cook, and between the use of his right hand, Cassie's use of her left, and Stevie using both, he figured he could present a decent ham with sweet potatoes, green beans, mashed potatoes and a tossed salad.

At her no, his spirits drooped. "I want to be home Christmas morning when Stevie opens her gifts," she explained. "But maybe you'd like to spend Christmas with us?"

"The answer to that is, yes."

"We can still make that ham with sweet potatoes and everything else, and we can still do it by putting our hands together." She laughed, holding up her left hand and pointing to his right. He loved her humor. "I'll make cream puffs for dessert," she added. Stevie can whip the batter and add in the eggs, one at a time. I'll do the filling."

Cassie had never seen Walter smile like that. "Sounds great, Cassie. I'd really like that. And I'll bring the wine."

"Not too much," she laughed, "or we won't be eating dinner. I get a bit tipsy on more than one glass."

"Fair enough," he said.

"How's 1:00 o'clock?"

"One is fine."

He left, feeling euphoric and wondered if Cassie felt, in any way, the way he was feeling about her. It was a feeling he had not felt in many, many years.

47

DEC 14, THE LADIES PRESENT OPHELIA

By Monday morning, while she was getting ready for work and swaying to "I'm Gonna' Miss You Girl," Cassie was more ebullient than she had been in years. Spending most of Saturday with Walter had been wonderful. The three of them had decorated the tree and had laughed almost the entire time. Then they took a break and made pasta with meat balls and sausage for an early dinner. Stevie had tied her Mom's Christmas apron around her and was supervising the meal as though she were head chef. It hung below her knees and Stevie anticipated the day she'd grow into it.

Dinner, with a tossed salad, garlic bread, and a chunk of sharp provolone cheese on the side, was delicious. A little cleanup and they were back working on the tree. Cassie was selecting each ornament with care and pride, and when a loving memory was attached, Cassie indulged in a nostalgic narrative. Everything she related gave

Walter deeper insight to her past and he felt rejuvenated just listening to her. Moments that resurrected memories of Brian, she handled delicately, and Walter was patient and sensitive enough to know he could never, would never, and should never encroach on those. But she was sharing her life with him, so was Stevie, and he could not have been happier. Tree finished, they wove garland and lights around the banister and tacked it over doorways. Walter couldn't remember a time since his divorce when he had felt so contented and alive. Cassie could have said nothing and he would have felt the same.

Later in the evening, Cassie put out cheese and crackers, hummus and pita, olives and baba ganoush, one of Stevie's favorites. "It's eggplant, roasted or baked, then mashed with lots of the seeds removed and mixed with tahini, that's sesame seed paste, and minced garlic - Mom always uses fresh. You can add a touch of lemon, if you want." Cassie laughed. Stevie seemed to know something about everything. "Then you drizzle olive oil over it." Stevie glanced at her mom. "Did I leave anything out?"

"No, Stevie, you got it all just fine. Maybe you can make it by yourself next time; you just about did this time."

"I've never tasted anything so delicious," Walter interjected. "Why don't you make it for Christmas, Stevie?"

"Yes! Mom, can I make it for Christmas, all by myself? "

"As long as I supervise the blender." A nod from Stevie and it was settled.

And here it was Monday, Cassie still savoring feelings from the weekend as she walked into period one. When she entered, the lights were off, the tree was aglow, and her four young ladies were frenetically doing last minute preparations before their presentation began, getting prompt cards in order and fluffing up Rachel's costume that replicated royal garb from Elizabethan England. The 'boys,' Gloria, Emelia, and Elizabeth, were costumed in men's hose, slip-on soft leather shoes, mantles, and caps.

Cassie paused at this somewhat hectic scene before her. Reminiscing about the weekend had caught her off guard. Lesson plans aside, which were always meticulously done, Cassie had almost forgotten this was the last week of classes before Christmas break and the week for class presentations. She only had to bring oral presentation matrices and these were in her attaché.

The ladies had chosen to present first, and everything taking place before her was the prelude to it. Gloria, in her male garb replicating the Elizabethan period, with Emelia and Gloria similarly dressed, was tightening the laces on the stiff corset Rachel was wearing. Cassie was a bit stunned; she had never expected them to dress for the part, but here they were, in period costumes or as close to it as possible. Perhaps they had gotten these outfits from the backstage rack of some semi-professional acting company, maybe from an old trunk given to an antique store or, very possibly, from an authentic Broadway wardrobe. People in this area were well acquainted with very influential people.

Since women were not allowed on the Elizabethan stage, boys played the parts of women. Tight-laced garments like Rachel's could never have been intended for a female's curves during that era. With Rachel, who had been gifted with voluptuous curves, these tight laces could never hide her full figure, no matter how hard Gloria tugged. Cassie glanced at Samir, who was trying to contain a smile of admiration for his new bride.

The ladies were presenting Ophelia's character from the 20th century female's perspective. Intriguing. They would be turning Elizabethan gender roles upside down, too, because, while boys played female roles in Shakespeare's day, the ladies were playing male roles here. All this was published in the playbills Elizabeth was passing out, listed under cast of characters. Gloria was playing two parts, Hamlet and the king; Elizabeth was playing Polonius, Emelia was Laertes, and Rachel, Ophelia. It was time for Cassie to remove herself from the action and become a spectator; time to get to the pit and become a commoner in the Elizabethan Age. Let the ladies do their thing. She dragged her chair to the far corner of the classroom to make herself as inconspicuous as possible.

While waiting for the drama to unfold, Cassie admired the detail in the playbill. Title and intricate art work of the Globe were on the front, prologue and acknowledgements were on the second page, cast of characters on the third, and advertisements on the last. Unbelievable, Cassie thought, they even solicited ads from the community. How creative. The ladies had gotten discount coupons from Bagels and Bakery, one free bagel, their choice of spread, with the purchase of a dozen; Manicures for Men offered a half-price manicure; Scarbello's donated a 50% coupon for any meal on the weeknight dinner menu; 50% off one hot dog with everything on it from Pat's luncheonette, and Lina's book store offered a 30% discount coupon on any purchase over ten dollars. Cassie was impressed before the performance had begun.

The prologue on page 2, above acknowledgments, explained that scenes being performed focused on Ophelia and were rewritten from her perspective, unencumbered with Shakespeare's omniscience, and removed from Polonius,' Claudius,' and Hamlet's control. No manipulation by males for their agendas. The ladies intended to show what Ophelia would have been like as a young girl with thoughts and emotions of her own. Let's hear from her, was their mantra.

Seven young men seated around the table and their teacher sitting in the back, Elizabeth, her hat covering her dark brown hair, presents the performance.

[Elizabeth enters stage and addresses
the audience]

"Ophelia's emotions were no different from emotions felt by lovers today. She falls in love with a young prince who promises love and trust, and she believes Hamlet when he says he loves her. Our presentation asks, if she had lived now, in the 20th century, would she still have believed him?"

Elizabeth searches for audience reaction, but the young men were reticent, maybe assuming Elizabeth's question was rhetorical. She continues.

"Ophelia's independent nature is apparent when she stands up to her brother, as the audience will see when our play commences. If she had the courage for that, we doubt she would have obeyed her father and stayed away from Hamlet once she realized her father was using her to ingratiate himself with Claudius."

[She pauses, puts her hand to her ear to
gesticulate she hears something.]

"But hark, brother and sister approach. I must depart."

[She exits. Laertes (Emelia) and
Ophelia (Rachel) enter.]

LAERTES (Emelia): Sister, you must guard yourself. Do
not trust Hamlet's words of love.

OPHELIA (Rachel): Prattle and tattle, to make me aware,
Whilst you seduce women into your lair.

LAERTES (Emelia): Sister be guarded, your virtue at
stake,
Chastity once taken, cannot be replaced.

OPHELIA (Rachel): Hamlet is honest, I feel it in my heart,
Give counsel to your own dalliance, once you depart.

OPHELIA [Aside]: "Am I such a fool as not to see my
brother's hypocrisy, he who philanders himself with every
female who intrigues him yet warns me against Hamlet to
preserve my own virtue and chastity?"

[Laertes (Emelia) exits.]

The guys are loving this. Cassie's attempts to suppress
her own laughter fail, and a brief giggle escapes her lips,

spiriting the young men onward. Jason looks over his shoulder, sees his English teacher's hands over her mouth and laughs openly.

[Enter Polonius (Elizabeth).]

POLONIUS (Elizabeth): What did Laertes say to you, my child?

OPHELIA (Rachel): He warns me away from Hamlet, who hath made overtures of love.

POLONIUS (Elizabeth): Heed his words my daughter, as you are innocent in these matters.

OPHELIA (Rachel): My brother advises me, dear father, to guard my honor and my virtue against Hamlet's advances, while he goes walking the primrose path of dalliance like a reckless libertine. Would he have women to bed were they to follow the advice he gives me?

Good point ladies! Cassie gives a silent, yes! Nothing like hypocrisy. How will the ladies develop Ophelia's character from this point now that they've given her the courage to stand up to her brother and her father. Will they still present her as a lovesick young woman who deteriorates into depression that drives her insane and leads her into waters that claim her life? Shakespeare gave Ophelia a questionable death, preventing her from the full rites of a Christian burial. Let's see what Rachel and the ladies do with this.

POLONIUS (Elizabeth): Hamlet's unholy suit flatters and fawns, beguiling is he, 'tis all, 'tis all,

So to Lord Hamlet, talk to him not; obey me, your father; my words take to heart.

OPHELIA (Rachel): Were we in the age of Shakespeare and such, I would fain, dearest father, obey you much,

But since the twenty-first century is nigh, I will not obey you, I cannot deny.

> [Ophelia (Rachel) and Polonius
> (Elizabeth) exit.]

Uproar! The guys are hooting and whistling, laughing, pounding the table. Mason, Parker, Matt, all slapping hands. Jason, Connor, Zach, shouting "Way to go, Ophelia!" Samir is beaming with pride. He knew his wife would steal the show, and Rachel has done just that, rewriting Shakespeare with a 20th century twist. None of them, Cassie ruminates, are ever gonna forget this class. A girl of the sixteenth century openly defying her father? Unfathomable. She could hardly wait for the next scene.

> [Emelia enters and narrates: "Ophelia
> (Rachel) enters, sits in her room sew-
> ing. Hamlet (Gloria) enters, his cloth-
> ing is disheveled. He takes Ophelia's
> wrist, stares, shakes his head, sighs and
> turns to leave."]

OPHELIA (Rachel): My Lord, you upset me, whatever is wrong,

For you to behave thusly, in manner and song.

HAMLET (Gloria): I trust you, Ophelia, my love for you burns,

But I must know my father's murderer, for that my heart yearns.

If I do behave the madman or fool, would you keep my secret, although it be cruel?

OPHELIA (Rachel): You promise your love and so I comply,

To keep your secret, to others, I will lie.

> [Ophelia (Rachel) and Hamlet (Gloria)
> exit. Emelia remains, holding another
> placard. A room in the castle.]

"So, wait." Zach interrupts. "In your version of the play, Ophelia knows Hamlet's insanity is only an act, but she agrees to keep his secret because she loves him?"

Emelia nods and begins her lines. "Ophelia plays along because she loves Hamlet and he has told her his insanity is only a pretense." That answered Zach's question. "Our action jumps to the scene in the castle where Hamlet and Ophelia talk after Polonius and Claudius have set her up. For brevity, we've omitted the scene where Ophelia tells her father Hamlet came to her room, when Polonius says it's love and they must tell the king and queen because love may be the cause of Hamlet's mad behavior."

Emelia's bright blue eyes are alive with excitement. "We pick up the action after Polonius has read the king and queen the letter Hamlet wrote Ophelia. Polonius tells the king he will let loose his daughter so they can spy on Hamlet and Ophelia while they talk. The setting is a room in the castle. The king tells Gertrude to leave. He and Polonius have sent for Hamlet so they can watch his behavior towards Ophelia. Polonius has told Ophelia to read a book.

[Emelia exits. Ophelia (Rachel) enters,
reading, walking a hallway. Hamlet
(Gloria) enters.]

"Wait again. Another question," Jason says, before Emelia exits. "If Ophelia knows Hamlet is just pretending to be crazy, how do you get her to go insane and drown?"

"You have to watch our play to its end to find out," Emelia smiles. Her eyes twinkle with mischief and she straightens her posture even more, if that were possible.

"And I can't wait to see it," Cassie responds from the back.

HAMLET (Gloria): To be or not to be . . .

OPHELIA (Rachel): Is that a question?

HAMLET (Gloria): Sweetest Ophelia, once I did love you,
But now to a nunnery, go to go to.

OPHELIA (Rachel), aside to Hamlet: I do not believe you; I know that you lie.

HAMLET (Gloria): I know they are watching, I know that they spy.
Play along with me, or my plans go awry.

[Hamlet (Gloria) and Ophelia (Rachel)
exit.]

[Elizabeth enters, holding a placard:
Hall in the castle. The play to catch
the king begins. "The king and queen
enter to watch the play which will rep-
licate the murder of Hamlet's father.
Watch and you shall see the actor pour
poison in the actor king's ear, the same
method used to kill Hamlet's father."]

[Hamlet (Gloria) and Ophelia (Rachel)
enter]

HAMLET (Gloria): Ophelia, I lie down at your feet, and watch my uncle as the play proceeds.

OPHELIA (Rachel): The actor pours poison in the sleep-er's ear;
Look the King rises; something is wrong, I fear.
I must leave, Hamlet; they tell us all to depart.

HAMLET (Gloria): I look for Horatio, much to impart.

[All exit. Elizabeth enters with a plot
summary.]

"Polonius tells Hamlet his mother summons him. Polonius goes to Gertrude's room and hides behind the arras. Thinking Hamlet is going to harm Gertrude, Polonius cries out. Hamlet thinks it's the king and stabs him.

"The plot hastens to its climax. Claudius sends Hamlet to England with Rosencrantz and Guildenstern who bear letters telling the King of England to kill Hamlet, but he overturns their plot and returns to Denmark.

"Meanwhile, Laertes has arrived home from France, enraged that his father is dead and his sister may be going crazy.

"He and Claudius plot to kill Hamlet when they hear he is still alive and in Denmark. Laertes will poison Hamlet's rapier. One scratch from it will kill him.

"Ophelia, who has been overcome with grief after her father's death, has been wandering the castle halls. When she overhears Laertes and Claudius plot to kill Hamlet, she runs to warn him."

"So then she goes insane and drowns?" Matt blurts out.

"You're so impatient, Matthew," Elizabeth chastises with a hint of flirtation.

"You can chastise me any time, Lizzie," Matt retorts, with hoots from the guys.

"Nope," Cassie interjects, laughing herself, "not in class."

"Com'on, Mrs. Komsky," Parker retorts, "you were young once . . . weren't you?"

Cassie sits there, pretending to be annoyed, drumming her fingers against her leg. "It's hard to tell, isn't it, Parker? I mean with all the wrinkles and dry skin." With that retort, their laughter escalates. Her old personality is back; of that there is no doubt. Whatever is the matter with you? She wonders, but she knows. Despite Dr. O/B's disconcerting intrusions, she has regained a happiness she never believed she could ever recapture.

"Your interpretation and your craft are amazing, ladies. I love the poetry with the 16th century vernacular. Okay, gentlemen, focus on the presentation. Let's let the ladies finish."

[Enter Ophelia (Rachel)]

OPHELIA (Rachel): Oh that my heart were one more than one;
One for my father and one for my love.
For the words I have heard cleft my heart in two;
My brother and the king bring fears anew.
Hamlet, returned? To find him I must,
To warn him of poison, unholy and unjust,
To my father's house, I have been;
But to no avail,
Through the gardens, through the woods;
I go, not to fail.

[She exits. Then all reenter and bow to
tumultuous applause.]

"So she drowns," Zach asks, after the clapping and hooting have stopped, "but not accidentally because she's gone insane and becomes oblivious to her surroundings? Right?"

"She *was* oblivious to her surroundings, Zach," Mason answers, "and drowning *was* the end result, accidentally, but not because she goes insane. The cause of her oblivion was concern for Hamlet's safety. That's what caused her death."

"What do the ladies say?" Cassie asks. "Ophelia drowns one way or the other, but Shakespeare's cause is from complete loss of her mental faculties, while the ladies have her drowning from her devotion to the man she loves."

"And her dedication to save him," Rachel adds. She lost her life because she was dedicated to the man she loved. Even with her 20th century independence, she believed in Hamlet's love and never doubted it. Even when he said all those harsh things, she knew he was pretending." Did they notice Samir beaming with pride? Cassie glanced around. Maybe Parker, who had taken a sideward glance at Samir.

"That's pretty good plot development, Rachel," Jason acknowledges. I wouldn't have thought of that. You kept the same ending but changed the reason." He paused momentarily. "I like it. I like it a lot."

"I concur," Cassie says. In fact, I'd say it's outstanding plot development, and I would never have thought of it either. I am so impressed. What do you think, class? Could we offer their plot to an avant-garde theatre group?"

"And they'd jump on it," Mason stated emphatically. "They did a great job, Mrs. Komsky.   I'm glad Chelsea admitted girls."

That, followed by a roar of laughter, ended the class.

48

LAST DAY OF CLASS BEFORE CHRISTMAS PARTY

F riday, last day of classes before Christmas break. Her students were done. Everyone, in every class, had presented an outstanding oral report; either on his own, in pairs or in groups. The caliber was so outstanding, she would have put them head to head with any student from any university, Ivy Leagues included. The various approaches she had anticipated paled in comparison to the quality and creativity she had seen. As usual, she reflected on period one. Maybe it was Samir, maybe it was Parker. Who knows how and why a teacher focuses on one class or a few students more than others. But she did, and today was no exception.

The ladies' presentation this past Monday had been first rate, peerless. Presenting Ophelia from the 20th century perspective dramatically, writing their own 16th century dialogue adhering to 16th century character and in period costumes should have earned a high school

Tony award, if there were one. Sharp wit and poetry. Shakespeare would have been impressed.

Zach and Matt had followed. Their abstract had outlined specific weapons and the ultimate weapon. No indication, though, of what that one weapon would be. Cassie had assumed their presentation would have focused on actual historical weapons, and although it did in part, she was wrong.

They began with a brief reference to the threat of Norway invading Denmark which had been deflected by Norway's army marching off to reclaim a worthless strip of land in Poland. They touched on weaponry a bit, but the surprise was using Norway's invasion as the springboard to Sun-Tzu's philosophical treatise, *The Art of War*. Heck, she had never even heard of that book until Brian and his Marine training had introduced her to it. She couldn't pronounce the author's name at first without Brian correcting her.

Matt, Asian from his mother's side, was very proud of his heritage and had interwoven this contribution from his Chinese heritage into the West's, using *Hamlet* as the springboard. It was a perfect analogy. Zach had welcomed it and was impressed and inspired by what he had learned about Asian culture, Sun-Tzu's perspective of war and how perhaps his most famous credo, know your enemy, could be applied to all arenas of competition.

Jason and Connor presented next. They analyzed Hamlet's development from a psychological perspective, the study of Hamlet as a melancholy man, unable to, or not wanting to shed his mantle of gloom. Cassie thought they would have evoked Freud or one of his ilk, but the pair developed the premise that his melancholy became part of him after his father died and his mother remarried. Jason showed how melancholy affected his actions and reactions; Connor supported their statements from a 1910 booklet titled, "The tragedy of Hamlet, a psychological study."

"I've never seen that book, Connor," Cassie said, "Where'd you get it?"

"Princeton's library, interlibrary loan from the Library of Congress. Did you know there are three buildings in the Library of Congress, the Thomas Jefferson building, the James Madison Memorial building and the John Adams building? I learned a lot more than Hamlet from this research project." He glanced at Jason. "We both did." Jason nodded.

"Excellent job, both of you. That's what happens when you research; you look up one thing and it sort of mushrooms, and you spend the whole day digressing from your original point but lovin' every minute of it. I am very impressed." Cassie smiled and made a mental note to research that book herself. See if she could get it and read it in its entirety in her spare time, whenever that was. She was amazed at their in-depth hunt and the results it produced.

"Thank you, Mrs. Komsky. We really appreciate the compliment." Connor looked at Jason and both smiled. Her opinion meant a lot. They continued, supporting their premise from Hamlet's dialogue, placing the final emphasis on, "What a piece of work is man," Hamlet's discourse to Rosencrantz. 'but man delights me not,' Hamlet says, disillusioned with his parents and humanity."

An existential character struggling with the universal theme of feeling displaced in his world, Cassie thinks. Aren't we all, at times? Who of us, living and breathing and trying to make sense of life, could not relate to that?

Parker and Mason presented next and their theme was pretty gruesome - bloodshed and gore in *Hamlet*, emanating from Seneca, the Roman playwright, and his tragedy of blood. First they compared Seneca to the surgically clean Greek tragedy, in which no act of bloodshed was committed on stage. When Medea kills her children to avenge Jason, the bloody, horrible scene is reported by messenger. Seneca was different. His was blood and revenge in your face, as it was in *Hamlet*. Parker and Mason tore into that comparison with gusto and referenced *Gorboduc*, the first English tragedy, a chain of slaughter and revenge, then went to Kyd's, *The Spanish Tragedy*, blood, gore, murder, and ghosts, like *Hamlet*.

Their analysis was excellent and their analogy to modern times was right on. "Just Seneca? Just *Hamlet*?" They asked. If blood and gore were indigenous to past literature alone, why would we have horror movies today? Zach responded with "Friday the 13th" and "Nightmare on Elm Street." Rachel added "The Shining" and "American Werewolf in London." Emelia questioned how western culture could spawn a Jack the Ripper if we're all so civilized.

Obviously we aren't; obviously we have an evil side as well as a good side and it's just which side dominates and in which person. When Parker and Mason held up posters from a few horror films, Cassie balked, signaling a "T" for time-out. "Too graphic for me, gentlemen. I won't be able to sleep tonight." They put the posters down. The class agreed, especially the ladies. They concluded their research by reinforcing Hamlet's genteel nature amidst this tragedy of blood, his internal conflict between two clashing camps of morality, and how until the very end, it tore him apart.

Friday, last day of classes before Christmas break; Samir's presentation. His was last. He worked alone, even though the guys had invited him to join them. His theme might have fit, and he was certainly appreciative, but he wanted to, needed to, approach his topic in his own way. After his presentation, everyone realized what he had meant and why he had to present alone.

Like Zach and Matt, Samir began by referencing the twenty thousand Norwegian soldiers who had gone off to fight for a little strip of land in Poland that was completely insignificant to them. But they were ordered and so they marched, knowing they would die, die for honor. He compared it to the factions in Palestine and Lebanon who, knowing they are all branded fanatics and terrorists by the West, continue to fight for dignity and what they believe is right. Then he segued to the universal theme of good and evil, and hit the ball out of the park.

What does a good person do when he's presented with evil? How does he react? If he's a good person, does he even recognize evil when it's happening? Maybe not; at least not at first. And then what does a good person do when he finally realizes that believing in goodness or the people you've trusted and loved, have committed an evil act, or are evil themselves? Hamlet, a good person who trusted his uncle, must first believe this man murdered his father. Difficult enough in itself, because the only proof is his father's ghost. But he is forced to admit it after the players force his uncle's guilty reaction. Then he must accept him as the murderer. But even then, what does he do, this young man who doesn't have the stomach for murder?

But Samir goes beyond the evil individual, summoning evil in the aggregate, and he calls it up not from fiction, like *Lord of the Flies*, and not from his people in the Middle East, but from a consummate evil as indigenous to America as apple pie. Samir holds up a print-out of the title page of a little known, but vastly profound book, titled *A Century of Dishonor.*

"Never heard of it," whispered Parker, many heads turning to each other for validation. Cassie included.

"Sorry guys, I've never heard of that one either. Please Samir, go on."

This book, completely unfamiliar to both Cassie and the class, covered a subject no one references in history books, a subject Americans never question, never contemplate: the horrific treatment and utter destruction of the American Indians, complete and utter ethnic cleansing, committed by Expansionist Americans and our own government.

Samir gave an abstract of the book. Published in 1881 by a woman activist for Indian rights, the book, by Helen H. Jackson, written as a polemic, was an attempt to appeal to the hearts and conscience of the American people. It had minimal impact then, but she could never have imagined that a young man in the 20th century would apply her book and its theme of broken promises, lies and deceit perpetrated upon entire tribes of American Indians, people labeled subhuman, to the Israeli/Palestinian 'question' hundreds of years later.

Jackson had begun her book with a legal brief on the original Indian right of occupancy. Then she delineated how irresponsibility, dishonesty and broken treaties on the part of Americans and the U.S. government devastated the Delaware, Cheyenne, Nez Perce, Sioux, and more.

Samir's analogy took this position into the decades of lies, broken promises and treaties that worked against the Palestinians, beginning with the McMahon/Hussein correspondence, then Balfour, Sykes-Picot, the British Mandate, the recognition of Israel, and its continual decimation of the Palestinian people for land. He quoted line after line of horrific treatment of North American Indians in our government's insatiable quest for land, and equated it to more and more Palestinian land being confiscated and settled by Israel, with U.S. support, using justification or denial, while our government condemned other countries committing these same atrocities. "Is this not hypocrisy, to condemn in words but support the practice, letting ethnic cleansing creep onward like a silent fog?"

When Samir had finished, no one moved; no one spoke. Silence. Photos of atrocities and mountains of corpses that marked the American Indian extermination hung side by side with photos of Sabre and Shatila massacres, which hung side by side with mountains of corpses showing victims of the Armenian Genocide, which hung side by side next to victims of Auschwitz. All, side by side.

"Are we not all human?" Samir asked. "Without the labels, can you not see there is no difference in the dead?" He ripped the labels off each photo, shuffled their positions; there was no difference. Mountains of corpses all looked the same.

Sighs of sadness punctuated the silence. As the American Indians were non-people to Americans, as Armenians were non-people to the Ottomans, as Jews were non-people to the Nazis, so too were, and still are, the Palestinians, a non-people to Israel and America today.

"So we fight," Samir concluded, "and we die, but we die for dignity, for humanity, and for honor, like the twenty thousand Norwegian soldiers who marched to their death."

You could hear faint sounds of breathing; that was all. Samir's eyes held a thin veneer of tears, as did Rachel's, who looked at her husband with sadness, with love and pride. Cassie glanced around this silent room. She could detect a touch of moisture in everyone's eyes, not just the ladies. The young men too, had been overcome with emotion.

These young men and women were compassionate. They saw the world for its beauty, but they also saw the world in its evil shroud. They'd be taking the reins of this country in little more than a decade. Maybe they could make a change on the side of good. She said a silent prayer that they would.

And the young ladies making history now, each of them part of the very first class in Chelsea's almost two hundred years of existence. Surprisingly, or maybe not, these women had already taught her a few things about courage. Rachel. Look at her. Facing down some of her peers, her background, everything, because she trusted and loved Samir. These young women were role models for her and Stevie, not the other way around. She would never regret having been part of this, this beautiful 1987 class at Chelsea Academy. These kids, these kids she would take with her for the rest of her life.

49

SATURDAY MORNING, DECEMBER 19, STUDENTS LEAVE FOR CHRISTMAS BREAK

A school is a building, mortar, steel, wood and frame, shingles and insulation; it's all that and just that and nothing more, until you fill it with life, until you fill it with life and spirit, until you fill it with the breath of young life and young minds who jump through the hoops of life, uncontained, unrestrained, mischievous, curious, imaginative, breaking all bounds by questioning 'why' and 'why not.' Until you have that, it's just a building.

But ah, once you have it, you transcend limits of the adult world, its routine, its boredom, its jaded apathy and its paltry satisfaction of living for another "I want …" Once you have that, you can exist on fumes. Inhale. It surrounds you, infects you, and cleanses you. It's an epiphany; a rebirth. Makes you feel alive again at any age.

Thus, when Saturday morning dawned and the crackle of ice-crusted trees splattered on roofs and sidewalks from rising temperatures, Cassie dressed and hurried outdoors. There was electricity in the air. Kids were going home. Home for Christmas break. Two weeks of home. Home to decorate trees, Christmas shop, attend church services, sing Christmas carols, bake cookies and breads, cakes and desserts, turkeys and hams, and to every special family tradition. Home to collect for the needy; volunteer for charities; visit aging grandparents; to do all those things, and more. Even kids whose home-lives needed mending, they were going home.

Young girls in Cassie's house contributed to that electricity. You could feel it in the halls. It seeped out from cracks under the doors, wafted throughout the house and into her home. Almost palpable; it was everywhere. It was in suitcases being packed or being slammed shut; it was in loud squeals of taking this or leaving that or, My suitcase won't close or, My shampoo bottle broke.

"Home" permeated the hallways, crept through Cassie's outer office, around corners and behind doors. Everyone was going home. Cassie felt like a kid. She had never stopped feeling like a kid at Christmas time until Brian had been killed. Now it was back. She hugged herself, letting the crystal morning wash over her, then she ran inside, up the stairs to Stevie's room where Stevie was holding on tenaciously to last minutes of sleep, jumped in her bed and gave her a great, big mom/daughter hug.

Stevie admitted defeat and snuggled into her mom's arms. They held on to each other long and hard as though each knew an inner peace had worked its way into their hearts and into their lives. The sounds of life sung their sweet song outside Stevie's window, finally prompting them to get up. From there, they could see the lines of cars queuing up to transport their daughters home. Down the road, cars were doing the same in front of the senior boys' dorm, and this same scene was being enacted in front of every house. Parents were hoisting heavy luggage amidst groans and pseudo complaints like, Whatcha got in here, or, There must be rocks in this suitcase, carping as they lugged their kids' belongings, loving every second. Their kids were coming home.

From their second floor window, Cassie glimpsed a long, black stretch limo bearing flags of Lebanon and the UN, flanked by smaller limos, slowly wending their way through the winding drive to the senior boys dorm far down the drive. Samir's uncle himself, coming to take his nephew home. Of course he would not be lugging Samir's suitcases. Knowing Samir, he would most likely be lugging them himself. No pretense, no privilege expected because of his uncle's position, just Samir, full of love and compassion and hurt, slowly overcoming it. Maybe this break would be perfect for him and Rachel.

Suddenly Cassie felt a shudder. Samir and Rachel. How would they do this? How would they handle their marriage, going home to two separate homes? Problematic? Cassie shook it off. It'll work out; it has to.

"Stevie, hurry and get dressed. I want to say goodbye to some of the kids before they leave. Shower when we come back in."

"Gotta brush my teeth and hair. I'm not going anywhere looking like this, Mom."

"Okay, I'll be outside. But hurry or they'll all be gone." She glanced out the window. "Oh, Stacy just got into their car. Hurry before we miss Rebecca."

Cassie rushed outside. Parents and students were milling about in complete disarray, exactly the way it was supposed to be. Cassie remembered the last day of school before Christmas break when she was in high school, even in college. It was magical, like some fairy had descended upon the school and sprinkled pixie dust and jingle bells over its roof, inside the hallways and stairwells.

Decorated door contests, a Christmas tree in the main lobby, Christmas card boxes with repository slots, Secret Santas, a Christmas party, if your teacher still had a touch of childhood in her, or him, every kid eating Christmas cookies, then rushing home to the aroma of Christmas; it was all Christmas. She missed her mom so much during this time of year, so very much. Only as she got older did she realize how much her mother had sacrificed, and her aunt, trying as hard as she could to make a home for Cassie, an impish, recalcitrant and rebellious teenager, the perfect definition for those years.

"Mrs. Komsky! Mrs. Komsky!" In the distance, almost impossible to discern, Rachel, Gloria, Elizabeth and Emelia were shouting and waving to Cassie, the four of them, bound together tightly, curbside. Generic parents from across the way zoomed in on her and waved. Cassie waved back.

Senior boys were on her left, at the very end, closest to the campus entrance, even harder to recognize than the ladies. Samir stood at Ambassador Aboud's limo, which had parked at the curb, but he was facing Rachel's house. He placed his hand over his heart and offered his upturned palm towards her, assuming she could see him.

From the limo's interior, a tall man emerged. Samir glanced in Cassie's direction and his arm went up. Not a wave; he was too reserved for that, but half a wave, his arm bent at the elbow. Cassie nodded; his uncle turned and gave a slight bow, placed his fingers on his lips, then to his forehead, then gracefully outward, arm outstretched. Salem Alleikum. (*Peace be to you*), in a sign of respect. Cassie returned the bow, a symbol of honor.

Stevie was by her side after cars had filtered to a few stragglers. By now, all the freshmen girls in Cassie's house had gone; Stacy had left before Cassie had come out. Rebecca, one of the last stragglers, hugged Cassie goodbye on her way to her limo. Her driver had already loaded her bags; then they headed to Rachel's house. Millie Thompson was last to leave. No older siblings, she took her time bringing her suitcases downstairs. She gave Cassie a warm, goodbye hug. "Mrs. Komsky, I'm sorry Stevie couldn't stay with us tonight. We didn't realize the faculty party was the day Christmas break began."

"Neither did I, Millie, so please do not apologize; I should have realized it myself. Besides, we'll be fine. I spoke to the manager at King George's Seal; he has no problem with Stevie attending. She'll be with me, and the faculty I'm sitting with is happy she's coming. They're very pleased to have a little Komsky with them." Millie laughed, and Stevie gave her mom a big smile. "So don't concern yourself one bit. Have a wonderful Christmas, Millie."

"You too, Mrs. Komsky." The Thompson's driver collected Millie's bags and Millie ran to her parents, who hugged her and waved to Cassie. The last Sanders House resident had departed for Christmas. Cassie curled her arm around Stevie. "Dancing partners, right Hon?"

Stevie nodded. Yup, she'd get on the dance floor with her mom, and hopefully, someday she'd be as good a dancer. But at this age, for Stevie, now was all about shopping for the outfit she would wear. For Cassie, it was all about being with her daughter and Walter, who was reappearing in her thoughts more often. She realized she was looking forward to a lot lately, and that was good.

50

TO THE FACULTY CHRISTMAS PARTY

"Stevie!" Cassie shouted. "Stevie, are you ready? Dr. Goodman is here!" This was a first, Cassie thought, a nine-year-old takes longer to get ready for a party than her mother.

"Coming, Mom," Stevie hollered back and the sound of quick footsteps ran through the upstairs hallway and down the stairs. And there she was, a beauty, her honey blond hair in an intricate braid that began just above her forehead and spanned the length of her neck to several inches below her shoulders. Cassie had interwoven a thin thread of red lace studded with tiny cranberries, gold balls and green poinsettia leaves, beginning with a small cluster at the top of Stevie's forehead and going all the way down the braid, as tiny natural curls framed her face. Stunning. Her features were astoundingly beautiful, a mix of her mother's high cheekbones and exotic eyes, with a bolder, more defined chin. Definitely Brian. Tall for her age, without one ounce of fat, Stevie was gorgeous, and the black long-sleeved, heavily sequined lace cocktail dress with a hemline of crinoline ruffles that she wore accentuated a frame that would develop into a model's figure as she matured.

Cassie wore a black slinky wool and polyester blend sleeveless cocktail dress with multiple spaghetti-thin straps that created a V-look neckline. Its sweeping knee-length skirt flared slightly at the hemline and moved as gracefully as she did. Her golden shoulder-length hair was pulled back at the forehead and sides, slightly back-combed to create a little height, and curled where both sides met the center back. The back hung loose, curled into cascades. A single diamond choker set in white gold that Brian had given her on their first anniversary accentuated her neckline, diamond stud earrings and a touch of eyeliner, mascara, and a soft mauve lipstick were all she needed to look exquisite.

"Wow," Walter offered in admiration, "And I'm escorting both of you?!" He looked at Cassie and smiled. "How lucky can a man get?"

"Down, boy," Cassie chided, almost flirtatiously, "watch your manners."

Walter was ecstatic. "I will be the best behaved escort you have ever had."

Cassie laughed as Walter helped her on with her coat. If only he knew how very few of those there had ever been.

51

DECEMBER 19, FACULTY PARTY AT KING GEORGE'S SEAL

King George's lit up the evening skyline with the magical glow of Christmas. Most restaurants had transitioned from multicolored lights to white for a classy touch, but King George's had kept the 'Ho! Ho! Ho!' joviality of red, green and gold mini lights, which enveloped every tree, every bush, every column, gable, every everything as though the acres of grounds on which the restaurant were situated had been enveloped in a gossamer chrysalis dipped in three colors.

"Beautiful," Cassie commented as the car traversed the winding drive. Walter pulled under the portico for valet parking, and a doorman, dressed meticulously in a crisp tux, red carnation in his lapel, replaced him in the driver's seat and another doorman escorted the ladies out and opened the massive door to a grand foyer. A Christmas tree that could have rivaled the tree at Rockefeller Center dominated the expansive entranceway, its height almost touching the vaulted ceiling that reached to a second floor balcony. Set against a musical backdrop of Christmas carols, the scene was breathtaking. In addition to its height, the tree was symmetrically perfect and beautifully decorated with huge red, green, silver and gold glass Christmas balls, crystal angels playing harps or blowing bugles, reindeer in Christmas livery, hand blown glass elves and Santas holding naughty and nice lists, some sitting at workshop benches, others inspecting toys. A multitude of exquisite decorations on an exquisite tree, enhanced by the light scent of pine. She inhaled deeply. Who could not appreciate this?

First floor, Arcadian Room, Southern Mercer County District Schools and Chelsea Academy. "That's us," Walter confirmed and led the ladies forward.

"Other schools?" Cassie queried, as Walter ushered them through crowds of guests.

"Chelsea used to celebrate Christmas in a smaller restaurant a few miles from here, because we only had thirty-five, forty people max, not enough to command a room big enough for a dance floor and a DJ. About ten years ago, we were invited to partner with several local school districts. We went with it, and we have never been sorry. We reserve our own little enclave, but we also mingle with everyone else from the community. Believe me, this party will be great – food, music, dancing; you'll love it."

Like a champagne bottle being popped, effervescence greeted her as soon as she walked through the doorway. Food, umm, inhale the aroma . . . and music. The DJ was playing soft rock for now, but its tempo would increase soon. For centerpieces, a small Christmas tree sat at every table, decorated with miniature silver and gold balls. Garland draped from the chandeliers, like silver and gold moss hanging from willows on a southern plantation from long ago.

The room, immense, glistened. Women were adorned in sequined dresses, lots of reds and greens; men in crisp suits, some with festive vests; wait staff in tuxedoes, serving trays of colossal shrimp, lamb chops, scallops nestled in bacon, and what else could she not see that was passing by on filigreed silver trays, hungry hands stretching out to claim canapés of one kind or another, trying to slow the server down. Conversation hummed with excitement.

"We'd better find our table and become part of the feeding frenzy," Walter spoke close to her ear. "The cocktail hour is the best part for me."

Cassie shook her head emphatically, "me too." She glanced at Stevie. "For both of us, right kiddo?"

Stevie nodded.

"There. Over there." Walter pointed subtly. "Melissa and Tasha are waving us over. Jeremy's there too."

Cassie wove through pockets of people and glimpsed the football crew. They were all there. "Guess we're the last arrivals," she said.

"As the adage goes, 'Save the best for last.'"

"You are in rare form tonight, Dr. Goodman," Cassie emphasized.

"Hey, it's a party, and a great one at that! You ready to party? Stevie? You ready to have a lot of fun."

"Most assuredly, Dr. Goodman," Stevie stated, emphatically.

Most assuredly, Walter chuckled, controlled his laughter and led them forward.

52

TABLE TALK

Jeremy welcomed Cassie with open arms and a light kiss on her cheek. "Hi, Stevie. Happy to see you again."

"When's the next cook-off, Dr. Harper?" Stevie asked hopefully. "My culinary skills have improved tremendously in the last two weeks. I've made meatloaf with gravy, roast chicken, *and* my own spaghetti sauce, with Mom's supervision, of course." Her complete self assurance elicited laughter.

"After New Year's, Stevie," Jeremy smiled. "Way after New Year's. I'm going to need weeks of serious dieting after the holidays to work off the catastrophic results of gluttony.

"Make that several *months*, Jeremy," Walter shot back, nodding towards the full plate of lamb chops, beefsteak, and mounds of shrimp overflowing on Jeremy's plate.

Neither embarrassed nor shy about Walter's quip, Jeremy countered, "Two plates. That one's mine as well."

He pointed to a second plate, just as full, that Walter had mistaken for Joe's.

Joe pushed the second plate closer to Jeremy. "Just so there's no confusion," he quipped.

"Good one, Joe!" Ronnie joined in the repartee. The table had been jumping before the three had arrived, most of the group had already finished at least one glass of wine and were working on a second or third.

"Crescendo to fortissimo!" Joe shouted and raised his wine glass to toast.

"Let's *de*crescendo to pianissimo," Tasha Meyer, admonished, "before we get thrown out." She interjected. Tasha wore a sequined cherry red dress and looked divine.

"So," Joe turned to her mischievously, "calculus plays piano? I never knew that."

"Seven years," Tasha quipped back.

"Same here," Ronnie, Samir's previous advisor, added. Her graying hair was pulled back in a very stately top knot and studded with rhinestones, matching the collar of her black knit mock turtle dress.

"Anybody else?" Walter interjected and glanced at Cassie." Cassie's hand crept up with four fingers extended, bandages removed; Alicia Walsh, Walter's guidance partner, wearing a green sequined dress, held up eight. Stevie held up two.

"Impressive," Jeremy remarked, turning to Joe. "See Joe, talking music does not make you distinctive in this group."

Joe nodded. "I can see that." He looked at Jeremy and smiled, "but eating does do that for you." At this, the group broke into irreverent laughter. This was going to be some night. Forget the festivities; they would be creating enough fun at their own table.

As the cocktail hour grew to a close, the wait staff solicited each guest for their order, and the DJ pumped up the tempo. "Upside Down," Diana Ross," Cassie squealed, spontaneously moving in her chair to the "round and round" refrain.

"Hit the floor, Cassie," Tasha prodded. "Go ahead." Her hand gestured Cassie forward.

"Dance with me?"

"Hell, no. I'm not getting out on that dance floor." Tasha glanced at Stevie. "Oops! Sorry Stevie.

Stevie smiled. "That's okay, Mrs. Meyer, I hear that word a lot at home." Tasha laughed. "Go ahead, Mom. Dr. O/B isn't here." And that was all it took for the Chelsea football crew to explode, leaving other Chelsea tables staring at them curiously. Everyone in the football crew understood Stevie's reference. They'd have to make her an honorary member after this.

With that, Cassie leaped from her seat and grooved her way to the dance floor, solo. No one else had wanted to be the first on the floor, and after Cassie began to move, no one else wanted to dance in her shadow. She moved slowly, keeping to the edge of the floor so as not to be too noticeable, but how could anyone not notice that. Her black slinky dress accentuated her grace, but had she worn a housedress, nothing could have hidden her rhythm and her shape.

Her dancing caught the DJ's attention; he had no intention of letting her escape when the song ended. He segued to "Get Down On It," a Kool and the Gang hit.

Cassie could *not* sit down; she was in the groove, and she sure could move! The DJ had a captive.

Walter was captivated also. His eyes could look nowhere else; and he entered his own private zone. Tasha watched him with a smile; Melissa looked at Tasha, then at Walter, back at Tasha. Neither said anything. Stevie was with them. They'd talk later.

Salad was served, but Cassie was still soloing on the dance floor until Stevie waved her over. Good thing Stevie was here, Walter thought to himself, or Cassie would never have been at the table. Penne with vodka sauce followed. Stevie offered hers to her mom, who, more thirsty than hungry, declined. Both moved their plates towards Jeremy. "Never let good food go to waste. That's my motto." He accepted both plates gladly.

Conversation became energized when the group talked about Christmas plans. Melissa would be with her sister in Connecticut, Alicia's daughter was flying in from California, from a heat wave to chilling cold, ugh; Ronnie and Joe would be traveling to London and Vienna, respectively. Tasha would be with her daughter and young grandchild. And Jeremy? "I always go to my older brother's in North Carolina for Christmas, but this year, they're heading to Oregon. His daughter, my niece, has just had her first child. So, I am a great uncle!"

"Congratulations, Jeremy! That's wonderful. But," Cassie paused, "where will you be spending Christmas?"

"I might go into the City. Spend a few days taking in the sights, you know, a little of this, a little of that. I'll be fine."

"Absolutely not!" Cassie stated adamantly, making her decision instantly. "Not on Christmas." She shook her head. "You'll spend Christmas with us – me, Stevie and Walter."

"To hit something with strong or great force" is one of several definitions of "impact" from Mirriam-Webster's dictionary, and impact is exactly how this statement landed, with tremendous impact. The table went from loud and boisterous to absolute silence, intensified by ambient sounds of laughter that surrounded them. What they had heard was tantamount to water flowing upstream or life being discovered on some distant planet. Thankfully, the aroma of fillet mignon, mushroom gravy, broiled grouper and almond sauce with a touch of dill permeated the room.

"Dinner's served," Walter said quickly, relieved he could change the topic. He wasn't going to talk about his visit to Cassie's, his Christmas invitation to her, her counter-invitation to him, his feelings, maybe her feelings, he hoped there were some, and other personal stuff.

Ronnie came to his rescue. "I hear Samir has made substantial progress in class," she said casually, the subject and attention transferred from Walter to Samir.

But the question bothered Cassie. She would have preferred talking about Christmas. It had most likely emanated from sincere concern, since Ronnie had been Samir's adviser before she and Cassie had done a drop/add for Samir, but Cassie became guarded.

"He presented an outstanding oral report yesterday," she responded succinctly, steering any discussion away from personal stuff, and any hint of Rachel and Samir's relationship. The two of them as a couple were not something Chelsea Academy could fathom, since women weren't even on campus, in dorms or in classrooms until five months ago. A marriage between two students would blow the lid off Chelsea's decision to have admitted females, and all who had said it would distract the young men would have been crowing.

"That's wonderful," Ronnie replied, cutting into her grouper. "But none of us ever doubted his academic ability. His records clearly show that. I meant beyond that, with his peers."

"Ronnie, I don't talk about any conversations I have with him, no matter how brief, and they have been brief, but I will say there *is* a bit more communication between him and his peers now. In fact, all the males in his class invited him to join them for his presentation."

"Wonderful! Who'd he work with?"

She shook her head slightly. "He declined their offers."

"Declined? Why?"

"Because his perspective on the topic was different and he needed to present it in his own way."

Ronnie continued to push. "And in what way was that?" She asked.

"It's a Christmas party, Ronnie, so briefly, very briefly, he used the Norwegian soldiers in *Hamlet*, marching to Poland – you know that scene?" Ronnie, Tasha and Jeremy all nodded. "Zach and Mason tied that scene to *The Art of War*, a great analogy, but Samir tied it to groups in the Middle East, branded terrorists by the West, who fight for dignity and honor, and for what they believe is right. He used that theme to segue to the universality of good and evil, and a little known, but vastly profound book, titled *A Century of Dishonor*. Anybody ever hear of it?"

All shook their heads, no. "Neither did I, but he used it to compare the lies and broken treaties of the American Indians with the Palestinian's plight, and he tied it all together with several horrific examples of ethnic cleansing in the 20th century.

"But, as I said, it's a Christmas party, and Christmas is the epitome of compassion and love. I wish these same feelings could be bottled and sprinkled over people all over the world. Since we can't do that, let's enjoy what we've been given tonight." Her smile was so ingenuous. Her innocence resembled Stevie's, thirty years or so older.

Dinner over, dessert and coffee were being served and Cassie, refreshed, was ready to dance again. She stood up and signaled to the DJ. He got the message, but she waved him off at his selection, "Girls Just Want to Have Fun." Lots of bodies hit the floor, shaking their heads, big hair flying all about their faces, jumping up and down, arms flailing. Not Cassie's style. She'd wait.

Two songs later, he got it right. Fine Young Cannibals, "She Drives Me Crazy."

"There she goes," quipped Joe. "Wish I had her rhythm." He sat back and relaxed, absorbing the sight, the sounds, everything about Christmas that he had loved since childhood, and he watched Walter, too. He watched Walter watching Cassie, eyes riveted on her, unable to relax. One sign from her that she considered Walter more than a friend, and Joe knew Walter's marital status would change in a heartbeat.

Suddenly Joe sits upright in his chair; his head jerking up. "Hey, I thought this party was for faculty?"

"It is," Tasha, Jeremy, and Alicia said in sync.

"I mean faculty only."

"It *is* faculty only," Walter reaffirmed, "except for Stevie."

"Then," Joe hesitated, "then why is Vaughn here . . . with an entourage?'

This time Walter jerked forward. "What?" They all turned and faced the doorway. Joe wasn't wrong. Vaughn, Taylor, Brett, and Hillary, of all people, walked towards an empty table that had remained empty all evening without anyone questioning why. Your plans change, you don't show up. But this empty table had obviously not been empty because someone's plans had changed. It had remained empty until its diners had arrived as planned.

"That son of a bitch," Walter said under his breath quietly; no one else heard. The others may not have known why Vaughn was here, with Taylor and his entourage as cover, but Walter knew. And Vaughn's focus confirmed it – his eyes were glued to Cassie as she moved on the dance floor.

She had come off the floor to grab Stevie, and the two of them were having a wonderful time dancing and laughing. Walter had been watching them with admiration and ease, thinking how nicely the evening had turned out, Stevie here to dance with her mom. She would be as great a dancer as her mother some day; she was so much like her. He was also wondering what Brian had been like. Honorable, honest, wholesome and genuine. In order for him to have volunteered for that tour of duty, he had to be. He had to be handsome too. Someday, he would ask Cassie to show him a picture. But it was way too soon to ask for something like that. In good time, in good time.

One look at Vaughn, though, Walter's relaxed demeanor evaporated and his pleasant ruminations vaporized. Without question, Vaughn was here to enjoy Cassie using Taylor as cover. How did he get her to agree to that? She had never accompanied him to any evening event related to Chelsea. Never. Worse, in Walter's mind, how would Cassie react to Vaughn's presence once she saw him? Not well, Walter was certain of that. Vaughn's table was situated apart from any faculty table, to play it safe, of course. Be present, but maintain your pretensions; don't mingle too closely with the riffraff. Hopefully, Cassie wouldn't notice him.

And she had not. She and Stevie had danced through two more songs and the "Electric Slide." Dozens of revelers were on the floor and the lines were long. Little personal room left, but Cassie and Stevie had eked out a spot at the opposite end of the dance floor, enough for Cassie to move in her own inimitable fashion. Every now and again, Stevie would miss a step, but Cassie was there to guide her into the next one.

After that, Cassie needed to sit out a few songs for more hydration. She just about collapsed into her chair. "Mom, you're getting old," Stevie jibed.

"I am not even going to respond to that. But, I could drink about a gallon of seltzer water real fast," she conceded.

"Don't pass out just yet," Joe laughed. "I'll get it." Anyone else want anything from the bar? Wine, scotch, vodka, soda?" He looked at Stevie. "A Shirley Temple?" His brown eyes twinkled while his hands rapped a quick drum beat on the table.

No, no, and no's all around. Just seltzer. "Not a drinking crowd, are we?" Joe asked rhetorically.

For no overt reason, Jeremy, who was sitting across from Joe, began standing up. "I said 'I'll get it,'" Joe affirmed, misreading Jeremy's reason. But Jeremy's gaze focused behind Joe and Cassie as he continued to rise. Confused, they glanced around. "What's going . . . ?" Then they knew.

Vaughn, Taylor, Brett and Hillary, waving hellos to the Chelsea tables behind theirs, were headed right towards them, only a few yards away. Having been the first to acknowledge their destination, Jeremy had begun to rise. As the O/B entourage reached their table, they were all standing, Cassie and Stevie with them. Vaughn extended his hand to Joe in Christmas greetings, then to Jeremy and everyone else until he got to Stevie standing next to her mom. "Having fun?" He asked, his eyes twinkling. Stevie nodded. "What about you, Cassie?" he asked, holding her hand a bit too long before he released it. "I saw you dancing." He paused. "The only difference between here and Homecoming is that here, your dean couldn't interfere."

Cassie was shocked. She hadn't seen Vaughn since last Friday when he had intruded on her with a Black Forest cake, telling her to call him by his first name as he left, saying they could be friends. Him, here with his wife, brother, sister-in-law, telling her boldly he had watched her dance, and smiling his captivating almost flirtatious smile directly into her eyes? His wife was right there! Cassie was confused. Was he being forward, was she missing something, or was she that naive? Before she could respond, Brett insinuated himself between them, took her hand and wished her a Merry Christmas.

"Too bad you have to teach *Hamlet* this time of the year. *A Christmas Carol* would be so much more appropriate, don't you think?"

"It would," she replied feeling uncomfortable and compromised, if the course were British lit." Brett was captivated.

Taylor, with Hillary, greeted the faculty with warm smiles and watched this three-way interplay with her husband, Brett and Cassie. When she got to Cassie, an icy glare had formed on her face. Her focus shifted to Vaughn, who was still gushing effusively at Cassie, then to Brett, whose smile bordered on lust, then to Hillary, her sister-in-law, whose smile and good will reminded her of Melanie in *Gone with the Wind*. Taylor, who had despised Cassie from Thanksgiving, riveted her cold glare on her now.

"Merry Christmas, everyone," Vaughn continued in jovial Christmas spirit, as though his vocabulary was programmed to regurgitate those three words. "It's nice to see my faculty in a completely different environment." He was trying to compliment the football crew without sounding patronizing but being the supercilious person he was, his tone ended up being just that. "Suits, Christmas ties, beautiful dresses, such a gala affair," he preened. Cassie couldn't miss Brett's seductive smile. Didn't Hillary notice? Hillary was a class act. Her smile was not only genuine, but exuded such warmth that Cassie actually felt sad the two of them came from such disparate backgrounds, because that dictated they could never be friends.

"Did you and Taylor come from the Club, Vaughn?" Melissa asked, her voice tight. She was more than surprised to see Taylor here. She had once told Cassie if

Vaughn ever showed up at a school function with his wife, something had to be wrong. Yet here she was. "You're both in party dress yourselves," Melissa added. The glare on Taylor's face held.

"Taylor, I love your dress," Tasha commented. "It's beautiful." Taylor, immaculate in every detail, wore a V-neck, silk, white dress with soft folds that crisscrossed along the bodice, fitted at the waist to the knee. Around her neck, she wore a double strand of green emeralds and red rubies set in yellow gold, a wide, matching bracelet on her wrist, matching cluster earrings, and a huge emerald ring on her third finger, right hand. All decked out for Christmas, except for the warm Christmas glow.

"Yes, Tasha, it's a Halston. I didn't want to overdress for a faculty party," her nose went up a bit, "Vaughn insisted on stopping by. Little affairs like this are so homey, but I can't imagine why my husband would want to intrude. This is your time to enjoy yourselves without the presence of your dean." She glared at Cassie with every syllable, every word she spoke.

Her glare was now obvious to everyone at the table, obvious and uncomfortable. Jeremy and Joe reseated themselves but Walter remained standing and, of all things, was glaring back, a bold response from a man who Vaughn and Taylor considered a friend, who had shared Thanksgiving at their house for almost two decades. But stare he did, at Taylor, then at Vaughn and Brett.

Why would Vaughn leave the Club to be here? They could understand the cook-off. That was casual and Jeremy's condo was situated on Chelsea Academy grounds. Moreover, they had been open enough to discuss the topic during the work day in Guidance and in the corridors en route to one office or another, asking what they were bringing, a dessert, an appetizer? It all fit there, but here?

Here, it did not. All Vaughn's Merry Christmas good-will seemed iffy, and to bring Taylor, his brother and sister-in-law? No one knew what else to say; so they waited for the O/B contingent to provide the next move, and that move did come, from Taylor, who, with complete impunity, issued a vicious and unprovoked onslaught that shocked them.

"Cassie, it must be so distressing for you this time of year," she began icily. Tasha, Melissa, Alicia, Ronnie . . . all squirmed in their seats, sensing this statement was a prelude to something horrible. Vaughn too, seemed cautious, or at least, perplexed. He had no idea what his wife intended to say. Only Cassie, ingenuous to a fault, remained unsuspecting, unguarded and unarmed, confused but with that warm smile on her face, until it was too late. She had sensed Taylor did not like her from the start for whatever reason, but not everybody likes everyone.

"But of course," Taylor continued seamlessly, knowing Cassie was completely focused, "to endure Christmas alone," she smiled diabolically, "without your *husband*," her smile had taken on a tinge of malevolence as she shot the word, husband, "especially knowing he had been blown apart at the Marine barracks in Lebanon? Horrible, I don't know how I would react if I ever lost Vaughn." Her lips had turned into a cruel, nefarious, joker smile.

Cassie reeled, her thoughts whirled, taking her equilibrium with her. She reached for the table involuntarily. Taylor was gloating. Why? How? How did Taylor know . . .

How? When? Then suddenly . . . suddenly she knew. The cook-off; Jeremy's condo. When she had left the dining room for the bathroom, Stevie, Stevie must have told. Oh, no. Oh no! That meant they all knew. They *all* knew.

Cassie withdrew, going within for protection, hiding inside her mental fortress, preventing herself from reliving memories, shielding herself from images, palpable specters, holding back tears. Lightheaded, her breathing increased and her heart pounded in her chest. Get a grip; get a grip. She grasped the table's edge for balance and steadied herself.

She held on and fought it off. Then, like an epiphany, she realized she had been viciously and unconscionably attacked, all the while thinking kind thoughts and warm wishes. God, she was so naïve. But no human with anything close to a soul or a conscience would ever have attacked someone as Taylor had just done. Forget that Stevie had revealed something personal amidst people she believed were hers and her mother's friends. Forget the nightmares, the empty days and empty years and the looking for herself without Brian and the quest to find inner peace. Forget Vaughn, her employer, who had gone way beyond breaking down professional barriers she had never sought to erode even though he had been instrumental in saving her life; forget Brett and the entire O/B dynasty; forget it all. Taylor had attacked her personally in the cruelest way imaginable, and she had attacked something sacred, a Marine's death, her husband's death and Stevie's father.

Now soundly entrenched behind her fortress, she countered. From somewhere deep, from a primordial instinct that had developed when she was a kid growing up in Paterson, when you know you've become a target, without reason, without provocation, when your instincts for survival take hold, you know, whatever the outcome, you do not back down. Win, lose, no matter. You do *not* back down. You take a stand and fight, for respect, honor, morality, for your reputation. Cassie's insides stopped quivering. Her eyes met Taylor's head on. She never blinked; she never backed down.

"You are correct, Taylor, it is distressing. To have to endure Christmas, nay, to have to endure every day, every minute of every day, without Brian, who was blown apart at the Marine barracks in Lebanon, as you so callously yet graphically state, but 'distressing' doesn't even come close to the raw, unabated horror of that attack, which shows your grasp of description and narration is merely superficial.

"However, having taught descriptive, narrative, expository and persuasive writing, I will suggest ways you might have expounded a bit. For example, your descriptive detail could have included the endless nights and interminable days of agony and tears, holding them back whenever you could to be strong for your child who did not understand and never would. You could have enhanced your imagery by highlighting the screams of torment as those Marines were blown to pieces or incinerated, or my husband's anguish as he found cover with his right leg ripped to pieces, crawling back to pull his burning colonel from a liquid incendiary that had become uncontained.

"But really, Taylor, why stop with description? You could have added to your narration with a day-by-day interview with the widow and child, as the press did for weeks. You know, with a microphone in your face, asking how the widow feels having lost her husband to the terrorists in the Middle East, how do I expect to raise my child, where do I go from here?

For exposition, you simply needed to include more facts: two hundred forty-one American servicemen killed: two hundred twenty Marines, eighteen sailors, and three soldiers, making this incident the deadliest single-day death toll for the United States Marine Corps since World War II's Battle of Iwo Jima.

Lastly, you could have included a touch of persuasion by introducing pros and cons as to why we were there, whether we should or should not have been, and whose interests our presence served. Your presentation, Taylor, although passable because it did achieve its purpose, could have been much more graphic. Perhaps a refresher course in creative writing or impromptu speaking could assist in those areas of weakness?

"But in response to the rhetorical part of your statement, the 'I don't know how I would react if I ever lost Vaughn'? Come now; I doubt you'd have much of a life-changing experience in that arena." Cassie gestured to Taylor's jewelry and her Halston dress. "As long as you didn't lose your fine accoutrements, your jewelry and your Halston dresses . . . oh, and, of course, your standing at the Club, I think your life would go on completely undisturbed, with one little hiccup - a few additional black outfits and accessories to add to your closets, you know, for mourning and little amenities like that."

Oh! My! God! Had Cassie just said what everyone had heard? Had everyone heard what Cassie had just said?

Had that obnoxious, smug, condescending smile just been ripped off Taylor's face? Did it just morph into a grimace, then a snarl, and then a defeated expression of horror that cowered this pseudo-immaculate lady and reduced her to the pitiful, worthless, empty carbon-based creature of a human she had taken decades to camouflage and perfect?

Taylor's countenance crashed. No one had ever spoken to her like this. No one! Although highly intelligent, she had never imagined a retort like this. In fact, she had never expected a retort at all! She was part of the O/B dynasty! She looked at Vaughn for support and tried her sexy pout; he had turned away. She looked at Brett, imploring assistance; Brett shook his head, giving her a "you have gone too far," look; and Hillary, whose look was pure, unadulterated sympathy, was directing that sympathy towards Cassie, not her sister-in-law.

Taylor's invective had gone beyond cruel and inhumane, and although Cassie had countered in the only way she could, she was sure there would be repercussions. Wealth was wealth, like wet, sticky glue, holding disparate pieces together even if it wasn't dry. Taylor was an O/B wife, part of the ruling class. They'd defend her. Vaughn had reacted viscerally when he turned away, which showed he had a touch of humanity. Give him a little time to become an O/B baron again, and Cassie was certain humanity would evaporate. In short, he would fold. Vaughn talked a good game as the dean, but in real life, he was an emasculated male. Always was, always would be.

53

THE O/B CREW HEADS HOME

They sipped cocktails on the drive home. Quiet, into their own thoughts. Vaughn had gone too far. He would never be able to repair his relationship with Cassie because he didn't have one. He never had; it had been a fantasy. She had been playtime so he could pretend he was young and seductive. In doing that, he had insinuated himself into her private life, where, as dean, he could have trespassed with impunity. At least, that was his assumption. But here he never should have tried. He realized that now, and his fantasy crumbled like a mortar demolishing a cement wall.

Affairs like St. George's Seal were beneath him, beneath all of them; it would never have been a casual night out for the O/B clan. If he had wanted to see Cassie, how she looked, what she was wearing, how she was dancing, he should have found a way to do it without involving anyone else.

It had all seemed so easy. Bring Taylor, who had agreed to go albeit reluctantly; ask Brett, who had jumped at the chance to observe this beauty, and Hillary would simply follow along. Simple, so what had gone wrong? What had prompted Taylor's attack? He couldn't figure it out, and Cassie's retort? Shocking. Absolutely shocking. How dare she insult his wife and hurt her feelings, no matter how callous Taylor had been. Vaughn would always be the aristocracy and people like Cassie would be the proletariat. Her counter-attack was an impeachable offense, not to be tolerated under any conditions. Might makes right, and wealth controls it all.

It didn't matter now; by doing what was best for him, he had created a situation he now had to salvage. To fix it, Cassie would have to fall. She deserved it, especially after that insult about his death meaning nothing except a few additional black outfits in his wife's closet. If Vaughn were 100% certain of one thing, it was his wife's devotion to him and the family name. Cassie would be held accountable for that statement alone. She had lived through an ugly tragedy; she'd have to live through more.

"We'll fix it, Dear," he said perfunctorily patting Taylor's hand as their stretch limo cruised homewards. "We'll fix it. She should never have spoken to you that way." He turned to Brett, who was deep in thought, and Hillary, who gaped at Vaughn, her mouth partially open in surprise. Only Hillary could understand how a human heart could be destroyed from external forces completely beyond your control and feel your whole life, your whole world, revolving around you without you in it.

"Care to stay over?" He asked his brother. "Save your-selves an extra forty minute ride? Breakfast at the Club? Wear something of mine for a change of clothes."

Whatever had been occupying Brett's thoughts va-porized. What a luscious invitation; what delectable pos-sibilities; he and Taylor – in the kitchen, a hallway or a bathroom, maybe in the gym or library, maybe both, may-be the entertainment studio . . . make their own steamy film? A glance at Taylor confirmed his thoughts. She was imagining the same thing and ready for it all.

"Sure, Vaughn. You and I still fit into the same clothes, except you have a little less bulk." He laughed. "Although, little brother, you do seem to be filling out a bit. Am I right?"

"Vaughn's been working out for over a month. Haven't you Darling?" Taylor gushed over her insipid husband. "Tell him, Darling. You should be proud he's noticed."

"Looks, good, Vaughn. Looks good. Yeah, we'll stay." He glanced at Hillary as an afterthought. "If it's all right with you, Hon."

Hillary nodded. Life had been empty, sterile, for so long she could only react robotically. What did it matter if she stayed at her disgusting brother-in-law's who could use and abuse someone kind and innocent like Cassie.

Hillary had come from wealth; she knew the game, its rules, its lack of rules, bending the rules when it meant winning, but for her, the trigger that had changed her from mildly unscrupulous, nothing close to Brett or Vaughn, had occurred with her stillborn, the cancer, and the final realization that she would never be a mother.

Things we just assume while we revel in our mammon; things we take for granted while we sit at the Club and blabber about petty little passions, shuffling the kids off to one nanny or another while we take our cruises or our tennis and golf lessons to fix our backhand or cure our slices and hooks; things we take for granted while we fly our private planes to destinations around the globe, then come back and preen about the sub-cultures' vagaries; when we vacation where the wealthy are supposed to vacation while taking everything for granted, until the external hand of fate, or God, as Hillary had come to believe, was refusing to give her the one thing she had always believed would be a concomitant to her marriage – kids.

Sure, they could stay over and she could pretend to be asleep when Brett left her bed to rendezvous with Taylor. She knew exactly what was going on, but she was too dead to care. Which is better, she wondered, to know what's happening and not care, or to be Vaughn and not know what's happening? Her kind, blue eyes glossed over as she duly nodded her consent to Brett.

But for Taylor, a night with Brett had revived her, a temporary catharsis for all her enmity, and she focused on where they could rendezvous and how many times, just as Brett was doing. A ten-minute session with Vaughn was all he would need to satisfy him and he'd sleep like a baby, believing she was his sweet, passionate and faithful wife, ha, for whom he would do anything, which included destroying Cassie.

Taylor could wait for that. Tonight, she'd spend delicious hours with Brett and revel in every minute. Every cloud has a silver lining. What a serendipitous start to the

Christmas season. She allowed herself to get lost in her heat and the myriad ways Brett would satisfy her. Cassie had become an afterthought, a toy for another time.

54

TAYLOR AFTER THE FACULTY PARTY

Taylor hated Cassie at first sight, and this paltry, plebeian, faculty Christmas party, where she had expected to eviscerate her, had backfired completely. She had never expected such verbal acumen from a commoner. Cassie's counterattack spiked Taylor's venom and forced her to reassess her enemy. If she couldn't bring her down one way, she'd do it another.

Her husband was interested in this woman. That was obvious. Cassie, a mere teacher, was being escorted from group to group Thanksgiving Day by her husband who was fawning over her and introducing her to the whole family, as though any Otis-Barrett would ever want to meet someone so lowly, as if Taylor's origins had not been Jersey City.

Taylor had discarded her humble origins decades ago from pride, not shame. Her entire career had been to marry a man like Vaughn, and she had succeeded. Aside from Brett and Muriel, Vaughn's mother, and Hillary, who for all intents and purposes was dead, Taylor was top dog on the O/B totem and at the Club. To watch Vaughn bring Cassie into their high society and shamefully allow her son to fraternize with this woman's daughter was repulsive.

But as angry as she felt because Vaughn, that whimpering, feckless male she called husband, had become infatuated with Cassie, what tormented her to her core was the realization that Brett was drooling over Cassie too. Taylor's lifestyle emanated from Vaughn, but her reason for living was Brett. He was her whole world, something she had never anticipated, something she could never rationalize and for Brett to lust after Cassie, real or virtual, didn't matter. Taylor would let nothing come between her and Brett. Because of this, Cassie had become Taylor's target.

The night of the storm had cemented it. Every time Taylor replayed that drama her hatred intensified. Vaughn's first call said he would be sleeping at Chelsea. Since he had done that twice before it was of no consequence. In fact, Taylor welcomed his absence - any absence gave her more time for Brett, who was with her at Manicures for Men.

His second call told her he was cancelling classes. Who cared? He'd call Brett to make sure she was all right or if she needed him to drive her home after she closed the shop. What irony, Brett was right there servicing all her needs. A lie about spilling her manicure tray ended the call quickly so Vaughn didn't hear her gasps. She threw her mobile phone on the counter and dug her fingers into Brett's shoulders as her insides exploded.

Another call to Brett, "Help Taylor if she needs anything," should have ended his absurd interruptions, but no, one last call minutes later to tell him he was going in search of Cassie because she had gotten lost in the storm. Taylor, her face fused to Brett's, had heard every word, and as abominable as it was knowing her husband was risking his life to search for this bitch, it was nothing compared to the hatred she felt when she sensed Brett's intensity. His kisses suddenly became more erotic, more passionate and lascivious. He explored her body with animal lust, insatiable, unquenchable lust. There, then, Taylor knew his thoughts were on fire with Cassie, not her. While Brett was inside her, he was mentally fornicating with Cassie. For that, Cassie was doomed.

Her green eyes were alive with jealousy then, and they were now. Her second martini should have been her victory celebration, but it wasn't. She was going for a third when Vaughn issued his luscious invitation to Brett and Hillary, stay the night. Immediately, the Cassie problem disappeared. There would be other ways and other times to get Cassie.

But Brett was staying the night! Her fantasies came alive with anticipation: which rooms, which hallways, which anywhere. Her husband had just given her Brett, the perfect Christmas gift. She'd not waste another second on anything else.

55

BRETT

After two calls to Taylor the night of the storm, Vaughn had made two calls to his brother. Brett should have left his mobile phone in the car, but he usually kept it close in case Hillary needed him. Maybe in this weather she would.

For all his infidelity, Brett cared deeply about his wife. They had been a couple through university years into their early twenties. When he had asked her to marry him, females wondered why Hillary? Why her? Maybe because he was the first man she had ever had. Maybe that was so uniquely special to Brett that he had been given something pure. He loved her and wanted to be with her for the rest of his life. If there had ever been an indiscretion, it would have been a one-time insignificant thing. He never thought then he'd become the man he'd been prior to Hillary.

And he hadn't at first, until Hillary's miscarriages, a still born and life-threatening illnesses told her she'd never be a mom. That's when she lost all reason for living. Despite their billions and the best doctors billions could buy, they couldn't buy her the one thing she wanted most. That would haunt Brett forever, but he would always be there to protect her until she no longer wanted him. And then Vaughn introduced him to Taylor and his relationship of faithful infidelity began. Until Thanksgiving and the night of the storm, he had never considered any other woman, just Taylor.

The night of the storm had been absurd, Vaughn calling to enlist his help if Taylor needed anything while Brett was right there in his wife's shop satisfying her needs. He had to control his laughter; his brother, such a joke, preferring the deanship of a private academy to running a multi-billion dollar enterprise. Oftentimes, Brett was almost ashamed to acknowledge him as his brother.

But the reason for Vaughn's second call piqued his libido. Vaughn was so concerned for his most recent staff member, Cassie Komsky, that sexual magnet who had gotten herself caught in the storm, that he was going after her. Brett remembered Thanksgiving and gave a silent, predatory hoot. This creature goes off in this storm looking for a reclusive Arab kid whose whereabouts after curfew were unknown? He had never heard that one before, and it aroused his primordial instincts to a pitch he had never quite experienced. His passion towards Taylor intensified. What an aphrodisiac! He would go all night on this and Taylor sensed it.

Brett could understand why his brother had such a fascination. He had been a wimp of a CEO who had never gotten any female who didn't want his money before they wanted him and that included Taylor. But why did Cassie excite him, a guy who considered women mere targets, targets and trophies and could get any one of them? It didn't matter; she simply did, and another opportunity to see her was fine with him.

Sure, he'd go to this faculty Christmas party, see the main attraction and super-charge his fantasies with this wildcat. She'd sure be that in bed, if a guy could get her there. Instinctively he knew she was a one-man woman, even though she had come without a husband. A few weeks later, he learned why - the Marine barracks bombing. Pretty bad, but it didn't matter; she was fair game and her history would make her even more vulnerable. Maybe test her, see what makes her break. She'd be worth it. Maybe that was Vaughn's intent. Otis-Barrett's always get what they want. Why exempt her? Sure he'd go to this plebian faculty party and see if something could develop. Nothing had; after Taylor's attack, the evening was over.

However, the ride home from an encounter that had gotten him nothing with Cassie had now gotten him more than he could ever have expected with Taylor. Nice. Inwardly Brett could have cheered. He had never seen Taylor emotionally compromised and it was quite sexy. But the best part, she was being handed to him on a silver platter by, of all people, her own husband, his own brother! Brett could hardly contain himself.

Vaughn was so consumed with palliating his wife that he had no idea how exciting his invitation had been. Sure brother, I'll stay at your mansion and bed your wife. This is delicious. He covered his mouth to control his laughter.

The evening couldn't have worked out any better if he had planned it himself. Taylor's spirits had soared instantly; she was sharing his thoughts. He bit his lower lip. Taylor would be his luscious dessert for the evening and how delicious she would be. Merry Christmas, everyone; Merry Christmas indeed.

56

CASSIE'S EVENING FOR REFLECTION

Soft traditional Christmas music played, "Silent Night," "Away in a Manger," "O Holy Night," "The Little Drummer Boy." All the classic carols Cassie loved. She loved everything about the season and the beautiful memories she had from childhood when her mother would take her to church and she'd get lost in the choir's mellifluent songs.

During the service, the choir responded to the priest like the strophe and antistrophe of a Greek chorus, but once the service was over, the choir would break out into song, one carol after another, and the congregation would join in. Tonight, these carols had a special purpose for her, to still her disquietude and mask the harsh realities that had interrupted what would have been a perfect evening.

Cassie swirled the few sips of wine still remaining in her glass. She indulged in a glass maybe three or four times a year, Christmas, Thanksgiving, maybe New Year's to celebrate the conclusion of another year or the beginning of a new one, with hope and anticipation of good things to come. Kindness shouldn't have to wait for a special day or a new year.

The residual pangs of this evening's party initiated the soft music and the wine swirling in the cut crystal glass, a shower gift from years ago. It had remained in the breakfront since 1983, but tonight, in the half light of darkness, muted by lights from her tree and flickering candle flames, the music and the wine in her special glass softened the harsh reflections of the evening.

Stevie had long been asleep. That's where Cassie should have been, in "sleep that knits up the raveled sleeve of care," but it was not to be. In soft sweat pants and an oversized thermal top, she had tiptoed downstairs to turn on the stereo, delicately caress the wine glass she had last held with Brian, and hope the tranquil ambiance of Christmas would put her to sleep. Instead, it drew her closer to Brian, a place of sadness, a place where she shouldn't have gone. She cried softly, like silent rain that falls so lightly you don't know it's there until you notice tiny, almost invisible droplets splattered on your sleeves.

She thought of Walter too. She liked him; she admired him, and she appreciated all he had done for her. She wondered, could they ever be more than friends? During their initial meeting, he had been so absorbed in his computer read-out that he had no idea his words were ripping her to shreds. Lebanon, Hezbollah, the American Embassy, the Marine barracks, they were his entire focus. He never looked up to see how his words were cleaving her in two.

Do you want some water? He had asked, when he noticed she was close to hysteria. Cassie smiled. He had no clue. How could he? But in the ensuing months, she had gotten to know him as the truly kind and conscientious person he was. Could she show him more than friendship? She had a feeling he'd be receptive if she gave him a sign, but was something holding her back? Was there something about Walter that was holding her back? Was it Brian? She doubted it. Dr. O/B flashed through her mind. No, that's impossible. What brought him to mind? She dismissed it instantly.

She should never have allowed Taylor's behavior to dominate her thoughts and shut her off from Walter and Stevie. The ride home should have been ebullient, happy and talkative. They should have been yakking about the food, which had been superb, the music and the dancing that had made the evening such a marvelous affair. But Taylor's attack had dominated her thoughts; Cassie regretted it.

She understood jealousy. She had witnessed it from the time she was a teen, when kids in high school with lots more made everyone aware of social standing even in Paterson. She had also lived it first hand and raw when she was a summer nanny for the upper class. When you're not needed for the role for which you are hired, you are invisible. Terse, succinct, just like that. But that was child's play compared to the vicious assault Taylor had issued.

Taylor was another breed, a species of unadulterated, unmitigated raw animus, and for what reason? Why did she show up with her husband at a faculty affair? How did Vaughn get her to agree to that? According to Melissa, Taylor never accompanied her husband to any evening event related to Chelsea, never, unless, Melissa had said, something was wrong. So what was wrong? With all their wealth, what could possibly be wrong? Cassie wouldn't begin to speculate, but she believed Taylor was not a happy person. You can't be happy inside and spew out such venom.

Brian always said she was naïve, naïve and innocent. Her first encounter at the Nor'easter Hotel made her aware of that, and she was as naïve, innocent and trusting now as she had been then, except with tragedy woven into her life. Cassie operated on the premise that no one would ever be out to do her harm, which is okay, until you encounter someone evil. Then, being naive and trusting are inadequate attributes for battle. Other than her ability to verbally rip an opponent to shreds, Cassie was defenseless.

If Taylor had made her a target, what recourse did Cassie have? None; she had no way to avoid Taylor's wrath. It was her husband's turf; his authority ruled on Chelsea grounds, and his money ruled off. Brian's death had taught Cassie that you can't control things you can't control. No matter how good a person you might want to be, there are forces you can't control. Cassie sensed Taylor was one of them.

I refuse to dwell on this now. I will continue to do the best I can. If there were do-over's in life, I'd be with Brian, and Stevie would have her father. So, I will take advantage of the time I have, we have, especially the good times.

And these are the good times. Forget Taylor's attack. It's done. Ink writes the past; pencil writes the future. And the present? The present isn't written; it's lived. I will focus on the present.

And she did. She focused on the present until "Leather and Lace" infused itself into the Christmas medley. The DJ was taking a holiday break. "And so for all you lovers out there, here's one for you." This one was definitely for her. Another sip of wine, she closed her eyes and drifted back.

The dirty white building on the corner that rounded wide at the intersection peeked out from her stored memories. She was standing outside in the not-yet-stifling heat of the Jersey shore, Memorial Day weekend, wearing white hip huggers that belted about an inch below her waist, exposing a hint of a pancake-flat tummy, an unbelievably tiny waist and a curvaceous mid-line that bared itself just below a navy and white horizontal striped three-quarter sleeved form-fitting top, with Brian telling her how naïve she really was, telling her right there as they stood outside the Nor'easter's bar. She didn't get it. Bars, alcohol, testosterone and estrogen reduced men to their biological alter egos. She still stared at him. She still didn't get it. Not something her aunt had ever told her. How many girls from her generation had been? A lot more than her, obviously, or she wouldn't have been the only female in the Nor'easter who had gone there to dance.

But Cassie, all twenty-one of her, brought up with a puritanical background in Paterson, what an oxymoron, had come here to dance. What a naïve, embarrassing fool, to think that was anyone's purpose in being here, anyone's except her own. Brian had laughed without inhibition. He had just saved her from being mauled, mauled by half a dozen guys who couldn't keep their hands off her, and the two of them standing outside the Nor'easter in the heat of a late May night. "You're here to dance?" He had guffawed, and laughed harder at her blank reaction. "I have *never* heard anything like this before!"

She fumed. She was so angry at him, and so inwardly embarrassed that she turned and started to walk home. "Hey, wait a minute," he had said, positioning himself directly in front of her. What was she thinking? "Hey, you can't walk home alone." He stood fast. He was so wide she couldn't go around him.

"Get out of my way. I am going home," five feet plus three inches had said defiantly, and she tried to push him out of her way. Seriously?

"Look, I'm sorry. I'm really sorry. I wasn't laughing at you, I mean, I *was* . . . I *was* laughing at you, but just the idea of a girl as beautiful as you coming here to dance, and actually meaning it." He put his hands out in consternation.

"What do other girls come here for?" she demanded.

Stunned, is she for real? "Look, you want to go home, I'll drive you. I can't let you walk home by yourself. Besides, you're going the wrong way." He pointed forward. "That's the beach." But he didn't answer her question, and he didn't until several years after they had been married. But there, standing outside the Nor'easter's bar, he knew she was the most naïve female he had ever met. The most naïve, without exaggeration, and the most beautiful, and the combination of the two made her completely vulnerable. Right then and there, he felt this yearning to protect her.

"Do you want to go home?" he asked; Cassie said nothing. "Come on," he said softly. I'll take you home."

Cassie remembered every word, every line, every crease of his eyebrows, every curve of his lips. "Do you want to go home?" he had asked softly. "Do you want to go home?"

"Yes," she had said finally. Yes, she mumbled now; her lips moved and a soft "yes," escaped. "I want to go home."

"Tomorrow, tomorrow and tomorrow, creep in this petty pace from day to day to the last syllable of recorded time...." Tomorrow had become today, and she drifted into sleep.

57

CHRISTMAS BREAK

hristmas was on a Friday, six days after the faculty party. Everything is like a dream. We spend countless hours and days waiting for and preparing for that special day, that special moment, only to turn around and find it occurred a year ago, five years ago, a decade or decades ago, until we're old, too old to make new memories, and we exist on the ones we've already made. Life is a dream. Her mother used to say, you blink and it's over, and so, she'd tell her young daughter, the reason for getting up each day was to help someone, give them a smile or a reason to smile, because a day without a smile is like a cloud without a sun to hide.

Two short months ago she had been existing from day to day, stoically plodding on, trying to do the best she could for herself and her daughter, and she had been doing a fairly good job of existing. Nothing spectacular, but making it, something to feel good about given the circumstances.

But never had she imagined this move and this job would have brought her back to life like this. Magic filled the air; magic she hadn't felt in years, magic she thought she had lost forever. She and Walter had been together every day, and she hadn't tired of it not once. Neither had Stevie. Stevie would wake up every morning and ask, Is Walter coming over today? Are we doing something with Walter? What did you two do last night? As though something secretive had gone on or she had missed something between the hours of 9:30 p.m. and 6:00 a.m.

Nope, Stevie had not missed anything, except, to Cassie's surprise, one very delicate good-night kiss Christmas Eve that Walter courageously bestowed. Life was going on, happening in its own way, in its own fashion, but it was happening, and it was a little scary. Strange, she was transitioning from sadness to happiness with a touch of fear, and the latter was kind of unsettling. Living alone was easier, a day to day bubble; never come out. But she had come to Chelsea to overcome that. I'm not backing down now, she insisted. Life would take her where it wanted her to go.

The three of them had prepared for Christmas day all week. Cooking, baking, putting their hands together and doing quite well. Cassie's bandages had been off since last Friday, so she was her old self in the kitchen, but Stevie would have been so disappointed if Cassie had taken over completely. Cassie would never do that, especially since Stevie's culinary expertise had leapfrogged in the last two weeks. Keep her motivated and improving. Walter still wore bandages for protection since sutures had been removed, but he lived up to his word; he was very good in the kitchen.

Christmas morning Stevie opened all her gifts, and there were plenty. Clothes, jeans, tops, boots, and pierced earrings, studs and hoops! "Mom! Pierced earrings? That means I'm getting my ears pierced?" She squealed.

"Yup," Cassie nodded. We have an appointment to-morrow, 3:00 p.m. at the boutique."

"Mom, I am so excited. Thank you." Stevie jumped up and kissed her with a tight hug. Then she finished opening her presents. Next she opened a ninth-grade edi-tion of *Pride and Prejudice.* Christmas gifts always included books, and *Pride and Prejudice* was one of Cassie's favorites. Literature was about life, and characters in a good book came to life; good characters could be anyone who had lived, anyone who'd ever felt excessive pride, fear, fear to commit, fear to admit, fear to face reality, anyone; any-one who felt jealously, revenge, love, love that builds or love that destroys. We're all those people. Cassie had also included a volume of poems from Rabindranath Tagore, an Indian poet she had inhaled from her college days. So much sensitivity and beauty imbued in his poetry.

When Stevie got older, Cassie would let her read an-other one of her favorites, Conrad's *Heart of Darkness,* the book she had referenced in class a few weeks ago, a book whose ending epitomized man's inhumanity and savagery and juxtaposed the raw and primordial against the pseudo-cultivated British: the one, guttural and hon-estly open; the other, the phony facade of proper British civility to which Jason and Connor had both remarked in the class' discussion about lies we tell ourselves so we can travel through life protected. Masks on, that's how we live. The civilized world is as cruel as the uncivilized; it's merely wrapped in a different package. But she wanted Stevie to get a touch of man's inhumanity and its savagery. Hopefully she'd grow up a lot less naïve than her mother.

Once Walter arrived, they exchanged gifts. He loved the soft but heavy texture of the flannel Woolrich shirt she had gotten him, its light gray and maroon plaid would accent his gray hair. Stevie had bought him a Mediterranean cookbook, paid for with her own money. "Now, Dr. Goodman, you can make hummus and baba ga-noush anytime you want."

"What about nemura?"

Stevie nodded, "Yup, that's in there too."

"Great gift, Stevie. It'll have a permanent place, open, on my kitchen counter. Can't wait."

"And wait until we make baba ganoush. Everything's ready. All we do is mix it together."

Cassie had roasted the eggplant early in the morning, sliced it; removed its excess liquid and a few big pockets of seeds. Then she had spooned out the flesh from inside the skin. Four bowls sat on the table: eggplant, mashed and at room temperature, tahini mixed with lemon juice, a small spice bowl of salt, cumin and chopped garlic, and one with finely chopped parsley. A cruet of olive oil on the side.

"Ready, Dr. Goodman?" Stevie asked excitedly moving into the kitchen.

"Let's do it," he said, following her. Cassie was already adding the tahini and lemon juice mixture to the egg-plant. After she stirred that around, she let Stevie add the salt, cumin and garlic and blended all of that together. Cassie took a serving bowl from the cabinet, spooned in the baba ganoush, drizzled olive oil over it and sprinkled chopped parsley on top. She emptied a bag of pita wedges into a wicker bread basket and passed the dip and pita to Walter. "Please. Enjoy."

Walter did not need further encouragement. Taking a pita wedge, he dipped it into the baba ganoush and scooped out a healthy portion. His facial expression showed his appreciation for the eclectic appetizer.

"This is delicious. I've never tasted anything like it. I'll just take the whole bowl and leave the rest of the dinner for you and Stevie."

"What about Jeremy?"

"If I finish this before he comes, he won't know he's missed it."

They laughed. Next was the hummus. "We used the processor for that this morning," Cassie said and brought out a bowl from the frig filled half way with mashed chick peas. "Chick peas blended with two cloves of fresh garlic." Stevie added the cumin, salt, a touch of pepper and tahini paste and stirred until the yellow of the chick peas took on a grayish tinge. "You've gotta taste this." Cassie said, placing the bowl next to the baba ganoush and sliding the tray of spinach and cheese phylo into the oven. "Jeremy should be here any minute; he's a bit late," she said, glancing at the clock, "and he's never late."

Just then, the bell rang; Jeremy gave his inimitable knock and entered bearing wine, dried fruits, a dessert he wouldn't divulge, plopped it all on the counter, and presented Cassie with her Christmas gift, beautifully wrapped. Cassie opened it gingerly and held the most exquisite glass tree ornament she had ever seen. A hand-blown glass deer, sitting with her sleeping fawn cuddled next to her. Each wore a green Christmas wreath on its head, decorated with red berries, noses tipped with 14k gold. So gossamer, so delicate, so exquisite it brought tears to Cassie's eyes. "Oh, Jeremy," Cassie choked with emotion. "It's beautiful."

"You trumped me," Walter chided. "Big time. I gave her a Lenox Christmas photo frame with a picture of her and Stevie hugging on the dance floor at the Christmas party. Nothing like this."

Cassie had been overwhelmed with Walter's gift, so lovely and thoughtful, never even knowing he had taken his camera to the party. At his self-deprecation, Cassie took his arm and gave him a little hug. No words; they weren't needed. Nothing could have surpassed that. He felt so strong; so protective; he felt what he believed was love.

While they waited for the phyllo to bake, golden brown and crisp, they munched on celery, carrots and cherry tomatoes dipped in hummus and baba ganoush or spooned onto crackers or pita bread wedges; they devoured olives, sharp provolone wedges, and scallops rolled in bacon that Walter had brought. Delicious. When the phyllo was ready, Cassie cut it into wedges. The group of four downed them one after another. Just as delicious. Sweet potatoes would go into the oven a little later and everything else was flowing into place. "You know what? No one's going to be hungry for Christmas dinner."

"We'll manage," Jeremy rebutted. "You don't stop eating Christmas dinner just because you're full."

By 4:30, they sat at the dining room table decorated with a lovely Lenox table cloth, Christmas place settings with a holly and berry relief, and a centerpiece interspersed with pine, holly and sea shells. Cassie had made it when she and Brian were first married and they'd walk the beach, collecting shells, only the most perfect and unique shells, which Cassie designed into her centerpiece.

Walter said grace and dinner was served. They devoured their Christmas feast, never remembering that they had just devoured mountains of appetizers. But no one noticed; they just kept passing one platter then another, enjoying each other's company and the scintillating conversation. Topics went from interesting people they had known to memorable events in their lives, to the history of Chelsea Academy and their future goals; "If you could have one wish, or change one thing . . . ." An hour later, they sat back and tried to breath. Stuffed. Cassie pledged to run four miles tomorrow instead of three; Stevie promised to accompany her, and Walter asked if he could join. "Of course. How's 10:00?"

"Ten's fine. Jeremy, you in?"

"As much as I would like to join, and as much as I need the exercise, I promised myself I would not begin to diet or exercise until the New Year. If I don't have that for a New Year's resolution, I won't have any."

In the evening, Stevie snuggled into the living room sofa with *Pride and Prejudice* and a dinner-sized platter of desserts on her lap. Jeremy had brought dried figs, apricots and dates, and a scrumptious blueberry strudel. Walter had brought a huge Lindy's cheesecake, and Cassie and Stevie had baked cream puffs. Maneuvering desserts with a book was awkward, but Stevie's hardest decision was which to eat first, the cream puffs, easy to handle, or cheesecake, which could be a little messy. Blueberry strudel was out of the question. Mom would only let her eat that at the table; one dropped blueberry would forever stain the couch.

The adults sat around the kitchen table drinking tea and nibbling dessert. Cassie picked at the strudel. Although she loved puff pastry and blueberries, she honed in on Lindy's cheesecake, baked perfectly with a cookie dough crust and sour cream icing. Since she had never made a decent cup of coffee in her life, the beverage was always tea, unless the male contingent wanted to make it themselves. Tea was fine with them, and Cassie poured cup after cup as they nibbled on dried fruits - dates were her favorite - and all the other scrumptious desserts as they talked. Conversation never hit a lull, and they segued from one topic to another.

"I know I'm changing the subject," Jeremy interjected amidst a discussion about ambitions and goals, "but I have a question. If you don't want to talk about it, just say so."

Cassie and Walter shrugged. "Go ahead Jeremy, ask it," Cassie offered.

"It's about the faculty party and a little thing called 'jealousy.' Did I notice that 'green-eyed monster which doth mock the meat it feeds on' or was I imagining things?"

Cassie gave a little laugh at Jeremy's reference to *Othello*. "Want to sit in on next month's classes? We're beginning *Othello* right after Christmas break."

"Just the facts, Ma'am; just the facts." Jeremy mimicked Sgt. Joe Friday from Jack Webb.

Cassie paused momentarily. "I don't think she stooped to Iago's depths, even though she was exceptionally vicious and cruel, but no one should have said that." Taylor's cruel reference to Brian's death played through her mind. "But jealous? Why? What for? Why would a woman as wealthy and as attractive as Taylor be jealous of me to have said something that cruel."

"You're the Shakespeare teacher. Emelia's words to Desdemona are?"

"About jealousy?" Cassie asked. Jeremy nodded. "She says jealous souls do not need a reason to be jealous. Her exact words are, 'They are not ever jealous for the cause, but jealous for they're jealous.'"

"There's your answer, Cassie. Jealously doesn't need a reason. It feeds on itself. But in your case," he interjected before Cassie could respond, "there's an obvious reason, don't you think?"

Cassie gestured with her palms up, shoulders shrugged. "She's beautiful."

"Yes, she's beautiful, but so are you; and you're sensual, Cassie, Taylor is not, and she knows it." Cassie blushed. "You may not want to hear it, and I apologize if I embarrass you, but it's true. May as well accept it."

Cassie retreated from the conversation and became introspective. Compliments and words of praise were foreign to her. In her childhood, she remembered anger and vitriol, criticism and condescension - you're good for nothing . . . good for nothing . . . good for nothing . . . . Derision imprinted on a child's mind does not erase, even when as an adult, she realizes the parents were wrong. "Well," Cassie recovered, "if it's true, what do I do about it?'

"With Taylor," Jeremy shook his head, "you do nothing; absolutely nothing. This is her domain, their domain, the powerful and the wealthy. They rule. All you can do is defend what's morally right, and, as I told you once before, stay the same kind and good person you are. We can't control what happens to us in life. You of all people know that. We make decisions for good reasons and we hope for a good outcome. We live our lives that way, but Taylor, Vaughn and their ilk, they don't. 'Some rise by sin and some by virtue fall.'" He chuckled. "The Otis-Barretts are the first part of that quote; people like us are the second. Taylor and Vaughn, for no discernible reason, *will* hurt you, and the irony is that they'll rise while you fall. Just never let them change you Cassie. That's the only way they'll lose."

"That's how they *lose*? It doesn't seem as though they lose anything." Cassie turned to Walter. "What do you think? You've known Dr. O/B for decades; do you see jealousy?"

Walter hesitated before he spoke; then nodded. "One emotion, yes. I've seen him go after someone because he's disliked them or because someone's offended him. Those emotions don't pertain to you. Quite the opposite, in fact: he likes you even though your sharp retorts *have* offended him. The jealousy I see is from Taylor, female to female, but jealousy from Vaughn . . ." he chose his words very carefully, "because you're something he can't own." Cassie almost gagged on Walter's statement, "and because I agree with Jeremy's quote."

"What, his quote from *Measure for Measure*?" Walter nodded. "You mean Angelo's proposition of lust and hypocrisy, right?" Walter nodded again. Cassie reflected on his response. She did not like his answer. Then, putting something aside she did not want to confront, added somewhat humorously, "Why was I hired? Any one of you could have taught Shakespeare."

Walter and Jeremy exchanged glances and laughed. "Not me," Walter retorted, "I love working with kids, but not in a classroom setting. Besides, people think a shrink gets to know a student and what motivates him or her better than anyone else? Not so. To me, a teacher, who sees a kid five days a week about forty weeks out of the year, knows a kid a lot better than I do. I see a kid five times a year. You see him five times forty weeks. Big difference. Most likely, that's one reason you got to Samir. But I like my way."

"I like the five times a week because I really enjoy being with young people and helping them prepare for life," Jeremy added, "but I'd much rather do experiments with elements on a periodic table, stuff with distillation and titration, than teach adolescents about life, hardship, and tragedy, which is what you do with literature. Jeez, how do you ever know if you're getting it right? That's much too hard. That's even too hard for me as an adult!" They all laughed.

"That's probably too difficult for any of us, and at this age, I have come to believe I'll live my entire life, no matter how short or long, wondering, but never knowing, aside from bringing up Stevie, what I'm supposed to do here with my life. And if I've come this far and acknowledge this, every other human must wonder the same thing at some point in their lives." Cassie paused, contemplating reality and how much of a genius Shakespeare was to have grasped the human complexities and the absurdities of life.

"Shakespeare was a genius," she stated without equivocation. "He knew there were no answers, only uncertainties, and he dramatized these absurdities and complexities with characters that embodied them. His characters give us a mirror image of ourselves and the uncertainties we live: excessive ambition, Macbeth; jealousy and revenge, Othello; jealousy and hatred, Iago; trust and the inability to see deception, Brutus and Othello; loyalty and unconditional love, Desdemona; inaction and idealistic justice, Hamlet; Lady Macbeth, and Cassius, more jealousy and the ability to influence; add Iago to that group. Shakespeare gave us all of them; he gave us ourselves." She finally realized that what she had been teaching for decades had manifested itself in her own life.

"Ironically, *Macbeth* fits perfectly here, the lust for power and the ability of Lady Macbeth to persuade her husband to kill the king, but jealousy in its most malevolent form does begin with Iago. The Moor's downfall is gonna hurt, but maybe it'll give me more insight into myself and how I could become a victim of such a nefarious person. Maybe at some later point in my life, I'll be able to face the other reasons you gave."

"*Othello* will give you insight into Taylor. Othello and trust will give you insight into yourself, but reread *Measure for Measure* for further insight into Vaughn." Jeremy paused. "And hone in on Angelo's character."

Walter nodded. "Yes, absolutely, relate him to Vaughn."

Cassie shook her head. "Not ready for that challenge," she said. She had avoided that aspect of life all her life, except for Brian. She didn't have the fortitude to overcome it again. Her father's rejection had taken on its own persona and had become her avatar, that little voice in her head that keeps you up at night and buries itself somewhere inside during the daylight hours. That little voice you know is there, but you refuse to acknowledge. Until Brian, Cassie had avoided, worse, she had run from believing anyone she desired also desired her. Brian's death had catapulted her deeper into her own insecure past, a past she couldn't change.

Teaching about hatred, jealousy and lust was easy; living it was hard; denial made it easier to hide.

58

CHRISTMAS EVENING

From all the excitement of Christmas day, Stevie had fallen asleep at 9:00 o'clock, on the sofa. Cassie nudged her awake and ushered her semi-comatose daughter upstairs. Bed time, young lady. Even nine-year-olds need their sleep. Stevie fell in line and dreamily pulled herself up each step, happy to put on her soft flannel pajamas, brush her teeth, mandatory in the Komsky household no matter how tired, and snuggle into bed, asleep almost before her head touched the pillow. She's just like her dad, Cassie reminisced, although Stevie would never know it. After tucking her in and kissing her forehead, Cassie threw on a pair of soft sweat pants and rejoined Walter and Jeremy, still sipping tea intermittently with a glass of wine, talking about Chelsea.

"Here's another question," Walter said, "again, for both of you: Do you have plans for New Year's Eve, because if you don't, I'd like you to spend it with me. My daughter's flying out from Oregon this Monday and I'd like both of you to meet her."

"Walter, that's wonderful!" Cassie exclaimed. "How old is she, when did you see her last, did she decide on her own?"

Walter laughed. "Slow down Cassie. One question at a time; one answer at a time. First, she just turned twenty-one last week, so we'll have to celebrate her birthday by doing something special; second, the last time I saw her she was twelve and her mother, Janice, had come back to Jersey for her father's funeral; and third, yes, she decided to come completely on her own. She even fought her mother to do it, but she insisted. That's the best part. I can't wait to see her. Maybe we'll spend a day or two at Resorts or Caesars, celebrate her birthday there; have dinner; see a show. Go to dinner New Year's Eve. Father-daughter." He beamed, and he didn't even know it. "So I thought you two might like to join us, and Stevie, of course."

"Walter, I can't speak for Jeremy, but for the exact reason you just stated, that it's a father-daughter thing, I have to say no." She glanced at Jeremy.

"Oh, I absolutely agree with Cassie. This is a time for you and," he paused. "What's her name? You never mentioned her name."

"Ashton. Ashton Jean."

"Pretty name, Walter," Jeremy said. Cassie nodded. "But this is a very special time for you and Ashton and you need to spend it together. Thanks for thinking of us, though, especially me."

"The invitation is open in case you change your minds. I've told Ashton about both of you, and she'd love to meet you. Her plane leaves Monday morning after New Year's, the only flight she could get; so if you change your mind or you want to spend time with us Sunday morning, maybe a late breakfast, call me, please. We can meet at my house, or I'll bring her here, show her the campus and we can meet at the Bagels and Bakery for a quick bite. They make a dynamite egg, bacon and cheese bagel with Swiss cheese baked into the crust. Delicious. Have you tried it?"

They shook their heads. "And that is surprising for me," Jeremy offered, "since I've eaten almost everything on almost every menu in almost every eatery in this town."

"Well, there's always a first, and what better way to spend the last day before you crash diet than with one of their breakfast specials."

"I'll consider it," Jeremy said. He looked at Cassie, who shook her head.

"I'm still a no on that one, but if I change my mind, or if Stevie really wants to go, I'll call you. Or, even better, I'll let you know tomorrow when we run, how's that?"

"That'll be fine," Walter concluded.

By 11:00, their repetitious yawns signaled the evening's end. It had been a glorious Christmas; one they would never forget. Walter and Jeremy said their good-byes to Cassie, each accompanied with a bear hug, and Cassie kissed Walter gently on his lips. They'd see each other for tomorrow's run. Jeremy vowed he'd be in for the day; he'd get his exercise cleaning out his frig.

59

LAST DAY OF CHRISTMAS BREAK

The day after Christmas, Cassie, Walter and Stevie had run three miles, dropped Stevie off at home; then Cassie and Walter jogged another two. A good workout but just a chip off the extra calories they had ingested Christmas day. Then they had gone back to Cassie's and lunched on left-over ham, hummus and baba ganoush. Jeremy declined an invitation. He had already eaten more from his frig than he had discarded and was nowhere near finished.

Sunday evening, Walter left in high spirits, anticipating his daughter's flight the next morning. Cassie was as excited for him as he was, and offered numerous tips for encouraging conversation, what a twenty-one year old daughter who hadn't seen her father in years might want to ask or say, might want to know about her dad, may even ask her father about his side of the divorce story.

"Who knows what she'll ask," Cassie stated, "but she wanted to see you against her mother's wishes; so there's got to be an interest in having a relationship with her father, and lots of questions. Just relax and answer honestly."

"So that's the sum total advice you can offer me, a phychiatrist, for my week with my daughter?"

"Uh-hum," Cassie nodded and laughed. "Relax, Walter, you'll be fine. If you get nervous or need advice at any time, remember, I'm really good at this for others, not so good with advice for myself!"

And here it was, Sunday night, last day of Christmas break, and only two calls from Walter since last Monday when he got Ashton from the airport for her one week stay. His first call was the Tuesday before New Year's to thank her for all her advice. His second call was New Year's Day. First he wished her a Happy New Year; then his thoughts became emotional when he told Cassie that he never should have let so many years go by without seeing his daughter. He should have insisted on visiting and should have been more motivated, more pro-active, despite knowing his ex would rebuke him and resist.

He and Ashton had talked about things his ex had never told his daughter, leading her to assume her father didn't want her or her brother. Now that she was older and understood rules existed in a divorce, she wanted to know if that was the reason. Turning twenty-one, she could finally see her Dad on her own without her mother's blessing or her approval, and find out for herself. And so they had talked, about everything past, present and future. Of all things, Walter added, she was following in her father's footsteps, becoming a shrink, as she termed it, to help kids, especially adolescents, her hardest time, adjust to divorce.

Life is such a crap shoot; you never know how the dice will fall – "pass, don't pass; come, don't come; 50-50 odds, hold, don't hold," as simple and as forthright as that. Life was a game of chance, for something much more precious than money.

Cassie was deep in thought as she packed dried fruit and nuts for tomorrow's lunch, the mundane routine of life, when a knock, no, a pounding at her door, her front door startled her. What's happening, she thought, her first reaction? Is it *my* door? Is it for me? The pounding became louder, more insistent. "Mrs. Komsky? Mrs. Komsky? It's me, Gloria. Please Mrs. Komsky, I need to talk to you. Mrs. Komsky, are you there?"

No doubt it was for her. What's going on? Way past curfew and tomorrow began a new school year. Why would Gloria be pounding on her door now? Instantly, she went for the door.

"I'm here, Gloria, what's . . ." Cassie did not finish. Anguish distorted Gloria's beautiful face and her deep blue eyes were swollen, stained with tears. She flung herself into her teacher's arms, clinging and crying. Cassie held her close. "It's okay, Gloria. It's okay. What's wrong? Tell me what's wrong?"

Gloria backed away to face Cassie. "Mrs. Komsky. It's horrible. You have to come. You have to help. It's Rachel. She's hysterical. I don't know what to do."

"Rachel? Gloria, what's happening?" Cassie could not comprehend. This was the last weekend of Christmas break and kids had begun signing in since 11:00 a.m.; it was 9:30

p.m. now. What could have happened since then? "Tell me, please . . . slowly." Whatever it was, it had to be terrible for Gloria to break curfew and seek her out instead of her own housemistress. She led Gloria to the sofa.

"We were okay when we first got back. I mean, we all thought Rachel was okay. I had spoken to her over the break lots of times, and we got together twice: the second time I slept over. She was upset then, but when she got here this afternoon, I thought she was the same happy Rachel we all knew. But I was wrong. She must have been hiding it, and now she's hysterical. She's been crying since she came back from dinner and she's just getting worse. She sat with Samir, alone; just the two of them. I think that's what triggered it. I can't console her, and I can't ask anyone else for advice." She glanced furtively at Cassie, adding, "No one, no one at all, knows they're married. I know you do."

"No one else knows, Gloria. I've told no one. Please, tell me what's happened."

"Rachel will only talk to you. Even if you can't help, she needs you." She sobbed back tears and wiped her eyes with her sleeves. Cassie would have reached for a paper towel or something but she wouldn't leave Gloria to get one, not for a second, not like this. "Her father threw Samir out of their house. He called Samir a dirty Arab and said if he ever saw him again or heard his daughter was with him, he'd kill him. He's calling Dr. O/B tomorrow to tell him to expel Samir."

"Oh my God," Cassie was shocked. More and more hatred. "Gloria," she said tentatively, "do . . . do her parents know they're married?"

Gloria shook her head. "No, Mrs. Komsky, "other than me, only you know."

"Who was the second witness at their wedding?"

"Samir's uncle."

"Thank God," Cassie uttered in relief.

"Does Stevie know? Gloria asked apprehensively."

Cassie shook her head. "Just you and me, Gloria, and Samir's uncle. I didn't want to put that responsibility on Stevie. No one else knows, and I'll keep it that way."

Gloria nodded. Emotionally distraught, she could only offer a weak smile, but it was good enough. "Thank you, Mrs. Komsky. Samir said you'd never tell. He was right. How'd he know?"

"They left the room so quickly that afternoon I didn't get a chance to promise, but he knew. Otherwise, he wouldn't have told me." She paused. "Samir and I have something in common that I'm certain he's never repeated. That's why he knew."

Gloria understood. "They were going to tell her parents last week when he visited. They wanted to be together when they let her parents know. But it all went crazy." Gloria broke down again. "Rachel's father attacked Samir with the fire iron before they got a chance to tell him they were married."

"Physically attacked him?"

Gloria nodded. "Slashed his leg. Samir had to leap over the sofa to avoid him. Rachel was hysterical. She grabbed her father's arm and tried to hold him back. When she did that, her father hurled her away. She hit the dining room table and lost her balance."

"No!" Cassie gasped. She knew what happened next.

"Samir went beserk. He grabbed her father's arm and forced the poker out of his hand. Rachel was screaming. Her mother was screaming, telling her father to stop, and all the while, her dad was calling him a filthy Arab who had killed his people and ordering him to get out of his house. Except for our phone calls, Rachel's been alone. I thought she was okay, but I was wrong. Rachel was just trying to be strong, but that's impossible. She's scared because her father's a major donor to the academy. When he calls Dr. O/B and demands the Trustees expel Samir, Rachel thinks Dr O/B will give in. Rachel can't deal with any more, Mrs. Komsky. Please go see her."

Cassie rose quickly. "I'm getting my coat, and I have to tell Stevie I'm leaving. She can be alone for an hour or so as long as she knows where I'll be." Cassie ran upstairs and hurried down with her coat a few minutes later. "It's really cold out, isn't it?" There was a touch of angst in her voice.

"Very cold, Mrs. Komsky," Gloria said. "Please wear gloves because . . ." She stopped, not wanting to refer to Cassie's falling down in the storm. "Do you have a flashlight?" Cassie dropped it on the sofa to put on her coat. "I'll walk back with you."

Cassie was afraid. She felt it in the quickening beat of her heart, but she wouldn't let Gloria know nor would she let Rachel endure this alone. She shook her head. "No thanks, Gloria. I could never let you do that. Call me thirty minutes after I leave your dorm. If I'm not back here by then, call Mr. Harper." At least, she thought, at least there's no snow.

60

CASSIE AND GLORIA HELP RACHEL

The temperature had dropped drastically since the afternoon and the night was frigid. Cassie realized how daring Gloria had been to sneak out to come get her. Facing freezing temperatures alone was not something she'd encourage anyone to do; that, she knew from experience. Since Gloria had, and had broken curfew to seek her out, Cassie knew this situation was serious.

To make it worse, an icy wind blew from the north. It hugged their coats and slapped their faces. Cassie pulled her woolen scarf over her face and shoved her gloved hands into her coat sleeves like a turtle retracting it's extremities to protect itself from danger. The trip back would unnerve her; she'd be doing this when it was later and colder. Worse, she'd be alone.

They entered Roosevelt House through the dormitory entrance. Quietly, Cassie motioned to Gloria to remove her coat and gloves, in case Gloria's housemistress was in the back office and saw her. She doubted she would be there, since curfew was almost two hours ago. Who would want to be outside on a night this cold? But just in case. Even more, since Gloria had broken curfew, she'd be subjected to consequences if caught.

Cassie pulled on the heavy double doors and slid inside. The housemistress's door was completely closed. Safe. Cassie motioned the go-ahead for Gloria, watched her walk down the empty hallway and turn left. Then she tapped lightly on the office door. Ms. Marino, a full-bodied woman in her late forties, with hair dyed brown, roots badly in need of a touch-up, opened the door a crack.

"Hi, Ms. Marino, I'm Cassie Komsky. I took over for Steven Draggert . . ."

"I know who you are. We haven't met formally, but I saw you dancing at Homecoming."

Oh, well, that helped Cassie thought sarcastically. "I'm here to see Gloria and Rachel for a few minutes."

"Now?" She stared at Cassie, then glanced at her watch. "What can't wait until tomorrow?"

"I'd rather review what I need to review while it's fresh in my mind, before classes start tomorrow. And I'm right here, passing by, on a longer than usual, and later than usual, and much colder than usual," Cassie added to defuse the situation with a bit of humor, "walk?"

Judy Marino knew Cassie's excuse was a total fabrication. Who'd be out on a night like this? Not Cassie, especially after her near fatal accident. But Judy shrugged indifferently. "You don't need my permission; go ahead."

"It's more professional if I ask; it's a courtesy." Cassie nodded. The door closed and Cassie followed the path Gloria had taken down the hall. Most doors were closed, but whether partially open or closed, excited chatter emanated from inside each room. Excited young ladies talking about their glorious weeks home or abroad. Down the hall, left at the corner, three doors down, Gloria was peeking out the room motioning Cassie inside. Gloria pushed the door open a little more. In the shadows, Cassie saw Rachel's crumpled figure on the bed, soft muffled sobs emanating from deep in her soul.

Oh no, Cassie thought. Oh no. She hurried to her bedside. Rachel looked up in fear, recognized Cassie, and threw her arms around her as bottled up anguish and emotional pain burst forth and she sobbed into Cassie's shoulder. Cassie held on tightly and rocked her gently, as she did when Stevie had cried for her daddy who would never come home, as Cassie's mom had done when Cassie, at three, realized her daddy didn't love her, didn't want her, and never would. She just held on and rocked her. Gloria, halfway between the doorway and the room, backed out silently and closed the door.

61

CASSIE COMFORTS RACHEL

Rachel's universe had imploded. All the good she had been taught to believe, all the love and trust she had felt in people, in her parents, who had professed to love, be kind, to understand others and help, all that had been a phantasmagoric dream. None of it was real; it was all a lie, all a sham, from another dimension far away; the people she had loved all her life – strangers now. For her, her life had ended, as all the evil and hatred in the world had suffused itself into her father's persona and targeted Samir, her husband.

How could this have happened? Her parents had taught her to be open and tolerant of other views, to help people who had less; not just less money, but less fortunate; help people who hurt. Show compassion. Be a good steward of the world. All of their teachings had melted into hypocrisy. Both of them, hypocrites, especially her father, who hated Samir without knowing him; who hated Samir because of a name. Montague, Capulet, Gibran,

Greer. What's in a name?   To some people, plenty.
Nothing changes.

Despite all his posturing and all his preaching all her
life, her father was as prejudiced as any of the warring
two factions from *Romeo and Juliet,* so much so he had discarded his own daughter. The epitome of trust, betrayed.
She could have believed this if one of her friends had said
this about their father, but *her* father? He had been her
sun, and he had risen and set in her eyes. For the first
time, she truly understood the unwarranted hatred Samir
and his countrymen had experienced and still experience
throughout their lives. It was a hatred bred from, and
perpetrated through, indoctrination.

Today's world was supposed to be civilized, was supposed to fight for goodness to free people from tyranny
and oppression. How could we have evolved into the
greatest civilization and still allow, still feel, still foment
and proselytize hatred of such magnitude?

"We're only people, Rachel." Cassie spoke softly and
held her close. This young, beautiful woman needed,
more than anything, comfort, trust and assurance and
to know that someone who had taken a stand would
not betray her. "Whether we're in the first century, the
sixteenth or the twentieth, we're still only people. We
just mask it differently. Once the mask comes off, we're
all the same, same emotions, same loves, same hates.
Shakespeare's plays say that."

Rachel looked at her a bit surprised. Shakespeare
was taking on a more powerful dimension. "Well, did
it matter that you wore a costume from the seventeenth
century? You were still the same person, the same

good person. *Don't let yourself change.*" Jeremy had said these same words to her after Taylor's charge. "Rachel, don't succumb to hate. It'll destroy you just as it has destroyed all the Montagues and the Capulets of the world. Remember *your* words, words you've said: you pick yourself up and go on."

Rachel shook her head, "I can't," she cried. "I can't go on anymore. My world is falling apart and I don't know how to fix it."

"Rachel, you *are* the 20th century Ophelia you portrayed. You *do* have the courage to face down your father and stand up for what you believe is morally right. It doesn't matter that *he* couldn't; it matters that *you* can. Very few people have that kind of courage, Rachel, very few. You do not follow; you lead. You did not get caught up in ignoring or dismissing Samir, or even discarding him, as many of your peers and even some faculty did. It would have been easier to have gone along with the masses, but you didn't. You spoke out for what was ethically and morally right, and you'll continue to do so because that's you."

Cassie had Rachel's attention. She looked at Cassie. "You think so?" She asked apprehensively, gulping back her tears.

"Without a doubt! You may make a lot of enemies as you go along, and you'll experience some hardships, some severe, as you've just witnessed, but you'll live without compromise. That's freedom, as long as this country allows us that precious right."

Her sobs stopped. What remained were intermittent whimpers and a few silent tears. Her father cared more about his hatred than about her. Samir thought only of her. How did the lines get so crossed? A man who she was supposed to hate loved her more than the man who was supposed to love her unconditionally. A paradox.

"Rachel, you *have* had the courage to oppose the brainwashed masses. You love for what is right against the popular narrative, and you've chosen not to hate or stereotype, not to be indoctrinated and brainwashed by our government and our press. You *can* get up and go on, no matter how hard. You and Samir; you *both* can.

"Think about your future and your lives together," Cassie encouraged. "You've got college ahead of you and your whole life to live. You'll succeed. And remember, always remember, Samir will never let you fall, Rachel. Never. He loves you and will love you forever. His uncle will not let you be hurt either. It'll work out. Samir is your road taken; defeat is the road you've left behind.

"Your mother may come around, in time. If she defended you against her husband in her own house, she may have the courage to refute your father. But if not, you've chosen your own path, and Rachel, it's a beautiful one."

"I wish I had your confidence, Mrs. Komsky."

Cassie smiled. "It's more determination than confidence, Rachel. None of us know where life is going to take us, but wherever it does, whether up or down – and lots of times it's down – we pick ourselves up and go on." Rachel smiled weakly. They were her words, words they had talked about in class. "Because if we don't do that, we'll stay down. And who wants to do that?"

Rachel's tears had stopped. Disappointment would linger, so would hurt, but it would wane. The love she and Samir had for each other would keep her going. This she knew, and she knew Cassie was right. Samir would never let her falter. He'd find a way to see this through.

They were eighteen; they'd graduate in May and go to college. Ironically they both had applied to Princeton, early acceptance, before they knew each other, before Samir attended Chelsea. Fate plays strange games. Rachel's father had wanted her to go to Yale, his alma mater, but she would not even apply. Jersey was as far north as she had wanted to go. She was relieved she had rejected Yale then; she would never have considered it now. She and Samir would go to Princeton and find a complex for married couples. They'd overcome this struggle, as traumatic as it was, and they'd overcome it together.

62

CASSIE FINDS SAMIR

"Give me an hour before you call," Cassie told Gloria as she left their room. I need to see Samir. I want him to know I've seen Rachel." Gloria nodded; Cassie walked into the bitter night for Damon House and Samir.

If Cassie had thought the temperature was cold when she had gone with Gloria, she was shocked to the bone once she left the warm dorm. She covered her face with her scarf and vapor trickled out from its sides; the heat of her breath caught inside her scarf and moistened her nostrils. She sniffed it back, dug in her head and hid her gloved hands inside her coat pockets. Even with outerwear and layers of clothing, she was cold. Full moon, clear sky, twinkling stars, bright enough without a flashlight. If only this could be like the starry night from Homecoming. But it wasn't. It was cold, brutal and bitter. This would be a fast trip. Be careful; don't fall.

With an "I'm here; gotta talk to Samir," and a smile to Jeremy, she headed to Samir's room. But he wasn't there; nor was he in the game room. Missing? Again? Impossible! Come on, where could he be now? "He's here," Matt said. "He's in the building. I saw him come in; saw him drop his bags, punch a hole in the wall," he nodded towards the indentation next to Samir's desk "go to dinner, come back and punch another hole in the wall." He nodded to the hole in the plaster behind the door. "Then he disappeared. He gave his word he'd never leave after curfew again, and when Samir gives his word; he keeps it. If I've learned anything about Samir in the past four months, it's that he keeps his word, but where could he be?" Matt shrugged. Cassie wished she had had time to ask him how he spent Christmas, but she didn't. She had to find Samir and get home.

"Thanks, Matt. I'll look around."

"And no going outside unless it's straight to your house!"

"What?" Cassie looked at him. She couldn't believe what he had just said, but he wasn't backing down. He remembered all too well the last time Cassie had gone looking for Samir. Matt was completely serious and concerned for his teacher's safety. No way could she be offended. If anything, it was an expression of caring. Cassie smiled. "I promise, Matt. I will never leave the building to search for Samir again. And since we both know he'll never leave after curfew again, we're both safe. So please do not worry about me, but thank you for your concern."

He smiled and she was off. Had to make this quick. It was getting late. She had ignored the dorm rooms all occupied with chatter; he'd never be there. She had by-passed the game room with a quick glance, knowing he would not be there either, and she had opened and closed each of the vacant rooms in the wings – lights on, lights off, and hit the second floor. Nothing. The third floor, nothing, but yes! Foot prints in the dust. Good work, Cassie, she patted herself on the back until she examined them further and saw where they led. That's impossible. There were work orders for this, one from Jeremy; another from Dr. O/B. Both had confirmed this.

So where's the lock? Where's the bolt? With trepidation she opened the door leading to the roof. He wouldn't, he couldn't, but he had. Footsteps led upwards, heaviest at the top step which opened to a little attic, which led to a heavy door that led to the roof. The roof. Oh my God. She opened the door slowly. A blast of frigid air slapped her face and she recoiled. If he's up here, she thought, he's lost all reason.

Darkness enveloped her. Frigid air made her shiver. It would have made anyone shiver, and after being in a warm dormitory, her body had adjusted to it, welcoming it gladly, and it was telling her it did not want to be here in this torturous cold.

But as the ambient light from the attic seeped into this icy hell and her eyes adjusted to night, she saw his outline, sitting on the edge of the roof, staring in the direction of Rachel's dorm, yearning for her and hope in the world.

"You can't stay here," she stated calmly, without ambiguity. You will get sick, you will hurt yourself, *and* you will hurt Rachel." He turned and faced her in this blackness.

"You know?"

"I know."

"You have been to see her?"

"I have. I will tell you everything once we're sitting inside and we're warm! Warm, not freezing to death, where you will do her no good. Please, come inside." She lighted his path with her flashlight. "And be careful." She shone her light over long wires that coiled like snakes.

Samir placed his flashlight on the edge of the roof and pulled himself upright with unbelievable agility.

"Try to hurry. I'm standing in the doorway where it's much warmer and my joints are locking up already." Cassie's breath vaporized around her like a diaphanous cloud.

He passed his flashlight over the wires, stepped over them and started down the steps. Cassie sighed with relief and followed.

63

FIRST DAY BACK AFTER NEW YEAR

First day back after Christmas break. First office memo of the New Year: today's faculty meeting, cancelled. Nice. Get home early. The first day back after Christmas break and the New Year should have been a time for ebullient, non-stop chatter before class. It should have been an effervescent interchange of "Where'd you go," and "What'd you do?" And for nine students in her first period class, it was. But not for Samir and Rachel, who sat together and smiled with their friends, but who could not talk about their Christmas break. To Rachel's credit, no tears surfaced. If she were crying, she was hiding it well. Samir sat next to her, and this morning, his pinky was touching hers discretely, letting her know he was with her every step of the way.

Eight o'clock came and went without any cessation in their chatter. They had become oblivious to time. After a few more minutes crept into class time, Cassie rapped on the table with her pencil, a steady, monotonous tempo that finally got their attention and made them look at the clock and their watches. "Make haste and get seated before I decline into my 'vale of years.'"

"Oh, Mrs. Komsky, that's a good one," Jason exclaimed. "Was that a planned introduction to *Othello*, or an impromptu, because I remember that exact line." Connor gave him a derisive glance, ready to tease him mercilessly if he had read the play over Christmas break. "What?" Jason responded, "I read it over the break." His classmates laughed.

"Only you would read an entire Shakespeare play during Christmas break," Connor quipped. "Good," he said decisively, "I know exactly who to go to if I get stuck."

"What's new about that?" Jason retorted. "You *always* come to me when you get stuck!" The class was enjoying this.

"That's what happens when you have an eidetic memory; you get used. Don't act surprised. You're supposed to get used; that's part of being a brainy nerd." Connor gave Jason an affable shove. Surprisingly, this stocky, tough, muscular jock and this nerdy brain had transcended roommate status and had become very good friends, almost inseparable.

"No, Mr. Abrams," Cassie feigned formality, bringing the class back to academics. "This is *not* the way I intended to introduce the play. But since this situation related perfectly to that line, I used the analogy. And I'm still waiting for all of you to settle down so we can get started." Her pencil thumped against the table again and they quieted.

"Okay, since we've alluded to this passage, let's begin with it. Act 3, scene 3, read the full passage and interpret it as you see it out of context from the rest of the play. After we've read acts 1 and 2, we'll reread this scene and see if our interpretation or its significance has changed. I've referenced one line from this passage; maybe the rest of it will have more significance for you."

"Do you think there's much to interpret, Mrs. Komsky?" Jason asked, trying to get Cassie's perspective, "because, to me, it's just a simple feeling sorry for himself."

"You sure that's all you think it is?"

"Well, sort of. How much more is there?"

"We'll let the class decide before I interject, so let's not influence them. Pair up, everyone," she instructed. "Consider how Othello views Iago. Begin reading from line 155, where Iago stresses the importance of his good name. Othello's complete trust in Iago is the basis for him believing Desdemona is unfaithful. In the 'vale of years' soliloquy, Othello makes bold statements about race and his station in life. Are his assumptions justified, not just in his life, but in relationships and marriages today? Consider everything from a universal perspective, an individual perspective etc., etc., etc." She rotates her hand indicating consider everything. "Fifteen minutes in groups, then we'll discuss your ideas."

At this point in the semester, the class had delineated its own group dynamic. Emelia, Elizabeth and Gloria came together as did Jason and Connor, Mason and Parker, Matt and Zack. Gloria looked forlornly at Rachel and Samir, who nodded his wife forward to work with her group. Reluctantly, she joined the ladies. Samir opened his notebook and his text; he worked alone.

64

OTHELLO'S VALE OF YEARS

"I used vale of years to hurry you along, implying I'd get old before you settled in. Does Othello use it in the same way and for the same purpose?"

"Same way," Parker blurted out; different purpose."

"Elucidate."

"He says he's old; okay, he's old, but not by much. I guess in the same way you're old, but not old by much." That comment broke up the class.

"Oh my God, Parker," Elizabeth said, shocked, "you just implied Mrs. Komsky is old. Didn't you do that once before?" Her dark, almond eyes danced with anticipation. She couldn't wait to hear him get out of this one.

"No, no, no, Mrs Komsky," Parker flatly denied Elizabeth's charge. "If it sounded like that, it's not what I meant."

"Hmm," Cassie had a not-so-pleased expression on her face. "I've just gotta hear how you worm your way out of this." The ladies were holding their hands to their mouths, the guys were laughing without inhibition; even Samir was smiling. Cassie could take the jibe if it brought a smile to Rachel and Samir. "Please, Mr. Otis-Barrett, by all means, continue."

"It's not like that, Mrs. Komsky. What-I-meant-was," Parker enunciated each word in an attempt to redeem himself, " that Othello uses his age as one reason Desdemona may be cheating on him, then he contradicts that reason by saying he's not old by much. That's all; that's all I meant." He looks around for support. "And I added that comment about you because how we view age is relative, anyway, isn't it?"

Cassie nodded. "Good save, Parker, and you know I wasn't really insulted." Parker smiled.

"Mrs. Komsky, am I wrong or does the play mention the age twenty-eight?" Jason asks.

"In the beginning of the play, twenty-eight is mentioned, but by Othello?"

"Guess I'm not eidetic," Jason says apologetically. "I can't remember."

"Cheer up, Buddy," Connor slaps his back good-naturedly." We like you when you're just one of us."

"I agree with Parker," Mason enters the conversation. "I don't think Othello's age matters and I think Othello believes that too. Anyway, age *is* kind of relative, isn't it? I think my father's old, but he doesn't think he is. He thinks my grandmother's old, and at seventy-nine, she's just starting to agree. So when Othello adds that he's not that old, he means it. I think race is a more valid reason, maybe even social status."

"Good analysis," Cassie comments. "Anybody else?"

"Social class, that may affect their relationship," Zach offers. "Othello says he doesn't have soft parts like courtiers do. He's a general, great in battle, but not with courtly manners or gentle conversation."

"Does that make Othello a folly to Desdemona because of his adventurous life? Was he bolder, daring, maybe more 'masculine' than the other suitors who had courted her? Think that attracted or intrigued her?" Cassie asks, developing that point before having them search for another line that showed Othello's background.

"Maybe," Zach adds with uncertainty.

"Of course, Zach," Gloria says. "Would you get a lot more dates if you played football than if you were a bibliophile like Jason?"

Cassie nods. "Good analogy."

"Yes he would, Gloria," Jason says. "Parker gets a lot more dates than I'd ever get, but I don't agree it's only because he plays football. You play football, Mason, and you're an outstanding player, but I'll bet you don't get as many dates as Parker does." He paused and waited. Mason held back. Parker was his best friend. "Do you?" Jason pressed for an answer.

Mason looked at Parker. "No, I don't."

"Why not?"

"I can answer that," Parker added objectively, "Because of my family's social position, despite my playing football, and despite my dad being dean."

"Yup," Mason replied. Their ability to see analogies and to voice them was outstanding. "Everyone knows I'm a day student. There's no money in my family for room and board; there's just brains," he added humorously. They all saw it; they were not naïve. To be an Otis-Barrett meant prestige, control, power, and those were traits people feared and coveted. Even if Parker didn't play football, even if he were a nerd, he'd still be popular.

"So, from this soliloquy, Othello has reason to be jealous?" Cassie asks.

"No, Emelia says, posture-perfect. "These are the reasons he gives for what he *perceives* may be his wife's infidelity. They're not factual. His age is inconsequential at this point. He's not that old and he's still an able-bodied general. Being black? If the racial thing is anything like it is in this country and in this century, maybe. But Desdemona married him anyway. And his social class, which is not low, he's a general, or his lack of finesse? Again, she married him anyway. Othello's problem is he's naïve; he's too trusting. 'Honest' Iago, Othello calls him. He can be duped by Iago because he trusts him. It's that same trust and betrayal problem we talked about with *Hamlet*, and it seems Iago is a master at that. But if Othello didn't trust him so completely, he would have ignored his insinuations about Desdemona, or told him to shut-up."

"Yeah, Emelia's right," Parker interjects. "It is about trust, not social status. My mother grew up in Jersey City, and my father has nothing but praise for her ability to fit right in. He didn't care about her social status when he asked her to marry him, but he trusts her, completely."

Cassie reeled. No one in the football crew had ever mentioned Taylor's Jersey City roots. Could this be a reason for her jealousy? If Taylor had come from nothing and had married her way up, would she view Cassie as a threat, someone who wanted to do the same thing? Since

Vaughn had deviated from social protocol to marry her, a Jersey City girl who was light years away from his social class, could he do it again?

Of course he could. But would he? Maybe, but it would never be with her; Cassie would never let herself be the catalyst. But maybe from Taylor's perspective it was possible. Vaughn may not have been concerned about Taylor's social status when he asked her to marry him, but Cassie was now certain Taylor had been well aware of his. Anyone who would mention her Halston dress at a Christmas party for middle-class faculty had to be acutely aware of class distinction.

So, to Cassie, there was a reason after all, and Emelia's words to Desdemona, that jealous souls are "not ever jealous for the cause, but jealous for they're jealous," were not completely accurate in Taylor's case. Inadvertently, Parker had given Cassie Taylor's reason. Jersey City, huh? Very possibly Taylor *did* think her lifetime goal was in jeopardy, and whether perceived or real, that would have given her a reason to make Cassie her target.

Cassie was glad she had not referenced the beginning of the play where Othello tells Iago that his life and being come "from men of royal siege." Knowing Othello had come from royalty may have swayed the conversation to a different path, and Parker may never have mentioned his mother's roots. But he had, and it gave Taylor's jealousy a palpable motive.

65

CASSIE SUBMITS FORM TO MELISSA, MONDAY, JANUARY 4

Oh, for December's freezing temperatures and cold blasts of wind. This weather was so much worse. Last night, when she had walked home from Samir's House, it had been bitter cold. This morning had been no better and after four classes, the day held little prospect for double digits.

She remembered frigid temperatures like these in Manasquan, when howling winds would slam against their little cape with a fury so strong she'd think the gods on Mt. Olympus were battling for some coveted title. Sleet and hail would blacken daylight. Sometimes a few horrific storms would carry the ocean's mist to her door and attempt to beat it down. Flags would fly perpendicular to their masts from winds well over thirty-five miles an hour, and if the temperatures were freezing, they would be frozen in place as if Jack Frost had zapped them with icy magic. They'd stand like symbols of nature's might, saying, here's what I can do; now bow.

That's what Chelsea had become overnight, a frigid wind tunnel, temperatures close to zero and icy air currents slaloming between frozen branches and buildings hunting for human prey. No one was safe from this. She was surprised Dr. O/B hadn't canceled school, but then he'd had no way of knowing how horrific the weather would become as night turned to day and Yukon winds left their beds to sojourn south.

Cassie entered Smythe Hall with the wind pushing her into the building and slamming the door shut! Done with you, it had said. One deep breath, then a few more and she removed her heavy sherpa-lined gloves and threw back the hood on her coat, glad she had worn a coat that afforded such protection from the merciless weather.

She mushed forward to Guidance and familiar faces to submit her most recent report about Samir. Only what concerned his safety, and in this case, Cassie was positive this report, unequivocally, honed in on that. No lock? Samir on the roof? No one, no one, should be out on the roof of their dorm, or of any building, in warm weather, cold weather, or in any weather. She had told him she'd have to report it; he understood, but his grief from his father-in-law's assault, and Dr. Greer's gross mistreatment of his own daughter, Samir's wife, had created such deep despondency in Samir that having Dr. O/B know he was sitting up on the rooftop's ledge was insignificant, as long as Cassie didn't tell Dr. O/B why.

And this she would never do. Samir knew she would keep their unspoken bond. Like childhood: You don't know why you trust someone; you just do. Same with old age. She trusted Samir, and he trusted her, like that. And all the in-between years that had just about destroyed her she'd fight through. These same in-between years were close to destroying Rachel and Samir. She wouldn't let them go it alone.

Cassie opened the door to Guidance and entered a room pumping heat. She inhaled; smelled it. It warmed her nostrils. Everyone was occupied, concentrating on work, desperately doing catch-up after almost two absent weeks. First day back; must be tons of paperwork and forms to complete, and here she was about to give Melissa another one. She propped her attaché on the counter in front of Melissa's desk and pulled out the paper. Melissa hadn't glanced up.

"Hi, Melissa," Cassie said cheerily, "I have another form regarding Samir; we had another visit. Hope you had a nice New Year's," Cassie continued, handing the form to her friend who continued to work frenetically searching one stack of papers then another, perhaps for one obscure file she had misplaced before Christmas break. Cassie remained oblivious to Melissa's lack of response. "I see you're busy; you must have a backlog a foot high after ten days; I need your signature and date on this and a copy for my records; then I'll let you work."

Now Cassie glances around. No one is looking at her; no one is smiling; no one is talking. Cassie continues to look around. "Melissa . . . Melissa . . ." she whispers. "Is something wrong? It's like a morgue in here."

Without glancing up, without a hello, without a hint of a smile, Melissa takes the paper from Cassie, scribbles her signature and date on it, leans over to her copier, passes the sheet through and hands it back to Cassie. "Is everything all right?" Cassie asks, nonplussed, glancing at Melissa's signature, "because it's strangely quiet in here. Something happen?"

"I'll get this to Dr. Goodman as soon as he comes in."

"Dr. Goodman?" Cassie asks with consternation. She laughs uncomfortably. What's happened to "Walter?" She wonders. Her stomach begins to churn; there's a knot in it, a growing knot she refuses to admit is real. No one is talking. No one is talking to her! Not even Melissa from the football crew! What's happening, Cassie asks herself; with feet a little wobbly; knees a little weak. What's happening? Must be my imagination; must be my paranoia. "Okay, I've gotta go. Gotta get ready for next period. See you." There was no response.

Cassie pushes open the door, half delirious; half stupefied. What's wrong? Something I said? Something I've done? Is it me? She sniffs back a few tears. No, it can't be; I haven't said or done anything, or even seen anyone since the faculty party, except Walter and Jeremy.

And that's when the half-opened door became a fully opened door and smacked Dr. O/B's shoulder. "Oh, I'm sorry, Dr. O/B," Cassie drew back. "Hope the door didn't hurt you . . ." Her voice trailed as Vaughn walked by her as though he had felt nothing, as though she did not exist. She had become invisible.

66

AFTER MELISSA'S SNUB, JANUARY 4

Cassie's feet left the ground one step at a time, but she was unaware that she was walking; she arrived at Rand Hall in a stupor. The wind, the bone-chilling cold, no longer affected her. She'd become immune. She hadn't eaten before she left for Guidance, thinking she'd have plenty of time to grab something from Landon Hall afterwards. If she had, she might have thrown up; her appetite was gone, and she felt sick. Her stomach churned, telling her it didn't want a thing now, not one bite, even if she had had a full lunch period and she were starving.

Her thoughts reeled. Melissa? Was this the same Melissa she had come to trust, come to call a friend, treating her like a stranger? This same Melissa who had introduced her to the football crew and had called her one of them? Melissa, who had helped Cassie after her students and Jeremy had brought her in from the snow, helped her and given her warm, dry clothing to wear the day after? This same Melissa who treated Stevie like a daughter after two short months? How naïve can I be? How naïve and trusting and stupid can I be to have been so duped, like Othello under the influence of "honest" Iago.

And Dr. O/B? All his fawning and breaking protocols to intrude into my personal life, to treat me as though I were invisible? He saw me. He knew I had opened the door – it had hit him in the shoulder, but he refused to acknowledge my presence.

Cassie barely held on throughout the day, focusing on her afternoon classes and the lesson as her classes fell into their groups and analyzed Othello's vale of years passage. What causes jealousy? Who cares? Does the cause matter? No, it's just there. It was a little of what Jeremy had referred to from *Othello*: "They are not ever jealous for the cause, but jealous for they're jealous." But with Cassie, Taylor's jealousy had to do with what Parker had mentioned in class. Taylor's Jersey City roots and her innate fear of losing all she had gained had made Cassie her target. This evil woman's tentacles had now reached into Cassie's career and her interrelationship with her cohorts. Where would it end?

At the end of the day, Cassie sat alone in her room as always, but she did not do lesson plans or reread act 1, tomorrow's assignment. She sat alone and thought about life, friendship, trust and betrayal, about Hamlet's agony and Ophelia's and Desdemona's betrayal. Both women used and abused by men they had trusted and loved.

Not different for Rachel, a loving and trusting eighteen-year-old who had believed in her father's teachings and loved unconditionally, only to be disavowed by him when she did. Cassie hurt for her, for Samir, lastly, for herself. There was no justice in the world. "Some rise by sin and some by virtue fall." Shakespeare, right again.

Cassie pulled out the report she had submitted to Guidance, signed and dated by Melissa. It would go through channels and get to Dr. O/B's desk. She hoped someone in administration would address this situation quickly. That lock should have been there weeks ago. Dr. O/B had stated this at the cook-off; he had affirmed a work order had been released and that Maintenance would be on it. Yet, as of last night, no lock, no bolt. An oversight? Maybe, but a dangerous one. Samir, drowning in his own tragedy, just might go up there again.

She put the report back in her bag. She'd make a copy; file one here and another at home. She packed her attaché, dressed for the frigid weather and headed out, so glad the faculty meeting had been cancelled. With the door open to the merciless elements, Susan Dawson, secretary in Rand Hall's office, called to her. "Mrs. Komsky." She caught up to Cassie, handed her an inter-office memo, and wrapped her arms about her as a strong blast of Arctic wind smacked at her. "It's from Dr. O/B. He wants to see you in his office."

"Now?" Cassie responded uncomprehendingly. Susan glared at her. Another warm face turned cold.

Cassie read the message; it had been logged in at 3:32. She looked at her watch and held out her wrist towards Susan so its face turned to the secretary. "It's 3:34, Susan. My school day officially ended four minutes ago, earlier, since the faculty meeting had been cancelled. Kindly tell

Dr. O/B that if he had gotten this message to me five minutes ago, I would have reported. But this is my time now,
and I'm going home. I'll report to his office at whatever
time is best for him - tomorrow." She left, not caring if
Susan's dropped jaw would ever close.

Nope, she thought, no justice in the world, and no
empathy either. She'd call Walter later. Maybe he could
ease her depression, but nothing could extricate her from
this ineluctable cataclysm that was engulfing her. Would
there ever be any escape?

67

VAUGHN POUNDS ON CASSIE'S DOOR

Cassie had hoped, had believed Chelsea Academy would be the catalyst that would bring life back to her empty shell, breathe life and spirit back into her body; give her hope, inspiration after Brian's death, a nightmare from which she had never completely recovered. For a little while she thought she had achieved that here. Now she knew it was a matter of time before it all ended. She could fight Vaughn and the O/B dynasty; but she could never win. Might makes right, not principle, not morals, not ethics, just pure, unmitigated might. And in that arena, she had none. Hers would be a very brief tenure at Chelsea, very, very brief.

Her greater sadness, though, was for Stevie, who Cassie had yanked from her comfortable life and her friends in Manasquan so she could search for her own rebirth, a rebirth that would never occur. Cassie had believed a different place, a different home would remove her tragic memories, but that had been an illusion. She had actually believed she had made friends, had been accepted, and maybe even had a future with Walter – the Christmas party, Christmas day, long conversations about life, his history, hers, his invitation to meet Ashton. She had actually believed she knew him and that he had become part of her life.

But not even that. Her calls to Walter had cemented it; he had not returned one. Uncharacteristic? She had known him for little more than two months. People can spend a lifetime together in two months, but obviously it wasn't enough for her to get to know the real Walter, and it was certainly not enough to know the real Vaughn.

What was life all about, anyway, this passage through some absurd dimension where time travels and we simply exist as we grow old? What was this thing called life? Did any of us have the answer? Not at all. We may think we do; we may busy ourselves to hide from its inexplicable outcome; lose ourselves in one pompous, self-absorbed quest after another; live one fad after another to hide from our impending mortality, but that wasn't knowing life; that was running from it.

Cassie wiped back tears that fell despite efforts to hold them back. She didn't want Stevie to hear her cry. Stevie knew something was wrong when she got home, but Cassie would only tell her that people she had come to trust had turned away and her job could be in jeopardy. At nine, Stevie understood a lot. After supper, she helped Mom clean up and get lunches ready for tomorrow. Then she went upstairs to do homework and give her mother some quiet time alone.

Ten minutes of silence; ten minutes of reflection, then, bam! One horrific, loud bang against her door, and Cassie jerked up from her chair. She didn't have to ask herself who; she knew. It wasn't Walter; he hadn't answered her calls; nor was it Melissa, nor Gloria, nor Samir, nor any student. Nor was it Jeremy, who she could identify by his quick, repetitive "Let me in" rap. This was an assault, one angry, belligerent assault ordering her to open his door. No she told herself, this will not stand.

She used the peephole. "Go away; leave," she ordered. "This is not your time; it's mine, and it's my apartment."

"This is *my* apartment. Everything at Chelsea is mine. I instructed you to report to my office and you defied that order!"

"Order? You *ordered* me?" She opened the door to the full extension of the chain lock, which wasn't much. He was wearing a long cashmere coat over the same suit he had on when he had walked past her in the hall this afternoon. He had not gone home. "You do not own me, Dr. O/B, especially after the school day ends. Your behavior is not only unprovoked but unprofessional. On what grounds do you charge my door at night, during my own personal time and in my own personal space?"

"I told you, I own this place, he seethed. "You answer to me and I expect an answer when I demand it. Dr. Greer is coming to my office tomorrow morning, demanding to know why his daughter is dating an Arab student in this academy. Can you answer that question?"

"Why should I? Why should you? His daughter can date anyone she likes at this academy. You vet all students before you admit them, do you not?' Vaughn did not respond. "As

I thought, Samir was found acceptable to Chelsea, and his uncle's money found acceptable to Chelsea. He is on equal footing with every other student in every way, including his right to choose who he dates. Correct?"

"Do not twist the issue." His face contorted in anger. "No, he is not on equal footing with every other student. He's Lebanese . . . and he's dating Dr. Greer's daughter!"

Cassie feigned confusion. "Did you not know he was Lebanese when you admitted him? That information was in his bio when he was admitted; I read it. Didn't you? And I was informed of his history during my first visit to Guidance; so I don't see the confusion here, unless you're concerned about Dr. Greer's influence with the Board of Trustees?"

"Enough!" He shouted and pushed on the door. "I could break this chain with one shove, and be in *your* house in five seconds. Then where will you be?"

"Should I get a knife to defend my life and my daughter's?" Cassie shot back, visibly shaken. This was getting out of hand. Suddenly, Vaughn realized how maniacal he was being.

"I'm sorry." He backed away. "I didn't mean that, and I shouldn't have said it." He put his palms out, showing capitulation. Then in a cold and authoritarian tone, "You are required to report to my office at 10:30 tomorrow morning. Dr. Greer has cancelled appointments to be there and I expect you, as Samir's adviser and as a faculty member of this prestigious academy, to comport yourself in a professional manner. Am I making myself clear?"

"I assure you Dr. O/B, my deportment will be much more professional than yours has just been."

473

Vaughn gasped. "I can also assure you that I will answer Dr. Greer's questions and concerns as candidly as I can."

Vaughn leveled his eyes at her and he glowered. "I will fire you," he said vehemently, if you show him any disrespect."

"And what will you do to *him* if he shows *me* any disrespect?"

He fumed. His hands balled into fists and his teeth clenched so hard she heard them grind. "Not one thing!" He retorted.

"It is excellent to have a giant's strength, Dr. O/B, but it is tyrannous to use it like a giant."

"You're no Isabella, Cassie." Vaughn countered sarcastically.

"No, I'm not," she countered, "but *Measure for Measure* has the same theme of hypocrisy and without a doubt you are using your authority as Angelo used his," Cassie shot back. "Isabella's line fits perfectly here. If you can't recognize it, then identify yourself with Macbeth. That should be pretty easy for you." She watched Vaughn go red with fury. Was she implying that he was a coward, simply doing his wife's bidding? "I can tell you this much Dr. O/B: you may fire me, and you'll still have your power, your money and your lifestyle, but I will still have honor."

He laughed in her face. "You think honor matters, Cassie?" He asked smugly, a sneer on his face."

"Not to someone like you, but it does matter to me, and it did matter to my husband, and all the other soldiers who died for this country. And I'll spend the rest of my life looking for that small cadre of people who still think honor matters, and I'll cherish those I find. And people

like you? You'll stay locked behind the doors of your phony world and never have the courage to come out where
it's real. And for someone as intelligent as you, more's
the pity." She slammed the door shut, heard his footsteps
stomp away, and let herself cry.

Stevie stood at the bottom of the staircase, frightened
and trembling. She had heard much of the interplay between her mother and a person she had admired. As soon
as Cassie saw her, she held out her arms and Stevie ran
into her embrace. "I'm so sorry, Honey. Coming here was
such a big mistake. I've taken you away from a home and
friends for my own selfish needs, and brought you to this.
This won't last much longer, Stevie. We'll be forced to
leave." She kissed her daughter's hair and her forehead,
looking into Stevie's red eyes. "I'm sorry."

Stevie hugged her tightly. "It's okay, Mom. It's okay.
You always tell me not to feel sorry for myself. Pick myself
up and keep going on, right?" She smiled weakly. "You
had to try. We can go home, can't we?"

Cassie played out the scenario in her mind. "Maybe,
but not to our house, not just yet; it's rented through June.
But we'll find something. There are good people in this
world. Something will come up. Don't worry. As long as
we're together, we'll be fine. I love you, Honey . . . forever."
And the memory of her mother's words from thirty-nine
years ago played in her head. They were the same.

68

CLASS, TUESDAY, JANUARY 5, JON'S AND DAN'S ANALOGY

Cassie had never experienced a more hostile or threatening encounter as last night's with Vaughn, but she began the morning as well as she could even though she had been awake most of the night. Not a good way to meet with Dr. Greer today, but she focused on her classes and introduced *Othello* the way she had originally intended before her spontaneous 'vale of tears' intro yesterday. Hopefully, her fears were in her mind and Greer would display some semblance of professionalism.

The analogy she had used from her first day in class; Jonathan, the idealistic football captain's friend, and Dan, the jealous counterpart, fit in almost as perfectly here with *Othello* as it had with *Julius Caesar*. Mason had analyzed it perfectly then; he had been the only one to hone in on Cassius influencing Brutus for his own gain.

"That analogy was a perfect fit for *Julius Caesar*, and almost a perfect fit for *Othello*, but why did I insert 'almost'?

No one responded. "Consider this point: When Cassius talks Brutus into betraying Caesar, Brutus is directly involved in killing Caesar – 'Et tu Brute;' Brutus stabs Caesar along with the other Senators, but with *Othello* . . . ."

"'I know; I know!" Jason shouts, "I remember; I read the whole play."

"We know," Connor retorts. "You've already told us; say what you're gonna say."

"The jealousy theme is the same, and the antagonist in each is similar, but no other character in *Othello* brings about his downfall as Brutus does with Caesar. In *Caesar*, Cassius instigates Brutus who actually takes part in the killing. In *Othello*, Iago destroys Othello directly by having him kill Desdemona, but there's no third party. It's a fine point, but it's there."

"Your analysis is correct, Jason, and your explanation is perfect. "Now, everyone, relate to Iago's line, 'I am not what I am,' act 1, scene 1. Where have you heard something similar?"

"You mean compare it to another play?" Emelia asks. Cassie nods. "He says it after Othello appoints Michael Cassio to be his lieutenant instead of him. Iago's 'friend,' Roderigo, tells Iago he shouldn't follow Othello. Iago says he's only pretending to be loyal to Othello for what it can get him. 'In following him, I follow but myself,' Iago says, and at the end of that passage, adds, 'I am not what I am.'"

"Good explanation, Emelia; that's how Iago sucks him in. Now compare that one line to something or someone else."

Emelia shakes her head. "My brain needs another cup of coffee, Mrs. Komsky. I only see it as more deception."

"Anyone see a definite comparison?"

Matt's hand went up, then down. "Go ahead Matt; say it anyway."

"Well, I was just thinking . . . it is more deception, but it's also pretense. That line sounds like Hamlet when he tells Horatio he's going to put on an antic disposition, you know, pretend he's not who he is, act like he's crazy, that line after he's seen his father's ghost."

"That's the same thing I thought when I read that line," Mason concurred, his smile waking up his freckles.

"Me too," Connor interjected and Zach followed.

"And there's another line in that scene that reinforces this." Jason adds, "When Desdemona's father goes to look for her, Iago says he's gonna leave now to 'show out a flag and sign of love, which is indeed but a sign,' lines 157-158. Both statements sound like Hamlet."

"Good response, guys. You all need to *say* what you think. Come on, it's January. By now, you should know I am not telepathic." Cassie's wit kept them sharp and showed them she cared about their performance. "Anyone *not* see how Iago's words relate to Hamlet's?" She asks again, not expecting anyone to disagree. "Ladies? None of them respond, and Rachel, still much too quiet, looks pale. "Okay, let's continue chronologically and see what relates to what."

"I can do that," Connor interrupts enthusiastically with an ear to ear smile. "Iago and Roderigo wake up Desdemona's father, Brabantio – I think that's the way you pronounce it – in the middle of the night, and Iago tells him that . . ." He pauses and looks at the guys. "And Iago tells him . . ."

"Come on, Connor, Iago tells him what?"

"An old black ram is tupping your white ewe," Parker just about shouts out with a gleam in his eye and a grin from ear to ear. The guys roar.

Cassie sits there wondering why she never saw it coming. No wonder Connor was so eager to summarize this passage. Oh, well; they were eighteen, males, females, with strong libidos. Of course they'd get that line. She should have summarized the scene herself if she had wanted to avoid the quote. But many lines in Shakespeare's plays contained sexual references. She had sidestepped Hamlet's sexual discourse with Ophelia as they watched the players perform "The Murder of Gonzago," but she hadn't avoided this one.

They had transcended the stiff language and the four hundred year old setting to hone in on the universal aspects of sex. She'd have to be very careful when they discussed *Measure for Measure*, a blatant sexual proposal in exchange for a brother's life.

"Men can't keep their thoughts away from sex," Elizabeth interjects, looking at Matt with feigned criticism, "no matter how old they get."

Class was over. Whatever they'd say in the next two minutes would be irrelevant and forced. She didn't bother to get into Iago's and Roderigo's motive for waking Desdemona's father, being jealous and unhappy with themselves. They wanted Othello's marriage to backfire in his face. They wanted to hurt other people because they were jealous and unhappy with themselves.

She'd end the class right here, with Elizabeth's response, and wonder how old guys did have to get before they stopped viewing everything in terms of sex.

Cassie reflected on Taylor and Vaughn. Unhappy people hurt other people because they're unhappy with themselves. True for both Taylor and Vaughn, and the sex part had to factor in somewhere here, too. "No matter how old they get," Elizabeth had said. Amazing, that Elizabeth knew so much more about life than she ever did.

69

TUESDAY, JANUARY 5, MEETING WITH DR. GREER

Period two came and went. Fifteen minutes into period three, Ron Swenson, British lit teacher, walked in to cover her class for her 10:30 meeting with Drs. O/B and Greer.

"Focus on reasons Iago hates Othello and Cassio and analyze what Desdemona's father says about parent-daughter relationships. Do you agree? Do any lines relate to characters we've already discussed? Any questions before I leave?" No one had any. "Okay, work in groups for twenty minutes; then it's all individual."

They could do this easily, and Ron could always motivate discussion using interrelated themes from Dickens or Bronte. *Far from the Madding Crowd* would fit in nicely, but Ron would cover the material his way. She collected her things, bundled up and left for Dr. O/B's office and her confrontation with Dr. Greer. The most painful part was walking past Guidance, knowing people she had once called friends would never be that again.

Cassie announced herself to Charlotte and was told, coldly, to go in. She didn't expect the man she saw. She had never identified Joel Greer as Rachel and Rebecca's father when their parents had picked them up for Christmas break. They had been too far away and too many parents had been melded together around limos. She never knew which parent Dr. Greer was or how tall and broad he would be. And because Rachel was only a few inches over five feet, Cassie had expected him to be medium height; he wasn't. From Rachel's age, Cassie had also expected him to be in his late forties, as most parents with late teen-aged children were; but he wasn't that either. His wrinkles, sagging facial skin, and triple chin pegged him in his early sixties, and his stocky frame, sitting upright in his chair, put him close to Dr. O/B's height, over 6'3," and wider.

Neither man stood when Cassie entered. When Dr. O/B introduced them, Cassie extended her hand which Joel Greer ignored. So this is how it's going to be, she thought. Dr. O/B sat at one end of the rectangular table; Dr. Greer sat to his right, and Cassie sat opposite him, so they were face to face, eye to eye at all times, locked in constant battle mode.

Dr. Greer wasted no time. "I want him gone, Vaughn, do you hear? Gone, immediately! I don't want him anywhere near my daughter. No Arab is going to date my daughter. It's disgraceful. I'd be the laughing stock at the Club, at my temple, everywhere. Get rid of him. Now!" He glared at Cassie.

He had made his position ultimately clear, an un-equivocal order which Vaughn could not easily refute, since Joel Greer's money had funded at least one of the ladies' dorms. Samir's days at Chelsea would be over if Cassie couldn't intervene successfully. Quite an impossible task, especially since Vaughn had already capitulated. He would not be advocating for Samir.

But for Rachel's sake and Samir's, Cassie would do her best to reason with him. Maybe, for his daughter, his heart could melt just a little. "Dr. Greer, there's such animosity in your tone. I'm wondering if that's the way you've raised Rachel, to hate someone because of their ethnicity, because I don't sense a bit of hatred in her."

Dr. Greer was shocked. This nobody of a teacher wasn't genuflecting to him. "How dare you challenge me? What business is it of yours how I've brought her up? It's obvious that she has no sense of hatred, or she wouldn't be dating someone whose people are killing mine, killing hers."

Cassie was startled. Another stereotypical attack against Arabs. The press had been doing its preordained job. Defiant as usual when attacked, Cassie shot back, "Isn't it ironic then, that she cares deeply for someone who cares deeply for her, whose people are being killed by yours?"

Vaughn blanched. Dr. Greer blustered, almost unable to speak and stood. His full height had to top 6'3." Outraged at Cassie's audacity, he slammed his fist on the table like a gavel, leaned forward, palms intruding on Cassie's space, and glared. "How dare you, Mrs. Komsky.

How dare you make such an anti-Semitic statement?" His fist pounded the table again.

Cassie recalled Vaughn's vicious attack at Homecoming, but Dr. Greer's was worse, because he refuted truth with the anti-Semitic charge, meant to silence anyone who would speak openly. And the meeting had just begun.

She reacted with defiance again. She rose from her chair, her 5'3" standing straight. Tilting her head upward to face Greer eye to eye, she countered. "That's a spurious charge, Dr. Greer. There's nothing anti-Semitic at all in my statement. You're telling me your daughter has no sense of hatred or she wouldn't be dating an Arab, someone whose people are killing hers. I reversed it. I told you that her people, your people, are killing Samir's people, yet, despite that, *he* still loves *her.* An Arab loves a Jew.

"You're defending an Arab, an enemy of Israel! That's my anti-Semitic charge."

"I'm defending what's right, not whose side has the popular narrative, which is what you've been brainwashed to regurgitate. Based on your logic, Samir's uncle could argue that Israel is an enemy of Lebanon, or of Palestine, two countries Israel has invaded, but he hasn't. It's perspective, Dr. Greer. Further, neither Arabs nor Jews were enemies until Zionists plotted with the British to take Arab land, which they succeeded in doing, and continue to do. There was no institutionalized hatred before that. Yet, now that there is, despite all the destruction and hatred, neither Samir, nor his uncle, hate Rachel. I only see hatred in you."

Dr. Greer's face turned red and his jaw was clenching. She could hear his mandible grinding against his upper teeth. "You listen to me," he commanded, his forehead knotted with anger, "you are a defiant woman who does not know her place, and you do not belong at this academy." He turned to Vaughn. "I will not, do you hear me, will not have my daughter anywhere near this Arab boy whose country threatens the existence of Israel."

"It's the other way around, Dr. Greer, Cassie shot back, "If you read something other than mainstream media, you'll learn that Israel was and has been the aggressor nation from way back, well before the UN recognized it as a state. Zionists contrived the Balfour Declaration and began bringing in settlers before and during the British Mandate, well before the UN recognized Israel's statehood. Settlements continue to this day. Four years ago Israel invaded Lebanon, Samir's country, and still, Samir loves Rachel. If he can love her without resistance from his uncle, why can't you show your own daughter the same respect, and honor her decision?"

"How dare you! How dare you make accusations like that after all the persecution the Jews have been through; Israel has been forced to defend itself for decades."

"I agree with the first part of your statement, Dr. Greer. Jews *have* been persecuted, but instead of learning from it, Zionists have persecuted another ethnicity, stolen their land and killed their people. Zionist Jews did that. The second part of your statement is unequivocally incorrect: Israel has been an aggressor nation for decades, and the Palestinians counter-attack to stop the aggression and end the occupation. Simple truth.

"I stand by my analogy. You demand Samir be expelled because he is dating your daughter while Ambassador Gibran has not demanded Rachel be expelled for dating his nephew. Your argument is spurious and hypocritical, and you refuse to see it."

"Enough, Cas . . . Mrs. Komsky. Enough!" Dr. O/B exploded. Completely enraged, he leaped to Dr. Greer's rescue. "Dr. Greer is right, your statements are anti-Semitism." Unable to refute her logic, he attacked her with the same illogical charge.

Cassie ignored him. "Do you ever criticize the United States, Dr. Greer?"

"Of course; who doesn't?" Momentarily caught off guard, Dr. Greer responded honestly.

"Well, if you can criticize the U.S., I can criticize Israel. Israel's a state, not a sacred cow."

Dr. Greer's mouth dropped and his eyes popped open. "How dare you!" He shouted again. He seemed unable to say anything else. Cassie deduced he wasn't used to being defied, that he had always won his points from power, not logic. Greer and Vaughn, both from the same mold.

"I stated facts, facts you can get yourself if you read something other than the mainstream media, which would never print what I've said, and since it doesn't, our country remains ignorant of these facts.

"If Israel were not an aggressor state, Dr. Greer, it wouldn't be forced to 'defend' itself from Arab 'terrorists,' but that's what it is. It has conquered and occupied Palestine for decades, and it has used its tentacles and its military money from the U.S. to confiscate more and more of their land. It's counter-attacked by Palestinians because they want their land and their homes *back*. Israel may be a sacred cow to you, Dr. Greer, but it's not a sacred cow to me. Nor is it a sacred cow to many Jews and rabbis who do not believe what Israel is doing is right."

Dr. Greer sputtered, his hands went to his head and he glanced back and forth between Vaughn and Cassie, unable to speak. Vaughn intervened with venom. "Mrs. Komsky," he bellowed, "you are insubordinate, and you will be dismissed!"

"Why? I'm not insubordinate; you simply can't refute my response. My analogy about whose people are killing whose is sound. I didn't name the country first; Dr. Greer did. And yet again, he still hasn't justified his demand that Samir be expelled when Ambassador Gibran has not made the same demand. That's the purpose of this meeting, isn't it?"

"Because Arabs are terrorists!" Vaughn shouted. "*That's* your reason!"

"*All* Arabs?" She looked directly into Vaughn's eyes. She was reminding him of his charge against Samir at Homecoming; he remembered. She could see it in his eyes. Shame on him. He knew she wasn't anti-Semitic, and he also knew Samir had nothing to do with terrorism. "You've done the reading, Dr. O/B. You know who the original terrorist gangs in the Middle East were but it's not reported. You know that, too. To the American people, Israel innocently popped up in the desert forty years ago and was instantly attacked by crazy Arabs.

"Palestine never existed until the Jews wanted that land in the late 19th century," Greer countered.

"That's grossly incorrect, Dr. Greer. Palestine has existed for centuries."

"Never! It never existed until we wanted it."

"Zionism began at the turn of the 1900's. I'm sure you can check that." Dr. Greer did not refute her. "Then I only have to go back to the 19th century to disprove your statement and I can do much better than that." She opened her attaché, pulled out *Othello* and handed it to him."

Dr. Greer was confused. "What is this?' He demanded. "You think this is funny? You're giving me *Othello*? Is this some kind of a joke, Mrs. Komsky, because I certainly do not see the humor."

"I would never joke about such a sensitive issue, Dr. Greer, but you demand proof that Palestine existed before Zionists wanted that land. In giving you *Othello*, I'm giving you your proof. *Othello* was written in 1603, hundreds of years before the Zionists formed their organization, yet Shakespeare was well aware of Palestine's existence when he wrote it. Emelia, Iago's wife, relates a story to Desdemona about a lady in Venice who would have walked barefoot to Palestine for a touch of her lover's nether lip. Reread *Othello*, Dr. Greer. You'll find your proof. I have another copy. I also have my college text. I'll lend that to you if you'd like."

Cassie could understand why Rachel would tremble, especially having been raised by a man she had seen only as warm and loving transform from a Dr. Jekyll to a Mr. Hyde. Cassie assuredly understood that. He sneered diabolically. "Then we'll just have to change the text, won't we?"

Even Vaughn reeled at that. Cassie could see it in his face, an adulteration of Shakespeare for the expediency of someone's political agenda? Dr. Greer glared at her smugly, a demoniacal sneer. How powerful was he? How far and into what recesses did his agenda infiltrate? She was one person; she could do nothing but maintain an ethical stance. "Who controls the present controls the past," she countered defiantly. "Did you *read 1984* . . . or did you *write* it?"

Dr. Greer turned to Vaughn, seething. "Get rid of her, Vaughn. Get rid of her immediately!"

"I'll see to it, Joel; I assure you," he said, but Cassie detected a touch of trepidation in his voice, perhaps Greer's threat about rewriting classical Shakespeare had unnerved him.

Cassie knew her intercessions were pointless. Dr. Greer would never accept reason. Her days here would be short-lived, but she'd make one final attempt to help Rachel and Samir. She faced Vaughn, "Dr. O/B, I need to use your phone. I have to make an important call that will assuredly clarify a few issues here for both parties. If you refuse, I'll leave and make the call from my home."

Vaughn stalled. He glanced at Greer. The man, a cardiologist, looked as though he were about to have a heart attack. Vaughn looked at Cassie, still fuming, still intractable, and a hint of reason touched him. "Use the phone on my desk."

Cassie pulled a small piece of paper from her jacket and dialed what seemed to be more numbers than necessary. Finally a voice picked up at the other end. "Esafeer Jibran? Hathahee Kassee. Ma'tharah, min fudhlak sayy-eedee. Hal istatteea' an aakhathoo bidha'daqaiqa min waqatooka?" (*Ambassador Gibran? This is Cassie. Please, excuse me, sir. Can I take a few minutes of your time?*)

Vaughn was stunned. Dr. Greer froze, shocked. He recognized Arabic and was dumbfounded. Cassie was speaking Arabic to Ambassador Gibran. Was she Arabic? Had he been speaking to an Arab? He was speechless; they both were speechless.

The call was brief, maybe two minutes, and it ended when Cassie said, "Shukran, maa' salama," (*thank you, good bye*) and returned the phone to its cradle. Then she faced the two doctors with conviction.

"Ambassador Gibran says, emphatically, that he wants his nephew to finish the semester. He says if you take any action against Samir, such as expelling him or changing his class, he will press charges against you, Dr. Greer, for your assault on his nephew with your fire iron. That will not look good on your record, doctor, and most likely, you will be convicted. Tests confirm the blood on your fire poker is Samir's."

Dr. Greer, still reeling from a fact about Cassie's ethnicity he could never have imagined, blustered nervously at this charge. "Charge me with assault? How . . . how did Ambassador Gibran get *my* poker iron?" His voice was challenging, but his behavior less defiant. He paused, as though he had been hit with a numbing blast of wind. "And just who," he continued, now with a tone of apprehension, "who will testify against me?" His tone was no longer arrogant and a hint of uncertainty was evident in his voice.

Cassie made direct, glaring eye contact, then, quietly but emphatically, stated, "Your daughter."

70

AFTER GREER LEAVES

D r. Greer backed off: Samir would stay; a small victory that wouldn't alleviate Rachel's estrangement from her father, but at least she and Samir would be together.

Cassie went back to class, well into period four, but barely finished the day. Her stomach ached and her heart ached even more. To think it had all come to this, all this hatred, all this animosity. Where, how had it begun, this beautiful ideal that had turned a lifeless young man to joy, and had given this heartbroken forty-one-year-old woman respite from despair. What was the purpose of hope if it would be dashed to pieces by incessant acts of inhumanity? The melancholy Dane was not alone. He spanned centuries; he transcended time. He was all humanity and represented man's inhumanity to man at its worst, and it manifested itself right here with Samir almost four hundred years later.

The meeting played out in her mind over and over, like some 8mm film caught in a loop, repeating the same pathetic scene, spouting out the same pathetic dialogue, the same eternal hatred. Dr. Greer had stormed out, fuming like a petulant child who had not gotten his way. He had never anticipated Ambassador Gibran being brought into the game. He had assumed he had controlled every aspect in every way, but he had been defeated by his own machinations, "the engineer hoist on his own petard." Thank you, Hamlet.

Seeing a father hate from indoctrination more than he loved his own daughter was heartbreaking and it was destroying Rachel. Cassie had to be strong. She just had to. Other than Samir who was suffering himself, Rachel had no one else to turn to except Cassie, who was being assaulted on all sides as well. No help from the faculty, not one, not Melissa, not Walter. They had become cohorts to Vaughn. Who would support her rather than the great and powerful Oz?

She'd give Walter one last try, but if he hadn't returned her calls yesterday, why would he return her calls now, now that gossip about her counter-assault against Dr. Greer had spread through the main office into Guidance. If Walter had been covering his ass, he would need more covering now. And to think she had believed he was his own person. But no one would have the courage to stand up for a principle after this news circulated.

What had followed after Dr. Greer had left Vaughn's office had been a seething, vicious exchange, culminating in Cassie's diatribe which Vaughn had provoked. He vowed he would get her, not hard to do since he was the dean, but a very unprofessional statement, one of animosity and vengeance. Was it his true character? Yes, no one could act that out if it weren't somewhere inside.

A simple, You're fired, would have sufficed, but simple wasn't Vaughn's goal. After today and this meeting, he would not toy with Cassie for his own gratification, his own titillation, which he had finally come to realize had been his objective. He could no longer do this because Taylor had faced him down and would make his life utterly miserable.

Thus, his goal now was to punish Cassie, to punish her severely for what had become his own frustration and unhappiness. He had charged her with insubordination, and a mean, vicious side of him had emerged, a side he had never shown before, but a monster to be reckoned with.

"What infraction have I committed," Cassie challenged. The Dr. Jekyll she had believed Vaughn to be had morphed into a monster. "What heinous crime against you, to transform you from the affable person who was so eager to be overly friendly that you transcended bounds of propriety and professionalism to insert yourself into my personal life, to now become this, to actually threaten me?" She fought to quell the quiver in her voice.

Vaughn's anger enveloped him and his countenance distorted into a snarl. "I tried to be personable to you, to befriend you, as you put it, because you were new. That's why I showed you consideration. Yet to thank me for this, you viciously attack my wife in front of your peers, peers near the lower end of the social spectrum, I might add. You attack Taylor, who welcomed you into our home Thanksgiving because you had nowhere else to go."

His was the epitome of arrogance and bombast. She was gone anyway, this she knew. Be yourself, Cassie; don't let them change you. She wouldn't. "*You* showed *me* so much consideration?" She shot back without equivocation or trepidation. "*I* embarrassed *your* wife? *She* welcomed me into *her* home? You have it backwards, Dr. O/B; so let me be perfectly clear. First, I never asked you for any special consideration or any friendship, as *you* tell it, because I was new. I never invited you to my home my first night at Chelsea. Your decision to bring me that student handbook and to invade my privacy was yours, yours alone.

"Nor did I ask you to Scarbello's when we happened to meet at the mall before Thanksgiving. I resisted repeatedly; you insisted, repeatedly. Nor did I invite myself to your house, your mansion, for Thanksgiving dinner. That was your invitation, unexpected and unsolicited. And I never asked you for your mobile phone number. You initiated that, too. And the cook-off at Jeremy's? You most definitely invited yourself, and you insisted on walking me and Stevie home when I adamantly refused.

"But the worst thing you did was to knock on my door on a Friday evening bearing a Black Forest cake! That was all *you*. I did not want you to come in - you were not welcome, but you used your position as dean and tempted Stevie with her favorite dessert to get in. Then you tell me to call you by your first name?" He turned away on that charge. He couldn't face her; couldn't look in her eyes. As much as he told himself no, the little rationale he had left told him yes. Yes, she was right on every count.

"You have initiated every single overture in your definition of personable, none of which I encouraged. But you're the dean, and as you say, you own just about everything, even people, so you get what you want, any way you want.

"But to your second point, that I attacked Taylor, your wife, at the 'lowly' faculty party, a place you, the dean, should never have been. Again you twist the truth for your convenience: I didn't attack Taylor, I *counter*-attacked. No one, absolutely no one, is going to use my husband's death, in the service of his country, as a weapon to hurl against me and my daughter. No one! Ever! The cruelty is all hers, and you should realize that. You might also wonder why she had to say something as vicious as that, for what reason, when I have never done or said anything to hurt her in any way. *Maybe you should think about her motives instead of talking yourself into believing I was the perpetrator.*

"I know I will not be at Chelsea next semester. I doubt I'll finish this one, but if my choice is to subordinate my ethics, my principles and my honor, and my husband's honor, to patronize or palliate your spurious accusations, I choose to maintain principles, honor and character, qualities you are sorely lacking, and let the outcome determine itself."

She left his office shaking, went back to class and struggled to finish out the school day. Hopefully she'd be able to hold on until 3:15 and cry later.

71

By the time Cassie got home that afternoon, she was sobbing uncontrollably. She tried to calm herself but failed. She needed some human kindness, but there was none, no mother, no aunt, no friend, and worst of all, no Brian. She couldn't make it through this alone. In desperation, she called Walter again. Maybe he hadn't listened to his messages; maybe he had been delayed taking his daughter to the airport yesterday; maybe, maybe . . ." On fifth ring, it went to voice mail. All she said was, "Hi, it's Cassie. I need to talk to you. Please return my call."

That was all. Two months of believing he had cared only to realize he was as dependent on his master as they all were. Stevie hadn't come home yet so she let herself cry to the walls. She put on her music, thinking it would soothe her, but it was tied to Brian, "Oh, Girl," "Earth Angel," and most of all, "Leather and Lace." That's when she really cried; she'd always be alone.

She'd never have the confidence to love another man after this. Her father had cemented that decades before Brian who had come from nowhere, a serendipitous situation that had thrown him into her life, a kind, trustworthy man who would not let her run away, a man who had the determination to stay in her life knowing how frightened and insecure she was, and to never, never betray her hard-won trust. That's what had put Brian into her life. No other man before him had been so patient and understanding, and she was certain, now, after Walter and Vaughn, there'd never be trust again.

Then a faint rapping at her door. Was she hearing things? Was there another sound tapping into her music and her crying? Yes, there was and more insistent rapping confirmed it. Quickly she dried her eyes; nothing could get out the red, but who cared. She looked through the peep hole. Then she quickly opened the door to face Jeremy's frightened countenance. Seeing her red eyes, he stared with anguish, concern and empathy. Then he held out his arms and she fell right in.

"Cassie, oh my God, I just heard. You poor kid; you don't deserve this." She hugged him tightly. She had needed to commiserate with another human, someone she had believed was sincere, and here stood Jeremy, real, offering assistance. For a split second, she wondered if someone had sent him to find out what she was thinking. What an absurd thought. No one needed an insidious way to find out what she was thinking; she had already made her thoughts clear to everyone, loudly and boldly, exactly what they were afraid of, exactly why they had turned her into a pariah.

When she composed herself, she pulled arms length away. "Even Walter, Jeremy, even Walter." She teared up again.

Jeremy shook his head sadly. "I'm sorry, Cassie. I thought he had more courage. I thought he would stick to his convictions."

"Am I right? Is it all about Taylor and jealousy?"

He nodded. "Looks that way. Everybody likes you Cassie. Everybody. Even some people who shouldn't."

"You're talking about Vaughn. If you're right, I never did anything to initiate it. I didn't even recognize it, and I sure didn't realize he had such a cruel side. He kept that hidden. My problem has always been trust, who's sincere and who's acting, with Walter too. I'm more disappointed in him; I began to trust enough to actually believe we had a future. I never thought he'd abandon me like this." They were in the foyer with the door ajar and the freezing cold was beginning to bite her fingers and face. "Come in; I'll make some tea; we can talk and be warm. Stevie's upstairs with Rebecca and Stacy; so we'll have time."

She closed the door and ushered him into the kitchen. "I'm very glad you came over." She put the kettle on, took out cups and saucers; then reached into the freezer for a container of sugar cookies and tassies she had made for Christmas. "Want some? I know you're on a strict diet and I don't want to entice you by putting these out, but tea and talking go better with cookies."

"Tea and talking definitely go better with cookies, and I've only eaten seven hundred eighty calories all day. Lots of veggies and juice for five days, and I'm maybe ten pounds lighter. A few cookies mixed with much needed conversation won't kill me."

Cassie put cookies on a plate and got out teabags, milk, napkins. "Talking will do me a lot of good too. I'm starved for honest conversation."

"I used to talk out my problems years ago, and I'd always feel better afterwards. When I heard what Vaughn had done to you, his edict, and Greer's meeting, I didn't have to ask myself how you'd feel; I knew, and I couldn't desert you because the last thing in the world I'd want would be to have everyone desert me if something like this ever happened to me. So here I am."

"Thank you, Jeremy. I'm so glad you are. That's exactly how I was feeling, completely abandoned by the world, like being alone on an ice float." She put her hands to her face and her elbows on the table. "Any suggestions what I should do about life, about Vaughn . . . Walter?"

"You're asking me? I haven't done such a great job making decisions for my own life. I don't think you'd want me to give you suggestions about yours."

Cassie nodded. "Yeah, I do."

Jeremy's shrug said, okay, here goes nothing. "I think Walter loves you." He stopped her when she tried to disagree. She let him continue. "But his personality doesn't run on courage when it affects his lifestyle. Walter's not concerned with money or things. He's a pretty basic guy. But he sees things only from the way he operates his life, and in the only direction he wants it to go. He doesn't see it from any other perspective, and he won't adapt."

"I don't get it, Jeremy. I wouldn't ask him to change his life for me, but just from his own professional perspective, isn't he supposed to help people in an emotional time of need?"

"Cassie, I've known him since I've been here; that's about eighteen years. You're the first woman he's even let himself get close to. With everyone else, he just backs away. He's disagreed with Vaughn at times when it's from a professional perspective, Walter as the shrink, but never from a personal one where he would take a stand for someone he loves. He came closest when Taylor attacked you at the faculty party. He glared at her and at Vaughn. You probably didn't notice. I did. That's the most aggressive I've ever seen him on a personal level."

"What did he do when his wife left him?"

"He let her go. He claims she left him because she wanted the glitz and the money that comes with the doctor image, but I don't believe that. I think she left because he never discussed the decision with her." Cassie's expression registered disbelief. "True, he's said it casually several times. He never asked her for her input because he didn't think it had anything to do with her. He quit his practice, sold it, took the job here, and then told her."

Cassie exhaled. "Unbelievable. He did all that behind her back and never even let her be part of a lifetime decision." She was stunned. "No wonder she left, and in all these years, he's never realized he should have?"

"That's one possible explanation. Another is he didn't have the courage to admit it. Maybe that's why he didn't go after her; he didn't have the courage to apologize. That's the way I see it."

"No wonder she wanted nothing to do with him," Cassie concluded. "He made his decision as though she didn't exist."

"I've never been married – engaged once – but we made all our significant decisions together. I'm not talking about having a ham sandwich on white or rye," he chuckled. "I'm talking about significant decisions, and when a significant decision had to be made by one of us, at least we had discussed it as a team first."

"Jeremy, I'm learning so much about people here that I never knew. I never knew you had been engaged. You've never mentioned it until now. If I'm not being too personal, why didn't you marry?"

Sadness enveloped him. "She died," he said quietly.

"Oh, my God," Cassie whispered. "Jeremy, I am so sorry, so very sorry, and I'm sorry I asked."

"Something I live with every day, a little like you, just not as severe. So," he rallied, "if I had any advice to give, the only thing I would say is what I've said before, stay strong and never let them change you."

"Easier said than done."

"But you've had lots of experience, Cassie, more experience than most."

"That's part of the problem, Jeremy. I don't know how much more I can take. My childhood didn't give me much confidence. I always fight the world and my upbringing. When you're brought up with the 'You're good for nothing' mantra, it kind of gets imprinted on your brain."

"I understand what you're saying, but I can't empathize because I never experienced a dysfunctional childhood. I just know you've got to stay strong. You know that too; you know you have to go on . . . there's no other way out of life except death, and we've both experienced that through loved ones. You've got Stevie to raise, so don't lose your character. You're all about character. If you lose that, you've lost yourself. It'll turn out the way it's going to turn out, and if you need a friend, I'm here." He paused. "Does that help?"

She smiled. "Yes, it does, because a friend said it, and that would be you. I know I have to do that, if not for me, for Stevie, but corroboration helps and friendship makes it so much better." Jeremy's face lit up.

"Oh, I almost forgot. You hurried through the hallway so quickly Sunday night when you came looking for Samir that I didn't get a chance to mention Samir had requested a parking permit for the student lot behind Damon House. That may not be significant, but I thought you should know."

"Interesting," she said, "I'll give it some thought." She poured more tea and they each grabbed another tassie. "Love the nuts," she said, popping one into her mouth. Jeremy followed suit. They talked into early evening when Stevie came home. After Stevie made a roast turkey sandwich and scoffed it down in five minutes, she reached for the cookies. "Still good, Mom. You're a good baker."

"What about being a good cook?"

"That too." She grabbed a handful and went upstairs.

Cassie had been miserable when she got home. Amazing what family, friendship and faith in your fellow man, even one, could do.

72

VAUGHN'S REFLECTIONS ON MEETING WITH GREER

Vaughn stayed in his office for the rest of the day. He didn't eat or take calls, not even Taylor's. Most likely, she'd want to know how the meeting went and if he had destroyed Cassie enough for her. Yes he had, albeit with resistance, and he would continue to destroy her, push her face into the mud and make her suffer. But through it all, something bothered him that he couldn't quite identify.

He wasn't familiar with the vicious person he was becoming. Vaughn was not confrontational and had never been. Throughout his lifetime, he had usually deferred to Brett, a nine-year difference made Brett more than an older brother; he had almost brought him up. Vaughn was usually submissive to Taylor's wishes also, if not submissive, deferential, but being a good husband, he didn't mind.

But her last directive, this ultimatum, gnawed at him. It went against his nature: I hate her; she's hitting on you; destroy her. Could he be vicious, adamant, angry, dominating? Sure, when he wanted something to go his way, but never to completely and utterly set out to destroy someone; yet, this was his intent now.

Taylor's attack had been inappropriate; her cutting remark about Brian had been cruel. Vaughn realized that as soon as she had uttered those words. You don't use the death of a soldier to attack his widow and child.

Despite that, Cassie's retort had shocked him and his pride. Vaughn was the aristocracy; Cassie was and would always be the proletariat. He'd make her suffer for that alone, but to destroy her completely made him uncomfortable. He pondered this as he worked with a pile of forms on his desk; sign this, read that. He couldn't concentrate.

He kept rehashing everything Cassie had said that had disproved Taylor's charge. God, how he hated her for being right, but she was, beyond a doubt. Cassie was never hitting on him. In fact, now that he was man enough to analyze his feelings more objectively, he had been hitting on her. Her diatribe this morning had presented the evidence, loud and clear.

Everything she had said, every action he had taken *had* been initiated by him. He had been hitting on her under the guise of feigned professionalism. The reason? Obvious you idiot, she's beautiful, intelligent, enjoys scintillating conversation and is so sensual. I could watch her move all day, and she's kind, sincere, and almost innocent. What a combination. How could any male not be interested? Hell, his own brother talked about her after she and

Stevie had left Thanksgiving. In fact, if he didn't know Brett adored Hillary, he would have thought he'd try to seduce her himself.

But to please Taylor, early yesterday, first day back, he had called an office meeting and informed everyone that conversation with Cassie, other than the barest, curt response when business prescribed, was terminated, and violations would incur severe penalties. Walter had been the only absentee, and Vaughn had gotten to him late in the afternoon just before the school day ended before Walter received Cassie's first call.

That was the first step and it was working well. Today's meeting with Joel Greer had not. Vaughn knew Cassie was feisty with a spitfire personality, but he never imagined she'd go back at Greer like that. Coupled with Ambassador Gibran's ultimatum, he and Greer had backed down. Knowing his daughter would testify against her own father had a big impact on Greer, especially since she was siding with a young man she had been dating a few months. Vaughn couldn't imagine Parker ever testifying against him, and for Rachel to side with an Arab boy against her own father was unimaginable.

After Greer stormed out, Vaughn's personal vengeance kicked in, but this had not worked the way he had thought either. Things we play out in our heads play out differently in reality. Cassie had not shown subordination in any way. He would get her for that. He'd ruin her career; she'd never teach again; she'd never get another job in anything after he was finished with her.

But, as hard as he tried, as much busywork as he set his mind to, as many papers and forms as he read and signed, he could not get Cassie's words out of his head: *Maybe you should think about her motives instead of talking yourself into believing i was the perpetrator.* She had countered with venom. Vaughn could not get these words out of his head.

Was there something about Taylor's motives he was missing, because her charge was dead wrong: Cassie had never been hitting on him. Vaughn had shown Cassie more attention than he should have on Thanksgiving Day. Maybe going after Cassie in the storm had annoyed Taylor, but these things did not indicate Cassie was hitting on him. Nothing in Taylor's charge could justify it.

Taylor had no evidence for her accusation. Vaughn had been showing Cassie the attention, not the other way around. Where did Taylor's assumptions come from? He had deferred to her because women have intuition that men don't about matters involving emotions. But Cassie's words had merit. So, if there was no validity in Taylor's charge, then what *were* her motives?

The afternoon came and went, and still Vaughn sat. He sat while the day disappeared, while it sneaked behind a corner and didn't show its face again, taking all light out of the sky and allowing the moon to tiptoe onto the horizon. Vaughn sat. He'd get rid of her. He wasn't going to let Greer think a faculty member could challenge them. She was history, and he'd do it in the worst way he could. Yet he could not extricate the unsettling feeling that churned in his gut.

73

TAYLOR WINS

S mug. The perfect word for Taylor and she gloated in it. She could not have been happier. Vaughn hadn't come home yet; wonderful. She had defeated Cassie. Plus, Vaughn hadn't returned her calls; that had cemented it. He had overcome that miniscule bit of conscience that had been gnawing at him this weekend and had carried out her demands. She'd make sure he did until she was satisfied.

She could manipulate him so easily. How could any wife be happy knowing another woman was in a position to hit on her husband every day? *How could I ever feel comfortable, Darling, knowing some teacher is one building away, waiting to seduce you at any time? And you, Vaughn, you're so trusting; you'd never see her scheme.*

Appealing to his masculinity and his ego was even more gratifying. *You're handsome, strong, and virile. Don't you see it, Darling? She already has you mesmerized.* And if flirtation and deception didn't work, she'd go to the core: she'd leave. Subtle implication was enough to make Vaughn aware how angry and hurt Taylor really was.

Taylor had loathed going to that lowly faculty party, but she had gone for another look at the woman her husband was fawning over. What a low-class affair. Shower after that.

Taylor had watched Cassie dancing. Men were glued to her at one point or another, while their wives were looking in another direction or were in the restroom. But to see Brett, her entire world, drooling over this woman, literally in heat over someone other than herself drove Taylor to a frienzied pitch of jealousy.

Poor Hillary noticed nothing. She was completely unaware that her husband was salivating over Cassie, but then, she had been unaware that her husband had been sleeping with his sister-in-law for almost two decades. So how could she be aware of an inconsequential teacher she was seeing for the second time in her life?

But enough of Cassie. Tonight Taylor had things to do, places to go, and finishing touches for Hillary's 25th anniversary gala to plan. Plans were coming together quickly. Her extra services with Trevor Stauer after his last manicure had secured her a great excuse to justify garage parking. He would drive his own car rather than the limo, park it in the queue before the O/B limo arrived, pretend to search for something that had slipped behind the seat or on the floor. Then, when Vaughn's limo pulled up, Trevor would make sure he and his wife got out so Taylor could see her, refuse to be anywhere in her presence and instruct their driver to park underground. Perfect. That would force them to use the elevator and mistakenly go to the second floor for Hillary's gala after dinner. Two dinners within two hours would be a problem for digestion. They'd have to eat light.

5:00 p.m. She wouldn't wait for Vaughn. She'd listen to his inane prattle tomorrow morning. Taylor had dismissed her cook after she had made a tray of meat lasagna for whenever Vaughn came home. Despite gourmet meals at his fingertips, Vaughn would sit down to spaghetti and meatballs rather than lobster stuffed with crabmeat. Taylor didn't care what he ate tonight or any night, as long as it made her getaway easy, and this would be easy. So he would eat, workout, and relax in his recliner with a book, like a satisfied lap dog, and she'd be off to rendezvous with Veronica, Sharon and Brett at the Club.

She gloated, sipping her martini and getting dressed, partially dressed, for the Club and for everything else that followed. Although most of the details for Hillary's gala had been completed for a while, she and Brett had sabotaged incidentals which required another meeting, another visit to the Club, another rendezvous that provided alone-time after.

It was easy. Sharon and Veronica had both been widowed in their mid-fifties. They were always off somewhere after these meetings, ready for dancing and sipping cocktails in the lounge. They never knew how long Brett and Taylor stayed, where they went or what they did. They didn't care. What Brett and Taylor did afterwards, whether together or separately, was of no consequence to them, a very important reason why Taylor and Brett had brought them in on the planning. They were perfect cover. They simply adored Hillary and were happy to be part of her anniversary celebration; that's all.

Taylor finished dressing, downed the last sip of her martini, devoured the olive and grabbed her coat. She was off to her meeting, gloating all the way. Her life couldn't be any better.

74

WALTER REACTS TO HIS INACTION

Word spread through Smythe Hall like a spark on dried brush. It lit, electrified, sparked and sputtered, from one office to the next, hitting Guidance as soon as it had left Vaughn's outer office. In fact, reports of the altercation arrived in Guidance before it had left the dean's outer office. People in that office knew people in this office and wanted to be the first to announce juicy gossip, biting gossip that would sting and destroy another person's life. That was the best kind.

It hit the secretarial staff then bounced to Alicia Walsh via Melissa, then settled in at the desk of the Guidance head, Walter Goodman, who had been pensively staring out the window, gazing at a barren football field, reminiscing about metaphors for life and how just a few months ago, so much energy and life existed out there, right before his eyes, and how a beautiful and feisty Shakespeare teacher had walked into his office and into his life searching for information about a reticent young man who concerned her.

And here he was, two months later, aware that his entire world would never be the same. It had changed drastically once before, and he had let it; now he had let it again. She had called, what – five times, had left message after message. She was distraught; he could hear it in her voice, and yet, after all the unspoken and spoken assurances he had given her, all the days they had shared together, he had returned none of those calls.

He glanced up at Alicia, heard her words, saw the shocked look on her face and the glint in her blue eyes as she related each detail of the Greer/Komsky match like a soap opera that was being played out at Chelsea, and she was eager for the next episode. Tune in tomorrow: Will Vaughn fire Cassie on the spot; will he toy with her like a cat toys with a mouse before it's devoured? Will Cassie break down? Don't miss tomorrow's episode. Just like that. It was all just like that, and just for that. Alicia left, high on anticipation, her red hair bouncing from her shoulders.

Walter felt more alone than he had ever felt in his life. He realized the agony Cassie must be experiencing, and he was well aware of his medical oath, to help someone in need, empathize and comfort; but what had he done to adhere to his oath and help her through this? Nothing. He had abandoned every principle, every intrinsic mandate, every ethical aspect of it. His Hippocratic Oath had become his hypocritical oath. He had run from everything he was supposed to do professionally and what he should have done as a friend; he had run and hidden.

The Mediterranean cook book Stevie had given him for Christmas and had paid for with her own money was propped on his kitchen counter. He had found a special place for this very special gift given to him by this very unique child, whom he had come to regard somewhat as his own. Danger in that. He had placed the book equidistant between his coffee pot and his toaster, upright, open and ready to read, one recipe at a time at a moment's notice.

In fact, every day since Christmas, he had thumbed through it, considering what he could make. What ingredients did he have on his shelves? After he checked, he and Ashton had shopped, making sure he had tahini, cumin and garlic for hummus, his first endeavor. He couldn't wait to make it, then tell Cassie how it had turned out. So much anticipation. Then Vaughn's edict, and he backed off. He backed off because it was easy, easy to live life the way he had been for decades rather that meet resistance now. As much as he cared for, maybe even loved Cassie, he liked his life the way it was.

Ashton's visit had been better than expected. Getting her from the airport, unpacking, showing her around, having breakfast, lunch, and dinner together for a whole week, seeing a Broadway show, all had been wonderful. They had spent two day at Resorts playing roulette, craps and seeing two shows. But after almost a week of father-daughter time, the serious questions had begun.

There were things Ashton wanted to know, things about divorce kids never know, never see when they're young, one-sided stories that leave gaps on the other side, the side they're not supposed to care about or question.

And if questions were asked, they wouldn't get answered, or at least not honestly. But the questions remain, and once asked, have that horrible way of bringing the past right back to the present.

"Why did you let Mom go, Dad," Ashton had asked New Year's Day as they drove back from Resorts. "You never went after her; you never came after us. Didn't you love us?"

It's hard to reassure your daughter that you loved her then, and still do, when you can't dispute her charge. Ashton was correct; he hadn't gone after them. He had allowed himself to believe Jan had left because she had wanted their previous life style, the galas and the glitz. But he had fabricated that to make avoidance easy. Bottom line; he *had* let his wife go; he had let her take his kids and leave without any resistance on his part, and he never went after her because his lifestyle was first and foremost, more than his wife, more than his kids. He just sent her checks and closed the books, literally and figuratively.

Twenty years ago he had wanted a more simplistic life. He had wanted to teach here at Chelsea and he wanted no objections; so he made the decision on his own. Don't ask Jan. Maybe she'd agree, but why take the chance? He was going to make the change whether she agreed or not.

His thoughts drifted back to the faculty party, Christmas Eve, Christmas Day, jogging the day after, asking Cassie to meet Ashton and share New Year's Eve with them. Damn but she was easy to talk to, easy to look at, and so kind. Yet, one day back after Christmas and all they had done together, all his talk about the future had dissolved like melting ice cream dripping down its cone; you couldn't stop it fast enough.

Ashton's questions had forced him to look in the mirror. Answer her questions, Walter. Look yourself in the mirror and answer the question you've been avoiding for decades. Finally, without excuses, without rationalization, without lies, he did. The answer was simple: he was a coward.

And this undeniable truth had reinforced itself when Vaughn issued his persona non grata ultimatum against Cassie and he, Walter, the shrink who could solve other people's confrontational problems, but not his own, had let her go, same as he had done with Jan twenty years ago. This undeniable truth slapped him in the face again as Alicia revealed the juicy gossip in his ear and stepped lightly out of his office. He had lost Cassie, and any hopes of any future with her. She would reject him from this point on. Who wouldn't?

There was no way he could avoid his cowardice. Cassie was not his wife who had left him after he had given up his medical practice. He couldn't use the excuse Cassie had wanted more glitz. For one, Cassie didn't leave him, he left her; furthermore, she had come into his life here, at Chelsea, where there was no glitz and she had no expectations there ever would be. No, you fool; you let her go because you're still a coward.

Ashton's challenge had caused him to reevaluate his divorce; Vaughn's ultimatum had forced him to face reality in the present: he had been a coward then; he was a coward now. Cowardice had cemented him in a world of isolation for twenty years; it would condemn him to

isolation for the rest of his life. If he didn't have the courage to go after Cassie, someone he could have lived with
until he died, he would never have the courage to go after
anyone. He had doomed himself to a life of loneliness.

75

CLASS, THE DAY AFTER
VAUGHN & GREER

Wednesday. Cassie was in her classroom exceptionally early. So many thoughts running through her head since Monday that she simply couldn't sleep. An hour or two here and there, up at 1:00 a.m., 3:30, and again at 5:00. It was just no good. She had lost all the people she had come to believe were her friends, all but Jeremy. Thank God for Jeremy.

Her meeting with Dr. Greer had been a nightmare. How could he disown Rachel? How could any father do that to his daughter? From her own childhood, she knew how it felt and how it never leaves you. You grow up but you don't leave it behind. It becomes part of you and anybody who doesn't believe it has never experienced a childhood of rejection. Fortunately, Rachel was older than Cassie had been. Good thing Greer didn't know she and Samir were married. Between Greer's encounter and her follow-up meeting with Vaughn, Cassie was fortunate she had gotten the little sleep she had.

Vaughn had made himself very clear: he would not only fire her, he'd make sure she never taught again. She still had resources from her widow's insurance, which she had handled prudently. Mathematically she computed how much she'd have if she lived on a budget of x amount and didn't get another job until y number of months had passed, but she'd need an income to take her to retirement. She needed a monthly check. Having her career destroyed would hurt her and Stevie immeasurably, and after seeing the vicious Vaughn she never believed existed, she knew his threat was real.

She trembled at the thought, sometimes with shaky hands. She had meant what she had told Jeremy; she would not give up her principles. But the thought of never finding another job was frightening. Where would they live? Even if Vaughn fired her without ruining her teaching career, where would they go this time of year? Their house on Meadow Ave. was rented through June. A new job, new home, new school for Stevie would all have to mesh in a relatively short time. She had to get started.

What plagued her the most, though, was leaving Samir and Rachel. More than anything, more than any other time in her life, Rachel needed support, someone she knew cared for her and loved her. Cassie couldn't imagine her mother deserting her; she just couldn't. But until Mrs. Greer found the courage to refute her husband's edict and be a mother to her daughter, if she ever did, Rachel needed a surrogate.

So, at 5:00 a.m., she had dragged herself out of bed and gotten ready for school, but that boomeranged because inadvertently, she had wakened Stevie. Since sitting in the house waiting for the school bus made them antsy, Cassie drove Stevie to school; then headed straight to class. She settled in a good forty-five minutes before 8:00.

Quiet. Absolute quiet. She listened to the stillness and the quiet, interrupted only by intermittent flicks from tree branches hitting the side windows, and the ticking clock, which seemed exceptionally loud juxtaposed against silence. She looked around as she had on her first day. Life can change in a day, an hour, a second, a heartbeat. She knew that. At Chelsea, it had taken little over two months for her world to soar to new heights, and in less than twenty-four hours, come crashing down.

Everything that had filled her with hope, everything that had indicated her revival, she now looked upon with despair. The posters of Elizabethan England were still there. Shakespeare's birthplace, Anne Hathaway, Caesar, Cassius, Brutus, Macbeth, Othello, the queen, and the Globe replica in the corner, they were all still there; Hamlet and Ophelia, still there. Still life was still there.

But everything else had changed. Fiction: a story about people and events which are seemingly real, 'seemingly' because the words are still flat on the page. Once those words jump off that page, once they become the real drama in real people's lives and you live them, your world changes, sometimes for the good, sometimes not. For her, Rachel and Samir, Shakespeare's words had jumped, had leap-frogged off those pages.

Chelsea had become Cassie's second cataclysmic event. No, if she faced her past stoically, she would have admitted Chelsea had become her third. Her first, the cataclysm that had shattered her self-worth and directed her life, all her life, had been her father. Had she overcome his effects sufficiently? No, and most likely never would. Had she overcome her second cataclysm, Brian? Absolutely not and absolutely never. Would she have the strength now to deal with and overcome this? She sure hoped so. She had to, for herself, for Stevie, Samir and Rachel. "For I have promises to keep, and miles to go before I sleep." She would not give in to despair; she had too many promises to keep, too many people counting on her. There was more fight left in her. There had to be.

Time passes quickly when you're deep in thought. Sooner than she had anticipated, she became aware of footsteps. Almost time; almost 8 o'clock. Get ready. The boys filed in first, six of them, Matt, Zach, Jason, Connor, Mason and Parker. Then Emelia, Elizabeth, Gloria, and shortly after, Samir and Rachel, holding hands until they crossed the stile.

She remembered her first day, how stiff and uncomfortable she had felt with them, eleven strangers avoiding her as they took their seats. How they must have felt towards her, an interloper replacing a time-honored professor here at Chelsea.

Now, after two short months, she had grown to appreciate and love each of them as individuals. Emelia, who spoke only when she had something necessary or important to say, who sat up so straight to state her opinion; Elizabeth, feisty and quick to retort, whose black exotic eyes could bore right through you and hold you captive, and who had obviously captivated Matt; Gloria, Rachel's dearest friend, who had played a very good Hamlet to Rachel's Ophelia and who cared more about loyalty than perhaps the Dane, and Rachel, a young woman with unbounded passion for humanity and loyalty to her convictions and feelings. These were the young women she had come to know and love.

The young men, too: Parker, who had taken an immediate dislike to her, but had transformed into a person who enjoyed sparring with her, the woman whose life he had helped save. He was honorable and courageous, not at all like his father or mother, not yet; hopefully, never. She'd say the same about Matt, the Asian component of the group, and Mason with freckles and red hair, who had an inherent appreciation for Shakespeare and Mirriam-Webster, three of the four who had saved her life. Factor Connor in also, the stocky spark plug who tenaciously guarded his nerdy friend Jason, an unlikely friendship that proved people are people, ignore the stereotypes, and Zach, whose military bearing she'd never forget, because memories of Brian were mixed up in that.

But of all the young men in her class and of all the young men she had taught throughout her teaching career, never, never, would she forget Samir, as long as she lived. When the time came for her to leave their lives, how would she ever find the courage to tell them she had to go?

"What's on the agenda for today," Parker stated loudly and unabashedly.

"I don't know, Parker, what do you think?" Cassie stated flippantly. "*Wuthering Heights, Pride and Prejudice,* maybe *Last of the Mohicans*? Eleven students laughed, even Rachel, even Samir.

"She got you, Parker," Matt quipped, "Today's lesson has something to do with Shakespeare," he shouted as though he'd had a revelation.

"Good one, Matt. In fact very prescient, even telepathic," Elizabeth continued the sarcasm. Obviously, it was a day they wanted laughter.

Matt gave Elizabeth a wide smile and she blushed. "Lizzie, you have to read *The Art of War.* There's so much more to fighting than fighting. Plain and simple, it says you have to know your enemy. How well did Othello know his enemy . . . how well do you know me?" He added flirtatiously.

Elizabeth, prepared to defend herself, almost stood up from her chair, while Matt's Asian eyes twinkled. Their affection for each other was obvious.

"Make your point, Matt." Cassie interrupted, quelling their repartee.

"Well," Matt put on his serious face, "you told us to analyze act 1; so I did, you know I never miss an assignment," he added, facetiously, and he never had. None of them had. "Anyway, I think the military component in this scene is as intriguing as Desdemona's father who screams for retribution just because Othello's married his daughter. I mean, it's all legal, isn't it, so he claims Othello must have drugged Desdemona so she'd marry him. That's ridiculous. But the part about the war reports intrigued me because you see how one man who knows his enemy, in just one sentence, got it right."

Cassie was intrigued. She had never given this section much thought despite having taught Shakespeare for years, but maybe Matt saw something she had missed. "Explain your point better, Matt, because I'm not quite seeing how it relates to Brabantio or Othello."

"The original reports all show that the Turks want Cyprus, right? Okay, they want Cyprus, but they head for Rhodes. Why? One report says one hundred twenty galleys were heading there, another says two hundred, the duke's letters say one hundred forty. The numbers don't really matter; what matters is they all think Rhodes, except for this one senator, the First Senator, who says it can't be Rhodes because Rhodes is not a prize to the Turks and it can counter-attack. Cyprus can't."

"Yup, the dialogue does say that," Cassie corroborates."

"Well, that senator was right. He believed the Turks didn't want Rhodes and he tells the duke before they learn the Turks had joined with another fleet and turned back to attack Cyprus."

"I'm still not following you, Matt," Zach said. "What does that have to do with Brabantio making a lot of noise about his daughter's marriage to Othello? He tells the duke he's lost his daughter – she's dead, he says, maybe not in those exact words. How does that fit in?"

Rachel blanches and Samir puts his hand over hers. What was Rachel thinking when she read this scene? How closely did it relate to her life? Very closely, Cassie realized, and wondered how Rachel would get through today's class. But Zach, Matt and the rest of the class, except for Gloria, had no idea what kind of hell Rachel was going through.

"I get what Matt's saying about knowing your enemy. We did our presentation together and we both read Sun-Tzu's book," Zach said, "but so what? The First Senator is right, but how is that significant to Othello eloping with Brabantio's daughter, and a father saying his daughter's dead to him?"

"It's not significant to Brabantio," Matt states adamantly, insisting on having his point understood. "It's significant to Othello, because it's all about knowing your enemy. The senator knew his enemy; Othello didn't know his."

"How? How do thirty galleys meeting the Turkish fleet that turns back to Cyprus relate to Othello not knowing his enemy? Othello wasn't even in this scene yet. Besides, it's war; Othello's a great general. He'd go meet the Turks at Cyprus and defeat them, except the storm did it for him."

"No, Zach, think about it. There's an analogy here, 'Know your enemy' from *The Art of War*. You have to know your enemy even when it's *not* a military confrontation, and that's what Othello missed, big time. He never knew Iago. He never knew how jealous and vicious he could be, and as great a military general as he was, he didn't know his enemy when he wasn't on the battlefield, and because of it, he lost everything."

The class sits, stunned. Elizabeth looks at Matt with new admiration and Cassie is speechless. It takes her a few seconds to digest all of this, to see not only how Matt was right about Othello not knowing Iago, but how she didn't know the people she had thought had become her friends, and how Rachel never believed her father was the person he actually had shown himself to be. Matt had just presented her with the perfect example of how the student could surpass the teacher, because Cassie would never have made the connection Matt just did.

"Matt, I have been teaching *Othello* for years, and until your analysis right now, no one, including myself, has ever made this analogy. No one. I am so impressed."

Matt shies away. "Thanks, Mrs. Komsky." Elizabeth looks at him, beaming with pride, and Emelia and Gloria look at Elizabeth. Matt smiles.

"I never thought of that either, Matt," Zach said as the revelation of his friend's analysis sinks in. "You're right. That's exactly what we did in our presentation. We applied it to Hamlet because our reports were tied to that play, but I never took it further and applied it to Othello. You did. Great job, Buddy."

Cassie nodded in admiration. "This class never ceases to amaze me."

76

DID CASSIE KNOW HER
ENEMY?

Know your enemy, Cassie thought. Amazing analysis from Matt, and so apropos her own situation as it was unfolding. Othello didn't know Iago was his enemy. He didn't know how vicious he could be. He was too good and too trusting. Honest Iago. Othello never thought he was anything else, and that trust allowed Iago to outsmart him.

Cassie, too. She didn't recognize how vicious and calculating Taylor could be because she didn't know her and never had the opportunity, but she did believe she had known Vaughn. She didn't. She didn't know him at all, and she didn't know Walter either, although she had thought she had. She had even visualized a future with him, being a couple. She had been so wrong. The only person she really knew was herself. After years of soul searching, she had finally come to know herself. And that was it.

And her 'self' told her that her life was about Stevie, Rachel and Samir. Stevie was doing fine, and Cassie had come to believe that she was much more malleable than she had anticipated. She had given her mother attitude when they had moved from Manasquan, but she had fit into her new life smoothly with school and with activities and friends. As much as she wouldn't want to move again - who would? - she would adapt because she could. As long as Cassie was there for her, she could walk through the fire.

Thus, in the order of exigency, her priority was Rachel. Rachel was not doing fine. She was still grieving, still caught up in a maelstrom that was sucking her down without her mother or father there for her. You could see the anguish in her eyes. That perky spark that had lit up her face for months, maybe for all the years before Cassie had come to know her, was gone. She was fighting to hold on.

Samir was right there for her, every second he could be without breaking curfew, because that would get him expelled, and he would never risk that, and no one better than he understood the loss of parents. The only difference between his loss and Rachel's was that his parents had been taken from him in a vicious and horrific attack. His parents had been killed; there was no way they could have been there for him. Rachel's parents were alive and well, and they had chosen to reject their daughter. That was the part that was tearing Rachel apart.

Thus, despite Samir being with her every minute he could, Rachel wasn't responding well. They'd walk in to-gether every morning, Samir holding her hand, not letting go until they crossed the threshold, then he'd sit next to her with his fingers intertwined in hers. Still, she was pale, sometimes ashen, and Cassie was very concerned. Would she become ill? Cassie knew Rachel wasn't sleeping, but was she eating? She resolved to ask them.

Today after class, she asked them to stay, because class had ended with Brabantio's words, "Fathers, from hence trust not your daughter's minds by what you see them act." It was the biggest blow so far for Rachel.

"Rachel, don't relate Brabantio's words to your father. There's a big difference here. Your father doesn't hate Samir because he's your husband. Your father hates Samir because he hates his entire race. He doesn't even know he's your husband." Thank God, Cassie thought to herself.

"Brabantio thinks Desdemona betrayed him. He thinks she was opposed to marriage because she had turned away so many suitors. Maybe that's why he invited Othello to his house so frequently, because he never thought his daughter would fall in love with him. But she did, and he fell in love with her. Brabantio misinterpreted her actions; that's not what your father did. He assumed you'd bring home the man you loved, but he never expected that man to be an ethnicity he hated. When he went after Samir with the fire poker, he didn't know you were married, but he still reacted with hate."

"I know that, Mrs. Komsky. I see that myself, but I'll never accept my father's rejection, his complete hypocrisy. That's what's eating at me." She grew pensive, head down, "How do you throw away your own daughter because she grew up to be the loving person you taught her to be?

My father always taught me to help people and be open-minded. He always told me to learn from the Holocaust, and never let prejudice stand in the way of justice. But he meant be open-minded if that person wasn't an Arab. I learned the theory behind his teaching too well; I didn't see the hypocrisy in him. But I do now." She looked up with fierce determination. "And I won't accept it."

"Samir and I have gone through enough to know you don't throw away even a second of loving the person you love." Samir smiled at Cassie's reference. "Perhaps, hopefully, your father is using it as a ploy, thinking you're dependent on him and that you'll eventually come around."

"And leave my husband for that to happen? Never. My father needs to reread the lines where Desdemona tells her father she owes her allegiance to her husband, just as her mother before her preferred her husband to her father. That scene hurts me, and it's difficult reading it and discussing it in class, but, like Desdemona, I love my husband first, before my father, even though he never gave us the chance to tell him we're husband and wife. Maybe if we had, he would have reacted even worse, if that's possible." She paused. "I guess Desdemona is the 20th century Ophelia I portrayed in my presentation." She looked at Samir, and he embraced her. "After everything my father's said about my husband, if he ever came around, I don't think I would accept him."

Cassie considered Rachel's words; they paralleled her own feelings. Had she ever forgiven her own father for the horrible way he had treated her when she was growing up? Her situation was a little different from Rachel's because Cassie knew her father had never loved her; so

LORETTA J. KRAUSE

she felt no betrayal there, but she did feel betrayed at the way a father was supposed to feel towards his child. He had handicapped her emotionally for her entire life by destroying every happy moment childhood had given her, by crushing every little thing that made an innocent child smile, by stepping on her, making her feel worthless, making her feel "good for nothing, good for nothing, good for nothing." A father's not supposed to do that. If only he had left sooner, she thought, before his destruction had become so ingrained.

"It's hard to trust someone after they've betrayed you," Cassie began. "I don't think I could either, not at this point in my life. Your decision will be determined by what's yet to unfold, Rachel. You'll know in your heart." She paused, hesitant. "On another topic, Rachel, which is none of my business, except I'm concerned about your health, are you eating?" Rachel looked at her, then at Samir and shook her head.

"She is not, Mrs. Komsky," Samir answered. "This concerns me greatly."

"You've got to eat. Please don't let yourself get sick. Who will that hurt?' She looked at them. "It'll hurt you and it'll hurt Samir. As you've just said, you owe your allegiance to your husband, not your father. If you need someone to talk to when you can't be with Samir, I'll do my best to fill in; you know, like a surrogate. I wouldn't try to take the place of your mother, I would never do that, but if you need mothering, I know how. I think Stevie will give me fairly good grades in that category." She smiled.

"Thank you, Mrs. Komsky. You've helped me, us, so much already; I don't know what I'd do without you."

"It's the other way around, Rachel. I thank both of you."

They started to leave when Rachel paused. "Mrs. Komsky, there's a rumor going around that you might lose your job. Everybody's talking about it. Is it true?"

"That's another thing I can't control. It's what it is, and I'll do the best job I can until someone no longer lets me."

"It is because of me, is it not?" Samir asked intuitively.

"Actually, Samir, it's because of me. I am who I am, and I will not become someone else to keep a job."

He bowed. "Thank you for not becoming someone else because of me."

She looked at him compassionately. She had to be herself, which meant she would not discard her principles, the principles both she and Brian had lived by, that they had wanted for their daughter. "Samir, if I become someone else, then who am I?"

"You're too good for this school, Mrs. Komsky," Rachel said sadly.

She shook her head. "I've come to know too many of you who have the same ethics, the same principles. I'm looking at two of you right now. If I throw away my principles to keep this job, then what have I taught you? To have a principle when it's convenient? Then we will have lost another principle to convenience. That's the easy way, and it makes it harder for people who want to hold on to principles. So to keep my vow to Brian, my husband, I will be who I am, and life will take me where it wants me to go. As you've said, Rachel, we pick ourselves up and go on." Rachel smiled. "You do that too."

"I will, Mrs. Komsky. I promise." She looked at Samir. "We both will."

As Samir and Rachel walked out, Samir turned and looked at Cassie. "*In shaa' allah,*" (God willing) he said softly. And they were gone.

77

FRIDAY, RACHEL BOLTS FROM CLASS

"**H**er father wants nothing to do with her. That's a little harsh, especially after he's the one who invited Othello into his home to hear his war stories and exploits. It's not Desdemona's fault she fell in love with him. Her father shares some of the blame. Othello's a general, good enough for him to invite into his home to narrate his war stories, but not good enough for his daughter. That's a typical hypocrite." Elizabeth's anger surfaces.

It was Friday and they were still going back to Brabantio rejecting his daughter. Cassie had hoped they'd be done with that section for Rachel's sake, but the class saw more and more in that scene.

Yesterday, they had reviewed the section where the duke had heard Brabantio's side of Desdemona's marriage; then Othello's side; then, Desdemona's, but they carried it into today. It couldn't be easy for a young woman of that time to tell her father she's choosing loyalty to her husband over loyalty to her father. She is definitely not Ophelia. At the turn of the 17th century, Shakespeare is writing about a courageous daughter's defiance to her father. They wished Ophelia had had the same courage.

This section also sets the stage for Desdemona's downfall. Mason was the first to see that. Desdemona's father refuses to have her in his house while Othello goes to war; Othello won't have her live there anyway, and Desdemona refuses to stay there too. So, where to go? In whose care? Ironic, Mason says, that she goes to Emelia, Iago's wife. Emelia might be okay, but Iago's got the advantage now, big time. Desdemona is being sent into the devil's lair. Irony, cruel, dramatic irony.

"You can almost hear the audience gasp, clutch their hands to their open mouths, and say, 'Oh, no! Don't send her there,'" Emelia interjects.

Their vituperation against Brabantio continued. His pride and spite set the stage for his daughter's downfall, and it was obvious to all of them, even though, except for Rachel, they were not living it.

The guys attacked Roderigo, too, and shouted him down as though they knew him personally. "He's gonna drown himself if he can't have Desdemona?' Zach comments. Zach now had another Shakespearean character to hate. "Get over it! What a wimp! Like Iago says, 'Be a man!'"

The guys laugh. "Be a man! Yeah, com'on Roderigo; be a man!" The women contravene: Why can we accept Ophelia drowning when Hamlet and her father betray her, but not Roderigo saying that? Zach and Connor jump on that at the same time. Because Ophelia was depressed; she was distracted; she was young; she's a female; Roderigo's a man, and a Venetian gentleman. That's why!

Is this a male-female thing? The ladies ask, contentiously. Yeah, the males retort; it sure is. No doubt, men can handle tragedy better. Those are fighting words for Emelia, Gloria and Elizabeth. Even Rachel perks up, that old argumentative spark peeking though. The young women counter: maybe impossible for a man like Iago, who cares for no one, but very possible for a man like Roderigo. Okay, the men concede, not all males. Not real men, anyway! Cassie loves this. She is so glad Chelsea opened its academy to women. They'd never be having a discussion like this if it were all males.

And so the debate had raged, cantankerous at times, guys versus the ladies, perceived weakness versus perceived strength, Thursday to Friday, and they still weren't letting the father-daughter conflict and its repercussions go, and they hadn't even begun Iago's soliloquy. So Cassie lets the discussion take its course because it's real, real life being argued out here. All kids have fathers, whether good, bad, indifferent, in their lives, never there, whatever, and many personal references filled this passage they couldn't or didn't want to ignore. Maybe the discussion was a catharsis in some way. Maybe they were verbalizing what each had thought at one time or another. Didn't matter; let it flow and go where it will.

Gloria picks up where Elizabeth's initial point had left off. "Roderigo's obviously a 'wimp,'" she glares at the guys who had used the word, "and Othello's obviously a 'real male,' but what makes someone good enough to marry? Elizabeth's right. You can't help who you love, and as long as that person is a good person, and not a complete loser, it shouldn't matter. My mother thought she had a wonderful life with a wonderful husband who had great social status and made tons of money. But my father, with his great social status, dumped her, he dumped her, me and my sister, for a young tramp who came from nothing and was working her way up, one guy at a time."

"How do you know that, Gloria? Maybe she wasn't as bad a person as you make her out to be. Maybe they just fell in love." Zach said.

"You can't be a nice person and destroy a marriage because you just fell in love with a guy who already has a wife and a family." Gloria faced Zach head on; her violet blue eyes blazed. "Does a nice person do that? What if you were on the receiving end and it was you who got dumped, divorced and left with the kids? How would you feel then? That some nice person just happened to steal your wife and destroy your marriage?"

A very long pause. Zach was careful to respond. Having the situation turn so that he was forced to deal with it as the victim presented a new twist to his original answer. "No, Gloria. I don't think I could accept it if I were the one who got dumped. Sorry. Maybe we need to look at something as though it were happening to us to see how we'd feel before we judge the situation."

"Maybe that's what we all need to do *before* we do something we want just because we want it, without caring how the other people involved will feel." Gloria fumes.

"Isn't that what Gertrude and Claudius do to Hamlet?" Mason says. "They just think of their own desires without thinking or caring how their actions will affect him."

"Then Brabantio should have had more concern for his daughter's feelings than for himself," Emelia interjects. "He didn't have to lose a daughter. He threw her away because of his ego and his pride; he had lost control over his daughter's decisions and he didn't like it. Instead of having a daughter and a son-in-law, and a nice one, he just threw her away and disowned her."

Uh-oh, Cassie thinks instantly and in that same instant Rachel breaks from her chair and bolts out the door with Samir on her heels. The class is stunned. They glance at each other, right, left, at the person in front of them. Whispers follow: What happened; why'd she run; is she okay; is Samir okay. "What's wrong Mrs. Komsky? Is Rachel all right?" Emelia asks.

Cassie jumps up and grabs her coat. "Find the line that shows Othello's lineage. We'll change the topic. Find it on your own. I've gotta make sure Rachel is okay."

Cassie grabs Rachel's coat in case they've gone outside. She checks the immediate hallway; not there, and only one other class further on down past the office; she guesses which way she would go to get away as quickly as possible. Then she heads for the side door.

She sees them before she pushes it open. They are together, halfway down the path near a huge oak tree, facing a tall man in a black full-length coat who's carrying something in his hand, a clipboard? His back is towards

Cassie. She heads after them but pulls up short once she realizes it's Vaughn.

He turns, faces her with a grimace and glares. "Is this what you call classroom supervision, Mrs. Komsky? Two of your students are out of class, outside the school building during class time, and you've left the rest of the class unattended. This is lack of control and inadequate classroom management." His demeanor is confrontational, his voice, malevolent; his face contorts into a snarl.

"No, Dr. O/B, Rachel begins, shaking from cold . . ."

"It's okay, Rachel," Cassie says, putting her coat over her shoulders. "Let's go back inside. Too cold out here."

They walk back to class; Vaughn follows. They enter the room; he's still behind them. She had expected him to veer off towards Smythe Hall; he didn't. Instead, he stands in the doorway looking at the class, pauses, takes out a pen, writes as all eyes stare at him, then leaves.

For a few seconds, Cassie is confused, baffled, as they all are, until she suddenly realizes he has documented the incident on her chart. He had been heading for her classroom all along.

78

C assie had been observed many times during her teaching career; it was a concomitant of the profession. Three times a year prior tenure year, four times during her tenure year, then yearly as a tenured teacher, a principal, supervisor, or department chair would set up a time when they would come into the class, sit in the back and observe the lesson for a full period. He or she would be judging the teacher on her presentation of the lesson, her motivation, preparation, student/teacher interaction, a big one, and classroom management. Cassie knew all this; it was the process that maintained teaching standards and offered remediation to ameliorate any perceived weakness in performance.

When Vaughn walked into her first period class Monday, unannounced, after he had encountered Samir, Rachel and Cassie outside class last Friday, she was quite certain this was not the usual observation to determine any weaknesses for the purpose of remediation. This observation was to collect evidence Vaughn could put into an evaluation he didn't need to dismiss her. No teachers' union in a private academy, no tenure, no need to even give a reason for dismissal. None of it needed at Chelsea. All he had to say was, "You're fired."

But for Vaughn, there was one reason he was coming into her classroom, unannounced, and that was to rattle her. He knew before he hired her that she was an outstanding teacher, and he had told her numerous times since her first day. She was doing a great job; her students had come to admire and respect her; she had communicated with Samir when no one else could. Vaughn's reason, under the pretense of an official observation, was to harass her, make her feel uncomfortable, tense, ill at ease, make her sweat, destroy her ability to conduct a normal class; in short, make her pay for her rebuttal to Taylor and for standing up to Joel Greer. Seeing Samir, Rachel, and Cassie outside an unsupervised classroom had given him one final bit of ammunition. Vaughn pulled up a chair, dropped his coat over the back, sat, crossed his legs, using them as a table for his clip board, pen in hand, and cavalierly began to observe, glaring straight at her, freezing discussion mid-sentence.

Friday's class had ended with a discussion about Othello's royal lineage and his statement about boasting. They had gotten caught up in this because most admitted they had been guilty of boasting at one time or another. Both Parker and Mason had said they had bragged when they were younger to increase their popularity, although neither of them had to. They were both liked, and for obvious reasons. "I stopped bragging by the time I got to sophomore level," Parker had said facetiously, and Mason one-upped him by telling the class that he had outgrown the need for bragging by 8th grade.

Their assignment for today had been to study Iago's lines, "Tis in ourselves that we are thus or thus," compare them to lines from another Shakespearean play; then ana- lyze his soliloquy in act 2, scene 1 after Roderigo leaves. Summarize for today.

Rachel had walked into class with determination cloaking her sadness and began a tirade against Othello for having been so naive and trusting that he left his wife in honest Iago's household.

"But that's dramatic irony, isn't it?" Connor asks "Because we know Iago can't be trusted, but Othello doesn't. As Rachel just said, he let's his wife stay in Iago's household."

Enter Vaughn, center stage, five minutes into class. Speech halts; Connor's question goes unanswered; Rachel's diatribe gets put on the back burner as all motion halts and they face the door, watching him drag a chair to the table without a hello or any acknowledgement. They watch him sit, prop his clip board on his crossed legs, and glare, like a poster tacked to the wall with a facial expres- sion frozen in time, an animate object without inertia, simply there, occupying space.

Cassie recovers somewhat, so she thinks, and asks, "Anybody remember the play that has similar lines to 'tis in ourselves that we are thus or thus,'" without realizing Vaughn had distracted her so much she skipped Rachel's and Connor's points, jumping to last night's assignment, a glaring metathesis.

She realizes it a second after she asks her question. She feels her throat tighten. Vaughn's eyes penetrating, piercing, shoot right through her. She can almost feel his hatred, his vitriol, palpable to the touch like Macbeth's dagger. Her breathing increases, her heart pounds; her stomach summersaults. Heat creeps up her back into her neck, climbing like some creeping, crawling insect, climbing up her spine into her neck, tingling into her arms, no way to stop it.

Emelia sits straight up in her chair. *"Julius Caesar,"* she offers, sensing Cassie's discomfort. "'The fault, dear Brutus, is not in our stars, but in ourselves, that we are underlings.'"

"Excellent Emelia," Cassie recovers somewhat and beams, realizing what Emelia has done for her. "Can you take it a step further and compare their meanings?"

Most of them hadn't even heard Cassie's question. They were still staring at her, their focus shifting from her to their dean, or to the table or wall. Vaughn's focus remained riveted on Cassie, his glare boring right into her, resurrecting the memory of the person that used to be encased in that outer shell, the man who had visited her home, wormed his way into the cook-off, into her life, giving her his mobile phone number, offering to change her bandages and help decorate her tree . . . and so much more.

This person looked like the other person, but he wasn't. He was not the same person who had insisted on walking her and Stevie home after the cook-off; not the same person who had told her to call him Vaughn. This Dr. O/B looked like that man, but that man was gone; only his shell remained. She tried to maintain the discussion, but Vaughn was killing it as each second ticked away.

"Iago is telling Roderigo the same thing Cassius told Brutus," Connor responds again; ignoring his previous question about dramatic irony, knowing it had gone unanswered because the dean was here staring.

Anyone disagree with Connor?" Cassie thought she sensed a tremble in her voice. Did anyone else hear it? God, she hoped not; maybe it was in her mind. "Come on, class. Stay focused; try to ignore the distraction." Oh my God, had she just called Vaughn a distraction? What the hell. He was.

So she was telling them to stay focused when she could barely do the same. "Okay, we have Iago telling Roderigo he has the power to be who he wants to be and Cassius telling Brutus to achieve what people dream they can achieve, if only we control our own will. Remember Cassius saying we have the power to control our destinies, to become something better than what we are? Well, how much control do we actually have over our own destinies? Any, or are we all just puppets no matter what we do or what decisions we make? Will our puppet-masters put us where they want us to be regardless?" She couldn't have made the point any clearer. Courageously, she looked directly at Vaughn.

"Maybe we will; maybe we won't, but we'll never know." Rachel responds to Cassie's question. "That's why we should make decisions that we think will be good ones, kind decisions without any intent to hurt ourselves or others, which is what too many people don't do." Her sorrow is obvious.

"You once told us, Mrs. Komsky, if we make decisions for good reasons, the rest falls into place, the way it was meant to be. Do you still believe that?"

Vaughn winced, imperceptible to the class, but not to Cassie. His shoulders drooped a bit, and it kept her alive. Dr. Greer's daughter had the ability to reason on a more profound level than her father, more profound than Vaughn, too. And, although his presence was ruining the class, Cassie was glad he was here to hear her.

"Yes, Rachel, I do. I still believe we should make our decisions for good reasons. If we do that, then even if something goes wrong or tragedy results, we can't chastise ourselves for having been malicious."

Rachel smiled. If she had the spirit to go on, that validated Cassie's determination not to buckle to Vaughn or Dr. Greer. She'd go on, too, with Samir and Rachel, for as long as she could.

79

VAUGHN'S BATTLE PLAN

C assie's mettle would be tested from this point on. Not only had Vaughn observed period one, but periods four and six, same clip board, same vitriolic stare, same numbing effect on discussion. Worse, it was not a one-time observation or an occasional one, where he'd stay out of class for a few days or a week, returning for another. Nope, Vaughn observed her every day this week, Tuesday through today, Friday.

He had become a permanent fixture, so when he walked into period one today, as Cassie now expected, no one was surprised. But the down side was that his presence had stifled all spontaneous discussion, the nucleus around which literature classes thrived. Without discussion, you weren't experiencing the theme, plot, or characters. You were simply reading about them.

At this point, too, he was affecting Cassie's fortitude. Harassment and intimidation were justifiable formal complaints in public schools, but in this academy there was no recourse. No wonder her faculty 'friends' had deserted her. Who'd want to be subjected to this? As long as it hurt her, Vaughn didn't care.

Her classes' reticence was justified; no one wanted to interact or discuss anything while their dean was sitting in the room, glaring at their instructor malevolently. Drawing analogies between plot, characters and themes and their own lives made literature dynamic, but compare something personal in their own lives to Othello's or Iago's while the dean was in class? Not a chance. Vaughn had told Cassie she was history her first day back from Christmas; so let the kids have a decent discussion.

Yesterday she had begun scanning newspapers for mid-year teaching jobs. If she were lucky, there'd be a temporary position available. Maybe a teacher would need a leave of absence for illness or pregnancy, requiring a replacement on short notice. This weekend, she'd begin in earnest with the classified section of *The Star Ledger.*

She'd search for apartments, too, some place available at the shore, the home she had left for this. For this! What a fool she had been. You can't run from the past. It travels with you. She should have realized it then. What would she include on her resume, she wondered? Chelsea Academy, two months? Dismissed because of the dean's wife? Nah, she'd substitute before she'd ever put Chelsea Academy on paper. She couldn't excise it from her life, but she could excise it from her teaching career, if she still had one after this.

Today's class began because it was 8:00, for no other reason. It had taken them a full week to discuss Iago's soliloquy about how he'd use Othello's trusting nature and

Desdemona's father's warning to him – careful Othello, she has deceived me; she can deceive you too. Maybe this warning is what makes Othello believe Desdemona is being overly friendly to Cassio. Remember, Othello trusts Iago. He trusts him! Cassie ran her hand through her hair at that thought. Trust and deception, the bases for Iago's plot. It worked against Othello; it'll work against her too.

Cassie presents the position that people who trust are fools, doomed to become victims of evil, powerful people who have no conscience, people who destroy without remorse. Today, Friday, almost a full week after Dr. O/B's torture had begun, thoughts and comments were still not forthcoming; her students were still too constrained to speak spontaneously; in fact, even more so. But her statement did elicit a slight response from Vaughn. She could tell from his raised eyebrow. Good. She couldn't tell him to leave, but she could focus her comments towards something unethical he was doing.

"I don't get something, Mrs. Komsky," Zach's voice broke the silence, "Iago tells Roderigo to use reason and to control his emotions, but Iago can't practice what he preaches. Roderigo's emotion is love; Iago's is hate; they're different, but they're both emotions, and Iago has as much trouble controlling his hate as Roderigo has controlling his love."

"Great point, Zach. Iago can't control his hatred even though he tells Roderigo he should control his love. He's such a master of duplicity and wears his mask so well that no one suspects his emotions or his intentions or that he's plotting. When 'honest' Iago speaks or advises, everyone believes he has their best interests at heart, especially Othello."

She had been facing Zach on her right. At the end of her response, she turned and faced Vaughn on her left. "The ultimate power of deception," she affirms, controlling her trepidation, "occurs when a person can wear one face so well that you believe, beyond a doubt, he . . . or she, is that person, until you realize he was the exact opposite. Is that not perfect deception?"

Now it's her turn to stare. "Have any of you ever known an evil person who has destroyed an innocent person, without provocation, because of jealousy?" She marshals all the courage she has and continues to stare directly at him, never blinking. He pales, blinks and sits up stiffly in his chair.

"Anybody *you've* ever known, Dr. O/B?" She actually addresses him! "Sorry, Dr. O/B, I have to apologize for excluding you from the conversation this week. I never realized you had intended to be part of the class." She offers a wan smile, "but since you are here, perhaps permanently, we'd love to have you engage in the conversation."

"I have no intention of getting drawn into your rather weak conversation, Mrs. Komsky," Vaughn responds with venom. "That is not the purpose of my observations." His stare becomes acid; his face distorts into animosity. Silence . . . heart-beating, pulse coursing silence, interminable, as the clock ticks and the class shuffles its feet.

Then, breaking this roaring silence, one loud voice, clearly, and boldly says: "Then why *are* you here, Dad?" An icy, long pause. Did the clock stop ticking? "I could talk about people wearing masks easily if my father weren't in class."

Parker's salvo visibly startles Vaughn. Vaughn blusters a little but retains his authority, "This is a formal observation, Parker. You need to stay out of it."

But Parker would not stay out of it. "Dad, this is my Shakespeare class. It was a great class until you started coming in four days ago, but you're ruining it. No one wants to discuss anything with the dean sitting in on a conversation that's meant for senior students. I don't. I've seen you observe faculty before, but you've never been in a class four days in a row, and you've never glared at the teacher. What's going on? I want my old class back, the class I was in before Tuesday. Don't you have other administrative things to do?"

Oh my God! Only Parker, only Parker could have delivered that blow. What a shock! Nobody could see that coming, especially Vaughn. He had no retort. Reprimand his son during class? Tell him to keep quiet? Why? How? Parker was right. Should he remain in class, continue his bogus observation and keep targeting the instructor? How professional could that be if his own son had noticed? Cassie breathed a sigh. Thank God Parker was in her class.

Tick-tock began again. Its rhythmic beat sounding in the room like Poe's swinging pendulum, every swish burning its victim's ears as it swung lower and lower to excruciating death.

Suddenly, Vaughn rises, yanks his coat from the back of his chair and storms out.

Everyone breathes.

80

MONDAY, CASSIE ASKS PARKER FOR HELP

Next Monday morning, she walked into her classroom and sighed with relief. Vaughn was not
there. She waited, her stomach in knots, but by
8:20, she was sure he wasn't coming. Period one settled
into their familiar, energetic discussion and gradually returned to the rapport Vaughn had destroyed. But Cassie
would soon discover he had simply substituted period 2
for period 1 to avoid a repeat confrontation with his son,
and he would continue his routine for periods 3 and 6.
She would have period 1 to enjoy, but he would still cru-
cify her throughout the day.

Discussion in periods 3 and 6 remained dormant,
and in period 2, the class Vaughn now observed instead
of period 1, discussion became a forced trickle. Proof of
his destructive force showed in period 1's renewed energy.
By the end of the week, they had finished act 1 and were
into act 2. They had analyzed Iago's plot to destroy Cassio

and Othello. First came personality and character: "The Moor is of a free and open nature that thinks men honest that seem but to be so; and will as tenderly be led by the nose as asses are." Honest Iago? No, that's not you.

After that, discussion focuses on act 2, Cyprus, the setting. The Turkish fleet had set out to destroy this little island but was wrecked at sea. The Venetian fleet comes into port one by one, Cassio's ship first, then Iago's bearing Desdemona and Emelia, Iago' wife; finally, Othello's, a final gunshot confirming his ship's arrival. Here is where Iago sets his villainous plan in motion.

While Iago, Emelia, Cassio and Desdemona wait for Othello to disembark, Cassio kisses Emelia in greeting. Iago sees an opportunity. A light banter between Iago and Emelia draws Desdemona in, and she asks Cassio to comment on Iago's wit. Cassio smiles at Desdemona, takes her hand and kisses it. Another opportunity! Iago's evil scheme becomes corporeal. Devise a little here and a little there and he will undo both Cassio and Othello.

Shakespeare has transcended time again. Every student related Iago's lines to their own lives. Cassie loves this class. She loves the students, loves their rapport, thrives on their discussions, which keep her going as the week grinds on, and she empathizes with Rachel's depression because Cassie is living hers again. The senseless pain, the futility of hope, looking for reality not to be what it is, wishing you could step back in time and have what you once had, what you believed you'd have forever, for something you believed you'd always have with you until it wasn't.

The strain of Vaughn's relentless harassment and intimidation was wearing on her. Her stomach churned whenever she thought of the next day, the next class, his next onslaught, no friends - no, one friend. But she stopped noticing the wind playing through the trees, sunbeams decorating classroom walls or filtering into her townhouse, rain pattering on her roof, and the glitz of a starlit sky. She stopped glancing up into the heavens, looking for Orion, Pegasus, or Hercules, constellations that twinkled on that nighttime panorama at Homecoming; stars that had made her heart leap. She even stopped gazing at the moon and the beauty of its refracted light. She was enmeshed in sorrow, tension and fear.

What kept her grounded was Stevie, Rachel and Samir, her classes, her lessons, and her friend, her one friend whom she talked to every few days. But how often could she turn to Jeremy? He had his own classes and his own life to deal with. She didn't want to bother him and drive him away, so she had to make sure she called him only when she was desperate for adult companionship. And he was always there for her. Always.

Rachel and Samir. If any two young people needed help, if any couple was being treated unjustly, it was them. Samir had gone through so much during the past four years. To have all the beauty he had found assaulted every minute of every day by the specter of his father-in-law's hate was too much for an isolated man of eighteen. He had crawled out of his own darkness so recently only to be assaulted with more. Happily though, they could look forward to college together.

Ironic how both Samir and Rachel had applied for early acceptance to Princeton before they had even met and both had been accepted. Rachel wondered how she would get there without her father's financial support. Would her trust funds kick in for higher education or were they locked until twenty-one? How far would Ambassador Gibran go to help his new niece? Cassie figured, without knowing facts, he'd go pretty far.

But how much can a heart endure? Where's the respite? When does it get easy? Why is it so easy for some, and so difficult for others? Some people have so many blessings, yet they throw them away recklessly, while others would cherish a small percent of what another was blithely discarding. Distribution isn't equal. Never was; never would be.

Cassie persevered one day at a time. She met with Samir and Rachel whenever she could, individually in their dorms, a little while after classes. Sometimes she'd sit with them before dinner in Landon Hall and encourage them with the little stamina she had left while she continued to search the papers for housing and temporary positions anywhere and everywhere near Manasquan, as far north as Freehold; as far south as Waretown, further if she had to.

As of this past weekend, one possibility emerged, a middle school math position to replace a teacher with a high-risk pregnancy. This had possibilities. Math teachers were always in demand and not easy to come by. Cassie was certified in both English and math, a very unusual combination, and she had taught 7th and 8th grade math after she and Brian had made Manasquan their permanent residence and she had given up tenure at Passaic. This one, she'd pursue.

So another week had begun. Monday, January 18, 5:30 pm, after an early supper, she sits in the kitchen and explains the entire situation to Stevie. Stevie understands; she knows her mom has been very upset recently, and now she knows some of the reasons. She had been there when Dr. O/B had pounded on their door after Christmas break; she had seen him angry and she had been frightened. "I'll be ready, Mom, whenever you say."

"Thanks, Hon. Thanks for understanding. I know I've moved us to the other side of the state looking for something, or running from something. I'm sorry. I'm sorry I moved us here. It was a mistake." Cassie sighed. January 18, she thought sadly, of all days.

"It's okay, Mom, really it is. I won't be as upset leaving here as I was leaving Manasquan." Stevie looked around the kitchen, on the counter and table. "Mom, did you get the mail?"

A strange question, Cassie thinks and shakes her head. "No Hon. I didn't. I had too many things on my mind. I can get it now if you're expecting something." Who, she thought, would be sending Stevie something in the mail? Maybe one of her friends?

"No, I'm not expecting anything, Mom, but you've been so upset I mailed you a card. I wanted to cheer you up. I want you to smile again and be happy. Don't worry, Mom; we'll be okay."

Cassie's heart melted. Here she was, so distraught that Stevie felt compelled to cheer up her mother. "Stevie, what a beautiful thing to do? I love you so much, Honey." She hugged her hard.

The doorbell shocks her. She jumps. The last time anyone rang that door bell, a Black Forest cake was at the door carried by a man she no longer knew. "I'll get it, Mom," Stevie echoes, hurrying for the door.

"Stevie, use the peephole, Hon."

Too late, a voice was coming in. A happy voice. What's going on, Cassie thinks.

"We have two hours and then I turn into a pumpkin." Jeremy, followed by Stevie, strolls into the kitchen, carrying a cake box.

Cassie was completely confused. "What? What is. . .?"

"Happy birthday!" They say in unison, and sing. Then Jeremy presents the cake. "An ice cream cake, best in two towns." He puts it on the table. "So we've got to eat it real fast!"

Cassie was so surprised and happy, she cried. "But how. . ."

"I sort of called him last week." Stevie smiled, going for plates, forks, and napkins.

"You 'sort of'?" She asks, smiling at Jeremy and giving Stevie another big hug. "I never thought you'd remember, Honey, not with all this insanity going on."

"Mom, it's your birthday. That's what's in the mail, your card. Somebody has to remind you you're forty-three."

"Forty-two, young lady, and you know it." She began to unwind, laugh, and eat cake; they all did, to the last melted drop.

81

MONDAY EVENING, JEREMY'S SURPRISE

One eight-inch ice cream cake got devoured in one sitting. Stevie cleared the plates and went to her room for homework. "How many calories did we just eat?" Cassie asked as she and her stomach groaned. She put the kettle on for more tea.

"I don't know, but I sacrificed my diet for it; nineteen pounds down since New Year's Day and I've just put back two, or more!"

Cassie was moved. "Jeremy, this is so thoughtful. You really are a true friend."

"At least you've got *one*," he said shyly." He exhaled before he spoke. "You're not gonna like this, but I'll tell you anyway so you know what's going on." He sighed. "The football crowd is having a Super Bowl party, at Pete's Pub and Grill." He points south. "Down College Drive, if you've ever been down that far. They've reserved a back room."

"That's what . . . two weeks from now?" Cassie extrapolated quickly. He nodded. "You're invited, of course?"

He nodded again. "Yup."

"You can tell me all about it, if you want to. Feel free to talk about it. My feelings will not be hurt. I'm sure everyone will have a wonderful time."

"I won't be able to tell you a thing; I'm not going." She looked at him quizzically. "When I asked Walter if you were invited, he put his head down. I told him he was a coward and I walked away."

"You did what?!" Cassie uttered in shock. "Jeremy, you've got to work with these people. Please don't avoid them because of me."

"I'm not avoiding them because of you. I'm avoiding them because they're not the people I thought they were. They fooled me too. I can understand someone being frightened to get in Vaughn's cross-hairs. That makes sense, but I can't accept all of them shutting you out, especially after the school day.

"Come on, Cassie, we're all busy, but Melissa or Alicia, or Walter? They could have called you after school or on a weekend. Even if they didn't want Vaughn to know, they could have said that, and you would never have said anything. But they didn't. They just dropped you as though you didn't exist. They were told there'd be consequences and they just caved. My thinking is that if they can do that to you, they can do that to any of us, they can do that to me. I don't want to be part of a group that can do that."

Cassie was thunderstruck. "But, but how, who will you have for a friend, other than me, of course." She forced a laugh. "But you know I won't be here much longer.

Then who will you have for friendship. Everybody needs a friend."

"Between you and me," he laughed, "not that you talk to anyone anyway, but between you and me, I won't be here much longer either."

"What?" Cassie was shocked. Why not?"

"I found another job."

Cassie's mouth dropped. "You've been here almost two decades."

"Then maybe it's time for a change."

"And you got a job that quickly?" He nodded. "In less than two weeks, from the day we talked here after my meeting with Greer?"

He nodded. "Rutger's, teaching advanced chem."

"Advanced chem. At a university? Jeremy, I'm missing something here. A university just doesn't hire a high school chemistry teacher and that quickly."

"Yes they do, if they are desperate for a fully qualified chem instructor who has a PhD in chem and in physics." He said sheepishly.

"What!?" Cassie almost screamed it out. "When did you fit all this in?"

Jeremy gave a little shrug. "Started college, MIT, at sixteen. PhD in physics at nineteen; Poly Cal at nineteen; met Sharon there, PhD in chem by twenty-two. I stayed for a while after she died. Then I came here. I wanted to hide; I needed to hide. I've done that for the past eighteen years. When I realized how courageous you were, what you had to overcome after your husband was killed, and I learned that, we all learned that, from Stevie at the cook-off, which you now know, I realized you had gone through a hell of a lot worse than I had. And if you were still trying to start over, I could try for the same reason. Rutger's approached me over the Christmas break, an MIT friend instructs there, but I didn't put it into action until Vaughn's edict, when everyone abandoned you because of it."

Cassie needed a few minutes to digest this. Not only was she talking to a genius, but this genius had so much more courage than she had ever imagined. She remembered him at Homecoming when he and Tasha were howling out "Hungry like a Wolf," and Cassie was thinking he was a geek. Wow, talk about first impressions being wrong. Someday she'd have to confess this and apologize to him, big time.

"Cassie you can't stay here. They'll kill you, figuratively. They'll grind you into the floor boards and sprinkle dust on you, and they won't give a damn. You've already walked through hell and come out of it; no way you can let Vaughn repeat that kind of tragedy." He passed his cup to her and she refilled it, added a new teabag, a little sugar and a hint of half and half. "Fifty more calories, at least," he chuckled then got serious again. "I assume you're looking?"

Cassie nodded. "I have to. Vaughn's made it very clear I'm history, with his statements and now by his actions. I can't stay in this environment, even if he kept me. He's using intimidation and emotional torture, and quite well. But it's the timing, when everything will come together, and it's Rachel and Samir; I have to find a way to help them."

"Cassie, I will never pry, and I never want you to tell me, especially if my knowing will in any way make things worse, but find a way to help them and find a way fast."

"I will, Jeremy. I understand. By the way," she changed the subject, "you have two PhD's, one in chem. and one in physics, and the kids call you 'mister'? Why?"

Again, Jeremy shrugged sheepishly. "It's a little like Othello's line where he says he'd talk about being from royalty when boasting becomes honorable. Who cares how many degrees a person has? Degrees don't make us honorable. Courage in the face of horrific obstacles does."

Cassie had trouble holding back tears. "I have one hell of a friend," she said quietly and ran her hand over her eyes. "And I never would have known it if all this hadn't happened. Maybe in one way, it's good that it did."

82

THURSDAY INTO FRIDAY, PEER PRESSURE AND DECEIT

Another week done. Friday. Even though each day seemed to be an eternity, paradoxically, time seemed to be flying by. Every class, every day, stress increased. That was the negative, but not having Vaughn in period one had given her back that class, and that was the positive.

Full potential; power on. It had been a week of dynamic discussion. One topic after the other had electrified them. Thank God. She could have hugged Parker. Had he not challenged his father, some of the best dialogue and character interaction would never have surfaced.

Monday morning, act 2, scene 3, Iago persuades Cassio to drink, knowing Cassio can't hold his liquor. Have a cup of wine; our general wants us to celebrate, come on, have one cup. So you've already had one, have one more. Of course you can hold your liquor. Come, drink.

Iago succeeds; Cassio drinks, followed by a drunken brawl. When Othello learns what's happened from his trusted Iago, he strips Cassio of his rank. "Consequences," Cassie remarks. "Whatever we do, there are consequences. Jason, give it all you've got."

"Iago sets Cassio up to fight with Rodrigo who taunts him intentionally. And being drunk, Cassio falls for it and goes after him. That part of Iago's plot works perfectly, proving there are consequences to going against your better judgment."

"Excellent analysis, Jason. Now, . . ."

"Wait, Mrs. Komsky," Jason interrupts, "I'm not finished. The important part is about consequences, and that brings Cassio's problem into the present. The way I see it, it's all about the consequences of peer pressure. You're invited to a party. All the popular kids will be there, all the popular kids and alcohol. You want to be with those kids, so you go. Can you go and not drink when all the popular kids are drinking and they're shoving drinks in your face? That's what happened to Cassio. Everyone there wants him to drink; so he drinks. It's the same with today's peer pressure."

"Excellent analogy, Jason. Absolutely excellent." He beams with satisfaction. "What do you think class?" Cassie is asking them to dig deep into their hearts and think about peer pressure, the bane of every teen-ager's existence, and after. Peer pressure does not disappear because we age. It manifests itself throughout college, the right fraternity or sorority, the right sport; it manifests itself in the workplace, in your neighborhood, having the right house, the right car, the right dinner-parties.

"I agree with Jason." Connor concurs. "Just about everything he said depends upon how much of yourself and your principles you want to give up to be part of the crowd."

"Yup, me too," Mason adds. "Peer pressure manifests itself throughout life, only in different guises. When do you walk away?"

"'Manifests?' 'Guises?' I'll have to warn Stevie; you're gaining momentum."

Mason smiled. He sure was studying the dictionary.

Thursday, with Friday on the back burner if they needed or wanted more time, the discussion was riveted on peer pressure and examples, how it manifests itself and the psychology behind it. Why do we let people talk us into doing things against our principles, against things we know are not good or not safe? Why get talked into doing or saying things that are not morally or ethically right? Is the need to be accepted or have friends so overriding that we'll risk it at any cost?

With Cassio, he loses his position and his reputation because he drinks against his better judgment, and worse, he shames himself in Othello's eyes, the general he reveres. Consequences. Do we think of the consequences before we act?

"I don't think any of us do, not all the time, and not when we're offered something we really want. We can all succumb to something tempting," Elizabeth offers and nods to Mason while stressing 'succumb,' "whether we're seniors, younger, or older. That's the scary part.

"We can all get sucked in by someone we trust, by someone we think has our best interests at heart, while all they care about is using you for what they can gain from you. That's Iago, master of deceit. Deception allows Cassio and Othello to trust Iago and he destroys them. They think he has their best interests at heart, but his only objective is revenge, sick, distorted revenge. We can all get sucked into something dangerous if we believe someone is our true friend."

"I agree with Elizabeth," Gloria says, but from a different perspective. I don't understand how people who are so dishonest and so deceitful can actually gain someone's trust. You have to be one great hypocrite to play one role and be another. Why can't anyone see the real Iago? Psychologically, I think he hates but mostly I think he hates himself. He's jealous of everyone because he's unhappy with himself and who he is."

"Lizzie's right," Matt says. "I think the guy's insane. His soliloquy in act 1, after Roderigo leaves, says he thinks Othello has slept with his wife. He's not sure, but he'll assume Othello has and he'll hate him anyway. He says this again in his soliloquy in act 2, scene 1, and now he says Cassio has slept with his wife too. You've got to be kidding me! This guy is a nut case, and Othello trusts him."

"Matt was right when he said Othello doesn't know his enemy," Zach says. "He doesn't have a clue."

"Zach and Matt are both right," Mason concurs. "And I agree with Elizabeth because I don't get how so many people are fooled by deceitful people, either. What is it that let's good people get sucked in by someone this devious, this nefarious?"

"Another good word, Mason. Keep your dictionary open."

"I will, Mrs Komsky," Mason beams. "If your daughter can do it, so can I." That provided a little humor, but if Vaughn had still been in class, it would never have happened. Nothing could compare to a good teacher-student rapport.

"And he's also diabolical," Mason throws in another, getting very confident with his newly acquired vocabulary, then finishes his point. "It's scary to think this devious guy gets Othello's complete and unquestioning trust, very scary. If being good and trusting means you can get duped like that by someone you trust completely, where's the hope? Gee, Mrs. Komsky, I trust Parker with my life. Does that mean I shouldn't?" His voice actually quivered, and his head bowed. Everyone became pensive with the gravity of his statement.

It was a moment of complete silence. Mason's analogy had brought the reality of Iago's duplicity home, right at their doorstep. Mason and Parker had been best friends since day one at Chelsea. Could this ever happen to them? Mason's question was as real and as frightening as Shakespeare could get. How would Cassie respond? It had happened to Hamlet; it would happen to Othello; it had had happened to her; and it had happened to Rachel. Mason was asking if it could happen to him too.

"I've asked Mrs. Komsky that same question," Rachel's soft voice broke the silence. "None of you know this, and maybe it's time you did, but none of you, except Gloria, know that I brought Samir home with me over Christmas break to introduce him to my parents, parents I've loved and trusted every minute of my life. A mother, and especially a father, who had brought me up to be open-minded and to accept and love people because they were kind and good, not because of race, nationality, ethnicity or religion; *regardless* of ethnicity and religion," she emphasized, "and my father threw Samir out."

She looked at Samir and gulped; tears filled her eyes. Samir put his arm around her and she continued. "My father not only threw him out, he attacked him, physically, with the fire iron. And when I intervened, he threw me across the room. That's how much he hates Samir, because he's an Arab. He attacked him . . ." she broke into sobs. Samir held her close, cradling her in his arms. Her classmates had frozen in their seats, trying to grasp the hurt, the horror of what Rachel had just said and of what the young couple must be feeling. Rachel dried her tears with her sweater. "So you ask how you trust someone you've trusted all your life only to find out they're not what they presented themselves to be? When you find the answer to that, let me know, please, because I'll never figure it out. But it changes you. It changes you for the rest of your life."

The girls rose, reached out to Rachel and hugged her. She stood up and they embraced. One by one, they held their dear friend, cried with her, and understood why she had changed. Samir stood by her side, protecting her, and so unexpectedly, after hugging her best friend, Gloria went to Samir and hugged him unabashedly. One after the other, all the girls did.

At first, he was confused, not knowing how to respond, until his awkwardness made Rachel smile. Then he returned their hugs, one after the other, and felt part of a family he had missed for years. That was the ladies.

Then the guys got up and hugged Samir as men hug –
close, with slaps on the back that echoed. A guy's embrace
had to have back-slaps or it meant nothing. But they all
came forward, each one, and hugged Samir, whom they
had come to respect and in their own way, love.

It was beautiful. One of the most moving moments
Cassie had ever witnessed. This was the epitome of life,
and the universality that brought mankind together.

For the few minutes that remained of class time, Cassie
was hands-off. She let them mingle, talk, empathize, express their feelings, share their grief amongst each other.
Nothing about Shakespeare could have surpassed this.
This was the apex of teaching literature. They were living
it. They could have written their own story or play about
the experiences they had shared in this class, in this year,
the first year for young women at Chelsea. They had been
living a drama all year, a drama not yet written.

At 8:50, the class waved a goodbye to Cassie and began walking towards the door. Cassie positioned herself
next to Parker and caught his attention. She had been
thinking about this all week, since Monday, when she and
Jeremy had discussed ensuing events that were unraveling
quickly. She had given very serious thought to this and
had realized she needed help. Yes, she needed help, but
she needed help for Rachel.

"Hold back just a bit." She motioned for him to let the
others pass.

Mason turned at the doorway looking for his pal. "I'll
catch up, Mason. Give me a minute." Mason motioned
okay.

"This'll just take a minute, Parker," she exhaled with determination and began. "I need a favor, not for me, for someone else."

Parker glanced at Rachel's empty chair; he knew exactly who Cassie meant without her saying a word.

"Does it have something to do with my father?" Cassie turned away. "Maybe indirectly?" He asked. Cassie nodded. "What do you need, Mrs. Komsky?"

"If I'm not here in the near future, I need to know this person can turn to someone for help. I need to know that Parker." She focused on him intently. "What I need is for you to ask your Aunt Hillary to call me. I would sincerely appreciate it. She seems kind, Parker. I believe she would assist a student who's going through a very difficult time. I'm sure she would, if she's asked. Would you please ask her to call me so I can explain the situation to her?"

The overly-confident, somewhat egocentric young man she had first met in November was gone. He stood with sad eyes. "'I'll do whatever I can, Mrs. Komsky."

83

Another Monday, the week of Super Bowl. As Cassie approached her classroom, voices, laughter, light seeped into the hallway. What's going on, she thinks. She reaches the doorway; she knows. Lights on, every male in the class was hanging posters, even Jason, who was not an athlete, and shock of all shocks, even Samir! Cassie was stunned. Samir working with his classmates to hang football posters, with Rachel sitting in her seat, looking on with admiration. It was amazing.

Obviously, it had been a well-planned endeavor, kept secret from her alone, holding her to the promise she had made after Thanksgiving to let the guys decorate the classroom for Super Bowl. Posters only, that was the deal, and posters it was.

They had kept their word. Cassie surveyed the scene while one of the last posters, the Redskins team, was going up over Macbeth. John Elway had replaced Cassius;

Doug Williams covered Hamlet, Super bowl XX11 replaced Queen Elizabeth. "Oh no," she groaned, "over the queen?" And a Broncos poster covered Stratford on Avon. That she could live with.

"It's okay, Mrs. Komsky. It'll all come down after this weekend," Mason said, seeing the disquieting look in Cassie's eyes.

"Who you rooting for? Parker asks. "Giants aren't playing so you gotta pick Redskins or Broncos."

She thought about it. The Giants were last year, Super Bowl XX1. She loved the catchy tune they had written; it went something like the Giants being number one and going to Pasadena for some fun. The deep bass voice that sang it gave it just the right touch. Nothing catchy like that this year.

"Well, since the Giants aren't playing, guess I'll go with the Redskins."

"No way, Mrs. Komsky! Broncos are the favorites. You know you're gonna lose. Why are you picking the Redskins?"

Cassie shrugged. "Don't know. Gut feeling, but we'll know a week from today, won't we?"

The ladies had arrived. "Ooo, I like this," Gloria commented, appreciating the muscular guys. "Me too," Liz commented, glancing flirtatiously at Matt.

This was a fantastic idea. Hope Vaughn's not too distracted today, she thinks, but if he doesn't like the lesson, he can always focus on the football wall of fame.

Okay, 8:00, everyone settled in with difficulty. They were phyched; maybe she'd be too as it got closer to Sunday.

"End of act 2, scene 3, Cassio mourns his lost reputation. Iago's response is that reputation is an idle and false imposition, often got without merit, and lost without deserving. What do you think; guys? . . . ladies?" Silence. They were still looking at the walls.

Now how can I relate these lines to the Super Bowl, she thinks. "Parker, Mason, you play football; Matt, Connor, you wrestle, right?" They nod. "Zach? Jason?"

"Track and Field," Zach responds.

"Chess . . .?" Jason responds apprehensively.

Cassie turns to Samir. She doesn't want to pressure him, but he was with the guys this morning. Maybe he'd participate in the discussion.

"Fencing," he bows, "and boxing."

Everyone turns to Samir. "You fence?" Mason asks? "I'm impressed."

"Ditto from me. That's an art form," Parker says.

"If you wish, I will teach you some drills," Samir responds, reaching out to his classmates.

They are all stunned. "Thanks, Samir," Parker replies. "I'd like that." Mason and Matt follow Parker's approval.

"Ladies? Field hockey?" Three hands went up. "Elizabeth? Any sport?"

"Swimming."

Absolutely, Cassie thought. She has the height and she's thin with broad shoulders. Perfect build for it. Sports it is. "While you're in training, aside from parents' and school rules in general, you are restricted from any indulgences, like drinking, that could compromise your athletic or mental ability, yes?" They all nod, even Samir, whose religion forbade alcohol.

"Two lines at the end of act 2, scene 3 address this exact issue in the early 1600's. The first is Iago's response to Cassio as Cassio mourns his lost reputation. Iago tells Cassio that reputation is an idle and false imposition. The second line is Cassio's response to Iago, 'God, that men should put an enemy in their mouths to steal away their brains! That we should with joy, pleasure, revel, and applause, transform ourselves into beasts.'

"Think of the gravitas in that statement: 'That men should put an enemy in their mouths to steal away their brains.'" She punctuated each word to let its significance sink in. Cassio means alcohol. You're all involved in sports; how does Cassio's line from four hundred years ago relate to you?"

That was all the motivation they needed. They tied drinking to being popular; then they tied it to hiding from reality; they related drinking to destroying a person's ability to think and destroying a person's potential; they related it to addiction and how it can destroy a person literally, harming themselves and others. They included real-life experiences they had had, almost had, or their friends, or friends of friends had had. Almost every one of them knew someone directly or indirectly whose life had been destroyed by alcohol, or some stronger drug. Samir contributed with peers mocking him because his religion forbade it. It took strength to ignore them.

The discussion segued to psychological reasons why people would need to be liked by a group that most likely wouldn't give a damn about their welfare. That discussion, the curse of inebriation, carried into the next two days when they tied it with Iago's statement about lost reputation.

Cassio had gotten so drunk he remembered nothing, one of the curses of inebriation. He had put an enemy into his mouth that had stolen away his brain and had transformed him into a beast. To Cassie, that brought back the Nor'ester Hotel and its revelers doing the exact same thing. They had lost their reason, transformed into beasts, yet they repeated this every weekend. She still didn't understand it and never would.

Ethics and morality come together when Cassio realizes what he's done. He despises himself for it because he has ethics and morals. Why have those qualities when so many people you meet do not? Isn't Iago's line, "got without merit, lost without deserving," closer to the way people conduct themselves today than the punishment Cassio imposes upon himself for having morals and ethics?"

And when that aspect of the conversation came up in periods two, three and six, the classes where Vaughn was still soundly entrenched, Cassie looked right at him, her stomach pounding, and drew him in. As much as he tried to stare her down, as much as he attempted to bully his way out of the question, to use his authority to claim he was an observer, not a participant, she encouraged the classes to invite their dean into the discussion since he might feel more comfortable joining in. And wouldn't they want to hear from him and get his perspective, since he could offer so much to the discussion? At that point, he gathered his things and walked out. Two days before week's end, four days before the Super Bowl, five days before February 1, 1988. No, this would never last until June.

The next day, Thursday, Parker made sure he was the last to leave. Just before he exited, he gave Cassie a thumbs-up. He had made contact with his aunt; she had agreed to call.

84

SUPER BOWL SUNDAY, JANUARY 31

This was not your typical hot wings, club sandwiches, meatballs, chips, dips and beer Super Bowl party. Nope, the football crew wanted something special this year. For the past ten years, Walter had hosted the party, either for the close-knit football crowd or a few more. His house could accommodate twenty guests easily, allowing plenty of room to pace around, jump up and hoot or stretch out and relax in front of the brick, wood-burning fireplace. Everyone would contribute a tray of food and Walter would make two trays of lasagna, one meat, one cheese. As Cassie and Stevie had witnessed Christmas day, he could handle himself in the kitchen.

As of December, he had expected to do the same, but as of January, Walter would not host the party; he wasn't motivated. When Alicia suggested a bar atmosphere, it was yes by acclamation. Two days after

Christmas break, they had secured Pete's Bar & Grill. The ambience of beer on tap, tables for six or eight and their own private room fit the bill. Two large TV's and an affable owner hosted the event, but the big difference was food. This year they had wanted classy, and the owner offered them a fantastic spread, thirty bucks a head, thirty bucks per person for a lavish buffet of shrimp, spare ribs dripping with BBQ sauce, hot wings, crab-stuffed clams, Italian meat balls, cheese lasagna, sliced brisket plus pitchers of beer.

Not your typical bill of fare for a bar and grill, especially with a cascading fountain of dark chocolate and fresh banana chunks and strawberries for dunking, but a great deal. With one extra staff needed to butler, another to pour and another to clear, the proprietor of Pete's Brill, as the locals had abbreviated it, welcomed the group with its desire for a classy flair. Typical bowls of chips and dips, nuts and pretzels were already on each table.

There was one big difference between Pete's Brill and what would have been Walter's Super Bowl festivities: Cassie, someone he had had by his side for three months, either with her physical presence or being a phone call away, was not here. Even more glaring was Jeremy's absence, Jeremy, who had been hired almost two decades ago, same as Walter. He had become a staple at Chealsea, like pen and paper, flour and sugar in your pantry, always expected to be there. But he wasn't, and the reason he wasn't stood in stark juxtaposition to Walter's personality. Jeremy wasn't here because he had adhered to honor and doing the right thing. As a shrink, wasn't that, or shouldn't that have been Walter's line?

Less than two minutes into the game, the Broncos score. "If it keeps up this way, Broncos are gonna run away with it," Joe De Biasso shouts. "Odds are in their favor."

"Let's see what happens," Ron Swenson counters. "Players don't play a game based on odds."

Everyone settles in to watch what will turn into a major upset. But the revelry had begun, great food, unending beer, some hard drinks here and there, and the football crowd with a few additional faces. Ron had never been with the crowd before, but he had always wanted to be. After he had covered Cassie's class when she met with Rachel's father, he had made some inroads through Melissa. Art teacher, John Atkins, was a new face; so was Trevor Russeau, who taught Constitutional history. Charlotte, Vaughn's secretary, had never seemed interested in football until this year, but she sat at Melissa's table with pad and pen, taking notes. Two secretaries from the Guidance pool had also signed up. Chris Devon, who taught biology, and Sam Atkins who taught American lit had eagerly said yes. The new faces had jumped at the opportunity.

Laughter, hooting, oh's, damn it's, and other expletives peppered the room as the game found its rhythm. Yet, amidst the festivities, Walter sat alone at his table, picking at a full plate of shrimp and spare ribs, nursing a shot of vodka, watching, watching his friends of almost twenty years glued to two TV's positioned strategically for optimum viewing, alive with action and time outs, penalties and replays. Despite all of it, Walter sat alone, feeling isolated and desolate. Here he was surrounded by decades of friends, feeling completely alone, and he wondered how, if Cassie had become invisible to them, how she could possibly be feeling, especially about him, who had offered her unsolicited verbal assurances she would be in his world and in his future. He had never returned one call. Not one.

A failed attempt by Elway causes Alicia to turn in frustration. Noooo! This was not a Redskins crowd. Spying Walter all by himself, she moves towards his table, grabs a shrimp, smothers it in cocktail sauce before she approaches and sits. "Walter?" He nods, offering a silent response. "Walter, what's wrong? Everybody's having a great time; everyone except you. It's a great crowd. Mix in a little. Everybody's here." She looks around, "except Jeremy. I don't see Jeremy. Where is he?"

Walter flicked his hand in a cavalier gesture. "He's not coming."

"Not coming? Why not, is he sick?" Walter shakes his head. "He's at another party?" Walter shakes his head again. "Then where is he?" Alicia asks.

"Home."

"Home? He stayed home instead of coming here? I don't get it; the entire football crew is here watching the Super Bowl. Why would he miss this?"

"Maybe because someone else is missing."

"Who else?" Alicia asks, missing Walter's import. Then she realizes he means Cassie. "Walter, if you mean Cassie, she's only been here three months. Our crowd's been together almost twenty years. You're saying Jeremy refused to come here because someone who's been here only three months isn't here?"

"All the more reason to respect him, don't you think? He walked away from friends he's known almost twenty years for a principle, an ethic, for someone who's only been here three months. What does that say about us?"

"Come on Walter. Who's going to risk Vaughn's wrath for someone who's only been here three months?"

"Would you risk Vaughn's wrath for someone who's been here longer than three months?" She looks at him. "What's the time limit, Alicia, a year, two years, ten years? Would you risk Vaughn's wrath if Vaughn suddenly turned on me? Should we risk his wrath if he suddenly turned on you?"

She gasped, not wanting to imagine something so fearful. "We're all apprehensive, Walter. No one wants to lose their job."

"That wasn't my question, Alicia. I asked you what your time limit would be before you stick your neck out and risk Vaughn's wrath for someone we considered part of our football crowd. She didn't invite herself in; we invited her. And now, she's been ostracized and turned into a pariah because she's not one of us, or she hasn't been here long enough. So I'm asking you, what's long enough?" Alicia turned away. "We're all scared, Alicia, but that doesn't make what we did, what I did – I'm not speaking for anyone except myself – right. Fear doesn't make it right. And it makes Jeremy, who's only known her for three months also," he puts his head down, "a guy with more guts than I have. For me, a psychiatrist, that makes it even worse."

At that moment, Vaughn walks in. Walter and Alicia watch him scan the group and saunter over to Charlotte, Melissa, Joe and Tasha. "Tell me Alicia," Walter asks, "if his life is so perfect, so wonderful with all his friends and his money at the Club, why is he here? It's not a school function; his son isn't here, and he has the Club. So why is he here?" Alicia doesn't respond. "And why did he push his way into the cook-off? That wasn't a school function either."

Alicia's face takes on a chagrinned countenance and she shrugs. "Guess he just wanted to be there?"

"Yeah, he did. He wanted to be there more than at the Club with his wife, his brother, his sister-in-law, his mother, his super wealthy friends. Think about it Alicia. People go where they're happy because they want to be happy. And for Vaughn, that was the cook-off, and the faculty party, and now, here. I may not be the best psychiatrist in the world, but I know why he insinuated himself into a faculty party, a place he's never been before and never wanted to be before. And he's here now. Look at him; he's looking at everyone, one person at a time, almost as though he's looking for one special, one particular person. As if he hasn't destroyed her enough."

"Don't beat yourself up, Walter. You didn't make her Vaughn's target."

"No I didn't, but I sure as hell stayed out of his firing range," he stated angrily and balled his fist. "We all did; all of us, except Jeremy. Jeremy," he snickered, "who'd a' thought."

85

SUPER BOWL AT JEREMY'S

Super Bowl at Pete's Brill was a lot different than Super Bowl at Jeremy's. Jeremy was still tenaciously adhering to his diet and Cassie refused to be a spoiler, well . . . not completely. She had prepared a huge platter of vegetables – sliced carrots, celery, radishes, mushrooms, and endive, with hummus for dunking. Then a platter of shrimp and chicken salad made with fresh chicken she had boned yesterday, adding finely chopped onions, cilantro and parsley surrounded by sliced tomatoes. Delicious. And in case dessert was needed, Cassie had brought over a small plate from a fresh tray of nemura, with apologies. Just in case, she had said.

Jeremy had made beef stew, with chunks of rump roast, potatoes, onions and carrots, a few cloves of garlic added for flavor. Who was going to eat all this? There was enough for another cook-off, which would never happen again. When she handed him the plate of nemura, Jeremy reproached her. His scale weighed in at a twenty-two pound loss, which was becoming obvious. He was not about to destroy success, but when Cassie pulled back the pastry dish, Jeremy yanked it from her, vowing he would eat only one piece. He would do without food rather than do without one piece of nemura. That set the tone for a great Super Bowl evening, just the two of them.

Stevie was watching the game on the second floor of Sanders House with Rebecca, Stacy and tiny Millie Thompson, the three friends she had come to really love here at Chelsea. She would miss them when she and her mom left, and that would be soon.

Cassie and Jeremy talked about Rachel and Samir without Cassie feeling she was mentioning something she shouldn't with Stevie present. Rebecca had never mentioned her father was angry with Rachel, so Cassie continued to keep that situation to herself, herself and Jeremy, even though Rachel had recently confided in her classmates.

So she and Jeremy talked, watched the game, watched the game and talked, but mostly talked. Cassie couldn't wait to tell him her fantastic news and she was so glad she had a friend to tell it to.

Cassie is on cloud nine, she says, because Hillary called her late yesterday morning to get together to talk. Parker had told his aunt what he knew and what he surmised, that a classmate was in trouble and Mrs. Komsky had hoped his aunt would help. "He told her someone might be forcing me to leave. Hillary figured my problem had something to do with the family, and that could only be Vaughn."

And basically that's what had happened. Hillary, working with the little information Parker had given her, figured his request, coming from his teacher, had to be important to him because Parker had never seemed interested in anything except his own life or comfort. Hillary had considered her decision carefully. She hadn't involved herself in anything for a long time. At her nephew's request, maybe it was time she did. She also wondered how this change in Parker had occurred. His concern piqued her interest; she'd make the call.

It was brief; could they meet and talk somewhere in person, face to face. Was Cassie surprised? Oh yeah. They couldn't meet at the Club; Cassie sure as hell didn't fit in there and if anonymity was paramount, a nobody in the Club with Hillary Otis-Barrett would cancel that out immediately. Hillary suggested her house, but she couldn't guarantee Brett wouldn't be in and out after a morning at the Club.

"I'd come to you if you wouldn't mind," Hillary had offered. Someone as entrenched in the upper crust as Hillary would come to a three bedroom condo on Chelsea's campus? Is she kidding? But Hillary wasn't kidding and indeed she did arrive with her driver who dropped off his Miss Hillary at the walkway to Cassie's townhouse, then discretely parked the limo around back. How discrete can that be, having a limo parked in the space adjacent to hers? Cassie felt a bit apprehensive as she stood by the front door.

"I apologize for the limo," Hillary said sincerely as she approached Cassie's door, "but I don't drive much anymore. I didn't want Arthur to reposition all the other cars just to take something smaller." Then she almost blushed, realizing she had said, "all the other cars." Hillary wasn't ostentatious, but it was an inherent lifestyle she couldn't avoid.

"That's okay, Hillary," Cassie responded good-naturedly. "All my other cars are at the junk yard being used for parts." Her humor put them both at ease. Cassie ushered her inside, put on tea, took hazel nut cookies and nemura from the frig along with the fresh hummus and egg salad she had just made when Hillary had suggested her condo. Cassie included a wedge of cheddar and crackers. It wasn't the Club, but Hillary wouldn't go hungry.

Hillary and Cassie drank tea, nibbled at the egg salad and hummus, and each took a piece of nemura. "I love this," she said. "I can't believe you can make it yourself. Does it take a lot of time?"

Cassie nodded. "I rarely make it because it is very fattening," she smiled, "but I do make it as a stress-reliever. When I was a kid, I'd sit in a chair at the kitchen table and watch my mom spread layers of phyllo into a baking pan, brushing each one with melted butter. I'd watch her heat the cream, add corn starch and check its consistency. Other Arabic pastries are delicious too, but my mother would make these, which are filled with cream, because she knew I loved cream. When I make this, I feel warm and nurtured, like most kids feel." She turned her face away. She didn't want to bring sentiment into this conversation. This conversation would be sensitive enough, and that emotion would focus on Rachel.

As they nibbled, they talked, and Cassie explained the situation as much as she could without mentioning names or hinting that the couple was married. Hillary understood the gravity of Cassie's concern without proper nouns, although from her brief conversation with Parker, Hillary thought she knew who the young lady might be. Parker had mentioned a doctor's daughter. There were lots of MD's in the area but not too many who had sent a daughter to Chelsea the first year it had admitted women and as a senior. If this doctor had sent both daughters to Chelsea, it had to be Joel Greer, who had made munificent donations for renovating and building the women's dorms. He had clout.

Parker had also said Mrs. Komsky didn't think she would be at Chelsea much longer because of a conflict with administration. Cassie confirmed an administration conflict would be forcing her to leave. It had to be Vaughn. Hillary remembered the confrontation between Taylor and Cassie at the faculty party. Now, it appeared that conflict was affecting another person's life, a student's, a young woman who Hillary might be able to help, if she'd let her.

This student trusted Cassie but that didn't mean she'd transition her trust automatically to another person. This, Hillary and Cassie both understood. But Hillary vowed she would help in any way she could: time, transportation, comfort, housing, money; whatever I can do, whatever this young woman will let me do for her, she had said.

From their conversation, Hillary also realized why a student, any student, every student, would confide in Cassie or seek her help. Now, she understood why Parker had called. Cassie was more than a classroom teacher; she was a teacher for life, and an example of compassion. She cared, she empathized, and she exuded love. A woman who had gone through the tragedy she had experienced could still love, while Hillary's own husband, her sister-in-law and brother-in-law, who had everything imaginable, and then some, were filled with egos and lust for more. What a difference. Where had she not seen the emptiness of their world?

When she was young, her life was one of expensive trinkets and baubles just like Brett's and the family she married into. Her tragedy changed all that, but she was never able to convince Brett that life meant something much deeper. After so many miscarriages and illnesses, she had retreated into her own universe, inside her own little bubble and watched the superficial life she had ascribed to whirl by. Life had lost meaning. She had known and accepted Brett's infidelity for decades, but she didn't care. For the family's sake, she maintained the semblance of propriety. Brett never suspected she was aware.

But when she saw Cassie's passionate concern over this young student who desperately needed help, even though Cassie had only skimmed the surface, what Cassie had told her was enough. A young Romeo and Juliet couple, from different ethnicities and religions, loved each other and were hated by one set of parents, being devoured and destroyed. What about the other set of parents? How did they fit in?

Hillary would wait for Cassie to explain. Patience was important. Don't inquire about this; don't ask Parker; don't ask at the Club; don't ask friends; don't ask anyone. Wait until Cassie is ready. Hillary would need this young lady's trust to replace the teacher she trusted completely. Hillary would never get it or keep it if Cassie or the student learned she had ferreted out information. It didn't matter who the couple was, what mattered was that the transition worked.

Hillary had cringed when Taylor attacked Cassie at the faculty Christmas party and had inwardly applauded when Cassie countered. Cassie had been more than justified; she had been noble. Hillary wished she could speak her thoughts as Cassie had. In the limo riding home, Vaughn had vowed he'd make Cassie suffer for her vicious response to Taylor, even though it was more than deserved. Most likely, this was what he was doing.

So, a young Romeo and Juliet couple from different ethnicities and religions loved each other and were hated by one set of parents. Hillary assumed the girl was Jewish; so the boy had to be Christian. That could fit into an explosive situation with some families, although interfaith dating and marriages were becoming much more common. That would qualify for different religions, but what would the different ethnicities be and why would ethnicity matter?

There was more to this. There had to be if it factored into Cassie's conflict with Vaughn. Obviously, Cassie was preparing for a quick departure. When this occurred, this young lady would need help, and Hillary would not hesitate to be the surrogate.

When Hillary left, Cassie felt the universe rise from her shoulders. She had made the right decision. Hillary would be her perfect replacement. What Cassie had to do now was present this scenario to Rachel and Samir and explain that when she was gone, and it would be soon, Rachel would need someone, an adult, to get through the rest of the school year, even through college.

Cassie had a gut feeling Vaughn was waiting for mid-March, right before the start of spring break, to fire her – leave, collect your things, go, don't come back. Rather than wait passively until he fired her, she was searching for a job and housing now. With luck, she'd find both and leave first. Without waiting for him to use his ace, she'd use hers. Either way, the situation would explode soon enough.

86

MORE TO TELL

"That was yesterday, Jeremy," Cassie took a sip of wine, a gulp of tea, downed a few more shrimp and chunks of beef stew. She had just talked, non-stop, over fifteen minutes. Her throat was dry and she was still hungry. "All of this happened yesterday. We talked from lunch time until late afternoon, and she gave me her word she'd help. I believe her Jeremy. I hope, for Rachel's sake, she's telling the truth. Do you think she is?"

Jeremy shrugged and nodded. "Yeah, why not? Hillary doesn't have to lie. You think she wants to get into your head so she can gossip at the Club?" He smiled.

"You're right, and I have no other option. I have to trust her for Rachel's sake and I have to get Rachel to trust her enough so she can take my place. But that's not all that's happened this weekend," she added happily, filling a small plate with veggies and hummus. She paused, smiling.

"So?" He questioned, implying, are you gonna tell me or keep me in suspense? "What else happened this weekend?"

"Listen to this." Another small sip of wine and a wedge of pita dipped in hummus. "Early this morning, Stevie and I drove to the shore, one town over from our Manasquan house on Meadow. That's our old address. I don't think I ever mentioned it, but that doesn't matter because why would it matter or why would you care where my old house is."

"Cassie! You're rambling, and if you're doing it to pique my interest, you're doing a good job!" He looks at her in frustration.

Cassie finds this amusing. Jeremy has put her in a light mood. "I went to Point Pleasant to look at a townhouse, and . . . I took it!" She slams her fist on the table jubilantly.

Jeremy leaned forward. "You took it; you rented it, without a job?"

Cassie nodded. "Uh-huh."

"You *are* a gutsy lady."

"Rent from my house is still coming in; the lease lasts through June. So that'll help. And, I have a job interview coming up, tomorrow in fact. If I get it, I'll fill you in, and I have applications for subbing in three contiguous towns. God willing, something will come up until I can find a permanent job.

"But I can't, I won't, stay here. He's making me sick and he knows it. I can hardly teach. He's in three of my classes harassing me every day and has been for the last three weeks, just glaring. Even after school. If Chelsea were a public school, he'd never get away with that, but Chelsea is not a public school."

"That would be harassment in a public school, harassment and intimidation. You're right; he'd never get away with that in a public school, but here he can do whatever he wants. I remember telling you to pick the big issues before you fight back, remember, at the cook-off, might makes right and that's the way the world works?" Cassie nodded. "Well, you've picked the big one, and you're fighting back. Give it all you've got. I'll help as much as I can, but eventually you will lose."

"I may need a shoulder to cry on every now and then. And you're leaving when?"

"Monday, March 7."

Have you told Vaughn?"

"No reason. I'll give him two-weeks notice, a lot more than he'd give you. But," he paused, "what did you mean when you said he harassed you after school?"

"I never told you he came to my apartment and pounded on my door the night before my meeting with Greer?" Jeremy's jaw drops.

Cassie nods. "When I wouldn't let him in, he threatened to break the lock and force his way in. He only backed off when I threatened to get a knife and defend myself and Stevie. But I was pretty scared. He's a big guy. One step over the edge and he would have broken in. Most likely, he'll never do that again, but I don't trust him."

"Cassie, that's assault. You should have called the police."

"And tell them what? There were no witnesses, only me and Stevie. He didn't break the chain; so there's no visible forced entry. So what do I charge the dean of Chelsea with in a town he owns? Remember, might makes right?"

Jeremy bowed his head. "He's losing it, Cassie. He's not the man I thought I knew. Something is eating him up inside that he can't control." He looked up, sighed and changed the subject and his tone. "So, how'd it feel going home?"

"You mean going back to Manasquan and the shore?" He nods. "Exactly that; I was going home. Stevie and I passed our house; then we walked on the beach until my fingers and feet ached, which wasn't long." She became melancholy. "It's peaceful there.

"Jeremy, I was so wrong. I never should have left. I thought the only way I could leave those horrific memories behind was to leave physically. I thought I had wrapped them all up with brown paper, tied them with string and put them way back on a closet shelf. She laughs. "I thought they'd be sealed away and I'd be safe. Leave, start a new life." She shook her head. "All I did was jump from one nightmare to another. Not as bad; losing Brian was the worst, but bad.

"Nobody can seal things away forever; you have to come to terms with tragedy, accept that it happened, tuck your tears somewhere inside one of your heart's tiny chambers, lock it up and come out into the real world. Epiphanies after cataclysmic events are not guaranteed simply by exchanging geographic locations. They have to occur from within." She stopped talking and sighed. "It just took me so long to realize it."

"You realized it in what, four years? Me? It's taken me twenty, so don't beat yourself up, Cassie, and I was only able to realize it because of you. For what it's worth, Cassie, I'm glad you came to Chelsea. You, my friend, have changed my world, and I will be forever grateful."

87

It had been a great weekend, depending on how you looked at it, and Cassie took the glass half-full approach. Not only had she met with Hillary with very positive results, not only had she secured an apartment for the remainder of the year, beginning March first, moving in as early as mid-February if she wished, not only had she enjoyed Super Bowl Sunday with Jeremy and was going to an interview this afternoon - keep your fingers crossed, girl - but the best part of the entire weekend, the best part, was watching the Redskins beat the Broncos in an upset, giving her bragging rights to hurl at Parker, someway, somehow, for teasing her for her pick.

No, wait, strike that. That wasn't the best part of the weekend. The absolute best part of the entire evening was the knock on Jeremy's door late in the evening, during the third quarter of the game, a knock that Cassie hardly heard after she had finished one glass of wine, something she hardly ever did, a knock which put her face to face with Walter.

She had been feeling a little like Cassio without his belligerence, but she sure knew the effects of wine on the biochemistry of her brain. One glass was absolutely her limit and she'd never make Cassio's mistake. Nevertheless, that one glass did make her uninhibited enough to go to the front hallway when she heard Jeremy talking to a male voice at the door.

"No, you can't. This is my home and you are no longer welcome here. Go back to your party and leave me to mine."

Cassie saw the pained expression on the visitor's face when she poked her head into the doorway. "Well, well, well, if it isn't the shrink of Chelsea Academy. What are you doing here, Dr. Goodman," emphasizing his professional appellation. "Don't you have a football crowd, Super Bowl party to attend? You know, that crowd with all those special people and special friends I got to meet a few months ago? I'm certain that party started at least two hours ago, as it did here. It's eastern standard time here as well as at Pete's Brill, as I've heard it's called."

Walter hung his head. "I'm sorry, Cassie. I didn't know you were here. If I had, I would never have intruded."

"So now that you do know I'm here, you no longer have to intrude. I can't tell you to leave; it's not my home," she glanced towards Jeremy, "but I certainly have nothing nice to say to you, nothing at all, that I would have gladly said to you four weeks ago when I called you five times, in tears, five calls you chose not to return."

Cassie," Walter blustered, "wait . . . I'm, I'm sorry. I've been thinking about what happened and what I should have done, and my behavior was inexcusable. I want to apologize; I need to apologize. Please, forgive me. I'm sorry."

"You want to apologize? You need to apologize, when you didn't know I was here? Isn't that somewhat illogical?" He looked down at his feet, unable to respond. "But since I am here without your knowing, and you *have* apologized, are you sorry for being a coward, or for abrogating your professional oath?"

He breathed heavily. His gray hair plopped on his forehead in a somewhat unkempt manner and his face seemed haggard with a few more lines than she had noticed when they were happy together. "Sorry for both, for not living up to my professional ethics and for behaving cowardly. I thought of my own comfort level instead of standing up for what was right."

"Yes, you did," she shot back, a touch of sadness tugging at her heart as she recalled promises about their future. "You reneged on both . . . and both hurt. If that was your goal, you achieved it. Nicely done, Dr. Goodman. Since that's over, your path is clear. You can go back to your own comfort level with my blessings.

"But now that you've admitted to abandoning your ethics, and having been a coward, go see Jan and apologize to her for having been a coward way back then, for having let her walk out decades ago when you were too cowardly to discuss your career change which you made without even mentioning it to her, your wife, mother of your two children, and for not having had the courage to go after her and apologize. And when she slams the door in your face, go back and apologize again, and again, until, hopefully, she may realize you care more about her believing you're really sorry than you do about your own bruised ego." She walked back into the family room to drink tea for the rest of the game.

Jeremy stood at the door, waiting for a chagrinned Walter to make the first move and leave. When he didn't, Jeremy politely but boldly bid him a good evening and closed the door. "You okay?" He asked Cassie, who had repositioned herself in the armchair, sitting up straight and pouring herself more tea.

"Very okay," she said, happily. "Thank you, Jeremy. Thank you for everything."

88

MONDAY AFTER THE SUPER BOWL

So that was the absolute best part of the evening, and she was almost on a high when she entered Rand Hall and saw the opened door to her classroom. What now, she thought.

It was like the Christmas decorating brigade that had come in early to decorate the room, but this was even better. Not better because posters were coming down, although that was a plus; not better because all the guys were helping to remove them; but better because the entire class had shown up to remove them, even the ladies. They were all meticulously peeling tape from the wall, and the young men were directing the ladies to pull carefully from one tiny edge or another, so they wouldn't tear the poster or its edge. Once down, each was carefully rolled into a long tube secured with a tiny piece of tape at its center.

"Don't want to ruin a precious piece of art work, fellas?" Cassie commented facetiously.

From Zach, she got, "These are important works of art, Mrs. Komsky. Would you want your posters to tear?" And from Mason, "What if we ripped Shakespeare or the queen in her famous gown, or any other poster on this wall? Bet you'd be pretty mad." The ladies hooted and called them whiners.

"Mason, you're correct. If you have the same reverence for these posters I have for my Shakespeare collection, then you should take as much care with your posters as I take with mine."

"You agree with them, Mrs. Komsky?" Gloria and Emelia replied somewhat stunned. "You actually think their posters are as valuable as yours?"

"To them they are. There's really no monetary value to any of them. What does each cost to replace, ten, maybe twenty dollars? Maybe mine cost a little more 'cause they'd be harder to get, but it's what they represent that makes the difference."

"That's right, Mrs. Komsky. It is. It's what they represent," Parker emphasized.

"So what do they represent to you, Mrs. Komsky," Elizabeth asked.

"Well, Elizabeth, I can't say they represent dirty jocks and cleats, something Gloria referenced way back in November," Cassie nodded to Gloria, who was smiling from ear to ear, "so to me, Elizabeth, I'd have to say," her impish smile peeked onto her face as she stated boldly, "these posters represent the undeniable fact, that if I had bet Mr. Parker Otis-Barrett money that the Redskins would win when he had ridiculed my choice, I would have had enough to keep my gas tank full for the rest of the year!"

Ouch! She got him good. Uproarious laughter as Cassie grabbed a piece of chalk and wrote 42-10 in large print. Parker smiled. She had bested him and he raised his hands in surrender. The last poster was rolled, taped closed, and placed in a vertical pile alongside the wall. They were ready for Shakespeare.

"Okay, on to more consequences of misplaced trust and getting drunk. Othello dismisses Cassio when he finds out he's gotten drunk and started a brawl, and Iago, the dear, sweet, loving friend," she says so sarcastically, "will now advise him how he can get back into Othello's good graces and reclaim his rank, by cozying up to Desdemona. Kind of him, isn't it? What a friend.

"Someone give us a quick plot summary that takes us to Iago planting the seeds of that green-eyed monster, jealousy, in Othello's mind, where it latches on and grows like a cancer."

"From the end of act 2," Jason began, "as briefly as possible, Iago tells Cassio the general's wife is now the general, which is a pretty good analysis of most marriages, don't you think?" He smiled; the guys smiled; the ladies did not. "Anyway, he tells Cassio to talk to Desdemona because she can help him get his position back. Cassio never realizes Iago's gonna convince Othello that his wife wants him to reinstate Cassio because she lusts after him, but that's what Iago does. Works like a charm."

"Ladies, what do you think?"

The ladies agree with Jason, and Elizabeth adds how Iago gets Othello away from Desdemona while she's talking to Cassio, so when Othello returns and sees them together, Iago can say, 'Ha, I like that not.' "It's hard to believe Othello falls for this so easily."

Matt agrees with her. He listens to her every word. If she were reading a grocery list, he'd hear music. Then he criticizes Desdemona's incessant pleas for Cassio's reinstatement. "Desdemona's innocence dooms her and makes it easy for Iago to convince Othello something's going on. "'Will it be shortly, will it be tonight at supper, tomorrow, dinner, will it be tomorrow night or Tuesday morning or Tuesday noon, or night or Wednesday morning.' Desdemona doesn't stop. If that were me, I might think the woman I loved were interested in this guy." Then he adds, "Not only that, but her incessant pleading would drive me crazy."

"Oh it would, would it?" Elizabeth gives him a look that makes Matt blush, and the guys tear into him.

"Okay, fellas, leave Matt alone. He has more than enough to handle without any assistance from you."

"Mrs. Komsky is on your side, Matt!" Zach shouts.

"Plot development, guys; back to plot development, before we get carried away."

"You're worse than we are, Mrs. Komsky," Elizabeth counters.

"I know," Cassie nods. "I have to admit I am guilty of that charge. Sometimes Stevie acts older than I do. But," she shakes off her playfulness, "back to the serious stuff, because this is where the intrigue really takes hold and you want to shake Othello and say, 'Wake up, you idiot.

You have a fantastic wife and you're listening to this piece of garbage?'" When they laugh at her word choice, she changes it to 'scoundrel.'

Connor attacks Othello for being so gullible, especially when Iago fills his head with the idea that Cassio and Desdemona had something going on before Othello married her.

"Hey, that's not so hard to believe, Connor," Zach says. "Cassio was the go-between when Othello was courting Desdemona. I've known a few situations where a guy has gone off somewhere for a while and he comes back to find the best friend is now the boyfriend. Am I the only one who's seen this happen?"

Zach's question sparks an energetic discussion. Matt's brother's friend; Parker's cousin on his aunt's side, Emelia's older brother, who experienced that when he enlisted in the army; Elizabeth's friend's brother when he went to the U.S. Military Prep School for a year before getting into West Point. One after the other, they knew someone; they had seen it first-hand, and their life-experiences let them understand how Iago's line of questioning could easily plant the seeds of jealousy in Othello. And because Cassio had been Othello's intermediary when Othello and Desdemona were courting, Iago's insinuation that maybe Cassio had been courting Desdemona for himself made complete sense.

"And Iago, master of hypocrisy, has the gall to say 'he that filches from me my good name robs me of that which . . . makes me poor indeed.'" Mason reads the lines. "He who robs his good name? Iago *has* no good name. The only good name for him is hypocrite, dissembler, or just plain liar. Now we're back to the same argument about who to trust. Like Rachel said, you can't know."

The pause was long; eleven students were pondering the same problem they had discussed previously. It seemed there would never be a concrete answer, only abstracts and opinions based on morals of the day, and the hope they would never be the victim of such deceit.

"But can we be anything other than ourselves?" Samir's voice broke the quiet. The class pauses, surprised by his contribution, and waits. "Can Othello be anything other than honest and trusting? Can we be or should we be, anything but ourselves, even if, by being ourselves, we get hurt?" Samir was so ingenuous, and his question made everyone focus on their inner selves.

"I get it, Samir," Matt responds to his roommate. "You're wondering if, once we recognize the goodness in ourselves that allows us to be hurt, we should stop being good to avoid being hurt. You think we should be ourselves anyway?"

Samir became pensive. When he spoke, his words reminded Cassie of Plato. "If we light a candle, should we hide it under a rock or use it to brighten a dark world?"

"Maybe we should never light it at all," Parker counters to offer a defense against a world of hurt.

"Then we would all live in perpetual darkness. My parents were killed when the American Embassy in Lebanon was bombed four years ago. I surrounded myself in a world of perpetual darkness, until now. For me, I know now I would not want to live in perpetual darkness if I could live in light, knowing I am vulnerable, knowing I could sometimes be ill-used. Is it not better to have one hour of sunshine in a dark day, than never to have any sunshine at all?"

This time, Rachel put her hand over Samir's, as the rest of the class swallowed the intensity of his words. He had alluded to his past once but in very general terms. This time it was in depth, the portrait of his family tragedy. It was beautiful to see him now open up in class and confide his life's worst hurt with his classmates. And it made the analogy to Othello much more powerful because Samir had lived it.

The class was silent, absorbing the intensity of his statement; Samir, who had suffered so much and who now had the courage to come into the light. Finally, Matt whispered, "That's profound, Samir. You've been through hell. I hope I could be as good a person as you if what had happened to you had happened to me. I'm honored to know you."

Without speaking, the rest of the class agreed.

89

C assie turned onto Chelsea's campus at 6:34 exactly, singing along to "Hey Now." Not bad, she thought; she had made very good time, driving to the other side of the state, having her interview, which she felt had been very positive, then driving back to Chelsea. For all the negativity she had experienced these past four weeks, she was happy, singing along to words that spoke of holding on to dreams and love.

Stevie had been with Rebecca and Stacy since the bus had dropped her off after school. She always enjoyed being with them and felt as comfortable in Sanders House now as she had with her friends in Manasquan. Even though the girls were almost four years older, which concerned Cassie at times, Stevie balanced their friendships with several girls from public school. It also helped that Rebecca and Stacy viewed being with Stevie as part friendship and part sitter, although every time Cassie had offered them money or given it to Stevie to leave on their desks, they'd run downstairs and return it. At first, they would knock, but when Cassie refused to let them in, they'd either slide it under her door or leave it on the office desk when they signed in the next evening.

What they did accept, thankfully, were the Christmas gifts Cassie bought each of them. She had given Stevie the task of finding out what they would want, and both had inadvertently said they would love to get their hair done at Tres Chique, the state-of-the-art beauty parlor at the mall. That was it, a gift certificate to Tres Chique.

Cassie's total trip had taken about four hours and it had been well worth it. Mr. Hastings, principal of the middle school, was very impressed with her resume, her total teaching experience, and most of all, with her math certification and almost five years teaching middle school math. Even better, the texts they were using were recent editions of the same math books Cassie had used years ago. The interview had gone very well. Mr. Hastings had a final interview tomorrow; he'd make his decision then; nothing 100%, but very promising. So, it was good news all the way. Cassie was coming back to life while she drove home.

When she started back after the interview, dusk was painting pink streaks over puffy clouds that morphed from one monster face to another. Dragons, gargoyles, lions, a snarling raccoon, were all rising before her as she drove, decorating the dark blue sky. Halfway home, wisps of orange and violet airbrushed this pink, night-time spectrum. She gazed up romantically, captivated by the muted stars and the moon's brilliance as clouds over-lapped and drifted by. It had been too long since she had looked up at the stars and the sky. She was happy she had caught herself doing it now.

Cassie was anxious to get back to nature; it was the one thing she sorely missed since leaving Manasquan - the sky, the salty air, the harsh breezes and the walks on the beach, even in winter when layers of thermals and her windbreaker coat and pants were vital for protection. She was looking forward to that again, staring out over the Point Pleasant breakers as night fell and the surf assaulted tremulous beaches.

She turned onto Chelsea's campus with a smile, music and her voice infusing the car. Happy thoughts played in her head. Tomorrow she'd meet Samir and Rachel. She had much to say. She navigated the car around the circle, made one right and a final left, slipping her car into her parking space. She braked, put the car in park and exhaled.

A very good trip, except she wondered, why was a car parked one space from hers? Each house had ample room for the housemaster or mistress and three or four additional spaces for visitors, family or company. But no one was visiting her. Could this car have been Samir's? Jeremy had mentioned a while back Samir had requested a permit for a car, but even if his permit had been granted, his car would be parked at Damon House in the student lot, not here, at Sanders.

Look carefully before you unlock the doors. Brian's advice was kicking in. It always did now that it was Cassie alone, Cassie and Stevie. Give strange situations close scrutiny; look before you leap. Nothing. No one in the car; no one in sight. She grabbed her attaché, got out and walked briskly to her door, key in hand, ready for the lock. Whew. Safe. I'm here.

Suddenly strong hands grab her, like a vice, knocking the breath out of her; her attaché dropping to the ground. Her assailant spins her around and slams her against the door; his face so close she can smell the liquor, inhale its residual fumes. His fire eyes bore into hers, his hideous contorted face, demonic, the charming smile that had once decorated it now distorted, twisted into a maniacal snarl. His hands pin her arms against the door, his body slams against hers and his forehead pushes her head back.

She is trapped, imprisoned, with every effort she makes to extricate herself, he forces his body harder against hers. He is strong, stronger than she had imagined.

"You little bitch," he spews, his face so close his mouth spits into hers, "you dare miss a faculty meeting without my permission. You dare defy me; you defy everything about this institution and you mock its rules." He hissed. His saliva splattered her face, his mouth wet her hair. This savagery for a faculty meeting? He was crazy; he had reached a point of insanity.

She twisted; she writhed, turned her head side to side, away from his face. Whichever way he faced her, she moved opposite, but she was powerless. Her heart pounded; she was being assaulted. This man who was destroying her career, destroying her emotionally, was now destroying her physically. Might made right, emotionally, mentally or physically, and he was stronger than her in every way. Might made right in a savage world and in Vaughn's present world, he had reduced himself to a savage. Fear shot through her; she was no match for him. She had defied him and she was suffering the consequences. His face was viciously suffocating hers; she couldn't even scream. She thought of Stevie; she thought of Brian, her life flashed before her. In abject fear, she wondered, how would this end?

Finally, she twisted her head so she could open her mouth enough to scream, not a muted scream or bursts of forced breaths or powerful grunts, part of her physical battle to pull away. Not those, but enough of an opening for a full open-mouthed scream. His senses on adrenaline, Vaughn saw it and preempted her. As her mouth opened, he forced his mouth onto hers, covering hers completely. She forced her head to the side, anything to separate her mouth from his. She moved her head side to side, but his mouth, his face, cemented to hers, followed with such force and slammed her head into the door, cutting into her scalp. She could not move; she could not escape; she could not come up for air. She was drowning; she was slipping away, and still he forced himself onto her, this vicious, demented man.

Suddenly, his tongue pushed into her mouth. Her mind whirled. He was choking her, cutting off her oral and nasal air supply, but, but this could be her salvation. With her last gasp for self-preservation, with the one weapon that remained, she bit down hard, so hard she felt his warm blood in her mouth. Her teeth had opened a wound. She bit, and kept biting, biting harder, harder, until blood filled her mouth and drooled from its sides. She had become the vicious incarnation of the savagery he had begun.

In agony, he began pulling away. She held. He fought for release but she held on. His vicious grunts that had been filled with anger and hatred now became panicked squeals of fear; he was squealing for mercy, for life. Still, she continued to rip him apart. He tried lunging away, but her grip was so fierce, she was tearing into his tongue with every outward thrust.

She hated him. At that moment she hated him and wanted to destroy him as he had been destroying her. She wanted to destroy him for the hypocrisy and the lies, for the hurt, the emotional destruction he had willingly and intentionally caused her, for the trust he had nurtured then betrayed, destroy him for the destruction he was hurling upon her, her and Stevie, this man she had once trusted, once welcomed into her life. Now she wanted to devour and destroy, just as he had been destroying her. She wanted him out of her life forever, even if he had to die for it. In this very moment, when her compassion for humanity left her body, she had become the same savage, primordial beast he had become. She had taken a page from *Heart of Darkness*. "Oh the horror! The horror!"

In that instant, he had transformed her into someone as evil as himself, and in that one instant of recognition, she loosened her bite. One instant; that was all he needed. He wrenched away, she wrenched backwards, blood splattering from their mouths, spraying the night air, their mouths running with blood, the savagery of it all dripping from their mouths as though they had hunted their prey, made their kill and were feasting on raw flesh.

Their faces were covered with blood dripping from their mouths, their clothing bloodied and stained. Vaughn stumbled back, his hands covered his face, drenched in his own blood; his throat gurgled with it. Howling in pain and fear, he stumbled and fell. Cassie, awash in this phantasmagoric scene, looked on as an observer locked behind a glass shield. She watched, but it wasn't her; in all her years of torment, all the horror she had experienced, she had never witnessed anything as primordial ands as barbaric as this.

Was this what Brian had seen, this primordial battle for survival? Was this the specter that had been thrust upon him, upon all the young men our nation sent off to fight for some idealistic figment a brainwashed public had believed was righteous? Was this hideous scene before her a splinter, a sliver, of the devastation at the Marine Barracks where Brian had been killed, or at the American Embassy where Samir's parents had been blown apart? Easy to read words in a newspaper, not easy to live them, while military brass and elected officials sat snugly on their safe seats of power, issuing ultimatums of war.

In this moment of horror awash with blood, and intense panic sucking her down, with echoes of Vaughn's footsteps running for his sanity, Cassie's trembling hands found the keyhole and she escaped to safety.

90

VAUGHN AFTER HIS ATTACK

Blood. Blood on his shirt, cuffs, suit jacket, tie; his overcoat. Blood covered his face, hers too, a testament to the horror of what had actually happened. It was no nightmare, no bad dream, no horror film; it was real. He had actually done what he had just done, he, Vaughn Otis-Barrett, the epitome of propriety. Yes he had.

Would she press charges? Would there be enough evidence to have him arrested and have the charges stick? Most likely there was; forensics could easily match the blood on her clothing and hair to his. But would she? I've got friends, powerful friends and judges who would dismiss any charges at the snap of my fingers. She knows this, so would she chance it, or would she go public and let the community know what he had done anyway? Who would it hurt, her, me . . . both of us? She might; she hates me. He hung his head. I don't blame her.

For the first time since he began his personal assault against Cassie, he actually thought of her feelings and the pain he had been causing her, and he wondered who he was, this insane man, this forty-three-year-old man driving this Porsche in the late evening of a school day, having just accosted a member of his faculty for what, for missing a faculty meeting. He had kidded himself long enough; he had lost it for a reason he could no longer ignore. For the first time in his life, he had fallen in love. Vaughn Otis-Barrett had fallen in love with a woman he could never have. Forget being married. If he were not married, he still couldn't have her because, despite his billions, she wanted nothing to do with him. Maybe she would have if his vicious side had not surfaced, maybe not even then.

From the time he could reason and be an independent thinker, he had let life take him where it was easiest to go, like a stream that follows its path. Boarding school, college, multiple degrees, marriage, he rolled with whatever fell into place; yes, even marriage, when the situation had presented itself. Taylor had simply been there, stunning, fawning over him, impressed with his every word, every deed. Had she really married him for his title, his money and his prestige? He had never allowed himself to believe that, yet, despite an iron-clad pre-nuptial agreement, she'd still get a fortune. Was it all for that?

Even if it were, he believed he had made a good bargain. She looked good on his arm, a trophy to show off to other men, and they did look. Taylor was beautiful, intelligent, a good conversationalist, a good wife and mother to their son. But did Vaughn love her? No. Did he ever love her? No. Did he ever love anyone? No, not until now, and love had been so new to him, such an anomaly, that he never even recognized it.

Cassie was vivacious; brilliant, well-read, beautiful, sensual and challenging. She was a spitfire and courageous under attack, but most of all, she was passionate, passionate about life, passionate about humanity, and it showed. Because of her passion, people loved her in return. You couldn't help but fall in love with her, unless you were jealous.

Like Taylor? Could jealously have motivated Taylor to have contrived this entire scenario? Perhaps Taylor saw what I refused to see. Perhaps she noticed all the books about the Middle East Cassie had suggested. Did she see the books about Arab culture and history on my desk?

Vaughn had read everything Cassie had recommended – King-Crane, Peel Commission, Partition Plan, the McMahon-Hussein letters. He had read books about Israel's origins, its land grab and acts of inhumanity, things that never appeared in our press. The assault upon the USS Liberty was next on his list, the top book on the pile in the bedroom. But he had read these books for her, to talk to her, to see her. It was a reason he had never allowed to surface before, but he let it surface now.

He'd let it surface now because it no longer mattered, because he had destroyed his relationship with the person who had motivated him to pursue the topic. She was the person, the only person with whom he ever discussed this topic. Now that any interaction with her was over, most likely he would never read the book. It remained unopened on his desk.

Cassie stood apart from any other person, any other woman he had ever known. She cared nothing about advancing her social status; she cared about ethics and morality, doing the right thing and helping people, she of all people, who had suffered an indescribable tragedy, an almost insurmountable one. Maybe that's what came through, her tenacity, her empathy, her endurance. Having gone through the hell she had experienced, how could she not empathize with people who hurt? How could she not have empathized with Samir and the tragedy he had suffered? She touched people because she touched life, while all he tried to do was destroy her.

He glanced in his rear-view mirror. His mouth oozed blood. The wad of tissues he had stuffed into his mouth when he had gotten into his car was soaked with blood, despite swallowing gulp after gulp. He was frightened. Would he need stitches? Did doctors stitch tongues? How bad were these lacerations? He couldn't open his mouth to look, but he had to do something, and fast, before the pain became overbearing and his tongue swelled so much he couldn't talk. Will I be able to talk at all, he wondered. He grabbed his mobile phone and dialed, his heart racing, his speed well over the limit.

His head had cleared a bit and his adrenaline was receding. Funny thing, he thought as he dialed, with all the consequences running through his head, he never thought of Taylor or how she would react.

"Sarah? Sarah?" He tried to shout to his cook to no avail. His voice seemed weird; his words seemed garbled. Sarah was confused. In desperation, he wrenched the bloodied tissues from his mouth and blood gushed out.

"Sarah," he shouted quickly, knowing he had little control over the way the twisted words sounded, "it's me, Mister Vaughn. I bit my tongue badly and I'm having trouble talking. Sarah, is Miss Taylor home?"

No, Taylor had gone out for the evening and had told Sarah to take the evening off after she had fixed his dinner. "Good, you and the staff are dismissed for the evening. Everyone. Evening off. I need absolute quiet."

First phone call done. Tongue really hard to control. Wobbly, uncontrollable; just how bad were these bites? Had Cassie almost bitten his tongue off? He shook off the thought. Taylor's not home. Staff's dismissed. That part is good. I can go home, change, shower and think. Second call was to Mike, his golf buddy, an orthopedic surgeon. He'd help. Mike picked up on the third ring. "Mike, I need your help. Can you come to the house?"

Not if stitches were required. Mike had never stitched a tongue before. Cuts that deep were extremely rare, but if Vaughn believed they were that severe, he'd have to come to the office. Vaughn changed direction. He'd be at Mike's office in fifteen minutes; no other patients, no staff, hopefully, not too many questions. Good.

Another problem almost solved. He doubted he'd be able to side-step all Mike's questions, lacerations don't lie, but he could whittle the story down to bare minimum and Mike wouldn't press it. They'd been buddies too long.

Vaughn's third problem: If Cassie pressed charges, everyone would know what had happened. But he could discredit her; have everyone laugh at an insignificant teacher who he'd claim was infatuated with him. She could have induced him to go to her home and then seduced him.

But why would he be at her home at night? Come on; come on, Vaughn, think . . . to do her a favor. Would that work? He'd come up with something, and to cover all bases, he'd get legal counsel. No reason to have loose ends, not when you've got so many resources on your side.

Last call to Wayne, another friend since childhood. Whenever one of them had wanted a special favor they'd want kept secret, each would confide in the other. And into adulthood, they still sought each other out for their individual expertise, Vaughn with real estate or finance, using Brett as backup, while Wayne reciprocated with legal.

Vaughn's call went through quickly, second ring. Wayne was having dinner with a friend, but he'd get free. Medical and legal, Vaughn would have both bases covered. He felt relieved. His tongue had become more uncontrollable as he had made that last call; his speech garbled badly. How long would it take for swelling to come down? Could you ice a tongue? What if he couldn't swallow or eat? Hillary's anniversary gala was less than two weeks away. His final fear was how this would affect his performance in bed? Taylor would know something was wrong if it affected him that way.

Too much to think about now. He'd wait until the doctor and the lawyer advised him.

91

CASSIE TO JEREMY'S AFTER VAUGHN'S ATTACK,

"Charge him with what, Jeremy?" Two paper towels, folded in fours, pressed against the cuts on her lip with the back of her hand. Her fingers trembled in fugues of hysteria. Cassie was sitting in Jeremy's kitchen trying to regain some composure as the nightmare that had played out a few minutes ago swirled in her head and the scent of Vaughn's aftershave lingered on her face and hair. Was this real? Had this happened to her? She shivered and wiped her tongue on her sleeve to remove the last remnants of his scent.

As soon as she was positive Vaughn had gone, she had run to Jeremy's. When she saw the expression on his face as he opened the door, she shrieked. If what Jeremy had seen had caused such a horrific reaction, what did she really look like? His expression would remain with her a long time.

He had run for paper towels, covered the blood oozing from her mouth and wiped off her face as much as
he could. Then he had sat her down, gotten his camera
and made her remove the dressing so he could take pictures. Just in case, he had said. "And charge him with
what?" She importuned, still crying. "I'm not a lawyer
and I don't know any lawyers. My father never finished
third grade; we're nobodies, Jeremy. Do I call the police
and have forensics take swabs of his tongue? See if his lacerations match my teeth marks? Guaranteed, the blood
on my clothes and my face will match his blood. Then
what? He'd make a call to someone at the Club, and my
charges would be dismissed, or I'd be discredited in some
way. Then off to a round of golf and a good laugh.

"A little golf, a few cocktails, some laughs. That's the
way the game is played. You said that yourself. That's the
way it's always been played and always will be. Taylor was
smart to marry into it; once you're in it, you never lose.
Me? I'm not in it. I'm not even close to the periphery.

"The only chance I'd have against someone like him is
his conscience, and Vaughn doesn't have one; none of his
kind do." She shook her head. "I have to leave Chelsea as
quickly as possible. That's my only choice. Maybe teaching math will be the best thing. Shakespeare is becoming
much too real. I've got to get away from Hamlet, Othello,
Iago . . . Ophelia and Desdemona, and that entire cast of
characters Shakespeare created, because I'm living them."
She rotated her hand in a circular motion. "I'm living
all their tragedies. Maybe he lived them too. Maybe he
wrote about them from experience. All I know is *I'm* living

them, and they're killing me. This, this place, this academy, this has become a nightmare." She let the paper towel fall from her mouth and clasped her hands to her face, trying to shake the demons from her thoughts. "Jeremy, I can't even imagine what he would have done, could have done to me, if I hadn't gotten that one-second opening to retaliate."

She shuddered involuntarily. Her eyes spoke the hurt, the anguish and fear that still coursed through her veins. Jeremy held out his arms and she cried against his shoulder. He said nothing because there was nothing to say. She was right.

Cassie longed for Brian, for his comfort, his advice and protection. If he were here, this never would have happened. None of it would have happened. If anyone had even come close to hurting her, Brian would have pounded the life out of them. He wasn't upper class like Vaughn; he was Jersey City and he played the game of life the way Jersey City guys played the game. Somebody hurts you or someone you love, you beat the crap out of them, and they think twice about going after you again.

But no matter how much she wished for Brian, he was not here to protect her. He had been lost to her in the service of protecting someone else. In her life now, for as long as she lived, she was her own last line of protection, for herself and for Stevie. How would she ever get through this? Her final thought - thank God Stevie hadn't been home.

92

Next morning, she awoke disoriented. Where was she, what had happened the night before? Had it been real? Yes, it had been. She walked stiffly to the bathroom and hesitated before looking in the mirror. She was afraid of what she'd see.

When she looked, she was somewhat relieved. Not as bad as she had thought. Two cuts marred the right side of her mouth. One measured about a quarter inch in length. It was thin and had almost scarred over; the other was a good half inch long and still red, not just red, but ragged at the end, close to her mouth. Hmmm, she thought; this one's worse than I thought. This must have been where Vaughn's teeth cut into my mouth when he forced his mouth against mine. She spit into the sink in disgust. She could almost vomit. The only positive was that there was no swelling; ice had taken that down. Hopefully, a little extra foundation should hide whatever remained.

When she passed her hairbrush through her hair she squealed in pain. Her scalp had been badly bruised where Vaughn had crushed her head against the door; gashes must have continued to bleed after she had showered. During the night, they had caked, leaving her with scabs. She'd have to by-pass that part of her scalp, leave the knots, and brush around that area. She could do that. Her major concern at this point was what Stevie would notice now that it was morning.

After Cassie had gotten back from Jeremy's she had showered, gotten into pajamas and held a bag of frozen peas to her bruised mouth. Only then had she called Rebecca's room for Stevie. Stevie enjoyed being there, and Cassie was so glad she was with them now. It had given her time to recover. Her hope was that, by the time Stevie came down, Mom would appear normal.

It had worked. Cassie had kept the lighting dim, made herself tea, sat on the sofa, and hugged a pillow. Stevie ran in as usual, kissed her mother quickly on her cheek as usual, ran upstairs to shower and never took a close look at her mother's still-swollen eyes, the puffiness around her mouth and the quiver in her hands. Luck had definitely been on Cassie's side; Stevie had noticed nothing. In fact, as she had run upstairs, she shouted down that Rebecca's birthday was less than two weeks away and could we buy · her a gift. Wonderful!

But that was yesterday evening; this was morning; this was daylight and Stevie would surely notice the cuts now, especially the jagged one, unless Cassie got ready for school super fast from dressing to makeup and really caked that on. Cassie stared in the mirror evaluating her predicament. Forty-two. Damn, she sure felt old, old and scared. As frightened as she had been after Brian's death, knowing she'd be on her own for the rest of her life and that she'd be the sole provider and protector for herself and their daughter, this fear was completely different.

Brian's death had taken him from her world, but it had been a pretty safe world, a traditional world, with a routine: get up, get dressed, go to work, food shop, do laundry, cook, hold hands, be playful, and love. A safe world, with Brian so entrenched and ingrained as her last line of defense that she never gave external danger any thought.

Now, for the first time ever in her life, she had been the victim of a real assault, a real physical assault, with her assailant, someone she had trusted completely, now intent on doing her bodily harm. How could she have foreseen this? What was wrong with her that she couldn't? Well, what was wrong with Othello that he couldn't? Was she any different from him? He never saw his antagonist coming; neither had she.

Vaughn showed her what it was like to be completely powerless in every way, emotionally, mentally, and physically. And, also for the first time, she had experienced something else - primordial instincts; raw, primitive; primordial instincts that had instinctively allowed her to counter-attack and save herself from serious injuries, or worse.

Vaughn had devolved from civilized behavior to a wild savage who had ceased his attack only because she devolved into a wild savage too. He was the theme from *Lord of the Flies,* proper British kids who devolved from the apex of civility and propriety to wild savages, hunting human prey with spears. That is what Vaughn had become, and that's what she had become in self-defense to survive. If she hadn't fallen to that same level of savagery, she would not have been able to inflict such savage and tortuous pain. She shuddered at what they had both become, and the thought of facing him another day sent a chill through her.

And here it was, another day. She would have to face him again, this savage monster who was still sitting in three of her classes day after day under the pretense of observation for academic integrity. Academic integrity? Ha! She'd face him as courageously as she could, she with her bruised mouth, him with his lacerated tongue.

She'd fight through each period and each day until she could leave. Things were falling into place. She already had a new address. She'd change it officially at the post office next week and have her mail delivered to her new address in Point Pleasant instead of her mailbox here. And she was one day away from knowing if she'd have a new job. She prayed everything would come together quickly enough so Vaughn would not have another opportunity to hurt her again. She'd have her guard up, no matter where she was.

Quickly, she applied a thicker than usual layer of makeup, then made it even thicker. Stevie might think the look was overdone. Cassie was okay with that, as long as she didn't notice what was beneath it. She'd face her with her good side as often as she could. As she brushed her blondish hair away from her face, she pulled down bangs for camouflage. That would help. It was early and Stevie did not like early. Maybe she wouldn't notice; hopefully her classes wouldn't either. If they asked? She'd make up something - a zipper had scraped her mouth as she pulled off her parka. Plausible, and better than telling the class the dean of Chelsea Academy had assaulted her outside her home, especially if it were the class where she was teaching the dean's son.

93

TUESDAY'S CLASS AND THE HANDKERCHIEF

Yesterday's discussion had ended with Samir saying if you have to become someone else, someone who lives in the dark in order not to get hurt, are you really living at all?

This thought had consumed Cassie after last night's attack. She had become someone she didn't recognize after Brian had been killed and had just begun to feel sunny days inside her heart. Now, she wondered if she ever should have come out of her cave. She should have stayed there, grown as old as she was meant to get, and died. She shook off the thought. No, that would have set a horrible example for Stevie. She had to be herself, even if it was getting harder and harder to know who that was.

Obviously, though, the class had thought of these lines and Samir's statement too, because Gloria's comments began before 8:00. First, she let loose a diatribe against Othello for telling Iago to have his wife watch Desdemona, which she said was disgraceful; it was like a husband hiring a private investigator to tail his wife. But she followed with an apology, because she realized Othello could not have been anything other than what he was, the Moor, great in battle, but lacking in social graces and confidence towards his beautiful wife, which made him susceptible to Iago's scheme.

Emelia sat up straight in her chair. She agreed with Gloria, but saw Othello's downfall turn on Iago's wife, Emelia, stealing Desdemona's handkerchief. "It's not hers; she knows it's not hers, but she picks it up when Desdemona drops it and keeps it because her husband, *honest* Iago, has asked her to steal it over a hundred times. And she only asks him why he wanted it so badly after she gives it to him and he treats her like garbage."

"Emelia is despicable." Rachel was always pale now, but her tenacity still compeled her to participate. Good, it kept her focusing on something other than her father. "If Emelia hadn't kept Desdemona's handkerchief, Iago would never have been able to plant it in Cassio's room, which gave Othello tangible proof Desdemona had cheated on him. Worse, Othello never gives Desdemona a chance to explain. He asks her for the handkerchief *after* he decides she's guilty and sentences her to death."

Parker agrees, then he looks around, "Is it me or does anyone else think it's coincidental that Iago's Emelia and our Emelia have the same name?" Everyone pauses. Maybe. Maybe they had without mentioning it. But Parker was correct: Iago's wife and Emelia Bronston did have the same name.

"But I like our Emelia a lot better than Iago's," Zach shouts out.

"Yeah, me too," Connor adds. The others smile and nod; so does *their* Emilia.

"Anyway, not to digress, Mrs Komsky," Parker offers a slight nod of apology, "Iago's Emelia gives her husband the handkerchief to please him without knowing why he wants it. That was wrong, but maybe, just maybe, her one saving grace is she tells Iago she'll give the handkerchief back to Desdemona if he didn't have a good purpose for wanting it."

"No way, Parker," Matt counters. "So if you don't have a good reason for keeping this diamond pendant my friend dropped and I kept because you had said you wanted it, then give it back to me and I'll give it back to her? That doesn't justify what Emelia did. She even says Desdemona will go mad when she can't find the handkerchief, but keeps it anyway and gives it to Iago. That's more than unethical; that's theft. She doesn't redeem herself with that one, Parker. Not to me anyway. What do you think, Mrs. Komsky?"

"Think about the next few lines. Does Desdemona mention her handkerchief to Emelia and where she could have lost it?"

Connor finds the answer in act 3, scene 4. "Desdemona asks Emelia where she could have lost her handkerchief and Emelia says, 'I know not, madam.' It's a deliberate lie. I can't excuse her either; not in any way."

Heads nod; no one can excuse Iago's Emelia, not even Parker who had tried to find some extenuating circumstance for her actions.

"The damning point is that right before this, Othello and Iago swear both Cassio and Desdemona will die, and right after this, Othello asks Desdemona for the handkerchief and she doesn't have it. If Emelia had had the courage to tell Desdemona she had taken it and given it to Iago, his plot would have been exposed and Desdemona would have lived."

"You're right, Jason, but," Mason contradicts, "Shakespeare didn't want her to live. That's the point. She had to die, just like Ophelia had to die. Shakespeare wanted to show how jealousy, lies and deceit could destroy people."

"Just another innocent life lost to jealousy and hatred." Rachel interjects sadly, her words coming from her heart."

Nothing about Rachel's situation had improved; that was obvious. Cassie had to talk to her and Samir about Hillary today; it couldn't wait. She had to ask Rachel to let Hillary step in for her, try to persuade her it was vital. Vaughn's relentless observations had been bad enough; after his attack, she had to get out as soon as possible. This would leave Rachel with no one. Cassie had to convince her that she needed someone and that Hillary would be the perfect replacement.

94

CASSIE'S PLEA TO RACHEL AND SAMIR

Period two, Cassie awaited a man who had become a monster, a Mr. Hyde to his once Dr. Jekyll, but as the clock ate minutes away from period two and Vaughn didn't appear, she began to relax, as did the class. The last twenty-five minutes had actually been refreshing, and stimulating, without the dean for the first time in almost four weeks. Wonderful!

Period three, no dean either, nor in period six. Was this an anomaly? Would he appear tomorrow to intimidate her again, or had yesterday evening been as devastating for him as it had been for her? Perhaps this paragon of propriety had given his conduct a second thought and realized he had committed assault and battery. Maybe his lacerations had set him back a bit. If she were lucky, he'd stay away long enough for her to be gone.

She tried to relax and enjoy the free-flowing discussions about Othello and Iago, Desdemona and Emelia, the handkerchief and life - her life, Rachel's life, everyone's life. Every class talked freely about their own experiences with jealousy and how Othello's gift fueled the plot.

The day passed with lively discussion. After weeks of Dr. O/B watching and glaring at their teacher, spontaneity and freedom filled the classroom. At the end of the day, Cassie breathed a sigh of relief, not only great discussion, but not one student had noticed the gash on her mouth; at least no one commented. Good. She had gotten through the day 'normally.' Now she set to work clearing the table and her desk. Rachel and Samir were due any minute. She had told them she needed to talk; they would meet her here. Cassie needed to explain the situation as candidly as possible and stress how important a replacement for her would be.

At 3:15, this beautiful couple walked in, hand in hand. Even though they knew Cassie was about to tell them something upsetting, they smiled bravely.

"You wish to explain something to us we will not like." Samir stated.

Cassie nodded. "Unfortunately, yes. And she began. She presented the situation delicately but realistically. "Do you remember a while back you said you had heard I would be losing my job?" It was their turn to nod. "It has come to that."

She referred to the number of observations Vaughn had done, rumors they had heard that were materializing and that other circumstances had occurred she couldn't reveal. The conclusion was that she had to leave, and it would be very soon. "Rachel, you need someone to replace me, and I believe I've found someone who can take my place. I've met with her, given her generalities, nothing specific, and she is willing to help you in any way she can. She's kind and trustworthy. I think, I hope, you will like her. Please, I'd like you to meet with her."

Rachel was reluctant. How could she trust another woman, a complete stranger, to take Cassie's place? Cassie embodied warmth and trust from experience. Who was this person Mrs. Komsky wanted her to meet? "Who is she, Mrs. Komsky?" Rachel asked apprehensively.

"Hillary Otis-Barrett, Parker's aunt, Dr. O/B's sister-in-law."

Shock. Beyond belief, Rachel was shocked. "Hillary Otis-Barrett?" She uttered and sat straight up in her chair. "Parker's aunt? Dr. O/B's sister-in-law? How can I trust *her*, Mrs. Komsky? If it weren't for you, Dr. O/B would have expelled Samir even though my father attacked *him* with a poker iron and then went after me. And if it weren't for you, he would have let Parker and Mason beat Samir at Homecoming. Now he's making you miserable, and you still want me to trust his sister-in-law?"

Cassie nodded emphatically. "Yes, Rachel, I do. After you've met her, I believe you will feel the same way towards her I do. She's not like Dr. O/B at all; she's kind, very kind, understanding and compassionate. She's gone through her own personal hardship in her life and I think that's why she'll be able to help."

"An ultra wealthy person from that family has gone through hardship?" She shook her head, "That's impossible."

Cassie's turn to shake her head. "Rachel, would you say you come from a pretty wealthy family?" Rachel took a few seconds then nodded. "And wouldn't you say you're going through hardship?" Another pause, and Rachel nodded again.

"I have to leave, Rachel," Cassie implored. "I don't want to; I *have* to, and I don't want to leave without knowing there's someone here for you, someone you can go to when you need an adult to help in whatever way you may need help. She's kind, not pushy; she won't force herself into your life, and she won't pry. You can tell her as much or as little as you want. At this point, she doesn't know your name or who you are. She may surmise, but until you agreed to meet her, I wouldn't reveal your name. Despite this, she'll help." Rachel was still apprehensive, but Cassie's words were making her reconsider.

"I've met with her, Rachel. We talked for a long time, and I honestly believe you can trust her. I wouldn't recommend her if I didn't, and I would never leave you if I didn't have to. I wouldn't leave any of you, not Samir, not my classes; but I can't stay, I can't." Cassie almost burst into tears when she said this. She gulped hard.

The room was quiet, quiet and still. They looked at her forlornly; this time it was their turn to be understanding. They knew something was tearing her apart and they knew it had to do with the dean, somehow, some way; it had to do with him. Cassie had defended Samir when Vaughn had wanted to expel him and when Vaughn and Walter had held him down at Homecoming so Parker and Mason could go after him. It was a vivid image that would always haunt them. Cassie had risked her job to help them and to stand up for what was right. It had taken its toll. They knew her well enough to know she would never leave unless she had no alternative.

And she had no alternative. While Parker had become an understanding and honorable person; his father had changed for the worse. Hate exuded from his pores. Every student who sat in Cassie's classes and watched him glare at her saw this. Dr. O/B was hateful; Rachel's father was hateful, and it would never end. Cassie admitted that now; so did Samir and Rachel. Fortunately, they would be leaving their albatross behind when they started Princeton; Cassie had to leave hers behind in her own way.

Samir gazed at her with penetrating eyes; then motioned to her face. "*Man?* (Who?)" He asked. Cassie was startled. What was he saying; what was he referring to? "*Man fa'l hatha bikee?* (Who did this to you?)" He repeated, and motioned again.

She never expected the question. She thought she had avoided it. The entire day had gone by and no one had asked her about scars she had covered up so well in the morning. Maybe her makeup had worn off. Her face flushed. She turned, avoiding his gaze. Rachel was glancing from Cassie to Samir, wondering what her husband had said and what Mrs. Komsky was avoiding.

Cassie was beaten; too tired to conjure an excuse or to deny, but too stoic and professional to admit what had really happened. Tears came to her eyes and she covered her face with her hands. Almost in a whisper, she uttered, "I have to leave Samir; I just have to."

Samir's hand balled into a fist. His assumption was correct even though Cassie wouldn't provide verbal confirmation. He turned to Rachel and nodded. "We must meet Miss Hillary soon, together, or you alone."

It was done. Cassie would make the call and establish a mutual meeting time. If it had to be at Rachel's dorm, where Samir was not allowed, then it would be Rachel alone. But it would be soon, as soon as possible.

95

FRIDAY, OTHELLO STRIKES DESDEMONA

Friday. Waiting for Saturday's meeting between Hillary and Rachel had made the week drag, but that was the earliest they could manage. A school night wouldn't work, and Hillary's Friday schedule was filled with appointments she could not postpone.

After Rachel had agreed to meet Hillary, Cassie had given Hillary her name. Now Hillary knew; it *was* Joel's daughter. Now, she was all the more determined to help Rachel, since she considered Joel to be a troglodyte despite his money, influence and wealthy upbringing.

Good week. Class discussions had been focused and engaged, like old times, before Vaughn had insinuated himself into her classes, and they were reveling in freedom from his oppression.

Cassie thought of the Palestinians and couldn't imagine the horror of their occupation, an army everywhere; loaded weapons and military gear interspersed among mothers shopping and kids playing in the streets. Would they ever be free? She doubted it, not if the narrative the mainstream media proselytized was creating more and more Dr. Greers.

Wednesday's discussion had continued with Desdemona's handkerchief, the catalyst that had brought about her death and propelled the plot forward; then it segued to spousal abuse.

"What spousal abuse," Gloria had asked.

Connor was first to find it, but unsure, his hand crept up and down. "It's February, Connor," Cassie says, "just say it."

"Yeah, Connor, just say it," Zach teased. "We can handle it if you're wrong."

"And if I'm right?"

I'll do your laundry for a week," Parker interjected, sure of himself but in a good–natured way."

"You are gonna be so burned," Connor retorted. "Okay, as long as you get it out of the dryer immediately. I don't like wrinkles."

"Connor!" Cassie said impatiently.

"Sorry Mrs. Komsky, then he addressed his classmates. "You are all gonna be so burned. It's act 4, scene 1. Othello smacks Desdemona. You all missed it, didn't you?" He stares at them with glee. He has nailed this and his answer sends them flipping pages, muttering to themselves, "Where? Where is that statement? Did Othello really do this?"

"Yup, you all missed it," Connor teases staring at Parker, who would be doing his laundry for a week. He'd be sure to strip his bedding and his comforter and take advantage of a bet fairly won.

Yes, they had missed it. Elizabeth is the first to find it. "He *does* hit her," she squeals! "How did I miss this? Act 4, scene 1, he strikes her after Lodovico's letter orders Othello home and puts Cassio in charge of Cyprus. Desdemona is happy. Othello becomes so furious he strikes her and tells her to get out of his sight." She looks up from the text. "I can't believe I missed this! This is horrible! He's horrible! Poor Desdemona, she's an innocent victim in this."

Cassie reverts back to being three years old when she reads this line. She wonders what Rachel is thinking. Is she recalling her father attacking Samir with a fire iron or hurling her across the room? How is she relating this scene to her own horror, and what are Samir's feelings when he remembers his father-in-law attacking him and his wife?

"Good call, Connor," Jason compliments his buddy. "So, do you use fabric softener in your wash?" He looked at Parker who was being a good sport about all of this while the class hooted.

"Good one, Jason. Okay class, we'll pick this up Monday. Have a great weekend, everyone." As they saunter out, Cassie simply could not let this go. "Parker?" He turns. "Make sure you use stain remover on the collars."

Bested by his teacher, again, he loved it. For all his popularity and his bravado, Parker had never felt as accepted as he did since Cassie had come to Chelsea. No other teacher had ever ignored his pedigree or his father's position. Cassie was the only one who had ever put it to him; he loved her spunk and her courage.

He was sorry he wouldn't be here in the fall. But then again, Mrs. Komsky most likely wouldn't be here either. Was it all tied to his father? He wondered how much of those rumors were true, and if he could do something to stop it.

96

CASSIE HAS GOTTEN THE JOB.

I f anyone had told her twenty-five years ago that her life would have turned out like this she would have laughed, flicked the idea away with a shoo of her hand. At forty-two, she would have been married for twenty years or so, lived in a relatively quiet white picket-fence community and been raising three kids, maybe four.

But not even close. Here she was, forty-two, widowed at thirty-eight by an attack that had been front-page news for weeks, living in a townhouse with her young daughter, on a private school campus where she was close to being terminated for having defended a young man left orphaned at fourteen in an attack that had also hit the papers for weeks and whose ethnicity the world hated.

Never write plans in pen, she had read somewhere. You better believe it. Here it was, Friday evening, a month after her life had seemed to be regerminating, and it was all falling apart. Except for revitalized classes with Vaughn no longer present, the only positive was that she was very close to departure. It was a bittersweet testament to plans gone awry. Here, a place she had thought would have been her salvation had turned into another indelible cataclysm in her life.

Cassie sipped cold tea, listened to the Ronettes, and reflected on her life and Brian, Walter, and Vaughn, the men who had come and gone. Brian she had loved; she always would, but God had taken him out of her life. Walter, she thought she had loved, and today she didn't even know who he was. How weird was that? And Vaughn, what had Vaughn been to her? Inspiration? No. A mentor? No way. A reawakening for life? Maybe. A source of fantasy? Now that was an interesting perspective, and she wondered why the thought popped into her head. Just like that, appearing out of nowhere. Had she ever thought about him that way? Not consciously, but subconsciously? She shook it off. Maybe she'd revisit it again when there was distance between her and his attack, but not now.

And there would be distance between her and this academy and soon because she had gotten the job! The news was wonderful, fantastic, supercalifragilisticexpialidocious, the best adjective ever. Mr. Hastings had kept his word, his phone call one day late, to tell her she was hired.

According to him, she had been by far the most qualified candidate he had interviewed. She'd be teaching math, seventh grade, pre-algebra, beginning March 7, with a higher salary *and* great health benefits. Much better for both her and Stevie. No more Shakespeare, no more literature, with all its analogies to life, her life, Rachel's life and Samir's. She'd be working with x's and y's and finding unknowns that had a concrete solution, not with abstracts that could never be resolved.

She would be close to her old home, too, where she, Brian, and Stevie had lived with the ocean, the surf and the breezes with attitude. A change most welcome, and unless external forces beyond her control didn't disrupt her life in some other disastrous way, she'd live there for as long as she was meant to live.

Cassie was ecstatic. She had gotten Mr. Hastings' call Wednesday after school, and had all she could do Thursday and Friday not to let on in any way during her classes. The discussion had been exciting enough, and if her own inner anticipation had surfaced with a few witty comments about Connor's laundry, they wouldn't make the connection to anything that had occurred in her life. Her students were used to her wit.

The job would change everything. She'd miss her students so much, and she'd miss teaching about life through literature, but her life was hurting so much and literature was making it worse, especially when you could see yourself in the characters. Math? Math would be good after this.

Wednesday evening, she and Stevie had celebrated with garlic popcorn drenched with butter. They had plopped on the sofa and watched "Growing Pains" with the Seaver family, followed by "Magnum, P.I." Tomas Magnum, a man very easy to look at. Such a good mental break. She needed to relax and savor the good news.

Thursday evening, she had finalized two possible dates with the movers who didn't care which day she picked; she'd be piggy-backing from Princeton to Atlantic

City with them either way. Next weekend, she'd firm it up and be gone by the end of February. That would leave her a week to unpack and settle in, much more time than she had had when she had come to Chelsea. She told Jeremy the news after school. How ironic that they'd be starting new jobs the same day. He hugged her so tightly she thought he'd dislocate a rib.

This weekend she had lots to do. Tomorrow, she and Stevie would shop for Rebecca's birthday gift. Her roommates were giving her a party Saturday and her parents were giving her a party Sunday at some posh venue in Short Hills near her home. She'd get Rebecca something Stevie suggested; something a thirteen-year-old who had just about everything would want.

Also on her agenda, she'd make sure her grade book and her kids' averages were completely up to date. She'd leave with no loose ends. Leaving abruptly was bad enough, but her students would lose two teachers during their senior year. Not the best experience for any class. She'd put every effort into their grade point average and academic standing. Their grades were all excellent. They were all tomorrow's leaders.

And tomorrow, Hillary would meet with Rachel. If all went well, Cassie would leave knowing Rachel would have an advocate. She'd leave and never worry about facing Vaughn and the horror of this past Monday night again, only the memory, which would always be with her. There would always be the horror of Brian's death, and now there would always be the horror of Vaughn.

But she was free, and she reveled in it. A switch inside her head had turned on once she knew she had the job, and her renewed energy had become infectious. Her students sensed something. Most had thought it was Dr. O/B's absence from class, which certainly created a better environment, but Samir and Rachel knew it went deeper. Samir watched her closely when the discussion segued to physical assault. Rachel and Samir related to this completely, but Samir noticed Cassie wince when Elizabeth asked how someone could attack such a kind woman who was loving and sincere. She meant Desdemona; Cassie related it to herself and Samir knew.

Cassie had been a victim of an attack and Samir was almost certain who the perpetrator was. Only one person in this academy had the power to do something like that to Mrs. Komsky and get away with it. When Cassie tore into that scene, Samir empathized. She was reliving her nightmare as they were reliving theirs. But when she summarized the discussion, he sensed something had changed, something positive, for her, sorrowful for them. She would be leaving them very soon. "We feel sorrow for that which has been our delight." She had been his salvation, his and Rachel's. He would always mourn her loss from their lives.

97

Hillary's Rolls pulled in behind Roosevelt House. Arthur helped Hillary out and she walked to the front door where Cassie was waiting. Both walked past Ms. Marino whose mouth dropped when Hillary presented herself at her office. Judy Marino knew exactly who Hillary Otis-Barrett was and wondered why she was here, especially with that Shakespeare teacher the faculty and staff had been warned to ignore. But she directed them to Rachel's room as requested.

Word of this would spread through the campus like an electrical fire. By tomorrow morning, the campus, the faculty, Rachel's sister, and Vaughn would know that Hillary Otis-Barrett had been here to see Rachel. Maybe they'd know by tonight. Dr. Greer would know a phone call later.

Gloria left the room when Hillary and Cassie appeared. Even though she'd know what had transpired as soon as Cassie and Hillary were gone, she always waited for Rachel to seek her out for advice and emotional support.   If only Desdemona had had Gloria to watch over her instead of Iago's wife.

Rachel was barefooted; she wore jeans and an oversized sweatshirt with a "Peace" logo on its front.   Her hair was a bit messy – a typical scene for a girls' dorm on a weekend.   The troubling part was the tension on her face.   She had been agonizing over Cassie's imminent departure.   She loved Cassie and trusted her unequivocally. Hillary was a complete unknown.

Haggard from all she and Samir had endured, Rachel's face showed its strain more than ever and there were dark circles under her eyes.   According to Samir, she still wasn't eating and she didn't want to either.   Not good, Cassie thought.   Rachel's nightmare had begun over Christmas break and it had not abated.   That was over a month ago.   Here it was February, and she was facing a woman with kind eyes whom she and Samir would have to trust.

Samir had told his wife his suspicions for the cuts on Cassie's face.   Rachel had been appalled.   At first, she refused to believe it.   That can't be, she had said.   Dr. O/B? But the more she thought about it, the more it seemed possible.   None of what was happening made sense, just people hating people.

Hillary walked towards her and sat on the bed, straight posture, like Emelia's, with a softness that surrounded her, almost like an angelic glow.   Rachel felt as though she had been wrapped in a soft blanket and she warmed to Hillary that moment.

"Whatever you want to tell me will be your decision," Hillary began. Mrs. Komsky has told me your father has," she pauses, knowing what she was about to say would hurt, but she said it, "disowned you because you are dating someone he finds unacceptable." Rachel did not interrupt to explain that "unacceptable" couldn't come close to describe its severity. "I can help; I will help, in any way I can."

"Why?" Rachel asked succinctly. It was a blunt question from Rachel, but, even though she was drawn to Hillary, she had been pushed to her limit and had to test Hillary herself, even at the risk of losing her only possible salvation. Hillary understood. Why should an eighteen-year-old with a father who had betrayed her, trust her?

"Fair question," Hillary replied, not offended at all. "This is what Mrs. Komsky has told me: you brought your boyfriend home during Christmas break to introduce him to your parents and your father went after him with a fire iron because he wasn't the 'right' ethnicity or religion. She told me you defended him, and when you did, your father pushed you across the room and you hit the dining room table; your boyfriend went after your father, who tried to have him expelled, unsuccessfully, thank goodness. She told me you've been traumatized ever since, and I can easily understand that. In fact, I would be surprised if you weren't. You love your parents, who've brought you up to care about people; you believed they'd respect your decision, but you got a horrific reaction instead.

"That's what I know; it's what Mrs. Komsky has told me, nothing else, and I will ask nothing else. But I will still help you any way I can, because I know Mrs. Komsky is honorable and I respect her. She has also told me she has to leave . . . not the specific reason, but I believe whatever she has to do is valid. That leaves you without an adult to advocate for you and help when you need an older person," Hillary smiled and followed with, "and I am a *lot* older."

Rachel smiled. Miss Hillary had a sense of humor. She liked that, and she was carefully considering everything Hillary hadn't said. So Hillary didn't know her boyfriend was her husband; she didn't know he was an Arab, the Arab whose parents had been blown up in the Embassy attack over four years ago. Hillary knew none of this, yet she was still willing to help. A wealthy Mrs. Otis-Barrett didn't need to offer; she didn't need to spend her time helping someone despite only knowing the skeleton of the truth, and yet she would. Maybe she was for real. Rachel looked into Hillary's eyes and nodded. Cassie exhaled. This might work. At least Rachel would give it a try.

After Hillary left, Cassie remained. "Thank you. I'm happy you're willing to give Hillary a chance. "She'll be a good advocate for you. She has clout, something I don't have, and she has principles. Will you see Samir later on?"

"After I shower and dress." She smiled. "I can't let him see me looking like this."

Cassie returned the smile, remembering when she'd get dressed so meticulously to meet Brian, before and after they were married. She loved that look in his eyes when he checked her out from head to toe and was very pleased with what he saw, in addition to her spunk and sharp wit. He loved that she was so well read, always researching one thing after the other. "Okay, tell Samir that both of you have made me very happy, and tell him . . . tell him I love you both."

Cassie couldn't believe she had just told two students she loved them. But she had, and she loved the universality of loving people who were good and kind. If that was wrong, then the whole world was upside down. Cassie hugged Rachel, then put on her coat to leave. It was February and still very cold. "Almost forgot," she said as an afterthought, "do you have a copy of your marriage certificate?"

Rachel nodded. "We've requested two copies. We filled out forms last month when Samir couldn't get a permit for a car. We couldn't get back to Philly to pick them up; so they're being mailed. They should be here any day."

"Good. Keep them in a safe place. You may need them."

When Cassie left Roosevelt House, Hillary was waiting for her in her limo. She motioned Cassie over. "She's lovely, and so frightened. I know there's a lot going on you can't tell me, but I promise you, I will do everything I can to help her. And if *you* ever need me, *ever*, here's my mobile phone number. You can always reach me on that."

Cassie held Hillary's number in her hand, staring at it and committing it to memory, overwhelmed by her kindness. When she had been introduced to Hillary on Thanksgiving, she had thought it sad that they had come from such disparate worlds because she had sensed the goodness in her. After they had spoken last Saturday, she was convinced of it. Hillary had alluded to a lifetime of no children and illness. Sorrow is sorrow. Maybe the degree didn't parallel Cassie's or Samir's, but her life hadn't been the silver-spoon fantasy typical of the Club set.

Cassie thanked Hillary as Arthur started the Rolls and, as she watched the car exit the academy, felt that same sadness. Two people so similar in ideals and principles lived so far apart on the socio-economic ladder, making friendship impossible. Rachel's background was much closer to Hillary's. Maybe later in life they would have the kind of friendship Cassie could only imagine.

For now though, the biggest obstacle had been surmounted. Cassie could leave whenever, knowing Hillary would be there for Rachel, who had no idea how much she would really need her. First Rachel would have to tell her that her boyfriend wasn't her boyfriend; that he was her husband; that she, a Jew, and Samir, an Arab, were married. Cassie imagined Hillary's reaction when that piece of the puzzle filled in.

But, if that shocked Hillary, Cassie would love to be a fly on the wall when Rachel gave her the news that would shock the hell out of Chelsea, this staid establishment, because, whether Rachel knew it or not, that girl was pregnant, and those dark circles around her eyes were all the proof Cassie needed.

98

S unday evening; Vaughn had been trying to read the same book for a week, but in complete frustration and anger, he threw it across the room with such ferocity that it hit the fireplace mantel forty feet away, ricocheted off and landed upside down on the plush snow-white carpeting. He didn't care. He was consumed with last Monday night and had been unable to eat or sleep since, first from his tongue, which was healing, and then from his emotions, which were not.

Aside from the first few days of intense pain and swelling after Cassie had had almost severed his tongue, he had healed more quickly than he had expected. He had ordered lobster tails at the Club last night and found he could bite, chew and swallow with only a hint of pain and an annoying skin tag on the side Mike had stitched, and that would be snipped tomorrow. Six days after the stitches and he was doing great. So, eating was no longer a problem.

Talking wasn't much of a problem either. With the exception of 'r,' 'n,' and 'l,' he could pretty much speak normally. 'W's' were a little problem too, but aside from that, Mike's expertise and lots of salt-water rinses had done the job so well that Taylor hadn't noticed.

He sighed; his tongue was not the reason for his inability to eat or sleep. And as interesting as the attack on the USS Liberty might be, if he could get past page twenty-nine, it was his attack on Cassie that was gnawing at him. He could not shake off the shame of what he had done. Vaughn Otis-Barrett ashamed? Yes, ashamed, for his loss of control and, more than that, for its reason.

Try as he might, he could not focus on much of anything, least of all a book Cassie had recommended before Christmas. Concentration seemed fruitless, because, every time he picked up the book, bittersweet memories of Cassie wafted through his mind. She was all he could think about, her beautiful face, her sensual body, and the scintillating, sometimes biting interaction they had shared. But to avenge Taylor, he had relegated Cassie to invisibility a month ago. That, plus all the acts of vengeance he had hurled upon her, had resulted in one thing: alienation from a person he had come to thoroughly appreciate and enjoy.

He missed her. Bottom line, he missed her more than he could ever have imagined. He missed her sharp repartee, the tilt of her head just before her biting wit unleashed itself upon him or anyone; her furrowed brows as she went into deep-thought mode; he missed her vivacity as she extemporized on the Middle East, the spark in her eyes and the sorrow in her tone. In short, he missed her company in everything they had ever shared. He would have welcomed any small encounter now, a brief hello, a sharp comment if she opened a door and it hit him in the shoulder, or her, "Dr. O/B, are you following me?"

And in a way, he had been. He had instructed Mary, the receptionist whose desk was positioned behind Melissa's, to dial his extension any time Cassie walked into the office. Mary suspected nothing, so he thought, and any glimpse of Cassie at any time brought sunshine into his day. For Vaughn, Cassie decorated any office, any classroom, any place. Sometimes he wondered what her husband had been like; how he'd gotten through to her when he, Vaughn Otis-Barrett, the wealthiest man in Jersey, maybe throughout the tri-state area, had to work to get a smile.

But he was married, and it was obvious Cassie was not one to ignore that. He had initially contented himself with what he had, but he had wanted more, and in searching for more, he had destroyed it all by forcing Taylor to that faculty Christmas party. He had ruined everything, and it had made him crazy. Now, Cassie wanted nothing to do with him. After Monday night, he was certain she despised him. He was surprised she had not pressed charges.

He winced at the savagery of his attack. If she had had a man in her life, he would never have dared that. But Cassie didn't have a husband; so Vaughn had acted with impunity. No male to challenge him; he was thinking on a primordial level, and he wasn't wrong. Even though he wasn't good at it, he believed subtle sexual innuendo was inherent in almost every encounter between a male and a female. The smart women knew this and knew how to play it to their advantage. The naïve ones like Cassie would always get it wrong.

So, here he sat, attempting to read the attack on the USS Liberty, June 8, 1967, thirty-four Americans dead, one hundred seventy-four wounded in international waters, an attack never fully investigated because the aggressor had been Israel. His fourth attempt to read something about a topic he had become interested in because of the anticipated follow-up, an innocent, innocuous way to get into a conversation with a delightful member of his faculty, had failed. She had always been willing and eager to talk about the Middle East, the place where her husband had been killed. But she would converse with him no more.

As he pondered how he could change this, heal the damage, get her to soften, get her to forgive his attack and be lured into a discussion about anything, his phone rang. Taylor was out, putting final touches on Hillary's anniversary celebration one week away. He answered the phone and sat straight up in his recliner. "My sister-in-law did what?' He shouted, and forgot all speculation about Cassie.

99

"**A**m I missing something here or was the person who called me yesterday misinformed?" Vaughn had called Hillary last night, demanding to know why his sister-in-law had visited Rachel Greer in her dorm Saturday afternoon. Hillary, usually passive and deferential to her husband and her brother-in-law, had, surprisingly, not been intimidated. She'd see Vaughn at Chelsea in his office tomorrow to discuss whatever he wanted to discuss, face to face. From the tone of her voice, Vaughn sensed a very determined Hillary, someone unfamiliar to him.

And so, while Cassie's classes were discussing infidelity, spousal abuse, a handkerchief, and the complexities of *Othello*, Hillary sat opposite Vaughn at the conference table in his office, posture straight, hair meticulously coifed in a top knot, makeup immaculate but not ostentatious, wearing a stunning aqua pants suit with a self-belt loosely secured at the waist and a matching scarf knotted around her neck. She had nodded when she walked in; aside from that, she hadn't uttered a word. She was here at Vaughn's request, not hers, and his opening to her was rude. She'd wait. Her reply would come when she was ready.

"Okay, Hillary, you're here, I'm here. Did you, with Cassie Komsky, the woman who insulted your sister-in-law about a month ago, show up at Rachel Greer's dorm and have a private conversation?"

Now, Hillary was ready. As usual, Vaughn had twisted the incident to reflect his interpretation, his needs. That will not stand, she thought. "Your source is correct Vaughn. I *did* visit Rachel in her dorm Saturday, but it was not with the woman who insulted my sister-in-law. It was with Cassie Komsky, the woman who my sister-in-law, your wife, viciously attacked at a faculty Christmas party, not the other way around, as you describe it." Vaughn avoided her penetrating gaze. "But who are you to challenge what I do and with whom I speak? Nothing I've ever said or done has ever concerned you before." This was definitely a new Hillary. "And since you are seeking information from me, exactly who was this person who called you yesterday, informing you of my whereabouts yesterday afternoon?"

"No, Hillary, tell me why you were there first."

Hillary stared at her brother-in-law sitting opposite her. It had been a difficult weekend for Hillary, not only because she had seen the distress in Rachel's eyes, her gaunt face and her austere countenance, but because Rachel had called her yesterday afternoon to talk; she needed to tell Miss Hillary more about her situation than she had the day before. If Miss Hillary was extending her unconditional support to her, knowing only meager essentials of her situation, Rachel had thought it only fair to tell her more. And it would help Rachel ascertain how much more she could tell her in the future.

What Rachel had told Hillary made her aware of her brother-in-law's reprehensible behavior. You don't observe a teacher in three classes every day for almost a month, staring and glaring at her, because you find her outside with two of her students, one who had been completely distraught from a scene in *Othello* that related so closely to her father's rejection. You don't do that every day, three periods a day, unless it's a calculated retaliation for a well-deserved retort from Cassie to your wife. Hillary was pleased to learn that Parker had courageously challenged his father's observations and forced him to leave class.

Hillary was also upset that Vaughn had tried to have Samir expelled. So Samir was the young man Rachel had brought home over the Christmas break to introduce to her family, the young man she loved, and yes, he was an Arab and a Muslim, whose parents had been blown-up at the Embassy bombing in Lebanon four years ago.

Hillary had skipped a breath at that one. How horrific, yet Rachel's father hated him instantly because of his ethnicity and his religion and had gone after him with a fire iron before he threw his daughter across the room. Horrible. Rachel and Samir, they had gone through so much torment, and this is how they were being treated.

Cassie had not been wrong; they did need help, and Hillary was so glad she had agreed even before knowing this. Now she was more determined than ever. And here she sat face to face with her brother-in-law, who had been guilty of so much in this situation. To think he had met with Joel Greer and was intending to get Samir expelled after the horrible things Greer had done to him. Thank God Cassie had intervened and had gotten Ambassador Gibran to intervene also. She had indeed put herself on the line for these two young people who deserved none of this.

Hillary was stunned while Rachel was informing her of this. Hillary accepted Samir, the man in Rachel's life, being an Arab and a Muslim. The Jew/Muslim combination had never entered her mind when Cassie had said this couple was from different ethnicities, different religions. Hillary had pictured Jew and Christian, but never Jew and Muslim; that was a shock. Two young lovers from ethnicities in the Middle East in perpetual war, one the aggressor, the other retaliating to hold on, could be a culture shock. But she looked for the good and the love, and it was there.

The older Hillary got, the more she looked for the good in all people regardless of religion, regardless of ethnicity, and with the Middle East situation, regardless of the media's slanted presentation. Rachel's father's hatred made sense now, especially because it was Joel Greer, a person Hillary knew from the Club, more from a distance, by choice, than Brett and Vaughn. His personality grated on her. He was brash, disrespectful and became belligerent when he didn't get his way, no matter what it concerned. He was also very outspoken about his allegiance to Israel, preferring that country to the U.S, his place of birth. Hillary acknowledged, happily, that she and Cassie had a common value – neither liked Dr. Joel Greer, but his munificent donations made him a man to be placated and reckoned with.

Once Hillary knew the ethnic and religious combination, she understood the problem Samir and Rachel had been facing and she reinforced her conviction to help them against all odds, even against her brother-in-law. Unbelievable, Vaughn observing Cassie every day, three classes per day and glaring. Unprofessional wasn't the word. And Parker's calling him on it in her defense? Wonderful. She swelled with pride. She was certain much of the change in Parker's personality had something, a lot, to do with Cassie Komsky, a woman who seemed to have more honor and more guts than any of them, a woman who must be going through hell. No wonder she had to leave.

Hillary was determined to stand up for what was right, regardless of the outcome instead of regurgitating the self-serving Otis-Barrett mantra of hedonism, or retreating from it all. "Why I was there? No, Vaughn, not why I was there. Why I am *here*," she stated emphatically, looking at him face to face. "And I am here to demand you account for your horrific behavior towards Cassie and everything you have done to her."

Vaughn recoiled in horror. Impossible! Impossible! She knew?! How? How did she know? How *could* she know? Did Cassie tell her? Had Cassie told her what he had done? How much had she said? Did she tell Hillary everything, even forcing his tongue into her mouth? Had Cassie told her that? My God, no! He had been found out. Almost as bad as Cassie pressing charges, she had told his sister-in-law!

"No, Hillary. No, it's not how it looks," he backed off, going into defensive mode. "I didn't attack her, not intentionally. I . . . I was angry because she had missed the faculty meeting without my permission. I confronted her; that's all. Things got out of hand. It wasn't a real attack; nothing was intentional. It wasn't right, I know, but her head hit the wall harder than I had intended." He flushed with shame. "I lost control, I was angry . . . my tongue . . ." He turned away. "I didn't realize my tongue was in her mouth. I wanted to punish her, hurt her; let her know I was in charge. She had defied me! Damn it!" He pounded his hands in anger. "That's all, Hillary, honestly. That's all I wanted to do. Whatever else she told you is a lie, a lie!"

Hillary stared at him, shocked. She glared at her brother-in-law, digesting the horror of what he had confessed. The horror of what she had thought Cassie must have been experiencing from Vaughn's observations paled in relation to his horrific attack.

Cassie should have gone to the police. Vaughn should have been arrested. He should have been arrested! Why hadn't Cassie called 9-1-1? Why? Because Vaughn held all the cards; he owned all the politicians, the lawyers and the police. Promise them something if they'd look the other way and they would, even in this town.

What else could Cassie have done? So, this was the real reason Cassie was leaving, why she had to get away. It was the dean, her brother-in-law. When did he become so crazed? When did he turn into such a monster? I'll definitely help her, Hillary thought; if she'll let me, if she needs me, in any way I can.

She rose stoically. As she stood to her full height, not much over five feet, a feeling of revulsion, futility, vulnerability, whatever, awakened in her and she glared at him, looking for a sincere sign of sorrow for what he had done. She found sorrow only for himself. She backed away in disgust, ready to leave, when suddenly, she moved towards him, raised her hand involuntarily and slapped his face so hard his head turned 180 degrees. Vaughn reeled. Hers was a guttural, purely guttural response, unplanned and inexplicable, and it shocked them both.

Hillary's breath came hard. "You are despicable! So is Joel Greer, and you can tell him I said so. He's lucky, blessed to have been given two beautiful daughters and he's throwing Rachel away because she doesn't hate the way he does. Someday he's going to regret what he's done; someday, you're going to regret what you've done to Cassie."

"Hillary, please, please, don't tell Taylor."

"Don't tell Taylor? You've committed assault and battery, and a sexual assault at that, and your only response is that I not tell Taylor?" She shook her head. "You disgust me." She walked out.

Vaughn rubbed his stinging cheek, wringing his hand through his hair, wishing he had never hired a woman named Cassie.

100

HILLARY REFLECTS AFTER MEETING WITH VAUGHN

Hillary was so distraught, so lost in her thoughts after hearing Vaughn that she by-passed her limo. She didn't see the car, she didn't see Arthur, nor did she hear him call to her the first time. She was consumed with images of Vaughn's horrific attack, and how traumatized Cassie must have been then and still. How was she getting through the day? What a heinous, despicable thing for Vaughn, her brother-in-law, to have done.

She had noticed scars on Cassie's upper lip when they had met at Sanders House Saturday, but she had attributed them to an inadvertent scratch, maybe with a fingernail. Since Vaughn's attack had occurred days before Hillary had seen Cassie, scabs would have healed and faded into thin lines. Covered with makeup, they were hardly discernible.

But hardly discernible to the eye is no indication of the internal scars they must have left. They'd remain indelible in Cassie's mind for the rest of her life. How she could stay at Chelsea and still function in her classes was inscrutable. If Hillary had proof, if she had evidence, she would press charges herself. But that would do nothing for Cassie, especially if she wanted to keep it from her daughter. That had to be a major factor. How do you tell your daughter someone she admired and viewed as a mentor had physically attacked her mother?

Arthur held the door open and Hillary slid into the back seat deep in thought, reflecting on decades of having known the Otis-Barrett family. She had known Brett from early adolescence to dating in college, to marriage. This handsome, sexy guy had been every girl's dream, every girl's target, every girl's perfect guy, perfect husband, and he had picked Hillary. She had been flattered and so honored that she never thought to refuse him or contradict him in any way. She never took the chance of losing him, even though her family had limitless resources. When everyone's wealthy, wealth becomes relative and you look for other traits.

Wealth only becomes a priority to someone like Taylor, who had hooked her claws into Vaughn for that one purpose, no, two. Hillary had seen Taylor look at Brett the first time she met him, shortly before she and Vaughn had become engaged. Brett had returned the look, the passion and lust. There was something between them shortly after she had been diagnosed with cancer, when her dreams of adopting had been completely shattered. She had handled the first two miscarriages stoically. After the third, followed by her stillborn, when pregnancy had become futile, her emotional fortitude had collapsed. She turned to adoption, her last chance, but cancer, chemo and radiation ended it all. She had shut herself off from everyone after that, the world, and Brett. Maybe that had sent him to Taylor more frequently, but it had begun before that.

From then on, she had lived a life without purpose, shutting her eyes to Brett, Taylor, Vaughn, and, except for Mildred whom she adored, the whole Otis-Barrett family, even Parker, who had been brought up overindulged in every way.

But suddenly she felt renewed. Rachel's plight had touched her heart. Hillary understood heartache and isolation. She understood and empathized with a young woman who had been disenfranchised from her father for a hateful reason when no rational reason existed.

After Rachel confided in her yesterday, telling her who she had brought home to meet her dad and how viciously he had responded, she became more determined than ever. She was ecstatic that Rachel had called her. Maybe in time, she'd confide more, but now, after this encounter with Vaughn, after she learned what he had done to Cassie and how this was forcing Cassie's departure, she dedicated herself to helping her too, in any way she could.

Hillary had a renewed purpose for living, and woe to anyone who got in her way.

101

THE CLASSROOM WHILE HILLARY & VAUGHN TALKED

"**C**onnor?" He glanced up, thinking Mrs. Komsky would be asking him a question about the week end's assignment. "Did Parker get your collars clean?" That was not the question he had expected, but Cassie was in a playful mood. She was still floating on last Wednesday's phone call from Mr. Hastings.

"Needs lots of work on stain removal," he gave a 'so-so' shake of his hand and smiled, "but he'll get it; he's got five days to go."

Parker slumped his six feet, three-plus inches as far down into his seat as he could possibly slide, while his classmates teased him mercilessly.

"You'll get the hang of it, Parker," Gloria encouraged.

"It's not easy for some upper crust guys to get away from their maids and housekeepers," Mason teased, jabbing Parker on his shoulder.

Parker withstood it all. He had left his ego behind a few months ago and he didn't mind the jibes. He didn't even mind doing Connor's laundry. The playful banter was worth it, and maybe, someday, in a fantasy world, he may have to one day do his own laundry.

Cassie began the lesson with a quick reference to spousal abuse from Friday, then jumped to act 4, scene 2, Othello's 'subtle whore' comment, where Emelia defends Desdemona to Othello. But no one believed it redeemed her for stealing the handkerchief. "It's too little, too late. She still stole the handkerchief," Elizabeth stated. "Without it, Iago's plan couldn't have worked."

"So, Othello slapping his wife and vowing to kill her both pivot on a handkerchief?"

Elizabeth nods. "Without that handkerchief, everything Iago accused Desdemona of doing would have been hearsay. Othello wanted tangible proof that his wife had been unfaithful. Iago, with his wife's help and that handkerchief, gave him that proof."

"Yup," says Parker. "The irony of it all is seeing Desdemona ask Iago, the master-mind behind this scheme, what she should do."

"She's trusting and naïve, same as Cassio," Gloria says, "and Iago is nothing but a sick, unhappy person whose only goal is to hurt someone who's happy because he's not."

Rachel sat up straight in her chair, looking at her classmates, Cassie, and Samir. "Oh my gosh," she uttered, "that's the reason my father's so angry. It's what Gloria just said: Unhappy people want to destroy happy people because . . . they're not happy! We talked about this before, but I never had a family situation to relate it to until now. My father's not happy, so he doesn't want me to be happy either, especially with someone who symbolizes what he hates.

She nods towards Samir, "All he cares about is making us as unhappy as he is." She shakes her head. "I never would have realized it if he hadn't done what he did – *and* if we had not had such in-depth conversations about Othello and life."

"Shakespeare can do that to you. You'll always find something about Shakespeare in yourself. His characters can be you, me, any of us. As I said during my first week here, and as Professor Draggert must have said many times, Shakespeare's characters and his four-hundred-year old plays are timeless. No matter what the century, they give us a mirror to ourselves and other people, people who have lived before us, with us, or after us. Past, present, or future doesn't matter; his plays are in our lives. For you, Rachel, Iago let you understand your father."

"Big time, scary, Mrs. Komsky,' Connor reflects. "We know what happens to them; we don't know what happens to us."

A long pause, then Mason says. "This may have nothing to do with the play itself, but I think this play is tough reading. It's the only play I had to read and reread just to keep track of the plot and figure out who Iago was setting up, and how he ties it all together to destroy Othello, Cassio, Desdemona and anybody else who got in his way. Not an easy read."

"Same for me," Jason adds. "I had to reread some lines twice, sometimes more."

"Twice? More than twice," Connor teases. "You? For you, that's not normal."

"Funny, Connor, and no, for me that's not normal, but I discovered, as I read the play, that so much intrigue in the dialogue seems irrelevant when you first read it, but as you go along, you realize a line you glossed over is very relevant; then you have to go back, find it, and reread it."

Elizabeth liked the play because it revolved around ordinary people. "There's no royalty, no court, no country whose fate is at stake." She empathized with Othello because he was a regular guy who fell in love with a genteel, beautiful woman who he couldn't believe had fallen in love with him.

Zach stressed insecurity as the reason Othello believed Iago so easily and got sucked in by his lies. "He's insecure, like all of us at one time or another, and he's betrayed by a friend, a friend he shared his life and his way of life with in battle and off the field. "You're right, Mrs. Komsky, Shakespeare can happen to any of us. For me, more than any other play, it's through *Othello*." He sits back in his chair and closes the book.

"What about you, Mrs. Komsky?" Connor asks, "Which tragedy do you relate to the most?"

"This one," Cassie responded immediately. "In a way it's *Macbeth*; I like the collusion between him and his wife, and the irony: she talks her reluctant husband into murdering the king, yet she's the one who goes insane from guilt. I also appreciate Macbeth's "tomorrow" soliloquy more than any other, but for character interaction, I relate most to *Othello*. It's about the common man, me, and one little gift, one trivial handkerchief that causes unmitigated jealousy in such a noble, yet common man. This play would find an audience in any age."

"Yeah," Matt mutters. "No regicide, no ghosts, no weird sisters, just real people fighting their emotions and failing, and Desdemona gets caught in the middle."

"Sad, isn't it? Sometimes life just grabs you and sweeps you into a tragic situation you can't control. No matter which way you turn to make it better, it only makes it worse."

This was Cassie's story, Samir's and Rachel's, here at Chelsea Academy. "It's life, the way life happens to each of us, and the lives we get mixed up in as we go along. Some people we'll like, love and remember forever. Others we'll wish we had never met." A little stab jerked at Cassie's heart for the man she missed and the man she never wanted to see again.

"Next topic is also timeless and fits right in to our contemporary world; it's the conversation Desdemona and Emelia have about infidelity. Before we begin that though, I'd like your thoughts on the adjective I used to describe the handkerchief. I said it was trivial, and no one contradicted me. Should I assume you all agree?"

A bit of silence then Mason asks, "You want us to tell you if we think a handkerchief is trivial or not?"

Cassie nodded. "This handkerchief in this play, yes, I do."

"Of course it's trivial," Mason says. "It's just a handkerchief, and a handkerchief would be considered a trivial gift. The only reason it's not trivial is because it caused a lot of people to die. So it can't be trivial if it did that."

"Good answer Mason. It's not trivial because it did cause a lot of deaths, but any other reason why this particular handkerchief," she points to the opened text, "would not be a trivial gift?"

Zach responds. "Just like Mason said, as a gift, any handkerchief would be trivial. But this particular handkerchief would not be trivial because, in addition to causing a lot of deaths, it was Othello's first gift to Desdemona."

"Two reasons why it's not trivial. Good. Is there a third?"

They all shook their heads, except Samir.

"Reread that section again, and do some research if you need it."

"For another reason? It's just a handkerchief, Mrs. Komsky," Matt comments, "and we gave two reasons why it's not trivial. Why would we need research to find a third?"

"Read that section carefully. You might find another reason. Besides, not all of you agreed that there were only two. Samir didn't respond. Maybe you'll see something that'll change your mind." Cassie glances at her watch. "Time to go. See you tomorrow."

They collect their books and shuffle out, wondering why they'd need research about something as trivial as a handkerchief.

102

"So, is there a third reason why this handkerchief is not trivial?" It was Tuesday and that had been yesterday's assignment. "Ladies, if your boyfriend had given you this very handkerchief, based on the text, would you consider it a trivial gift?"

Elizabeth looked at Matt. "None of us found any other reason. It was Othello's first gift to Desdemona; it caused a lot of deaths and that's it. If a guy gave it to his girlfriend in today's world, it would be trivial."

"This exact handkerchief? This one, that's in *Othello*?" Cassie questions in consternation, wondering how they missed the vital significance.

Matt shrugged his shoulders. "Yeah, this one; I wouldn't give it to Lizzie and expect her to think it was special, except that I had given it to her." He looks at Lizzie; then asks the shocker. "If your husband had given you this handkerchief, Mrs. Komsky, would it be trivial to you?"

Samir is startled. He looks at Cassie, who feels like she's been struck with a hammer. She had never expected that question, never. If her husband had given her any handkerchief, she would have treasured it forever. She would have used it through laughter and tears and she would never have given it away, and heaven forbid if she had lost it. But this handkerchief, this very same handkerchief Othello had given Desdemona? This handkerchief was an irreplaceable treasure, but none of them knew why. Well, maybe one; yes, one.

"Perhaps Mrs. Komsky considers this her personal life? Perhaps we should retract the question?" Samir says, trying to run interference for Cassie from having to answer Matt's question. Only Samir knew Cassie's husband had been blown up in the American Embassy attack. He was trying to protect her from the emotional pain of reliving her tragedy because he knew how much hurt he felt whenever he relived his.

"It's okay, Samir," she rallies and responds to Matt. I'll answer it, but no digressions, okay guys? This is not an invitation into my personal life, just this one question." She gave it a few seconds to orient her response. "If my husband had ever given me a handkerchief, I would treasure it always, because he had given it to me even though, in comparison to the materialism and glitz we are inundated with in our society, a handkerchief would be a trivial gift. How-ev-er!" She breaks down each syllable for them and keeps the class focused on the topic, "If he had given me *this* handkerchief, this very handkerchief," she stabs at the textbook, "it would never have been a trivial gift. I used verbal irony when I used that word, and I asked you to tell me why. After you reread the scene and researched whatever it is you researched, do you know why I said this about Othello's handkerchief." No response.

"Okay, you missed it, or you didn't read closely enough, or you didn't research. Here's a hint, and if you can't answer my question after it, you didn't research: Think of Shakespeare's universality and the way this handkerchief ties us to his past, which carries all the way into the present."

"Huh?" Jason had hardly ever used that word, but he used it now. "Mrs. Komsky that is the most convoluted question I've ever heard, from anybody."

"Shakespeare's our past; he ties his era to his previous era, his past, then his play comes down to us through the centuries into our present. Not confusing to me. Come on, think. Here's my last hint: Focus on a proper noun."

All of them had their faces in their texts. Zach mutters, "That's our last hint? Some hint."

He draws his finger under each line and criticizes the lack of footnotes. All have their heads down in the text, all except Samir. "I don't understand this at all, Mrs. Komsky," Gloria says.

"Don't understand what, Gloria?"

"I've reread this scene over and over, and it seems kind of supernatural. It says an Egyptian gave the handkerchief to Othello's mother who gave it to him on her deathbed. It was supposed to have magic in it?" Gloria shook her head in consternation. "And she told him to give it to his wife when he married." Confused, she looks up apologetically. "Isn't this just some hocus pocus stuff Shakespeare threw in? You told us to research those lines, but I didn't even know what to look up."

"You got part of it: An Egyptian gives it to Othello's mother; she gives it to him on her deathbed, and yes, it supposedly had magical powers. So if it does have magical powers, it wouldn't be trivial. And the explanation for why it wouldn't be is in the proper noun and the part that follows."

Gloria moves her finger along each line then stops. "Sybil? Sybil is a proper noun? Othello says a Sybil gave it to his mother." She shakes her head. "What's a Sybil?"

"And nobody looked that up? Why not? I was going on to the next topic and realized no one had asked about this, which made me think you all understood it." She looks around. "Then I thought, no, what if no one mentioned it because you were hoping I'd avoid it?" A broad smile appeared on her face. "Am I correct or can someone, anyone, answer my question . . . and Gloria's?"

Cassie smiled her gotcha smile which always made them squirm. This time was no different. She waited for a response. "My instincts, from decades of teaching, are telling me that none of you know the definition of Sybil, unless someone's not talking." She looks around and pauses at Samir for a moment; then moves on. "None of you asked; no one consulted an encyclopedia or a dictionary. Senior students just let this go?" Now she was grinning mischievously from ear to ear.

"I give up, Mrs. Komsky, Matt capitulated, throwing his hands in the air. "I don't know what a Sybil is; none of us do, so please tell us, what's a Sybil?"

"You want me to give you the answer, Matt? Just like that? No quid pro quo?" Her humor put them at ease, but they had a feeling this was not the finale, that some ball was about to drop. "Matt, think. You said none of you know what a Sybil is, but an Egyptian gave it to Othello's mother. Based on that, don't you think someone here might know the answer?

He paused and took a quick look around the table. "Who? Why would anyone in this class know what a Sybil is?"

"I'll bet someone in this class knows," she said as Samir turned away. Think, think of the word 'Egyptian.'" Samir squirmed. "Did you ask your roommate? Betcha he knows."

Matt was confused. "Samir? Why would he know?" Then suddenly the class got it.

They got it like a light switch had been flipped, and all heads turned towards Samir, who actually blushed. Now, they know he knows. "Come on, Samir," Parker urges, "tell us what it means or she'll have us do a five page paper on something connected with this."

Cassie shakes her head. "Ten," she quips. "A ten page paper, and we'll make it a third of your fourth quarter grade."

Agonizing groans filled the classroom. "No, not a paper. Come on Samir, please . . . save us."

Samir came to their rescue. "Sybils are women the ancient Greeks believed were oracles, prophets, women who were able to predict events from the gods. Legend dates them hundreds, thousands of years before Christ."

He paused for a second; then offered more. "The Egyptian Sybil is also known as the Hebrew Sybil. She was brought up by a Palestinian. Some say she was Egyptian; others say she was Babylonian – they took their names from the shrines they visited. The Egyptian Sybil was two hundred years old when she wove that handkerchief, and she wove it from the silk of sacred worms, the source of its magical power. To lose it or give it away was perdition, eternal punishment and damnation. This handkerchief would not be considered a trivial gift."

The class looked at Cassie. Would she accept Samir's answer and spare them a ten page paper? She had to; it was a great answer. Cassie looked at them stone faced, prolonging their agony. Then she smiled, and looked at Samir, "You have saved your classmates hours of research and writing."

Samir smiled. His status amongst his peers had just increased exponentially. They leaped from their seats and gave him a standing ovation. Rachel beamed. What a difference from his first weeks in November when Samir spoke to no one and no one spoke to him. Emotion filled Cassie with happiness and pride, for him, for Rachel, for the entire class. Had Vaughn still been entrenched in the classroom, this would never have happened. Thank God he was gone.

"Notice the history in Samir's answer. She's a Hebrew Sybil from the Middle East, also known as the Egyptian Sybil, perhaps Babylonian, brought up by a Palestinian. The history of these places, which originated thousands of years ago, ties us all to one universal lifeline, a lifeline we find in Shakespeare and in this play. Shakespeare connects the Egyptian Sybil and her history to Palestine and to the Moor in *Othello*.

Emelia sits up straight and asks, "In act 4, scene 3, Iago's wife says something about Palestine. How did Shakespeare know about Palestine way back then?"

"Indirectly, your question asks why we *don't* know about Palestine in our culture and in our country, except in a negative context. Shakespeare knew about Palestine the same way he knew about Sybils, Venice and their wars with the Turks, which introduce *Othello*. The Ottomans and Venice vied for supremacy for the Spice and Silk trade after the Ottomans conquered the Arabs.

"Shakespeare's generation knew about these wars, just as the great masters of the Renaissance knew about Asia Minor and Sybils. Shakespeare was born in 1564. Michelangelo painted his frescos on the Sistine Chapel in the early 1500's. If you look at the ceiling of the Sistine Chapel, you'll see five Sybils. The Persian Sybil, the Delphic, and the Libyan Sybil are three of the five. I can't remember the other two. You might want to research this on your own, but they connect past and present right there on the Chapel's ceiling." She glanced around. "Fascinating, isn't it, yet we, in our culture are so cut off from all of it.

"If we exclude Shakespeare from our world we would maintain only part of our culture. We'd be throwing away everything we imported from England and Europe, and everything they imported from the Middle East. It would be a little like burning all history books except those written about American history, which would leave us disjointed from our past and more than half the world that influenced us in some way directly or indirectly. Whether we realize it or not, we're all cut from the same cloth, just from a different part of the design."

"You have a nice way of saying things, Mrs. Komsky," Gloria said. "I can almost see a pair of scissors cutting millions of pieces of cloth from an endless piece of fabric. It's a nice image." Cassie nodded.

"Do we have time to talk about the barefoot to Palestine image Iago's wife mentions?" Emelia asks dreamily. "That's a beautiful image." Rachel perks up when Emelia quotes that phrase.

"I'd like to talk about the dialogue between Emelia, Iago's wife, and Desdemona first," she smiles at the coincidence of the two Emelia's, "because it's a topic any two women could be discussing today while they're in a restaurant eating a salad or having tea, but we can interweave them both into tomorrow's discussion."

"Great," Elizabeth says, "because I love that line too; it contains such beautiful imagery."

Matt reacts playfully. "Beautiful imagery? I can't wait to hear this." Zach and Mason laugh. They know Matt's in trouble now. Elizabeth glares at him and he sinks into his seat.

Cassie crosses her arms and taps her foot. "Can we grow up now?"

The guys love it when she does that, but they calm down so she can continue.

"We'll start tomorrow into Thursday if we have to. Into Friday if we need additional time, because the topics are multi-faceted. We'll blend 'barefoot to Palestine' in with Desdemona's and Emelia's discussion about infidelity and it doesn't matter which topic comes first. We'll let it flow after we discuss what I definitely want to discuss first."

She pauses. "You *will* need research and a map, because I want to include more about the history I just mentioned. So make sure you know the locations of Venice, Cyprus, Rhodes, Turkey, Palestine and that whole region. Got it? Research, with a capital 'R'! Geography with a capital 'G'! That's tonight's assignment. Any quick questions?"

"There are no quick questions in this class," Connor retorts.

"Not usually, but it sure makes the class interesting, doesn't it? Anybody? Questions?" None. "Okay. See you tomorrow for another gut-wrenching episode of Othello the Moor, that naïve, trusting man who throws away the most precious gift a man can have."

"I have a quick question now, Mrs. Komsky," Mason asks, gathering his books, "What's the most precious gift a man can have?"

"A good wife, Mason. A good wife.

103

FEBRUARY 10, SPICE, SILK, & BAREFOOT TO PALESTINE

N
ext day, before class began, Cassie was at the board drawing lots of what looked like squiggly lines. Eleven students glanced at her as they walked in; then focused on what she continued to draw. Her 'artwork' took on the semblance of an area, then a region, then a very big region, until they realized she was drawing a map and recognized the coastline of China. As Cassie filled in the lines westward, they identified India, then Iran, Saudi Arabia, the Levant, into Turkey. She continued westward through the Mediterranean, past Italy and the European coastline, ending with England.

She stepped back and took a good look. Not bad, she thought, redrawing a few lines for Syria and Italy, making it more like a boot. Once completed to her satisfaction, she drew a solid red line for an overland route beginning with China, and a dotted blue line that crossed from the China Sea, through the Mediterranean, and up the

Adriatic. Chalk down. "Most of you, maybe all of you, can identify the countries outlined here. The important thing that relates to the dialogue we're discussing in *Othello* are the red and blue lines. Why? If you did some research, as I *strongly* suggested, you'd know."

All hands went up. She pointed to the blue line first. "Don't need hands. Just shout it out," and from everyone at the table, she heard, "Sea Route, blue line, spices; land route, red line - silk . . . and spices."

"Great. Now, before I ask a more specific question about these routes, name the major cities, countries or city-states I've drawn."

Jason identified Alexandria, Egypt, southern part of the Mediterranean Sea. Connor and Gloria located Venice, north coast of the Adriatic Sea, one of the two settings of *Othello*. Mason honed in on Cyprus, the main setting for the play; Zach found Rhodes. Parker identified Italy and India; Elizabeth located Genoa; Samir identified Arabia, Damascus, and Turkey; Rachel went around the coast of Spain and Portugal and stopped at England.

"Excellent!" Cassie exclaimed; I'm impressed. So, in relation to the scene we're discussing, we have the key players," she nodded. "But, we need one very important aspect regarding these two routes. Let's break these down. The land route, red line, along which silks were transported, this originated where?"

"China," Mason responded. "At the far right side of your *map*." He smiled and the class laughed. Cassie's drawing was good, but it did leave a lot to the imagination.

"Stop laughing," she feigned anger. "There was a reason I didn't major in fine arts." She traced the red line, Silk Road. Notice anything?" Nothing was forthcoming. She traced it again then traced the blue line, the Sea Route, which carried spices. "Think," she insisted. Nothing. "Okay, think math."

Think math? They muttered as Cassie traced them both simultaneously. "What is she talking about . . . ?"

"Point of intersection!" Rachel shouts, spontaneously and happily.

"Fantastic, Rachel. "Yes! And where is that point of intersection?"

"Damascus. Damascus is where the Spice Route and the Silk Road meet. Damascus is the heart of both trade routes leading to the Mediterranean, up the Adriatic Sea, then to Venice! I can see it clearly with your map." She hesitated. "It's really not that bad, Mrs. Komsky. They laughed. "Actually," Rachel countered, reproaching her classmates, "it's pretty good. But wait, I have a question . . . isn't Lebanon next to Damascus? How could Damascus lead to the sea when merchants had to go through Lebanon?"

"Very observant, Rachel." Cassie looked to Samir. "Samir, explain please?"

Samir nodded in respect. "Damascus no longer leads to the sea as a result of the direct intervention of British and French powers after World War 1. They divided Arab lands arbitrarily for their own interests and profit. Promises to Arab leaders were broken. France controlled Syria, the French Mandate, and in 1920, Lebanon was created from Syria. This blocked off the sea route Damascus once had during its glorious age of trade with China and Europe."

"So Damascus was important during the Middle Ages because it had access to the sea?" Elizabeth and Gloria ask.

Samir nodded. "Both trade routes – spices and silks, water and land, intersected at Damascus, as Rachel has observed." He smiled at her. "The Far East brought their goods to Damascus. Europe, the West, went to Damascus and brought them back. They met in the middle, the Middle East."

Mason followed. "It's easy when you explain it like that. It's also easy to understand when you see it on a map, and it is a pretty good map, Mrs. Komsky. I was just teasing before."

"I appreciate that," Cassie smiled. "If I can give it, I have to be able to take it. But, back to the map, and the spices and silks that followed. Trade between the East and the West was conducted for centuries, with Venice as the primary power until the Ottoman Turks conquered the Arabian Empire around 1450 and shut down Venice's source through heavy taxes the Ottomans imposed on merchandise headed for the West. The West wanted their spices, their cloves, cinnamon, pepper, and their silks, but they didn't want to pay those taxes. And as a result?"

"Portugal, Columbus, the discovery of America. He thought it was India," Zach answers. "He thought he had found a new trade route. Boy, was he wrong,"

"Money, power, trade. Anything change in five hundred years?" They shook they heads. "Nope," Cassie concluded, "Just the players. But, to get back to *Othello* and why or how Shakespeare would know about Palestine . . ."

"Because it's right below Damascus, where both trade routes intersect," Rachel completed the thought. A spark of the old Rachel was showing through.

"Exactly. So Shakespeare absolutely knew about the existence of Palestine in his history as did those who lived during and after the Renaissance, and he referenced Palestine both with the Egyptian Sybil, and, as Elizabeth commented, his poetic use of imagery. When Iago's Emelia tells Desdemona she knew a lady in Venice who would walk barefoot to Palestine for a touch of her lover's nether lip, Shakespeare's audience knew Palestine. This allowed him to reference Palestine and create a beautiful image showing the power of love.

"Look where Palestine's situated." Cassie points a little southwest of Damascus, the capital of Syria. "Look where Venice is situated." She traces her finger up the Adriatic Sea to the little nook in which Venice sits. "Look at the distance; the countries between Palestine and Venice. Think of the terrain, the sand, the heat, the sun. This would be an impossible trek. To walk across the Eastern shoreline of the Adriatic, through Greece into Turkey and down into Syria and then to Palestine? Now think of Emelia's, our Emilia's, appreciation for imagery. 'Barefoot to Palestine;' why does Shakespeare say 'barefoot' to Palestine? Close your eyes . . . what image do you see when you say or hear these words? Barefoot to Palestine; she'd walk barefoot to Palestine for a touch of his nether lip?"

Elizabeth, Emelia, Gloria and Rachel close their eyes. Smiles appear on their faces as Cassie describes the image that plays in her mind. "Imagine the desert, hot, dry, powerful sun beating down, pulsing heat, and in the midst of it all, a lone woman, dressed in long white garb from head to foot, face covered to protect against the broiling sun and gusting sand, walking step after step, barefooted, feet torn, burned, an impossible journey, plodding, plodding onward, never stopping. She'd die before she'd let herself stop, one bare foot in front of the other, never stopping until she reaches Palestine and her lover."

The ladies are too enraptured to break the spell and come back to reality. "And why is this woman walking barefoot to Palestine? What makes this woman attempt such an impossible and tortuous journey?"

Everyone is silent, quiet. The young men accede. They are quiet, submissive as they watch the young women imagining the beauty of a woman loving a man so much she would walk barefoot to Palestine, "For a touch of his nether lip," Rachel whispers.

Finally, after a lengthy silence, perhaps feeling uncomfortable, Parker breaks the trance. "Come on, Mrs. Komsky. Let's be realistic. No one would do that for someone they loved; no one *could* do that. It's impossible, physically impossible. They couldn't; they physically couldn't."

"It's the image, Parker, the image. Close your eyes and imagine the image, then ask yourself that question, 'Who would make that torturous journey for one delicate touch of her lover's nether lip'? What woman would love a man so much she would walk barefoot to Palestine for him?"

Parker was quiet. The men were quiet. The ladies, completely silent in their reverie.

Finally, the silence is broken. "I would," Rachel whispers as if it were a prayer, "for Samir. I would walk barefoot to Palestine for Samir."

104

Yesterday's barefoot to Palestine image dominated the discussion until it segued to infidelity, the topic Cassie had intended to talk about first, but, she was right, it did follow nicely. The question they struggled with now was how a woman who loved a man so much she'd walk barefoot to Palestine for him, be unfaithful.

Desdemona's answer was simply, she couldn't, even after Othello had treated her horribly. She loves him despite his cruelty, despite Emelia wishing Desdemona had never met him. But Desdemona doesn't believe any woman could be unfaithful and asks Emelia if she thinks there are women who could be. Of course there are, Emelia says, no question about it. Even knowing that, Desdemona stands firm; she would never be unfaithful to Othello for all the world.

The class picks up the discussion with Iago's Emelia proposing that, if you could get the whole world as payment, why not? Be unfaithful, earn the whole world, your prize, and once you have it, undo the wrong you've done. You can change any wrong and make it a right once you control the world.

"At least she puts a high price on infidelity," Gloria comments. "It's what you can get for it that makes it worthwhile."

Elizabeth disagrees. Cheating for all the world goes way beyond a discussion about infidelity. It's about power and changing ethics, not cheating for pleasure or revenge."

"Expound a little more, Elizabeth." Cassie wants to see more cause and effect.

"Emelia, Iago's Emelia, says cheating on your husband is a small price to pay to earn the world. If you controlled the world, you could do anything. You could make wrong right and right wrong. That goes way beyond being unfaithful just to cheat on your spouse. 'Who would not make her husband a cuckold to make him a monarch - to be a king, a ruler, or a monarch?' Emelia says this near the end of act 4, scene 3. That statement is pretty profound, and it's scary."

They're all thinking now. What Elizabeth has said did go way beyond infidelity; it was the universal might makes right mantra. If you had power, you could have one set of morals when it suited you, another set when it didn't. "You can do whatever you want once you control the world," Mason says, "whether it's infidelity, theft or murder. People would do a lot more for a lot less, but anything, wrong or right, becomes right if you rule."

"You think power makes anything right?" Rachel responds. She was thinking about her father and the power he was wielding to hurt her and Samir.

"I'm not saying I'd do this. I'm saying you would have the power to do this." Mason defends his position. "Iago's wife says a wrong is only a wrong in *this* world. If you got the whole world for your deed, if that was your reward, you could make the wrong a right; you could *change* what's considered wrong today."

"Then you wouldn't have 'this' world," Rachel rebuked. "You'd have another world, where *our* morals and *our* ethics no longer mattered. You'd have a world where all morals could change at the whim of the ruler. What would happen to mantras like "Do unto others as you would have them do unto you," or moral absolutes like the Ten Commandments?"

Rachel was thinking like Cassie. Wrong is only wrong until you can change it. If you got the ultimate power, you could make the wrong a right. People in power today were doing that; Vaughn and Joel Greer were doing the same thing in their world; our government was doing whatever it wanted in the Middle East because they had the power. All of it being done because those who had the power . . . had the power.

That's why she had lost Brian; that's why so many other wives and children lost their husbands and fathers. It was an upside-down immoral world, starting at the top, and transcending so much more than sexual immorality. People who made decisions based on ethics and morality in a world that eschewed them became the weird ones;

they became the prey. Ultimately, they were doomed. Rachel's comment said it perfectly, from Shakespeare to the present and into the future, it was true.

"Guess Shakespeare had no idea how profound this concept could be," Zach reflected, bringing Cassie back to the discussion between Desdemona and Emelia.

Cassie shakes off her thoughts and tilts her head. "Sure about that? Maybe he knew *exactly* how profound this concept was in his world, just as it is in ours. Maybe that's why he wrote this scene. In fact, a perfect example is *Measure for Measure* which he wrote shortly before *Othello*, which we might read next, but you read the abstract last year. What's the theme of that play?"

"It's a quid pro quo. I'll release your brother from his death sentence for fornication if you'll fornicate with me." Good answer from Jason.

"Well, there you have it. Way back at the turn of the 1600's, when the duke of Vienna chooses Angelo to replace him in his absence. New ruler, new rules, *his* rules, and he'll do exactly as he pleases. He's just changed morality to suit himself."

They thought long, intently. "Yeah," Parker adds casually, but follows with, "that's why humanity has to have a higher moral code, so humanity doesn't change just because our ruler changes. We're all fallible; we can all be tempted by something we want, something lustful, like Roderigo with Desdemona. Look at what he did when he thought he could get her. He knew he was wrong, but he did it anyway to get what he wanted." Parker looks at Cassie for confirmation. His analysis is perfect. Look what Vaughn had done to punish and control her, and he could because he ruled.

She nodded. "When you start turning morals upside down or chipping away at them, it works like a drug, especially if you're successful the first few times; then you're hooked and it's hard to get off." She became quiet and pensive again, thinking of Vaughn when she shouldn't have; thinking of his absolute power, and thinking of Brian and the powers that sent him off to a war from which he never returned. "Sometimes the only way we get off is to leave; sometimes that doesn't even work. Sometimes it doesn't end until we die." She almost chuckled at that thought, but it was a stifled chuckle, a sad one, filled with sorrow and suppression of tears.

The class sensed her withdrawal. They sensed how far away her thoughts had wandered and wondered where she had gone. Why had she said that? What little cubby did Mrs. Komsky hide in when her problems surfaced and bubbled over? If Shakespeare had taught them anything it was that we're all human, them, at their stage of life, and their teacher at hers. What did this person who seemed to devote herself to all of them and her daughter do when the world fell in on her? And how badly had her world ever fallen in on her?

"Mrs. Komsky," Gloria's shaky voice permeated the silence of Cassie's hideaway. "Why aren't you married anymore?"

Samir gasped! Rachel looked at him, startled; he had never told her what had happened to Cassie's husband. He looked at Gloria and shook his head trying to warn her off. No, no, he indicated with his eye contact and facial expression. Do not ask her that; take back that question, take back that question.   Tuesday's question about the handkerchief was nothing compared to this.

Cassie watched him with sadness, this fine young man who had suffered so much, trying to protect her, trying to protect her from her world of sorrow. She watched the others watch Samir with consternation.   Yes, Gloria had asked a personal question and she shouldn't have, but to her, what could have been so bad? They could never have imagined.

Cassie waved him off gently. "It's okay Samir. It was a momentary lapse into my past, into my sorrow. I should not have succumbed. But I'll answer the question. Maybe I should have included it when Matt asked me how I'd feel if my husband had given me the handkerchief Othello had given Desdemona.   Maybe I should have, but I didn't. I ask you to dig deep and you all respond; no reason why I shouldn't do the same every once in a while, especially when it relates to our discussions."

She inhaled deeply and began. "You all know I corrected Parker during my first class when he told me I was pronouncing Samir's last name incorrectly." She looked at Parker and smiled. He returned her smile with sincere affection. "Well, the reason I knew how to pronounce 'Gibran' correctly is because I am an Arab. Most of you do not know this; I sure don't fit the stereotype, but I am, and Samir knows.   He knows this because I spoke to him in Arabic when I first saw him at the Homecoming game. So, Samir and I have something personal in common."

They took furtive glances at each other. They had never considered this, but it made sense.

"Samir and I also share beliefs regarding Israel's invasion of Lebanon and its take-over of Palestinian lands. Aside from the political aspects of that invasion, the Palestinian situation gave us our second personal aspect, the one that hurts, because this invasion answers Gloria's question." Her chin fell to her chest and tears actually fell. Tears she didn't try to conceal or hide.

"One of the horrific outcomes of Israel's occupation of Palestinian lands sent its people to Lebanon, which encamped PLO fighters there and disrupted that country's political balance. Lebanon's president asked America for military help. We went in with a multinational force, but after thousands of civilians were killed, certain factions no longer welcomed us. Because of this, our Embassy in Lebanon was bombed. Sadly and bravely, Samir has told you his parents were killed there." Samir is visibly distraught. Rachel places her hand over Samir's.

"A horrible, senseless tragedy left him an orphan and changed his life forever." Cassie inhales deeply. "This is where Samir's life and my life are inextricably linked, because," she gulped, "because my husband, Stevie's father, was a Marine, and six months after our embassy was bombed, our Marine barracks were bombed. That's where my husband was stationed; that's where he was blown apart." She was choking with tears now. "My husband . . . his name was Brian . . . was killed there. Stevie was four, and I . . . I was a lifetime younger."

No one moved, not a finger, or an eyelid, stillness engulfed the room. Cassie retreated to her world far away.

Wherever they had imagined she had wandered mentally, they could never have imagined this. Finally, her voice quivering, she spoke, sorrow in every word. "I will not be here much longer. You may have heard rumors. Certain things are beyond my control, as Othello has shown us, as we've discussed many times. The powerful make the rules, and we are but pawns in the game." She tried to smile; nothing surfaced.

"But I want you all to know, should I not get another opportunity, that I will never forget you. You are the most beautiful, the kindest, the most courageous young men and women I have ever known and I will miss you dearly, for the rest of my life."

She glanced at her watch while they remained seated like stone pillars. "Go," she motioned softly with a tilt of her head, "class time is almost over. Take a few minutes for yourselves. See you tomorrow, and I'll be the same teacher you've known me to be, so no easy-on-the-teacher attitude. I can still beat your butts."

Samir led the group. He stood up, nodded in respect, took Rachel's hand, and led her out. The rest of the class followed, not knowing what else to do. There was nothing else they could do. It was time to go; time to leave Cassie to her own thoughts before her next class came in. This class for her, for all her lifetime, would be enough. Thursday ended.

105

"We got sidetracked yesterday." She was weary and her eyes were puffy, evidence she had been up much of the night crying. "I'm sorry; I'll try never to do that again. We did discuss 'might makes right' changing the rules; so let's go to the dialogue where Emelia justifies the reasons why a wife would cheat on her husband; then we'll go on to act 5, scenes 1 and 2.

"Emelia says a woman is equal to a man in senses, desires, feelings, sport, frailties, etc, so if he's going to treat her unkindly, she would be justified in being unfaithful to him for revenge, she adds. Do you agree ladies? Gentlemen?"

No one responded. They weren't there. Mentally and emotionally, they simply weren't there. They were having trouble with the question; actually, they were having trouble being their old selves. Cassie's revealing something so personal and painful about her husband had changed them in some way, in some strange way they couldn't put into words, but they weren't the same people they had been twenty-four hours ago.

Their phones had rung all night. They had talked all night. These eleven students had developed more than a bond between themselves and their teacher, and more than a bond amongst each other. They were no longer a group of isolated individuals sitting in a Shakespeare class, taking notes, answering questions, or commenting on something that had happened in a scene here or a scene there. They had become one cohesive unit; in some ways they now thought the same thoughts and felt the same feelings. Cassie's revelation had brought them together in a way they had never experienced, and they all shared and experienced the same heartbreaking emotions.

The young men had talked for hours in their dorm amidst periods of silence when they didn't talk at all. They had started in the game room where they could get lost in ping pong or an arcade game; then they headed to their rooms as night fell, drank cokes and talked more. Mason stayed overnight with Parker and slept on the floor; he couldn't pull himself away and go home. In the morning, he wore Parker's clean clothes. Samir had remained in his room alone until Matt and Connor had come in and pulled him into Parker's room where all seven of them, even Jason, had settled in for the night. Each expressed his grief in his own way, Samir mostly through reticence. Not one of them asked him why he had never disclosed this. They knew he never could, never would; he was the most trustworthy friend they had ever known, and yes, they called him friend. They had for a long time.

Parker reflected in his own personal way. What he had come to see in Mrs. Komsky was a teacher, a person, a human being, a kind human being who cared so much about others that she put her feelings aside for them. He thought of all she had done for Rachel and Samir, while all he, Parker, had done for years was think of himself and what he had wanted, materialistic things, gotten with the money and power of being an Otis-Barrett. He was glad this teacher had come into his life. He was realizing more and more that life was not all about him, and he felt satisfaction that he had followed his gut and reached out to his aunt when Mrs. Komsky had asked. He wished he could have done more.

Mason, that shock of red hair kid who had appreciated his teacher's compliment from the first week in class, loved her wit and had begun studying Latin roots and prefixes and the dictionary because of Cassie and her daughter. He had blossomed and matured so much mentally, along with the additional inch or two he had grown in the past few months. He was now almost as tall as Parker. He had confided his sadness in Parker and both wondered what kind of a hell this life and its power-people were all about.

Connor and Matt, the other two who had helped bring Cassie in from the cold, had melded with Parker and Mason and had become a unit ever since they had carried her lifeless body back to warmth. Cassie's revelation this morning had cemented their bond even more. Their respect and admiration for Mrs. Komsky had soared after yesterday's class, and it had been pretty high after she had risked her life for Samir because they knew she had placed him above herself, even though it had been a foolish thing to do in the midst of a storm. But after yesterday they understood why. She and Samir would always have Lebanon. That country was their nucleus and it magnetically kept them in each other's sphere.

Jason was with them. Jason, the nerdy kid who had found his confidence because Mrs. Komsky had encouraged him and urged him on, the kid who now had a friend he trusted in Connor. He had left his room to seek out Connor, but he didn't have to – Connor had been heading in his direction to drag him out, just in case Jason had felt a residue of shy. There was no need, they all would have dragged him into their room if he had stayed away too long. Connor was the first student Jason had come to call friend. Now there were five more; for him, they had all become friends.

The ladies dealt with Cassie's revelation in their own way. They had talked and cried and passed around boxes of tissues, balling one after the other into tight wads, then tossing them into the waste basket. Elizabeth and Emelia had begun in their individual rooms until they converged in Rachel's and Gloria's room. After all the discussions they had had in class, all the times Mrs. Komsky had shared life's philosophy and encouraged them to get up and go on after hardships, they had never imagined she could have experienced something as horrific as this and had actually gotten up and gone on, day after day for the rest of her life. Their problems were insignificant and paled in comparison to hers.

Emelia, the feisty outspoken young lady with dirty-blond hair and blue eyes, whose posture jumped up at you whenever she spoke, and who either responded perceptively or didn't respond at all, concluded that Othello and Hamlet had nothing on their teacher. Their lives were no more horrific than Cassie's or Samir's; they just didn't realize it because they hadn't known. Nobody confides in people about experiences they've suffered unless they've come to trust. And that was the happy part, if any, because Emelia, almost as shy as Jason at first except for her candor, now trusted. She trusted her friends and Mrs. Komsky, and the most beautiful thing was that Cassie trusted them, or she would never have revealed her secret.

Elizabeth amazed herself; she had grown up more in the four months since Cassie had arrived at Chelsea than she had in her prior eighteen years. When she had turned eighteen in August, she had thought she was pretty profound. She thought she had seen just about everything there was to see, and that she couldn't possibly learn much more than she had already known. But after this class and after Mrs. Komsky told them about her husband, Elizabeth realized she didn't know much at all. Elizabeth had come to realize how little she knew about life, and that she was just a tiny speck in the universe. Weren't we all, just specks in the universe? We don't know it until we get older or until something really traumatic happens to us or to someone we really care about.

"I've been beating myself up and feeling sorry for myself since my mom and dad got divorced," Gloria said teary-eyed, her face was almost as red as her swollen eyes and her red hair. "I've thought of myself as the deserted and unloved daughter who deserved pity, but look at what Mrs. Komsky has lived with for the past four years, and I've never seen a poor-me attitude from her. And Stevie, look at Stevie, losing her father at four. How do you explain to a four-year-old you'll never see your father again because he got blown up in a terrorist attack in some far-away country we never had to be in. That little girl will never see her father again, a father who loved her. Mine didn't love me enough to stay; hers did. He just couldn't come home again. How sad."

Rachel had beaten herself up too. Samir had never told her about Mrs. Komsky's husband. Now she understood why. It was something they alone shared, and unless something had made it surface in its own way, its own time, it wasn't something Samir should have revealed.

But now that it had surfaced, now that she did know what Mrs. Komsky had experienced, she couldn't imagine the horror her teacher had lived with and would continue to live with for the rest of her life. Rachel thought of Stevie too. Stevie wanted to see her father again but never would, while Rachel still had a father who she never wanted to see again. Mrs. Komsky was right; Shakespeare was right. Some things you can't control. You just have to go on and the end will resolve itself. That's what Mrs. Komsky was doing; that's what Rachel would have to do. "I can't imagine the kind of hell she experiences day after day; yet she helps me and thinks of me first while she goes through all this?"

"Maybe that's why she can, Rachel, because she's gone through all this."

And then there was Samir, always Samir. Cassie adored Samir; at first the empathy drew them together like magnets, but as she had come to know him and as he had come to know her, she had become the mother he had lost. No one had ever cared about him, not since his parents had died, the way Cassie had cared about him. He thought of the football game, where she first spoke to him, and in Arabic. She had braved his rejection when she had first come to his room and left him the Khalil Gibran quote; she had confided in him about Brian when he shouldn't have asked, and she had risked her life to look for him in that horrific snowstorm when he had sneaked out to be with Rachel.

Everything she had done for him and then for him and Rachel. And now she had revealed her pain and her tragedy to the class, and she had told them she would be leaving soon. He knew it would be very soon, any day, any day they'd come in and she would be gone. He was certain he knew why, but it was just another example of might makes right, and those in power who can change the rules.

He hadn't allowed himself to think of his parents for so long; he had shut himself away from that devastating day in his life when his uncle had searched him out to give him the horrible news. So much hatred, so many innocent lives destroyed, and now, this one person who had been his salvation, his and Rachel's, the woman he loved and had married, was leaving; she was leaving with the pain of loss ever present. Her pain would never leave; neither would his.

Maybe it was good she had told the class. Maybe there was some good in their having seen her pain, felt her inexplicable loss because of something uncontrollable, because people with power surgically signed edicts of war that sent people to their deaths – husbands, fathers, mothers, children, all dead. Would it ever change? Involuntarily, he shook his head.

After Rachel had talked with the ladies, she had called Samir, the man she'd walk barefoot to Palestine for. No doubt, she'd love him until she died. They had talked into early morning about Mrs. Komsky's tragedy, their sadness and their future. In the end, their resolve was Cassie's resolve: We pick ourselves up and move on because there's nothing else we can do, until the end.

And that was the aura, the specter in which eleven students had left class yesterday, and the specter they had walked in with this morning. They could not extricate that haunting specter from their minds or continue their discussion about infidelity or if it mattered whether wives had the same senses for sweet and sour, or the same desires or frailties, or the same sport as men. They simply could not respond.

Cassie just about bit her tongue and spoke. "Let's talk," she said candidly, hoping her old casual self would bring back their happy personas. "I am sorry I let my feelings take over my professionalism. I should never have told you about my life and why I don't have a husband, even though . . ."

"We're not, Mrs. Komsky," Parker's determination interrupted her. "Don't be sorry. You made us think about other people and other problems apart from our own. We know people get hurt all the time, but I never imagined it could have been so bad. Samir telling us about his parents was bad enough: Who here can ever imagine that? And now you've confirmed it can happen to people we think are living life just like us, only they're not. Don't apologize, Mrs Komsky. You've given us the best all-nighter we've ever had."

They looked at each other and smiled. Cassie looked at them, puzzled. "You mean you've all been up all night?"

They nodded; Gloria and Elizabeth yawned. I sure could use a cup of coffee," Gloria added, her strawberry blond curls covering her eyes. How could she even see through all those fringes?

"Seriously?"

They nodded again. Cassie replied spontaneously, "Well, then let's go get one." They perked up and looked at her skeptically. Was she okay? "Come on, collect your things, put on your coats; let's go get a second breakfast, or first for some of you." The class hesitated; then Mason began collecting his things. Everyone followed his lead. Cassie looked at Rachel. If she were still having trouble with food, it wasn't from depression. Rachel wondered if Mrs. Komsky suspected. She herself hadn't been certain until yesterday afternoon and, after Mrs. Komsky's announcement, it was not the evening to tell Samir.

"We'll start the last act in Langley Hall. It won't be Homecoming, but it'll be just as memorable."

That's what they did. Eleven seniors and their teacher converged on the cafeteria and staff, who had stopped serving breakfast, but not for them. Suddenly more pancakes appeared in the trays, more scrambled eggs and more bacon. They carried heaping platters and steaming cups of coffee to one of the long tables in their section, passed around cream and sugar, and pulled out their books. Zach had found a lone bagel in the bread basket. Mason and Parker had asked for buttered hard rolls while they were devouring a huge plate of pancakes, with side plates of bacon and eggs.

How could they eat so much? Where did it all go? Elizabeth gave Matt a penetrating glare when he got up to get a second plate. He sat down immediately. According to her, one high stack of pancakes, with a side plate overflowing with bacon and eggs was enough, but her criticism had been issued with deep affection and Matt sure didn't mind. Surprisingly, Gloria and Zach sat together, with signs of warm camaraderie. For Gloria, that was a major step.

They ate; sipped hot coffee and talked about Shakespeare, Othello, Desdemona, Iago's wife defending Desdemona, too late though, and the incubus of the handkerchief, that ever present handkerchief. By the time class ended, their spirits had returned. They were good to go.

As they all packed up and started out, Cassie called after them. "Have a great weekend everyone."

"I should," Parker called back. "It's my aunt's 25th anniversary gala.

"Oh, I didn't know," Cassie responded. "She never mentioned it."

"It's a surprise, Mrs. Komsky. She's not supposed to know."

"Then after she does know, congratulate her for me. Tell her I hope she has a wonderful night."

106

S aturday morning refreshed the Chelsea campus with bright sunshine and temperatures unseasonably warm for a February day. By 8:00 a.m., the thermometer read in the low forty's, climbing steadily to the high forty's, low fifty's. Most kids had abandoned coats and hats for a sweatshirt, relieved to be rid of heavy clothing, even for a day. Kids walked to or from breakfast slowly, strolled leisurely from dorm to dorm, lingered under still-leafless trees, visited classmates, headed to the library or gym, or walked for the exercise. This day was the harbinger of spring.

Cassie watched from her kitchen window while frying eggs and guarding toast so it would not burn. As always, a bowl of fruit topped with yogurt sat on the table. Today it was bananas; usually it was apples. In the summer it would be strawberries, blueberries, or diced cantaloupe. She smiled as couples passed her window walking hand in hand.

Rebecca's on-campus birthday party was tonight, and the dorm had become electrified. Her family birthday party was tomorrow in some exquisitely posh place in Short Hills, but tonight would be a sleep-over for eleven girls, all stuffed into Rebecca's and Stacy's room on the second floor, and one of the eleven would be Stevie. She was excited.

Of course, the dorm's head mistress, Cassie, had to approve this, and she had. According to the regulation handbook, lights-out on weekends for freshman was 10:30, but Cassie wasn't expecting anything close to that. The girls had ordered pizza scheduled for a 10:30 delivery and Cassie would have to unlock the doors to accept it. 10:30, no one eats pizza at 10:30 unless they intend to stay up until 12:00, at the least. Cassie would not be surprised if the girls yakked until 2:00 or 3:00, or if they got any sleep at all. But Stevie had instructions to be downstairs by 12:00 at the very latest. Cassie would be waiting up; she'd listen to her tell her all about the party when she got in, every word.

After breakfast, mother and daughter headed to the mall. Stevie bought a new pair of jeans at Old Navy; then they bought a gift certificate for Rebecca at Tres Chique. She'd like that. But the best part was for Cassie. As they passed Bayber's Jewelers, she spied a scarab bracelet displayed in a case too close to the window to ignore. It was reminiscent of a bracelet her mother had given her one Christmas when she was young. The stones hadn't been set in gold, as these were, but it had been special to her. In the frenzy of her mom's passing and that crazy time of being displaced, it had been lost. Cassie never saw it again, and she had always missed it. This one would never be the one her mother had given her, but it would remind her of her mom whenever it was on her wrist.

She walked in to have a closer look and walked out with the bracelet on her wrist. The price tag took her back a bit, actually it took her back a lot, but the jeweler negotiated it down and it was a done deal. For the memories, it was worth the money. Its sturdy clasp was a lobster-claw, holding five pastel-colored scarabs each set in ten-carat gold, one pink, one pale turquoise, a tiger-eye, a fourth that was light gold, and the fifth, pale blue-green. Beautiful colors. Stevie loved it too, so it would be a great hand-me-down for her.

Shopping finished, they headed home for a late lunch. By 2:00, they were starving. Cassie diced fresh chicken over a bed of baby lettuce, added chopped onions, chick peas, half a tomato and avocado, drizzled it with extra virgin olive oil and apple cider vinegar. Cassie had a lunch she could eat any day of the week. Stevie had peanut butter and raspberry jelly.

The afternoon passed; Cassie put some last minute touches on her lessons, and speculated about beginning *Macbeth* after *Othello* instead of *Measure for Measure*. *Macbeth* might be easier for a new teacher; maybe a lighter discussion would be a better. *Macbeth* was also an easier play to read, at least to her. Maybe the kids would think so too. The guys would love the witches, their prophesies and the bloodshed, and the ladies would have lots to talk about when Lady Macbeth tries washing out that damned spot. More discussion about morality and fornication for a quid pro quo, as Jason had described *Measure for Measure*, might be a little much.

But she wouldn't be here for either play. All she'd have time for would be an introduction. She had two weeks to go before the movers would whisk her away, as though she had never been here. Just a speck of dust in the universe. Yeah, let's do *Macbeth*, she thought, as I watch each day creep in this petty pace to the last syllable of recorded time.

107

SATURDAY EVENING, FEBRUARY 13, TWO PARTIES TURN BAD

Arthur held the door open for his Miss Hillary and Mister Brett. Her 25th anniversary celebration would begin in less than an hour and it was to be the night of nights. A surprise - yes, no? Hillary had an idea something was going on because Brett had been slipping away more evenings than usual, using excuses that Vaughn needed advice about family business, or his will, or getting back into the partnership, as if Vaughn would ever want that. But after learning what he had done to Cassie, Hillary wondered if there wasn't some truth in that, although none of that needed 'slipping away.'

She dressed for the evening with total ennui, checking her look without a hint of enthusiasm. Although stunning in her black silk dress, peplum waist, hand-painted with silver fronds and leaves around its border, all she thought about now, all she had thought about for over a week, were Rachel and Cassie, and how Rachel would make it through each day when Cassie, because of her cowardly brother-in-law, was no longer there. No one would have been able to stay after Vaughn's perverted assault, but would Rachel be able to transition from Cassie to her smoothly? Hillary said a little prayer all would work out well, but deep inside, she felt as though God would be testing her again.

Daytime had been unusually warm for February, but the evening had turned cooler. Bring a coat, she thought. She threw on a sable jacket before heading to the limo and thanked Arthur as he opened the door. They passed Chelsea and sped through contiguous towns. Arthur never crawled to his destination unless Miss Hillary told him to slow down. To Arthur, red meant stop; green meant go; and yellow meant go faster, and he was never inhibited about doing that. He had been her driver for more than two decades, and both had a professional affection for each other, but he held no special loyalty to Brett. Brett's destinations took him to places and people Arthur cared not to know, proving 'discreet' was only a word. But tonight was Hillary's night, a twenty-five year remembrance of the day she and Brett had said "I do," and Arthur swelled with affection for her, and pride that he was her driver.

One stop to get Vaughn and Taylor, whose all silver-beaded, V-neck showed so much cleavage its spaghetti straps were working overtime to hold everything up and in; then they were on their way. Parker would follow in his own car. If Hillary had known he was home for the weekend, she would have suspected something, since football and friends kept Parker firmly entrenched at Chelsea.

But his aunt's celebration took precedence this weekend. Seeing his aunt and his grandmother, whom he adored, would certainly bring him home. Just in case there was a little too much family for him to endure the entire evening, he'd take his own car. He'd get to the Club well before everyone yelled surprise, most likely get his grandmother, and be able to leave whenever he wanted.

The Otis-Barrett limo arrived at the Club five minutes early. As they pulled into the queue, Trevor Staur's Bentley was blocking everyone else as he searched his car for who knows what that had fallen who knows where. The poor guy had to listen to his wife's harangue for not having taken the limo instead of driving in this plebian fashion, but true to his word, he was holding firm, searching the front, then the back for some obscure item only he could have devised. As soon as the Otis-Barrett limo spun out of the queue and headed for the garage, he miraculously 'found' whatever it was and turned his car over to the valet. His part was done and he had played it well. Taylor would thank him profusely for that.

Everything moved along as planned. Elevator 'up' to the dining hall, ordering light, at least three of them had, two hours later, elevator 'down,' nothing special for Hillary, Brett's wallet forgotten in the cloak room, and it was elevator up again, passing the dining hall inadvertently to the second floor, to open doors and a deafening 'surprise!' Hillary's reverie and her state of ennui shattered.

Everyone she had remembered throughout her life stood as one monolithic memorable collage. Everyone from private elementary school, to riding, golf, and tennis lessons, piano and flute concerts, through college, from monthly cruises and the Club, seemed to be here. Was everyone she had ever met with, lunched with, confided in since boarding school, here? It was all a blur. Parker, escorting his grandmother, emerged from the crowd and gave Hillary the tightest hug. What a surprise! He had come home for this. Hillary would be forever grateful to him for having encouraged her to call Cassie. He would never know how much it had meant to her. She planted a kiss on his cheek and returned his hug. Then she embraced her mother-in-law, Muriel, matriarch of the Otis-Barrett clan. Muriel and Parker were the best part of the Otis-Barretts and she loved them both deeply.

Brett escorted his wife, still shaky from the ebullience of it all, from table to table, group to group. She stopped at each to talk to people she had lost touch with as she had steadily withdrawn over the years, but they were here, all here to welcome her and offer their admiration and congratulations. Veronica and Stacy, ensconced close to the head table since they had played such a pivotal role in bringing this celebration to fruition, were radiant. They had shunned dates, devoting all their attention to their dear friend. They loved Hillary and were so happy Brett acknowledged their assistance in making the night a success.

As Hillary greeted each table and moved on to the next, guests dispersed to eat, drink and dance. Three, maybe four tables to go, then two and now the last, where Hillary squelched a gasp. Joel Greer, Dr. Joel Greer and his wife stood ready to greet her with proper decorum. Joel Greer, of all people, was certainly not her friend. Which of the Otis-Barrett brothers had invited him? Her obsequious brother-in-law? Only Vaughn would use her anniversary celebration to ingratiate himself with that disgusting man, especially after she had told Vaughn both he and Greer were despicable, or had Greer's invitation been mailed by then? Ironic though, Vaughn's money could have bought the entire institution outright. He didn't need to be gratuitous to such a monster.

"Dr. Greer," Hillary said politely, "I am surprised you were able to attend my anniversary celebration." He nodded affably, either not recognizing or acknowledging Hillary's omission of 'honored.' "Am I correct that both your daughters attend Chelsea and are doing exceptionally well?" He blanched. "Such a distinct honor, to know they're doing so well in an institution that opened its doors to women only six months ago. You must be so proud."

"Thank you," he replied stiffly, "I am; we are," he turned to his wife who remained mute.

The sight of Greer turned Hillary's stomach. Her conversations with Cassie and Rachel were assaulting her head on. Everything Rachel had said about her father's hatred towards Samir and the attack with the poker iron reverberated in her mind. This was the man who was throwing away the children and the family Hillary had never had. She shuddered at the thought and fought back tears. Keep the past in the past, she admonished herself, but Greer's presence had brought it all into the present.

Hillary excused herself politely, and tried to mingle with other guests, but the glamour had waned. She extricated herself from the crowds and walked directly to the head table for quiet time. How could this man disown his daughter because he hated all Arabs? He should have gotten down on his knees and thanked God he had her, her and her sister, two examples of everything a parent could do right. He had let hatred destroy it.

Hillary walked to her table without pausing for shrimp, lobster, or caviar, her favorite, or for paper thin slices of fillet mignon or Nova Scotia salmon. On any other evening, she would have speared a few strawberries and drizzled them under liquid dark chocolate. Joel Greer's presence had zoomed in on Cassie's and Rachel's problems. Hillary needed some alone time to think, but here, with over four hundred guests? Either that, or . . . leave? She spied Muriel sitting alone at the head table. Muriel was not only kind and compassionate, qualities she did not pass on to her sons, but Hillary could think in Muriel's presence.

She headed in Muriel's direction while the orchestra was magnetically drawing everyone onto the dance floor. They had begun with the 40's for all the swingers still alive and able to kick up their heels and were now honing in on the 50's and 60's. Any 50's group that expected respect had to have a fantastic sax player, and this band had one of the best Hillary had ever heard. Hillary thought of Cassie and how she had moved with the music at the faculty Christmas party. Cassie would have devoured this group.

As dinner was served, Hillary sat quietly and lost herself in her own thoughts. She could hardly eat a thing. Had she not been brought up in high society, she would have asked for a doggie bag and taken her dinner home.

"Having fun Darling?" Brett asked, turning to her with a broad smile. Without a doubt, he had surprised her completely, despite Vaughn and Taylor saying it couldn't be done. Now, knowing he had pulled it off gave him bragging rights to an indisputable victory. He was more bombastic than usual.

Hillary nodded politely. Brett's ego centered on putting another feather in his cap and getting another accolade. He loved the attention Hillary was getting, but even more, he loved the attention he was getting for having achieved his goal. But even if he hadn't surprised her, he wouldn't have lost – not with his side benefit being Taylor. He was looking forward to more of those benefits tonight.

Dinner over, the orchestra picked up the tempo and moved into the 80's. Brett pulled Taylor onto the dance floor leaving Hillary to watch the show. Brett and Taylor always danced together at the Club, but for some reason it bothered Hillary tonight. Maybe it was because it was her evening; maybe it was because there was something so flagrant about the two of them. Maybe it was because Joel Greer, the last person she had ever expected or wanted to see, had been invited. Blame it on anything, but suddenly she didn't want to be here.

She felt sad and empty, and she wished she were home. She would have preferred being in a condo on Chelsea's grounds talking with a Shakespeare teacher she knew was sincere, or sitting with a young eighteen-year-old woman who was light years away from a father she had believed in, a father who was here, when he should have been there. Wherever it was Hillary had wanted to be, it was anywhere but here.

Sensing Hillary's discomfort, Muriel leaned over, "My sons can be jerks, sometimes."

She said it so casually that Hillary laughed out loud, so hard her stomach hurt. Thinking she was having a wonderful time, Veronica and Sharon came over and hugged her.

"We are so happy for you, Hillary," Veronica said. Sharon nodded. "You are the nicest person we have ever known. We wish you would come out with us sometime, for lunch or a play. We miss you; that's why we would never have missed this, and we are so thankful Brett and Taylor brought us in on the planning. They did an outstanding job."

"Yes, an outstanding job," she mused. "Maybe . . . maybe I should start getting out again."

"You certainly should. We'll call you, Hillary. We'll drag you out." Veronica preened. "Come on, Sharon, let's hit the dance floor."

"You should Hillary," Muriel concurred. "You should go out with them." Muriel sometimes wondered why Hillary had married Brett. Hillary was a beauty in her own right. When she was young, she was very reserved, modest and classy, a little self-indulged, but not even close to the young ladies Brett had dated before honing in on her.

Muriel had been ecstatic when Hillary accepted Brett's proposal, but as years went by, she realized Hillary had deserved better. Having a son that was too good looking to be away from the ladies had always disturbed her, but to cheat on Hillary with his sister-in-law was insufferable. It was low-class; it was reprehensible. Hillary should have dumped him decades ago.

A sister-in-law who would do that was not worthy of respect. She certainly was not worthy of Muriel's. Sex for money had been Taylor's goal. She had wanted the 'whole world' as in *Othello*, and she would have gotten it had it not been for the iron clad pre-nuptial Muriel had insisted upon. Had Taylor not agreed, Muriel would have cut Vaughn out of her will. This left Taylor with claws into half of Vaughn's personal millions, but the Otis-Barrett dynasty would be out of her grasp.

"You're too good for him," Muriel whispered, shocking Hillary. Why had she said that? What did she know? And if she did know, then others knew too? And all these years, Hillary had remained silent to keep a semblance of propriety in the family. Muriel leaned over and gave her daughter-in-law a hug, a very tight hug and Hillary began to cry.

"Muriel, I don't want this lifestyle anymore," Hillary confessed. "I want to be with real people who care about me because I'm me, one or two people who didn't attend this event because my last name is Otis-Barrett."

Muriel hugged her tighter. "Then go find them, or go be with them if you already have, because that's the real wealth in life."

The evening was passing quickly. Time moves on its belly while you're waiting for a special event; once it's here, four or five hours evaporate like vapor, leaving you wondering if the event had ever happened at all. Hillary's gala was just like that. By midnight, the cake had been cut and doors opened to a Venetian table and every confection imaginable. The orchestra would be playing until two, held over longer if guests desired.

Hillary thought about Muriel's words, her encouragement, her spirit, and watched the entire evening dance around her. She shivered. She needed her coat or another hot cup of coffee. Hell with sleeping tonight. But where was Brett? She scanned the horizon. Women and men in formal attire were dancing their hearts out on that capacious floor, but no Brett, and no Taylor.

At this point, Hillary's teeth were close to chattering. She motioned to the wait staff for coffee and they poured the steaming liquid into her cup, and a second cup on the side. Vaughn and Parker appeared just at that moment. "Parker, please be a dear and get my jacket. It's my black sable." She fumbled in her purse and handed Parker her coat check stub. He was off in a flash. "If this ballroom's maiden voyage is tonight, either the air conditioning or the heat is malfunctioning."

"Maybe you should dance a little, Hillary; then you won't be so cold." Vaughn searched the dance floor. "I don't see Brett . . . I don't see Taylor either."

Neither of them noticed the expression on Muriel's face. "You go Vaughn. Don't let Parker get Hillary's jacket. You go."

Vaughn looked at his mother perplexed. "He can get it Mother. He's eighteen. He knows how to retrieve a coat from a cloakroom."

Just another smug response from my dolt of a son, Muriel thought, but she dared not say what she thought. If her suspicions were correct, his wife would be in that room, and she would not be alone. Parker was returning empty handed, shaking his head.

"It's locked, Dad. I tried the knob, knocked at least three times and called in. Nothing. No staff working the cloakroom."

"Okay, you stay here. I'll get it; I have a master key."

108

FEBRUARY 13, REBECCA'S
BIRTHDAY PARTY

"**H**appy birthday dear Rebecca . . . Happy birthday to you!"

Ten freshman girls and one fifth grader packed Rebecca and Stacy's room singing, screaming, their hearts out for their friend. Rebecca Greer had turned fifteen. She sat up straight against her headboard surrounded by dorm mates wearing smiles from ear to ear, and empty paper plates stained with red sauce and flecks of gooey mozzarella that had seeped off pizza slices when it had been hot.

Surprisingly, pizza delivery had been punctual, 10:30, as planned. Cassie had unlocked the door and accepted delivery. Ten boxes of pizza, four plain, three with pepperoni, three with extra cheese, piled high on Cassie's office desk as four teenagers waited impatiently, ready to grab two or three boxes and head upstairs. Rebecca was feeding the entire dorm. Stacy paid with the money the girls had collected and Cassie added in an extra five dollar tip. After all, Stevie was upstairs eating too. Stacy had insisted Cassie take two slices, extra cheese. Cassie took one.

By 12:00, Stevie called down and begged for another hour or even a half. The girls had just finished the last pizza, and Rebecca had yet to open cards and gifts. Cassie gave her wide latitude. Enjoy yourself; she'd stay up. Rachel had called earlier to wish her little sis a happy birthday today, her actual birth date, and for her family party tomorrow. The reminder that Rachel would not be there was the only downside to Rebecca's special day, she so wanted her sister to be part of it, but Rebecca's dad wouldn't budge and Rachel no longer wanted anything to do with him. She would be out with Samir tonight and tomorrow.

Just as the evening sped for Hillary at her anniversary gala, it had hustled along for Rebecca. By 12:30, finally, after all the talking and giggling fourteen year-olds could do, after all the talking about boys and boys and boys, which fascinated Stevie, too young to empathize but certainly not too young to understand, Rebecca was ready to open her gifts. Gift cards to one side, she opened presents first, and there were plenty of those, from new portable stereos to jogging outfits to the very latest in sartorial designs. But the most amazing gift had been hidden in Stacy's closet behind all her clothes, where Rebecca would never have seen a thing even if she had looked. Stacy and Millie T had pooled their resources and, with their parents' help, unveiled a new LCD television with a 32 inch screen, large enough for Rebecca's friends to see no matter how many converged into their room. What a gift. Kids went really big at this academy.

Cassie heard their squeals of excitement down the stairwell and into her living room. "Hunter" had long been over, and she had shut off the TV in search of a book. She hadn't read a decent book in a long time and had spent much of the evening finishing interim reports and doing three loads of laundry, which should have been done during the week. Now she sat in comfy sweats, sneakers off, with the book open, trying to focus but not succeeding.

She called Jeremy. It was a perfect opportunity to catch up on a one-week hiatus and their conversation went well over an hour. Things were happening quickly. He had three weeks to go before his title changed from chemistry teacher at Chelsea Academy to Professor of Organic Chemistry at Rutgers. Cassie was two weeks away from leaving the academy and one week after that she'd start her new job. Jeremy was not flustered or nervous or experiencing any of the trepidations Cassie was experiencing. But, according to him, he had less to lose. He was single; he had no one depending on him for sustenance of any kind.

He'd give his two-week notice at the end of next week and then he'd be gone. He'd miss his students and most of them would miss him, but not the way Cassie would miss her students or they would miss her. In eighteen years of teaching here, he had never bonded with anyone, faculty or students alike, the way Cassie had. Or the way he had bonded with her. Apart from her, everything else had been just another drip in the pool of time.

Cassie's scheduled move to Point Pleasant was February 27th. In two weeks, she and Stevie would be gone. Stevie's transcripts would be transferred and she'd begin classes in her new school Monday, the 29th, another 'new' school, and accepting life's changes stoically. Wow, Cassie thought, Stevie is growing up, and I, at forty-two, am getting old. Maybe Brian looks down every now and then and watches over us as life passes. I hope so.

She glanced at the mantle clock bordered by two framed photos; one was the three of them taken by a passer-by when Stevie was two. Brian was standing in the surf, wearing a pair of Bermudas, shirtless, with Stevie hoisted on his shoulders; Cassie was peeking out behind his shoulders, wearing her favorite bikini. Waves lapped around them; gulls flew overhead while others rode the waves. A perfect day; a perfect memory.

The other photo was in the Lenox frame Walter had given her for Christmas, the picture of her and Stevie dancing at the Christmas party. Another beautiful memory, but it all seemed so far away, so distant. She wondered if any of it ever happened. Brian was gone; Walter had become invisible; and Vaughn, he had become a nightmare. Thank God there was Jeremy.

When their conversation ended, Cassie sat dreamily, her book closed, listening to the monotonous hum of the drier as it lulled her to sleep, and waited for Stevie to come down and tell her all about Rebecca's fantastic party.

Suddenly, loud hysterical screams shattered her reverie, shrieks that made her bolt upright. Oh my God, she thought, what's happening? She leaped up, raced through her office as Stevie came rushing though the door, breathless. "Stevie? Stevie, what's wrong, Honey? What's wrong? She glanced upstairs as the screams permeating the house, and began racing upstairs.

"Mom!" Stevie uttered breathless, as her Mom dashed for the stairwell. "Mom! Rachel and Samir are married!"

109

THE CLOAK ROOM

aster key in hand, Vaughn walked to the coat room to retrieve his sister-in-law's jacket. He had avoided her as much as possible all evening, still stinging from the slap she had inflicted on his face and the shame of knowing he had revealed what he had done to Cassie. He had tried to force it from his mind without any luck. Every so often, from nowhere, a stabbing vignette of that night surfaced and he'd hang his head.

What Hillary thought of him was clear. That bothered him somewhat because he knew he deserved her disdain, but what upset him more was that he had succumbed to such a base and barbaric attack, an instinct he never knew he possessed. Since that evening, he had gone about his daily routine pretending things were as normal as possible, with two exceptions: One, he didn't leave his office until his tongue had healed and he could talk fairly normally, which had taken about a week. Second, his relentless observations ceased.

His objective to fire Cassie before spring break had not changed. He would carry through with that to placate Taylor and keep his marriage strong. What he couldn't put to rest was how his anger had manifested itself towards Cassie. Unimaginable, that he could have been capable of such an assault.

But he had, and now Hillary knew. Only with her was his secret no longer a secret. Hence he'd avoid her as much as possible. She must have felt the same because her reticence in the limo had been more egregious than usual. Avoidance would be best for both of them. Had Brett still been on the dance floor, he would have told him to get his wife's jacket, and Vaughn would have maintained his distance, but his brother had not been around and the damn door was locked. He'd get her jacket and be done with it.

As he walked across the immense ballroom, the music infused his senses. He became lost in the rhythm of "I'm Gonna Miss You Girl." The image of Cassie swaying to it was titillating, a lovely, sensual thought. It was a memory that might never leave him, and he admitted honestly, he didn't mind. Something beautiful to remember as he walked through life.

He chuckled at life's irony, in big things and in little, like the triviality of his workouts. He had been working out daily since November and now it showed. It was more than a comment Taylor had thrown at Brett a while back when it was hard to tell. Now it was obvious, but no one noticed, not Taylor, not Brett, no one, and the one person he had wanted to notice was no longer in his life. What made life significant anyway?

As he approached the coat room, he saw the closed door. He wiggled the knob. Parker was right; it was closed and locked. "What the . . . ." He uttered, shaking the handle harder. This door shouldn't be locked. What if someone needed to leave? Good thing he had a master. He'd talk to Maurice about this before the night was over. He knocked; knocked harder; then called in. No response; no answer, no nothing. Who was on duty here?

He turned the key and swung the door open, cursing that he'd have to find Hillary's coat himself through conveyors of outerwear. Coats of all sizes, shapes, fabrics and furs were on lines of conveyors going up and down like some ride in an amusement park. This was not a task Vaughn was suited for. He pulled Hillary's coat tag from his pocket and read the number, 432. Damn, were there that many guests here tonight? Most likely there were, since Brett liked this type of affair, including its planning stages. Most likely there were *more* than four hundred sixty-two guests here in the maiden voyage of this new ballroom, the epitome of palatial. I can do this, he thought. Three PhDs . . . I can find a coat. Three switches on the wall. Obviously, one went up, the other down and the third, what . . . pause, go slower, faster? Let's see.

He reached over the counter to flick a switch when he heard a moan, a distinct moan. He listened. Nothing. Then again, another, more guttural moan, stifled, but obvious. Human instincts demand investigation, so, quietly, almost on tip-toe, he trod lightly around the counter; then down its entire length, thirty feet at least. He wove through and around hangars of coats, wraps, shawls, anything people wore to fend off cold, the sound increasing in frequency and intensity. What, who was that and if it was what he thought it was, they'd better go somewhere else to enjoy their pleasures, not in the Club and dishonor its reputation.

He was close, very close. One more turn and he'd be face to face with whoever had chosen to have sex in the cloak room of this prestigious establishment. He turned the corner, acknowledging their heat and passion with the reprimand, "Kindly get out and get a room so guests can get their . . ." and he froze.

Disoriented, the familiar mingling with the unfamiliar, he recognized the couple instantly, or thought he did. It was a scenario so foreign, a place so strange, not home but it should have been, and not the male it should have been. He reeled, his stomach lurched as he staggered back, trying to fathom this scene and hold on to reality, hold on to sanity. His wife, and . . . and . . . his brother?! Taylor and Brett, fornicating their brains out? She, on her back, Brett sucking her breasts pushing himself in, into his wife!

Suddenly Brett became aware of someone's presence. How could anyone have gotten in? Brett had tipped the coat-check girl handsomely. She had left and locked the door. Brett had let Taylor in after the young staffer had gone and he had relocked it himself. The only way in was if you had a master key and that would be himself and . . . Oh my God! He panicked. For perhaps the first time in his life, Brett panicked. My brother! He pulled away from Taylor, revealing her half naked, legs splayed wide, with her green eyes wider, wider than Vaughn had ever seen them. She was shocked, utterly shocked, for what, for having been caught? For having been caught by her husband? For never having imagined she could have been caught? The great scheming Taylor never, ever believing her devious escapades could have gotten her caught, especially by her nitwit husband?

Brett, having recovered some semblance of decorum, defended himself. "Vaughn, sorry brother, it just happened. It's not what it seems; things got out of control. I came in for Taylor's coat – it's freezing out there – and she followed me in. We lost control. Too much partying and all that." He tried an ineffective smile.

Vaughn couldn't think; he couldn't talk; his words didn't come; his voice didn't follow; he was choking, drowning in the horrific spectacle of what he had just seen. His wife and his brother, fornicating!? No! Impossible! She was his faithful wife, his wife whom he never doubted; his wife, whom he trusted completely, doing this? Had it really, 'just happened,' or had it just happened before? How big a fool was he? He doted on Taylor, believing she was the paragon of fidelity. What kind of betrayal was this?

The rage he had felt when he had assaulted Cassie was nothing compared to this. Trusting Cassie was never relevant. She had done the trusting and he had betrayed her. With Taylor, his wife, he had trusted her completely and now she had betrayed him. Betrayal hurts like hell.

Vaughn's hands ripped at his hair, emitting groans of agony, anguish, anger, explosive anger he could not contain. His fury ripped coats from the racks, tore them from their hangars and hurled them from one wall to the next, not caring whether anyone ever found them again. Then he focused on Brett, his smug, deceitful brother. With one powerful swing, his fist connected with Brett's jaw. Brett was thrown back, slammed against the wall in shock and pain. Stunned, he was caught off guard as Vaughn continued his assault with the full force of his newly acquired strength. Brett protected his face sheepishly, pulled himself up and attempted to counter.

He had always been the stronger of the two and was shocked when his defense was stymied by a brother he had believed was such a weakling. Vaughn side-stepped Brett's counter and issued a new onslaught, throwing his brother against the wall then pummeling his stomach and face. Taylor, screaming, lunged at Vaughn, clawed at him, scratching his face with acrylic nails. Vaughn had become crazed. He threw her off, backed away, and stood panting. He passed his hand over his face and saw his own blood. He didn't care; he had seen much more when he had assaulted Cassie. He had lost every shred of rational thought then, and he had lost all rational thought now. Every pretense he could ever have believed important to preserve, gone.

"Too much partying, huh?" He rasped. "You came here to get Taylor's coat, huh, with the door locked from the inside, with the coat-check staff missing? How much did you tip her to disappear?

"And you, my *wife*, the one person I trusted completely. You bitch!" His hands went to his face in agony. He couldn't think; he couldn't comprehend. Taylor, this woman he had believed was the paragon of virtue, devotion and fidelity, screwing with his brother! "No, no," he uttered, trying to will the demons from his mind. Twenty years of trust, twenty years destroyed. If he could turn back time . . . but he couldn't, no one could. He had seen what he had seen and he had to deal with it, someway, somehow.

He flung Hillary's coat check stub in the air. "Get your own wife's jacket," he uttered with venom, trying desperately for control, "and get my wife's jacket while you're at it. And get your own ride home, Taylor. I'm leaving." He faced them with ferocity in his heart and cold blood in his veins. "My house, in an hour. We're having this out, tonight!" He turned and walked out, leaving Brett to wonder where Vaughn had ever gotten such courage. Inwardly, he suddenly and for the first time admired the guy.

Neither Hillary nor Muriel questioned Vaughn when he approached the head table without Hillary's jacket. Nor were they surprised at "I'm leaving, now!" The raw, bloody skin on his face, his ferocious look, his clenched fists, and his disheveled appearance, told them what they needed to know.

"Hillary, I apologize for leaving early, but I can't stay, not another second." I'll call Thomas to come and get me. I'll be waiting outside."

"Vaughn," Hillary protested, "you and I have differences, and you know what they are, but I will not stay either." What she had known for decades, in theory, had now become palpable. It burned in Vaughn's eyes. She had avoided Brett's infidelity because of the family but here, at her anniversary celebration, Brett and Taylor together here, in the cloak room? She had given herself her last excuse. She knew exactly what Vaughn had seen, and would have known even without the gouges on his face.

"Arthur will drive us both home. Brett can find his own transportation."

"I'm going to my house Hillary. Brett and Taylor are meeting me there. We're having this out tonight."

"Then the four of us will have this out, tonight. Brett is my husband of twenty-five years." She paused, thinking of vows and commitment and the decades of deceit, thinking of tonight of all nights. "He'll meet both of us at your house."

Vaughn scanned the ballroom for Parker. He had brought Muriel. "Parker's still here, son," Muriel said, nodding to the dance floor where Parker was enjoying the music with a dancing partner, a very pretty ingenue` from a very distinguished family. "He'll take me home. You go and get your house in order."

Vaughn was surprised. Had his mother been aware of what he had just witnessed for the first time? Was he the only, stupid, trusting, naive fool? Vaughn wove through the dancers to his son and spoke a few words. Parker nodded.

"Let's go, Hillary," Vaughn said, not as the cavalier, callow dean of Chelsea, but the undisputed head of the Otis-Barrett clan. Mentally, he had finally deposed his brother. He kissed his mother good night and he and Hillary left her 25th anniversary gala as Brett and Taylor emerged at the far side of the ballroom.

110

Ordinary people believe wealth solves all problems. They believe the obscenely wealthy live in a dream world, untouched, unscathed by tribulations that beleaguer their lives. They believe the wealthy live a life of ease, a pampered existence, free from the travails of those who work through each day and struggle to stretch a paycheck, to give their kids a decent life and a decent education. That's what they believe and for the most part they are correct; but that is not always correct. Sometimes the obscenely wealthy have problems that transcend the power of money and the easy solutions money often provides. Tonight, Vaughn had had his first experience with this.

Thirty-five minutes later Vaughn and Hillary sat facing each other on soft leather sofas in his study. He had poured himself a double scotch, no rocks, and sat quietly, pensively, sipping. Intermittently, he balled his hand into a fist, slammed it on the armrest in anger or ran his hand through his hair in agony. His thirty-five minute ride home had afforded him too much time to replay the image of what he had seen, to zoom in and replay it in color, to fast forward or replay in slow motion, again and again, until it had made him sick.

Thoughts of Taylor's accusations against Cassie played in his head and he finally came face to face with the reason for her verbal attack. Consider Taylor's motive, Cassie had said when she had defended herself against Vaughn's diatribe after their meeting with Joel Greer, that pompous self-absorbed man who would throw away his child to satiate his hatred. Vaughn finally understood Taylor's motive: She, his wife of twenty years, was jealous of Cassie, not because Cassie was hitting on him, but because Brett wanted to hit on her. Vaughn recalled the way Brett had leered at Cassie Thanksgiving Day and how he was so quick to accompany him to the faculty Christmas party. Taylor saw what he, Vaughn, had dismissed.

She didn't even love me enough to care if she lost me to another woman, he agonized. Her only concern was that she'd lose my *brother*!" He shuddered at the horror, the horror of this realization, this epiphany, and his stomach roiled. He had never lived in reality, but he was being forced now.

Vaughn stood and paced. It was 2:30 a.m. Silence had become interminable, and when he finally spoke, it was with remorse. "You know what I did to Cassie, and I know what you think of me because of it. I did it for Taylor. She had convinced me Cassie was hitting on me. I was a fool. I *am* a fool. Cassie's a kind, naïve, and beautiful woman with whom I had become infatuated, no, with whom I had fallen in love. It wasn't the other way around as Taylor had charged. My brother would have hit on Cassie in a heartbeat, and obviously, my wife knew it. As harsh as that sounds Hillary, it's the truth, and I'm sorry."

Hillary remained quiet. Her brother-in-law had worn blinders since the day she had met him. Telling him would not change the past, and it would not change a sexual assault that could never be excused or erased. But his words held contrition. Perhaps Vaughn was seeing clearly for the first time.

Vaughn looked at her with so much sadness. "How long have you known?"

Hillary shrugged. "Before you proposed, Vaughn; I knew then."

He broke down. Not sobs or shrieks as a woman cries, but his body heaving while he covered his face to hide renegade tears. Hillary understood. She remembered nights when Brett would contrive some excuse to leave well before chemo treatments had rendered her too sick to protest, or the finality of being denied adoption had left her dead. Then, she had cried, not now, but she understood why Vaughn would. Betrayal comes in many guises. A brother betrayed by a brother. Hamlet would understand.

Brett and Taylor arrived. Taylor's heels clicked on the Italian marble tile in the foyer. Brett entered Vaughn's study with Hillary's jacket in hand. His face bore a sheepish look, perhaps because Hillary was here, seated opposite Vaughn. Had he not expected her? Where else would his wife be, waiting at home for the reprobate husband to arrive? And this was to have been a happy anniversary celebration.

Taylor, having regained a semblance of her usual arrogance, followed on Brett's heels. Not this time, Darling, Vaughn thought. One look at her silver beaded dress with her breasts half exposed made him realize who she had been dressing for all these years. "Before you sit, go upstairs and change into something decent," he commanded in a voice he had never used before.

Taylor's usual response would have been condescension or ridicule, but his demeanor and his tone took her back. She halted, mid-step. The gashes she had inflicted might have given her pause, but the daggers in Vaughn's eyes stopped her cold. She started upstairs with a pretense of bravado, but returned wearing a long-sleeved V-necked black cashmere sweater, black tight pants and open-toed heels, not exactly modest, but much more de rigueur.

Brett had taken the seat next to Hillary who moved to an armchair instantly, a move that told him exactly where he stood. He got up to make himself a drink. "Bar's closed to you, Brett. Sit down; this is no social visit."

"Then what kind of visit is it, Vaughn?" Taylor asked, somewhat affronted.

"This is a let's-tell- the-truth visit, Taylor. So let's tell it, shall we?" He rose from his seat and paced. "We've been married twenty years," he stated, looking directly at her, "twenty years during which I trusted you completely. But now, it's apparent I was deceived." Taylor avoided his eyes, her body language saying, yes, you were. "So, Taylor, when did sex with my brother start?"

Taylor paused. The standard question from the spouse who had been cuckolded would have been, "Did you ever love me?" That would have been easy. That response would have been, "Darling, I have always loved you, only you. Tonight just happened." Most likely Vaughn would have believed her. But asking when she and Brett started having sex? That was not an open-ended question; this question assumed guilt and simply asked for a time line. A truthful answer would admit her guilt throughout her entire marriage.

What the hell, she thought. Her prenuptial never gave her access to the Otis-Barrett fortune, so her answer would not affect that, but she'd always have half of their joint accounts if he filed for divorce, so let's get this over with.

"If you need to know, if it'll make you happy, your brother and I began having sex, as you so properly put it, before you and I were married, the very week after you introduced me to the family, if you remember." Brett turned away, visibly uncomfortable. "One look at your brother and I devoured him with my eyes. A week later I was devouring him in other ways." She licked her lips salaciously. Hillary turned away. Brett took one look at his wife and became painfully aware how cutting Taylor's words were.

"Was there anyone else?"

"Anyone else?" Taylor laughed diabolically. "Everyone else. Brett loved to hear about my sexual exploits and how many customers I'd bed on my back-room counter in one night, after of course, giving them the best manicures they'd ever had. How do you think Trevor Stauer was persuaded to hold up the queue so we could justify garage parking? Favors always come with a price."

Vaughn stood. His eyes showed regret, sadness, betrayal, and conviction. He had been pushed far enough. His wife had been cheating on him for decades, with his brother, and for fun with dozens of other men. Her little shop, Manicures for Men, had served its purpose. It's where Vaughn had first met her and where he had first seduced her, so he had thought. She excelled at making him think he was seducing her while all the while she was seducing him, making him think he was virile, so desirable.

Manicures for Men had been their salacious hideaway. Alone with Taylor during his manicure, he would drool in anticipation of the back room, on the counter or the floor. Did he think it was used by him alone? Yes, he did. What a stupid, ignorant fool he had been, but no more.

"Pack a bag," he said decisively. Pack one, pack two, pack however many you'll need because you are not staying in my house, not ever again."

"What?!" Taylor was shocked. *Your* house; this is *my* house too."

"Wrong, Darling, it's mine. It's in my name; it's always been in my name, and that little prenuptial you signed, thanks to my mother, not only says you get nothing of what I had before we married, but it itemizes every item that's excluded; every one of them enumerated, like the Constitution, and this house is one of them. This house, the cabanas, the pool, tennis courts, stables, the servants quarters, the plane and the yacht, to name a few, are mine, all mine. So, get out of my house!"

Now Taylor emitted a nefarious chuckle, low at first, then louder and louder until she laughed openly and without shame, or remorse.

"You find this funny? What's funny about this?"

"You, Vaughn, you! I find *you* funny, so proper, so formal, so stuck in your patterns and your rigidity, your propriety. You're a joke. You think I care that it's your house, your pools, your stables, your everything? Oh, I'll admit I did believe that, being married to you, they were all mine, but with all your grown-up toys, you've missed out on all the really good things in life.

"You play by the rules, never deviating, not a drop of emotion or passion, while I, your wife, and your brother, have not been just having sex, we've been fucking our brains out for twenty years, everywhere, at the shop, the Club, this house, this mansion, your mansion, in every room, anytime you weren't around or anywhere I could get away, and getting away was easy. You can keep your house, Vaughn; I'll get enough to keep me in luxury for the rest of my life, and believe me, I have enjoyed the fucking and I'll continue to enjoy all the fucking that will follow.

"While you, you pathetic male, will waste away wondering if you'll ever find another woman, or find anyone you can ever trust again. Poor, victimized Vaughn. You are a pathetic male, you are, were, and will be. You'll live alone for the rest of your life because you'll never figure out what you did to lose me or why you made such a mistake in the first place.

"Ha! You can have your mansion, Vaughn, your stables and everything else, but your life will be empty, empty, and you will live in complete isolation."

"Wrong, Taylor. I'll have our son. When he learns what you've been doing, he won't want anything to do with you. You were never there for him anyway. Now I know why."

"You're right," she licked her lips lasciviously. "I was spreading my legs and loving everything that went between them."

Vaughn turned away. "You're a slut! A slut, and I never saw it."

"A Jersey City slut who satisfied every desire you ever had, and you loved it. You saw what you wanted to see, and you wanted to believe it was only you," she uttered in contempt. "You saw the devoted wife, who assimilated herself right in with the Club, where snobs of all shapes and sizes meet to strut like peacocks on display. And while I was looking good on your arm, which is all you wanted for your ego, my son was growing up just fine without me."

"My son, Taylor, *my* son, the son I watched at all his games and at all his activities. I was there for him. You? You just admitted what you were doing instead of watching our son. You repulse me."

Taylor laughed diabolically; her eyes glowed like a demon's. "You fool, Vaughn, you blind fool." She hated Vaughn. She had tolerated him for Brett and the Club, but she hated Vaughn, the obsequious man she had married. Now she'd be rid of him and the pretense, and be with the man she loved. "You see nothing except your own ego. Hubris got you through life. Hubris. Without it, you'd wallow in failure. You, a dean; three PhDs and all you could handle in life was the deanship of a private academy. How pathetic! Your own brother ridicules you. And you think being a father gives your life validity."

"Taylor!' Brett interjected. He saw where she was going. "Leave it! Let's go!"

But Taylor would not leave it. She had whipped herself into a frenzy whose hatred had finally overflowed. "Well, swallow this one. If being a father gives your life validity, then you have no validity, because you are *not* Parker's father! He is *not* your son! You may have raised him, but you didn't father him. I am Parker's mother, and Brett is his father. You've been bringing up a child whose only DNA comes from your parents' genes. You had nothing, *nothing* to do with creating him, you stupid, stupid fool!"

Silence. Silence. It hit each one of them in its own devastating wake. Vaughn staggered. He couldn't believe her words, couldn't process them. He couldn't move. Brett, shocked. Taylor had disclosed their long-kept secret. Eighteen years they had kept it theirs, talked about it, laughed about it, but never, ever divulged it. Taylor, sanctimonious, had cut Vaughn with a dagger deeper than any wound she could have inflicted. She had killed him, while letting him live.

And Hillary, quiet ladylike Hillary, sat like marble. She had looked into Medusa's eyes and had turned to stone. Taylor's words chiseled shock around her eyes, horror around her mouth and a crypt around her heart. Brett had a son? Her breath stopped. Her stomach lurched. Dazed, Hillary slowly rose from her stone chrysalis, like a puppeteer had put her on strings that would allow her to rise on wobbly legs. She staggered, fell back and righted herself.

When she could move, she stepped back from the horror of the Otis-Barretts, away from Vaughn, from Taylor, from Brett. She whimpered, not realizing she had. She could not control the horror of what she had heard; what she now knew was undeniably true.

"You . . . you have . . . a . . . son?" She uttered softly, the agony of it all drowning her. Brett turned to his wife, a woman who could not conceive, could not hold the fetuses she had conceived. "You have a son?" She uttered again, her face contorted with grief. "All these years, you have a son? And you never told me? I never knew?"

"He wasn't yours, Hillary, so what difference does it make?!"

Brett looked at Taylor with savagery, knowing her words had cut his wife more deeply than anything else could have. "Shut up, Taylor!" He shouted. "Shut up!" At that moment, he could have killed her.

Hillary left her jacket; grabbed her purse and fled the house in agony. "Don't come home, Brett. Don't ever come home again!" She stumbled backwards, righted herself then raced into the night, not knowing where to go, what to do, what to think, how to think, where she was, how to get home. Arthur, always on watch for his Miss Hillary, had seen her exit. She was in trouble. He had no idea why, nor did it matter. He started the limo, rammed the pedal to the floor and screeched into the cul de sac. He slammed the brakes, got out and opened the door. Hillary raced to him without decorum, threw herself into the back seat as Arthur closed the door, and unleashed decades of tears, in deep lugubrious wails. Reality is like a fog. Sometimes it engulfs us slowly, insidiously; other times it's suddenly in your face. Whichever way it arrives, it cuts to our very soul. From deep inside, Hillary cried for decades of hurt, anguish, betrayal, deception she could no longer deny. Arthur glanced back as he pushed the car to fifty down that winding drive and headed his Miss Hillary home. Damn Mister Brett. Hillary deserved so much better than her husband.

Suddenly her mobile phone rang. It had to be Brett; she wouldn't answer. But he had his brother and wife to face; why call her now? She peeked at caller ID and paused. Who else had this number aside from her family, and their numbers she'd recognize instantly? Who else, except, except, Cassie, except Rachel? Almost 4:00 in the morning? Suddenly she panicked. They had no idea she'd be awake, so why call now? Oh my God, she thought, something's happened.

She answered to hysteria, incoherent words and garbled sobs. She sat up straight. "Cassie! Cassie, please, calm down. I can't understand you. What are you saying? What's happened? Tell me, please!"

As hard as she tried, Cassie could not calm down, but she forced her shrieks to become sobs, allowing Hillary to understand five words: Samir, Rachel, help, pregnant, dead.

Hillary felt herself turn to ice. "Oh my God, no, no, no!' What, what kind of a nightmare was this? What had God thrown at her now?

"Help! Hillary! A doctor! Rachel . . . needs a doctor! Help, please! Help!"

Arthur reached the end of the drive and braked hard. Left, for home; right for Chelsea Academy. Without verbal direction from Hillary, he turned right burning rubber, heading for the academy. And tonight, no matter how fast he drove, he knew his Miss Hillary would never tell him to slow down.

111

C assie took the stairs two at a time, three when she could, Stevie's voice trailing behind her with an innocent, "Mom, did you know? Did you know they were married?" Oh yeah, she knew, and now the entire academy would know, and the Administration, the dean and perhaps Rachel's father.

Cassie couldn't answer Stevie; she couldn't think of anything except getting to Rebecca and finding out how much damage had been done. If Stevie knew, everyone in that room knew, and after those screams, everyone in the entire dorm would know. No one could sleep through that. Word would spread like wildfire, and that would mean to Rachel. Had Rebecca called her? How had Rebecca found out? Most of all, had she called her father?

Oh my God, no, she prayed. Please, God, don't let that happen. She barreled into Rebecca's room amidst the screaming girls and a wailing Rebecca, being held tightly in Stacy's embrace. As soon as she saw Cassie, Rebecca fell into her arms crying. "It's horrible, Mrs. Komsky, horrible."

"What's horrible, Rebecca? Tell me. Tell me how you found out."

Rebecca stopped instantly. "Mrs. Komsky, you knew?"

"That doesn't matter, Rebecca. Right now, I need to know exactly what happened, how you found out and if you've told Rachel."

Rebecca motioned towards the birthday gifts and cards strewn about on her bed. A tri-folded letter lay on top. Cassie grabbed it and read. Two copies of Rachel and Samir's marriage certificates. How did they ever get here?

"I thought it was a birthday card," Rebecca began. "It came with all the other mail and there were other long cards. I opened two and went for the third." She shrugged. "I never looked at the outside address; I just tore it open like the rest, expecting to see 'Happy Birthday' with some message.

"I was confused when I saw Samir's name and my sister's name on a form letter. When I read the heading, 'Certificate of Marriage,' I screamed and . . . ." She lowered her head.

"And what, Rebecca? And what? Did you call Rachel?" She nodded. "What did Rachel say?"

Rebecca burst into tears. "She didn't answer. I let it ring until I got her answering machine, so . . . ." She raised her head and looked into Cassie's eyes, hesitant to continue.

"You called your father?" Cassie asked, knowing the answer would be yes before Rebecca responded. Softly, Cassie asked again, "Did you call your father?"

Rebecca nodded. "I wanted to know why my sister and Samir were married and no one had told me, why they would keep this from me? When Rachel didn't answer her phone, I had to find out, so I called my dad."

Cassie exhaled. She feared what would come next. "I knew he and my mom were out, so I called his mobile phone. When he picked up, I was angry. I told him he had no right to keep this from me. Just because he's angry with Rachel for some reason didn't mean I didn't have a right to know my own sister was married. I started to ask if this was why he wasn't talking to Rachel, but he was so angry I never got a chance. He shouted obscenities and vowed he'd kill Samir. Then he hung up."

"Oh my God," Cassie uttered more to herself than out loud. What would he do? What could he do? Fear shot through her, but she squelched it. She couldn't let Rebecca see it.

"Mrs. Komsky, I've never heard my father so angry. He called Rachel and Samir horrible names, like he hates them, especially Samir. He's not the same person who brought me up, me and my sister. How could he change like this? How could he hate Samir because he's an Arab? A nice person is a nice person. Rachel and Samir got married behind his back, easy to see why." She trembled. "I'm scared, Mrs. Komsky. What's gonna happen now?"

Cassie wished she knew, but it wouldn't be good. Rebecca would have to find out for herself why her father hated Samir. It wasn't Cassie's prerogative to comment on that. Right now, somehow, she had to contact Rachel and Samir. She had to let them know Rachel's father knew, and was most likely heading this way at 3:25 in the morning. Greer would do that. Her thoughts whirled. Greer had Rachel and Samir at a disadvantage. He knew his daughter was married to the young Arab man he had attacked over Christmas break, but Rachel did not. She would be unprepared for his onslaught. So would Samir.

Were Rachel and Samir out for the weekend? Had they come back late and gone back to their dorms? If they had, why hadn't Rachel answered her phone? Why hadn't Gloria picked up? Whatever was happening, Rachel had to know. Cassie had to find Rachel before this situation exploded. How much time did she have?

Stevie had followed her mother to Rebecca's room and was standing in the doorway. "Stevie, Honey, I need you to stay here. She turned to Rebecca and Stacy, "I have to leave. I have to find Rachel." She turned to the young ladies who were still in the room. "Ladies, please go back to your rooms and stay there. If you can't sleep, that's okay, call your friends, talk from room to room, whatever you feel comfortable doing, but please promise me you won't leave your room, no matter what you hear or what happens." Their faces were grave. They realized something was very wrong. "Promise?" Cassie asked. They nodded.

"Stacy, call Security. Tell them I'm leaving and I need them to patrol Sanders House so no one goes in or out. I'll go out through my front door and lock it from the outside. If you all stay in your rooms, you'll be fine. But you have to make that call now, okay"?

Stacy went for the numbers pinned on their bulletin board, ran her fingers down a few, found the number she needed and dialed using their desk phone. Cassie scribbled a number on a notepaper on Rebecca's desk. "Stevie, this is Mr. Harper's number. After Stacy talks to Security, call him immediately. Tell him exactly what happened and that I'm leaving here for Rachel's dorm. Tell him to check for Samir, see if he signed in. Cassie turned to Rebecca. Rebecca, can I borrow your mobile phone?" Rebecca nodded.

Cassie turned to leave as Stacy was informing Security that Mrs. Komsky needed them to send a unit to patrol their house, but they were resisting. Cassie grabbed the phone. "This is Mrs. Komsky. I have an emergency and I must leave my house. I'm locking the doors. I need you to patrol this house, Roosevelt House and Damon. It's vital!" She listened. "Then wake someone up!" She shouted angrily. Wake up the dean and get his permission. Get someone else on duty. Do whatever you have to for safety. Just do it! I have to leave, now!"

She hung up. "I have to go. Rebecca, call 9-1-1; I'll call them from your mobile phone while I'm on my way." She ran for the door then turned. "Rebecca, how far is it from your house to Chelsea?"

"Almost sixty miles."

"Good," she said, relieved, "I've got time," she spoke to herself out loud. "That's almost an hour, even if he speeds." Cassie raced out the door and started down the stairs.

"Mrs. Komsky, wait," Rebecca called after her. "My father isn't home. He was at the Club tonight, at an anniversary party for Dr. O/B's sister-in-law. He's staying with friends, Mrs. Komsky. He's in Princeton."

Cassie's heart sunk. He's in Princeton? One second for that to sink in, and it was devastating. Oh my God, ten miles away! He was what – fifteen minutes from the academy, despite lights and side streets, and he would not be doing the speed limit. Cassie needed more than that; she needed a miracle.

112

C assie raced through her house, forced her feet into her sneakers, grabbed her purse, dumped it upside down, found her keys, grabbed her coat, shoved Rebecca's phone into its pocket, and raced out the front door, locking it behind her. Her young ladies would be safe. She doubted Greer would come here unless he wanted to see Rebecca, but that wouldn't be his priority. His anger would be focused on Rachel and Samir, and with Security patrolling Sanders House her charges would be safe. It was Rachel's and Samir's dorms that worried her. Only two patrol cars available at night? Unbelievable!

She ran cautiously. Except for a bright moon, darkness enveloped the campus, and street lighting was ineffective for running or dodging brush and trees at this hour. As she ran, she held Rebecca's mobile phone as steady as she could and dialed 9-1-1. The officer on duty picked up to a breathless caller. Between gulps of air, she explained the situation.

We need help, she implored, but 'Chelsea Academy' and 'Joel Greer' did not sit well with him. The academy was a staple in this town. Although Greer did not live here, the officer knew his name. Thus, he wouldn't dispatch a car without corroboration from the dean, even for an emergency. He couldn't respond to a supposition. What kind of response was that? He'd respond after something happened? Finally she got him to send the car that patrolled this sector of town for a closer look.

That was something. Something is better than nothing, and even though she found Vaughn repulsive, she would have called him if she had known his home phone number or had memorized his mobile number when he had given it to her. But it was a stray piece of paper thrown into her phone directory with the belief she'd never need it for any reason, ever.

A cold, clear night, clouds parting to reveal a perfect moon and bright stars. What irony, a beautiful sky, a beautiful night fraught with impending tragedy. She crossed the circle in less than ten minutes and banged on the doors. No response, exactly what she had expected. She knocked harder and called. Again, no response. Most likely at 3:37 in the morning, Judy Marino was sound asleep. Why wouldn't she be? Knowing the new dorms followed the same blueprint, Cassie ran to her front door and pounded, shouting Judy's name. She was about to throw stones at her upstairs window when the second-floor window opened. "Mrs. Komsky? Is that you? Are you crazy?! It's almost 4:00 a.m.!"

Ms. Marino, I don't have time to explain now; I need to talk to Rachel. It's an emergency, a real emergency! Please, let me in!"

"Go away or I'll call Security."

"I've already *called* Security!" Judy Marino paused. Obviously this *was* an emergency.

"I'll be down in two minutes."

In less than two minutes, Judy, hugging a bathrobe around her middle, was unbolting her front door and leading Cassie through her house to the office door. "You've been here before with Dr. O/B's sister-in-law; you know the way. I'll expect you to leave through the dormitory doors on your way out. I'm going back to bed."

A quick thank-you and Cassie ran to Rachel's room, knocking and calling her name. Finally, the lock turned and Rachel's pale, sleepy face peered through the opening. "Mrs. Komsky?" She asked in a daze. Cassie's knocking had awakened her. "What are you doing here; it's after 3:30." Then the realization sunk in. Why would Mrs. Komsky be here at this hour if something weren't wrong? "Oh my God! Mrs. Komsky, what's wrong? Something's wrong . . . what? What is it? Is it Samir? Is it my sister?"

Cassie ushered her into her room and glanced at Gloria's perfectly made bed. "Gloria's in the City with her mom," Rachel said, then became breathless. "Please tell me what's wrong?"

"Rebecca tried to call you about a half hour ago; you didn't answer." Rachel thought back a half hour and avoided Cassie's gaze. "Her call went to voice mail." Rachel went for her phone. "You might want to hear this from me, first." Cassie pulled Rachel onto the edge of her bed and sat beside her. Rachel could see the almost panic in her teacher's eyes. Something was very wrong.

"Rebecca was opening birthday gifts and cards. A few were letter sized; she didn't know one of them was addressed to you; she thought they were all cards for her." Rachel paused, somewhat confused. What would birthday cards have to do with her, and why would that be so traumatic? Cassie continued. When she described how Rebecca opened one, read it and screamed, Rachel realized it had something to do with her. She wasn't expecting anything in the mail . . . except . . . "It was from the Department of Vital Statistics."

Rachel gasped. Her hands went to her mouth. Instantly, she knew what Rebecca had opened. "Our marriage certificates? Rebecca opened our marriage certificates? How did she get them? Why were they mailed to her?"

"They weren't mailed to her, but the carrier delivered them to her by mistake. He must have read the last name and put it in her mail box instead of yours."

"Oh my God, now Rebecca knows!"

"Not just Rebecca – everyone at her birthday party."

Now Rachel's eyes opened wide with fear. If Rebecca knew, and all those freshmen knew . . . how much longer would it be before her father found out? "She could tell my father! I've got to talk to her before she tells my father!"

Cassie's look told her what she didn't want to hear. She screamed, hysterically. "No! No! My father knows? He knows? He'll kill Samir! He'll kill him. He won't care if he goes to jail; he won't care! He hates him!"

Rachel raced to her phone and dialed Samir. She let it ring until his voice mail came on. "Samir, pick up! Where are you, Hon? Something horrible has happened – be careful. My father knows. Oh my God, he knows! You've got to get away from him. If he comes after you, you've got to get away!"

She dialed Matt's number. He had to be awake; he had to. Nobody sleeps through a ringing phone. But where was he? Suddenly Matt's voice, groggy beyond recognition, answered. "Matt! Matt, it's Rachel! Where's Samir; where is he?"

"Rachel? Wha . . . What time is it?" Matt was trying to shake off his confusion and reorient himself. Rachel was calling him at this hour asking for Samir? Something was wrong. "Samir? He's . . . not here. But he is because his bed's unmade. What's, what's wrong, Rachel?"

"Tell him my father knows. Just tell him, Matt. Samir will know."

"Mrs. Komsky," Rachel implored, "you've got to get to Samir. You've just got to."

"I'll do what I can." As Cassie started out the door, she looked back at Rachel who was holding her stomach and crying. "Were you in the bathroom when your sister called?"

Rachel looked up. She nodded shyly. Should she tell or not, or did Mrs. Komsky know?

"Does Samir know?"

How? How did Mrs Komsky find out? She had told Samir tonight.

"Congratulations, Rachel. You will be wonderful parents."

Then she was gone.

113

Jeremy was waiting for her at Damon House, doors open wide. He was unkempt, a rumpled T-shirt and a pair of jeans thrown on. Cassie rushed in breathless. "What's going on, Cassie?" Jeremy shut and bolted the doors. "Stevie called a little while ago; Security passed a few minutes later, then again right before you got here. There's too much happening, Cassie. Neither of us can deal with it all." She could hear the tension in his voice, "Least of all Samir and Rachel. They're too young. Hell, we're too old." His face collapsed onto his chest. "So they're married. How long have you known?"

She lowered her head. "The week after I went looking for him in the snowstorm. I'm sorry, Jeremy; they told me in confidence. I couldn't violate that trust."

"I wouldn't have either, but you're in one hell of a mess. Greer's on his way? If he acts anything like your meeting with him, he'll kill Samir. The police?"

"I've called them. They need Vaughn's permission to investigate. The best I could get them to do was reroute the patrol car that covers this area.

"I called Vaughn." He shook his head. "No answer. I left a message then told Matt to contact Mason to get through to Parker. I didn't tell Matt they were married even though most of your freshmen must know." Cassie nodded. By now her whole dorm would know. "I stressed Greer is on his way to hurt Samir, that Mason had to get to Parker fast. If anyone can get to Vaughn at this hour, it's Parker."

"Is Samir in his room yet?"

"Uh-uh, but he's signed in. He and Matt talked earlier in the evening for quite a while; then they went to bed. Until Rachel called, Matt was sleeping. He thought Samir was too."

"I have to find him, Jeremy. He knows nothing about what's just happened. If Greer gets here before Samir knows, he'll be completely off guard. I've gotta talk to Matt too. Come on Jeremy; we're wasting time."

They hurried down the hall, Jeremy leading. He had lost over twenty-five pounds and was surprisingly agile. Cassie had to walk quickly to keep up. One hard knock, a 'Come in,' and they faced Matt, sleepy-eyed from lack of sleep. Cassie doubted he'd be able to sleep after this. She looked at Samir's unmade bed, not like him at all, and looked questioningly at Matt. Matt faced her with upturned hands and a shake of his head. He had no idea where Samir could be.

Samir, however, was on his roof, appreciating the beauty of life and loving every minute of it. He was going to be a father. He never knew how powerful that feeling could be until tonight when Rachel had announced their miracle.

Despite being tired, he could not sleep. Tossing, turning, thinking of renewed life, he had made his way to the roof and the serenity he always felt there. He wished his parents had been here to experience his joy. They would have been grandparents. His uncle was ecstatic enough for all of them, even relatives in Lebanon. He told the expectant couple that he would provide anything they needed. Samir hugged himself with joy. A father! He was going to be a father! And Rachel, his beautiful wife was giving him this miracle.

Who would the baby look like? What would they name him, or her, if it were a girl? Where would they live? There was sadness too, because Rachel's parents would not be in their lives, and she had cried from the senselessness of it all - hatred from her father, cowardice from her mother who would not confront him.

Rachel would never let them in their lives. Maybe Miss Hillary would be a surrogate grand-mom, maybe Mrs. Komsky too. They knew Cassie would be moving soon, but maybe she'd be close enough to remain in their lives.

So when Rachel had called a short while ago, Samir had been up on his rooftop looking at the sky, the stars and the moonlit night, admiring the splendor of it all, mesmerized by the twinkling and the glow of the moon, thinking of their baby and names for a boy or girl. He had no idea what was happening below.

Flashing lights interrupted his thoughts. Flashing lights on the ground had passed once before, now a second time, red and yellow lights moving slowly, so un-like the beauty of the stars. He had ignored the first pass, thinking it was a routine patrol. Perhaps Security always passed his house and he had always been asleep. He had never sat up here this late before. But this was the second time a car passed, and he took notice.

Had something happened? He wondered. He should go downstairs. He wouldn't want someone to find him up here. Not that anyone had ever seen him up here ex-cept Mrs. Komsky. That's why she had requested the at-tic door be bolted. If he were discovered here, it might reflect badly on her, even though Maintenance had never completed the job. Holes on one side of a door do not constitute a lock.

He arose effortlessly, his strong arms picking his lithe body up from a sitting position in one liquid motion. He stood and looked over the circle towards Rachel's dorm. He could not see it, but even if he could, her room was on the opposite side, so he would never have known she was throwing up again, in between trying desperately to get dressed so she could rush to him, hold him in her arms and tell him to be careful, tell him let's run away; my fa-ther is hunting you down. But the heaves kept coming no matter that she had eaten nothing for lunch or dinner, the vomit forcing her delay, forcing her to change from one stinking, soiled shirt to another while trying to get into her jeans and swollen waist.

Samir walked quickly and quietly; he didn't want to make noise and wake someone. He walked through the attic, down the steps, through the derelict room, down the stairway to his floor, almost on tiptoe, and just before he turned into his room, he paused. His door was open, the lights were on, and he heard voices. Voices? Mr. Hartman's and, and Mrs. Komsky's? What was Mrs. Komsky doing here? Why were either of them here, talking to Matt at this hour? Something was wrong.

Immediately, he connected the patrol car with their presence; something was definitely wrong. Rachel? His wife? No! No! He rushed into his room and almost careened into Jeremy, his panic palpable.

"What has happened?" He blurted out, startling both Cassie and Jeremy. "What has happened to Rachel? What has happened to my wife?" Through his panic, he commanded an answer.

Matt stood, shocked, confused, his sleepiness gone instantly. "Your *wife*? Rachel is your *wife*? You and Rachel are married?"

"Rachel tried to call you." Cassie addressed Samir. "Your certificates of marriage were put in Rebecca's mailbox by mistake along with her birthday cards." Cassie paused. "When she saw them, she became hysterical. She called Rachel, who didn't answer – she was in the bathroom and never heard the phone." Samir realized Cassie knew why. "When Rachel didn't answer, she called her father for an explanation." Samir's hands went to his head. He understood. He knew exactly what that meant, what was about to happen.

"He's on his way, vicious and out for blood. That was about twenty minutes ago. He's staying in Princeton tonight. He should have been here by now. Maybe he already is. Security is patrolling, but doing it half-heartedly, as is the local police patrol. You have got to get out of here."

Samir was in agony. "Does he, does he know . . . anything else?" He asked apprehensively.

Cassie shook her head. "Only me."

Jeremy looked at her. What else was she not telling him, but before he could ask, a horrific pounding assaulted the front doors.

"Oh my God, he's here!" Cassie screamed.

"He can't get in. The doors are bolted."

Seconds later, Greer's pounding morphed into something harder than his fist. He was pounding the glass with a heavy rock, and the shattered glass told them he had assailed their only defense. Their fortress had been compromised. "Go! Go, Samir! Leave! You must leave!"

Samir could not move. His emotions had choked his rational thought. Greer bellowed as he made his way down the hall, pounding on one closed door then the next, assaulting its sleeping denizens. He rampaged through the hallway, intimidating every student sleeping peacefully in his bed, believing no harm could ever come to him at the academy. They were wrong. Tonight, no one was safe from this maniacal predator.

Jeremy shook off his shock. "This is my dorm and these students are under my protection. Matt, call 9-1-1. Tell them the threat is real. Tell them to get their cars and whatever else they have over here immediately, or someone might be dead by the time they move their asses."

Suddenly a huge imposing shadow blocked the door, a mass large enough to occupy every cubic centimeter of space. Greer, his eyes flaming, his look insane, stepped over the threshold. "Get out!" Jeremy commanded with more courage than Cassie could have imagined. "Get out!

You are guilty of breaking and entering and I will press charges!"

Greer flicked off the challenge like you'd flick a mosquito. His fiery eyes honed in on Samir and he charged. Jeremy met him head to head, like a Sumo wrestler. With all his might, he pushed into Greer's chest, arms under Greer's neck for maximum strength, but compared to Greer's, it was feeble. For an instant, Jeremy pushed Greer off balance. He recovered quickly and threw Jeremy aside like a rag doll.

There stood his target, that hateful creature, that filthy Arab who had stolen his daughter. "I'll kill you!" Greer shouted, eyes blazing, paralyzing Matt, who stood, phone in hand, unable to dial. "I'll kill you!" Then he lunged.

Samir leaped to the far side of the bed and pushed the desk between himself and Greer. Greer, with strength like Goliath, grabbed the end of the bed and hurled it upside down, forcing it to swing at Samir, pinning him and Jeremy behind it. An easy target for Greer now, but with the width of the desk between them like an invisible barricade, Samir leaned towards Greer with his long arms, raised powerful fists and punched his face. A sharp crack, a flow of blood spurting from his nostrils and Greer howled. Seeing his own blood, the raging monster became more ferocious, a deadly animal.

Forcing his bulk into the sliver of space between the bed and desk, and, putting all his weight behind him. Greer swung at Samir who sidestepped the blow. Greer's punch by-passed Samir's face, connected with the plaster board behind his son-in-law's head, and punched a hole through the wall.

Seizing that moment as Greer, stunned, realized his error, Samir leaped over the bed frame and mattress. Greer's cumbersome weight and mass detained him a moment too long. Samir rained powerful blows against the injured side of Greer's face, intensifying his already wounded nose, disabling and disorienting him.

This was Samir's opportunity to run. But run where? Wide-eyed classmates, including Connor, Zach, and Jason blocked his escape. Wondering who and why this man had forced his way into their rooms, they had gotten out of bed and gathered outside Samir's room. Shocked by everything they had seen and heard, they stood, like Matt, like cement pillars frozen in place, blocking Samir's path. When Samir turned to leave, a wall of dorm-mates blocked the doorway and hall. He could not break right for the exit.

Suddenly, Cassie attacked from the rear. Samir needed an opening, even if it meant this monster would turn on her. In frustration and fear, she had watched Greer throw Jeremy, his leg still pinned at the far side of the bed frame. She had watched Samir protect himself valiantly against his impregnable foe and had seen Matt and his dorm-mates immobilized, watching this phantasmagoric spectacle in horror as it played out before him. For them, this was a scene more traumatic than any from *Hamlet* or *Othello*.

Desperate for a weapon, Cassie grabbed the heavy goose-necked lamp from Matt's desk, yanking its cord from its socket. Holding the lamp tightly in both hands, with one devastating blow, she smashed it against Greer's jaw. He never saw it coming. A loud, unequivocal crack told her she had broken his jaw. Good, let him suffer! While he was dazed and she had the advantage, she smashed him again, and again.

In pain beyond imagination, he roared like a wild animal speared on all sides. No matter how this played out for her, she'd bring this man, this manifestation of evil and hate, down. He would not get away unscathed. Her attack gave Samir a few seconds.

In those few seconds, Samir bolts. He has only one way to go - up. "No, Samir!" Cassie shouts. She knows where he's going, but that door is bolted; he'll be trapped! Samir hopes that if he can't run, maybe he can hide, hide until Security or the police arrive. At least then, this nightmare would be over, and he and Rachel and their child would be forever free.

Greer would be punished in some way after this. No one, no matter how influential he was, no one could invade a dorm on the academy's campus, attack its house master, a faculty member, a student, trash their room and get away with it unscathed. Too many other influential families had children here and they would not tolerate this. His uncle would never tolerate it, and his uncle was very influential. As he races for his rooftop, peaceful and serene, he thinks of the stars and their message of hope, symbolic of renewed life

He races upstairs, through the empty, dust-filled hallway, up the second flight of stairs through the derelict room once used for stage-rehearsals, throws open the door punctured with holes for a lock that had never been installed, up the narrow attic stairwell, through the dark attic and out the door to the stars and the beauty of life.

He stands, panting, gulping in air; his lungs desperately needing air. He leans over, hands on his knees, knuckles raw. Then he plops down, sitting cross-legged on the roof, his roof, inhaling deep gulps of air.

Sirens wail, becoming louder. Finally some sense of sanity arriving. Where had they been all this time? Were they that slow, or simply that unresponsive? And had anyone contacted the dean? Samir had no respect for that man, a spineless man of no honor and little character, but this was his academy. He should have been here to take charge. At least help was on the way now. A revolving ball, whirling and screaming like a strobe, careened down the road to Damon House. Any second, the car would brake at their door.

He gets up, paces in circles to get oriented then hunkers down again, this time behind the old brick chimney no longer used after the advent of oil heat followed by gas. From here, he has a perfect vantage point; he can see the attic door. From its inner light, he'd know exactly who'd be walking through it. They'd be moving from light into darkness. No one would be able to see him; but he would see them.

Suddenly, everything converges: the patrol car screeches to a halt in front of his house; another car slams its brakes. Loud, booming footsteps pound through the attic in his direction. Does he feel floorboards quivering? Does he hear Mrs. Komsky screaming, calling his name, telling him Greer is coming after him?

After he had bolted, Greer turned on Cassie. Jeremy had pulled himself free and Matt, defensive instincts finally kicking in, threw down the phone and grabbed his hockey stick. Unwilling to waste time fending off these petty gnats, Greer ploughed through the wall of students in pursuit of Samir.

Suddenly, his monolithic mass lunges from the lighted attic onto the roof top. Surrounded by blackness Greer is blinded while his eyes adapt to night. He has no idea where Samir is; he bellows his name. "Samir! Samir, I'll kill you! I'll kill you! You're dead. You will never have my daughter, you filthy Arab!"

Samir leaps up. He will face this man, one on one, be done with him once and for all. This man will not ruin their lives. Greer sees his outline. Cassie, right behind him, heavy desk lamp still in hand, slams it into his back before he can lunge. Jeremy, right behind Cassie, pushes her aside and grabs Greer, securing him in a headlock.

Light still streaming from the attic, Samir sees Greer's bloody broken nose and the gash Cassie had inflicted. He sees Mr. Hartman and Mrs. Komsky valiantly trying to ward off their assailant to protect him, risking their lives to protect him.

Greer rips out of Jeremy's headlock, grabs his shoulders and hurls him down. Jeremy spins and struggles to his feet. Greer goes after him. Knowing Jeremy is completely vulnerable, Cassie attacks from behind, pounding Greer with the lamp gripped tightly in her fists, giving Jeremy time to get out of Greer's path. Success. She has deflected his attention from Jeremy to herself. For a brief instant, Greer forgets Samir, his primary target, and hones in on another Arab, the one who had prevented Samir's expulsion. He turns on her like a feral cat, a ferocious tiger, stalking, each step bringing him closer and closer as she backs away.

Samir grasps this in horror; he must prevent this. Somehow, he must prevent Greer's attack. He respects Dr. Hartman; he loves Mrs. Komsky and everything she has done for him. He cannot let Greer harm them because of him. He lunges for Greer.

At that same instant Rachel, dressed in an old sweatshirt and whatever jeans would fit, reaches the dorm. As soon as her last heave had stopped, she had thrown on whatever was clean and dry and had rushed out of her room to warn Samir. Thirty feet away, she hears screams from above. She stops, looks up and sees the moonlight outline the horror on Samir's roof. Her father, Mrs. Komsky, Dr. Hartman, and Samir? Samir on that roof? In a second, she realizes her father's intent and her curdling scream pierces the night. "No!" She shrieks. "No, Dad, stay away from my husband! Stay away from Samir! I love him. Samir, I love you!"

In that same instant, as Greer hears his daughter professing unabashed love for this Arab he hates, he turns from Cassie and lunges towards Samir. Cassie runs at him and swings the desk lamp at his face. With one hand, Greer punches through it, making contact with the bulb; his fist shattering it into thousands of tiny shards that explode with the force of a burst balloon, thousands of shards propelling into his side, his neck and the right side of his face. Shards penetrate his eye, destroy his sight. In a now partially blind state, blood oozing from his eye, he turns to the blurred outline of the man he hates and attacks with full force.

In this same instant, Samir hears Rachel's voice, "Samir, I love you!" She has told him, her father, and the world. She has told them all she loves him. Not since his parents died had anyone told him publically they loved him, but here, here, braving her father, campus protocol, academy rules, she has broken them all, to seek him out and tell him, everyone, of their love. He turns instinctively and his heart leaps when he sees her in the moon's semi-glow. It is the East, and Rachel is even more beautiful than the sun, his everlasting moment of love, beauty and perfection.

And in that one everlasting moment of perfection, while he is gazing at Rachel who is carrying his child, Greer attacks, his powerful shoulder hitting Samir's chest, pushing him backwards to the edge, close to the edge, close to the edge and over. Samir struggles for balance; struggles to plant his foot on solid surface, struggles to live for Rachel, his wife, the woman he loves, and for his unborn child. He falters; his life is over. In his heart, in this one millisecond of life, he knows this is the last time he will look upon his wife. He cannot regain his balance, and in that one millisecond of life's passing, he captures the complete essence of her love and compassion, of love and tragedy, and falls.

In slow motion, Cassie, Jeremy, and Rachel watch the beauty of life and the horror of death. Samir takes his last breath in this world, in this beautiful yet cruel, cruel world, leaving Rachel and his unborn child behind, his unborn child who will never see his father.

Rachel's curdling shriek echoes through the campus. It hovers overhead; soars through treetops; rides the wind;

penetrates the early night sky, and travels to the heavens, towards the twinkling stars and the glow of the moon. All is silenced as Samir's body hits the ground, succumbing to gravity, flight's nemesis, his neck twisted, his body still, while the horror, the horror of the sight sears into Rachel's memory, forever.

114

GOODBYE

The scene replays in slow motion. Cassie watches Greer break from Jeremy's headlock, punch through the bulb as she swings it at his face, then careen into Samir. She watches him lose his balance, try desperately to hold firmly to the edge, his foot catching then missing in quick succession, take his last look at Rachel and plunge to his death.

Rachel's shriek drowns out the world, night sounds, tapping twigs, a hooting owl, the din of voices trailing through the attic, and the sounds of shock as Jeremy looks on in horror and Matt, who had trailed Jeremy in time to see it all, sinks into the doorway.

Cassie recognizes that shriek. She had heard it four years ago when the army brass had knocked on her door while four-year-old Stevie clung to her leg and Cassie collapsed. She had come here for a new life, a new beginning, free from gnawing, suffocating grief. No such thing. Not for her; not for Rachel.

Cassie collapses to her knees, unable to rise. Her gasps drown out life; sounds ricochet as though she were in a fog, until, until Rachel's keening gets through. Rachel is drowning in grief, like Cassie, but worse: Cassie had never seen her husband die. Samir's body was lying right there. Cassie has to get to her. She has to put aside her own grief and help this young woman, a widow, a pregnant widow at eighteen.

Cassie struggles to rise, leaning against the wall for support. Jeremy, tears in his eyes, takes her arms and helps her up. Cassie hurries past Matt, past students milling throughout the attic and stairwell, Security and the local police rushing up the stairs to the roof, too late. As quickly as she can in her disoriented state, she struggles to maintain her balance, feels the cold blast of air in her face and is at Rachel's side without knowing how she's gotten there, urging her to leave Samir, to leave his body.

His "body." The image of that ugly word is suffocating her. Here was Samir on cold ground under a halo of darkness, under stars and a cold moon. Here lay the body of a young man who had been living, breathing a few minutes ago, a young man dreaming of rebirth, life and his family, lying dead on this cold ground, the victim of hate, man's inhumanity to man, until the end of time.

Rachel is kneeling beside Samir's lifeless body, whimpering softly, choking back grief, hesitant to reach out and touch him. Cassie tries to avert her eyes, but they are riveted on Rachel, reaching out to touch Samir's hand then pulling back, alternating between courage and fear. Finally she grazes his finger and nudges it, as if to say, "Get up, Samir. Get up. Let's leave this place, this horrible place that has caused us so much pain. You'll be all right. We'll both be all right. Get up, Hon, and come away with me."

She leans low, caresses his face, and in one final gesture of deepest love for the man she would never see again or hold in her arms, her lips brush Samir's nether lip. Barefoot to Palestine, Samir. Barefoot to Palestine. Life as she knows it, is over. Then in utter despair, her hands fall to her sides; she looks to the heavens and emits one violent shriek that splits the sky. From deep inside her where her soul resides, she cries for the man she would always love, for the man who had brought beauty into her life and for the horror of knowing the man who had taken her husband's life had been her father.

Cassie crawls closer on all fours, urging her to leave. "Come away, Rachel," she whispers softly amidst her own tears, but Rachel could not. Blind with sorrow, she cannot hear, cannot see. Cassie touches her hand lightly. Rachel is shaking, quivering uncontrollably. Cassie has to get her away. Rachel has to keep Samir's baby. "Come, Rachel," she whispers. "Come. You will be a mother soon. You will be the mother of Samir's baby. You must protect his baby. Come." She embraces Rachel gently. Rachel hears; she understands, she wills herself to rise, to leave her husband's lifeless body. She will fight to keep their baby. She will not let her father destroy their child. Never.

Cassie helps Rachel up. They start for her dorm, unbalanced, knees quivering, each engulfed with tears, both shaking with grief. They need help. Rachel needs help. Holding Rachel with one quivering hand, Cassie pulls Rebecca's phone from her pocket and calls Hillary.

Disoriented, she screams for help. Seconds later, Jeremy catches up from behind and holds Rachel's arm. She does not resist. After they get Rachel to her room, Jeremy leaves. Cassie holds Rachel close, trying to console her. Minutes drag as though they were hours. They always would.

Minutes later, Arthur screeches to a halt in front of Roosevelt House and Hillary runs for the dorm, passing Judy Marino who moves out of the way. She has heard; she prays Rachel will be okay.

115

Vaughn had risen to the emergency after Parker had roused the man he had been brought up to believe was his father. Coming home sooner than expected after driving his grandmother home, coming in through the garage, Parker had heard it all. He had heard his mother, a veritable slut, hurl invectives at his erstwhile father, who in one breath had become his uncle, while his uncle had become his father. He had reeled in shock and revulsion, heaving his dinner into his mouth, his head screaming inside, unable to fathom the deceit, duplicity, and betrayal, being sucked into a whirlpool, until he got Mason's first call.

Parker had sequestered himself in his gym, crying. He sat on the edge of his workbench, his hands covering his face. This young man of eighteen, who had once thought he was king of his world, cried. A lifetime of deceit. He was his mother's mistake, conceived while she was fornicating with his uncle, his real father. Your 'father' will be there, was always her fall-back excuse. But his real father had never been there. He had always been with his mother. It had been his uncle who had always been there, his duped fool of an uncle. Parker had inherited Hamlet's tragedy.

He answered Mason's call because Mason had never called him at 3:37 in the morning. His buzzing phone would relate bad news, of that he was sure, but worse than what he'd just lived through? Impossible. Yet his own grief was put on hold when Mason told him Matt had called. For whatever reason, Rachel's father was on his way to Chelsea, vowing to kill Samir. Stevie had called Mr. Hartman, who couldn't get through to Parker's dad and told Matt to call Mason. Mason's words tumbled one after the other. "Something bad's gonna happen, Parker."

If Stevie had called Mr. Hartman that meant Mrs. Komsky was involved. She wouldn't be if it hadn't been serious, of that Parker was certain. He held back tears, willed himself to rise and began dragging himself through the hallway and up the stairs. His phone rang again. This call stopped Parker in his tracks. "They're married! Rachel and Samir are married! Rachel's father broke into Damon House and attacked Samir, Mr. Hartman and Mrs. Komsky! Samir ran off somewhere. Matt thinks they're heading for the roof! Security and the police are dragging their heels. Parker, you've gotta get your father!"

Stunned . . . stunned, Parker could hardly think. Get to his father, his uncle, whoever he is, get to him fast and get him to do something; get him to help Rachel and Samir who are married! Greer had attacked Samir, Mrs. Komsky and Mr. Hartman? Is this real?

Now, Parker is alert. He races upstairs through the center wing and checks his father's study. Vaughn is still there, slumped in his recliner, a drink in one hand and a bottle of vodka in the other. Parker kneels and shakes him, trying to pull him out of his stupor. He takes the vodka and the bottle from him shouting, "Snap out of it!" He shakes his shoulders. "There's an emergency at Chelsea; get up! Snap out of it . . . Dad!"

Mason's third call. Mason is crying, grief palpable, telling Parker Samir is dead. Parker drops the phone and falls backwards, unable to hold himself upright, unable to absorb Mason's words. Only then does Vaughn react, picking up Parker's phone to hear the words from Mason himself.

Greer, on the rampage, had broken into Damon House, fought with Samir, Mr. Hartman, Mrs. Komsky, run after Samir and pushed him off the roof. "He's dead, Dr. O/B," Mason could barely speak the word. "D. . . dead!" Finally, Vaughn pulls himself out of his stupor, realizing there was an emergency more important than his own.

"Come on, son," Vaughn said instinctively, helping Parker up. It would take years, decades, maybe his lifetime before it would register that Parker was not his son.

Getting their bearings, they both raced to the garage. Vaughn grabbed the closest car, the Volvo, keys in place. Parker raced to his Porsche. Both drove like hell out of their drive, Vaughn leading. Vaughn raced to save his academy and its students from the horror, the panic and grief of the unspeakable tragedy that had just occurred, and to see if he could redeem himself as a leader and a man. Parker was racing to save one person who would never be the same, wondering if he would ever be either. Both pushed the pedal to the floor, and wondered what kind of nightmare they were living. How had it all, all gone so wrong?

Father and son arrived on campus after the police had called the ambulance, after Greer was in handcuffs on his way to the hospital, after Cassie had taken a shrieking, hysterical Rachel back to her dorm, after Hillary had arrived, after Hillary's doctor had arrived. Hillary's doctor? Why not Walter? Why not a hospital? Why her room?

Married? Samir, her husband? When had that occurred and how had they kept it secret? God, seeing her husband fall like that, pushed like that, from the roof of his dorm? That door was supposed to have been locked. Heads will roll for this. They were all living a nightmare. Vaughn wondered who they would be when they emerged from it all, if they ever did.

116

RACHEL'S ROOM

Inside Rachel's room, Cassie hugs the young widow tightly, trying to calm both of them. Both are shaking. Rachel needs a doctor. Cassie prays Hillary will get here soon. Minutes later, a quick rapping at the door and a familiar voice calling Rachel's name.

"Hurry, Hillary; we need you!"

Hillary rushes in still dressed in her black silk cocktail dress from her anniversary gala, a night she'd never forget. She goes to Rachel's side and touches her shoulder. "Dr. Spears will be here any minute. He's turning into the academy now. You'll be all right, Rachel, you and your baby."

Hillary nods to Cassie. "Be strong," she mouths. Cassie wonders if Hillary knows how much strength it takes to be strong when profound tragedy strikes, but maybe she does. She had lost every baby she had conceived. That had to leave deep, horrific scars. Wiping back her tears, Cassie nods.

Dr. Spears raps minutes later and opens the door a crack. "Quickly, Richard." Softly Hillary tells Rachel Dr. Spears has been her doctor for more than twenty-five years and that his unparalleled expertise in trauma cases has saved her life and the lives of hundreds of high-risk babies. "Do you want Mrs. Komsky or me to stay?" Rachel does not respond. "He'll check your vitals, Rachel," she glances at Richard who nods. "Ask him anything you want to know or don't understand. His concern is for you and your baby, not for his pride – it won't get wounded, and he won't tell anyone you're pregnant."

When Rachel nods, Hillary and Cassie leave the room. Hillary leans against the wall, watching Cassie sink to the floor, gasping. "Cassie," she says softly. Cassie does not respond, the gaping memories she had tied up and stored in her closet had fallen off their shelf. When Hillary tries again and gets no response, she lets Cassie have her own space. Cassie had loved Samir. There had been a bond between them no one would ever share, nothing could ever duplicate. Hillary let's her grieve in her own way. She feels secure now that Richard has arrived. If anyone could help Rachel, he could. Hillary had miscarried three times, but Richard had saved her life, twice.

While they wait, Hillary realizes she hasn't been this tense in two decades. She has something to live for now and a new resolve wells inside her. Here were people who needed her. She focuses on Cassie, drowning in past and present memories. For a few beautiful months here, this widow had actually thought she had succeeded. Not even close.

Suddenly Vaughn rounds the corner. He sees the women before they see him. Hillary is standing, shoes by her side, her back against the wall. Cassie sits lifeless on the floor, hands covering her face. He marvels at their courage, their compassion and fortitude, especially Cassie, the woman he tried to destroy. He had never given either of them more than a cursory thought except when it had satisfied his ego or his needs. For the first time he saw them differently; saw how much they both cared beyond themselves, while all he had cared about was himself.

If he approached them now, would they accept his help? Hillary hated him for being an Otis-Barrett, and for what he had done to Cassie. Cassie despised him, hated him, for much worse, and she was justified. Betrayal does not manifest itself in infidelity alone.

But he had a crisis to deal with; what the women thought of him was secondary. If he didn't address their emergency, it would reinforce his feeling of cowardice when courage was required. Now that Damon House was safe, he turned to Rachel and Cassie. Regardless how they responded to him, he had to offer assistance.

He walked quickly to Judy Marino's office and hurried back with a chair, importuning Hillary to sit. She glared at him, but when she saw sincerity in his eyes, she thanked him tersely and sat. Cassie, still in shock, wasn't cognizant of Vaughn when he brought the chair; she hadn't looked up; hadn't reacted; hadn't responded to his voice or the few words he had spoken. Only a man's black shoes, that's all she had registered.

When he knelt beside her to offer help, she became aware of a voice. In tiny increments she realized this voice was familiar and it was addressing her. Slowly, she looked up and assimilated his face, his eyes, that smile that had charmed her, had caught her off-guard, letting her believe an ingenuous and sincere person lived behind it when he had presented her with a student handbook so many Monday's ago. Suddenly his identity sunk in.

Suddenly his betrayal and his assault from another Monday night regaled her. Like an onslaught. Suddenly this same person was slamming her against the door, choking off her oxygen with his tongue, hurting her and liking it! Here he was, next to her now, and the horror of it all overwhelmed her.

"No!" She shuddered in abject fear. "No! Not you! Not you!" She shrieked, pedaling backwards to get as far from him as possible. She struggled, her arms slipping under her. She fell backwards, unbalanced, disoriented, righted herself and frenetically continued to back away. "Get away! Get away from me!" She shrieked.

"Vaughn, leave her!" Hillary commanded, rushing to Cassie's side. "Leave her. She's scared to death of you!"

"I'm trying to help, Hillary."

Hillary rose and positioned herself confrontationally between Cassie and Vaughn. "It's too late, Vaughn. Why would she believe that after what you've done to her?"

He hung his head and avoided her penetrating glare. "I hope someday she'll forgive me for that," he uttered with remorse. "But I'm hoping she'll let me help, now."

"Vaughn, actions have consequences, even if you're an Otis-Barrett. You may have the power to bend rules and hurt people, but no one can control another person's emotions." She glared at him with invective; then glanced behind her at Cassie, struggling to survive. "If you want to help her now, just leave . . . please."

Defeated, Vaughn turned. "I'll have a mattress pulled out from another room. It'll be more comfortable than this cold floor."

Hillary nodded. It would be.

"Should I call Walter or an ambulance?"

Hillary shook her head. "Richard will treat Cassie. No need for Walter. Both of you have done more than enough *for* her." Her look said what her words did not. Both he and Walter had betrayed Cassie, each for his own interests. No reason she'd ever want them in her life again.

Vaughn bowed his head. "I'm sorry," he utters again. "I'm truly sorry." Silence. Hillary looks away; Cassie is wide-eyed with fear, sobbing. He turns forlornly and leaves, walking back to nothing. His marriage was over; his son was not his son; his brother would always be a stranger, and he had destroyed his honor and the only woman he had ever loved.

Hate, jealousy and betrayal gloated in triumph.

117

Denied access to Cassie and Rachel, Vaughn took up the challenge of being dean of his prestigious academy at a time of extreme emergency, and he responded gallantly to his students' needs. Cancelling classes until further notice, he recruited faculty from local towns and the university and provided empty classrooms throughout the campus for students who wanted to focus on academics or keep their minds off tragic events. Although it was Sunday, response throughout the town and neighboring communities was overwhelming, instructors and professors volunteering their time graciously to sit in whatever rooms Vaughn could provide.

Coordinating with Walter, who silently accepted culpability in Samir's death, Vaughn set up grief counseling cells in every house, several in the library and cafeteria. Any student who needed emotional support or wanted to speak with a counselor would have full-time access. Again, the community responded in earnest.

On Monday, all students would meet in Landon Hall. Vaughn would address the plenary student body and make them aware of available instruction and counseling. Chaplains would speak; then Walter, and any student who wanted to eulogize his thoughts or grief. Vaughn had done his job admirably and the Trustees acknowledged it.

Vaughn, again with Walter's help, also planned a gathering to commemorate Samir's passing. It would be Thursday. For anyone who hadn't known Samir, they had missed knowing one of the most selfless and beautiful people the academy had ever known, a young man who had overcome horrific tragedy, emerged from it through the love of the young woman he had married, and had it all destroyed because of hate. A gathering would allow his classmates to pay tribute to him, express their feelings and realize first-hand how jealousy and hate could destroy something so beautiful – the universality of Iago, four hundred years later.

But Cassie would not be at Monday's meeting in Landon Hall; nor would she be at Thursday's gathering. Cassie sought refuge in her house, her room, in her bed, unable to rise, except to a sitting position where, grief stricken, she'd place her hands on her forehead and cry.

The day dawned gray, but for Cassie it went unnoticed. Had she risen from her bed to glance out, she would have seen almost-black clouds running with an angry wind, the day, dressed in mourning for a young noble's death; Cassie saw nothing. She cared for nothing; she didn't eat; didn't sleep; didn't shower, didn't dress. For the second time in her life, she had died.

Stevie brought her food that went untouched; calls from Hillary and Jeremy went unanswered, her hair went uncombed. Jeremy knocked on her front door twice. Stevie met him, hugged him then shook her head in despair.

Only one simplistic ritual from childhood grounded Cassie to reality, brushing her teeth. It had been ingrained in her since early childhood when she would hurry into the bathroom, following in her mother's footsteps to grab her toothbrush, smear on the paste and brush her baby teeth before her father demanded the room.

Always brush your teeth, Honey, so they stay clean and strong and you won't get cavities. Her mom smiles and calls her "my little angel." Mommy always calls me angel. "I love you," her mom says, removing her potholders and sending a kiss to her little girl across the kitchen, to the little daughter with the golden hair, the almond-shaped eyes and the flecks of dimples when she smiles. The image replays in her mind like a movie caught in a loop.

Mommy loves me, something she just knows in her heart. When you're young, you know when somebody loves you and when they don't. Same when you're old. It's all the in-between years that get so confusing. These in-between years, the years she was living now, the years she had wished she hadn't lived, hadn't hurt, hadn't lost Brian, hadn't met a Walter or a Vaughn or hadn't messed up like this, like now. Mom . . . Mom, why did he have to die? Why did he have to die?

On the roof; she could see him now. Had she caused his death? If she hadn't gone after Greer with the desk lamp, he might never have turned on her; Samir might never have tried to defend her. Greer might never have punched the bulb, never have become blind. He would have gone after Samir anyway, but would he have pushed him off the roof? After all his threats, would that have been his intention? She'd never know; no one except Greer ever would. We make choices every day, and life takes us the way we're meant to go, discussions they had had many times. Yet, for all her reasoning, if she hadn't . . . if she hadn't . . . if she hadn't, she blamed herself.

Greer had been charged with manslaughter, first degree, punishable with a hefty fine and jail time if convicted, and there was a good chance of that. Parents were in an uproar. Respected doctor or not, his life was ruined. He was partially blind in his left eye, jaw broken in two places, nose broken, his reputation in his home community ruined and his reputation at the Club destroyed.

Worst of all, anathema to Rachel who would never see him again, he had lost Rebecca too. Samir, her brother-in-law, was dead. Rebecca would reject her father for the rest of her life. Both daughters withdrew from their mother as well, who it was rumored, was filing for divorce, too late to save her family. Hate punishes in its own way.

But Cassie was done. She would never walk into that classroom again. She would never teach Shakespeare again. She would never do a lot of things again, like hope and dream, like wake up each morning to a bright day even with a shining sun. She would always be gulping a tear; hiding sadness, walking through life in a daze, wondering how something so beautiful had all gone so wrong.

118

WEEK AFTER DEATH

nd she never did. She never walked into her classroom again and her classes never finished *Othello*. No one needed to read it when they had lived it. The tragedy that had befallen Othello and Desdemona was no worse than what had befallen Samir and Rachel and the other nine students who had sat in Mrs. Komsky's Shakespeare class that cold Monday morning, Nov 2, wondering what their new teacher would be like.

The classroom became dormant, stagnant, an empty room with neglected posters hanging lifeless on the walls, an empty room that remained a shell without students, without life and flesh and blood and happy youthful voices and the beauty of youth and hope, their yearning and thirst for knowledge. Only in a classroom could you get this, in a classroom full of eager young minds. But in this classroom, in this year, in this lifetime, that had died.

After the student body met in Landon Hall Monday for Vaughn's program, pockets of Cassie's students stayed while others left, only to be drawn back like a magnet. They stayed to sit in the makeshift classroom Vaughn had set up there. They didn't want to be alone. They wanted their old, safe world back. Knowing it was gone, they chose the next best thing, their friends.

Mason and Matt had walked in together and stayed. Matt had witnessed too much, had seen it from beginning to end, had stood in the attic doorway watching Cassie take that final swing, saw Greer punch the bulb, shatter his face and eye and charge Samir.

He had seen Samir lose his balance, try to regain it, and fall. He had seen the look in Samir's eyes as he realized his life was over. There was no fear, no panic, only serenity as he gazed at Rachel and fell. Matt would be forever traumatized. He would never forget the love he felt for the young man who had been his roommate then his friend. Like the phoenix, like Cassie, like Rachel, he would rise from the ashes a completely different bird, simply covered with the same plumage.

Elizabeth, eyes red, face puffy, had gone back to her room, but returned, looked around for Matt apprehensively, found him and sat next to him. His arm embraced her and her head fell onto his shoulder. She cried. She too, would never go into that classroom. She too, would never be the same.

Mason, the interlocutor between Matt and Parker who had been sucked into this drama through Matt, he too, would be changed for his lifetime. Vignettes of happy times interspersed with unthinkable memories.

Mrs. Komsky's first day, how she had addressed Samir and Parker about the Arabic 'G,' how she had gotten him to open up, how he and Parker had held Samir down at Homecoming because he was different. That memory cut like a knife. Would he ever shake off the guilt? Samir never held it against him. Quite the opposite; he had a way about him, a soft, gentle manner that had united them. No surprise Rachel loved him.

Parker left Landon Hall thinking he could handle it on his own; he couldn't. Like his friends, he returned and sat close. He had his own demons to sort and no one to confide in for help, not even Mason, not yet anyway. It would take a long time for him to confide in someone, to tell even his closest friend that his father was his uncle and that his mother was a whore. His own travesty. But he needed the closeness of his classmates he now considered family and always would. He sought them out, sitting quietly in his own thoughts.

Gloria and Zach, partnered in friendship and in grief, joined the table. As late morning passed, Jason, Connor and Emelia straggled in. The class in its entirety, now numbering nine, sat together, huddled together for protection, creating a shield against an evil world. A Princeton professor sat at the far end of the table but encouraged no conversation. He was there to talk Shakespeare or not to talk Shakespeare, to talk themes in life or to talk about nothing at all. A grief counselor had been assigned specifically to Landon Hall, senior level, in anticipation that Samir's classmates would have the greatest need. But, except for a muffled cry every so often, no one said a word.

Samir was gone; Rachel was gone, and Cassie. It was just a matter of days before she vanished from their lives, as though she had never been there. A shadow? Impossible. She would vanish from their lives, but never as though she'd never been there. She had most definitely been there, and had left her indelible mark of defying tragedy and living with hope. We pick ourselves up and go on. Could Cassie do it again, after this? Could Rachel? Could they? Only their tomorrows would tell.

The real-life consequences of hate had seeped insidiously into their pores, locking its destruction inside for as long as they would live.

119

WEEK CASSIE LEAVES

The week following Samir's death was a compilation of tomorrows: Samir's uncle had arrived Sunday afternoon and taken his nephew's body; Rachel and Hillary had gone with him. The full student body met Monday morning and the gathering was held Thursday, sad, but cathartic.

Walter's planning had been exemplary and he spoke, choosing the right words, the right sentiment. He had also chosen the right chaplains, and the students who spoke had been eloquent. In his heart he knew it was all futile. His cowardice had played a part in this tragedy, of this he was sure. To make up for it, he put his heart and soul into the gathering and prayed it would achieve its purpose.

It did. Mason, Matt, Gloria, all spoke of Samir's passion for life and his love for people. Matt quoted Kahlil Gibran: "When you are sorrowful look again in your heart, and you shall see that in truth you are weeping for that which has been your delight."

Gloria spoke of hatred and stereotypes, using the same photos Samir had used in his presentation. Four photos of mass graves, without headings or captions. "Are these people Native Americans, are they Arabs? Are they Jews? Are they Armenians? Samir showed us ethnicity and race do not matter; hatred and stereotypes can destroy us all. And he was right." They understood; they had learned.

On Friday, Jeremy submitted his resignation. He wished he had resigned sooner; he would have avoided the horror of what he had witnessed. Despite all he had done, it hadn't been enough.

The week after the gathering, a formal letter from the Board of Trustees required Cassie's and Jeremy's presence. The Trustees were holding a hearing to learn as much about Samir's death as possible. They demanded an explanation as to how something as important as a lock to an attic door could have been missing for how long, years? Although they appreciated Vaughn's emergency response, a missing bolt was something they would not tolerate.

Vaughn admitted he had been unaware, but one lock on an attic door in one dorm was not something he would have known. These dorms had been inspected before any student had been assigned to them and that inspection would have included a room by room, floor by floor search. In that respect, he was correct.

He also explained that once Mrs. Komsky had made him aware this bolt was missing, which allowed Samir access to the roof, he had issued orders to Maintenance that the omission be addressed and corrected immediately.

Questioning fell to Jeremy. Had Maintenance installed the lock? Jeremy produced the work order confirming its completion. Maintenance's foreman had left the completed job order on his desk the week after the cook-off. It validated the repair, but the job itself simply hadn't gotten done.

Eyes fell on Cassie, who had left her house for the first time since Samir's death. Gaunt and weak, a pall of despair engulfed her. Vaughn winced when he saw her and inwardly groaned when she was questioned. "Were you aware the bolt was still missing after Christmas break?" Downcast eyes, she nodded. "Why didn't you report it?" She did. To whom, came the question. To Mrs. Donelly, the day after Christmas break. "Mrs. Donelly has denied this; she has stated no such report exists."

Cassie glances at Melissa. "Perhaps she misplaced my report, which stated I had met with Samir the last weekend of Christmas break." Mrs. Donelly demurs. No such report was forthcoming, she insists.

Despite her grief, Cassie had come prepared. She reaches into her bag, produces a manila folder, opens it, and places a sheet of paper on the table. It was the copy of the report she had submitted to Melissa after she had come back from Christmas, when she had entered the office happy, smiling, and eager to greet everyone with Happy New Year, but had been rebuked by everyone, made invisible in one administrative fiat, the coldness permeating her pores.

That day, period five, after her fourth period when Melissa had been ordered to ignore Cassie, she had submitted her report, watched Melissa initial it, pass it through the copier and hand it back to her. Cassie had left the building in tears but had filed away a copy in her room and had made one for home. It was that day. Melissa in her discomfort and her obsequious need to attend to Vaughn's orders must have misplaced the original.

The Trustees each take the report and scan it. Yes, "No lock" clearly stated; Melissa's initials clearly written; January 4, 1988 on the heading. Cassie had written the report; she had submitted it through the proper channels, but it had been misplaced, tension, pride, arrogance, and vengeance taking precedence over the proper channels, getting the report to Walter then to Vaughn.

Taylor's jealousy and Vaughn's anger had indirectly caused Samir's death. What a waste, a complete and utter waste.

Cassie rose slowly. Ten pairs of eyes watched her. She had not been given permission to leave; she had not formally been dismissed. But Cassie was finished. She had said all she had to say; she had adhered to every prescription of a teacher's responsibility; she had followed every protocol and tried to balance her responsibilities against a barrage of hatred, unending harassment, ostracism, and a physical attack. She had no more to give and no reason to stay. She rose and nodded, her last gesture of respect, and turned for the door.

Vaughn called to her; she did not stop; did not turn; did not reply; did not hear Jeremy push his chair out. She only realized he had when he caught up to her. He opened the door for her as they both walked out.

120

CASSIE'S LAST WEEKEND

Last weekend in February. Cassie had hugged and kissed each of her twenty-six charges in Sanders House and had cried whatever vestiges of tears she had left. She had been packing intermittently as soon as she was able to force herself out of bed and begin focusing on life. Since no one, no one except Jeremy would ever walk into her house again, it didn't matter that boxes lay open and cluttered the floor. She and Stevie were ready to go.

Sunday afternoon the movers arrived. Three hours to load all her belongings, some of which she was leaving, and to begin the reverse trek to the Jersey shore. Route 133 to 33 to 34 then veer off to Point Pleasant instead of Manasquan, until their house on Meadow Ave. became vacant again and the sound of surf and breezes with attitude would play at her door. But she had no desire to play.

It was 5:30 when they started out. Stevie did not read. No *Narnia* this time or any other book; no conversation.

She let her mother grieve, hoping someday soon she'd come out of it. Stevie understood grief and loss now. At four, she didn't fully understand her dad wasn't coming home, but at nine she knew. She had loved Samir too.

She too, had been taken in by the football crowd, by Walter and Dr. O/B. She too had been taken in by Melissa who had hugged her when Mason and the others had brought their mother in from the cold. She remembered them all at the cook-off and couldn't understand how someone who had professed such loyalty could just cut you from their life like a light switch being shut off.

They had said goodbye to Rachel and Hillary. That was sad, so sad. Cassie and Stevie promised they would visit once a month if not more, as long as Rachel wouldn't get tired of them. Rachel had hugged Cassie, vowing she would never get tired of them. They'd be in her life, and Samir's baby's life for as long as they wanted.

Rachel would be privately tutored for the rest of the semester. She would be living with Hillary in two town house units combined into one. Brett had bought an eight-unit townhouse for Hillary and was gutting it for her – four units combined for Hillary, one unit for Arthur and his wife, another for Hillary's cook and her husband, and two units combined for Rachel, enough space for them to have their own lives, and enough closeness to be a family.

They said goodbye to Jeremy. In one week, he would be gone too. They had exchanged addresses and phone numbers and would contact each other for the rest of their lives. Jeremy would remain her lifetime friend, to talk to about "Whatcha been up to," and "How's work?" and a whole lot of other milestones in life that would occur as they passed through life's phases. Only Jeremy. Her mom had said a person was blessed to have one true friend who would stand up for what was right before taking the easy route. One loyal friend was all she needed, and that was Jeremy, and maybe Hillary; the irony of it all.

So for the trip back, back home to a home Cassie wished she had never left, Stevie would not be reading, the radio would not be playing, and she and her mother would not be sparring over Greek and Latin roots and prefixes. They would go back to the Jersey shore, with its beautiful beaches and its breezes with attitude. Cassie would go back to this, hoping someday she would appreciate the surf, walk in the sand, feel the ocean mist in her face and not cry.

Forever

How long is forever, a little child asked.
And the answer was always, past upon past,
Today and tomorrow, a life without end.
The little child listened,
And then asked again.

But how *long* is forever?
Her mother replied,
Well, not quite so long that nobody dies.
Not quite so long that it brings only joy,
Or laughter or comfort;
Sometimes it destroys.

How long is *forever*, she asked with a sigh.
Well, I was told it meant always,
But somebody lied.
Forever lasts only as long as we live,
As long as we want, as long as we give.

When a promise is broken,
Or a close tie is severed.
Then you will know,
What is meant by forever.

Loretta J. Krause

ACKNOWLEGEMENTS

Several people deserve thanks for their contributions to this book:

My husband, Mike, and my sons, Michael and Mitchel, provided their football knowledge to those "on the field," sections of the book. Their assistance was invaluable.

My very dear friend, Kay, checked the Arabic sentences. They could not have been written without her.

Guzide let me sit in on her Basic Arabic course at William Paterson University and eventually became a friend.

Michele, my daughter, never doubted I would complete my book even at times when I didn't think I could. Her positive thinking was wonderful motivation.

A final thanks to Carol B, who kept me in college so many decades ago when I had decided to quit. Without her, this book would never have been written.

My love to all.

ABOUT THE AUTHOR

Loretta J. Krause was born and raised and has long re-
sided in New Jersey, and she earned her BA and MA from
Montclair State University. A longtime educator, Krause
has taught everything from Shakespeare to journalism
to middle-school math. She blended her talent for both
math and narration in the children's book *The Beaver
Twins Learn about Subtraction*.

Barefoot to Palestine is Krause's first novel.